THE
DAUGHTERS *of*
MERSEY SQUARE

BOOKS BY PAM HOWES

THE MERSEY TRILOGY
The Lost Daughter of Liverpool
The Forgotten Family of Liverpool
The Liverpool Girls

LARK LANE SERIES
The Factory Girls of Lark Lane
The Shop Girls of Lark Lane
The Nurses of Lark Lane
The Midwives of Lark Lane

THE BRYANT SISTERS SERIES
The Girls of Victory Street
Wedding Bells on Victory Street
The Mothers of Victory Street
The Daughters of Victory Street
A Royal Visit to Victory Street

MERSEY SQUARE SERIES
The Girls of Mersey Square
The Mothers of Mersey Square
Secrets on Mersey Square
Dreams on Mersey Square

A Child For Sale

Fast Movin' Train
Hungry Eyes
It's Only Words

THE DAUGHTERS *of* MERSEY SQUARE

PAM HOWES

bookouture

Published by Bookouture in 2024

An imprint of Storyfire Ltd.
Carmelite House
50 Victoria Embankment
London EC4Y 0DZ

www.bookouture.com

Copyright © Pam Howes, 2024

Pam Howes has asserted her right to be identified as the author of this work.

First published as *'Til I Kissed You* by Cantello Publications in 2014.

All rights reserved. No part of this publication may be reproduced, stored in any retrieval system, or transmitted, in any form or by any means, electronic, mechanical, photocopying, recording or otherwise, without the prior written permission of the publishers.

ISBN: 978-1-83790-996-4
eBook ISBN: 978-1-83790-995-7

This book is a work of fiction. Names, characters, businesses, organizations, places and events other than those clearly in the public domain, are either the product of the author's imagination or are used fictitiously. Any resemblance to actual persons, living or dead, events or locales is entirely coincidental.

Dedicated to the memory of my very dear friend, Susan Frances Hooper, 1949–2010. Always in my thoughts, Sue, and I'm sad that we never got the chance to be those dotty old ladies we planned to be! Till we meet again. Xxx

1

ASHLEA VILLAGE, CHESHIRE, APRIL 1984

'Nick, where are you?'

Silence.

'Nick, for God's sake stop messing around.' The corridor was dark, long and narrow. She could smell him. Cigarette smoke and leather. Why wouldn't he answer? She crept down the corridor, one hand against the wall, the other outstretched. She could hear him breathing now. 'Nick, you're scaring me. I don't like this game.' Then she was falling and Nick was shouting.

'Hold on tight, Jess.'

Down, down, down like Alice in the rabbit hole, and then thump.

Her eyes flew open and she let out a sharp breath. She was in her bed – alone – drenched with sweat and tangled up in the duvet. That bloody dream, again. How many times was that now? What was it all about? She dashed a trembling hand across her face. Tears. She'd been crying in her sleep. Was she going nuts? Was it the spliff she and Nick shared last night? Surely not? Nick's mate wouldn't sell them dodgy gear and anyway, she'd had the dream before. She looked at her bedside clock: 7:30. 'Shit!' The Cantellos were picking her up at 8:00, she'd never be ready at this rate. She leapt out of bed and hurried into the en suite. Still shaking, she turned on the shower and stepped in. The soothing hot water relaxed her and she remembered last night's date with Nick, when his eager hands and lips had had the opposite effect.

She grabbed a towel, wrapped it around her middle and sat in front of the dressing table mirror, rubbing at the dark circles under her eyes. She must start going to bed early, but then there was the dream. Nick laughed the first time she told him about it. Said she had an overactive imagination. She dragged a brush through her long hair, blasted it with the dryer, then slapped blusher on her cheeks and rimmed her eyes with kohl. She pulled on jeans and a tight white T-shirt, pushed her feet into Doc Martens and clomped downstairs.

* * *

Sammy Cantello checked her watch. She called up the stairs, 'Roy, for the last time, get a move on – and give Nick and Jason a shout. It's after seven. We promised Jess we'd pick her up at eight.' She hurried back into the kitchen, poured a mug of coffee and loaded the toaster. Her boys were hopeless at getting up and her husband even worse. They'd been roped in to help clear out the house in Brighton that their friends, Eddie and Jane Mellor, had recently inherited from Eddie's Aunt Celia, but unless they got a move on, the first day would be wasted.

Clad in boxer shorts, dark hair glistening from the shower, Roy padded barefoot into the kitchen and bent to kiss the top of her head. 'Morning, Sam.'

'About time, too! Sit down and I'll pour you a coffee. Any sign of the boys?'

'They're styling their hair. Give 'em half an hour. Nick's bog-eyed after his late night. I guess he was out with Jess?'

'You guess right.' She handed him a mug. 'Help yourself to toast. It's probably cold now.'

'I'll do without. Pass me a fag, love.'

'Those boys take longer than I do over their hair.' She handed Roy his cigarettes. 'The bags are in the hall. Load the car when you've finished, please.'

'I'll put the roof rack on first.' He lit up, took a lengthy drag and coughed. 'I really must give up.'

'You say that every morning.'

He took another long drag. 'I'll take the keyboard and guitars. Ed's taken a couple of amps and Jess's bass with him.'

'You and Ed planning on doing some serious work then, or just jamming?' Sammy wiped up toast crumbs from the worktop and tossed the cloth into the sink.

'Both, if we've time. There's a couple of new songs to run through while we've got the kids under one roof.'

'You alright, Roy?' Sammy asked as his dark eyes narrowed and he stared out of the window. 'You look miles away.'

'Yeah – just thinking. Shame Livvy Grant's not coming with us. One of the songs is a real rocker and I wrote it with her in mind. It needs a stronger voice than Jess's.'

'Huh, don't fancy your chances if you say that to Jess! She doesn't want Livvy in The Zoo, she thinks the girl fancies Nick.'

'Nah, she doesn't – does she? Fancy Nick, I mean?'

'I've no idea. I heard Jess having a go at him last week for being over friendly.'

Roy stubbed out his cigarette and came and stood beside her. He gazed into her eyes and kissed her. 'I fancy *you*, Mrs C.'

'Do you now?'

'You can feel I do. How about a quickie while the lads have their breakfast?'

'Roy, for God's sake, do you ever think about anything else? Get dressed.'

Nick and Jason appeared; both yawning, dark hair blown and gelled to perfection.

'Grab some toast,' Sammy said. 'Then you can help Dad load the car. Get the roof rack out of the garage.' She was conscious of Roy hiding behind her, hands strategically placed over his boxer shorts.

'That was a bit too close for comfort,' he muttered as the boys headed for the door.

'Serves you right for walking around half-naked. Now get ready and load the car.'

'One kiss and I will.'

'Roy, it never stops at one kiss with you.' She pulled away. 'Go, now, or I won't be responsible for my actions.'

'Tonight then, promise?'

'If I'm not too tired.' She jumped as the phone rang.

Roy grabbed the receiver and pressed her against the cupboard. His free hand caressed her back through her linen shirt. 'Roy Cantello. Ah, the lovely Mrs Mellor! And how are you this fine morning? Good. Just a mo.'

'Jane.' He handed Sammy the phone.

'Hi, Jane. Saved by the bell,' Sammy said as Roy left the kitchen.

'What bell?'

'The phone. Roy's like a tom on the tiles, as usual, while I'm getting more and more agitated – as usual! Your timing is perfect.'

'Put him off his stride, did I? Not that much ever does. I've forgotten my locket. Can you get it when you pick up Jess, please? I've tried calling her but there's no answer. She must be in the shower.'

'Of course, anything else?'

'No, that's it. It's in my jewellery box. Thanks, Sam, see you in a few hours. Safe journey.'

'Thanks, see you soon.'

* * *

Roy glanced out of the bedroom window and shook his head as he watched Nick and Jason struggling with the roof rack. He opened the window and yelled, 'Leave it – you'll scratch the bloody car! I'll be down in a minute.' He checked his hair in the mirror and winked at his reflection. 'Not bad for forty-two, Cantello.' He picked up his leather jacket and car keys.

Hand on the doorknob, he paused for a minute. Sammy's earlier comment about Livvy Grant fancying Nick bothered him and he wondered why. Roy wanted her in The Zoo. Her voice had a strength the band needed. Not only that, she was a good-looking kid, didn't give lip and he liked having her around. He'd have to call a serious band meeting next week. There had to be a way of persuading Jess that it would be a very sound move to have Livvy on board.

* * *

Jane smiled as she dropped the receiver back onto the cradle. In the lounge her husband Eddie was reading the *Daily Mail* and her stepson Jon fiddling with a portable cassette recorder, trying to retrieve a jammed tape.

'I called Sammy,' Jane said. 'Roy's giving her no peace. He never changes.'

Eddie folded his newspaper and laughed. 'Don't suppose he ever will now.'

'Want a ciggie, Dad?' Jon held out a packet of Silk Cut.

'I'll have one later, son.'

Jon plonked his feet on the coffee table, lit up and blew a perfect smoke ring.

'Don't get too comfy.' Jane smacked his feet down. 'So, what's the plan of action for today?'

'Well, first off, me and Jon will go to the solicitor's to sort out Celia's will,' Eddie said.

'Okay.' Jane nodded. 'I'll have a wander around The Lanes, see if the bric-a-brac shops will be interested in any of the furniture and stuff.'

'I'll be sorry to see it go,' Eddie started to say, but something caused his voice to crack. Jane stepped in.

'End of an era, love, isn't it? I'm sure it will all find a nice home. Right, I'll have a tidy round and get the rooms ready. The boys can have camp beds in with you, Jon. Jess can sleep in the attic. While you're out, you can pick up some groceries for tonight. I'll write a list.'

'I'll cook,' Eddie said. 'I'll do Beef in Beer. Roy loves that.'

'So do I.' Jon was fiddling with the cassette recorder again. 'Especially when *you* cook it and not Mum.'

'Thanks very much, Jon. I'll remember that the next time your father's in London and you have to eat my burnt offerings, which, incidentally, you never refuse – or leave.'

'Even your burnt offerings are preferable to starving, Mum,' Jon teased. 'Dad just happens to be the better cook, that's all.'

'Pity he didn't realise that years ago,' she said, only half joking.

***

Sammy knocked on the door of Hanover's Lodge. Jess answered, looking bleary-eyed.

'Morning, Jess. You look tired. Not had much sleep?'

'I'm fine,' Jess said, smiling.

'Well, if you're ready, put your case in the boot. Your mum forgot her locket. I'll nip upstairs and get it.'

'Do you want me to go?'

'It's okay, love. You get yourself settled in the car. I'll lock up as I leave.'

As Sammy climbed the familiar staircase a million memories flashed through her mind. She passed Jess's bedroom door. The room had been hers and Roy's when they'd all lived together during the sixties and Eddie and Roy had been members of the chart-topping group, The Raiders. She opened the door next to Jess's room and peered in. The music room – walls adorned with souvenirs of the group's heyday. Awards, framed photographs and gold discs. A corner of the room had doubled as her studio when she'd started her own fashion design business. She smiled as she closed the door and walked along the landing to Jane and Eddie's bedroom.

She found the locket, dropped it into her bag and hurried out to the car. Roy slumped in the front passenger seat, his earlier friskiness gone. Jess was sitting between Nick and Jason, Nick's hand resting possessively on her knee.

'Alright now, Jess?' Sammy climbed in.

'She's fine, Mum,' Nick answered for her.

'Right then. We'll stop at the services in a couple of hours.' She started up the engine of the sleek BMW saloon and drove down the rutted, private lane towards the main road.

Jess chatted non-stop. She was very much her mother's daughter in that respect, while Nick, nodding and grunting only when he had to, was very much his father's son first thing in the morning.

Roy glanced at Sammy with pleading eyes that said, 'Can't you shut her up?' Sammy smiled. She enjoyed Jess's chatter. 'Did you have a good time last night, Jess?'

'We did, thanks, Sammy.'

Sammy looked in the rear-view mirror. She saw Jess squeeze Nick's hand and he winked at her.

'Go anywhere nice?' Roy asked.

'Pub in Didsbury with some mates,' Nick said.

'So, they've started all-night opening in Didsbury, have they?'

'Roy, stop it. You're embarrassing them.' In the rear-view mirror, Sammy saw Jess's cheeks flush.

'Sorry, kids, just envious. I wish I were your age again. Don't you, Sam?'

'Sometimes, but knowing what I know now.'

* * *

Jon dashed upstairs to get changed. While he dressed, he mulled over what he would spend his inheritance money on. A new car maybe, depending on how much Great Aunt Celia had left him. Jess had already spent hers a million times over in her head. He slapped on the cologne she'd given him for Christmas – she'd told him she loved the musky scent on him.

He felt his stomach tighten as he thought about her, then immediately felt guilty. She was beautiful and he ached to hold her and take her to bed. He shouldn't be having such thoughts about his sister, even though they only shared the same dad. It's not right, he told himself, but the feelings had started soon after she began dating his mate, Nick Cantello, and he couldn't seem to stop them. Nick was a lucky bugger and nowhere near good enough for his little sis.

He grimaced at his reflection and ran his hands through his thick, dark curls. In the mirror he didn't see his own green eyes, but the alluring blue of Jess's. Eyes you could fall into, eyes that you could fall in love with. 'Get over it, Jon,' he muttered. 'It ain't gonna happen.'

* * *

Jane called her mother to enquire after her and Eddie's younger children, Katie and Dominic, and Lennon their dog.

'They're fine, Jane,' her mum reassured her, after making

small talk. 'We're enjoying having them to stay. Have a nice holiday, see you soon.'

'Hardly a holiday, Mum,' Jane muttered as she wandered from room to room. 'There's so much to do.' Aunt Celia's Victorian home was packed with stuff. She looked at the array of ornaments, wondering why anyone could possibly want so many glass brandy balloons. They were on every surface, in every colour imaginable.

Apart from the glass collection there were many family photographs. Eddie's late parents, Dad, smart in military dress, and Mum, smiling up at him, her eyes large and dewy, and a little fox-fur around her neck.

Photos of a young Eddie, neat in his school uniform with no hint of the leather-clad rebel to come. Jane ran her fingers over his face and lovingly traced the dimple in his chin, leaving a trail through the dust on the glass.

She flopped down on the sofa next to the old radiogram and smiled as memories of her 1964 Bank Holiday trip to Brighton flooded back. It was the same sofa she'd sat on with Eddie, Roy and Sammy, smoking her first joint, while the Mods and Rockers riots raged on outside. She shook her head, thinking how her trusting mother would have had a holy fit if she'd known half of what her daughter got up to once she became involved with The Raiders.

* * *

Jess leapt out of the car and rang the bell. 'Hi, Mum,' she greeted as Jane threw open the door.

'Hello, darling.' Jane hugged her daughter. 'It's good to see you all. You did well for time.'

'We did,' Jess agreed as Jane stepped aside to let them in.

Roy and the boys carried the bags. They dumped them in

the hall and followed Jane into the lounge, where Eddie was sitting on the sofa. He jumped up to greet them.

'Blimey, it's exactly the same.' Sammy's gaze swept the room. Celia's house was a time warp, decorated in shades of orange, purple and brown. 'God, this takes me back a few years.'

'Twenty, to be precise.' Roy stood behind her and rested his hands on her shoulders. 'It's a shame to sell it, Ed. It's like a sixties museum.'

'It's in need of a major refurb,' Eddie said. 'I haven't the time to be dealing with it. Right, grab some wine glasses, Jane.' He uncorked a bottle of red. 'Let's have a drink before dinner. It's nice to be here again, even though we've got the kids under our feet this time.'

'Cramping your style, are we?' Jon walked into the room and gave Jess a hug.

'Son, believe me, you always did.'

'We'll leave you in peace after dinner,' Jess said as Jon winked at her. 'I fancy a dance.' She wiggled her slender hips. 'There'll be some good clubs in town.'

* * *

'Bring another bottle of wine through, Jane,' Eddie called as he and Roy tuned up the guitars in the lounge.

'Yes, your lordship.' Jane laughed and topped up the glasses. She sat down on the sofa next to Sammy.

Jess sauntered into the room, her black leather jeans and white cropped top fitting just where they touched.

'For God's sake, Jess,' Jane began. 'That top leaves nothing to the imagination and those jeans look as though they're cutting you in two.'

'Mum, quit criticising! Bet Gran never gave you a hard time about what *you* wore when you went out. Anyway, Nick likes my tight pants.'

'I bet he does,' Jane said. 'And believe me, your gran always gave me a hard time about my short skirts, you ask your dad.'

Eddie caught his breath as Jess flicked her long, dark hair over her shoulders and planted herself in front of him. She was the image of Jane at eighteen, except for her eyes. Jess's were blue as forget-me-nots and Jane's brown and soulful. 'Yes, Jess, what can I do for you?'

'Daddy,' she wheedled, dropping a kiss on his cheek.

'Can I borrow some money?' he finished.

'How did you know I was gonna ask that?'

'Because you usually kiss me when you want something and it's either my money or my car keys. Am I right, or am I right?'

'You're right. You usually are.'

He fished a ten-pound note from his pocket. 'Buy the boys a drink and, Jess, when we get home, maybe you could start looking for a part-time job.'

'Yeah, I will, but The Zoo will be making enough money to keep me soon.' She left the room as the boys clattered down the stairs.

Jane shook her head and took a sip of wine.

Roy grinned. 'Big ideas.'

'That's my girl,' Eddie said. 'We need to sort things out with the band when we get back. I keep telling her they'll do better with Livvy on board.'

'I agree,' Roy said. 'The lads want her in and so do I. Band meeting, Livvy included, as soon as we get home.'

'God help you,' Jane said. 'But you're right. Livvy's a fabulous singer, and if she doesn't join them soon, someone else will snap her up.'

Eddie nodded. Livvy's powerful vocal chords could be the making of The Zoo and were the perfect complement to Jess's soft and soulful voice.

2

'Let's have a drink on the pier before we find a club,' Jon suggested as they strode in the direction of the Palace Pier.

Nick slipped his arm around Jess's waist. 'Has your dad said how much Celia's left you yet?'

'No, and there's not been the right time to ask.'

'I know how much you're getting,' Jon said.

'Is it enough for me and Nick to live on?'

'Plenty.' Jon wished it wasn't. The thought of Jess living with Nick was almost too much to bear. 'You'll have to wait until tomorrow. Dad wants to tell you himself.'

'Tell me now.' Jess slipped out of Nick's arms and grabbed Jon's hand. 'Please, Jon.'

'No.' He looked into her eyes and felt his stomach lurch. He reached out, brushed her hair from her face and was conscious of Nick giving him a strange look. He pulled his hand away and carried on walking. They made their way to the white painted tables and chairs outside a bar and sat down. Jon went inside and came back with four pints of lager.

The bar was quiet. It was still early in the season and dusk was setting in as the bright neon lights of the fairground rides danced in their eyes. 'Relax' by Frankie Goes To Hollywood blasted from the overhead speakers. Nick sang along, smiling at Jess. She giggled as he leant across and whispered in her ear.

'Better not, Nick. We need to keep the parents sweet for when we tell them we're moving in together.'

'They wouldn't know. You're in the attic, they're on the floor below. C'mon, Jess, for me,' he whispered, giving her his special bone-melting smile.

'What are you two on about?' Jon said as Nick looked into Jess's eyes.

'Nick wants to share my room,' she said.

Jason raised an eyebrow. 'You'll have to be back in ours before Mum wakes up. Remember her speech last night about no hanky-panky between you and Jess?' He stood up, hands on hips in a camp fashion, and did a perfect imitation of his mother as the others laughed.

Jess rolled her eyes. 'It's ridiculous. We'd be living together already if we had a place. Why shouldn't we share a room?'

'You can, as long as Nick's back in ours before they get up,' Jon said. 'Try and keep the peace for once, please, Jess. You can borrow my travel alarm. Now stop sulking and drink up.' He downed his pint. 'C'mon, Jase, let's go and find us a woman.'

Jason smiled shyly and followed the others.

Jess linked her arm through his. 'You okay, Jase?'

'Yeah, I suppose so. Would have been nice if Jules could have come with us though.'

Nick turned. 'Don't you see enough of him at college? Jase, you'll never get a woman with him hanging around. People think you're a couple.'

'Leave it, Nick,' Jon said as Jason's brown eyes clouded. Nick was always goading him about his best mate and it really annoyed Jon. He and Jules were close, maybe a bit too close, but that was Jason's business and Nick should keep his bloody thoughts to himself.

* * *

Jon paused for a moment outside the pier entrance. 'So, this is where the infamous Mods and Rockers riots began?'

'Yeah.' Jess nodded. 'According to Sammy, this area was awash with Rockers and then The Mods rode up on their scooters, chanting and shouting. God, I bet it was such a thrill, just like a scene from *Quadrophenia*.'

'I wouldn't have fancied being stuck in the middle of it all,' Jon said. '*Quadrophenia* was bad enough and that was just the film. Mind you,' he smirked, 'I'd play the part of Jimmy any day, getting to shag Leslie Ash in that backyard!'

'Trust you.' Jess laughed. 'Those riots happened before we were born, but Dad often talks about 'em as though it was yesterday.'

'I was born, but I lived with Angie then,' Jon said.

'Do you ever wonder what she was like?' Jason asked as they set off for the town centre.

'Sometimes I do.' Jon nodded. 'It didn't bother me when I was younger. I mean, she died when I was three so I hardly remember her. But now, well... I'd like to know more. I'm told I look like her, green eyes and curls and all that. I was twelve when Dad told me Jane wasn't my mum and that my real mother had died in an accident. I thought they were joking at first.'

Jon smiled as Jess squeezed his arm. One of his earliest memories was of Dad telling him he always had to take great care of her. She'd been upset when they'd told him about Angie, she'd cried with him, but not really understanding what it was all about. He'd soon got over the shock and carried on as normal, putting it to the back of his mind until recently, when for some reason, curiosity had started to surface.

As far as he was concerned, Jane had always been Mum, but as time passed the need to find out more about Angie grew stronger. For years, birthday and Christmas cards from his grandparents and aunt had been the only communication he'd had with her family. Apart from making him write thank you letters for money received in his cards, Dad, for whatever reasons, didn't encourage contact.

'Listen.' Nick's eyes lit up as they turned into a side road. 'That's our kind of sound. C'mon, let's go in there.'

Music blasting through open doors further along the road reached their ears. They paid their entrance fee and walked past two burly, black-suited bouncers into a crowded, smoky room. The brick walls of the building, which had begun life as a warehouse, were painted a myriad of bright colours. Garish flashing lights assaulted their eyes even further and the music was so loud, it seemed to bounce off the walls.

'Get us a drink, Jon, I'll pay,' Nick shouted above the noise as they weaved their way through the sweating, gyrating dancers.

'Here, take this.' Jess fished in her bag and handed Dad's tenner to Jon. 'Lager for me, please, and whatever you lot want.' She made her way to a vacant table, followed by Nick and Jason.

As Jon lounged against the bar, he spotted a couple of girls standing to his left. They were looking across to where Jess and the boys were seated. One of them, a willowy blonde, made eye contact with Nick. Nick smiled and winked. Jess won't like that, Jon thought, as Jess pulled Nick to his feet and onto the dance floor.

She wound her arms around his neck. Nick held her, lips seeking hers. Then Jon saw his sister grinning in the blonde's direction. She got the message that Nick was not available and turned her attention to Jon as he carried the drinks over.

She smiled, revealing even white teeth, and tossed back her long, blonde hair. 'Hi, I'm Helen.'

'I'm Jon, that's Jason.' He gestured to an empty chair. Helen sat down and crossed her long legs, revealing lightly tanned thighs as her skirt rode up. Jon caught a glimpse of white lace and hoped this would be his lucky night.

Jason nodded, looking intimidated by Helen, who was eyeing Jon as though he were a stud bull at a cattle market. She beckoned to a small, dark-haired girl, who sat down beside her.

'This is Ronnie, my mate. Meet Jon and Jason.'

'Ronnie?' Jon said. 'Short for Veronica?'

'It's really Rhonda,' Ronnie said. 'Mum was a Beach Boys fan. You know, "Help Me, Rhonda". But I prefer Ronnie.'

'I'm not surprised.' Jon held out his hand. 'Nice to meet you, really, Rhonda.'

'You on holiday, Jon?' Helen asked.

'Not really.' Jon detected a northern accent. 'You?'

'Yeah, we're staying in Rottingdean with my aunt. We're from Stockport in Cheshire.'

'Bloody hell, there's a coincidence! We're from Ashlea Village,' Jon said. The DJ changed tempo and Lionel Richie sang 'Hello'. 'That's better, I can hear myself speak. Fancy a dance?' He led Helen onto the dance floor, leaving Jason and Ronnie staring after them.

Jon slipped his arms around her trim waist and she put hers around his neck.

'Who's the couple you're with?' she asked.

'My half-sister, Jess, and Jason's brother, Nick.'

'They're very into one another.' She smiled at the pair who were swaying, eyes closed. 'How old are they?'

'Jess is eighteen and Nick's eighteen next month.' Jon glanced at Nick and Jess and felt the familiar surge of jealousy.

'Have they been together long?'

'All their lives. They were born a year apart. Both families lived together at our home, Hanover's Lodge,' he explained.

'Hanover's Lodge? I've heard all about that place. Mum and

her mates hung around outside the gates after school. The Raiders used to live there.'

Jon nodded. 'Our dad Ed was their drummer. Jason and Nick's dad is Roy, their lead singer. The group's disbanded now but Dad and Roy are still songwriters and they manage our band, The Zoo.'

'Your band? You mean the four of you?'

'Yeah,' Jon said. 'I'm the drummer, Jess plays bass and sings, Jason plays keyboards and Nick's on lead guitar and also sings.'

'Wow! I'll have to come to a gig. Do you have a home down here, too?'

'Dad's aunt died and left her house to him. We're clearing it before he sells it. Right, now you know my life history, let's hear yours.'

'There's nothing to tell really.' Helen shrugged. 'Mum will be gobsmacked when I tell her who I've met. She was crazy about your dad. Bought all The Raiders' records and has a scrapbook full of cuttings and autographs. She used to say Eddie Mellor had the most gorgeous blue eyes she'd ever seen.'

'He still has,' Jon said. 'So has Jess. They look right into your soul. Would you like a drink?'

'Coke, please,' she said and went back to her seat. Jon frowned as he waited at the bar. With her tall, model-girl figure, sexily clad in a short white rah-rah skirt and skimpy black cutaway top, Helen looked about eighteen. He ordered a round of drinks and carried the tray to the table.

'How come you don't want alcohol?' He sat next to Helen, bumping thighs. 'How old are you?'

She leant forward and whispered, 'Sixteen – next month. And you?'

Jon sighed, thinking, *shit, jailbait, just my luck.* 'Twenty-two. Is that too old for you?'

She shook her head as Nick and Jess returned to the table. 'Lads my age are childish.'

'Do you think they'll have gone to bed yet?' Nick interrupted, looking at his watch.

'It's only just gone eleven,' Jon said. 'Give them a bit longer.'

'You don't have to go yet, do you?' Helen touched Jon's arm.

'No, these two have the hots for one another.'

Jess stared at Helen, eyebrows raised questioningly.

'This is Helen,' Jon introduced her. 'And that's Rhonda, or Ronnie, as she prefers. They live in Stockport, believe it or not. Helen's mum was a Raiders' fan in the sixties. She was into Dad and his blue eyes.'

'So was half the town, apparently,' Jess said. 'You should come to the house and meet him. Roy's down here, too. You'd better bring your camera though, or your mum might not believe you.'

Helen looked at Jon. 'Would that be okay?'

'Yeah. Come tomorrow. They won't bite. They're just dead ordinary parents, no different to anyone else's.'

'Then I'd love to. How about you, Ronnie?'

Ronnie smiled at Jason, who smiled back. She nodded shyly.

'We'll have one more dance and then chance going,' Nick said. 'Give me the key, Jon. I'll leave the catch on the door for you and Jase. Where's your alarm clock?'

'On the bedside table.' Jon handed the key to Nick. 'Knowing your luck, I bet they're still up singing.'

'Better not be.' Nick rolled his eyes. 'I'm going for a pee, back in a minute.'

Jon followed Nick into the gents'. 'Listen, mate, on second thoughts, I wouldn't risk staying in Jess's room all night. Dad'll kill you if he catches you.'

'Well, he won't catch me, will he?' Nick swayed slightly as he zipped himself up. 'Nobody's gonna stop me being with my girl. Besides, they'll never know. I'll be tucked up with you and Jason long before that lot surfaces.'

Jon stared after him as he swaggered away. It took all his self-control to stop him grabbing Nick and punching him.

* * *

Nick and Jess were back on the dance floor when Jon rejoined Helen. 'Let's dance.' Jon pulled her to her feet and held her close. She was a decent-looking girl and felt good in his arms. She'd take his mind off Nick shagging Jess, for now, anyway.

'Doesn't Jason like dancing?' Helen's voice interrupted his thoughts.

'Not really. He looks happy enough with your mate though.'

'Ronnie's not a dancer either. She's happier just to sit and talk.'

'They should get on well then. Meet me in front of the pier tomorrow night at seven.'

'Okay. I'm so glad we came into Brighton tonight.'

'Yeah, me too.' Jon looked up and caught Jess staring at him. He wondered if Nick had told her what he'd said. He bent to kiss Helen. When he glanced back, Jess was still looking and he saw something in her eyes that he hadn't seen before. She gave a forced smile and turned her attention back to Nick.

* * *

Nick crossed his fingers as he and Jess went indoors. They flicked on the lounge lights and found the room deserted.

'Yes, all quiet on the Western Front.' Nick sniffed the air as Jess hooked her fingers through the belt loops of his jeans and pulled him close. 'They'll be out for the count.' He pointed to an ashtray, where telltale joint ends remained. 'You can't leave 'em alone for five minutes.'

Jess stifled a giggle. 'They're worse than us. Go and find Jon's clock and I'll get into bed, but for God's sake, be quiet.'

They crept upstairs, hardly daring to breathe as they passed their parents' bedroom doors. Jon's warning came back to Nick and he half expected Jess's dad to appear at any moment, demanding to know where he was going. They turned onto the second staircase that led to the attic and Jess slipped into her room. Nick was with her in seconds, clutching the clock. He set it for six.

Jess groaned. 'Why so early?'

'It's either that, or I go back before we fall asleep. I want to hold you all night, so there's no choice.'

Jess peeled off her clothes. She tossed them onto the floor and pranced around, naked.

Nick pulled her onto the single bed. He kissed her while she unbuttoned his shirt. He wriggled out of his clothes and threw them down with hers. Jess ran her fingers through his hair. For the next half-hour, they kissed and explored each other. Nick was desperate to enter her, but held back because she liked lots of foreplay. As Jess moaned that she needed him, a noise outside on the landing made them jump.

'What was that?' Jess whispered.

'Don't know,' Nick began as someone tapped lightly on the door.

'Shit, what if it's Dad?' Jess held her breath, the door opened slightly and Jon popped his head in.

'Nick, your mum's downstairs, making a cup of tea. Didn't you hear her get up?'

'She'll go nuts.' Nick leapt out of bed. Jess tried to pull him back, saying it would be okay if they just kept quiet.

'I'd better go,' he said, throwing her a kiss. 'I'll come back later.' He wrapped a sheet around his middle, tripping over a dangling corner and pushed past Jon as he hurried from the room.

* * *

Jon felt a surge of heat as he looked at Jess; her lips swollen from kissing, face flushed with arousal. He averted his eyes from her naked body as she pulled a sheet over herself.

'Sorry about that,' he began, sitting on the edge of the bed. 'But Sammy saw me and Jason come in and asked where you two were. I told her you left the club before us. I was worried that she might pop her head in our room to say goodnight to Nick.'

'It's okay.' Jess touched his arm and he jerked away as though she'd bitten him. It was all he could do to keep his hands off her. He stood up as she looked at him, a bewildered expression in her eyes.

'Jon, what is it?'

'Nothing. I'm off to bed, see you in the morning.' He pecked her cheek quickly and hurried from the room. Outside on the landing, he leant against the door and sighed. He felt like crying and swallowed hard. He heard footsteps on the stairs and peered over the banister. Sammy was on her way up. She went into her first-floor room and closed the door.

Nick, draped toga-style in the sheet, was seated on the edge of his camp bed and looked up as Jon walked in. 'Is Mum back in bed?'

Jon nodded, unable to speak. The thought of Nick going to Jess again was overwhelming and he felt he might throw up any minute.

'See you in the morning then,' Nick said, slipping out of the room.

Jon sighed. Jason, already asleep, was snoring lightly on his bed in the corner. Jon threw off his clothes, lay down and stared at the ceiling for a long moment. His stomach was in knots. Jess, naked, was far more beautiful than he'd ever imagined.

* * *

As she lay in Nick's arms after making love, Jess's thoughts turned to Jon's earlier unfathomable expression. Why had he snatched his arm away? She also wondered why she'd felt a sudden and unexpected surge of jealousy when she saw him kissing Helen. Then she thought about last night's dream and what it meant. Why did she keep having these dreams? Was it a premonition? At least she wasn't alone tonight if she had the dream again. Nick was snoring softly now, drained after the long day. He usually had bags of stamina, but the late night yesterday had taken its toll, too. Never mind, she thought and cuddled up. They had a whole lifetime of loving ahead. She closed her eyes to picture Nick's handsome face, but it was her brother's intense green eyes that she saw and a strange unsettled feeling came over her.

3

Sammy stared with amusement as Roy and Eddie, sportily attired in navy designer shell suits and top-of-the-range trainers, slipped out through the front door. They wore natty blue sweatbands around their heads, Mark Knopfler style.

She joined Jane, who was in the kitchen, trimming the rind off several rashers of bacon.

'They spent a fortune on those bloomin' shell suits. I suppose I shouldn't mock their efforts to keep fit.'

'They do their best.' Jane grinned and tossed the bacon onto the grill. She wiped her hands on a tea towel and looked around. 'This kitchen could be really fabulous, fitted with new units and a fresh coat of paint.'

Sammy nodded and glanced at the dated olive-green cupboards and orange walls. 'It's huge. I don't recall it being this big when we came down for the Bank Holiday. Then again, the size of the kitchen was the last thing on our minds.'

'Hmm,' Jane said. 'I was more interested in the size of something else.'

Sammy laughed. 'You were always a hussy, Jane Mellor.

But yeah, waxed pine units and buttermilk walls, like yours at home, now *that* would look lovely.'

'Oh, it would,' Jane agreed. 'But I doubt Ed'll change anything. This house holds so many memories for him. He spent every summer down here until his teens. If he can't sell it as it is, then he'll have to think again and get it updated.'

'We should ask one of the antique dealers in The Lanes if they'll make an offer for the furniture,' Sammy said. 'Coffee?' She picked up the kettle as Jane nodded.

'I made a few enquiries yesterday. Ed and Roy can go out later to organise a dealer. Meantime, we can box up the china and coloured glassware.'

'Is there anything *you'd* like to keep, Jane?'

'The framed photos and Ed wants to keep Celia's wartime letters. I might take the brown furry rug from the lounge,' she added, almost as an afterthought.

'Why do you want that moth-eaten old thing? It's seen better days.'

'It's sort of sentimental – to me and Ed.'

Sammy frowned, and then smiled. 'Ah, so that's where the pair of you got up to tricks that afternoon. Roy and I wondered why you never followed us upstairs.'

'That rug could tell you a tale or two. It'll do for the dog to lie on in the back porch if anyone asks why I want it.'

Eddie and Roy arrived back, red-faced and coughing like consumptives. As they collapsed to their knees in the hallway, Sammy showed no sympathy.

'Get up, you pair of posers! It's all very well dolling up in that gear, pretending to keep fit. What you *should* do is give up smoking, or at least try.'

'I want to, love,' Roy gasped. 'But it would kill me.'

'It'll kill you if you don't. Jane's cooking breakfast, so crawl on through to the kitchen.'

'Sit down, you two. Eggs, bacon and sausages okay?' Jane said, grinning as they limped towards her.

'Please, Jane,' Roy said. 'I need coffee first. I'm hopeless until I've had caffeine. My hands shake. Look.' He held them out for her inspection.

'Roy, you're a mess,' Sammy said. 'You've got to start taking more care of yourself or you won't make forty-three.'

'I'm not that bad, I'm not overweight or anything. Perhaps I'll cut down on smoking and drink decaff. But I can only do one thing at a time. I'd be impossible to live with if I did both together.'

Sammy snorted. 'Too right! We'll start with the coffee, see how it goes. We should make the kids get up, Jane, or they'll sleep in all day.'

Jane handed Eddie and Roy their breakfasts. She placed a rack of toast and a pot of honey on the table. 'Right, tuck in while I go and call the lazy foursome.'

She bellowed up the stairs, 'Come on, get up. We've a busy day today.' Running up the first flight, she yelled again: 'Jon, Jess, Nick, Jason, up – now!'

Jon's sleepy voice called back: 'Coming, Mum. We'll get ready first.'

'Don't bother poncing around with your hair, you can do it later.'

'Alright,' was the weary response.

Jane strolled back into the kitchen, sat down and reached for a slice of toast, drizzling it with honey. 'Ed, you and Roy can go out and find a dealer this morning, while Sammy and I make a start on the cupboards.'

'Antique dealer, darling,' Sammy explained to a frowning Roy. She patted his hand. The only dealer Roy was familiar with was his old friend Mac, from whom he purchased his cannabis supplies.

'Ah, of course. Wasn't thinking.'

'Too early for you,' Sammy said.

* * *

Jason sauntered into the kitchen, bare-chested, hair standing on end. 'Hi, folks.' He sniffed the air. 'Smells good. Any left for us?'

'Sit down, son,' his mum ordered. 'Jane's making you some. Any sign of the others?'

'They're getting ready,' he replied, avoiding her gaze. He'd been sent downstairs half-asleep and half-dressed to create a diversion while Jon went to get Nick out of Jess's room.

* * *

Jon tapped on Jess's bedroom door and walked in without waiting to be asked. Jess and Nick were fast asleep on the narrow bed, wrapped in one another's arms. Jon's breath caught in his throat at the sight of her beautiful body. He averted his gaze and threw a sheet over the naked pair. 'Wake up, sis. Shh,' he warned as she opened her eyes. He shook Nick: 'Come on, everyone's downstairs having breakfast.'

'Whatsamatta?' Nick began as Jon clapped a warning hand over his mouth.

'Shurrup! Move it, Jess. Throw some clothes on and go. You can get ready properly later. The alarm mustn't have gone off, or you slept through it.'

Nick sat up, blinking. 'Fuck! Do they know where we are?'

'Not at the moment. You go down first, Jess. We'll follow in a minute.'

'Don't look then,' she said, not quite meeting Jon's eye.

She slid out of bed, pulled on jeans and a T-shirt, fastened her hair into a ponytail and slipped out of the room.

'I don't understand why the alarm didn't go off,' Nick said, grabbing his jeans from the floor.

'Did you pull the button out at the back of the clock?'
'No, don't think I did.' Nick yawned loudly.
'Well, that's why, you dope.'

* * *

'Morning, boys,' Sammy greeted Jon and Nick as they took their places at the table. They thanked Jane, who handed them laden plates.

'Morning, Mum,' Nick said and winked at Jess, who was buttering a slice of toast. 'Sleep well, Jess?' He held her gaze as she licked her buttery fingers.

'Like a baby,' she said with an innocent smile. 'And you?'

Sammy caught the look that passed between the pair. She raised her eyebrows, but remained silent. She'd tackle Nick later, rather than create a scene now. She wasn't stupid, that intimate look was exactly like Roy had given *her* so many times in the past. She excused herself and left the room.

'Any more toast?' Jane asked. 'No? Well, in that case bring your plates over here when you've finished and I'll wash up.'

'That'll be a novelty for you, Mum,' Jess said.

'*You* should offer to wash up,' Eddie suggested, looking closely at Jess, who had never washed a plate in her life, having been brought up in a home with a dishwasher.

'What about my nails? They'll get ruined.'

'Rubber gloves, Jess dear.' Jane flapped them at her.

'Ugh, God! They'll make my hands smell.' Jess shuddered, recoiling in disgust from the bright yellow rubber.

'It's quicker if I do it myself,' Jane said. 'At least they'll be done properly. We'll end up with salmonella or something if Jess does them. You can get some groceries from the supermarket later. I'll write you a list,' she said to Jess.

'Okay, I'll get ready then. Bagsy the bathroom first.'

'Don't take all morning, I want to wash my hair,' Nick said.

'Me too,' Jason echoed.

Sammy, who had just come back downstairs, said, 'When you've finished your coffee, Nick, go up to my room.'

'Why?' He stared at his mother, wide-eyed.

'You know very well why.' She'd taken a look in the boys' room and found Nick's sleeping bag still rolled up on his camp bed, as she'd suspected it would be. A further investigation had revealed his shoes, socks and boxer shorts on Jess's bedroom floor.

'What's going on, Sam?' Roy raised a questioning eyebrow.

'Nothing I can't handle.'

'Fair enough. Let's take our coffee into the lounge, Ed.'

* * *

As they went upstairs, Nick whispered to Jess, 'Mum's sussed where I spent the night.'

'Oh God!' Jess chewed her lip. 'Well, if that's the case we'll just have to brazen it out if she says anything.'

'Oh, she'll *say* something,' Nick said. 'Making love isn't a hangable offence though, is it?'

'Who knows?' Jess shrugged and squeezed his hand. 'Don't worry, we'll be fine.'

* * *

'What is it?' Jane gazed at Sammy over the pile of washing-up. 'Don't tell me, I can guess. Well, it's not as if it's a casual fling. At the end of the day, *we* were all guilty of the same crime.'

Sammy pursed her lips. 'Yes, but not in front of our parents, so to speak. We wouldn't have dared. We'll talk it over with Roy and Ed. Nick can stew for a while. It serves him right for being so bloody sneaky right under our noses.'

'What's up?' Roy looked up as Sammy and Jane strolled into the lounge and sat down on the sofa.

'I found Nick's clothes in Jess's room,' Sammy said. 'He spent the night with her.'

'Not necessarily.' Roy lit his third cigarette since breakfast. 'Granted, he was probably in with her earlier. Maybe he forgot to pick them up before he left.'

'He *did* spend the night with Jess. His sleeping bag's still rolled up on the camp bed. Both you and I know he isn't that tidy he would have rolled it up as soon as he got out of it. I warned him about behaving before we left home. He never listens to a word I say.'

'Oh, come on, Sam,' Roy said. 'You can't treat him like a child. They're past the age of consent, they know what they're doing.'

'Age has nothing to do with it. It's the sneaking about that annoys me. Winking at Jess over breakfast, asking her if she'd slept well, knowing full well how she'd slept, if indeed she slept at all. Randy little git! He must think we're all stupid.'

Jane and Eddie laughed at Sammy's indignant expression.

'You sound almost jealous, Sam,' Eddie said. 'I'll call them down, we'll talk to them. They don't need to sneak about. Why are we making a mountain out of a molehill?'

'You don't *mind* them sharing a room?' Sammy asked.

'*I* don't mind,' Jane said. '*You* obviously don't have a problem with it, Ed?'

'Have you forgotten what it was like to be young, Sam?' he said. 'At least we know who she's with and where he comes from. But we'll have a bit of fun, make 'em sweat first.' He shouted up the stairs. 'Jess, Nick, get your arses down here, now.'

Two anxious faces peered over the banister rail.

'Coming.' Jess stuck her chin out with determination.

* * *

As she and Nick walked into the lounge her dad stared so disapprovingly that Jess's heart sank to her boots and she grabbed Nick's hand. 'You wanted to speak to us, Dad?'

'Sit down, Jess. You, too, Nick, over there.' He pointed to chairs on opposite sides of the room.

'Where did you sleep last night, Nick?' Eddie came straight to the point.

'Jess's room,' Nick said, lowering his gaze.

'And whose idea was that?'

'Mine,' he said. 'I borrowed Jon's alarm clock. It was supposed to go off at six but it didn't.'

'So, that was the plan, was it?' Roy said. 'You were going to sneak back to your room and no one would have been any the wiser?'

'Yes, Dad. I'm sorry, it won't happen again,' Nick muttered, staring down at his feet.

'Too bloody right it won't. You're a guest in this house; you don't do as you please. Remember what your mother told you the other night?'

'Yes, Dad, I'm sorry, Mum.' Nick hung his head.

'And you, young lady, what have *you* got to say for yourself?' Eddie switched his gaze to Jess.

She stared defiantly back at him, arms folded. 'You're a hypocrite, Dad.'

'Jess! Don't you dare speak to your father like that.'

'Well, it's true, Mum, he is,' Jess said. 'You *all* are. It's one set of rules for you and another for us. At least Nick and I have got *some* morals, for what they're worth. Not like you lot!'

'Jess, that's quite enough,' her mum said. 'Now you apologise at once.'

But Jess was on her high horse and hadn't finished. '*I* won't get pregnant until I want to. I know for a fact that Dad knocked

Angie up before he married her, and you, too, Mum. Nick was on the way before Roy married Sammy. What sort of an example is *that* to set your kids?' She jumped up and stormed out of the room, slamming the front door behind her.

'Go after her, Ed,' Jane urged. 'You can't let her go like that.'

He flopped down on the sofa and shook his head. 'No, she won't want me. You go, Nick, bring her back.'

Nick, white-faced, stood up and left the room.

* * *

Eddie turned to Jane, who had an expression of shock on her face. 'I didn't realise she had such a low opinion of us,' he said. 'She makes it sound like we've the morals of alley cats. My first marriage has never been discussed with the kids, apart from telling Jon about his mum, so how the hell did she know that Angie was pregnant?'

'Maybe she and Jon talk about these things between themselves,' Jane said. 'Let's face it, not many get married from choice at eighteen. They've worked it out, they're not daft.'

Sammy sighed. 'What do we say to them now, when Nick finds her, I mean?'

Roy shrugged. 'I don't know. I wasn't expecting her to turn the tables on *us*. She's a feisty little piece.'

'She's never spoken to me like that before,' Eddie said. In spite of her wayward ways, his precious daughter meant the world to him. He hated falling out with her over anything. With shaking hands, he lit a cigarette and drew on it as Jon and Jason strolled into the lounge.

'What was all that shouting about?' Jason asked.

'You know damn well what it was, Jason. You both knew Nick was in Jess's room, so don't come the innocent with me,' Roy said.

'Don't take it out on Jason,' Sammy said. 'He might not have been aware what they were up to.'

Roy raised his eyebrows. 'For fuck's sake, Sammy, of course he knew.'

'Don't swear in front of him, either,' Sammy snapped back.

Eddie diffused the situation by suggesting Jason and Jon go and do the grocery shopping.

Jon nodded. 'Mum, I've invited a couple of girls over for dinner. We met them last night. They're from Stockport. I hope it's alright in view of what's happened just now?'

'Okay, Jon. Things should have quietened down by this evening. We'll make a curry or something.'

'Thanks, Mum.' Jon and Jason hurried off with the shopping list.

* * *

Jess ran up the road onto Marine Parade and down the steps to the beach. The pebbles crunched beneath her Doc Martens and her freshly washed hair flapped around her face. Tears ran unchecked down her cheeks. She walked towards the sea, sat down and watched the waves lapping rhythmically onto the pebbles. She felt terrible, wishing desperately that she hadn't said those things to her dad. He'd looked so hurt and hadn't deserved any of it. He doted on her and had given her everything she'd ever asked for, and Jess knew that she'd always asked for a lot more than her fair share.

Back there she'd felt anger at the unfairness of it all. Why couldn't their parents see how much she and Nick meant to one another? It's not as if they needed permission to sleep together – after all, they were old enough and Mum and Dad knew she was on the pill. But it would be nice to have their approval or blessing, or something like that anyway. Not to be reprimanded like a naughty kid caught stealing sweets in Woolies.

***

Nick walked along the promenade, scanning the beach for a sign of Jess. He spotted her slim figure as she walked along the sea edge and then dropped down onto the pebbles, shoulders hunched. She was crying; he recognised the stance. He ran down the nearest steps, sprinting across the beach to her side. He took her in his arms and hugged her.

'Come on, Jess, don't cry, please. One more month and we'll get our own place, I promise. Even if we have to eat bread and water all week. We can live on our love, can't we?'

She smiled through her tears. 'I love you, Nick Cantello. Don't ever leave me.'

'Never, Jessie-Babes. We'll be together forever, you and I.' He wiped away her tears with the sleeve of his shirt. 'Let's go back. Your dad's very upset, you owe him a big apology.'

She nodded. 'I do.'

They strolled hand in hand back to Dorset Gardens, where their mums were at the kitchen table, sorting through boxes of letters and photographs. They looked up and smiled reassuringly as Nick and Jess walked in.

Their dads were still sitting on the sofa in the lounge.

'Dad, I'm so sorry.' Jess knelt in front of him and wound her arms around his neck. She kissed him on the cheek.

He pulled her close and hugged her tightly. 'I'm sorry too, Jess. I should have spoken to you privately. Am I forgiven?'

'Of course you are. I shouldn't have said what I did about Angie and Mum, and Roy and Sammy, it was very wrong of me. You've always done your best for us, whatever the circumstances.'

'Well, maybe I deserved it, for the way I handled the situation.' He wiped her eyes and tilted her chin, a thing he'd done many times when she was younger and had run to him crying for comfort. 'Anyway, perhaps we were being a bit old-fashioned, so we've had a chat and made a decision. You and Nick have our permission to share your room. We have no problem with it and that includes your mothers.'

Jess was overwhelmed. She stood up and went to stand beside Nick, who put his arm around her shoulders. He looked towards their respective fathers.

'Thank you, Eddie, and you too, Dad.'

'Thank you, Dad.' Jess smiled and then walked across the room and kissed Roy, who gave her a reassuring hug.

'We all remember what it was like to be young, honestly. Hell, we still are, aren't we?' Roy said.

Jess grinned up at him through her tears. Uncle Roy could always cheer her up.

'Go and help Mum sort out the kitchen cupboards. Me and Roy are going out in a minute to see if we can find a furniture dealer. Nick can help Jon and Jason in the cellars.'

'Where *are* Jon and Jason?' Jess looked around.

'Shopping for groceries,' Jane said as she walked into the lounge. 'All sorted?'

Eddie nodded. 'Least said soonest mended.'

'Good.' She held out her arms to Jess, who moved into them.

'Thanks for being so understanding, Mum.'

'I almost started World War Three with Gran the day I asked permission to move in with your dad. It was "Not until you're married, Jane. I don't wish to discuss it any further!"'

They all laughed at Jane's perfect imitation of her mother.

4

Jane peered through a cloud of steam as she drained a large pan of rice. 'What did you say, Ed?'

'Have we enough wine?'

'Get a couple more bottles of white. We need poppadums and mango chutney, too. The boys forgot them this morning.'

Eddie left the house with Jon and Jason, who were meeting up with Helen and Ronnie.

Sammy picked up a handful of cutlery. 'Shall I set the big table in the dining room? There won't be enough space in the kitchen for us all.'

'Please, Sam.' Jane followed Sammy into the high-ceilinged room, with its ornate cornice and cast-iron fireplace. 'It's beautiful in here and we never use it.'

A large shelving unit, filled with photographs and ornaments, spanned the back wall. Jane picked up a pretty silver frame and stared at the photo of Eddie, Angie and Jon taken on Jon's christening day. She showed it to Sammy.

'Put it away. Give it to Jon when you get home,' Sammy advised.

Jane nodded. There'd been no love lost between her friend

and Angie, for try as she might, Sammy had never got on with Eddie's late ex. Jane slipped the frame into a drawer. She couldn't face answering any awkward questions that the photograph might prompt, especially with strangers coming for dinner.

Eddie arrived back with the supplies as Jon and Jason strolled in with Helen and Ronnie and introduced them.

'Nice to meet you, girls,' Sammy said. 'Take them through to the lounge and get them something to drink, Jon.'

'Coke okay for you both?' Jon asked.

They nodded and followed Jason and Eddie.

* * *

'Sit down, girls.' Eddie gestured to the sofa.

Helen smiled at her mother's former teenage heartthrob and said, 'I've heard so much about you. I feel I know you already.'

'Is that right?' Eddie grinned.

'So, your mum was a Raiders' fan?' Roy said as Jon handed out drinks.

'Yeah.' Helen nodded. 'A *big* fan. She's kept all sorts of press cuttings and pictures. She's also got a lock of Eddie's hair that her friend cut while his back was turned.'

'Was your mum one of the girls who hung around the gates of Hanover's Lodge?' Jane asked.

Helen laughed. 'She was.'

'Are we eating yet?' Eddie interrupted. 'Me and Roy are starving.'

Jane rolled her eyes. 'You two have got hollow legs! Go through to the dining room, everything's ready. Jon, shout Nick and Jess, please.'

Jon bawled up the stairs and Jess and Nick, faces flushed, came running down.

'Hi again,' Jess said, greeting the visitors with a smile. Helen and Ronnie smiled back and took their places at the table.

'Wine?' Roy held the bottle over Helen's glass.

'Just a drop, thanks.'

'Ronnie?' He waved the bottle in her direction. She nodded.

Sammy and Jane carried in two huge bowls of chicken curry and rice.

'Get stuck in,' Sammy ordered. 'Guests first,' she said as Roy's face lit up and he reached for the serving spoon. 'He's no manners,' she told Helen and Ronnie, who giggled, and the ice was broken.

'Are you two at college?' Jane asked the girls, pushing the rice bowl towards them.

'Still at school,' Helen replied, digging in. 'We're doing GCSEs. I start college in September.'

'And what about you, Ronnie, any plans?' Sammy asked.

'I'm hoping to do the NNEB,' she replied, picking up a poppadum.

'What's that when it's at home?' Jess asked, frowning.

'A Nursery Nursing course,' Ronnie said. 'I love kids.'

'God, why would you want to work with ankle biters?' Jess grimaced. 'I could think of better things to do with my life!'

'Jess, that's not very polite,' Jane said. 'At least Ronnie knows what she wants to do. It's time you thought—'

'Yeah, yeah, I know.' Jess screwed up her face. 'I'll do something about it when we get home.'

'You can help me and Sammy with our business,' Jane said, and helped herself to rice. 'Damn, I didn't put the mango chutney out. Nip and get it for me, Jon. Put it in a small dish and bring some teaspoons, too.'

Jon left the room as Jason turned to Helen: 'Which college have you applied to?'

'Hollings, in Manchester. I'd like to study dress design.'

'I go to Hollings – well, The Toast Rack as we call it,' Jason said. 'I'm doing art and design, but Mum did dress design there in the sixties, didn't you, Mum?'

'I did,' Sammy replied, 'for my sins. It's a good college – I met the nicest people. You get to go to all the fashion shows. I could have gone to Paris with my course, but Mum couldn't afford it at the time. Still, I've been plenty of times since.'

'Have you ever been to Paris, Jason?' Helen asked as Jon returned with the bowl of chutney and sat down next to Jess.

'Yeah, but not with college,' Jason replied. 'We go to France a lot because we have a lovely house there and occasionally we drive across to Paris for a few days so Mum can indulge herself.'

'Oh, it's my dream to go to a Paris fashion show,' Helen said.

'You met your best mate at The Toast Rack, didn't you, Jase?' Nick said with a hint of sarcasm in his voice.

Jason blushed and nodded. 'Yes, I met Jules there,' he told Helen. 'He's on the same course as me, but he's *really* talented. You should see the bronze sculpture he did last term. It's amazing.'

'Sounds impressive,' Helen said. 'You'll have to introduce me to him when I start my course.'

'Oh, you wouldn't be interested in Jules,' Nick said. 'Or should I rephrase that? Jules wouldn't be interested in *you*. He bats for the other side.'

'He does not.' Jason punched Nick on the arm. 'You've only met him once, so how would *you* know?'

'Nick, that's enough,' Sammy said. 'Behave yourself in front of our guests.'

* * *

Jon frowned at the exchange between the brothers. Why did Nick take such delight in having a go about Jules, knowing full well how it riled Jason? Jess tapped him on the arm.

'Pass me the chutney, bruv.'

'Certainly, sis.' He picked up the bowl and dug a spoon in. 'Where do you want it?' He grinned as she opened her mouth and he tipped a spoonful in, watching Nick's face closely. Jess licked the spoon clean while he held on to it. At least it had stopped Nick goading Jason. Two can play the teasing game. He looked around the table. Mum and Sammy were chatting to Helen and Ronnie about Paris, Dad and Roy were talking music. Jason was toying with his meal.

'More chutney, Jess,' Jon said after a while. She nodded and he popped another spoonful into her mouth.

Nick got up from his chair and pushed it back so hard, it hit the wall unit. Everyone jumped as he stormed from the room.

'What the hell's wrong with *him?*' Roy said as the door slammed shut.

'Don't know.' Jon winked at Jess, who blushed slightly. 'You'd better go after him. Don't think he liked me spoon-feeding you,' he whispered.

She got to her feet. 'I'll sort him out.'

Helen and Ronnie offered to wash up as Jess left the room. They carried the plates and dishes to the kitchen with Jane and Sammy.

'Fancy a bit of a jam?' Roy suggested. He and Eddie made their way into the lounge and Roy tuned up the guitars. Jason set up his keyboard and Jon grabbed a set of tom-toms.

'We'll run through the new songs,' Roy said. 'Somebody give Nick and Jess a shout.'

* * *

Nick lay on the bed in Jess's room, arms behind his head. He felt bad for teasing Jason –he was always touchy where Jules was concerned. He was well pissed off with Jon though. Spoon-feeding Jess the chutney like that. Why couldn't he have just lobbed it onto her plate? But it was her fault for opening her mouth. Jon was always hugging and teasing her, but then he was her brother and maybe that's what brothers did. But how the hell would *he* know? He hadn't got a sister and you don't hug brothers like that, or at least he didn't hug Jason, except on his birthday, but it was more like a pat on the shoulder than a hug.

The door opened and Jess slid into the room. 'There you are. Why did you dash off like that?'

He shrugged. 'Jon was being touchy-feely with you again. I don't like it.'

'Don't be so daft.' She sat on the bed and stroked his cheek. 'He was just messing, that's all. And you weren't very nice to Jason. You should apologise. Come on, sit up, give me a kiss and then we'll go downstairs. Dad's shouting us. They want to play some songs for Helen and Ronnie.'

Nick sat up and took her in his arms. He kissed her long and hard. 'I love you,' he said.

'Love you too.' She pulled him to his feet. 'Better now?'

He nodded and followed her out of the room.

* * *

Jess picked up her bass, Eddie handed Nick his Stratocaster guitar and the house was soon filled with music.

The Zoo gave their first rendition of the, as yet untitled, new songs, Nick and Jess's voices blending as perfectly as their respective fathers did.

'Any requests?' Eddie asked as the evening wore on.

'"My Special Girl", please, Dad,' Jess suggested.

'Okay, why not? Ready, Roy?'

Jane and Sammy looked at one another. The song always transported them back to the long-ago night when they'd first heard it. It still had the power to bring a lump to their throats. Written by Eddie and Roy while on the road touring, the ballad was dedicated to their girls and was The Raiders' first big hit.

Helen smiled. 'I've heard Mum play the record so many times, I know every note. It was lovely, thank you so much.'

After Helen had taken photographs of everyone for her mum, Jon ordered a taxi to take the girls back to Rottingdean and Roy handed over money for the fare. Jon promised to call Helen the following day and kissed her goodnight.

Jason shyly hugged Ronnie, who grabbed the opportunity to peck his cheek. He smiled and said he'd talk to her when Jon called Helen.

'What lovely girls,' Sammy said, closing the front door after waving the taxi off.

'They were.' Jane flopped down on the rug in front of the gas fire. 'I've a feeling we'll be seeing a lot more of them.'

'I'm off to bed.' Jon yawned. 'I'm shattered after that cellar clearing. See you in the morning. G'night, all.'

'Night, son,' Eddie said as Jane blew Jon a kiss.

Jason stood up. 'I'm off as well. See y'all.'

'Night, boys,' Sammy and Roy chorused.

Nick and Jess looked at each another and at their respective parents.

'Err, anyone mind if *we* go up?' Nick asked.

'Of course not,' Jane said. 'See you in the morning,' she added as they hurried out of the room.

'Yes, g'night everybody,' Jess called over her shoulder.

'Shall *we* hit the sack?' Roy pulled Sammy to her feet.

'What about you, Jane?' Eddie sat down beside her on the rug and put his arms around her.

'Let's stay down here for a while.'

'For old times' sake?'

She nodded, eyes sparkling as she kissed him.

'What am I missing?' Roy looked puzzled.

'Tell you upstairs,' Sammy said. 'Night, you two, have fun.

Come on, you.' She pushed Roy outside, turned off the main lights, leaving the room romantically bathed in the soft glow from the table lamps, and quietly closed the door.

* * *

Jane smiled at Eddie, gazing deep into his eyes. 'I love you more today than I ever did, if that's possible.'

'And I love you, too,' he said, unbuttoning her top.

'Do you think the kids will come back down?' She yanked his T-shirt off and ran her hands over his chest.

'I doubt it. Jon and Jason were knackered and Jess and Nick have other things in mind.' He pulled the cushions off the sofa, threw them onto the rug and lowered her down.

She cocked an ear. 'They're still using the bathroom. I can hear water running.'

Footsteps sounded overhead, doors slamming, then silence.

Eddie smiled. 'Do you think that's it?' He kissed her deeply.

'What was that?' She sat upright at the sound of feet on the stairs and pulled her top back on.

Eddie rolled his eyes as Roy called out, 'Only me. Sammy's forgotten her glass of water.'

Jane stifled a giggle. 'No peace for the wicked.'

They heard Roy running back up the stairs. Eddie pulled her back into his arms.

She unzipped his jeans and pushed them down. There came another bang from upstairs.

'For fuck's sake,' Eddie said at the sound of peeing, a loud fart and then another door shutting.

'Roy,' they said, laughing together.

'Push the sofa across the door, just in case,' Jane suggested. 'Then I can relax properly.'

He leapt up and shoved the heavy sofa across the room. 'That okay for you?' He dropped back down beside her. 'Now get your clothes off, woman.' He gazed at her in the light from the flickering gas fire. 'You're still so beautiful,' he whispered and bent to kiss her again. 'It seems only yesterday that we made love on this very rug. I can even remember the red top you were wearing, with those little buttons all down the front.'

She smiled. 'You used to like me wearing that top, if I remember rightly.'

'Because it was easy to take off,' he teased, raining kisses down her front. He moved slowly down her body, kissing and stroking.

In all the years they'd been together he'd never failed to please and tonight was no exception. Jane felt waves of orgasmic pleasure and cried his name. His breathing deepened as his pace quickened and, as always, he told her he loved her as he came. He collapsed on top and nuzzled her neck.

'We've still got it, babe,' he whispered, 'you and I, and it just gets better.'

She smiled, tears filling her eyes.

'What's the matter?' He touched her wet cheek.

'I just love you so much, that's all.'

'Women!' he said. 'Especially mine.'

* * *

As the week progressed, the house was slowly emptied of its contents. A dealer offered Eddie a job-lot price for the bigger items. Another dealer, who dealt solely in bric-a-brac and smaller pieces of furniture, was happy to take the rest.

The remainder of Aunt Celia's belongings was packed into the cars. A large box of newspaper cuttings and records of The Raiders that Celia had collected was handed to Jess. Jane had her own collection of Raiders' memorabilia at home.

Helen and Ronnie popped in early morning to say goodbye

on their way to the station and Jon told Helen he would call her that evening.

'Maybe we could meet up somewhere later, depending on what time we get home,' he suggested.

'That would be lovely. I'll look forward to it.' Helen kissed him goodbye and he stood on the doorstep waving until she and Ronnie turned the corner.

Eddie watched as a For Sale board was erected in the front garden. He put his arm around Jane and gave her a hug. 'End of an era,' he said. 'I feel quite sad really. I'll give it six months; if there's no interest, I'll have a rethink about what to do. Maybe we could get it refurbished and keep it. After all, it's a good investment.'

Jane nodded. 'Right, have we got everything?' She took a last look around.

'Well, if we haven't, it'll have to stay down here, the Jeep's loaded to the gills.'

'Oh, Jess, grab that black bin bag over there,' Jane said. 'I almost forgot it.'

Jess picked up the bag, peered inside and wrinkled her nose. 'This should have gone to the tip with the rest of the rubbish.'

'Your mother wants to keep it,' Eddie said.

'God, why? It's minging!'

'It's sentimental to her, that's why.'

'Yuck! How the hell can you get sentimental over a smelly old rug?'

'It's our love rug,' he teased, looking at Jane's blushing face.

'Love rug? Oh... I see. Was that during the riots? Well, if you were stuck indoors, I suppose you had to have *something* to do. I'll sling it in the back of the Jeep then, shall I?'

'If you can find the room. I'll give it to the dog to lie on in the porch,' Jane said.

'Hey, Jane, you can always bring it out and put it in front of your own fireplace when you fancy a session,' Roy teased.

'Jane's already got a nice furry rug in front of her fire, Dad,' Nick smirked, winking at Jess. 'Isn't that right, Jess?'

'Nick, stop giving our secrets away,' Jess said as her dad laughed.

'Come on, let's go home before this conversation takes a turn for the downright smutty,' he said. 'Meet you at Watford Gap for coffee. Drive carefully and thanks very much for all your help.'

'It's been fun, roughing it for a while without any mod cons,' Sammy said.

'And *I've* met Helen, who's a bit of alright if you ask me,' Jon said with a lustful grin.

'And Jason's met Ronnie,' Sammy said, squeezing his arm.

'Mum, for God's sake, we're just friends. Don't go reading anything into it,' Jason said. 'Anyway, she's not my type.'

'And what exactly *is* your type, Jase?' Nick teased. 'You've never been out with any birds. So how do you know what type yours is if you don't try a few for size?'

'Leave me alone,' Jason snapped and climbed into the back of the BMW.

'Oooh, sorry for breathing,' Nick retorted as Sammy raised her eyebrows. 'Trouble with you, Jase, is that you spend far too much time with that poncey Jules instead of going on the pull.'

'That's enough, Nick. Jules is a nice boy and he's a good friend to Jason,' Sammy said. 'Now get in the car and leave him alone.'

'You started it, Sam, by mentioning Ronnie,' Roy said. 'You know how bloody touchy Jason is about girls. Right, let's get a move on, or we'll never get home today.'

5

'Dominic, take Lennon down the lane, there's a good lad,' Enid called up the stairs.

'Do I have to?' Dominic called back. 'I want to finish reading my book before it gets dark.' Maurice Sendak's monsters were scary enough in the daylight; Dominic wouldn't dare read about them at bedtime. 'Why can't Katie take him?' he said, running downstairs. 'I did it this morning.'

'Katie's not here, she's playing at Lucy's. Come on, love, your mum and dad will be home soon. I haven't time to take him myself. I need to nip across to our house to switch the heating on and your grandpa's still bowling with Tom.'

Dominic sighed, called Lennon to heel and stomped out of the kitchen. Enid smiled and went back to putting the finishing touches to the evening meal. She was a plain cook, but justifiably proud of the chicken casserole simmering in the oven.

She checked her watch, placed a large pan of broccoli on the hob and wiped her hands on her apron. Ten minutes at the most. Eddie didn't like his veg mushy, preferring it something foreign sounding – al dente, was it?

She bent to lift a latticed-topped pie from the oven. It was done to perfection – golden brown on top, the delicate fragrance of cinnamon blending with the apples. She ran her hand across her face. That oven was bloomin' hot. A newspaper lay on the table and she picked it up and fanned herself.

Dominic and Lennon trailed back into the kitchen. Enid gave the young lad a glass of orange juice and a chocolate biscuit.

'Did you enjoy the walk after all that moaning?'

'Yeah. I was looking for conkers and acorns.' He reached for a second biscuit. 'But I couldn't find any.'

'Just the one,' she said, gently pushing his hand away. 'We don't want to spoil your dinner. And it's the wrong time of year for conkers and acorns, love. You'll have to wait until autumn.' She gave Lennon a Bonio biscuit and absent-mindedly patted his head. 'You're a bit grubby, Dom. Wash your hands and face when you've finished your snack. They won't be long now. Your mum said about two hours when she phoned from the services.'

'Is Katie coming back for dinner, Gran?'

'No, Lucy's mum will bring her home later. Ah, here's Grandpa.'

Ben strolled into the kitchen and dropped his bowling bag in the middle of the floor. He tweaked Dominic's ear and planted a kiss on Enid's cheek. 'Hello, love. Are they not back?'

'No, but they won't be long. Get yourself washed and changed and then we'll all eat together here. I've cooked enough to feed an army, so I hope they're hungry. Take your bowling balls with you before somebody trips over them. Dominic, you can help me set the table.'

* * *

Ben went next door to his barn conversion bungalow, Lennon on his heels. Eddie and Jane had presented him and Enid with the keys on its completion and they'd moved in five years ago.

He picked up a stick and chucked it for the dog. Lennon carried the muddy stick inside and dropped it on the kitchen floor.

'You'll get me shot if Enid sees that on her clean tiles,' Ben said. 'Now stay there while I get myself ready.' Lennon settled down on an old blanket Enid kept for him by the wood-burning stove and placed his head on his paws. He closed his eyes and began to snore gently.

Ben took a quick shower, pulled on a clean shirt and comfy slacks. He lit a cigarette and stood out on the patio at the back of the bungalow, enjoying the cool air. He wasn't allowed to smoke indoors any more. Enid thought she was the bee's knees with her new home and after years of living on a noisy estate, he was inclined to agree. Thanks to his son-in-law's generosity, he was also enjoying the luxury of early retirement.

Ben stubbed his cigarette out on the wall, put the butt in the dustbin and went back inside. 'Come on, Lennon, lad, let's go and get some grub.' The dog wagged his tail, jumped up, retrieved his stick and followed Ben across the communal gardens.

'Any beer in that fridge?' Ben asked as he walked into the kitchen. It was thirsty work playing bowls and all he'd had this afternoon was a cup of tea. Right now, he could murder a pint or two down the local, but he wouldn't dare suggest it without Eddie being around to back him up.

Enid had worked hard in the kitchen all afternoon and she'd no doubt begrudge him going alone to the pub. If he wasn't careful, she'd be finding him jobs to do when all he wanted was to relax.

'Have you ever known Ed not have beer in his fridge?' Enid said, draining broccoli over the sink. She tipped it into a serving dish and popped it in the oven.

'Don't suppose I have.' Ben scratched his chin.

'Well then, why ask daft questions?'

He winked at Dominic, who was grinning behind Gran's

back, and helped himself to a can. 'Why can't women answer a question with just a simple yes or no, Dom? It would make life much easier.'

Lennon whimpered and wagged his tail. 'Hey up, old lad, what's the matter?' Ben patted the dog's head and scratched his silky ears. Lennon ran to the door, barking excitedly. 'Are they here? Let him out, Dom.'

There wasn't a car in sight and indeed it was several minutes before the Jeep bumped up the private lane. But Lennon, with his doggy sixth sense, stood quivering on the doorstep: his beloved mistress was on her way home.

* * *

Eddie leapt from the Jeep to help Jane down. The dog shot towards them, barking and wagging his tail frantically, knocking him sideways.

'Christ, Lennon, be careful!' Eddie picked himself up from the floor. He brushed grass and twigs from his jeans, laughing at the over-excited animal. Mental as anything, he thought. Lennon only had eyes for Jane; his devotion, total. Even Dominic couldn't get a look in as his mum fussed over her pet, sending him crazy.

Lennon had been Eddie's last-year-but-one's birthday gift for Jane. She'd longed for a dog, dropping hints as her birthday approached. The look on her face, when he placed the cream, eight-week-old puppy in her arms, was one he would treasure always. Tears had tumbled down her cheeks and she announced she'd name him in memory of John Lennon.

She told Eddie he was the best present ever and had come at just the right time. She was feeling broody again. He'd smiled, offering up a silent prayer of thanks for small puppies and vasectomies!

'Have you missed Mummy, sweetheart?' Jane cooed. 'Oh, I've missed you too, my darling boy.'

Jess clambered out of the Jeep, eyebrows raised in amusement at the scene. 'Show him what you've brought him then.' She tossed the black bin liner onto the grass.

'What is it?' Dominic asked excitedly. 'Is it a very big present?'

'It's nothing really, Dom. Just something for him to lie on in the porch.' Jane emptied the rug out and gave it a shake. The brown furry pile was so moth-eaten, the shaking made little difference, but Lennon dragged the rug from her hands and carried it off across the lawn. He dropped it under a tree, lay down with a sigh and placed his head on his front paws, his expression one of bliss.

Eddie nudged Jane and whispered, 'He must be able to smell your body scent from the other night. No wonder he looks so contented.'

'Ed!' She blushed as her mother called from the doorstep.

'Hurry up and come indoors. Dinner's ready and waiting.'

'Won't be a minute, Mum,' Jane called back.

'Why did you bring Lennon an old rug, Mum?' Dominic asked. 'He's got blankets in his basket to lie on.'

'Ah, but, Dom, it's not just any old rug, is it, Mum?' Jess teased and gave her little brother a hug.

Eddie dug her playfully in the ribs before she could say anything else. 'Stop it, you, or I won't give you your inheritance.'

'You'd better,' Jess said, grinning. He'd told her yesterday that she and Jon were each to have ten thousand pounds from Aunt Celia's estate. Katie and Dominic would receive the same amount, to be held in trust until they were eighteen. Jess pulled her holdall from the back of the Jeep, calling over her shoulder as she went indoors, 'You and Jon can unload the instruments and amps, Dad.'

'Oh, thanks very much, Jess. Come on, Jon. Let's get this lot up to the music room and then we can relax after dinner. I won't feel like carting amps around if Gran's done one of her specials.'

* * *

Jess sat at her dressing table and brushed her hair, deep in thought. On the journey home, she'd told Mum and Dad that she and Nick were planning to live together when she got her money. They'd said that was fine, as long as it was okay with Roy and Sammy. Nick was supposed to be telling them on the way home, which was why she and Nick had travelled separately. Jon had been a bit cool with her after Mum and Dad had given their permission. He'd almost ignored her when they'd stopped at the services and had been really snappy with Nick. It bothered her. She and her brother had always been close, but since she'd been dating Nick, he'd been really odd. He'd never objected to any of her earlier boyfriends and Nick was his best mate, so she didn't understand why he wasn't thrilled for them.

* * *

Jon carried the largest of the amps upstairs to the music room. He'd been in a sunny mood for most of the day, which had as much to do with meeting Helen as receiving his inheritance. There'd been many girlfriends in the past, but never anything serious. Spending time with Helen this week had taken his mind off Jess, that is, until Jess told Mum and Dad that she and Nick were planning on moving in together and a rush of jealousy had overwhelmed him, yet again. He sensed he'd upset Jess by turning his back on her for most of the journey home.

'Oh well,' Jon muttered as he nipped back downstairs for his holdall. 'What Jess wants, Jess will get.' He dashed back upstairs, dropped the bag on the bedroom floor and kicked the door shut. Delving into the front pocket of the bag, he pulled out a silver frame and stared at the photograph, taken at his christening. Mum had given him the photo this morning, urging him to keep it out of Dad's sight.

He studied the pretty girl, his birth mother, who'd died so young. She was smiling proudly at the tiny baby in her arms. Even Dad, who had his arm draped around her shoulders, appeared to be smiling. Alright, it was a bit forced, but a smile, nonetheless.

'What on earth did you do that makes him hate you so much, he won't even talk about you?' he muttered. He slipped the photograph into the bedside drawers. He'd show it to Jess later, see if she had any thoughts on the subject.

* * *

Jane breathed in the delicious culinary smells in the warm kitchen. Dominic hopped from foot to foot in front of her and she bent to give him a hug. 'There we are, now I can get near you with Lennon out of the way.'

'Have you brought *me* a present?' he asked hopefully.

'Of course I have, sunshine.' She handed him a paper bag.

He looked inside and grinned. 'A boat, oh thanks, Mum.'

Jane kissed him. She'd rushed out that morning to look for gifts for him and Katie, but a collection of seaside bits and pieces was all she'd had time to grab. The Brighton rock would no doubt ruin their teeth and Lennon would probably pop the beach balls within the day, but Dominic could sail the little wooden yacht in his bath.

* * *

'Let's get cracking on that dinner.' Eddie strolled into the kitchen, smacking his lips. 'I'm starving. Have you made us one of your specials, Enid?'

'One of your favourites, Ed,' she replied, squeezing his arm.

Eddie smiled. Enid's cooking evoked memories of his mother's kitchen and his happy childhood, so whatever she'd made would be a treat. Whenever she baked a steak and kidney pie for Ben, she always made one for him, too. Her pastry was light as a feather and melted in the mouth, with gravy so rich, you could stand your fork up in it – bliss. Although he prided himself on being a reasonable cook, he hadn't mastered the art of pastry making and Jane had long given up trying. But between his mother-in-law and himself, he was well fed and contented with his lot.

* * *

'This looks and smells wonderful.' Eddie helped himself to vegetables.

'Have you decided what to do with Celia's place, Ed?' Ben asked, pouring wine for everyone.

'We've emptied it and it's up for sale. If it doesn't go, I'll update it and do holiday lets. The estate agent said the market's slow, so we'll have to wait and see what happens.'

'Did anyone ring while we were away, Mum?' Jane asked.

'There's a list of callers by the phone. I didn't give out Celia's number – I assumed you wouldn't want to be bothered unless it was urgent. There's a package on the dresser from Pat and Tim. It feels bulky. Might be photos. The label says "Do Not Bend".'

'Oh great, I haven't had a letter or call for weeks and neither has Sammy. We were getting a bit worried.'

Jane picked up the package from Nashville. She opened it and removed a bundle of photographs. A smiling Pat and Tim

Davis, lounging by their swimming pool, looked back at her. There were several shots of their daughters, Kim and Abby, sitting astride ponies.

The last photo was of Tim and a group of men standing around in a recording studio. Pat had written on the back, *Tim, and some guys you might recognise.*

Jane turned the photo over and looked closely at the bearded man, clutching drumsticks. Another man, standing next to Tim, was smiling and holding a double bass.

'I don't believe it. Ed, look who Tim's with!' she exclaimed.

'Ah, yeah, last time I spoke to Tim, he said he'd bumped into them. They were in the studio to do some recording the same time as Tim's band. I meant to tell you but it slipped my mind.'

'How could you forget something like that?'

'Well, what with the kids and dog, I get so mithered. You know how it is, a man's work and all that.'

'Oh God, get the violins out,' Jane said. 'How on earth do you think *I* managed with Jon and Jess? *You* were away with the group all the time and there was no Mum next door to go running to every five minutes.'

'You had Sammy living here,' Eddie said. 'She helped you with the kids.'

'Sammy was pregnant two years on the run. Then we had Nick and Jason to look after, too. It was no picnic, Ed. Especially with all those bloody fans hanging around the gates, waiting for you lot to come home.'

'Never mind, Jane.' Enid patted her hand. 'You've a nice little job now with Sammy. Eddie has all the hard work with the children these days.'

'Mum, honestly! Sammy and I run a business, we employ a lot of people. It's not a little job, as you put it. And Eddie does *not* have all the hard work either. You and the cleaner do most of it. He just messes about with Roy all afternoon in the music room while the kids are at school.'

'Jane!' Eddie exclaimed. 'That messing about keeps you in Porsches and leather coats. Roy and I write songs. It's a business, like the band was. It's our living.'

'Sorry, Ed, I'm tired. Mum always seems to think you're badly done to, staying at home with the kids all day. But you said you didn't want a nanny. It's your choice to look after them, I don't force you.'

'I know you don't, and I wouldn't do it if I didn't love it.'

'Are you two going to stop arguing?' Ben reached for the photograph. 'Put us out of our misery and tell us who this is.'

'It's The Crickets, Joe B and Jerry. Can you believe Ed forgot to tell me that Tim met them at the studio?'

'We were talking music. I said I was sorry. Anybody would think I'd committed a crime.'

'You have!' Jane's eyes twinkled. 'You just wait till later. I'll think of a suitable punishment.'

'Promises, promises,' he said, grinning.

Enid took the photo off Ben. 'Fancy that. Do you remember when Jane used to play "That'll Be the Day" over and over?'

'I do. Buddy Holly and The Crickets,' Ben said. 'I also remember the day she came home from school in tears after she'd heard Buddy Holly had died in that plane crash. That was the year after the Man United crash at Munich.'

'That's right.' Eddie nodded. 'He died on February the third, 1959. Some dates you never forget.'

'Like December the eighth, 1980,' Jane said, her eyes filling with sudden tears.

'Why, what happened then?' Enid said, frowning.

'John Lennon was murdered,' Jess said. 'Everybody knows that, Gran.'

'Oh yes, of course,' Enid said. 'That's when I realised just how vulnerable you boys had been on your American tours. I bet you're glad that's all behind you now, Ed?'

Eddie took a swig of wine and smiled. 'If I'm honest, I miss the band. Roy and I often talk of re-forming The Raiders, but without Tim, it's unthinkable.'

'Ed, I'd hate for you to be touring again,' Jane said quietly.

'Well, it's not likely to happen, love. Tim's in the States, Carl's happy working as a session pianist and Christ alone knows what's happened to Phil Jackson.'

'He's around,' Jane said, referring to The Raiders' blond rhythm guitarist. 'We always get a card off him at Christmas and his mum still lives in Stockport. You should get in touch with him again.'

'He was a good-looking lad, that Phil Jackson,' Enid said. 'Used to flatter me something shocking, he made me feel young again.'

Ben raised his eyebrows and passed his cigarettes round. 'The lad probably needed glasses!'

Jane laughed and picked up the letter. 'If you'll excuse me, I'm going into the lounge to read Pat's latest news.'

'Where's our Katie?' Eddie asked as Jane left the room. 'Shouldn't she be back by now? It's nearly bedtime.'

'She's still at her friend's,' Enid said. 'Lucy's mum said she'd bring her home about seven.'

'Okay, I suppose we should make the most of the peace. More wine, anybody?' Eddie opened another bottle of red as Ben, Jon and Jess pushed their glasses across the table.

'What's up with you two? You're both very quiet tonight,' Eddie addressed his son and daughter.

'We've a lot on our minds, Dad. Isn't that right, sis?' Jon said.

'I'm just keeping my fingers crossed that Roy and Sammy have okay-ed Nick and I living together,' Jess said, reaching for her wine.

'Living together?' Enid's eyebrows shot up her forehead.

'Yes, Gran. Mum and Dad have given *their* permission.'

'Well, it's very liberal of you, Ed, but don't you think they're a bit too young for that sort of commitment?' Enid pursed her lips in a manner that Eddie knew meant business.

'Jess is nearly nineteen. Jane was nineteen when you allowed her to move in with me.'

'I didn't allow her, she just did it,' Enid said. 'I gave her my blessing because you couldn't look after Jon on your own after Angie died. Those were exceptional circumstances and you two got married, eventually.'

'Jane and I were in love, we *wanted* to be together. Nick and Jess are also in love.'

'Well, there you are then,' Jess said, and smiled round at everyone. 'But Nick and I won't be getting married. He says we don't need a bit of paper to prove our love.'

'It's not just a bit of paper, Jess.' Enid folded her arms across her bosom. 'Your marriage vows should mean more than that. Oh well, I wash my hands of it. As I always said to your mother, you make your own bed. What will be, will be.'

6

Jane pulled the voile curtains across the French doors and switched on the lamps. She kicked off her shoes and flopped down on the sofa. It was good to be home, she thought as she wriggled her toes into the soft pile of the Flokati rug. Her mum had lit a fire earlier and the room felt warm and cosy.

She unfolded Pat's letter and settled back. Her friend had the knack of storytelling and her letters were always a joy to read. As she finished the first page, Jane's smile faded. She dropped the letter onto her lap and called out, 'Ed, come in here, quickly!'

He rushed into the lounge and she handed him the letter.

'What is it?' he asked as her eyes filled with tears.

'Read it,' she choked.

Eddie sat down next to her and read the page, shock registering on his face. 'Oh God, no!'

Enid, carrying a mug of coffee into the lounge, stared at their distressed faces. 'What's the matter?'

'Pat has breast cancer,' Eddie replied. 'She found a lump, had her right breast removed and she's having chemotherapy.'

He scanned the rest of the letter. 'She's lost her hair. That's upset her, of course. The photo of her and Tim was taken a week before she found the lump, she says, and wants us to remember her like that, just as she was.'

Jane was sobbing and Eddie took her in his arms. Enid had tears in her eyes as Ben walked into the lounge, Lennon on his heels as usual.

'What's going on?' Ben asked. 'One minute you're all smiles around the table, next minute, tears.'

Eddie handed him the letter. Ben read it and frowned. 'Will she make a full recovery?'

'I hope so,' Eddie said. 'Her letter is optimistic. She actually seems quite cheerful. We'll phone them later, Jane. You can speak with Pat, ask how she is. This letter was written over two weeks ago. She might be feeling more like her old self today. I don't understand why Tim didn't say anything to me when we last spoke. Why don't you call Sammy, see if she's heard anything?'

'I will,' Jane said, sniffing loudly.

Ben passed her his handkerchief. 'Here you are, pet, it's clean.'

'Thanks, Dad. I'll call from upstairs, it's more private.'

* * *

Enid watched her daughter leave the room. 'You don't know what's round the corner, do you? Pat's mother died young from breast cancer. That was before you met the girls, Ed. Her dad had married Sammy's mum, Molly, by then.'

Eddie nodded. 'I was puzzled as to how two sisters could look so different until Jane told me they were stepsisters.'

'Well, look at your lot,' Enid said. 'Katie and Dom are the spit of Jane, Jess is a bit of you both, but our Jon... well, he's nothing like you at all. I reckon Angie was having you on there and he's the milkman's.'

'I reckon you might be right.' Eddie laughed. 'I'll go up and see Jane. Jess can bath Dominic tonight. I'll leave you two to have your coffee in peace.'

* * *

What would Enid say if she knew the truth? Eddie wondered as he left the lounge. That with his thick, dark curls and vivid green eyes, Jon was the image of his late father, Richard Price. It was the most closely guarded secret of Eddie's life, how Angie had duped him into believing she was carrying his child. His thoughts returned to the day his life had been turned upside down.

When his seventeen-year-old ex announced she was pregnant and he was the baby's father, he'd told his parents, who urged him to do the right thing and marry her, even though he was in love with Jane. The marriage was unhappy. He and Angie separated when Jon was almost three. Eddie had resumed his relationship with Jane. Angie began dating Richard. Following Angie and Richard's deaths in a car crash, he was told by Jon's godmother, Cathy, that Richard had fathered Jon during an earlier one-night stand. But Eddie adored the little boy and couldn't bear to part with him.

Roy had taken charge when he went to pieces, suggesting they make a pact to keep the truth to themselves. Eddie had agreed; he didn't want to lose Jon to Angie's or Richard's families. The Raiders were high-profile at the time and the media would have loved a juicy story. Not even his late parents or Jane's were privy to the truth. The only parties to the pact, besides him and Jane, were Cathy, her husband Carl, Sammy, Roy, Tim and Pat. Eddie had told Jon that Jane was not his real mother. To this day, he was still none the wiser about his true parentage and Eddie hoped that was how it would always remain.

***

Jess and Jon were still sitting at the table in companionable silence, finishing off the last of the wine. Dominic, chin on hands, was staring at his big brother and sister, a look of adoration on his young face.

Eddie ruffled Dominic's hair. 'Bedtime, Dom. I'll come and read you a story as soon as I can. Jess, take him up and bath him, please.'

'Why, where's Mum? I heard her going upstairs. I presumed it was to run a bath.'

'We've had bad news from Nashville. Pat's got breast cancer. Mum's very upset. She's gone upstairs to call Sammy. Will *you* bath him, please, Jess?'

'Of course.' Jess's face registered shock. 'Will Pat be okay?'

'Well, let's hope so. She's having chemotherapy and she's lost her hair. We're calling her later to see how she's coping. I bet Tim's in bits over this. He worships the ground she walks on. It'll destroy him if anything happens to her.'

'You've known them such a long time, haven't you, Dad?' Jon said, shaking his head.

'All our lives, really. Me, Tim and Roy went to the same school. Mum and Pat met at infant school and then teamed up with Sammy at the grammar. We met them when they were fourteen and the rest, as they say, is history. Apart from my marriage to Angie, we've never been apart until Tim and Pat moved to Nashville. Right, on that note, I'm going upstairs. I'll leave Dom in your very capable hands, Jess.'

***

Jane lay on the bed, sobbing down the phone to Sammy. Eddie took the receiver.

'Hi, Sam, it's Ed. Is Roy there, love?' Sammy muttered something incoherent and called for Roy.

'Hi, Ed. Bad business, isn't it?' Roy said.

'Terrible,' Eddie agreed. 'Jane's heartbroken.'

'So's Sammy. We should be together at a time like this. We'll drop Jason at Jules's place and come over.'

'Please do,' Eddie replied. 'I'll call Tim when you get here.'

'See you soon, mate.'

'Katie should be home any minute.' Eddie pulled Jane into his arms. 'And Roy and Sammy are coming over.'

'Good.' She smiled through her tears as a car horn tooted.

Eddie looked out to see Katie waving goodbye to her friend. Seconds later, the bedroom door flew in and Katie hurtled into the room.

'Daddy,' she squealed, flinging herself at Eddie, who picked her up and twirled her round and round.

'Say hello to Mummy, Katie.' Eddie bounced his daughter onto the bed.

Katie frowned, looking closely at her mum's tear-stained cheeks. 'Mummy, why are you crying?' Her big brown eyes clouded with concern. 'Have you been naughty? Did Daddy shout at you?'

'No, of course he didn't.' Jane smiled at Katie's serious expression.

'Auntie Pat in America is poorly and Mummy's feeling upset by the news. But it's nothing for you to worry about,' Eddie told her.

Katie grinned. 'Did you bring me a present?' she asked hopefully.

'Yes, but it's not much, I'm afraid. Ed, nip downstairs and get me that little pink bag off the dresser, please.'

He was back in seconds, dangling the bag in front of Katie, just out of reach. 'Have you been a good girl for Grandma?'

'Of course I have,' Katie said, hands on hips. 'Why, what's Grandma been saying? Did she tell you that I haven't been good?'

Eddie laughed. 'Is that a guilty conscience, Katie Mellor?' He handed her the bag and she delved inside, pulling out a pearly shell necklace and matching bracelet.

'Oh, they're very pretty, Mummy. Thank you.'

'You're welcome, sweetheart. There's a stick of rock and a beach ball downstairs, too. Jess will help you with your bath when she's finished with Dom. Go and get yourself ready, please.'

Katie shot off the bed and ran out of the room. Jane turned to Eddie. 'I can't face going back downstairs at the moment, Ed. Make my apologies to Mum and Dad and tell them I'll catch up with them tomorrow.'

'Okay, love. I'll see them out and bring you a drink up.' As he walked across the room, Enid popped her head around the bedroom door.

'We're going home now, Jane. I'll see you in the morning and you can tell me how Pat is then. I'll phone Molly and Tom tomorrow. They've not mentioned anything to me, but perhaps they've kept the news to themselves for now. It'll take some coming to terms with. Anyway, we'll see ourselves out. Bye, love. Bye, Ed.'

'Bye, Mum, and thanks for everything. You're wonderful, I don't know how we would manage without you,' Jane said, smiling tearfully.

'Get away with you! It's our pleasure.'

* * *

Eddie let in Roy, Sammy and Nick, and led them upstairs. Jane and Sammy fell on one another in a fresh outburst of tears and Nick disappeared to look for Jess. Roy and Eddie hugged one another.

'Take a pew and we'll call Nashville.' Eddie gestured to the bed as Jon knocked on the door.

'Dad, can I call Helen? I promised I would tonight. I'll explain we've got a problem and you need the phone. I'll arrange to ring her back later – I don't want her to think I've let her down.'

'Go ahead. Give us a shout when you've finished.'

'Do you think we should go over to the States for a visit?' Roy asked, as the four made themselves comfortable on the large brass bed.

'I wondered that myself,' Eddie replied. 'Let's see what Tim has to say. He never said a thing about Pat's illness when I spoke to him recently. Have you called Tom and your mum tonight, Sammy?'

'Yes, I phoned them after I read my letter. They've known about Pat's cancer for a few months but she made them promise not to tell us until she was over the worst. That's even more upsetting, putting us first so we wouldn't worry. We've always shared our problems and there's poor Pat, thousands of miles away, keeping it all to herself.'

Jon popped his head around the door again. 'I've finished with the phone, Dad.'

'Thanks, son. If you're not going out, can you read the kids a quick story – if Jess hasn't already done it?'

'Helen's invited me over and we're going clubbing but I'll read them a story anyway. They can have one between them, it'll save time.'

'Katie won't like that,' Jane said, raising an eyebrow.

'Well, Katie will have to lump it. There's a sexy little bird waiting for me!'

'You just be careful,' Eddie warned, laughing at Jon's lusty grin.

'Dad, for God's sake, I'm twenty-two not sixteen!'

'Yes, but Helen's only fifteen. Watch your step, that's all I'm saying.'

'That Helen's bloody jailbait,' Roy called after Jon.

'I wish he'd find someone nearer his own age and settle down,' Jane said. 'He always seems to get involved with schoolgirls.'

'Trouble is,' Eddie mused, 'all girls look older than their years these days. Helen looks at least eighteen. I nearly dropped cork-legged when he told me her age.'

'Well, it's a girl thing to try and look older,' Sammy said. 'Me and Jane used to slap the make-up on when we were teenagers.'

'Yeah,' Roy's dark eyes twinkled, 'but I have to say I preferred you in your school uniform – without the make-up.'

'You're just a dirty old letch, Cantello!' Sammy smacked his leg.

'Right, let's phone Pat and Tim,' Eddie said. 'At least we're a bit more cheerful than we were. I'd hate them to think we've all gone to pieces, we need to keep strong for them.'

Tim answered after a few rings. 'Hi, mate, it's Ed. We got your letter and photos. We're very sorry, Tim. How's Pat doing?' He fell silent as Tim spoke.

'She's doing good, thanks. Needs more chemo and then she's having a reconstruction. She's optimistic about a full recovery – well, we both are. To be honest, she's more upset about losing her hair than her breast.'

Eddie remembered that Pat's long, blonde hair had been her pride and joy. Losing it would be such a blow to her morale. 'Is she able to come to the phone?' he asked.

'I'll go get her. Talk to you later, Ed.'

Tim went off to get Pat while Eddie relayed to the others

what he'd just learnt. Sammy and Jane nodded and held on to one another.

'Hi, Pat.' Eddie smiled into the receiver. 'How are you? Good, I'm so glad to hear that. Yes, we're all here at our place. We're sitting on our bed. No, it's not an orgy – well, not at the moment anyway.' He grinned broadly at the others. 'But we're always open to suggestions, as you know. I'm glad to hear that you haven't lost your sense of humour, girl. I'll hand you over to Jane and Sammy. Take care, darling. We love you and we're all rooting for you.'

Jane and Sammy pressed as close to the receiver as they could, both talking at once.

Roy rolled his eyes. 'Just like old times,' he said, smiling as the pair ooh-ed and aah-ed over whatever Pat was telling them. 'So, what do you reckon, Ed, will she get better?'

'Tim said she needs further chemo, then she's having a reconstruction. It sounds as though she's got the spirit to fight it all the way.'

Roy nodded and smiled at Jane and Sammy, both with tears running down their cheeks, as they said their goodbyes.

'Well,' Sammy said, 'she sounded really cheerful. Told us two to stop crying and not to worry. She also said she and Tim have decided to sell up and come home. The ranch is already up for sale. They realise how vulnerable they are out there without family support. Pat's feeling positive, but if anything goes wrong, Tim would be left to bring the children up alone.'

Eddie and Roy stared at one another over the girls' heads.

'You're thinking my thoughts,' Roy said, grinning at Eddie's animated face.

'Am I? You mean, re-formed Raiders? We were only talking about it over dinner.'

'The very same!' Roy said. 'Did Pat say when they'd be home, girls?'

'Hopefully in the autumn,' Jane replied. 'Pat said they'd

leave the ranch in the care of some friends if it hasn't sold and come home then anyway. They could stay here with us until they find somewhere to live. When Jess moves out, there'll be a spare room. Kim and Abby could share with Katie. It would be lovely to have them here.'

'Where's Jess going?' Sammy asked.

'You mean Nick hasn't told you?' Eddie said. 'Oh hell, talk about putting your foot in it.'

'Well, *you'd* better tell us,' Roy suggested. 'Forewarned is forearmed.'

Eddie outlined Nick and Jess's plans to move in together. He told them that he and Jane had given Jess permission. They presumed Nick had asked if it was okay on the way home from Brighton.

Sammy smiled. 'The dozy sod fell asleep after we met up at the services. We've had all this upset since I opened Pat's letter, so I don't suppose he thought it was the right time to say anything. Anyway, *I've* no objections. Roy?'

'Nor do I,' Roy said. 'They'll soon realise it's not a bed of roses. Nothing like a bit of practical experience for learning about life.'

'I'll go and tell them,' Eddie said, springing up off the bed. 'Where are they?'

'Jess's room,' Jane said. 'Don't go barging in, Ed. Knock first and wait till she tells you to come in.' She turned to Sammy and Roy: 'Don't know about you two, but I'm drained. Let's go down and get a drink.'

* * *

'Are you decent?' Eddie teased as he knocked on Jess's door.

'Course we are,' Jess called. 'Come in, Dad.'

'Why the glum faces?'

'We're worried about Pat,' Nick said, slipping his arm

around Jess's shoulders. 'We were thinking how it could just as easily have been Mum or Jane.'

'That thought had crossed *my* mind,' Eddie said. 'Anyway, at the moment I'm the bearer of good news. You can go ahead and look for a flat whenever you're ready. If it's what you both want, then we're all agreed it's okay.'

Jess stared at him. 'But, Dad, Nick hasn't had a chance to ask Roy and Sammy yet.'

'Ah well, your mum put her foot in it by saying that Pat and Tim could use your room when you move out. You can probably guess the rest.'

'So, Mum and Dad don't mind? Are Pat and Tim coming home? When? Will you re-form The Raiders?' Nick's questions tumbled excitedly over one another.

'They *are* coming home just as soon as Pat feels fit enough to travel. It'll be a good few months yet, but they're getting sorted out over there. And yes, we may re-form The Raiders. Right, I'll leave you two to make some plans.'

'Can Nick stay over tonight? I don't want to be on my own,' Jess pleaded.

'Of course he can.'

'Thanks, Dad, goodnight.'

As Eddie strolled down the landing, Jon rushed past, looking flustered.

'How come you're still here?' Eddie said as they ran downstairs together.

'I ended up reading two stories because the awkward little sods couldn't agree. Then I took a shower and my shirt needed ironing. I didn't like to pester Mum when she's so upset, so I did it myself. Does it look alright?'

'It's fine,' Eddie replied as Roy strolled into the hall. 'Now go on, get going or it won't be worth bothering.'

'Before you dash off, Jon,' Roy began, 'when you're next in work, tell Livvy to come here Tuesday for a rehearsal.'

'What about Jess? She hates Livvy coming here.'

'Err, I dunno, but you'll think of something to pacify her,' Roy said, going into the downstairs cloakroom.

'We'd both like Livvy in The Zoo,' Eddie said. 'She's got a bloody good voice and the band needs it. Now don't be too late home, you're back in work tomorrow. Sean won't be very happy if you don't turn up on time. Enjoy yourself. See you later.'

7

'Well, fuck *you* then!' Sean Grogan slammed the phone down. He turned as his sales assistant, Livvy Grant, ran upstairs to the record department.

'Problems, Sean?' She stared at her boss, who had a stubbly chin and a slightly dishevelled appearance. 'Night on the tiles?'

'I wish,' he grunted, lighting a cigarette. He tossed the packet and lighter in her direction. 'Help yourself then leave them on the counter for Jon. Ah, if it's not the divil himself,' he said as Jon puffed up the stairs.

'Less of the divil if you don't mind,' Jon quipped, mocking Sean's Dublin accent. He helped himself to a cigarette and took a lengthy drag. 'Ah, that's better.'

'Well now, it's grand to see you, Jon,' Sean said. 'We've been really busy the last few days. Livvy and I have been run off our pegs.'

'You look a bit rough around the edges.' Jon laughed. His dark-haired, good-looking boss was usually a stylish dresser and never less than immaculately turned out.

'I was about to tell Livvy that I didn't go home last night. It was Ian from Instruments birthday. We had a few bevies in

Tommy Ducks and a takeaway curry. I fell asleep at his place so I'm in the doghouse with Tina. She's just given me an earbashing for not letting her know I was staying out. How the fuck was I supposed to let her know, when I didn't even realise I was doing it? Bloody women, they won't listen, even when your excuse is genuine. Kettle's boiled. Go and brew up, Liv. I could murder a coffee. How was Brighton?' he asked Jon as Livvy disappeared into the staffroom.

'Good,' Jon said. 'I met a bird from Stockport down there. Saw her last night and took her clubbing.'

'Did you now?' Sean said, grinning broadly. 'You've had more birds than Disney has Dalmatians. So, come on, tell all. What's this one called and what's she like?'

'What's *who* like?' Livvy said, strolling back into the shop. She placed a tray on the counter. 'Help yourselves. There's a packet of biscuits, too, my treat.' Sean and Jon took a mug each and Livvy plonked herself on a stool behind the counter and nibbled the corner off a custard cream.

'Jon met a bird in Brighton,' Sean said.

'Another for your harem?' She rolled her eyes.

'Her name's Helen,' Jon began. 'She's tall, blonde, blue-eyed and sexy.'

'Bit like me then,' Livvy quipped, twisting a curl around her finger.

'Not quite, titch. Her hair's straight and she's at least six inches taller.'

'How old is she?' she asked.

'Erm, sixteen – next month,' he added, waiting for the ribald comments that were certain to follow.

'Holy BeJesus, Jon, she's jailbait!' Sean exclaimed.

'Yep, that's what Roy said. But she looks and acts a lot older.'

'Well, she's not so don't you go hiding the sausage just yet.'

'You sound like Dad.' Jon drained his mug and finished his

cigarette. 'By the way, The Raiders might be re-forming. Pat and Tim are coming home soon.' He related the story of Pat's cancer and the family's plans to return to the UK.

'Let's hope she makes a full recovery,' Sean said. 'But all clouds have a silver lining and it'd be great if the group *were* to re-form.'

'It's pretty much on the cards. Dad and Roy are really keen, they miss the buzz.'

'Did you rehearse any of the new songs while you were away?' Livvy asked.

'We did and they're brilliant. Roy wants you at our place next Tuesday night to have a run through.'

'What about Jess? I don't want to cause trouble.'

'Roy's adamant he wants you there. On the way to work, I've been racking my brains, thinking of a way to avoid upsetting Jess. We'll drop your car at your place after work. Then you come home with me and eat with us. When we go to the music room later, we'll say we'd planned to go somewhere after dinner, maybe something to do with work, then I'd remembered about the rehearsal on the way home. We'll already be at the house, so hopefully, Jess won't kick off. We can rehearse for a while, then I'll run you back to your flat later.'

'It sounds a wee bit long-winded,' Livvy said, frowning.

'Well, it also sounds feasible and saves falling out with Jess – it just makes life a bit easier.'

'Okay then, if you're sure. I'll look forward to that.' She smiled and took the empty mugs back into the staffroom.

Sean stared after her. 'She's done nothing but rabbit on about those new songs all the time you've been away. It's been Roy this and Roy that. She's driven me crackers, so she has. If I didn't know better, I'd swear she has a crush on him.'

'He always makes a big fuss of her and says she's a fantastic singer. He really wants her in The Zoo and we could use the extra voice. But Jess has a bee in her bonnet that she fancies

Nick and won't agree. It's a shame really, because Livvy's very good.'

'Ah well,' Sean mused, 'if she's *that* good, maybe she should try for a solo career.'

'Good idea. Maybe Roy could manage her?'

'No doubt your dad will be in touch with Phil and Carl about the group re-forming.'

'I'm sure he will,' Jon said.

'I must give Carl a ring sometime. We always got on well once he forgave me for enticing Tina away.'

'Carl bears no grudges. He's happily married to my Aunt Cathy,' Jon said. 'So all's well that ends well.'

'Indeed.'

* * *

The shelves in the upstairs music room at Hanover's Lodge groaned under the weight of Eddie's record collection. Beneath the window he'd installed a portable recording studio and on Tuesday night, The Zoo and Livvy went straight into rehearsal of the new song.

'I Need Your Love', the raunchy rocker written with Livvy in mind, was so much better with the extra voice than Eddie had dared hope. Her vocal range was amazing and tonight, she belted out the lyrics like a young Janis Joplin. Fired with enthusiasm, the group ran through The Zoo's complete repertoire.

'Bloody marvellous, Liv,' Roy said, beaming at Livvy, who smiled shyly back. 'One more time with the new one. Give it all you've got.'

Eddie mixed and recorded 'I Need Your Love'. 'I think that's cracked it,' he said as he rewound the tape. He played it back to them as Jess left to use the bathroom.

When she returned, Livvy, reclining on a beanbag near the

mixing desk, was talking animatedly with Nick, who knelt beside her, their heads close together.

Jess stiffened as she walked towards the pair and they sprang guiltily apart. Nick jumped to his feet. Jess had the knack of reducing Livvy to shreds and tonight was no exception.

'What the hell do you think you're doing?' she demanded.

'Nothing, we were just talking.' Nick frowned. He slipped an arm around her shoulders.

'Oh, it looks like it.' She shrugged him off. 'Did you need to have your faces so close together?'

'It was difficult to hear what Livvy was saying over the music,' Nick said. 'Cool it, Jess. Why do you always have to have a go at her?'

'I wasn't having a go. It's so bloody obvious that you fancy her.' She flounced out of the room, as only Jess could flounce, and slammed the door behind her.

Eddie switched off the tape deck and shook his head.

Nick looked apologetically at Livvy. 'Sorry, Liv, she's a bit touchy today. Probably PMT. I'll go after her.'

'Oh dear.' Roy raised an eyebrow. He and Jason were lounging on the sofa bed opposite and they smiled at Livvy, who was close to tears. 'Don't take any notice of Jess, love,' Roy continued. 'She's always on her high horse where Nick's concerned.'

Livvy nodded as Jane popped her head in the room. 'Stop slamming doors, you'll wake the kids. And can you call Helen, Jon? She rang earlier but I told her you were recording. Use the phone in our room.'

'That was Jess slamming doors, not us,' Jon told her. 'Those kids sleep through anything. We've been making a noise in here and they haven't stirred.'

'They're used to music,' Jane said. 'But that door sounded like a bomb going off. Why's she slamming doors anyway?'

'She's had a falling out with Livvy,' Roy said.

'I see.' Jane turned to Livvy, who was still sitting on the beanbag, wiping her eyes. 'I'm sorry, love. Would you like to come downstairs and have a cup of tea?'

Livvy smiled through her tears. 'No thanks, Jane, I need to go home in a minute.'

'I'll speak to Helen and then I'll take you home,' Jon said.

'Well, if you're sure you're okay, I'm going back downstairs,' Jane said. 'They're just showing Torvill and Dean doing their "Bolero" routine on telly.' She left the room as Roy stood up, stretching his arms above his head.

'Don't rush your call, Jon, *I'll* take Livvy. Perhaps you can take Jason home for me later, then I can stop off and have a pint. Come on, sweetheart,' he said to Livvy. 'I'll drop you off first. Do you fancy meeting me in the Royal Oak, Ed?'

'No thanks, mate. I'll stay home and relax with Jane. See you tomorrow about noon. Sorry, Livvy, Jess isn't usually that bad. Put it down to hormones like Nick suggested, but for God's sake don't tell her we said that,' he finished with a grin.

Livvy's smile was grateful. 'I won't. But, Roy, are you quite sure you don't mind giving me a lift?'

'Not at all. Let's go.' Roy led the way downstairs, calling goodbye to Jane.

***

Livvy sank back into the comfortable leather seat as Roy drove slowly down the private lane and out onto Ashlea Road. He turned to Livvy and said, 'You okay now?'

'Fine, thanks. This is a lovely car.' She admired the sleek BMW saloon. 'It feels enormous after my wee Mini.'

'Yeah, it's not bad. Don't use it very often, usually when I've got more than one passenger.'

'What do you drive when you're not using this?'

He looked at her, his face lighting up as he spoke. 'A bright red Lamborghini Jalpa. I love it. It's the most wonderful car to drive.'

'You sound like a wee boy at Christmas,' she said, laughing.

'I feel like a wee boy at Christmas when I'm driving it,' he said, imitating her Glaswegian accent. 'Now, where's your flat?'

'The other side of Stockport, near Jackson's Heath.'

'Oh, that's close to where Ed and I grew up. Have you home in no time. Let's stick some music on.' He leant across her and rooted in the glove compartment. 'Dire Straits okay?' She nodded and he pushed *Alchemy* into the tape slot. 'Needs rewinding, but it'll do.' He sang along to 'Romeo and Juliet', Livvy joining in with him.

'It's two roads down on the right,' she directed as they approached Jackson's Heath. She pointed to a three-storey apartment block. 'That's my Mini Cooper,' she said proudly as Roy swung onto the car park alongside the little red car. He stopped the engine and looked at her as she undid the seat belt.

'Thank you, Roy. It was kind of you to give me a lift.'

'You're very welcome.' For the rest of his days Roy could never fathom why he said what he said next, but say it he did, changing the course of all their lives forever. 'Aren't you going to ask me in for coffee?'

Livvy looked at him with startled eyes. 'Oh, erm, well, erm yes, if you'd like one. But I only have instant.' She got out of the car.

'Instant will do just fine,' he said, clambering out.

Livvy fumbled in her handbag for her key and opened the entrance door. Roy followed her inside, through the spotlessly clean hallway, with its troughs of exotic plants and framed local landmark prints, and up the equally clean stairs to the red door of flat number seven.

'Nice place. Not like some of the blocks of flats you see.' He followed her down the hall and into the lounge. 'Mind if I have a fag?'

'Of course not,' she said, kicking off her shoes. 'There's an ashtray on the windowsill. I'll put the kettle on and change out of my work clothes. Take a seat.'

'Thanks.' Roy lit up and sat down on the sofa. He glanced around the neat, feminine room. The dark-pink curtains matched the full-blown roses on the cream fabric suite. He leant back against the sofa cushions and stretched out his long legs.

As he blew smoke rings, Livvy came back into the room. She'd changed out of her black trouser suit and formal white blouse into tight denim jeans and a pink button-through top. Her long hair, released from its restraining clips, cascaded over her shoulders in a mass of golden curls.

Roy caught his breath and felt his stomach tighten as he stared open-mouthed at the petite, blue-eyed vision.

'Do you take sugar, Roy?'

'No, thanks.' He shook his head slowly. 'I'm quite sweet enough!'

'I'm sure you are,' she said softly. 'Won't be a minute.'

* * *

Livvy spooned Nescafé into two china mugs and topped them with boiling water and milk. She couldn't believe it and felt like pinching herself: Roy Cantello was sitting right here in her wee lounge, looking as though he belonged. Her best friend Sheena would never believe her, even if she were to tell her. And she couldn't, because... She shook her head. She wouldn't dwell on the whys and wherefores right now, or she'd be up half the night with nightmares.

She carried the mugs, balancing a small plate of Jaffa cakes on one, and put them down on the coffee table in front of Roy.

'Help yourself, either mug. *I'm* sweet enough too.'

'You certainly are,' Roy agreed as she blushed. 'Would you like a cigarette?'

She nodded, taking one. His hand shook slightly as he held out his lighter. She sat down next to him and smiled.

'How long have you lived here?'

'Almost a year.'

'Why did you leave Scotland?' He reached for a Jaffa cake.

'To escape from my past.'

'What do you mean, escape? Were you in bother with the law?'

'No, nothing like that,' she said, grinning shyly. He wouldn't be interested in her life story, would he? But he was looking at her with his head on one side as though waiting for her to continue so she took a deep breath. 'I'm adopted, you see. It was a private affair, done through the church. I was given to a couple who lived just outside Glasgow and brought up an only child. Mum went off with a lay preacher when I was ten and left me behind.

'Dad was a God-bothering nutcase, strict and overprotective. Wouldn't allow me out of his sight after Mum left. He'd wait for me outside school, lock me in my room when he went to his church meetings and I wasn't allowed friends over. It was awful.' She took a sip of coffee. 'You don't want to know any more, Roy. I must be boring you.'

He patted her knee. 'You're not. Carry on.'

'I got friendly with a boy called Danny McVey. One day we played truant, spent the time in the amusement arcades in the city centre. We missed the bus back to school in time for Dad picking me up. He went crazy when we got back. Punched Danny in the face and bundled *me* into the car.' Tears tumbled down Livvy's cheeks at the memory. She brushed them away with her hand. Roy reached into his jacket pocket and handed her a hanky.

'Thank you.' She wiped her eyes. 'I'll wash it for you.'

'Keep it.' He took a sip of coffee. 'Go on.'

'When we got home, he whacked me across the mouth and split my lip. A neighbour heard me screaming and called the police. Dad was arrested, I was taken into care. As the police took him away, he yelled at me, said that I was a whore and no better than my real mother. She was only sixteen, for God's sake, just a wee girl.' Livvy paused and looked at Roy, who was shaking his head.

She wiped her eyes again. 'I was allowed to have weekends with my adoptive granny. She died when I was eighteen and left me a wee legacy. It was the only security I had. I rented a flat with my friend Sheena and got a job in a music store. Then when I heard my father was being released from prison, I decided to leave Glasgow. The first train out was to Manchester so I chanced my fate. I stayed in a B&B while I found a job and this wee flat. Even Sheena doesn't know where I am, but I called her to let her know I'm safe.'

'And what happened to Danny?' Roy asked.

'He wouldn't come near me after the beating. Last I heard, he'd gone to London to work as an estate agent. Sheena and I used to sing in clubs back home and I was hoping to join a group down here. I was so happy to get the job at Flanagan and Grey's and when Jon told me his band could do with another female singer, I was over the moon.' She took a deep, shuddering breath. 'But, of course, Jess doesn't want me in The Zoo.' More tears tumbled down her cheeks.

Roy put down his mug and took her in his arms. 'Don't cry, Livvy. Jess will come round eventually.' As she raised her head, Roy looked into her eyes and held her gaze. He tilted her chin, hesitated momentarily then kissed her.

Surprised at first by his action, Livvy found it hard to resist his insistent lips and kissed him back.

He pulled her closer. Her arms crept up around his neck as she savoured his totally unexpected kisses. He undid the buttons on her top and she heard his gasp when he saw she was bra-less.

'Oh, Livvy.' He cupped her breasts; ran his thumbs over her nipples as she moaned and raked her hands through his hair. 'Oh God, what am I doing?' He jerked away. 'Livvy, I'm sorry, I'm really sorry. I shouldn't have done that.' He jumped up, snatching his car keys from the coffee table. 'I have to go, I'm so sorry.'

Livvy felt her cheeks warming as she fastened up her top. She followed him down the narrow hall.

'Please don't tell anyone about this,' he begged, backing out of the door. 'I don't know what came over me.'

'I won't tell a soul.' She touched his arm. 'Roy, don't worry, please.'

He nodded and shot off down the stairs.

* * *

Roy gripped the steering wheel for what felt like ages. He was shaken by his actions and the feelings he'd experienced as he kissed Livvy because nothing had felt so right and he'd wanted more. There was no doubt in his mind that he would have screwed her if he'd stayed. He'd *never* been unfaithful to Sammy since the day they'd met. She'd given him everything he'd ever wanted or needed. He'd fought the urge to seek it elsewhere, even though sex had been offered freely by groupies when he was with The Raiders.

He fired up the engine and shot out of the car park, swerving to avoid a small dog that ran out in front of him. 'Fucking idiot!' he said, shaking his fist at the elderly owner who ambled along, oblivious to the fact that his Jack Russell had almost met its maker. He loved Sammy with all his heart, so what the hell had happened to him back there? Putting his foot down, he drove home as quickly as he could.

Sammy was already in bed, curled up, reading. She smiled as he walked into the room.

'Hi, handsome. Good rehearsal? Nick called, said he's staying with Jess because she's upset about something. Jason got a lift home from Jon.'

Roy nodded, stripped off his clothes and chucked them on the floor.

'Roy, you untidy sod! Why can't you hang anything up?'

'Don't know.' He shrugged. 'Jess and Livvy had a falling out. Livvy was upset, too. I ran her home and then popped in the Royal Oak.' It surprised him how the lie came out so easily. 'I'll brush my teeth and then I want to show you something.'

'Oh, Roy, I'm tired. I've got to get up early. You should have come home sooner if you want to make love.'

'You were tired last night *and* the night before,' he complained. 'What about my conjugal rights?'

'What about them? I think *you've* had more than your fair share of conjugal rights. Probably more than any other man on earth,' she said, laughing at his disappointed expression. 'Oh – go on then – brush your teeth and hurry up.'

He needed no further encouragement. Shagging Sammy would block out the guilty feelings crowding his head.

* * *

Sitting on the sofa, chain-smoking, Livvy went over what had happened. Her cheeks burned as she thought of Roy's mouth on her lips and his hands on her breasts. He was her friend's father, for goodness' sake. She should have stopped him. How would she ever look him in the eye again, or Nick and Jason, come to that? Roy had been embarrassed, too. What on earth must he be thinking?

But, Livvy argued with her head, it felt so right and that was the scary thing. She'd had few boyfriends and had never allowed anyone to touch her intimately. Her father's preaching had had a profound effect on her and the way she reacted to men. With Roy, it had happened before she even *realised* it was happening. It was a good thing he stopped before they got too carried away. She switched on the TV but couldn't settle to watching anything and decided to go to bed.

All night she lay awake, unable to get Roy out of her mind. She rose at seven and ran a bath. As she was towelling her hair dry she remembered it was Wednesday, her day off. She could have done with work to take her mind off things. Now she had all day stretching out with nothing to do.

She lay on her bed and tried reading. If she could just doze for an hour or two she might feel a bit better. Then she could perhaps make a start on decorating the kitchen. She'd bought a can of bright-yellow paint weeks ago and it still stood unopened in the hall cupboard. Yes, she decided, *that's* what she'd do. Slapping paint on walls and watching it dry would take her mind off Roy, if nothing else.

8

Startled by the shrilling of the alarm, Roy mumbled and pulled the pillow around his head. Sammy slid quietly out of bed and crept into the en suite. To save Roy's slumbers from further disturbance, she collected her hairdryer and made her way to the spare room, knocking on Jason's bedroom door as she passed.

He opened the door, dressed, hair elaborately styled. 'Already up, Mum. I'm going down to make breakfast. Do you want toast and coffee?'

'Please, love. I'll be down in a few minutes. You look lovely, Jase.' She admired his stylish black jeans and crisp white shirt.

'Thanks, Mum. Jules always dresses nice, so I'm making an effort to look good, too.'

'Out to impress the girls, are you?' Sammy teased. 'You and Jules will knock 'em dead, looking like that.'

He blushed and ran downstairs. Sammy stared after him, smiling proudly. Unlike Nick and Roy, he wasn't concerned whether girls fancied him or not. He'd inherited the Cantello good looks but none of the confidence. Maybe that would come later, but for now, Sammy knew that Jason wasn't in the least bit bothered.

After a hurried breakfast, she rushed back upstairs and shook Roy by the shoulder.

'I'm going now, I'm giving Jason a lift to Jules's place. See you tonight.' She bent to kiss him as he opened one eye and mouthed 'I love you,' before shutting it again.

* * *

The front door slammed shut and Roy shot upright and rubbed his eyes. He didn't want to go back to sleep. His lusty dreams would put any erotic moviemaker to shame! After the frantic session with Sammy last night, he felt guilty for having such colourful visions. Livvy had danced naked, a nubile nymph, performing sexual acts that made the blood rush to his groin at the thought.

'Get a cold shower, you randy git,' he muttered. Before doing that, he leapt out of bed and padded into Nick's bedroom to look for his address book. It was in the cupboard by the bed and he looked under Livvy's surname. It wasn't there, but then again, Nick thought like him, so he turned to the L's and found it.

He scribbled the number on a scrap of paper and went back to his bedroom. Dare he call her? Maybe she'd already left for work? Before he changed his mind, Roy dialled her number and lay back on his pillows. She answered almost immediately.

He swallowed hard before speaking. Never had he felt so nervous and unsure of himself since his early teens. 'Hi, Livvy, Roy Cantello here.'

Much to his relief, Livvy's response was bright and cheerful.

'Hi, Roy; was just thinking about you.'

'Were you really?' He wondered if Livvy's thoughts mirrored his dreams. 'I want to apologise again for what I did last night. It was bang out of order and I'm very sorry. You must think I'm a dirty old letch.'

'I don't think anything of the sort. I'm as much to blame. I should have stopped you and I didn't. It wasn't your fault.'

'What time do you leave for work?' he asked, making small talk. He wanted to suggest she have a drink with him later, perhaps after she finished work.

'I'm not working today, I was planning on painting my kitchen walls.'

'Well, in that case, why don't I buy you a pub lunch first? Then you can paint your kitchen this afternoon and I'll go and do some work with Ed.' He crossed his fingers. She was silent for a few seconds before replying.

'Is that a good idea? I mean, won't your wife object?'

Roy screwed his face, knowing full well that Sammy would most certainly object. 'She won't know, will she? We can go out of town. There are some nice pubs in the Peak District. No one will recognise us up there.'

'They may well recognise you, but no one will know me from Adam.'

'Don't you mean Eve?' he quipped. 'Are you game or what?'

'Yeah, okay.'

'Collect you in a couple of hours then. It's a gorgeous day. We could take a walk before lunch.' He said goodbye, hung up and lay back on his pillows, hands behind his head. 'What the fuck am I doing?' he muttered. 'But more to the point, do I bloody care?' What harm would it do? It was only an invite to lunch when all's said and done.

* * *

'Morning, kids.' Eddie sat down at the kitchen table and helped himself to coffee.

'Morning, Dad.' Jess passed the newspaper across to Nick. 'Look, check the one I've circled, it sounds really nice.'

Nick cast his eyes over the advert. 'Yeah, sounds great. Phone the agent. Make an appointment to view this afternoon.'

'Found a flat?' Eddie asked, reaching for a slice of toast.

'Yep,' Jess said. 'A one-bedroomed in Alderley Edge. Can we borrow your car to go and view? Mum will be using *her* car for work. You'll need the Jeep to pick the kids up from school. If we take it, we might not be back in time.'

Eddie blew out his cheeks and sighed. 'I don't know, Jess. I've just had it valeted. Last time you left sweet wrappers and empty Coke cans lying around.'

'I won't do that again. Please, Dad, I promise we'll be *very* careful.'

'Oh, I suppose so, but don't be driving like an idiot. And remember, it's not insured for Nick. Make sure *you're* behind the wheel all the time.' His Ferrari 308 was his dream car, his pride and joy. It cost him a king's ransom to insure it for Jon and Jess. 'Bit of a pricey area, Alderley Edge. It's a yuppie place. You sure you can afford it?'

'Well, there's not much else and I refuse to live in a hovel,' Jess said. 'Anyway, Dad, you wouldn't see us starve, would you?'

'Don't suppose I would but there is such a thing as working for a living. The flat your mother and me shared with Roy and Tim in Wilmslow was considered a luxury apartment. We had to pool all our money for the bills and rent. I had two jobs, managing the record store *and* drumming with The Raiders, to keep us afloat. We had Jon; you were on the way, Jess. We knew what it was like to struggle before the band made it big, believe you me.'

'Oh God, here we go!' Jess grinned and rolled her eyes.

'I'll be looking for a job soon, Eddie. I'll be able to keep your daughter in the manner to which she's accustomed,' Nick said.

'Doubt you'll find a first-time job paying that much money, Nick,' Jane said, strolling into the kitchen. She sat down and helped herself to a mug of coffee. 'Pass me some toast, please, Ed. *You* need to get a job too, Jess.'

'I know. We've some gigs lined up over the next couple of weeks, and you and Sammy said I could help out at the factory. Let me know when I can start. We'll manage fine if we're both working. We'll buy furniture with my inheritance and pay the flat deposit with it as well.'

'The money won't go far if you keep dipping into it without putting any back,' Eddie warned, handing Jane a plate of toast.

'If we get stuck for money, I'm sure Mum and Dad will see us right,' Nick said, smiling confidently.

'You'll be okay if you avoid the patter of tiny feet,' Jane said.

Jess nodded. 'That's definitely not on the cards for at least six years. *We* don't want to be tied down with kids, do we, Nick?'

'No chance,' Nick said. '*I* want to do some living and travelling first.'

'Wise words,' Eddie agreed. 'But sometimes you get what you're given!'

Jess smiled. 'Not us. By the way, Mum, can we have the Brittany house for a holiday? We want to go sometime around Nick's birthday in May.'

'No problem. I'll let the caretakers know nearer the time. How many of you are going?'

'Us two, and Jon and Jason. Jon said he was going to invite Helen.'

'Have you not invited Livvy?' Eddie asked. 'Might be nice if you did. I reckon she gets lonely with no family living close by.'

'Well, she can stay lonely,' Jess said, scowling. 'There's no way she's coming with us.'

'That's not very nice,' Eddie said. 'And I wouldn't think for one minute that Helen's mother will allow *her* to go. She's too young. I certainly wouldn't let my fifteen-year-old daughter go off on holiday with a randy twenty-two-year-old.'

'Oh well, whatever, she'll be sixteen by then anyway,' Jess said airily.

'She's still too young for our Jon.' Eddie lit a cigarette and took a lengthy drag.

'You try telling *him* that,' Jane said.

'I wouldn't dream of interfering. But I know my son well enough to know that he's not going to be happy just sat holding hands and it bothers me.'

'Well, say something to him then,' Jane said, standing up. 'Right, I'm off to work. The kids are getting into their uniforms and Katie's hair needs fastening into pigtails. I'll leave her in your very capable hands, Ed. Are you working with Roy later?'

'Yeah, we're going to finish that new song for Perry's Dream.'

'Oh, James Perry's a real dish.' Jess smiled dreamily.

'He's a bloody poofter!' Nick said.

'No, he's not. He's soo-oo good-looking.'

'Yeah, in a pale, insignificant sort of way,' Nick said with a sneer.

'Oh, Nicky, I do believe you're jealous,' Jess taunted.

'I'm not. A man should be a man.'

'You sound just like your father, Nick.' Eddie grinned. 'Mr Macho!'

'Well, there's nothing wrong with that,' Nick said. 'Anyway,' he directed at Jess, 'I thought you liked me being all man. You never usually complain.'

'Nick, not in front of the parents,' Jess said, grinning.

'I'm off,' Jane said. 'I'll leave you lot to it.'

'And I'll sort out Katie's pigtails.' Eddie stubbed out his

cigarette and drained his coffee mug. 'Songwriter, pigtail-maker, multi-talented, that's me.'

* * *

Livvy looked in despair at the mountain of clothes on her bed. She'd tried on every outfit she possessed but couldn't decide.

It's only a pub lunch, you idiot. Anyone would think he'd asked you to the Oscars. What would Roy be wearing? Something casual, no doubt, she'd only ever seen him in jeans. But then, she only ever saw him at Jon's home or Flanagan and Grey's and they weren't places he would dress up to go to anyway.

She finally chose a denim skirt and a cream and blue long-sleeved top and pulled them on over black lacy underwear before she changed her mind again. She did a twirl in front of the mirror. The blue flowers on the top echoed the baby blue of her eyes and the short skirt showed off her shapely legs. She chewed her lip for a moment, pulled off her top, removed her bra and put her top back on. 'That's better,' she muttered.

She stroked blusher on her cheeks, slicked her lips with soft-pink gloss and mascara-ed her long fair lashes. Her hair had dried in Shirley Temple ringlets and she ran her fingers through to separate the curls. She checked the varnish wasn't chipped on her finger and toenails, a quick spray of L'Air du Temps and she was ready.

Taking a deep, steadying breath, she grabbed her new denim jacket from the wardrobe and slipped her feet into a pair of dainty black sandals. Her mouth felt dry and her palms sticky by the time the intercom buzzed.

Roy announced his arrival and Livvy released the door catch. She opened her flat door and as he strolled into the hall, looking so handsome, her stomach fluttered and her breath caught in her throat. In spite of a slight sprinkle of silver in his hair, with his dark good looks, tight denims and black T-shirt, he looked no more than thirty and could easily pass for Nick and Jason's older brother.

'Hi.' His smile was sexy, eyes sultry and as he kissed her chastely on the cheek, she felt she might faint. 'You look lovely.'

'Thanks, Roy,' she said. 'It's nice to see you again.'

'And you. Let's go.'

* * *

Roy glanced down at Livvy as they strolled across the car park. She was five-foot-nothing to his six-foot-two and looked as fragile as a china doll. Compared to Sammy, who at five-foot-seven was slender, but all legs and robust, Livvy looked as though a puff of wind would blow her away. Roy sensed she was feeling nervous and felt protective towards her. He helped her into the car and fastened the seat belt. 'You really *do* look beautiful,' he said and sank into the driver's seat.

He drove out to the Peak District and turned off towards Castleton, regaling her with stories about life on the road with The Raiders. She listened, enthralled with his tales, laughing at some of the antics they'd got up to. She visibly relaxed and Roy could see she felt at ease with him. He was driving his red Lamborghini today and she told him she felt like a film star, sitting beside him.

As they entered Castleton, he drove down the main street and swung into the car park of the Cheshire Cheese pub. He stopped the engine, ran round to open her door and helped her out. 'Shall we have a stroll around the village first and check out a few shops?'

She nodded. 'Slow down, Roy,' she puffed, trying to keep up with his long strides.

'Sorry, Liv.' He stopped and put his arm around her shoulders. Her closeness made his heart beat faster and when a flush crept over her neck and face as she gazed at him, he took her hand, lacing his fingers through hers.

'Roy, we really shouldn't be doing this.'

'You're right, we shouldn't. But I want to, very much.'

'So do I.'

'Well then, we're not hurting anyone.' He pulled her further along the main street, where they stopped to admire a window display in a craft and gift shop. Livvy's eyes lit up as she pointed to a large teddy bear on a display stand at the back of the window. The golden-haired bear sported a blue and white spotted bow tie and appeared to be smiling at them.

'Isn't he gorgeous?' she said.

'You like bears?' Roy said, grinning at her delight.

'I love them. I've a few wee ones sitting on my bed at home, but none quite as handsome as him.'

Roy ruffled her curls with his free hand. She was a delightful breath of fresh air and was doing things to him that only Sammy had done before. His stomach flip-flopped like a sixteen-year-old; his heart raced, not to mention the familiar twitching. *Down, boy*, he thought as he pulled her close. 'Come on, let's get some lunch. I could murder a pint.'

They strolled back towards the pub, Livvy giving the bear one last lingering glance. The Cheshire Cheese was cheerful and cosy with its densely beamed ceilings. In spite of the day being bright and sunny, a log fire crackled and spat in the open grate.

'A real fire! Can we sit by it?' she asked. 'We always had a real fire at home when I was a wee girl.'

'Bless you. Of course we can.' Roy smiled as her face lit up. She was still a wee girl. 'What would you like to drink?'

'White wine and soda, please,' she said, making her way to a table near the fireplace.

Roy ordered the drinks and while the barmaid busied herself, he turned to look at Livvy, who was draping her jacket over a chair. She pushed her hair back from her face and caught his eye. She smiled and his heart skipped a beat while his stomach tightened. Shit! He recognised that feeling. Was he falling in love? He carried the drinks over, handed Livvy hers and sat down beside her.

She took a sip then lifted her glass to his. 'Cheers, Roy, and thanks for bringing me out.'

'My pleasure.' He touched her glass with his pint pot, downed his lager almost in one go and wiped his mouth with the back of his hand. 'What would you like to eat? There's a specials board on the wall, or you can choose from the menu.'

She studied the specials board. 'What are *you* having?'

'Steak, I reckon. Sirloin if they do it. Would *you* like a steak?'

'Please. I *never* buy steak, I can't afford it.'

'Well, you shall have it today, my treat. Chips or salad?'

'Salad, please. And I'd like the steak well done.'

Roy strolled back from the bar after ordering the food and patted his jeans pocket.

'Damn it! I've left my fags and lighter in the car. Won't be a minute.' He dashed out of the door.

* * *

Livvy studied her surroundings. The pub decoration was in a traditional style with horse brasses on dirty-yellow walls, a shade attributed to nicotine rather than Dulux. It was fairly quiet, just a few middle-aged couples dining. There was no evidence of a jukebox, but an old-fashioned fruit machine and a cigarette dispenser stood against the back wall. An elderly man, standing by the bar, touched his cap and nodded. Livvy nodded back. The barmaid, collecting glasses, walked over and smiled in a friendly manner.

"Scuse me for being nosy, love, but that man you're with, did he used to be Roy Cantello?'

Livvy felt her cheeks heating. 'Err yes, actually, he still is!'

'Thought so.' She folded her arms with an air of satisfaction. 'I'd know that sexy smile and those sultry eyes anywhere. I was a fan of The Raiders, you see. I'll have to ask him to autograph a beer mat when he comes back.'

'He's just popped out to the car for his cigarettes.' Livvy finished her drink and looked at the door. Where on earth was he? The car park was opposite the pub and should only have taken a minute or two.

'Roy, where on earth have you been?' Livvy asked as he reappeared, gasping. 'Why are you so out of breath?'

'The packet was empty. I ran to the newsagent's down the road for more.'

'You could have bought some from here, there's a machine over there.'

'I didn't see it,' he said. 'Like another drink?'

'Please. The barmaid wants an autograph as well.'

'You're joking! Bloody hell, I can't go anywhere!'

The next couple of hours flew by as they enjoyed their meal and each other's company. The age gap fell away as she informed him she was just twenty-two while Roy told her that at forty-two, he was old enough to be her father.

As they left the pub, he announced he needed the gents' and handed her the car keys. She strolled across the road to the car park and unlocked the door to find the large teddy bear with the blue and white spotted bow tie sitting on the passenger seat. Tears filled her eyes as she picked him up. A little gift card, pinned to his front, bore the message, *Dear Livvy, I like plenty of kisses and cuddles, love Teddy. PS, so does Roy.*

She turned to face Roy, who had appeared behind her. The bear in one arm, she put her other arm around him and hugged him. Standing on tiptoes, she pulled his face down and kissed him full on the lips.

'Thank you so much. He's the nicest present I've ever had in my life. So that's where you disappeared to earlier?'

Roy grinned. 'Right, get in the car and we'll take him home. Find him a place on the end of your bed with your other bears.'

Livvy sat the bear on her knee as Roy turned to face her and looked into her eyes. She swallowed hard as his hand gently stroked her cheek. Then she was in his arms and he was kissing her as though his life depended on it. She responded, pushing against him, wanting more, but...

'Livvy, baby, I want you,' he whispered, holding her face between his hands.

She stiffened and pulled away. He wanted her? Did he mean...? Was that the reason he'd asked her to lunch, the reason he'd bought her the bear? Did he do this all the time, to amuse himself while his wife was working? He probably had a string of girlfriends around town and she was about to join them. Well, if that was the case, he had a shock coming: it would take more than a sirloin steak and a teddy bear to get *her* into bed.

Roy frowned, looking at her. 'What's wrong?'

'You said you want me.'

'I do.'

'But you're married.'

'I know,' he said with a heavy sigh. 'But it doesn't stop me wanting you.' He lifted her chin and smiled. 'I know what's going through your head. You think I do this all the time, don't you?'

She nodded. 'And do you?'

'I've never been unfaithful in all the years I've been married. Sammy has been the only woman I've ever wanted *or* needed – until now,' he finished softly. 'It's the truth, believe me.'

She chewed her lip and stared at him. What he'd said made

her feel better, made her feel special. 'Roy, I've never been with a man. I mean, I – err...' she faltered, lowering her gaze.

'You've never slept with anyone, not ever?' His tone was incredulous. 'Really?'

'Sorry,' she mumbled.

He tilted her chin. 'Why are you sorry?'

'Because I've no experience. Does that matter to you?'

'Not at all,' he assured her. 'But you won't want an old geezer like me to be your first.'

She touched his hand, feeling a strange tugging sensation in her tummy as he leant in to kiss her again. 'Yes, I do,' she whispered as they drew apart. 'Let's go to my flat.'

He started the engine and headed for home while Livvy held on tightly to her bear. Roy reached across and took her hand, squeezing it gently. He held it all the way home, letting it lie on his lap as he changed gear. In the car park at the front of the apartment block, he parked beside her Mini.

'You coming in?' she said, feeling suddenly unsure. What if he thought she was being easy? She couldn't fathom the look in his dark eyes as he stared into hers.

'Only if you want me to.'

'I do.' She got out of the car and Roy locked up and followed her indoors.

* * *

Livvy sat the bear on the sofa. She avoided Roy's eyes and rushed into the kitchen, muttering that she would make a coffee. He followed her and stood close behind her.

'Livvy.' He pulled her around, put his hands on her shoulders and bent to kiss her.

She responded, sliding her arms around his neck. He lifted her easily and sat her on the worktop.

'That's better,' he said. 'I won't get such a crick in my neck now.' He kissed her again, caressed her breasts through the fine cotton of her top and undid the tiny buttons down the front. He slipped it backwards over her shoulders. 'No bra again.'

'I hardly ever wear one. I'm so small, there doesn't seem much point,' she said. 'Pull the blind down, someone might see in.' She placed her hands modestly over her exposed breasts.

He smiled and yanked down the blind. 'Don't knock your boobs. They look pretty good to me. Perfect, in fact.' He bent to kiss her breasts, cupping them, his tongue flicking lightly over her nipples.

She sighed as his hand slid up her skirt and she moaned softly as he caressed her through the soft lace of her knickers. He picked her up, carried her to the bedroom and lay her down on the bed. He removed her skirt and sandals and quickly pulled off his own clothes.

'You sure about this? It's not too late to stop.' He could feel her shaking as he took her in his arms and guessed that she was terrified.

'I don't want to stop.'

'Relax a little. I won't do anything that hurts you, I promise.' He kissed each breast in turn, his eager mouth moving down her body. He peeled off her knickers and she gasped as his tongue searched. She arched to his touch as his fingers explored. 'That good?' he whispered and she nodded.

Desperate to feel her touch, he drew her hand to his erection and folded her fingers around it, moving them gently up and down. 'See, it won't bite,' he said, 'and that feels good to *me*, too.'

As he gently pushed into her, she flinched and cried out. He held his breath, terrified of hurting her. She was so tiny compared to Sammy.

'You okay?' He looked at her flushed face.

'Yes,' she whispered.

He moved slowly. 'Tell me if it hurts and I'll stop.'

'I'm fine.'

Roy felt her relax and he kissed her, pushing his tongue deep into her mouth. As he thrust into her, she pushed her hips against him. 'That's it,' he encouraged. 'You're getting the hang!' Her head tossed from side to side as she moved in rhythm. He cupped her buttocks, pulling her closer until she shuddered and cried his name. Roy built up speed and withdrew, ejaculating onto her stomach. He collapsed by her side, breathing deeply in her ear. Once he'd caught his breath, he looked at her flushed face, surrounded by a mass of tousled curls, and smiled. 'You sure you're okay?'

She nodded, wide-eyed. 'I wasn't expecting anything like those feelings.'

'*Those feelings,* my dear Livvy, were your first orgasm. It's what happens when you make love. Sorry I've made your tummy sticky, but we really should have used a condom.' He reached for a handful of tissues from the box on her bedside table and cleaned her up. 'I apologise for not being prepared. I'll get some for next time.'

She stared at him. 'You want a next time?'

'Of course. Do you?'

'Yes.' She smiled. 'But I wouldn't mind it being sooner rather than later!'

'You enjoyed it *that* much, eh? Share a ciggy with me then while I get my breath back.'

* * *

Roy left Livvy's apartment at 3:45 and drove to Hanover's Lodge at top speed. The wonderful time far outweighed the guilt and he felt on top of the world. He'd promised to call Livvy and see her again as soon as he could.

He pulled up outside the house and leapt out of his car as Eddie opened the door. 'Morning, Ed.'

'It's bloody afternoon! Where the hell have you been? I've been calling you all day.'

'Just out,' Roy said airily, following Eddie into the kitchen.

'Out where? You were supposed to be here just after twelve. You could at least have let me know you were going to be late.'

'I couldn't call, I was busy.' Roy lit the cigarette Eddie handed him.

'You've been up to something, Cantello. There's guilt written all over your face.'

'I haven't.' Roy lowered his gaze.

'So where've you been? Why won't you tell me?'

'I've been for lunch with Livvy Grant, if you must know,' he said, knowing that Eddie wouldn't give up until he told him.

Eddie's eyes widened and his jaw dropped. 'Why?'

'Because I wanted to, that's why.'

'So, you've been into Manchester? To Flanagan and Grey's?'

'No, it's Livvy's day off; I drove us out to Castleton. We had a walk and lunch in The Cheshire Cheese. Then I took her home.'

'Well, it's almost four now. Why on earth did it take you so long? I called you just after half ten. I wanted you to come over earlier so we could make a start. You've obviously been with her for most of the day, how come?'

'I was in the shower at half ten, didn't hear the phone. I picked Livvy up at eleven. I felt I owed her an apology for last night.'

'Oh, you mean Jess sounding off? Well, that was hardly your fault.'

'Well yeah, there was that and the fact that I kissed her when I took her home,' Roy confessed.

'Fucking hell! You did *what?*'

'I couldn't resist; she looked all lost and lonely and upset. It just happened.'

'And today, did you kiss her again today?'

'Yeah, but just a peck to say bye,' Roy lied. He couldn't tell Eddie he'd just taken Livvy's virginity. He wouldn't understand for one minute.

'Roy, you're playing with fire, mate. Next thing you know, you'll be shagging her! For God's sake, man, she's young enough to be your daughter. Sammy would bloody kill you if she even found out you'd had lunch with her.'

'Sammy won't find out, so don't worry about it.'

Eddie sighed and shook his head. 'It's too late now to do any work. I've got to collect Katie and Dom from their after-school club. Want to come with me for the ride?'

Roy shook his head. 'No thanks, Ed. I'll go home. I feel a bit tired actually, I might have an hour's kip.'

Eddie nodded and followed Roy out to his car.

'See you tomorrow then,' Roy called as he drove away.

* * *

As Roy sped off down the lane Eddie frowned and went back indoors. He had a gut feeling that Roy had shagged Livvy. Apart from oozing guilt, his mate was usually fired with enthusiasm and raring to go when they were writing new songs. Nothing got in the way of their work, least of all women. He wouldn't like to be in Roy's shoes if Sammy found out that he'd taken a very young, not to mention very attractive, girl out to lunch without her knowledge.

* * *

Livvy climbed back into bed after seeing Roy out. She felt exhausted, but mellow and contented. Roy had been an expert lover. Not that she'd anything to compare him with. Sheena had told her it was crap the first time and always hurt. Well, hers hadn't been crap and apart from the initial tightness when he first entered her, she'd enjoyed every minute.

She smiled as she thought of his firm body. His long legs straddling hers, the dark curly hairs on his chest brushing against her breasts and his wonderful, kissable lips glued to her own. She couldn't wait to see him again and remembered she'd made a promise as he left to consult with her doctor about taking the pill. In fact, if she called the surgery now, she might be able to get an appointment that evening.

She picked up the phone from her bedside table and dialled the number. The receptionist told her there was a cancellation at five thirty. Livvy promised to be there. She lay back on her pillows, thinking again about Roy and closed her eyes, hoping she might dream about him. She was semi-dozing when the phone rang, startling her.

'Hello,' she mumbled into the receiver.

'Hi, gorgeous,' a deep voice said.

'Roy, I was just dreaming about you.' She sat up, leaning back against the headboard.

'Were you now? Well, I can't stop thinking about you. I don't know what you've done to me, Livvy, but my mind's all over the bloody place.'

'Oh dear. Thought you were going to Eddie's after you left me. Are you calling from there?'

'No, I'm home, lying down. By the time I got to Ed's, it was too late to do any work. He had to do the school run. You've worn me out, you wanton woman!'

Livvy grinned. '*I'm* lying down, too. I feel so tired. I've arranged to see my doctor later. I'll take a shower in a wee while and wake myself up a bit.'

'That's good. Find out if the pill's the right thing for you and I'll get some condoms for the time being. I might be able to get over tomorrow night. Sammy's working late, they've a big order to finish. What time are you home?'

'Just after six thirty usually.'

'I promise I'll be there if I can.'

'Okay. See you very soon.' She hung up, smiling. He really *did* want to see her again. She got out of bed and padded into the bathroom, singing the chorus of the new song and feeling happier than she'd ever felt in her life.

9

'We'll take it,' Jess said as Nick nodded his agreement. The apartment in Alderley Edge was perfect. It was spacious, tastefully decorated, newly carpeted and had far-reaching views over The Edge from the lounge window.

The estate agent looked down his long, thin nose at her and Jess could tell that he thought they were penniless time-wasters.

'We will need to see a suitable reference, Miss, err,' – he looked at his clipboard – 'Mellor. We also require one month's rent in advance, plus a three-hundred-pound deposit.'

Wiping the supercilious look from his face, Jess brandished her cheque book and smiled sweetly. 'That's okay, Mr Hawthorn, money's not a problem. Six months up front do you?' The horrible man had shiny shoes, horn-rimmed glasses and a phony-posh accent. Jess hated him on sight.

'That won't be necessary, Miss Mellor. I presume you are both in regular employment? We prefer a reference from your employer.'

'We don't work. Not yet anyway,' Nick said.

'I see. Well, in that case, I'm not sure I can help you, Mr Cantello.'

'We could ask our dads to be guarantors,' Jess suggested.

Hawthorn pushed his heavy glasses up his nose and looked at her. 'So, can I assume your fathers would be able to provide suitable employment references?'

Nick shrugged dismissively. 'They don't work either; well, not boring work like *you* mean. They don't have employers, they're songwriters.'

Hawthorne's eyes widened with disbelief. 'Oh, really? And would their names mean anything to me?'

'They might,' Jess said. 'But I don't reckon their music would have been your thing. They had a lot of hit records when they were in a band called The Raiders.'

Hawthorn frowned as the penny dropped. 'Your fathers are Eddie Mellor and Roy Cantello?' he squeaked.

Jess nodded. 'Got it in one!'

His attitude towards them changed dramatically as he accompanied them back to the car park. His jaw hit the floor when he set eyes on Jess's dad's red Ferrari with its personalised number plate, EM 1.

'I'll have my secretary draw up the lease first thing tomorrow. You can sign when you collect the keys from the office.'

Jess and Nick grinned as he bowed and scraped his way back to his company Volvo. Jess stuck her fingers down her throat in a mock-vomiting gesture. Nick stuck two fingers up at the departing Volvo in a gesture *he* used all too often when people annoyed him.

'What a fucking arse-licker!' Nick climbed in the passenger side as Jess unlocked the car.

'Nicholas, you can't use that sort of language around here,' Jess said with a grin as she slid in beside him. 'Right, Habitat now to buy some furniture.'

'We only need a bed,' Nick leered, as she swung onto the main road. 'I hope the walls aren't too thin, or we'll be kicked out with the noise *you* make!'

'Behave yourself!' Jess giggled. 'Honestly, you're a bad boy at times.'

'But you love me, don't you, Jess?'

'With all my heart, Nick.' She glanced at him. 'You are sure about this? Living together, I mean. I know we've talked about it a lot, but now it's actually going to happen.'

'I'm positive. I want it more than anything.'

'So do I. We're not too young for the commitment, are we? Gran said we were.'

He reached across and squeezed her thigh. 'Of course not. Mum and Dad have been together since their teens and they're still very much into one another.'

'I guess we're lucky with our parents; they're well past the seven-year itch now,' Jess said.

* * *

'Shall we call into Flanagan and Grey's to see Jon and Sean while we're in town?' Nick suggested as they walked towards St Ann's Square and the Habitat store.

'Livvy will be there. Don't fancy seeing *her*.'

'She told me last night that she's off today.'

'Oh well, in that case, yes. We'll choose our furniture then go cadge a coffee.'

They wandered hand in hand around Habitat and chose a pine bed and a matching chest of drawers. Two comfortable-looking two-seater sofas, upholstered in a dusky-pink cord fabric caught Jess's eye.

'I love those, Nick. They'll go great with the beige carpet. We could have a cream Flokati rug on the floor in front of them.'

'What's a Flokati rug?'

'You know, like the one at home in front of our fireplace.'

'Ah, you mean the one we made...' he began as Jess dug him in the ribs.

'Yes, that one.'

'You said it tickled your backside.'

'Nick! Pack it in, I'm not coming shopping with you again. You're embarrassing me.'

He laughed and took her hand. 'Sorry, Jess, only teasing. Do we need a coffee table?'

'Yeah – a pine one, I think. We don't need a wardrobe, 'cos there's one built in. We'll ask your mum about curtains, she's good with that sort of thing.'

'What about stuff like cups and plates and sheets for the bed?' Nick said.

'We'll choose bedding from here and beg pots and pans from the parents. There are cupboards full at home and they don't use half of them. Mum's got tons of spare towels, too.'

They chose cream sheets and pillowcases and Nick picked up a terracotta and cream check duvet cover.

'I really like this. It's not too girly, I don't want flowers.'

'Okay then, we'll have that,' Jess said.

'There's just one problem as far as I can see,' Nick said as they stood in the queue waiting to pay.

'What's that then?' Jess rooted in her handbag for her cheque book.

'We don't have a duvet or pillows to put the bedding on.'

'Oh, we'll buy those from Kendals. Mum says they have the best duvets in town.'

'Quite the little housewife, aren't you?'

'You *are* joking? I hate washing-up and I haven't a clue how to use a washing machine. But I *can* make toast and coffee, so we won't starve.'

'We'll take our dirty laundry home. That's what mothers are for.' Nick smiled confidently, problem solved.

* * *

'What have you been buying?' Jon asked as Nick and Jess struggled up the stairs, arms laden.

'A bed.' Nick's eyes gleamed. 'But they're delivering it to the flat.'

'Ignore him,' Jess said. 'We've bought all sorts of things.'

'So, kids, what's the furniture shopping for?' Sean asked. 'You found somewhere to live?'

'Yeah. An apartment in Alderley Edge,' Jess replied. 'It's really lovely. You and Helen will have to come round for a meal as soon as we move in, Jon.'

'Alderley Edge? Bloody hell, that'll make a hole in Celia's legacy!' Jon said.

'Just a bit. But it's what we both want and the money's there to spend. You can't take it with you.'

'Grandma Molly's favourite saying is *there are no pockets in a shroud*! So we might as well enjoy it while we've got it and when we run out, well, there's always my dad,' Nick said as Jess shivered involuntarily. 'What's wrong, Jess?'

'Don't know. It was you mentioning a shroud, made me feel strange, that's all.'

'Jess, you *are* strange.' Nick kissed the tip of her nose and whispered, 'Let's go back to my place while there's no one home.'

'Okay. But we'll have coffee with Jon and Sean first.'

'I'll put the kettle on then, seeing as we don't have Livvy here to brew up,' Sean offered. 'Have you spoken to her today, Jon?'

'I called her earlier to see if she fancied coming into town for lunch, but there was no reply. I called again about half an hour ago and she sounded sleepy. Told me she'd been out to lunch with a friend and was very tired, said she was having a lie-down.'

'Lying down on her own, was she?' Nick said. 'Or was she with the friend?'

'Don't know. I never thought to ask,' Jon replied. 'Bit odd though, a girl Livvy's age needing an afternoon nap. Maybe she *was* in bed with someone. I've no idea if she's got a boyfriend. She's very secretive about her private life. But perhaps she hasn't and we're jumping to conclusions.'

'Well, if she has, it's obviously not someone we know. Because she'd be flaunting him around for us all to see,' Jess said. 'I hope she *has* got someone, at least she'll keep her claws off you then,' she directed at Nick.

Nick shook his head in an exasperated fashion. 'Jess, she doesn't fancy me and I don't fancy her. She's too doll-like and fluffy, I like something I can get hold of. I've told you that before. Ah, here's Sean with the coffees. Get it drunk and then we can go home before Jason comes in from college.'

Jess sat down on the stool behind the counter and sipped her coffee. 'Have you talked to Helen about France yet, Jon?'

'She's supposed to be asking her mum this week if she can come with us. But I don't hold out much hope, to be honest.'

'Well, you can hardly blame her mother if she says no, now can you?' Sean chipped in. 'I wouldn't allow my Charlotte to go off with a twenty-two-year-old bloke, no matter how much of a charmer Tina thought he was.'

'Charmer?' Jess raised an amused eyebrow.

Jon grinned sheepishly. 'Helen's mum thinks I've got charming manners and that I'm a lovely young man. Think she's disappointed that I don't have Dad's blue eyes though.'

'Never mind, Jon,' Jess said. '*I* think you're lovely as you are. Helen's a very lucky girl to have met you.'

Jon put his arm around her and squeezed her tightly. He took a deep breath. It felt good to hold her, even if it was short-lived.

'And *I'm* also very lucky that I've got *you* for a sister,' he said softly, aware that Nick was giving him a funny look. He let her go. 'Nick's also very lucky to have you,' he said pointedly.

'Right, come on, we're going.' Nick slammed his mug down on the counter, picked up some of the shopping bags and ran quickly downstairs.

'What was all that about?' Jess frowned at Jon.

'Me, giving you a hug. He can't handle it, makes him jealous.'

'Oh, for God's sake! You're my brother. See you later, Jon. Bye, Sean.' She gathered up her things and ran after Nick.

* * *

Nick hurried down Cross Street, fully aware that Jess was calling him, but too pig-headed to stop and wait. He couldn't bear it when Jon hugged and kissed her. He knew his fears were irrational; after all, Jon was her brother – well, partly – though he still felt that his feelings for Jess amounted to more than the normal feelings a brother should have for his sister. He'd seen the look in Jon's eyes when he thought no one was watching him. If Nick didn't know better, he'd swear Jon was in love with Jess. He turned as she caught up with him.

'Why on earth did you rush off like that?' she gasped.

'I don't like Jon hugging you. And he doesn't have to tell me how lucky I am to have you, I already know that.'

'But he's my brother, I love him. We always hug one another.'

'Forget it, Jess. I'm sorry, okay.' He leant over and kissed her. 'Come on, let's get back. I want to make love to you.'

'It's a deal,' she said, following him into the car park.

* * *

'Shit, Dad's home!' Nick exclaimed, spotting both of Roy's cars as Jess swung up the long gravel driveway of Jasmine House. 'There's no bloody peace for the wicked.'

Jess sighed. 'Well, let's unload the car, leave our stuff here and go and find somewhere to park up. I don't fancy doing it in your room in case your dad's next door in the music room.'

'There's not much space in your dad's car, Jess. We'll be like contortionists,' Nick said as they went indoors. 'Dad, are you in?' he called.

There was no reply as they made their way upstairs with their parcels. His parents' bedroom door was ajar and Nick popped his head into the room where Roy was curled up on the bed.

'He's asleep. Poor old sod, maybe he's ill. He never usually sleeps during the day. It must be his age catching him up.'

'Maybe he's been working really hard with Dad.' Jess smiled at Roy as he snored softly. 'And like you say, it's probably his age. He's not getting any younger.'

* * *

'Hope you don't mind a takeaway, Helen?' Jess said as she and Nick prepared to entertain Jon and Helen with a curry. 'We've ordered one of those banquets for four.'

'Not at all,' Helen replied.

'Well, it's that or Jess's specialty, coffee and toast. Or we could open a tin of beans as a real treat,' Nick teased.

'Nick and I will go and collect the order while you girls set the table,' Jon said as Jess bristled at Nick's teasing.

'We don't have a dining table,' Jess said. 'We can sit on the floor around the coffee table.'

Now the new furniture was in place, the apartment felt less spacious, but Jess loved her new home and the freedom it brought to her and Nick's relationship.

Helen took the cutlery and napkins through to the lounge while Jess opened a bottle of red wine.

'You okay with wine, Helen? I know you've got school tomorrow. Would you like Coke instead?'

'I'll have a small glass of wine then I won't be tiddly in front of Mum. She went mad the other night because I'd been out drinking with Jon.'

Jess raised an amused eyebrow. 'I hope he's not being a bad influence. Dad's warned him to behave.'

Helen smiled. 'He's not a bad influence. We have such fun together, I really like him.'

'Jon's a nice guy, but he's a randy sod. You watch out for yourself.'

Helen blushed and changed the subject. 'He's very striking to look at. Is he like his late mother?'

'Sort of, I suppose, in that she had curly hair,' Jess said, frowning. Why was Helen blushing, surely she and Jon hadn't... Jess didn't allow the thought any more space in her mind. 'I've only seen a couple of photos of Angie and they were old,' she continued. 'It's hard to tell really. Mum gave Jon a nice christening photo recently. You'll have to ask him to show you. Dad never speaks of his first marriage and Jon doesn't want to upset him by asking questions.'

'Is it really exciting, having a famous dad?'

'I never think of him as famous. He's just Dad, like Roy's just Roy. I suppose it has its advantages in that you get to meet stars. He's currently writing for Perry's Dream. Now I wouldn't mind meeting James Perry, I've really got the hots for *him*.' Jess grinned lustfully.

'Oh, *he's* gorgeous,' Helen agreed as the door flew open and Jon and Nick strolled in, arms laden.

'Talking about me again, Helen,' Jon teased as he put down the bags of food.

'James Perry actually, brother dear,' Jess said and went to get the plates out of the oven, where she'd remembered to put them to warm.

'He's a poser, if ever there was one.' Jon pulled a face. 'Still, if his records sell, then who am I to complain? More money in the family coffers.'

'Come and help yourselves,' Jess called from the kitchen. She put the foil containers out on the worktop and removed the lids.

Plates piled high, they settled down on the floor and tucked hungrily into the mounds of Indian food.

'I won't be able to move after this little lot,' Nick said, shovelling curry into his mouth like it was going out of fashion.

'Haven't you eaten today, Nick?' Helen asked in amusement.

'Course he has,' Jess said. 'He had toast and coffee for breakfast.'

'And *coffee* and toast for lunch,' Nick quipped, dodging the magazine Jess lobbed at his head. 'I'll look like a Warburtons sliced by the end of this year.'

'Any joy about the holiday, Helen?' Jon asked.

'I can't go. Mum went mad. Had a feeling she would, but it was worth asking, I suppose.'

'Can't you persuade her to change her mind?'

'No, and it'll cause more arguments if I bring the subject up again. It's not worth it.'

Jon frowned. 'So *I'm* not worth it? Is that what you're saying?'

'No, Jon, not at all. You know she really likes you but she says I'm too young to be going away with you and that's the end of it.'

'What if we tell her that you and Jess will share a room and you'll be quite safe?' he persisted.

'She'll still say I'm too young. I can't face any more arguments. She's always been overprotective towards me because of what happened to her.'

'Well, *I* won't get you pregnant!' Jon said indignantly. 'She need have no worries on that score with me. You tell her that.'

'Jon, leave it,' Jess interrupted, seeing Helen was close to tears. 'If Helen says she can't come with us then that's that. You're not being fair, putting pressure on her.'

'Sorry, Helen. I'm just disappointed.'

She smiled ruefully. 'I'm disappointed too, Jon. But there'll be other holidays.'

'More wine?' Nick produced another bottle.

'Not for me,' Helen said as Nick topped up the glasses.

'I'll get you a glass of Coke.' Nick jumped up and went into the kitchen. 'Why don't *you* go and see Helen's mum, Jess?' he said as he came back and handed Helen her drink. 'See if you can get her to change her mind. You can be quite persuasive when you try.'

'Would you, Jess? Please,' Helen said. 'I mean, it's worth a try, surely?'

'Please, sis,' Jon begged. 'I'll do the same for you. Well, I'll do you a favour anyway.'

Jess sighed. 'Okay then. But I'll feel guilty lying to her – about us room sharing, I mean. *You'll* feel guilty too, Jon, next time you see Helen's mum.'

'I'll cross the guilty bridge when I come to it. It's not like we'll be doing anything we haven't already done.' He pulled Helen close and kissed her while Nick raised his eyebrows and Jess shook her head. Just as she'd suspected, Jon *had* slept with Helen.

'Dangerous ground, Jon!' Nick exclaimed. 'Helen's underage.'

'She's sixteen next week. We didn't jump the gun by too much.'

Nick sighed. 'You're old enough and daft enough to know what you're doing, I suppose.'

'I'll clear the table then shall we have a game of cards?' Jess changed the subject, feeling strangely jealous at the thought of Jon sleeping with Helen. He'd had loads of girls and probably slept with most of them. She'd never felt jealous before, so why now? She began clearing away the empty plates from the coffee table and Helen got up to help.

'Let's play strip poker,' Nick said as Jess and Helen came back into the lounge.

'Nick! Honestly, what's he like?' Jess rolled her eyes as Helen giggled.

'What about a game of Trivial Pursuits?' Jon suggested. 'You brought the game from home, didn't you, Jess?'

'Yeah, I did. No one plays it these days, so I thought we might use it more here.' Jess rummaged in the hall cupboard and brought out the game.

'I've never played it,' Helen said.

'It's easy. I'll show you as we go.' Jon set up the board and tipped the coloured wedges onto the coffee table.

The game went on until almost midnight when Helen glanced at her watch and gasped.

'Jon, we'd better go. I'm supposed to be home by twelve. We need to keep Mum sweet if we're to get any favours from her.'

Jon stood up and stretched. 'Come on then. Thanks for a lovely evening, you two.' He shook Nick by the hand, swept Jess into his arms and kissed her full on the lips. She smiled as he looked deep into her eyes and she stroked his cheek affectionately.

Nick pecked Helen on the cheek as he watched Jon and Jess kissing. He forced a smile and waved them off.

Jess closed the front door and wandered into the bathroom. She turned on the shower, calling out for Nick to come and join her.

He walked into the bathroom as she stripped off. 'Come and have a shower with me, Nick.'

'You sure you wouldn't rather be having a shower with Jon?'

'What do you mean?'

'I mean, would you rather have a shower with Jon than me?' He leant against the doorframe, a mutinous expression on his face.

'Nick, that's a disgusting thing to say. Jon's my brother. For God's sake, what's the matter with you?'

'He kisses you in a very un-brotherly way. He looks at you as though he really wants to get in your knickers. I don't like it.'

'Now you're just being stupid.' She put her arms around him. 'Jon loves me; *I* love him, but not in the same way that I love *you*.' She unbuttoned his shirt and kissed his bare chest.

She unzipped his jeans and slid her hand inside. He groaned as she cupped him. 'Step out of your jeans and shorts,' she ordered, yanking them down as Nick slipped off his shirt. She pulled him into the shower cubicle and began soaping his body. He sighed blissfully and soaped hers in return. He kissed her, and picked her up, carrying her into the lounge. He lay her down on the Flokati rug and knelt beside her.

'The furry pile will stick to our bodies, we'll be all hairy.' She giggled. 'Am I forgiven for kissing my brother?' She looked into his eyes, seeing the love shining there.

'Totally,' he whispered. 'I'm sorry for being such an arse. Let's not mention it again.'

10

MAY 1984

'More champagne, Jess?' Nick swayed by her side at the entrance to the marquee, holding an almost-empty bottle over her glass.

'No thanks and anyway there's hardly any left. I don't think *you* should have more either. You won't be able to pick up your guitar later, never mind play.'

Nick was celebrating his eighteenth birthday in style. The DJ had got the evening's entertainment off to a good start, and later, The Zoo, along with Roy and Eddie, were to play. The marquee and gardens were overflowing with family and friends. The bushes around the patio had been strung with coloured fairy lights. Madonna's 'Holiday' blasted from speakers fixed onto a couple of large trees and caterers were handing out a hot buffet to the guests.

Halfway through the evening, Roy climbed onto the makeshift stage, where the instruments were lined up waiting, and invited Nick to join him.

Grinning and praying desperately that his dad wasn't about to embarrass him in front of his mates, Nick leapt up beside

Roy, who put his arm around his shoulders and spoke into the mike.

'Your mum and I would just like to say happy birthday, Nick. We're very proud of you, but there's one thing about you that drives us both mad!' He held out a small brown packet. 'I hope the contents of this envelope will put a stop to it.'

Puzzled, Nick took the proffered envelope. What had he ever done to annoy his parents so much that Dad had to announce it to everyone? He shook the envelope and a set of car keys attached to a Ford key ring fell onto the stage by his feet. 'Dad, a car?' He bent to pick up the keys.

Roy nodded. 'Yeah, a car. You see, the thing that drives us crazy is that you're always borrowing our cars and never put any petrol in them. Now we can do the same to you.'

Sammy appeared at Roy's side and handed Nick the garage keys.

'It's in the small garage,' she told him. 'Grandpa Tom cleared out all the junk to make room so it's now *your* responsibility to look after the garage as well as your new car.'

As everyone cheered, Nick thanked his parents and shot off the stage. Grabbing Jess by the hand, he pulled her through the revellers and across the garden to the garage block. His hand shook with excitement as he unlocked the door and pushed it upwards. His jaw dropped; standing in the middle of the floor was a brand new, black Ford Fiesta XR2.

For once he was speechless. His dream car! He'd been secretly hoping for one, but never for a moment had he expected to get it. His parents had already put a substantial sum into an account for him and Jess and he'd assumed that was also his birthday present.

'It's got a personal number plate, look.' Jess pointed as Roy and Sammy appeared at the door. '"NRC 18". Nicholas Roy Cantello, eighteen.' She laughed, looking at his delighted face. 'You'll never grow old, Nick. You'll always be eighteen.'

'I can't believe it! Mum, Dad, thank you so much again.' Nick hugged his dad and flung his arms around his mum and kissed her on the cheek as Jason and Jules strolled into the garage.

'You like it then, bruv?' Jason said, grinning. 'Pretty smart, isn't it?'

'Top of the range,' Roy said. 'You'll get your turn, son, in ten months' time.'

'I don't want to learn to drive yet,' Jason said. 'We don't mind jumping on the bus or train, do we, Jules?'

Jules nodded, smiling at Jason. 'It's a lovely car though, Nick. Nice alloys. You're very lucky. My mum could never run to something like this.'

'It's brilliant. Can we go out in it?' Jess ran her hands lovingly over the shiny bonnet.

'Not tonight,' Roy said. 'Nick's had a skinful of champagne *and* whatever else he's been knocking back.'

'We'll go out tomorrow, Jess. I'll take you, Jules and Jason somewhere nice for Sunday lunch,' Nick slurred and then hiccupped.

'We'd better get back to the marquee and play a few numbers,' Roy suggested. 'While you can still stand up!'

* * *

The audience cheered loudly as the group assembled on stage. Roy pulled Livvy out of the crowd to join them when they played the song he'd written for her. She belted out the lyrics with pride, smiling at Roy, who sang along beside her and Jess. As the song ended, Roy put an arm around each girl and pulled them close while the crowd shouted for more.

He looked back at Eddie, sitting at his drum kit, and grinned. Audience adoration, this was what they both missed, what they needed to get back to. He nodded as Eddie mouthed 'Summertime Blues' to him.

'One more for old times' sake,' Roy announced.

* * *

Stepping down from the stage, while the band performed a rousing version of one of her favourite Eddie Cochran songs, Livvy looked up at Roy, who winked at her.

She was head over heels in love with him and she was pretty sure that *he* was also in love with *her*. She'd broached the subject of his marriage and he'd told her quite truthfully that he still loved Sammy and probably always would. He'd also told her that theirs had to be a no-strings affair and that he had far too much to lose if Sammy were ever to find out about their relationship.

Livvy took everything on board, but in reality, none of it sunk in. She saw Roy needing her as his commitment to her and he needed her more and more as time went by. There was hardly a day now when they didn't meet up and make love. Livvy was convinced that it was only a matter of time before he left Sammy to move in with her.

* * *

As the song came to an end, Roy put down his guitar and thanked everyone for coming. A huge cake with eighteen candles was carried on stage and everyone joined in a rousing 'Happy Birthday' to Nick, who stood in-between his proud parents and next to Jess. He blew out the candles then amidst cheers, pulled Jess off the stage, out of the marquee and back into the garage.

He unlocked the passenger door of his new car and she climbed in. He clambered in beside her. 'I know we can't go anywhere tonight, but I wanted to sit in it for a while with you.' He took her in his arms and kissed her long and hard. 'Do you promise to love me always, Jessie-Babes?'

'For ever and ever, Nick.' She shivered as he looked deep into her eyes.

'You cold?' He rubbed her arms and pulled her closer.

'No. A little ghost ran across my grave, as Gran would say. Strange, really.' She smiled reassuringly and kissed him.

'You are staying tonight and not going back with your parents?' Nick ran his hands through her long hair.

'I'm staying. We're a proper couple now, I'm not leaving you on your own. But are you capable, Nick?' she teased.

'Of course I am. I'm a Cantello, we're always capable. Let's go and say goodnight to my guests and then I'll show you just *how* capable I am!'

They clambered out and he shut the car doors carefully, gave the bonnet a loving stroke and locked the garage door.

'Come along, Nick, your guests are waiting to go,' Sammy called out to him.

'Good,' he whispered to Jess. 'The quicker they go, the sooner I can drag you off to bed!'

* * *

Roy placed his arm around Sammy's shoulders as he watched Nick saying goodbye to his friends. 'The present went down very well, didn't it, love?' He looked into her cool blue eyes and added, 'I fancy you in this slinky dress, Mrs C.' He ran his hand down her back and caressed the top of her thighs through the fine fabric. 'It's so silky and soft, I can almost feel your flesh.'

'I chose this fabric and designed the dress especially with you in mind,' she told him.

'Is that right?' He grinned. 'Well, it works 'cos you look very sexy in it.'

'You know what I'd like to do, Roy?' she said, sliding her arms around his waist.

'No. What would you like to do?' he replied, eyes twinkling.

'I'd like to make love in the marquee when everyone's gone home.' She giggled drunkenly.

'Sammy! Actually, you took the words right out of my mouth. I was about to suggest the very same. Our minds obviously think alike.' He caught a movement to his right and turned to see Livvy observing him holding Sammy close.

'I'm about to leave,' she said, looking coolly at Roy. 'Thank you for a lovely evening, Mr and Mrs Cantello.'

'Roy and Sammy, please, no one calls us Mr and Mrs. It makes us feel so old,' Sammy said, smiling at Livvy. She was momentarily distracted by Jane, who came over to see if she could help with the clearing up.

Livvy turned and marched into the house. Roy seized his moment and followed her up the stairs to a spare room that was doubling as a cloakroom.

'Livvy?' He closed the door quietly.

'What?' She looked at him, eyes brimming with tears.

'Please don't get upset, love. You know the score.'

'Oh yeah, I know the score alright,' she spat. 'You still love her, don't you?'

'Of course I do. I've never lied to you and told you anything different, have I? I've always loved Sammy, I always will.'

'And me, Roy, what about me?'

'I love you, too; you know I do. You make me feel wonderful, alive, and young again. I *do* need you, Livvy,' he said with honesty.

She nodded. 'I need you, too. I can't be without you now, Roy.'

'I'll try and come over tomorrow night. Won't be able to stay too long, but we should have an hour or so and then I'll see you on Monday after work as usual. If there's a chance tomorrow afternoon to call you, I will. Might be a bit difficult with all the house guests, but I'll try.'

'Okay.' She nodded. 'Well, I'll leave you to make love to Sammy in the marquee then. Have fun!' She pushed him out of the way and left the room.

Roy stared after her, shaking his head. She'd obviously overheard every word he and Sammy had said to one another. He sighed, wishing he'd never started the affair in the first place. But he couldn't finish it; he needed her.

* * *

Eddie was standing alone in the hall as Roy walked slowly downstairs.

'Where did *you* disappear to?' Eddie asked, frowning.

'Just upstairs,' Roy said, eyes downcast.

'Livvy ran past me looking really upset. What do you know about that?' Eddie stared closely at Roy, waiting for a reaction.

'We had a few words,' he muttered sheepishly.

'About what?'

'I've been sort of seeing her, Ed. She got a bit upset tonight because I was with Sammy. She finds it hard to handle.'

'What, you mean seeing her as in shagging her?' Eddie raised an eyebrow.

Roy nodded and sighed.

'I knew you were up to something. You've been so bloody secretive lately and that's not like you. Is this the aftermath of that lunchtime session you had a few months ago? You're a bloody fool, Roy,' he said as Roy sighed again. 'You're really playing with fire. Put a stop to it right away. It'll destroy your marriage if you don't.'

'I can't just abandon her, Ed.' Roy pulled Eddie into the now-empty lounge from where Sammy's mother Molly had just emerged, shooting a curious glance at them, before going upstairs.

'You'll have to, mate. If she's upset at seeing you with Sammy then you can bet your life she'll be spilling the beans before too long. She'll land you right in the shit!'

'She wouldn't do that. She knows it's important to keep the affair secret. I don't want to hurt her, she's a lonely little soul. She'll go to pieces if I finish it.'

'Well, stop sleeping with her then. Be her friend, if you must. Be supportive, but encourage her to make friends of her own age.'

'She never goes out anywhere, apart from the odd drink after work with Sean and your Jon and even then, she goes home early. She's a bit timid around men.'

'Well, how the fuck did she get so involved with the likes of *you* then?' Eddie asked.

'That was my fault entirely and you're right, it followed on from me taking her out to lunch. I couldn't resist her and *she* wanted me. She'd never slept with anyone else.'

'Jesus, Roy! She's only a bit of a kid. How could you?'

'I can't stay away from her, Ed. I really think I love her,' Roy confessed.

'Fucking hell! You love Sammy.'

'Yes, I do. Christ, what a bloody mess.' He shook his head.

'What are you two looking so guilty about?' Jane asked, walking silently into the lounge, taking them by surprise.

'Nothing, Jane. We're discussing the new songwriting contract we're due to sign next week and whether or not we *should* sign it if we're planning on re-forming The Raiders,' Eddie fibbed.

'Well, you can do both, surely?' she said, frowning. 'You did before the band split.'

'Yes, but look how exhausted I was,' Eddie said, glad of the diversion.

'Well, the answer to that is don't do too many tours, pace yourselves. Anyway, Ed, come on, the taxi's waiting at the front door. Jon and Helen are already in it. Nick and Jess have disappeared upstairs and Sammy's on her way to the marquee to look for you, Roy.'

Roy smiled and nodded. 'Well, in that case I'd better go and find her. Wouldn't want to disappoint her now, would I? See you both on Monday when we bring the lads and their baggage over for France.'

'Jon wants a 7 a.m. start,' Jane said, 'so make sure you crack the whip as early as possible.'

'We'll be there. Goodnight.' Roy patted Eddie on the shoulder, kissed Jane on the cheek and waved them off.

* * *

Jon and Nick shared the long drive to Portsmouth. They'd borrowed Eddie and Jane's imported Cherokee Jeep and loaded it to the gills with bags and guitars. Jess, Helen and Jason were in high spirits, all looking forward to their two-week holiday.

Following Jess's visit to Helen's home, her mother had agreed she could go with them. Jess had reassured her that Helen would be sharing a room with her and that she would personally vouch for her daughter's safety.

Jon had been overjoyed when Jess returned home with the good news.

'Get her up the stick, Jon, and I'll never forgive you,' she warned. 'That woman was so trusting. I felt awful lying to her about the room sharing.'

'I promise you, Jess, I won't.'

Jane, overhearing their conversation, pursed her lips and started to lecture Jess that it was very wrong to deceive Helen's mother in that way. She caught sight of Eddie's raised eyebrows and blushed.

'Like mother, like daughter!' he muttered, referring to the time she and Sammy had done exactly the same thing, lying to their parents about room sharing in Brighton.

'Okay, I'll keep my mouth shut. Be very careful, Jon, that's all we ask. You don't want to ruin Helen's future, or yours either, come to that.'

'I will, Mum, don't worry,' he'd replied, laughing at Jane's crimson face. 'I promise not to make you a granny before you're forty!'

* * *

Jon manoeuvred the Jeep off the ferry in St Malo and, slightly less tired than Nick, drove the three hours to La Croix-Helléan, where the farmhouse was situated.

Jess stepped from the vehicle into pitch-blackness and switched on the flash lamp that her dad had advised her to bring.

'Jon, you're amazing. How on earth did you remember the way?' she said as he took the key from his pocket and unlocked the solid front door.

He smiled down at her tired face and put his arm around her shoulders. 'Dad's directions were pretty good, and I'm also dead smart!'

'Yeah,' she said, laughing, 'and don't you bloody know it.' She switched on the lights and looked around, sniffing the air appreciatively. The whole place smelt pine fresh and clean.

The flagstone floors gleamed and the old stripped wooden furniture showed signs of being recently waxed. Jess ran lightly upstairs and peeped in the bedrooms where the beds were made up, a welcome sight, ready and waiting. The elderly caretakers had obviously been very busy the previous day.

'Take a look in the fridge,' Jon said as she rejoined him in the kitchen. 'It's positively groaning with cheese and ham and salads and stuff. There's a big bowl of fruit on the table, fresh bread and six bottles of wine.'

'Well, we certainly won't starve for a few days,' Jess said. 'Oh look, this is for Nick.' She picked up an envelope from the table, addressed in a spidery hand to Nicholas. 'It's probably a birthday card from Madame and Monsieur Delabres. You'd better go and wake the others or they'll stay in the Jeep all night. Which bedroom would you and Helen like, Mum and Dad's or Roy and Sammy's?'

'Roy and Sammy's, please. I won't feel quite so guilty in their bed!'

'So, I've got to feel guilty in my parents' bed, have I?' She laughed as Jon put his arms around her and stared into her eyes for a long moment. He gently stroked her cheek.

'You never feel guilty, Jess,' he said softly. 'But I tell you one thing, I wish to God I was Nick tonight.' He bent to kiss her lips, but she moved her head as Jason staggered into the kitchen, rubbing his sleepy eyes, and the kiss brushed her cheek.

'Helen and Nick are awake. We wondered where you two were. Point me in the direction of my bed, Jess, I can hardly stand up.'

She nodded, her head reeling from Jon's statement. 'Either of the two singles, Jase. Take your pick.'

Nick and Helen strolled in, yawning loudly. 'Why didn't you wake us?' Nick frowned at Jon, who still had his arm draped around Jess's shoulders. 'How long have we been here? What are you two doing, coming in on your own? Why are you blushing, Jess?'

She sighed and extricated herself from Jon's arm. Nick's jealousy was rearing its head, and with good reason. 'I'm not blushing. I've a headache starting and I feel hot. We were debating which rooms to have. There's a card for you on the table over there.' Jess distracted Nick and shot a warning glance at Jon.

Nick picked up the envelope and opened it. 'It's a birthday card from Madame and Monsieur Delabres,' he said. 'That's kind of them. Your mum must have told them about my birthday.'

* * *

'Right, I'm off to bed! I'm so tired, I could sleep for a week.' Jason yawned loudly. 'G'night you lot.' He left the others standing in the kitchen and made his way upstairs to the front single bedroom.

He switched on the bedside lamp, collapsed wearily onto the bed, kicked off his boots, stripped off his jeans and lay back against the pillows. He was missing Jules already. Pity he couldn't have come with them and then he wouldn't feel such a gooseberry. But with five adults, the mountain of luggage and guitars, there hadn't been the room to squeeze him safely in. Jason had never met anyone like Jules before and they'd immediately hit it off the day they met and enrolled at college.

Jules wasn't from a privileged background like he was. He'd gone to a state school, his mum was divorced and he was an only child. But there was a connection, yeah, that was the word, Jason thought. Jules was like his other half, always knew how he felt and what he was thinking. Nick said that Jess was his soulmate. Well, if it was okay to have a male soulmate, then that's exactly what Jules was to him. Jason turned on his side, pulled the quilt up to his chin and flicked off the bedside lamp.

* * *

'Come on, Helen, let's hit the sack.' Giving Jess a last glance over his shoulder, Jon led Helen upstairs. He threw open the bedroom door, scooped her up in his arms and carried her over the threshold. She squealed with laughter as he bounced her down onto the old brass bedstead, the springs protesting noisily.

'It's lovely in here,' Helen said, running her hand over the white lace bedspread. 'Very rural France.'

'Yeah, it's nice. Mum and Sammy worked hard, shopping at local flea markets and antique shops to get the look.' Jon glanced around the attractive room. The windows were shuttered against the dark night, but in a few hours the early morning sun would be filtering through the cracks, throwing subdued light on the white painted walls and stripped wooden floors.

Jon kicked off his shoes and clothes and chucked them on the floor. He lay naked on the bed next to Helen. 'You leaving your clothes on all night then?' he teased.

She smiled shyly and slipped out of her jeans and T-shirt. Jon peeled off her underwear and gazed at her body. Although they'd had sex, he'd never seen her naked as their lovemaking so far had been conducted in his car in the dark. He leant up on one elbow, tracing her face with his fingers. She was a decent-looking bird with an amazing body and alright, she wasn't Jess, but he knew he was lucky that she was here with him. 'I'm glad your mum agreed to let you come with us,' he said.

'So am I. Although she would lay an egg if she could see us now. I'd have hated you being away for two weeks without me. You'd have found someone else.'

'I'm not like that.'

'Well, both you and Jess told me that you've had loads of girlfriends.'

'I have, but nothing serious.'

'Good.' She kissed him.

'Are you too tired to make love?' he asked, holding her tight.

'No, are you?'

'I'm never too tired. I'll make love to you properly tonight.' He turned off the light, took her in his arms and kissed her 'This is so much better than being squashed up in my car,' he said, trying to block out the thoughts of Jess with Nick in the bedroom next door.

* * *

Jess was sitting alone on the doorstep in the early morning sun, smoking a joint, when Jon came downstairs.

'All alone, sis? Where's Nick?'

'Asleep. There's fresh coffee in the pot on the stove.'

'Thanks.' He poured a mug and joined her. 'Nick been raiding his dad's tobacco tin again?' he observed as she handed the joint over. He took a long toke and handed it back.

'Jon,' she began, 'about last night and what you said.'

'Sorry, Jess. I was out of order. I shouldn't have said it. Forget it, please.' He put his arm around her and pulled her close, kissing the top of her head. 'What's wrong?' he said as she shivered.

'Don't know. I had that "falling" dream again and I keep having strange feelings that this can't all last. I shouldn't be so happy. Things are going too smoothly.'

'That's an odd thing to say.' Her serious expression told him she wasn't joking. She looked genuinely worried. 'Is it because of me? I know Nick's jealous of our closeness. Or is something wrong between you?'

'Everything's fine, most of the time anyway. Ignore me, I'm just being silly. How's Helen?'

'Sleeping, she's knackered after that long journey.'

'And you, dear brother, wouldn't be partly responsible for that, would you?' She handed him the remains of the joint.

'*Moi?*' He raised an innocent eyebrow. 'Not me, sis.'

Jason appeared in the doorway behind them. 'Bloody hell, I'm tired!'

'Didn't you sleep well?' Jess frowned.

'Not really.'

'But you were shattered when you went to bed.'

'Creaky bedsprings,' he said. 'Stereo creaky bedsprings at that!'

'Oh, I'm sorry, Jase.' Jess blushed and ruffled his hair affectionately.

'Yeah, I'm sorry, too,' Jon apologised. 'Promise not to do it again.'

11

'For you.' Sean handed the phone to Livvy and busied himself serving a young man who was clutching the sleeve of a Smiths album.

Livvy spoke into the receiver and then replaced it, a smile playing on her lips. She looked up as Sean's customer left. 'Did you say something?'

'Bloody hell, cloth ears! I said was that Roy Cantello on the phone?'

'Yeah. He invited me to lunch so we can talk about my rehearsing while Jon and the gang are away. He wants to take a demo tape to Abbey Road next time he goes. With The Zoo not being around, Roy said he and Eddie would back me instead.'

'I see.' Sean nodded, unconvinced. The animation on Livvy's face spoke volumes and quite obviously had more to do with her seeing Roy than recording songs.

Sean had had his suspicions for weeks now that something was going on between the pair. There'd been numerous phone calls and meetings and she was walking around as though the lights were on but there was no one home. Mind you, she was always what Tina called, *a bit fey*, whatever that meant, but it sounded kinder than Jon's choice of *not a full shilling*. Sean hoped his suspicions would prove to be unfounded. Roy surely wouldn't cheat on Sammy after all this time and not with a kid like Livvy, no matter how heart-stoppingly beautiful she was.

'Why do you keep staring at me like that?' Livvy's voice broke his reverie.

Sean looked at her for a long moment. 'Is something going on between you and Roy Cantello? Something other than the music, I mean?'

'Of course not. What on earth makes you think that?'

'Call it intuition.'

'Well, you're wrong, *very* wrong.'

'Okay. So why bite my head off?'

There was a welcome diversion as a delivery driver came up the stairs with the day's order of new stock. Livvy busied herself opening the box while Sean chatted with the man and signed for the goods.

Sean sensed he'd get no further with his questioning and left her to it. She filed the records on the shelves and disposed of the box in the stockroom.

Roy arrived and had a brief chat with Sean while Livvy collected her jacket and handbag.

'See you later,' she called to Sean, whose shrewd gaze followed the pair downstairs.

The way Roy stared at Livvy as she'd walked towards him and the look that passed between them had further fuelled his suspicions. He'd bet his life on it that they were lovers. Oh well, it wasn't his place to interfere though God help Roy if he and Livvy *were* having an affair and Sammy discovered his indiscretions. She'd have his balls on a skewer and serve them up to Jane's dog Lennon faster than you could blink.

* * *

Out in the street, Roy openly took Livvy's hand as they walked towards Tommy Duck's public house. 'You okay, Liv?'

She nodded. 'I am and I'm all the better for seeing you.' She smiled and he bent to plant a kiss on her lips.

'Same here.' He pulled her close as they walked into the pub.

'I've never been in here before.' She looked around the famous old pub and Roy grinned as she stared in amazement at the knickers-strewn ceiling.

'This place is quite a famous Manchester landmark for its knickers,' he said. 'Some have been up there since the year dot. We used to come in here regularly in the sixties to meet up with our dealer mate, Mac. In fact,' he said, looking around, 'I was hoping to see him today. That sod Nick's helped himself to my dope. I had an empty tin this morning. Ah well, I'll call Mac later. We can have a drink here and then I'll take you to a restaurant to eat if you prefer.'

'No, here's fine. I only get an hour for lunch, so we don't have too much time. I'll have a sandwich and a glass of lager, nothing fancy. It's just so nice to be with you.'

'I know.' He held her hand as they waited to be served at the bar. He placed their order and carried the drinks to a quiet corner at the back. 'Sorry I couldn't get over on Sunday night, but with the kids going to France the following day it was a bit difficult. Can I see you tomorrow morning?'

'Yep. I've got to work in the afternoon. With Jon being on holiday, we're short of staff, but we can have all morning together.'

'Shall we spend it in bed then?' he teased, grinning as she blushed.

'Roy, what are you like? Everyone will hear you.'

'So, they'll all be envious of an old fella like me, in-between the sheets with a pretty young lady like you.' He stroked her cheek. 'I don't mean to embarrass you – you're so shy at times.'

'I'm not any more.'

'Hmm. You're getting to be an insatiable wee madam. I'm having difficulty keeping up with your demands on my poor old body.'

'Oh yeah, I don't think so.' She smiled as the barmaid brought their order of sandwiches to the table. 'So, what's happening with the other new song? Have you finished it yet?' She took a sip of lager and picked up a sandwich.

Roy bit into his and nodded, cheeks bulging.

'You look like a hamster.'

He swallowed and laughed. 'I'm starving. I only had black coffee and a couple of fags for breakfast. I was hoping we could try the song tomorrow afternoon, but if you're working, it's going to have to wait. Leave it with me. I'll speak to Ed. Maybe we'll make it one evening instead. I could pick you up from your flat after work and then take you back later. That way we get to spend a bit of time together afterwards.'

'Sounds good to me. Have you heard from Jon and the others?'

'Yeah, Jon called Ed last night to let them know they'd arrived safely. They'll have a wonderful time. It's a pity Jason hasn't got a girl. He'll probably be feeling a bit left out. I was hoping he'd get it together with that Ronnie bird he met in Brighton when Jon met Helen, but nothing came of it.'

'He seems very shy.'

'To a point,' Roy said. 'He's comfortable around people he knows. Nick's a chip off the old Cantello block, a real Jack the Lad, but Jason's nothing like him. You can't even say he takes after Sammy, because she's like Nick and me, calls a spade a spade, although Jason gets his arty ways from her. He spends a lot of time in his room playing his keyboard or with that mate of his, Jules. Nick says Jules is gay, but I don't know. I can't make him out sometimes. He dresses a bit poncey, but then again, it's all this New Romantics influence.'

'Jason's a lovely lad. I don't think you've any problems with him.'

'You're probably right. At least he doesn't bring trouble home. Anyway, get stuck into your sandwich.'

They finished their lunch and Roy walked Livvy back to work. Outside the store he swept her into his arms and kissed her.

'Until tomorrow,' he whispered. He waved goodbye as she sauntered away with a dreamy expression on her face.

* * *

'I can't believe we've been here over a week.' Jess lay back on the tartan travel rug, squinting up at the patches of brilliant blue sky just visible between the dense green needles of the pine trees.

She and Nick had decided on an afternoon alone and had driven to Le Fôret de Lanouée. They'd parked the Jeep and carried the rug and laden picnic basket through the forest until they found a perfect spot to settle down. Although the day was hot and sticky, Jess hoped it would be cooler under the trees. They'd tucked into crusty bread, cheese and fresh fruit and then washed it all down with a chilled bottle of white wine.

'This is pure bliss, Jess. I could stay here forever with you.' Nick leant over to kiss her.

'I'd like to live here if The Zoo doesn't take off soon,' she said. 'But seeing as we both flunked French, we'd have to re-learn it. Good job Jon and Helen speak it fluently or we'd be really stuck.'

'What would we do for work if we came here?'

'We could sing in bars and clubs. We'd easily make a living.'

'I suppose we could,' Nick said. 'But if we decide to live abroad at all, we should go to the States. It's a pity in a way that

Tim and Pat are coming home. We could have stayed with them and tried to get singing jobs.'

'We could go under our own steam, work as a duo. Pat and Tim have loads of musical contacts and people they know who might offer us accommodation. Why don't we do it, next year?'

'Would you, Jess? Would you really come with me?'

She nodded and sat up. The last few days had been wonderful, but there had been times when she'd felt an undercurrent of tension between Nick and Jon. It would probably be the best thing all round if she and Nick went away for a while. Put some space between them all.

'If that's what you want, then yes, I'll come with you and give it a whirl.'

He knelt in front of her, eyes shining with love. He rested his hands on her shoulders and looked deep into her eyes. 'There's one more thing I'd like us to do.' His face was serious now.

'What's on your mind?'

'Will you marry me?'

Her jaw dropped. 'Nick,' she spluttered, 'you always said marriage isn't necessary if we love one another. Why have you changed your mind?'

He smiled and held her face between her hands. 'Because living with you has made me realise that I want to be with you forever. I want to make a commitment to you, to our relationship. Don't you *want* to marry me, Jess?'

Her eyes filled with tears and she blinked them away. 'Of course I do. You've taken me completely by surprise. I didn't think it was what *you* wanted at all.'

'Well, it is, more than anything in the world.'

'They'll all say we're too young. You know that, don't you?'

'But we're not, are we? I'm eighteen, you're almost nineteen. *We* know we're right for one another. I don't want anyone else,

I've only ever wanted you. Since we first started dating there's only ever been you for me.'

He spoke with such conviction that Jess knew he was being serious.

'And we're so compatible,' he finished, slipping down the shoulder straps of her blue sundress and giving her that special look. He pushed her down onto the rug and lay beside her, kissing her passionately.

'What if someone comes?'

'Well, that's the general idea,' he quipped, pulling up her dress to reveal her lightly tanned legs and skimpy white knickers.

'Nick! You're so rude at times, I don't know why I put up with you. You know full well what I mean. What if someone comes by?'

'They won't. There's no one around. We've been here ages and not seen a soul. Come on, Jess,' he coaxed. 'I want to make love to you. You never bother when we're doing it in Norman's Woods back home.'

'That's because we know no one ever goes to our favourite spot. We don't know these woods. The world and his mother could come charging through on horseback at any minute!'

'It's highly unlikely,' Nick said, grinning at her rationalising. 'Stop playing hard to get. You never refuse me as a rule. What's the matter with you?'

Jess smiled at his impatience. 'Nothing.' She unzipped him, freeing his erection.

'I need you, can't you tell?' He groaned at her gentle touch.

'Yes, and I want you too, but I'm keeping my dress on, just in case.'

'Okay,' he agreed and quietened her protests with a kiss as she responded to his touch in her usual wild fashion. Later, lying side by side, totally satiated, Nick turned his face to hers. 'Still want to marry me?'

'You bet, more than anything.'

'How about a Christmas wedding?'

'What, *this* Christmas? Isn't that rushing things?'

'Well, there's no reason to wait. We've got a home, money in the bank.'

She stared up at the sky for a long moment. What would Jon say? But then again, he seemed to be enjoying spending time with Helen, in spite of what he'd said the other night. 'Yeah, okay. Why not?' She leant over and kissed him.

'Christmas it is then,' he said. 'We can go somewhere wonderfully hot for our honeymoon. Let's go back and tell the others. We could all eat out tonight to celebrate. I'll buy you an engagement ring tomorrow.'

'I'd love an antique ring,' she enthused. 'But can we afford it?'

'I've just said there's plenty of money left in the account Mum and Dad gave us. You shall have the exact ring you want,' he promised.

* * *

'They want to what?' Sammy gasped, looking across the office she shared with Jane.

'They want to get married,' Jane repeated. 'Jess called last night. Nick proposed to her yesterday afternoon in some forest or other. It was very romantic and she said yes. They tried to call you and Roy last night, but got no reply.'

'We went to see Roy's mum and dad and then out for a meal. We must have missed their call.' Sammy shook her head in disbelief. 'I thought they were happy enough living together. Why do they suddenly want to get married? Is Jess pregnant?'

'Nope, *I* also asked that and nearly got my head bitten off. They love one another and want to make a commitment. They've decided on a Christmas wedding and want us to make enquiries at Ashlea Church for a free Saturday mid to late December. Jess said to ask if you'll design her dress.'

'So, they want the full monty? Church, white dress, the lot?'

'So it would seem.'

'Who would ever have thought it? The worst pair of rebels Manor Banks School ever had through its portals, according to the head,' Sammy said. 'Yet they're ready to settle down together. I must call Roy. What did Ed say?'

'He's delighted, now he's over the shock.'

Sammy dialled her home number. 'You still in bed, Roy? Right, well stay lying down while I tell you something: Nick and Jess want to get married. He proposed to her yesterday afternoon. No, she's not!' Sammy rolled her eyes at Jane and shook her head. 'Why? Well, because they love one another, of course. Why else? Yes, dear, I know it's a shock. But it's a nice one, don't you think? Okay, well, I'll talk to you later. Bye.'

'What did he say?' Jane asked.

'Is she pregnant?' Sammy grinned.

'So did Ed. Aren't we awful parents? Always expecting the worst. It'll be lovely to have a wedding between the families. We'll be related, just.'

'Well, we near enough are now,' Sammy said. 'You'd think Roy and Ed were married to each other, the way they go on.'

* * *

Jess chose a pretty diamond set in a circle of tiny pearls from an antique shop in Josselin. She couldn't believe her luck when Nick slipped the ring on her finger and it fitted perfectly.

'It's beautiful.' She looked at her left hand with delight.

'You want that one then?' Nick said, his dark eyes shining.

'Yes please, it's perfect,' she said, tears of happiness running down her cheeks.

Back at the farmhouse, Jess showed off her ring to Jon,

Helen and Jason. Helen smiled with delight as she looked at Jess's outstretched hand.

'It's lovely, Jess. I hope it's not true what they say though.'

'What's that?' Nick asked, frowning.

'Well, pearls for tears.' Helen chewed her lower lip as a flicker of alarm crossed Jess's face.

'It's a silly old wives' tale, Jess, nothing more,' Jon reassured her. 'Congratulations, sis, and you too, Nick. You're a lucky guy – my sister is one special lady.'

Nick beamed and hugged his fiancée. 'Course it's an old wives' tale. There'll be no tears for us, we're very happy together.'

Jess glanced at Jon and tried to fathom the look on his face as his eyes bore into hers. She shivered involuntarily, but smiled at him and pushed the strange feeling that crept down her spine away. She was proud to be wearing Nick's ring and silently told herself that any doubts she had about their future would be unfounded.

The remaining days of the holiday passed by in a haze of celebrations and last-minute gift shopping. On Friday morning the relaxed and suntanned friends loaded the Jeep, said goodbye to Madame and Monsieur Delabres and set off to St Malo to board the ferry to Portsmouth.

* * *

'So, what do you think, Gran?' Jess proudly stuck out her left hand.

Enid admired the ring on her granddaughter's finger. 'It's beautiful, Jess, really beautiful. And you say it fitted without having to be altered? Well, that's a good omen, in spite of what they say about pearls.'

'What do you mean?' Jess's eyes widened.

'Well, they do say, pearls for tears. That's what we used to say when I was younger.'

This was twice now that Jess had heard the tale relating to pearls and tears. 'That's a load of old wives' rubbish, Gran. Nick loves me more than anything in the world and he won't let me down. Any tears shed for us will be tears of joy, not sorrow.'

12

AUGUST 1984

By mid-August, Nick and Jess's wedding plans were well under way. The church in Ashlea village was booked, as was the reception at Mottram Hall Hotel. A three-week honeymoon in the Maldives was a treat from both sets of parents.

Sammy arrived at the factory on Monday morning with a portfolio under her arm. 'Hi, Mum,' she greeted Molly, already there, checking invoices.

'Hello, love, you're in earlier than I was expecting.' Eyeing the portfolio, Molly smiled. 'Are those the designs for Jess's wedding dress? I'll have a look when I've finished these. I've just made a coffee, would you like one?'

'Please, Mum, it might wake me up a bit.' Sammy removed her jacket and popped it over the back of a chair.

'You alright, Sam? You look a bit pale.' Molly handed her a steaming mug and went back to her desk.

Sammy sat down. 'Yeah, I'm okay. Didn't sleep too well last night.'

'That's not like you. You usually sleep like a log.'

'Roy didn't come home till the early hours and he slept in the spare room. I popped my head round the door this morning to see if he was okay. He was awake, so I sat on the bed talking to him, or at least I tried. He was shifty, like he didn't want me there.' Sammy paused and took a sip of coffee. 'Ouch, that's hot!'

'Give it here, I'll put some more milk in.' Molly reached for the mug. 'Carry on with your tale.'

'I asked why he came home late. He said he popped in to see John and Margaret Grey when he left Ed at the pub and lost track of time. When I asked why Ed didn't go with him, he nearly bit my head off. Said they weren't joined at the hip. I don't know what's wrong with him lately. He's so bloody moody.'

'It'll be the male menopause thingy they talk about on TV.' Molly passed Sammy's coffee back to her. 'Roy's coming up to that funny age. He probably slept in the spare room so he wouldn't disturb you. You'd have moaned if he'd come crashing in worse for wear and woken you like he usually does. Perhaps it's finally dawned on him you need your sleep.'

'Maybe,' Sammy said, running her finger round the rim of her mug. 'We could do with spending some time together. I've been so busy, we're like ships that pass in the night. I get the feeling he thinks I put the business before him. I'll have this coffee and call him. He said he's spending the morning in bed then going to Ed's later.'

'Why don't you have a night out with Jane and Ed? Go for a meal.'

'Good idea, Mum. We haven't been out as a foursome for ages and I bet Jane would be glad of a break.'

Leaving the portfolio for her mother to browse through, Sammy carried her coffee into the adjoining office she shared with Jane. She reached for the sketch of a jacket and placed it on her easel. She swept a pile of fabric swatches to one side, picked up the phone and dialled home. The number was engaged: Roy must be talking to Ed. She dropped the receiver back onto the cradle.

She wandered through into the factory, greeting the happy band of machinists and pressers who were already hard at work. Some of the girls were singing along to the latest Wham! song playing on the radio. Grinning at the bawdy comments she received from supervisor Ruby, about why she looked so tired, Sammy walked to the finishing table. She picked up a small pink and white striped dress that was waiting to be completed by the girl who did the hand smocking.

Sammy had designed the dress last year and it was one of her bestsellers, a real *Little House on the Prairie* style. She'd longed for a daughter to indulge all her ideas for pretty clothes. Instead, she'd had lads, one of whom wore through the knees of the toughest denim in record-breaking time. Some days she wished she'd not been so hasty in being sterilised after Jason's birth, but having two babies in just over nineteen months had made the decision easy at the time.

Putting the dress back on the table, Sammy returned to her office. She swivelled her chair round to face her easel and picked up a pale-green pastel from the box on her desk. Shading in the colour on the jacket, she became totally absorbed.

* * *

As Sammy left for work, Roy leapt out of bed and hurried across the landing to their bedroom. His head thudded and he felt bad for snapping at her. He'd made for the spare room when he got home because he felt guilty for falling asleep in Livvy's bed. God only knew how he'd managed to wake up, but when he did and realised the time, he'd never moved so fast in his life. Not even stopping to wash, he dressed, throwing sorry's at Livvy, and was out the door in seconds flat. He reckoned he'd successfully covered his tracks by lying to Sammy over his whereabouts.

After showering and shaving, he splashed on aftershave, dropped the damp towel on the floor and threw the T-shirt and boxer shorts he'd worn all night in the general direction of the laundry basket. He sat on the bed and dialled Livvy's number.

'Hello.'

'How come you sound so sleepy this morning, Olivia?' He grinned into the receiver as he pictured her lying naked, worn out from their lovemaking, blonde curls fanning the pillows, exactly as he'd left her.

'Probably because some thoughtless sod woke me up to go home!'

'Well, stay in bed and that thoughtless sod will be over in an hour to make it up to you. I've a couple of things I need to do here first.'

'Okay, sounds good.'

'See you soon.' Roy hung up and pulled a black T-shirt on. He picked up a pair of jeans from the back of the bedroom chair then put them down again. Livvy had said the other day that he never wore anything other than Levi's and T-shirts. Well, he'd show her. He could look a real smoothie when he tried; he had a wardrobe full of designer clothes, mainly chosen by Sammy. He only wore them when they went out, because she liked him to look nice.

He took a pair of smart black trousers from a hanger and put them on. They were a bit loose around the waist, he must be losing weight, but they looked okay with the T-shirt tucked in. Dare he wear his Versace jacket? It was just back from the cleaners, yet again. Cream was not the best colour for him, although Sammy said it suited his dark hair, but he never seemed able to keep it clean for very long.

There, he looked and smelt good. All he needed now was a black coffee, quick fag and a couple of tapes for Eddie that he'd recorded guitar solos on. He went downstairs, picking up the mail from the doormat on his way to the kitchen. He tossed the post onto a worktop without looking through it. They'd be mostly bills and Sammy usually dealt with those.

He sat with his coffee and fag and tried to forget Sammy's earlier hurt expression. He felt guilty all the time lately, convinced he would wake up one day with the word ADULTERER tattooed across his forehead. But he couldn't stop seeing Livvy, she was like a drug. The more he had her, the more he wanted *and* needed her. All he had to do was keep his cool and not screw up again like he'd nearly done last night.

He was leaving the house as the phone rang out. 'Oh, fuck it!' he muttered. 'It's probably some bugger selling double-glazing.' He jumped into his pride and joy, drove down the long gravel driveway and out onto tree-lined Jasmine Lane.

* * *

Roy parked next to Livvy's Mini and leapt out. He pressed the intercom and she answered immediately: 'Hello.'

'Hi, babe, it's me.'

'Come on up.' She released the lock; he hurried in and ran lightly upstairs. Her door stood open. He strolled in and closed it.

She appeared in the lounge doorway, a big smile on her face, blonde curls damp from the shower.

'You look really nice,' she said. 'Pity they've got to come off!' She reached up, winding her arms around his neck and kissed him.

'You shameless little hussy!' He enveloped her doll-like frame in a bear hug.

Her oversize white T-shirt rode up as she stood on tiptoes. He squeezed her bare backside and groaned as the blood rushed to his groin. He scooped her up, carried her through to the bedroom and dropped her onto the bed, where he quickly undressed and lay beside her, kissing her. The way she made him feel was unbelievable. He felt alive and ten years younger and there was the weight dropping off him too. After last night he didn't think he'd have the energy to shag again so soon, but he was raring to go.

She tugged eagerly at his boxer shorts and T-shirt.

'Patience, Olivia.' He sat up and yanked off his T-shirt and hers.

She pushed his shorts down and curled herself around him, kissing and caressing, then climbed on top, straddling him. She threw back her head as she rode him. He watched her face, her changing expressions and then flipped her onto her back. Her eyes were half-closed and she gave a low moan as he rained kisses down her front. He moved back up and she arched to meet him as he slid inside. She moved in rhythm and tossed her head from side to side. Her explosive orgasm sent Roy quickly to his own climax and he cried out her name and held her close. He rolled off and lay back on the pillows, eyes wide.

'Jesus, Olivia!' He smoothed her hair from her face and kissed her again. 'Oh, baby, I love you. I honestly didn't think I could do that after last night's session.'

She smiled and stroked his face. 'I love you too, Roy. There's still life in the old dog.'

He tickled her ribs and she squirmed. 'Little monkey! *I'm* no old dog. You wait a while, let me get my breath back. I'll show you how much life there is left in me. I used to shag all night, years ago. Bet I still could, given half a chance.' He saw a frown cross her face and realised he'd said the wrong thing. He sat up and offered her a cigarette. She shook her head, announced she'd make coffee and slid out of bed.

He followed her cute arse across the room with half-closed eyes. God, she was fit. Tiny but perfect. He shouldn't have mentioned the shagging all night though. She didn't want to know about his past exploits. He felt a pang of guilt as his thoughts turned to Sammy. He lit a cigarette and for the millionth time since the affair began, asked himself what the hell he was doing.

Sammy was his life, his friend, his soulmate and no one understood him better. He loved her more than life itself, but felt neglected when she put the business, the boys and even the bloody house before him. He took a long drag and blew a smoke ring. He loved Livvy, too. Not in the same way he loved Sammy, of course. But he couldn't be without her now. If Sammy found out about the affair she'd go mental, it would be the end of their marriage. It was a crazy risk to be taking. He jumped as the bedside phone rang. He heard Livvy pick up in the lounge. She came back into the room, carrying two mugs.

'That was Ed. He asked if you were here. I told him I hadn't seen you for a few days.'

'Good girl. I wonder why he thought I'd be here though.' Since Ed had warned him off at Nick's party, he'd kept it from him that he and Livvy were still lovers. Ed wasn't daft though; he'd no doubt put two and two together. Oh well, he'd wait and see what, if anything, he said later.

* * *

Jane strolled into the office carrying a small white box. 'Chocolate éclairs,' she announced. She took the box through to Molly, who helped herself and put the kettle on.

Back in the office, Jane took an éclair from the box. 'What's up, Sam? You look a bit glum.'

Sammy shrugged. 'Did Roy call Ed this morning? Was he at your place when you left?'

'Nobody rang and he's not at ours. Why do you ask, has he gone missing?'

Sammy explained what had happened. 'I can't put my finger on it, Jane, but I just have a feeling something's going on.'

Molly brought the coffees through, then left them to it.

Sammy took a sip and continued: 'I called him earlier to ask if he fancies going out for a meal later with you and Ed, but the line was engaged. I just tried again but he didn't answer. I'm sure he wasn't planning to go out before he meets up with Ed later.'

'Try again,' Jane suggested. 'He might have been in the shower and didn't hear the phone ring.'

Sammy dialled home again. She shook her head and hung up. 'No reply.'

'If you're that bothered, drive home and see if he's alright. He's probably gone back to sleep.'

'I will. I've been so busy these last few weeks, what with the wedding, and planning the summer fashion show, I haven't given him much attention. He's probably feeling a bit neglected. That's why a night out, just the four of us, would do him good.'

Jane nodded. 'It'll do all of us good. Take the rest of the morning off, spend it with him. Go on, Sam. Jess will be in later, she can finish shading in that design for you. You haven't taken any time off since Brighton.'

Sammy put on her jacket. 'Thanks, Jane, I owe you one. Take tomorrow morning off and spend it with Ed.'

'Sounds good to me.' Jane picked up the phone as it rang out. 'Go!' she mouthed at Sammy and pointed to the door.

Sammy popped her head around her mother's door and waved. 'I'm nipping home, back later. Bye.'

Molly looked up briefly. 'Bye, love.'

* * *

Sammy backed out of the car park, drove down the street and pulled onto the main road. She rummaged in the glove compartment for her *Double Fantasy* cassette and slid it into the tape slot. As the opening bars of 'Starting Over' filled the car, Sammy caught sight of Roy's Lamborghini turning a corner, two streets away.

At least it looked like Roy's car; the red colour was so distinctive. She glanced down the street as she passed but couldn't see anything. Maybe it wasn't Roy, although she knew that there were few, if any, cars like his in the area. She frowned and carried on towards home. The car wasn't on the drive, so it must have been him.

* * *

She ran upstairs to their bedroom, puzzling over where he might have been going. A discarded T-shirt, boxer shorts and a damp towel lay on the floor. She shook her head, picked them up and threw them in the laundry basket. The en suite was damp and the shower cubicle door open; the washbasin bore a tidemark of whiskers from a recent shave.

The smell of aftershave lingered in the air. Sammy picked up the open bottle of Van Cleef & Arpels from the vanity unit and held it to her nose. She'd bought it last month, loving the evocative, citrus scent on him. She screwed the top on and went back into the bedroom.

Standing by the window, she glanced around. The cream carpet showed every footprint in the deep pile. She could see where Roy had walked from the bathroom to his side of the bed and then across to the fitted wardrobes. His usual Levi's were dumped on the chair and she wondered what he was wearing instead. She opened his side of the wardrobe and peered in. He wasn't one for smart dressing, unless they were going out, or he was attending a music awards ceremony.

His cream Versace jacket was missing, along with his new black trousers. She tried to remember if they might still be at the dry cleaners, but she could have sworn she collected all the cleaning last week. So, wherever he was, he'd dressed up to go.

She picked up the phone and called Eddie.

'Ed, it's Sam. Have you any idea where Roy is?' She held her breath, her stomach churning, and knew for certain he was going to say no.

'I haven't, but he's coming later. Do you want him to call you?'

'Please. I'll go back to work, he can call me there.'

'Okay. Is he not at home this morning?'

'No, I'm home myself,' Sammy replied. She paused for a moment. 'Ed, he didn't come home until the early hours and he slept in the spare room. He told me he went to see the Greys after he left you and lost track of time. Something's not right, I feel it in my bones. The phone was engaged earlier when I tried to call him. Now he's out, dressed up, driving his Lamborghini, because I saw him coming through Jackson's Heath.'

'Well, if he was going towards Stockport, he may have popped in to see the accountant. I'll get him to call you as soon as he arrives.'

'Thanks, Ed.' She hung up. There'd be a simple explanation for Roy's odd behaviour – after all, they never kept secrets and as a rule, always told each other where they were going. She picked up her keys and bag, locked up and drove slowly back to work.

* * *

Eddie replaced the receiver and rubbed his chin. When Roy left him at the Royal Oak, he'd said he was tired and going straight home. Eddie thought it a bit odd for he and Roy were usually last to be chucked out at closing time. He sighed as he ran up the stairs; he had a sinking feeling that he knew exactly where Roy was.

Livvy's flat was in Jackson's Heath.

In Jon's bedroom he found his address book, located her phone number and dialled. It rang for a while before she answered.

'Livvy, it's Eddie. Have you seen Roy today?'

She seemed to hesitate before replying that she hadn't seen him for several days. He thanked her and hung up. She was lying. Roy was with her, he'd bet his life on it. He pulled on his jacket, grabbed the Jeep's keys and drove across town to Livvy's flat, parking around the corner. He walked the rest of the way and there it was: Roy's Lamborghini, parked shamelessly alongside Livvy's Mini. Eddie walked back to his Jeep, feeling sick. 'Now what?' he muttered as he sat in the car and lit a cigarette. 'Shit, Roy, what the fuck are you playing at?' He finished his cigarette, started up the engine and drove home.

* * *

Jane looked up as Sammy walked in and flung her bag and keys on her desk. 'You're back soon,' she said.

Sammy sat down. 'He wasn't there.'

'You said he was staying home all morning.'

'That's what he told me but he'd gone by the time I got back, freshly showered, dressed in his best and the Lamborghini was missing. Does that sound like a mid-week Roy to you?'

'No, it doesn't, and he never usually goes anywhere without Ed and *he's* at home. Well, he was when I left.'

'He still is. I called him. Ed doesn't know where he is either. He said he may have gone to see the accountant but *I* usually organise all that sort of stuff. Anyway, Ed said he'd get him to call me later.' Sammy picked up a pastel to finish the design she'd abandoned. 'Thought Jess was finishing this? Where is she?'

'Showing Ruby the wedding dress sketches.'

Sammy turned to her easel and Jane stared thoughtfully at her back.

* * *

'What are your plans for later?' Livvy asked as she and Roy drank their coffee, snuggled under the duvet.

'I'm recording with Ed. What are *you* doing with the rest of your day?'

'I promised Sean I'd go in to work,' she said, putting down her mug. 'Jon's taking the afternoon off. When are you and Ed going to finish that other song for me? You've been working on it for ages.'

'It's ready. I'll arrange for you to come over next Monday and we'll record it. We're in London sometime soon, probably later this week, so it won't be before then. It's a shame, because I wanted to take the solo tape to the studios with me. If I can get you a recording contract, I'll manage you.'

Her face lit up. He stubbed out his cigarette and drained his mug. 'That old dog you mentioned earlier, he's ready to perform tricks again!'

'You insatiable beast!' she cried as he pulled her down beside him.

* * *

Sitting by the music room window, Eddie watched as Roy's car bumped carefully up the private lane. He took a deep breath, ran downstairs and threw open the front door.

'Morning, Roy.'

'Hi, mate, how's things?' Roy grinned as he strolled into the house.

'Oh, fine,' Eddie replied, scanning Roy's face for signs of

guilt, but there were none. 'Sammy's been trying to get hold of you. Where've you been?'

'Home in bed. I didn't hear the phone.' Roy followed Eddie into the kitchen. He pulled a chair from under the table, turned it round and sat down, straddling his long legs either side of the seat. He leant his arms over the back.

'Don't lie to me. You and I have been mates forever. You've never lied to me before, why start now?' Eddie picked up the coffee pot, poured Roy a mug, pushed the milk jug towards him and sat down opposite. 'And you'd better know this: Sam went home from work this morning, she rang to see if you were here.'

Roy's eyes opened wide. 'What did you tell her?'

'Well, seeing as I wasn't sure *where* you were at the time, I said maybe you'd gone to see the accountant. She knows you're dressed up, because she looked in the wardrobe, and she's curious because you *never* dress up in the day. She also saw your car near Jackson's Heath. *I* know where you were. I drove to Livvy's place and saw your car parked next to hers.'

'Oh!' Roy stared at the floor. 'Well, there you go then. I nipped in to see Livvy to chat about the new song, that's all.'

'Yeah, sure!' Eddie raised a disbelieving eyebrow. 'She told me she hadn't seen you when I called. I knew she was lying. Why would she do that if your visit were legitimate?'

Roy said nothing and sipped his coffee.

'Roy, I know you fancy the arse off her. Did you screw her?'

'It just kind of happened,' he confessed. 'You know how these things are.'

'*These things?*' Eddie exploded. 'In all the years you were with the group, all the girls you could have had, you never touched them. Of us all I thought you'd be shagging left right and centre, but you didn't – you left that to Phil Jackson. You've never been unfaithful to Sam so what's so different about Livvy? Why do you want to risk everything for some twenty-two-year-old bit of skirt?'

'Livvy's *not* a bit of skirt.' Roy's eyes darkened. 'I love her, Ed. *You* of all people should know how *that* feels.'

'Oh, come on, you can't compare my awful marriage to Angie with yours and Sammy's wonderful marriage. You're a fool, Roy. Sammy will go mad. I wouldn't like to be in *your* shoes when she finds out.'

'She won't find out,' Roy said smugly. 'No one knows except Livvy and you.'

'Well, *I* sussed you out easily enough. While I think about it, where did you go last night? You said you were tired and going home when you left me. Sammy said you came home late and slept in the spare room.'

'I went to John Grey's,' Roy mumbled, lighting a cigarette and offering one to Eddie.

'And that's what you told Sam?' Eddie lit the cigarette and drew deeply.

'Yeah, it's the truth.'

'John and Margaret are in Portugal, have been for the last two weeks. We got a postcard today by second post. *You'll* probably get one, too, if you haven't already.'

Roy's jaw dropped. 'Fucking hell! I picked up the post this morning and threw it on the worktop, I didn't bother to look through it. If Sammy's been home and seen it, she'll know I lied about last night. Ed, what can I do?'

'Go home, check if it's there. It may come by the late post, which Sammy probably won't have seen. She told me you slept in the spare room. To be honest with you, she also told me you'd been at John's and lost track of time.'

Roy nodded. 'I didn't want to disturb her, she'd have had a go at me for being so late back.'

'So, I presume you went to Livvy's?'

Roy nodded. 'We, err, we fell asleep. That's why I was late home.'

'I don't want to know the details. How can I face Sammy now?'

'For fuck's sake, mate, don't say anything to Jane,' Roy pleaded.

'I won't. Now go home, see if the postcard's arrived and hurry up. We've got loads to do before the end of the week. I'll get everything set up in the music room. Ring Sam now before you go.' Eddie picked up the phone, dialled the factory and handed the receiver to Roy.

* * *

Sammy was on the factory floor chatting to Ruby when she heard Jane calling out that Roy was on the phone. She ran into the office and grabbed the receiver. 'Roy, where the hell have you been? I popped home earlier to surprise you.' She stopped as he spoke. 'Oh, right... and everything's okay? Listen, do you fancy going out tonight with Jane and Ed? Okay, I'll book us a table then. Italian or Indian? Okay, see you later. Love you, too.' She hung up and sat back on her chair, smiling as Jane hurried back into the office.

'Your mum's just gone home. She said goodbye and she'll see you tomorrow. Is everything alright?'

'Yeah, he had a call to go and see the accountant urgently. Something about a document that was missing his signature from when the books were done. He's with Ed now. He fancies Italian tonight. Is that okay with you?'

'Fine by me and Ed will eat anything. I'll call Jon, ask if he'll babysit tonight.'

Livvy answered the phone to Jane's call. 'Hi, Livvy, it's Jane Mellor. Is Jon there, please? Oh, right. Yes, now I come to think of it, he mentioned he was going out. Damn!' Livvy had just told her that Jon had taken the afternoon off and he and Helen were going to The Apollo to see The Eurythmics tonight. 'I was hoping Jon could babysit for us while we go out for a meal with Roy and Sammy.'

'Can I help? I'm not doing anything tonight.'

'Livvy, you're an angel. That would be lovely. We'll pay you for your time, of course. Will seven be okay? Brilliant, see you later then.' Jane said goodbye and hung up.

'Jon got a date?' Sammy asked.

'Yeah, but Livvy's offered her services. Wasn't that nice of her?'

'She's a lovely girl,' Sammy said. 'I can't understand why Jess doesn't like her.'

'Jess can be a funny bugger at times,' Jane said. 'She says there's something about Livvy that she doesn't trust. *I* think she's jealous because Nick pays Livvy attention.'

13

Roy hurtled through the front door. Nothing on the mat. Damn! He heard loud music blasting from upstairs as he made for the kitchen.

'That you, Jase?'

Jason popped his head over the banister. 'Hi, Dad. Why are you all ponced up?'

'I've been to the accountant's. Was there any post when you came in?'

'Yeah, I've put it on the worktop with the rest. There's a postcard from the Greys and a few bills.'

Roy dashed into the kitchen, grabbed the card and shoved it in his inside jacket pocket. He ran upstairs to get changed then popped his head around Jason's door to say goodbye. Jason was sitting on the floor, sifting through records. Jules was sprawled on the bed, sporting a new hairstyle – dark brown with a blonde stripe down the centre.

'Alright, Jules?' Roy said. 'Nice hairdo! You've a look of whatisname from Kajagoogoo.'

'Limahl,' Jules said and jumped up to shake Roy's hand. 'Thanks, Mr Cantello.'

'Roy, please.' He turned to Jason. 'How come you're not at college?'

'We've a couple of free periods, we thought we'd come and listen to some sounds. Jules is a fan of sixties music. I'm playing him some Raiders' outtakes.'

'I really enjoy your music, Roy,' Jules said politely. 'Mum was a big fan and I've grown up with your songs.'

'Good stuff. Right, I'm off to Ed's. See you later, Jase; see you again, Jules.'

Roy ran downstairs, shaking his head. Sammy was right – the New Romantics had a lot to answer for. Jules sported gold earrings and he could have sworn his eyes were rimmed with kohl. The new hairstyle was far more elaborate than Jason's and that was saying something.

Mind you, he thought, as he got into his car and shot down the drive, The Raiders had sported shoulder-length locks in the late sixties. Not to mention flowery shirts and velvet flares, so who was he to criticise?

* * *

Eddie tapped his fingers agitatedly against his chin and paced up and down the music room. He'd called Jane five minutes earlier, only to be told that Livvy was babysitting for them tonight. Why was life so bloody complicated? He might suggest they meet Sammy and Roy at the restaurant, but he didn't think the suggestion would go down well.

When they went out as a foursome they always left from The Lodge in one car, coming back for a nightcap. Best play it by ear, though God knew how he would be able to stop the conversation from getting round to the Greys' holiday and the postcard. Margaret had written that they were welcome to join them at the villa if they had a week free. There was no point in him hiding the card from Jane; her mother had been around when it arrived. She'd read it and would no doubt mention it to Jane. So even if Roy had chucked his and Sammy's card away, there could still be a problem.

The Lamborghini screeched to a halt. Roy leapt out and let himself in. He ran upstairs two at a time. 'Got it,' he puffed. 'I've hidden it in my jacket pocket. Right, let's do some work while we've still got time.'

'There's something you need to know first.' Eddie braced himself.

'What now?'

'Livvy's babysitting for us tonight.'

'What?' Roy's hand flew to his mouth. 'Oh fuck! Why can't Jon do it?'

'He's out with Helen. Livvy offered, Jane accepted. Nothing I can do about it. At least you're prepared.'

'Yeah, but will Livvy be? Does she realise we're going out with you?'

'I've no idea. This night out has nothing to do with me. It's Sammy's doing and from what Jane was saying, I think Sammy's got more up her sleeve for you than just the meal. I reckon you're in for a special treat when she gets you home.' Eddie grinned, watching the colour drain from Roy's face.

'You bastard! You're enjoying this, aren't you? I'm absolutely knackered – I couldn't perform again today if my life depended on it.'

'Pretend you feel ill or something. Anyway, you've always found the energy from somewhere. You and Sammy shagged for England most days *and* nights!'

'I was a lot younger then.' Roy sighed.

'Maybe this'll teach you to stop messing around. Right, come on, let's get this bloody work done. We've wasted enough time today as it is.'

* * *

Sammy put the finishing touches to her make-up. She felt relaxed after a long soak and was looking forward to the night out. Later, when they got home, she planned to leave Roy in no doubt as to just how much she loved him. The more she thought about it, the more she was convinced the gulf between them was mainly of *her* doing.

When the boys were babies she'd been so tired and was relieved that Roy was away for most of the time. When he was home between shows she'd always made an effort, knowing that if *she* didn't, there were hundreds of girl fans who would. But when The Raiders disbanded, he was under her feet all week.

He seemed oblivious to the fact that their sons needed her attention, too. When she and Jane set up Cantello Designs, Sammy had welcomed being out of the house. She threw herself into the growing business and raising her boys and although she tried to juggle everything, she was aware she was neglecting Roy. He rarely complained, but she'd seen the looks of rejection cross his face when he'd pulled her into his arms and she'd pushed him away, telling him she was too tired. What bothered her now was that he'd stopped coming to bed until she'd fallen asleep.

Roy walked out of the bathroom, dark hair glistening from the shower. He dropped his towel on the floor in a heap as usual. Sammy bit back the words, about not leaving damp towels lying around for her to pick up. Instead she stared hungrily at his body. He was still sexy and so handsome. He looked leaner lately and it was good on him. She shivered, realising that if *she* thought he was sexy then so would other women.

* * *

Roy caught Sammy staring and grinned. 'See anything you fancy, madam?' He walked over, pulled her to her feet and into his arms. Her satin camisole was cool and smooth against his skin. He rained soft kisses on her eyes, nose and lips. She responded, flinging her arms around him. He slid the shoestring straps of her camisole off her shoulders and let it fall. He pushed her gently onto the bed, lay down beside her and peeled off her French knickers. Sammy caressed his instant erection and slid down the bed to take him in her mouth. He moaned as her lips closed around and her tongue teased.

'Christ, Sammy,' he gasped. 'I love you!' Thoughts of Livvy left his mind as they made love with a renewed passion.

Afterwards, as they lay holding one another, she traced around his face with her fingertips. 'I want to carry this moment in my mind forever,' she whispered. 'I love you.'

Roy kissed her tenderly. 'I love you, too, more than you know.'

'Well, don't sleep in the spare room again,' she said. 'It makes me think something's wrong. I don't care about being woken up or whether you're drunk, stoned or whatever, I want you in bed with me. We spent enough nights apart when you were touring.'

'We did, and I promise not to do it again if *you* promise not to yell at me if I accidentally wake you. We'd better get ready, we're really late now. I'll call Ed. Let him know we've been delayed, while you redo your hair and put your knickers back on. Why are you blushing, Sam?'

'You're a bugger, Cantello. But don't ever change.'

'And don't you either.' He lifted the receiver and dialled. Jane answered. 'We're running a bit late, Jane. No, everything's fine, honestly. Sam had to have my body before we left. See you soon.' He hung up, dodging the cushion Sammy lobbed at his head.

'Swine!' she muttered, opening the wardrobe. 'Wear your Versace, Roy, and that new black and cream silk shirt I bought you last week. You'll look nice in those.'

'Black trousers as well?'

She nodded, slipping a black and white silk dress with a low-cut neckline and gently flaring skirt over her head.

'You look good in that dress,' he said, head on one side. 'Mind you, you look good in anything.'

* * *

Roy's stomach looped as he pulled up outside Hanover's Lodge. Livvy's Mini was parked on the drive. He took a deep breath, stopped the car and leapt out to help Sammy.

'Evening, Jane,' Roy greeted her as she invited them in.

'Evening, yourself.' Jane kissed him on the cheek and hugged Sammy. 'Go through into the lounge, Ed will get you a drink. He called the restaurant and asked them to change the time of our reservation. We've half an hour to spare before we need to leave. I'll finish getting ready.'

Sammy walked into the lounge, beaming. She greeted Livvy, Katie and Dominic, who were sitting on the rug, playing a very intense game of Junior Scrabble, with Katie changing the rules to suit.

Sammy flopped down on the sofa and Eddie handed her a gin and tonic. 'Well, that was a rush, to say the least!' she said, catching sight of Eddie's raised eyebrows.

He smiled and held out a glass of whisky to Roy, who took it with shaking hands.

'Sit down,' Eddie ordered, pushing him towards Sammy.

Livvy looked at Roy and smiled. 'You look tired, Roy. Had a busy day?'

He nodded. Shit, why was she asking him that in front of Sammy? She knew full well what sort of day he'd had. He took a swig of whisky and avoided her eye.

'Ed and I worked hard this afternoon so it's been quite hectic. And you?'

'Oh, *I've* had a lovely day. I worked this afternoon but this morning, I was lucky.' She looked pointedly at him. 'I got to spend it in bed, catching up on my sleep.'

Roy could feel his cheeks warming. Was it the whisky, the guilt, or the frantic sex he'd just had with Sammy? He signalled to Eddie with his eyes and sensing his friend's discomfort, Eddie came to his rescue.

'Livvy, the backing tracks are ready. Come over on your day off next week and we'll get the songs recorded. Not a word to Jess, please. Leave that to me, I'll pick my moment.'

'Okay, thanks a lot. Will you be here too, Roy?'

'Err, yes, of course. I can't wait to hear you sing them.'

She nodded, holding his gaze for a few seconds.

'Ready to go, you lot?' Jane popped her head around the door. 'See you later, Livvy. Bye, kids. No messing about, you go to bed when Livvy tells you.'

Katie, about to protest, caught her dad's eye. She sighed and turned back to the game of Scrabble.

Roy stood up. 'I'll just use the loo. You three wait in the car, won't be long.' He shot upstairs, closed the bathroom door and leant on the sink, staring at his flushed face in the mirror. He needed a minute alone to catch his whirling thoughts. A light tap on the door made him jump. He opened it slightly. Livvy pushed her way in.

'What the hell are you doing?' he said as she closed the door. 'Supposing one of the others saw you coming up here?' But Livvy wasn't listening; she reached up and pulled his face down. His lips responded and he crushed her in a bear hug. 'What am I doing?' he moaned, almost to himself.

'I love you, Roy,' she said. 'I overheard Jane telling Ed you would be late and why. Can you imagine how sick that made me feel after this morning?'

'Sorry,' he said. 'But in all fairness, I have to make love to Sammy occasionally, or she'll think something's wrong. Look, I love you, I really do, but I love Sam, too. All this is doing my fucking head in. I'm so confused. I'll have to go, they'll think I've fallen asleep on the loo. I'll call you tomorrow, I promise, and I'll come over.'

'I'm working tomorrow.'

'Shit! Can't you pretend you've got a doctor's appointment?'

'I'll think of something. I'll call you after nine to let you know what I'm doing. Will Sammy have gone to work by then?'

'She goes out between eight and nine. Any time after that will be fine. I must go.' He kissed her on the lips, dashed downstairs and out to the Jeep.

Eddie peered closely at him. '*You* were a long time.'

'My zip got stuck!' Roy fibbed, marvelling at how easily the lie came out.

* * *

The head waiter at Rozzillo's greeted them warmly. He showed them to their usual table in a quiet alcove.

Roy grinned at the tubby little man. 'Alright, Benito? Menus and a carafe of our favourite red, please.'

Benito waddled away and was back within seconds. He handed round the menus and hovered with the carafe. 'For everyone?'

'Half a glass for me, please,' Jane said.

Benito tutted and shook his head. 'You drive again, Miss Jane? You should let one of these men do the driving for a change.'

'Oh yeah, and that'll be the day,' she said, grinning.

'Now there's a title for a song,' Roy quipped, looking up from the menu.

'What?' Jane looked puzzled.

'Oh dear, Jane, wake up! It was your favourite way back

when. "That'll Be the Day",' he said, speaking slowly as though to a child.

'Oh, of course. Sorry, Roy, not with it – I'm very tired.' She sipped her wine and smiled at him.

'It's so nice to be out together.' Sammy raised her glass. 'Cheers, everyone.'

Roy clinked his glass against hers and nodded. 'It's lovely, but *I*, like Jane, am knackered. Sammy's worn me out. Haven't you, my love?' He squeezed her hand affectionately.

'I haven't finished with you yet, Cantello,' she said. 'You wait until we get home. I'm taking tomorrow morning off, too. We can spend it doing whatever takes our fancy.' Before Roy could reply, she continued, 'You have Jane to thank, because *she* was going to spend the morning with Ed. She's offered to take Wednesday instead.'

Roy gulped at his wine and choked, splattering it down the front of his jacket.

'Oh shit, now look what I've done!' He rubbed at the red stain with his napkin.

'Leave it, you'll make it worse,' Sammy said. 'I'll take it to the dry cleaners – it spends more time in there than it does in the bloody wardrobe!'

Roy nodded, his mind working overtime. Livvy would be phoning him in the morning and Sammy would be home. Shit! It was all getting just too complicated. Livvy would be upset if he couldn't see her tomorrow, but maybe it was no bad thing. What use would he be to a young woman after Sammy had finished with him? Once Sammy got the urge she was certainly a goer and tonight, she was *raring* to go. Her hand under the tablecloth roaming freely around his groin area told him that.

Following the main course, Jane and Sammy took themselves off to the ladies' and Roy looked at Eddie: 'You've gotta help me.'

'Bloody hell, what's up now?'

'You heard what Sam said: she's taking the morning off. Livvy's phoning me about nine. *She's* taking time off work tomorrow, too. Try and get her alone before she goes home. Tell her not to call me, I'll catch up with her later.'

Eddie sighed. 'I'll do my best.'

Roy's hand shook as he refilled the glasses. 'I'm a nervous wreck. This adultery lark's not doing me any good.'

'Well, it's your own daft fault for getting so involved. You've pinched my morning of lust with Jane to boot. You've had more sex in two days than I've had in a week, so don't complain to me,' Eddie said, grinning at Roy's pained expression.

'It's not all through choice, believe me. These things happen. Anyway, you've got Wednesday morning so what are *you* moaning about?'

'The cleaner comes on Wednesday. We can't act out our sexual fantasies in front of her, she'd have a coronary.'

'Get her to change her day, or go to Norman's Woods.'

Eddie's eyes lit up. 'Now *there's* a thought.' He knocked back his wine and caught Benito's eye.

'More wine, Mr Eddie?'

'Please, Benito, and can you bring the dessert menu for the girls.' He looked at Roy. 'If you have a dessert, you can tell Sammy you're too full to perform. She might let you off, if you're lucky.'

'She won't, but I'm having a dessert anyway.'

* * *

Livvy put Katie and Dominic to bed and read them each a story. She said goodnight and closed their doors. She wandered into the music room and looked at the memorabilia of The Raiders' heydays.

Gold discs, awards and framed photographs were neatly arranged in groups on the walls. She walked over to the mixing desk and picked up a framed black and white photograph. She reckoned it was one of the very first publicity photos taken when the group was still a trio. Roy, Eddie and Tim looked so young and full of hope.

She could see that even in youth, Roy had been blessed with striking good looks and not a pimple in sight. With his thick dark hair, high cheekbones and smouldering eyes, he bore a striking resemblance to a young Elvis. *Come to bed eyes*, she thought.

She traced a finger over his pouting lips. Those same lips had been on hers earlier; had been all over her, in fact. Livvy sighed dreamily and put the photo down. She walked out of the room and closed the door. She'd never met anyone like Roy before. She loved him totally and wished he felt the same about her. He said he loved her, but he couldn't leave Sammy.

But maybe he would in a month or two because Livvy had a scary feeling she might be pregnant, then again, maybe she wasn't. She'd forgotten her pill on a couple of occasions. It seemed to have mucked up her cycle. Perhaps she was worrying over nothing and it was normal to skip a period when your body was getting used to taking the pill. She wasn't going to bother Roy at this stage with her worries *or* keep mithering him about leaving Sammy either – she didn't want him to think she was being needy. She checked her watch and went downstairs. Lennon was waiting patiently by the kitchen door. He whimpered apologetically.

'Oh, Lennon, I'm sorry. Go on, wee laddie, do your stuff.' She opened the door and he ran outside, stopping briefly to cock his leg against Roy's sixteen-spoke alloy.

Livvy made a cup of tea and took a seat at the table. She looked around the comfortable family orientated room, which was dominated by a huge pine dresser. Photos, swimming certificates and paintings done at school by Dominic and Katie hung on the walls. Livvy envied Jane and Sammy and all they had. How wonderful it must have been during the sixties, knowing that almost every woman in the country fancied your man, but also to have the security of knowing it was *you* he came home to, *you* he loved.

Livvy had never experienced love in her life before Roy had taken her into his arms. Now she felt loved and safe, even though she shared him. He was the father figure she'd never had. She often wondered about her own dad. What he was doing and did he ever think about her. Did he regret giving her away? She could never give a baby away and she hugged her hands protectively around her middle.

She hardly ever thought about her mum – well, only sometimes. But whenever she thought about her real parents at all, it was her dad she tried to picture in her mind. He'd be thirty-eight now, as he'd been sixteen the year she was born. He was even younger than Roy. What on earth would he think, his daughter with a lover older than him? Roy had everything in life that a man could ever want. He'd travelled the world, had money in his pocket and still had his looks and talent. He also had two sons who were her friends and would be horrified to learn that she and their dad were lovers.

All she'd ever wanted from life, before she met Roy, was to be a singer. She thought she'd found her niche with The Zoo, but it wasn't going to work. Well, *she'd* show them all. With Roy planning to manage her solo career, she was determined to steal Jess's thunder in the singing stakes.

* * *

'Do you two want desserts and coffee?' Eddie asked Jane and Sammy.

'Tiramisu and a cappuccino for me,' Sammy said. 'No doubt Roy will have the same. Jane's suggested the four of us go to Brittany for the first two weeks of September. There's been a cancellation at the farmhouse, she'll keep it free if we fancy it. What do you think, Roy?'

'Brilliant, love – we need a break, you and Jane especially. You've both been working really hard lately.'

Eddie nodded. 'If we go away then, we'll be back a few weeks before Pat and Tim arrive home. That should fit in nicely with our plans to re-form the band. More wine, anyone?'

'When are they back?' Roy asked, pushing his empty glass across the table.

'Middle of October,' Jane replied. 'The flights are booked. By the way, talking of holidays, did you get a postcard from—' She got no further as Eddie dropped the wine carafe onto Roy's empty glass, shattering both and spilling the wine over the white tablecloth.

'Ed, you clumsy so-and-so!' Jane signalled to Benito, who ran over with a handful of tea towels.

'I'm sorry, it slipped,' he apologised, looking meaningfully at Roy, who raised a grateful eyebrow in response as Jane and Sammy helped Benito mop up the wine.

Roy asked Benito for the bill, paid it, tipped the little man generously and then joined Eddie in the gents'. 'I owe you one big time, mate, thanks.' He patted him on the shoulder.

'Well, let's just hope Jane doesn't remember what she was telling Sammy while we're in here or on the way home,' Eddie said.

'I'll keep Sammy occupied, don't worry,' Roy muttered. They rejoined their wives and said goodnight to Benito, who was sweeping shards of glass into a dustpan.

Roy helped a tipsy Sammy into the Jeep and slid his arm around her shoulders.

Jane started up the engine and pulled away. 'I don't know, Ed,' she began, 'fancy dropping the wine like that. Oh, Sam, I remember what I was starting to tell you...'

Eddie shook his head and pointed to the rear-view mirror.

She glanced over her shoulder at Roy and Sammy, who were locked in a passionate clinch.

'I hope they've got their seat belts on.'

'I don't think they care right at this moment.'

'We'll go straight home,' Roy announced as they pulled up outside Hanover's Lodge. 'I don't think I'm too much over the limit. If I drive slowly, I won't attract police attention.'

'That's fine by us, so long as *you're* sure you feel okay to drive,' Eddie said. 'Or you can come inside and I'll call a taxi.'

Roy shook his head and helped Sammy into their car. Jane kissed him goodnight, said goodnight to Sammy and went indoors. Eddie stood by the side of the car for a few minutes, talking to Roy.

'I'd rather not see Liv again tonight,' Roy whispered. 'Don't forget to tell her not to call me tomorrow.'

'I'll do my best. Go on, take Sam home. She's probably had a bit too much to drink, so you should be safe.'

Roy raised an eyebrow. 'You reckon? She was more than ready and willing in the back of your car. I had to keep reminding her where we were. Anyway, I feel raring to go again myself. God knows how, but I do.'

Eddie laughed. 'I don't know how you do it, Cantello, I really don't.'

'It's the Italian blood, it has to be. Right, I'm going before she goes off the boil. I'll talk to you tomorrow, sometime after Sammy's gone to work.'

* * *

Eddie went indoors, where Livvy was standing in the lounge with her jacket on.

'I've paid Livvy,' Jane told him. 'Go up and see Katie. She's had a bad dream about monsters and wants Daddy. Go on, I'll see Livvy out to her car and lock up.'

'Night, Livvy, and thanks very much,' Eddie called as he ran upstairs.

Katie was sitting up in bed, her face tear-stained, her lower lip pouting. He took her in his arms and cuddled her. 'That better, Katie?'

'Yes, thank you, Daddy. I had a horrible dream that a monster was chasing Lennon and me down the lane. It was awful,' she shuddered. 'It was just like the ones in Dom's book.'

'Shall I sing you a song to help you to go to sleep?' He lay her down and stroked her hair off her face.

'Sing "My Special Girl" for me,' she said, wiping her nose on her nightdress sleeve. '*I'm* your special girl now, aren't I? Now that Jess has left home.'

'Don't use your sleeve,' he said, handing her a tissue. 'You're *all* my special girls, you, Jess *and* your mum. I wrote that song with Uncle Roy a long, long time ago, before you were even a twinkle in my eye.' As he sang, Katie closed her eyes and drifted off to sleep. Eddie looked up to see Jane standing by the door, a smile on her face.

'Come on, Ed, let's go to bed. She'll be fine now.'

He rose, took her hand and led her to their room. 'Come and love me, Jane, I need you. All in all, it's been a pretty hectic day.'

'Well, *you've* been swanning around at home for most of it,' she teased as she took off her dress and hung it in the wardrobe.

'Don't you believe it,' he said as they sank down onto the bed.

It was only after making love to Jane, and before he drifted off into a much-needed sleep, that Eddie remembered he hadn't asked Livvy not to call Roy. 'Damn!' he muttered. Oh well, too late now – Roy would just have to take his chance.

14

Eddie stopped at the traffic lights and glanced across at Katie, who was frowning beneath the brim of her school hat. 'Something bothering you, Katie?'

'I've been thinking,' she began.

'Have you now?' He knew that tone, he was about to be interrogated.

'That twinkle in your eye, the one you told me about last night when you sang to me.'

'What about it?'

'Was Jess a twinkle when you wrote the song?'

Eddie rubbed his chin thoughtfully as the lights changed and he moved off. 'Err, no, Jess was already growing in Mum's tummy by then.'

'I knew it.' She folded her arms across her chest. 'She always gets to do things before me. You could have done two twinkles in one go if you'd shaped yourself.' She pursed her lips, exactly like Jane's mother, as Eddie tried to hide his amusement.

'Lucy's mum had two twinkles at once from Lucy's dad,' she continued. 'They got Lucy *and* Grace. Her daddy did it properly, not like you.'

'Well, it doesn't always happen that way, Katie. I'm sorry if I don't quite measure up in the twinkles department. I did my best, really.' He patted her knee.

She turned to look at him. 'Well, I s'pose it's alright. It's just that Jess's left home now *and* she's going to marry Nick. If I'd been borned a twin with Jess, Nick might have wanted to marry *me*, not her. It's not fair.'

'Well, *I'd* have been committed to the loony bin with two of you like Jess in one go,' Eddie said as he indicated to pull up outside Manor Banks. 'It's better this way, Katie. I hardly ever saw Jon and Jess when they were little. That's why Mummy and I chose to have you and Dom later. We can enjoy you both now that we've got more time on our hands. And, Katie, don't tell Mum or Jess this, but you're really my *very* special girl. Now that's our secret. Mum thinks it's her, Jess is quite sure *she* is as well, but *we* know that it's really you.'

'Thank you, Daddy.' She kissed him and got out of the car, beaming. She skipped off to join Lucy, who was waiting for her by the school gates.

Eddie watched her go, feeling pleased with his diplomacy.

Dominic, sitting quietly on the back seat, rolled his eyes. 'Women,' he muttered and clambered out of the Jeep.

Eddie leant out of the window and ruffled his hair. 'Son, if you've any sense at all, you'll avoid women like the plague when you grow up. They get you into all kinds of trouble.'

* * *

Jane looked up from her paperwork as Sammy flung her car keys and handbag onto the desk and collapsed in the nearest chair. 'Enjoyed yourself, then?'

'Wonderful, apart from the bloody phone ringing every half hour. Each time I answered, the caller hung up. Roy said it was probably kids who'd managed to get our number. Anyway,' she continued, 'I told him I'm going to organise myself better and not neglect him so much. Why don't you take a lunch break, Jane? I'll get on with things here.'

'I will. I need to get a sandwich, go to the bank and collect my dress from the dry cleaners.'

'Oh, in that case, would you mind dropping Roy's cream jacket in for me? It's in the car. Here's the key. I think the pockets are empty, but just check to make sure.'

* * *

Jane smiled as she made her way to the bakery. It was a warm and pleasant day and her thoughts turned to Brittany. It would be lovely to spend time at the farmhouse again. It would do the four of them good to get away for a couple of weeks. There was no need to worry about leaving Katie and Dom behind. With her parents' help and Jon and Jess, there were enough hands on deck to look after them.

She bought a chicken sandwich for lunch and a box of strawberry tarts for afternoon tea break. She reached the dry cleaners, collected her dress and handed in Roy's jacket, pointing out the red wine stains.

'Have you checked the pockets?' the assistant asked.

'I'll do it now.' The outer pockets were empty except for a couple of coins. She reached into the inside pocket and pulled out a postcard, smiling to see it was from the Greys. Roy must have picked it up and forgotten about it. She'd give it to Sammy later. 'There you go.' She handed the jacket to the assistant, who gave her a collection ticket, and left the shop.

On the way back to the factory she popped into the bank, bumped into her mother's ex-next door neighbour and had a chat. By the time she arrived back at work, she'd forgotten all about the postcard.

***

After Sammy left for work, Roy called Livvy. She answered immediately.

'Liv, I'm so sorry,' he began. 'Sammy took the morning off. Didn't Ed tell you last night?'

'He went straight upstairs to see to Katie. Jane saw me out to the car. I've tried calling you all morning, but Sammy kept answering the phone.'

'I know and I'm sorry.'

'So am I. I took the day off sick. Can't you come over now?'

Roy sighed. Sammy had worn him out, he couldn't face it. 'I can't. Sammy asked me to do a few jobs for her, then I'm working with Ed. Sorry about your wasted day. I'll see you later in the week, maybe before we go to London.'

'Okay, I love you,' she said tearfully.

'Love you, too. Don't get upset, please, it makes me feel bad.' He hung up, lay back on his pillow and sighed. What a hectic last couple of days. He couldn't go on like this. He should finish with Livvy before he got in too deep and *really* hurt her, and more importantly, before Sammy found out.

His thoughts turned to last night and Ed's well-timed diversion with the spilt wine. It was only a small thing, but could easily have been a disaster. He reminded himself to throw that postcard away, before Sammy took his jacket to the cleaners. In fact, he'd do it now. As he leapt out of bed, the phone rang. It was Eddie, calling to apologise for forgetting to tell Livvy about Sammy's morning off.

'It's okay, Ed, don't worry. She rang about four times. Sammy got there before me. Livvy kept hanging up and Sam wondered what the hell was going on. I told her it was probably kids messing about – I think she bought it. I've just spoken to Liv and I've made a decision: I'm gonna finish it, I can't cope with all the worry. She's lovely, but so is Sam. I don't want to jeopardise our marriage any more. We're getting back on track. I want it to stay that way. I'd still like to help Liv get her singing career off the ground and I'll try to encourage her to meet someone her own age.'

'That's the best idea all round. Finish it before it blows up in your face. Can you do me a favour? Will you collect Katie and Dom from school? I'm mixing down the Perry's Dream tracks and I want to get them finished, then I can relax tonight with Jane.'

'No problem, consider it done.'

'Thanks, mate, see you later.'

Roy looked at his watch. If he got a move on, he could be ready in ten minutes. He'd pop over to Livvy's, tell her the affair had to end and then collect Ed's kids. He took a quick shower, pulled on jeans and a T-shirt and reached into the wardrobe for his leather jacket. His eyes searched the rail of clothes: his cream jacket wasn't there. Fuck! Sammy must have taken it when she left for work. Now what? She'd be sure to check the pockets. Roy sat down on the bed, his mind working overtime.

Where the hell could he say he'd been on Sunday night? Obviously she'd realise he'd lied about being at the Greys. He felt sick. There was absolutely nowhere he could think of that would excuse him for being out till the early hours on his own. He'd have to enlist Ed's help.

Livvy's Mini wasn't in the car park. Bloody hell! She must have decided to go into work for the afternoon. He hadn't the time now to drive into Manchester and then get back for Ed's kids and anyway, he couldn't say anything to her at work in front of Jon and Sean. It would have to wait until he could see her alone.

He drove slowly around Stockport town centre to kill some time, through Mersey Square where they'd all caught buses home up after school and dates, then down Broadgate, where The Roulette Club used to be. Roy stopped the car and looked up at the old Victorian buildings that were now offices. As he sat quietly for a while, a host of happy memories came flooding back. The club had been the first place where The Raiders had played in public, over twenty-five years ago. It had been a small coffee bar called Mario's then. He'd been a cocky sixteen, Tim and Ed both fifteen, but they thought they knew it all, that the world owed them a living. Happy days. He grinned and drove out of town towards Manor Banks School.

* * *

Roy parked the car and sat down on a garden wall opposite the school gates. He stretched his long legs out in front of him, lit a cigarette and relaxed for the first time that day.

A woman, wearing a white cotton coat, walked briskly down the road and smiled as she passed him. She crossed over and disappeared through the school gates, emerging two minutes later, carrying a lollipop crossing stick. Roy stood up and put out his cigarette. He crossed the road and lounged against the school wall, observing the woman through half-closed eyes as she put on a black peaked cap.

He'd always had a thing about women in uniform. He would hazard a guess that she was about forty. She had nice legs, was slim and didn't appear to be wearing anything other than underwear beneath her coat. She turned round and caught him staring. He smiled.

'Aren't you Roy Cantello?' she asked, smiling back.

'For my sins.'

'I thought I recognised you when I saw you sitting on that wall. I was a Raiders' fan in the sixties. Have you come to collect Eddie's children?'

'Yeah. Now how did you guess that?'

'Well, he and I usually have a little chat. He told me you

still work together. *He's* not here and they certainly don't go home on their own. I just put two and two together.'

'Smart as well as pretty,' Roy teased and she blushed slightly. 'Eddie's working so he volunteered me for collecting Katie and Dom.'

'Here's Katie now.' She nodded towards the little girl, who was struggling down the steps with her navy-blue blazer half on, her lunch box and school bag in her hands. 'Dom's nearly always last out. It was nice to meet you, Roy. Now I'd better get on with my job. Give Eddie my love, won't you?'

Roy nodded as Katie launched herself at his legs, holding out her Victoria Plum lunch box. 'Uncle Roy, why are you here? Where's my daddy?'

'He's at home, Katie,' he said, taking hold of the lunch box. 'He's mixing some music. *I've* come to collect you instead.'

'No Eddie today?' a voice asked in his ear. He turned to see a pleasant-faced young woman standing behind him, holding a small boy by the hand.

'Err no, he's busy,' he replied, smiling at the woman.

'Well, tell him Katrina said hi,' she said with a smile.

'Oh, I will.' Roy grinned.

'I've got a mastiff bone to pick with Daddy when I get home,' Katie told Roy with a serious face.

'Why, what's he done?' Roy could hardly contain his amusement as the miniature version of Jane placed her bag on the floor and her hands on her hips, hat cocked at a rakish angle.

'He's told me big lies about twinkles!' She screwed up her nose and sniffed.

Roy scratched his head in bewilderment. 'Twinkles?'

'Where's Eddie today?' another woman asked him.

Thankfully, Dominic arrived at that moment, creating a diversion. 'Where's Dad?' he demanded, looking around.

'At home. Come on, let's go and get in the car.

'But we always go for sweets to the paper shop after school,' Dominic said.

'Well okay, we'll go for sweets then. Lead the way.'

'You have to carry our bags.' Katie thrust her Barbie school bag at him. 'I'm full of arms.'

'Full of arms?' Roy scratched his head again.

'She means her arms are full,' Dominic said. 'I'll carry mine for you, Roy. Then you only have to carry hers.'

Roy followed the pair down the road, carrying Katie's bright pink lunch box and bag. The diversion took his mind off his immediate problems of the postcard and how to end it with Livvy.

The small shop was crowded with kids and mums, but Katie and Dominic quickly made their choices and took the sweets to the counter. Roy dug in his pocket and handed a fiver to the young female assistant.

'Where's Eddie today?' she asked, handing him his change.

'Working,' he replied.

'Oh, that's a shame, he always makes my day.'

'Does he really?' Roy said dryly. 'Yours and a dozen others, it would seem. Come on, you two, let's go.'

* * *

Eddie put the kettle on and sent Katie and Dominic to their bedrooms to change out of their uniforms.

'You were missed down at the school gates and in the sweet shop,' Roy said with a lewd chuckle. 'No wonder you don't object to this bloody house husband malarkey. Your harem wondered where you were. Katrina says hi and the lollipop lady sends her love. Oh, and Katie's got a mastiff bone to pick with you.' He pulled a chair out from under the table and sat down.

'What have I done now?' Eddie groaned, spooning coffee

granules into two mugs. 'Instant do you? Saves me brewing a pot.'

'Instant's fine. Err, do twinkles ring any bells?' Roy raised an amused eyebrow. 'Here she comes,' he added.

Katie bounced into the kitchen and faced her father with her arms folded, a stern expression on her face. 'Daddy, you told me mastiff lies,' she began.

Eddie held up his hands in a gesture of protestation. 'I'm not with you, Katie. I *never* tell you lies.'

'Well, you did this time,' she retorted. 'Babies do *not* come out of twinkly eyes, they come from men's naughty bits and ladies' bottoms!'

Stifling a grin, Roy stood up and walked over to the sink, turning his back on father and daughter.

'Katie, who told you that?' her dad exclaimed.

'Lucy did, she said daddies plant seeds in mummies' tummies and that they do it with their naughty bits. I know babies grow in ladies' tummies 'cos Mummy told me. You said they get there from twinkly eyes but you're wrong, Daddy. Perhaps that's why I wasn't borned when Jess was. I told you that you did it all wrong.'

Roy's shoulders shook helplessly as Eddie looked at Katie's serious face. 'Get out of that one, mate!' he directed at Eddie.

'Well now, it looks like I did,' Eddie spluttered as Katie pursed her lips. 'But you know what? You're here now and that's all that matters. And, Katie, remember what I told you this morning, about you being my *very* special girl?'

Katie's features softened slightly. 'Don't worry, I won't tell Mummy or Jess our secret. We don't want to make them jealous, do we?'

'Of course we don't. Now why don't you go and see Grandma Enid? Take Dom with you. I believe she's made some chocolate crispy cakes. Go on, I need to talk with Uncle Roy privately. And, Katie, don't mention twinkles or men's naughty bits to Grandma, she might not understand.'

Nodding, Katie called Dominic and the pair hurried off.

'See, we each have our cross to bear,' Eddie said with a grin. 'My eight-year-old just informed me that I don't do it properly.'

'Obviously not.' Roy wiped the tears from his eyes and sat down at the table. 'That's the best laugh I've had in a long time.'

'Jane needs to explain things a bit more clearly to Katie,' Eddie said. 'That's her department.'

Roy shook his head, still grinning. 'Thank God mine are boys.'

'They can be just as bad. Although having said that, Jon knew what was what when I attempted to explain the birds and bees. They learn it all at school now. Not like us, having to pick it up as we went along.'

'Yeah, but it was fun finding out,' Roy reminded him. 'We were mean, moody and magnificent, not to mention randy.'

'Some people never change.' Eddie looked at Roy over the rim of his coffee mug.

The laughter left Roy's eyes as he handed Eddie a cigarette and lit up himself. 'I've got another problem, Ed.' He inhaled deeply and coughed out a cloud of smoke.

'Oh God, now what?'

'That bloody postcard. Sam's taken my jacket to the cleaners. Guess what was in the pocket?'

'Oh, fuck! Well, that ought to do it.'

'Help me, Ed. Where can I say I was on Sunday night that would cause me to lie to Sammy about my whereabouts?'

Eddie screwed up his face. 'I'm damned if *I* know. Can you think of anyone she wouldn't approve of you going to see?'

'I've racked my brains till my head hurts and still come up with nothing.'

They sipped their coffees, minds working overtime. Eddie spoke first.

'I've got it. The one person Sammy isn't too keen on is Mac.'

Roy's eyes lit up. 'Brilliant, Ed! *Bloody* brilliant, in fact. Why didn't *I* think of Mac?' He scratched his head for a few minutes, deep in thought. 'How does this sound? I was out of dope, nipped into town, bumped into Mac in Tommy Duck's, got talking, went back to his place and lost track of time.' Roy took another drag on his cigarette and continued: 'I didn't wanna tell Sam I was at Mac's. I made up the tale of being at John and Margaret's, not realising they were away until the postcard came. I panicked and hid it to avoid a row. Does that sound feasible?'

'Perfectly feasible. It's a far safer bet than telling Sammy you were in bed with Livvy. If necessary, Mac would cover for you. He's cheated on Jackie often enough to know the score. Anyway, come up and listen to the tracks, they're pretty good. We're off to Abbey Road on Thursday. I spoke to Spencer Phillips today and he needs the tapes for Perry's Dream pronto. I'm taking The Zoo tape, too, see what he thinks. We'll go in my car, stay over a couple of nights and then you can drive us home so I can get plastered the night before.'

'Sounds fair enough.' Feeling positively light-headed at the solution to his problem, Roy followed Eddie up the stairs to the music room.

* * *

'Mum, are we coming for dinner tonight?' Jess asked as she put on her jacket. Her culinary skills were showing no sign of improvement and she and Nick looked forward to dining with their respective families.

'Of course. Your dad's promised spaghetti bolognese,' Jane replied.

'Again?' Jess frowned.

'Well, it's your own fault. You and Nick always tell him

how much you enjoy his spag bol and he thinks it's your favourite. He's only making it because you two are coming.'

'Jess, anything's better than coffee and toast three times a day,' Nick, who had come to collect her from work, teased.

'Cheeky thing. You had beans yesterday and bacon the day before. Anyway, you're no better; you burnt our boiled eggs last week,' she retorted.

'I won't ask how you managed that, son, the mind boggles.' Sammy shook her head at the pair. 'See you tomorrow, kids.'

'Yes, Sam, see you tomorrow. See you later, Mum,' Jess called over her shoulder.

* * *

Sammy strolled through the factory, checking the machines were off and the irons unplugged. Jane locked Molly's office and collected her handbag and dry cleaning. The pair made their way out and Sammy locked the doors, dropping the keys into her handbag. She rummaged around in the bottom of the bag, frowning.

'Where the bloody hell is my car key?'

'Oh... I've still got it.' Jane opened her bag and took out both her own and Sammy's keys. 'And this was in Roy's pocket.' She fished out the postcard. 'I forgot to give it to you earlier. That's what I was about to ask you before Ed dropped the wine last night. Did you get a card from John and Margaret? We got one, too. They're at their new villa in Portugal for a few weeks. Margaret suggested we all join them but it's not convenient to go away at the moment.'

Sammy took the postcard and turned it over to read it. 'Trust them to post the cards at the last minute. Pointless inviting us over when they're already home.'

'They're not home until the weekend.' Jane stared at Sammy as her face drained of colour. 'Is something wrong?'

'They *are* home. Roy was with them until the early hours on Sunday.' Sammy turned the card over and stared at the picture of a fisherman mending his nets.

'You must be mistaken. Are you sure he said he was with John and Margaret? Not Sean and Tina maybe?'

Sammy nodded slowly. 'He definitely said John and Margaret. The lying bastard! I knew he'd been up to something by the way he avoided eye contact on Monday morning. What time is it now?' She looked at her watch. 'Five fifteen – right, come back inside with me.'

'What for?' Jane followed Sammy back into Molly's office.

'You'll see.' Sammy reached into her bag and pulled out a small address book. 'Accountant,' she muttered, running her finger down the first page. 'Here it is.' She snatched up the phone and dialled a number.

'Ah, yes, this is Sammy Cantello. Could you tell me if my husband left a set of house keys on your premises when he came in to see Mr Atkinson on Monday? Thank you, I'll hold.' She waited patiently, shaking her head at Jane, who was staring at her with a look of bewilderment on her face. 'I must have been mistaken then. Sorry to have troubled you. Goodbye.' Sammy slammed down the phone, her eyes wide in her pale face.

'What's going on?' Jane demanded.

'The lying bastard! I'll bloody kill him.'

'Who? Why?'

'Roy, of course. He's lied to me. He wasn't at the accountant's on Monday at all. Nor could he have been at John and Margaret's on Sunday night. He wasn't home until the early hours and slept in the spare room. He deliberately hid that postcard from me. He disappeared soon after I left for work, dressed up to the nines. Then those phone calls this morning and the caller hanging up every time I answered. What do you make of it, Jane? If that was a list of things Ed had done, what would you think?'

'To be honest, I'd suspect he was having an affair. Oh, but Roy can't be, Sammy. That's a ridiculous notion. He's been all over you the last couple of days and you've both been so happy.'

'Well, *I've* been *very* happy, but you can bet your life that for Roy, it's guilt. God, I feel so bloody angry. I've had my suspicions for a while. I didn't mention it to you because I thought I was being paranoid. There's been the odd thing. Like, he's not really listening when I'm speaking to him and there's a faraway look in his eyes. I thought it was because he'd got lyrics going through his head. You know how temperamental he *and* Ed can be when they're working on new songs. So I dismissed it. But now I'm wondering if I was right to be concerned.'

Jane chewed her lower lip. 'Go home and talk to him before you jump in with both feet and accuse him of anything,' she advised. 'You're probably barking up the wrong tree entirely. I'll ask Ed if he knows what Roy's been up to – discreetly, of course.'

Sammy snorted. 'They're as thick as thieves. I bet Ed's covering for him.'

'He'd better not be or I'll have a thing or two to say about that.'

'I tell you, Jane, if he *is* having an affair, I'll castrate the bastard. He'll never perform again. Not with me, *her*, whoever she is, or anyone else for that matter.'

15

Roy stretched his arms above his head. 'Those tracks are brilliant. Let's hope that Perry's Dream bunch can do 'em justice. Have you got any dope, Ed? I could murder a spliff before I face the wrath of Sammy.'

'On the shelf above the mixing desk.' Eddie pointed to a tin box. 'You roll up, you're neater than me.'

'It'll give me Dutch courage.' Roy expertly rolled a fat joint. He lit up and inhaled deeply. 'Ah, bloody hell, that's lovely! Here you go, Ed.'

They sat back in their respective chairs, sharing the joint and chatting amiably.

'If even one of those tracks is a hit, it'll keep us afloat for a bit longer,' Roy said. 'When Tim's back, I fancy going straight into the studio. Do a Raiders' hits album or something.'

'That reminds me, I spoke to him earlier and he's really excited about re-forming the band,' Eddie said. 'We need to contact Phil and Carl, see what their thoughts are. I'll call them when we're back from London.'

'Count me in. How's Pat?'

'Doing great apparently and looking forward to coming home.'

They sat in companionable silence for a while. Eddie stubbed the joint end out and stood up. Hearing car tyres on gravel, he looked out of the window.

'Shit, it's Jane! Is it that time already? Jess and Nick are coming to eat with us and I haven't even *started* dinner. A man's work, and all that crap.'

* * *

Jane was standing by the Welsh dresser as Eddie and Roy strolled into the kitchen. Mellow from the joint, Eddie caught her in his arms, whirled her round and kissed her. 'You look tired, sweetheart. Had a busy day?'

'So, so,' she said, looking at Roy. 'I think *you'd* better go straight home.'

'Oh!' Roy raised an innocent eyebrow. 'Why, Jane?'

'I'm not at liberty to say. Just go, Roy, please.'

'Okay. See you tomorrow, Ed. See you, Jane.'

Eddie closed the door after Roy and turned to Jane as she muttered, 'He'll be lucky.'

'What's that supposed to mean?'

'If he sees you tomorrow, he'll be lucky,' she repeated.

'Why? What's wrong?'

'As if you didn't know.'

Eddie shrugged. 'Haven't a clue what you're on about.'

'What's he been up to? I want the truth, don't you dare lie to me.'

He shook his head in mock bewilderment. 'He's not been up to anything. He just picked the kids up from school and we've been working. He was home with Sammy all morning.'

'Where was he yesterday morning and Sunday night until the early hours?'

'He was with the accountant yesterday and then he came over here. I don't really know where he went on Sunday night after he left me. He might have gone into town for supplies.' Eddie wasn't going to perjure himself by saying that Roy was with Mac in case he'd thought up a better excuse on his way home.

'He'd have told you if he was meeting Mac. You're lying, Ed, so's Roy. He wasn't with the accountant at all, Sammy checked. Have *you* been up to something, too? Are you covering for one another?'

She was getting really angry and Eddie put his hands on her shaking shoulders and pushed her gently down onto a chair.

'If I find out that you've been cheating on *me*, Eddie Mellor, I'll never forgive you as long as I live.'

'Jane, for fuck's sake, love, I haven't and I never will. You know that.' *Damn Roy*, he thought, *now I'm getting accused of something I would never dream of doing*. 'I love you. Didn't we have enough problems at the beginning of our relationship? Do you honestly think I would jeopardise what we have now for a cheap fling?'

'I hope not,' she sniffed. 'But Sammy's certain Roy's having an affair.'

'What reasons does she have for thinking that?'

Jane told him what Sammy had deduced and he shook his head.

'Admittedly it sounds a bit dodgy but don't you think Roy would tell me if he was having a bit on the side? He usually tells me everything.' Shit, he hated lying to her, but he and Roy went back even further than him and Jane. There was a certain amount of loyalty they owed one another. But if this mess jeopardised his marriage, Eddie would find it very hard to forgive Roy.

'There must be a simple explanation.' Jane sighed. 'Anyway, no doubt we'll hear from Sammy later. We'd better get dinner ready. Jess and Nick are expecting your spag bol and they'll be here soon.'

* * *

Roy entered the house and strolled through to the lounge. He casually flung his leather jacket onto a chair.

Sammy was sitting on one of the cream sofas in front of the marble fireplace, clutching a brandy glass, her face, pale and tear-streaked.

'Hi, Sam, everything alright?' He ducked as the glass sailed past his left ear and smashed against the wall.

'You tell me!' she yelled. 'You waltz in here without a care in the world and ask me if everything's alright, when you know full well you've been screwing around.'

'Sorry? What the fuck are you on about? I haven't been screwing around. Where's that notion come from?'

'You lying bastard!' She launched herself at him and slapped him soundly across the face, sending him flying backwards onto the other sofa.

Roy protected his face with his hands as the blows rained down on his head. He grabbed Sammy's wrists and wrestled her to the floor, pinning her down with his body while trying to dodge her feet as she lashed out in a vain attempt to kick his nether regions.

'Stop it, Sam, stop it. Stop it right now!' he yelled, shocked by her extremely out-of-character hysteria. Her body went limp beneath him as she sobbed.

'Who is she? Some tart you picked up in the pub?' She wriggled into an upright position and pushed him away.

'I don't know what you mean.'

'Yes, you do. You're having an affair.'

'I'm not. What makes you think that?'

Between sobs, Sammy presented him with her evidence.

Roy was ready with his excuse for Sunday night, but for Monday morning, he had none. Christ, he was well and truly up shit creek without a paddle. Should he just get it over with? It couldn't get any worse, could it? He decided to tell her the truth.

'It's Livvy Grant,' he muttered quietly, putting his head in his hands.

'What?' Sammy gasped.

'It's Livvy,' he repeated, looking at her.

'You must be joking?' Sammy got up off the floor and sat back on the sofa, eyes wide with horror. 'How could you? She's only a kid. For God's sake, you're old enough to be her father.' She looked at him, his eyes holding her gaze. 'Do you love her?'

'I do,' he replied truthfully. 'But not in the same way that I love you.'

'How long?'

He shrugged. 'Since May.'

'Is she better in bed than me?' she choked. 'Is that it?'

'Of course not, she's just... different,' he finished lamely.

'You don't know where she's been or who she's been with. Kids change partners all the time. You could catch all sorts and pass it on to me.'

'She's not like that, Sam. She's never slept around.'

She looked at him aghast. 'You mean you were her first? Oh, God, that makes it even worse.'

Roy clapped his hands to his head. 'Well, I can't fucking win either way!' he exclaimed. 'So what does it matter?'

'I hope to God she's on the pill. She is... isn't she?'

'She is.'

'Do you want to be with her? Are you planning on leaving me?'

He got down on his knees in front of her. 'Do you *want* me to go?' He took her hands in his. She was cold and shaking, tears running freely down her cheeks.

'Of course I don't want you to go. After last night and this morning I thought everything was perfect between us. I was so happy and now this. Oh, Roy, you were with her yesterday morning and then you made love to me last night. How could you do that?' Sammy sobbed. 'And she was at Jane's last night. What must she have been thinking? I bet she was laughing at me behind my back.'

'Sam, please don't think like that. I'd already made up my mind to finish with her and I went to do that this afternoon, but she wasn't home. I'll do it tomorrow, I promise you.'

Sammy shook her head. 'You won't. You don't see her again, or you're out of that door for good and there'll be a part of you missing, because I'll chop it off! *I'll* call her now and tell her that it's over. Was that her phoning this morning?'

'Yes. I'll have to tell her, not you, that's not fair. She'll be so upset.'

'Well, tough! If you go to her, you never set foot in this house again. I mean that, Roy. It's your choice.'

The door between the hall and lounge opened and Jason's worried face peered around it. 'I heard shouting. Is everything okay?'

'Oh wonderful, Jason, absolutely bloody wonderful! Your father's only been screwing your friend Livvy for the last few months!'

Jason gasped, the colour draining from his young face. 'Dad, no! You haven't... have you?' His tone was incredulous.

'Yes, he bloody well has,' Sammy answered for Roy, who hung his head, unable to look Jason in the eye. She spoke again, quieter this time. 'Just leave us alone, love. We've a lot to discuss. I'll come up and see you later.'

Jason nodded. He left the room and closed the door quietly.

'Did you have to tell him like that?' Roy said.

'Well, why not? He's a grown-up. You're always telling me not to baby him. I'll tell Nick later too when he phones. In fact,

I'll phone him at Jane's and tell him now. Let him know what sort of animal he's got for a father, seducing his young friend. I'm surprised you haven't made a play for Jess, you're always ogling her when she's around.'

'That's uncalled for, Sam. Jess is Ed's daughter, my son's fiancée. I would *never* do that.'

'Only because Ed and Nick would annihilate you if you did,' Sammy responded tartly.

'Sammy, this is getting ridiculous. I'm going to go now and tell her it's over.' He picked up his jacket and made for the door.

'You go to her now and you don't ever come back to this house,' she said.

'Fine, here's the fucking house key! I'll stay at Ed's or Sean's tonight.' He wrestled the key from his key ring, threw it at her, and walked out.

* * *

Why the hell didn't I keep my big mouth shut and think first before confessing all? Roy thought as he sat in his car and lit a cigarette. Now what? If he went to Livvy's, who knew what Sammy might do? She could be fiery and unpredictable when the mood took her.

He revved up the engine and drove over to Hanover's Lodge. He spotted Nick's car parked on the drive as well as Jon's and sighed; that meant Ed and Jane had a houseful. Still, he'd nowhere else to go apart from his elderly parents and his mother would give him hell when she found out what he'd been up to. Sammy would no doubt make it her business to tell them. She was very close to them, closer in fact than he was. She was probably calling them right now.

Eddie let him in, a wary look on his face. Nick, Jess and Jon were seated around the kitchen table, finishing their meal. Katie and Dom were in their pyjamas, about to go up to bed. Jane was on the phone and judging by the cold look she gave him, Roy guessed she was talking to Sammy.

'Say goodnight to everybody,' Eddie said to the kids as he tried to shepherd them out of the room.

'I want Uncle Roy to read me a bedtime story.' Katie folded her arms across her chest.

'Not tonight. He'll read you one another time. Now move it, Katie, or you won't get a story at all. Sit down and help yourself to a glass of wine,' Eddie said to Roy. 'See you in a few minutes.'

Jon got up. 'I'll take 'em up, Dad. You stay down here with Roy.'

'Thanks, son,' Eddie said as Katie flung herself at her brother and he hoisted her onto his shoulders. He left the room, Dom following.

There was an uneasy silence as Roy took a seat. He poured a glass of red and took a sip, his hand shaking. All eyes were on him and he felt his face warming.

'I've just talked to Mum,' Nick spoke first. 'I hope you haven't come here looking for sympathy, Dad, because you sure as hell won't get any from me.' He scraped his chair backwards on the quarry-tiled floor and stood up. 'I ought to punch your fucking lights out for what you've done.'

'Your mother's already done that,' Roy replied, touching his throbbing cheek.

'Good for her,' Jess said. 'How could you, Roy? How could you do that to Sammy, and with that little slapper? I knew there was something about her that I didn't trust.'

'Cool it, Jess,' Eddie warned. 'I think Roy's had enough for tonight.'

'We're going over to see Mum in a minute,' Nick said. 'She needs us.'

Jane finished on the phone, hung up and looked at Roy. 'Well, you've really done it this time. Why, Roy, why now? Why didn't you just get it out of your system while you were on the road? Why play around now under all our noses *and* with a bit of a kid? That little madam was here last night as well. The two of you together in the same room and neither of you batted an eyelid. How bloody brazen can you get? I can't believe it of you *or* Livvy, I really can't. I'm going over to sit with Sammy for a while; she's devastated. Try and talk some sense into him, Ed,' she finished as she left the house, closely followed by Jess and Nick, who didn't waste a backward glance on his father.

Jon returned to the kitchen shortly after the others left. He sat down and handed Roy a cigarette.

'What on earth made you tell Sammy the truth?' he asked. 'Wouldn't a white lie have been better?'

Roy smiled wearily. 'Believe me, I was all ready with my white lies. What I didn't bargain on was Sammy checking out my alibi for Monday morning. It fell flat on its face so I decided I'd better just get it over with. She'd guessed I was having an affair, she just needed a name. I can't believe I managed to get away with it for over three months and then blow it all in one fell swoop.'

'An unfortunate set of circumstances.' Eddie sighed. '*I* got accused of being in cahoots with you. Jane thought I'd been up to something, too. She doesn't know that I know, by the way, and she thinks that's really odd, considering how close me and you are.'

'I'm sorry, mate. I shouldn't have dragged you into this bloody mess.'

'So, what now, Roy?' Jon asked.

He shrugged. 'I don't know. Sammy told me not to come back if I go to Livvy's, so I threw the house key at her and walked out. I've got to warn Livvy that Sammy knows. I need to finish it with her. Sammy wanted to tell her, but I can't let her do that, it wouldn't be fair.'

'*You* should be the one to tell her it's over,' Eddie said. 'Go and do it now, get it out of the way, then go home and try and talk to Sammy.'

'If I go to Livvy's tonight, Sammy's threatened to cut off my tackle. I wouldn't put it past her to try either,' Roy said as Eddie and Jon exchanged amused glances. 'It's no bloody laughing matter, you two.'

'We know that,' Jon smirked. 'But you have to go and see Livvy. She came into work this afternoon and she was really miserable.'

'That's because I let her down this morning. I was supposed to be seeing her, but Sammy took the morning off, so I couldn't get out. Hey, don't you let on to Sean why she wasn't in work. She told him she was ill.'

'She didn't look well actually. Said she felt a bit off colour,' Jon said. 'I had a feeling she'd got mixed up with a married man, but I had no idea it was you, Roy. She's not an easy nut to crack. I took her out a couple of times and got absolutely nowhere, in spite of my charms. You're a lucky sod,' he finished with a grin.

'You reckon? I'm hardly lucky if I've lost everything. I suppose I'd better go and get it over with. I'm not looking forward to this at all. Shall I come back here afterwards or go home?'

'Go home to Sammy,' Eddie advised. 'She won't cut your bits off. Mind you, she did ask Jane to bring the meat cleaver.'

'Don't even joke about it,' Roy said, shuddering as he stood up to leave.

'Well, good luck, mate,' Eddie said as he accompanied Roy to his car. 'And when you get to Livvy's, try and keep it zipped up.'

* * *

Roy pressed the intercom and lounged against the wall.

'Hello.' Livvy answered immediately.

'It's me,' he said.

'Hi you, come on up.' She released the catch and he dragged his feet up to the first floor, feeling sick inside. He knew once he saw her he would find it hard to say goodbye. She opened the door with a smile and his heart thudded. Her hair, piled on top with a few escaping tendrils, along with her big blue eyes, gave her an almost waif-like appearance that made him want to sweep her up in his arms and carry her off to the bedroom. She was wearing her denim skirt and a little white top, her feet bare, and he could smell her perfume.

'It's lovely to see you and so unexpected. Come through to the lounge.' She took his hand and led the way, gasping as she caught sight of his face in the light from the window. 'Roy, what's happened to you?' She reached up and caressed his cheek.

'Can we sit down, please?'

'Of course.' She gestured to the sofa.

He flopped down with a weary sigh and she sat next to him, tucking her legs up underneath her bottom. Her skirt rode up slightly and she pulled it down, a demure gesture that made him smile. He put his hand on her knees, absent-mindedly stroking them.

'So, are we going to sit here all night, or are you going to tell me what's happened to your face?'

'Sammy hit me,' he replied.

'Oh, my God! Why?'

'Because she knows about us, that's why.'

'Who told her?' she gasped.

'Me!' he said. 'Me and my bloody big mouth.'

'But why would you do that? We're supposed to be a secret.'

'She guessed I'm having an affair. All she needed was a name. I couldn't see a way out, so I told her,' he replied.

'So what happens now?' Livvy asked, her eyes searching his face.

'Well, that's it; it's over. I'm sorry, Livvy,' he finished helplessly as her eyes filled.

'But I love you, Roy. What will I do without you?' she cried.

'Livvy, you're beautiful. You'll soon meet someone else, someone nearer your own age,' he said, pushing straying curls out of her eyes. The thought of another man pawing at her made him want to retch.

'I don't want anyone else. There's only you, who I can really trust,' she sobbed.

'Not all men are like your father, Livvy.' He pulled her into his arms, comforting her. 'You'll learn to trust people – it can take time, but you will. You didn't know if you could trust *me*, did you?'

'I did. I knew from the first moment I met you that I could. That's why it felt so right when you kissed me. I knew you'd be back before too long and I'm glad I lost my virginity to you.'

'Thank you for trusting me. I feel guilty for taking it. You should have waited, saved it for someone special.'

'You *are* someone special.' She put her hands up to his face and moved closer.

He pulled away. 'Don't, please. This is so hard for me.'

'One last kiss, please, just one last kiss.'

Roy knew he was lost. He couldn't fight it and kissed her gently as she knelt up beside him, kissing him back for all she was worth. He squeezed her so tightly that she squealed. He pulled her onto his knee, looking deep into her eyes.

'What are you doing to me?' He could feel a familiar twitching and tried desperately to stop it, but knew he was losing the battle, one that Livvy quickly realised she was winning.

She yanked his T-shirt out from the waistband of his jeans and slid her hands underneath to stroke his stomach. She unzipped his jeans and slipped her hand inside, smiling at the way he responded instantly to her touch.

'You shouldn't be doing that, Liv,' he moaned and his wandering hands soon discovered that underneath her skirt she was wearing the skimpiest pair of knickers. They tumbled onto the carpet and Roy undressed her. As usual she was bra-less and her pert breasts were a delight to his eager mouth.

She tugged down his jeans, releasing his erection, while his teasing of her nipples sent her crazy. Time stood still as they made love all over the flat until Roy chased her down the hallway before carrying her squealing over his shoulder into the bedroom.

As they lay on her bed, totally satiated, Roy looked down at her flushed face and smiled. 'Who am I kidding? I can't stop seeing you. I love you so much and I can't live without you.'

'So, what are you going to do?' she asked, sitting up with her back against the headboard, her knees tucked up under her chin. Her hair had tumbled down over her shoulders, giving her the appearance of a vulnerable cherub who Roy wanted to protect with his life.

'I don't honestly know. Do you mind if I have a fag?' He climbed out of bed and went in search of his jacket. He found it in the lounge, grabbed his cigarettes and lighter and made his way back to the bedroom, smiling at the trail of clothes that lay around the place.

'Do you always smoke after sex, Mr Cantello?' Livvy giggled, looking at him.

'I don't know, Miss Grant, I never look,' he quipped, adding, 'The old ones are always the best.'

'Give *me* a ciggie, Roy.' He passed her the one he'd lit and took another for himself.

'Liv, I know that this might sound a bit like shutting the stable door after the horse has bolted, but you *are* still taking the pill, aren't you?'

'Of course I am,' she said. 'Don't you trust me?'

'I trust you implicitly. I was just making sure, that's all.' His mind had wandered back to the confrontation with Sammy when she'd asked if Livvy was on the pill. 'The way we are with one another you could get pregnant anytime and that's one complication I really don't need at the moment.'

'We'll be fine, Roy,' she said, staring up at the ceiling. 'Don't worry about it. What you *do* need to worry about is what you're going to do now.'

He sighed. 'Christ only knows. Would you mind if I call Ed? I know I should be able to think things through for myself, but Ed's my other half in one respect and I always trust his judgement.'

'Feel free. He's a really nice man, isn't he? How can someone like Eddie have a lovely son like Jon and a bitch of a daughter like Jess?'

Roy raised an ironical eyebrow and grinned. 'You'd be surprised how that happened. Jess's not that bad really. Ed and Jane spoilt her rotten. Jane's ex kidnapped her as a baby. The guy had lost the plot, thought Jane and Jess were his wife and daughter and did a runner with Jess while The Raiders were in France on our first European tour. They got her back safely, but you can see how they would want to give her everything as they thought they'd lost her. She was a beautiful baby and that's how *we* ended up with Nick. Sam got broody and decided it was time we had one of our own.'

'Were you and Sammy married then?'

'We were living together. We got married after that European tour. Sammy was already pregnant, but Nick was planned.'

'There's hardly any age gap between Nick and Jason. Was *he* planned?'

Roy grinned. 'Nope. Sam read an article that said you couldn't conceive while breastfeeding. When she went to the hospital for her six-week check-up, they told her she was pregnant again.'

'God, I bet she was horrified.'

'She went absolutely ape-shit!' Roy sighed. 'I got the blame, of course. Sammy had insisted it was safe and who am I to argue? I'd been away on tour, we hadn't seen each other for weeks. I missed Nick's birth by fifteen minutes and was back on the road the following day. We were all over one another like a rash after the tour and that's how Jason happened.'

Livvy smiled and patted his arm. 'Did it bother you? I mean, Jason wasn't unwanted, was he?'

'It didn't bother me in the least,' he said. 'I don't think any baby is unwanted. Sometimes they come along at the wrong bloody time, but they're never really unwanted.' He looked into her eyes. 'Why are you asking these questions? Are you wondering about yourself? I'm sure your parents wanted *you*,' he continued as she blushed slightly, 'but felt they were doing the best for you at the time by having you adopted. They probably think about you every single day, you know.' He smiled at her reassuringly.

Livvy nodded. 'I'm sure they do, but I could never give a baby away to strangers.'

'There isn't always a choice. After Jason's birth, Sammy was sterilised; she said enough was enough. But she's regretted it ever since. When Ed and Jane had Katie, she'd have loved another. Sam's one regret in life, up to discovering she has an adulterous husband of course, is not having a daughter. We've even talked about trying to adopt a baby girl in the past, but we've never got around to doing anything about it.' Roy had a faraway look in his eyes. He was conscious of Livvy looking thoughtfully at him.

'I shouldn't be telling you all this, should I?'

She touched his arm gently. 'Go on home to Sammy. I can tell by the way you talk about her and your life together that you still love her. You have a whole load of memories that you're not ready to walk away from. I'll always be here for you if you need me.'

'I'll always need you. I love you. I'll tell Sam we've finished, but I'll try and see you when I can. We'll have to be careful though, we can't take any further chances.'

She kissed him. 'Do you realise you've reached a decision without speaking to Ed? That's a sure sign you're growing up at last.'

He smiled and went in search of his clothes. He kissed Livvy one last time, threw his jacket over his shoulder and promised to call her as soon as he got back from London.

* * *

Livvy stepped under the shower and soaped her body. She smoothed her hands over her flat stomach, stroking it gently. No baby was unwanted. That's what he'd told her. And she still wasn't sure anyway. But at least she now knew that if there was a baby, Roy would want it. He didn't even have to leave Sammy, she would manage on her own. All she'd need was his support and for him to be a father. The panicky feelings she had every time she contemplated the possibility of being pregnant didn't seem so bad now. She'd give it another couple of weeks and if nothing happened, she'd go and see her doctor.

* * *

'How do you feel?' Jane asked Sammy as she sat beside her on the sofa.

'In a word, Jane, gutted.' Sammy sighed. 'I just can't believe it.'

Nick and Jess strolled in and Nick put his arms around his mum and hugged her.

'Have you seen your dad?' she asked.

He nodded. 'The bastard's with Ed!'

'Nick, there's no need for that. He *is* your dad after all and no matter what he's done, he's always thought the world of you and Jason.'

Nick shrugged. 'Doesn't excuse him for his behaviour with Livvy though, does it?'

'I can't blame him totally.' Sammy sighed. 'I've neglected his needs when I shouldn't have done. He's been unfaithful, but he's admitted it and I hope he's going to put an end to it.'

Nick bristled. 'For God's sake, Mum, you can't just forgive him like that! He doesn't deserve it.'

'I bet it was all *her* fault,' Jess retorted. 'If it hadn't been Roy, she might have made a play for Dad. She obviously likes older men as well as Nick.'

Sammy shook her head. 'No, Jess, I doubt very much it was Livvy's fault. Roy will have done the chasing. The poor girl wouldn't have stood a chance. It makes me wonder if he's not done it before. He's had plenty of opportunity. Me at work all day and him… well, he's been free as a bloody bird to do his own thing for years.'

'You're wrong there, Sam,' Jane said. 'When they were touring, they had all that freedom to play around. Apart from Phil Jackson, they say they didn't and we really have to believe them. Otherwise it'll eat away at us and destroy any trust we have. I'd rather not know, to be honest.'

'Well, I've no trust in Roy at the moment,' Sammy said. 'How could I after this? I should divorce him, I've got ample grounds.'

'Don't make decisions like that yet, Sammy,' Jane advised. 'Your head's all over the place at the moment. One breath you're willing to forgive him, next, you want a divorce. You have to talk to him without shouting and screaming at one another.'

Sammy nodded tearfully. 'Shall I phone him, ask him to come home so we can talk?'

'That's better.' Jane smiled encouragingly. 'Yes, you should.'

Sammy turned to Nick. 'Listen, I know you want to be here for me and I really appreciate that, but I would rather be alone if, and when, your dad comes home. Take Jason back to the flat with you and Jess. Let him stay for a couple of nights.'

Nick began to protest, but Jess put her hand on his arm. 'Your mum's right. Let's go home, she can call us if she needs us.'

Nick put his arms around his mum. 'I'll call you tomorrow. You sure you'll be okay?'

Sammy nodded. 'Go and pack a bag, Jason. I'll see you on Thursday.'

'Call Nick's flat if you need us.' Jason hugged her and followed Nick and Jess out of the room.

Jane picked up the phone, dialled her home number and Jon answered. She asked to speak to Roy. Jon told her he wasn't there. 'Well, where is he then? A walk? Oh well, it's a pleasant enough evening. Tell Roy to call Sammy as soon as they come back. She feels ready to talk. Thanks, Jon, see you later.' She hung up and turned to Sammy. 'Eddie and Roy have taken Lennon for a walk to clear their heads. Jon said he'll get Roy to call when they come back.'

Sammy smiled wearily. 'Okay. Shall we have a coffee?'

Jane stood up and stretched. 'I'll make it, you stay there in case he calls.'

* * *

Jon replaced the receiver and turned to Eddie. 'I hate lying to Mum.'

'So do I, but thanks, Jon, that was quick thinking. I bet Roy's still at Livvy's. I'll drive over there, see if I can hurry him along.'

'Knowing Livvy, she'll be really upset. Maybe he's comforting her, or something.'

Eddie raised an eyebrow. 'And knowing Roy, it'll be more like something!'

'No, he wouldn't, *would* he? He's supposed to be finishing it.'

'He's besotted with her, he'll be finding it really difficult. Right, I'll see you later.'

* * *

Eddie pulled onto the back of the car park. He checked his watch: Roy had left Hanover's Lodge over an hour ago, so surely he wouldn't be much longer? He was certainly dragging out the goodbyes. He lit a cigarette, looking up at the apartment block and wondering idly which window was Livvy's. From where he was sitting, he could observe Roy's car without Roy being immediately aware that he was being watched. Eddie wished now that he'd asked Jon which number apartment she lived in and then he could have pressed the intercom and ordered Roy to get a move on.

A young couple strolled arm in arm past his car, going towards the entrance door. He leapt out and caught up with them. 'Excuse me, do you by any chance know Olivia Grant?'

'Yes, she lives opposite us,' the young man replied, staring curiously at Eddie. 'Flat number seven. Hey, aren't you Eddie Mellor?'

'Not me, mate,' Eddie replied. 'I'm told there's a bit of a likeness though.' He followed them in and up the flight of stairs. The couple paused outside the door of number five and pointed towards the end door on the opposite side of the landing.

'That's Livvy's place,' the young man said.

'Thanks.' Eddie crossed the landing, his hand poised to knock on the red front door when a noise from within caught his attention. Just the other side he could hear Livvy squealing with laughter and Roy's deep voice promising what he planned to do now that he'd caught up with her.

He stood rooted to the spot, hand in the air. Should he knock, or just go away? He heard another outburst of laughter and Livvy pleading with Roy to put her down, before the sounds seemed to disappear deeper into the flat. He shook his head and turned away.

The young couple from number five was still watching him. He smiled as he passed them. 'I changed my mind,' he said by way of an explanation and hurried down the stairs and out to his car. Now what, sit and wait for Roy, or go home? He decided to wait. Roy needed to be told that Sammy was in a talking mood. If he went home with any sort of attitude, he would blow all chances of reconciliation.

Five cigarettes and an hour later, Eddie felt more and more conspicuous. People passing by eyed him with suspicion as he sat in his red Ferrari, wearing sunglasses, looking for all the world like a wealthy pimp. He breathed a sigh of relief as the entrance doors to the apartment block opened and Roy bounded jauntily through them. Leather jacket slung casually over his shoulder, cigarette dangling defiantly from his lips, he looked as though he hadn't a care in the world. Eddie observed his smiling face as he unlocked his car and got in. Roy threw his jacket on the passenger seat and turned to close the door only to find it wouldn't move.

He looked up in alarm. 'Jesus, Ed! I thought it was Sammy with the meat cleaver.'

'What the hell have you been up to?' Eddie began. 'You've been in there well over two hours.'

'Saying goodbye to Livvy,' Roy answered sheepishly, not quite meeting his eye. 'She was upset, it took longer than I thought.'

'I came up to the flat, Roy. Heard you behind the front door. Strange bloody way of saying goodbye.'

Roy had the grace to look embarrassed. 'We were messing around. I chased her down the hall and I... well, never mind what I did.'

'So, after you finished shagging one another senseless, did you tell her it was over?'

'Of course. That's it now, I won't be seeing her again. Not like that anyway. I'd still like us to help her get her musical career off the ground though.'

Eddie shook his head. 'Not a chance. You're on your own if you do that. We're through as a partnership if you go near her again and I really mean it. Now get off home. Sammy's waiting to talk things over with you. Go and make her some promises you mean to keep. Oh, and by the way, we've been out walking the dog if she asks. I'll see you on Thursday morning about six thirty. Spend all day with Sammy tomorrow. Sort yourselves out, because if you don't, you're heading for divorce. You'll lose everything, and for what? It's not even as if you don't get it at home.'

Roy opened his mouth to protest, but Eddie hadn't finished: 'You'll ruin all our plans. Pat and Tim are coming home. Pat doesn't need upsets like this while she's still recovering. She'll never forgive you for hurting her sister. You'll split the family and we certainly couldn't re-form The Raiders, because Tim probably wouldn't want to work with you. Think seriously. You're my best mate and we've always been there for one another, but I can't handle covering up for you over this. I think the world of Sammy.'

Roy sighed. 'Okay, Ed, enough said. You're right. It's just that Livvy's hard to resist and I really do have feelings for her, but it's over. What you heard... well, that was just our way of saying goodbye.'

Eddie sighed ruefully and patted his shoulder. 'I told you to keep it zipped up! Now go on, get off home to your wife and get things sorted.'

***

Roy helped himself to a brandy while Sammy saw Jane out. He sat down on the sofa, nervously twisting the stem of his glass. Sammy walked back into the room and sat down opposite him.

'I believe you want to talk?' he began.

'Well?' She stared at him, cool blue eyes glittering with something he hadn't seen before.

'Well what?' He turned away from her gaze.

'Have you seen her?'

He nodded. 'I popped round after talking to Ed. It's over.' He looked at her. 'Do you believe me?'

She shrugged. 'I want to.'

He put down his glass and went to kneel in front of her. 'You have to trust me, Sam.'

'I've always trusted you, Roy. I can't believe you've been unfaithful to me.'

'I'm sorry. I don't know what else to say. Can you forgive me?'

'I'll try, but it won't be easy. You can sleep in the guest room tonight, I couldn't bear you near me at the moment. The thought of you in bed with her makes my flesh crawl.'

'I understand; whatever you want. I'm willing to try anything to save our marriage. I don't want to lose you; I love you, you know that.'

'You have a bloody funny way of showing it.'

'What more can I say?' He hung his head contritely. 'I said I'm sorry.'

'I think you've said enough for now. At least you've admitted you want to try again and so do I. But it doesn't mean I forgive you. It will take time. You've hurt me more than I ever thought possible. You can't wipe that out with a quick sorry, or an, I love you. I can't take any more tonight, let's see what tomorrow brings.'

He nodded. 'Let's have an *us* day. Go for a long walk, leave the cars at home. We can talk and have a pub lunch. What do you say?'

'Sounds nice,' she said. 'I'm taking tomorrow off anyway. Jane's offered to hold the fort again.'

'Oh shit!' Roy rolled his eyes. 'Ed will kill me. He was planning a romantic morning with Jane. I'm fast trying his patience at the moment.'

'Jane said she'd take Thursday or Friday morning off instead.'

'Ed and I are going to London on Thursday morning. We won't be back till the early hours of Saturday, or even later if we stay three nights, which looks likely. Oh well, not to worry.' Roy smiled wearily, leant forward and kissed her lightly on the lips.

She recoiled backwards, her eyes widening with horror. Shocked, he put his hand over hers. 'Sam, what was that for?'

'I can smell her on you,' she said, pushing him away.

'No, you can't. I wore this T-shirt the other day; it must be her perfume from then.'

'It's not, Roy. You slept with her again. I can smell her all over you and it's *not* just perfume. You smell of sex! Go away, you make me feel sick.'

She ran out of the lounge and up to their bedroom, locking herself in the en suite. Shocked by her reaction, Roy ran after her. She was retching as he knocked on the door.

'Go away,' she called in between sobs.

He shook his head and walked out of the room. He crossed the landing and went into the guest room. Damn it, if only he'd taken the time to shower before he left Livvy's apartment. He lay down on the bed; he was back to square one.

* * *

Sammy glanced at her bedside clock: four twenty. She was surprised she'd slept at all, considering, and she felt drained. She pulled on her silk robe and went downstairs. In the kitchen the dim glow from a cigarette told her Roy was sitting in total darkness at the table. She switched on the light. An empty whisky bottle and an overflowing ashtray sat in front of him. The sweet smell of cannabis hung heavily in the air. He glanced at her, his tired eyes giving her the smouldering look she usually found so hard to resist.

'Sammy,' he faltered.

'Save it for the solicitor. You slept with her again last night and I can't even *begin* to forgive you for that. I hope it was worth it, because that one fuck alone is going to cost you everything!'

She made a mug of chamomile tea, turned off the lights and went back upstairs. She couldn't even cry. Her heart felt like lead. If he'd just gone to the flat and told Livvy it was over, then yes, she might learn to forgive him in time. But Sammy knew he'd screwed her, his face had given it away when she'd recoiled backwards from him. In her heart she knew that Roy would no more be able to stay away from Livvy than he would give up smoking and she wasn't prepared to share him. Her mind made up, she decided that tomorrow she'd consult her solicitor for advice on her rights and set the ball rolling for a quick divorce.

16

Jane dropped the phone onto the cradle and frowned. Sammy had strolled into the office unannounced and flopped down on a chair. Usually immaculate, with her smart tailored suits and expensive silk blouses, today Sammy was wearing sunglasses, faded Levi's and a crumpled white T-shirt. Her shoulder-length hair was scraped back into a casual ponytail, her pale face devoid of make-up. She whipped off her glasses and her cool blue eyes were ringed with dark circles.

'Sam, what on earth are you doing here?' Jane said. 'You're supposed to be taking the day off.'

'I've been to see my solicitor,' Sammy replied. 'I'm divorcing Roy on the grounds of his adultery with Livvy.'

'You can't!' Jane exclaimed.

'You just watch me.' Sammy's lips quivered.

'But you were going to talk last night and today. Surely you've managed to sort it out?'

Sammy shook her head. 'We *did* talk. I almost felt I could forgive him. He said the affair was over. Then he leant in and kissed me and I could smell her on him, and I don't just mean her perfume. He went to see her after he left Ed and screwed her again. He won't stay away from her, even though he swears he will. I can't handle that. I'm not sharing him with a twenty-two-year-old. She can have him and she's bloody welcome to him. But he's gonna pay big time for this. He won't know what's hit him once I start and neither will she.'

Jane sighed. 'I don't know what to say.'

'There's nothing *to* say, Jane. If she thinks she's found a sugar daddy then she's in for a shock. Roy's worth a fair bob or two, same as Ed, but what's his is also mine. I'm going to sting him for every last penny.'

Jane nodded. Once Sammy made a decision, she rarely changed her mind. 'My advice, for what it's worth – I think you're rushing things. It's one affair. He said it's over. It was wrong of him to sleep with her again and I bet he wishes with all his heart that he hadn't. But he did and you have to deal with it.'

'That's exactly what I'm doing. I can't forgive him for last night.'

'Why don't you ask him to move out for a while? You need some space to think things through. He's off to London with Ed tomorrow. Then he can come and stay with us until he sorts himself out. I think you're making a big mistake. You'll push him into Livvy's arms right away.'

'I'm not backing down.' Sammy folded her arms. 'He'll be getting a letter from my solicitor and so will she. No matter what happens, I won't be able to forget last night. He knew what was at stake.'

'Come and stay over tonight,' Jane suggested. 'Maybe we can talk some more.'

'Thanks for the offer, but I've things to do at home. Jason's back tomorrow night and Jess and Nick are coming for dinner on Friday.'

'What about the weekend, what will you do then?'

'I can't come to you. *He'll* be there. Don't worry. I'll be in touch over the weekend. I'll be back in work tomorrow and Friday anyway. Perhaps we could do a bit of therapeutic clothes shopping, have lunch out on Saturday, spend some of his money.'

'Good idea.' Jane stood up and put her arms around Sammy. 'I wish we could turn the clock back to 1959 and know what we know now, don't you?'

'Yes, I do, and I know who *I* would have avoided like the plague. Just look at all the bloody scrapes he got me into in the past.'

'Yeah, and you loved every minute of it,' Jane said as Sammy's eyes filled. Jane reached for a tissue and gently wiped the tears that tumbled down her friend's cheeks.

'I love the lying, cheating bastard to bits, Jane. But I'll never be able to forgive him. I'd make our lives hell.'

'You would, in time. Why don't you go and see Livvy, ask her what happened last night and if he's definitely told her it's over?'

'I plan to, but not today. I'd kill her if I got my hands on her right at this moment. Anyway, I'm off. I'll see you tomorrow.'

'Okay, take care.' Jane hugged Sammy and kissed her goodbye. 'See you soon.'

* * *

Sammy ate an early dinner and spent the rest of the night holed up in her bedroom. She locked the door and told Roy, who knocked several times to ask if there was anything she needed, that she was busy and to get lost. She called Nick and also spoke to Jason, assuring both her worried boys that she was fine and planning to have a relaxing bath and a read. She'd brought a bottle of white wine upstairs. She took a glass into the bathroom and lay back in the Jacuzzi, a self-satisfied smile playing on her face.

* * *

Early the following morning, Roy knocked on the bedroom door. There was no response so he tried the handle and it opened. Sammy must have unlocked the door sometime during the night, he thought. He crept into the room to get some clothes for his trip to London. Not daring to put on the lights for fear of disturbing her, he opened the wardrobe and reached inside. Trying to do everything in the dark was proving difficult. He grabbed several hangers and carried them into the bathroom to see what was what.

'Fucking hell! What the... SAMMY!'

Sammy stirred as he continued with his angry expletives.

'Sammy, what the fuck have you done to my clothes?' He shook her by the shoulder and threw the remains onto the bed. Although still on hangers, everything had been cut into ribbons. He snapped on the lights and went back to look in the wardrobe. Not a single item was untouched, no tie, shirt, jacket or trousers. He opened the dressing table drawers and peered inside. His socks and underwear were also massacred. In the bottom of the wardrobe, every pair of shoes he possessed had been filled with shaving foam. Each and every bottle of aftershave and cologne, empty. Scrawled across the dressing table mirror in foot-high letters and bright red lipstick was the word *ADULTERER*!

He shook his head in disbelief. 'Sammy, you crazy cow! Wake up. Why have you done this? You know me and Ed are going to London this morning, it's important.'

'So was our marriage.' She sprang up, a dangerous glint in her eyes. 'I've only done to your clothes what you've done to us – ruined them.'

As he lunged at her in fury, she whipped a large pair of dressmaking shears from under the pillow and waved them in the air, opening and closing the blades in a threatening manner.

'One more move like that, cradle snatcher, and I'll cut it off, balls and all!' she warned, appearing to be enjoying every minute of his fear.

With trembling hands, Roy picked up the bedside phone and dialled Eddie's number. 'Morning, Ed. This is an emergency. Can you bring me a T-shirt, socks and boxer shorts or underpants, please? I'll explain when we're on our way. See you soon.'

He shot Sammy a look of pure venom, stormed out of the room and back to the sanctuary of the guest bedroom where, fortunately, his Levi's and the pair of boots he had worn yesterday were safe.

He stomped downstairs wrapped in a bath towel, taking what was left of his clothes with him. His leather jacket was still on a chair in the lounge where he'd left it and appeared untouched.

Eddie arrived and helped himself to coffee while Roy pulled on an assortment of his own and Eddie's clothing.

'Bloody hell, these pants are a bit snug!' Roy grumbled, tugging at the skimpy black briefs.

'Sorry about that. We can't all be blessed with the appendage you've got.'

Roy smiled weakly. 'They say size has nothing to do with it.'

'Precisely, and I've never heard Jane moaning, apart from with pleasure,' Eddie quipped. 'So, are you gonna tell me what happened and why you need my clothes?'

'Wait till we're on the way.' Roy looked nervously over his shoulder as Sammy appeared behind him, thankfully empty-handed.

'Morning, Ed,' she greeted him with a weary smile.

'Morning, Sam. Did you sleep better last night?'

'Much better, thank you,' she replied. 'It's surprising what a spot of revenge can do for your morale.'

'Come on, Ed, let's go.' Roy pushed him towards the door,

desperate to get away. 'I'll see you Saturday,' he called as they left the house.

* * *

As the door shut behind them, angry tears sprang to Sammy's eyes. She went through into the lounge, collapsed on the sofa, buried her face in a cushion and sobbed. The revenge had been sweet, but short-lived, and she knew it wasn't the answer. She hated Roy going away without a kiss goodbye and them saying, 'I love you and be safe.' 'Oh, Roy, what have you done to us? Why was I no longer enough for you,' she moaned broken-heartedly, punching the cushion and wishing it was Livvy's head.

* * *

'I'll just check the alarm's on.' Roy strolled round to the side of the house where he'd parked his Lamborghini.

As Eddie unlocked his car he heard a howl of utter anguish and dashed to Roy's side. The car had four flat tyres and the paintwork on the bonnet was blistering and peeling.

'The mad cow! She's slashed the tyres and poured paint stripper on the bonnet. Oh, how could she do this? I'll kill her!'

Eddie caught hold of him as he hurtled towards the front door. 'Leave it! Sort it out when we get back. Let her cool off a bit. She's wreaked her revenge on your favourite toy. She probably won't do anything else just yet.'

'She's fucking crazy!' Roy yelled, waving his fists at the house as Eddie pushed him into the passenger seat of his car. He started the engine and quickly drove away.

* * *

Shocked into silence by Sammy's actions, they were halfway down the M1 before Roy could bring himself to speak and tell Eddie what Sammy had done to his clothes.

'What did you expect? Sammy's no wimp and you know that. Did you also know she's seen a solicitor? She told Jane yesterday. She's divorcing you on the grounds of your adultery with Livvy.'

Roy's eyes opened wide. 'Divorcing me? She hasn't told *me* that.'

'Well, I expect you'll be hearing something soon and so will Livvy. You were a bloody fool the other night. You should have told Livvy it was over and then taken yourself off home. That couple of hours of lust has cost you the lot – I just hope it was worth it.'

Roy's shoulders sagged and he let out a huge sigh. 'So, what do I do now? Sammy will probably kick me out.'

'No doubt she will. You'll have to rent somewhere until everything's sorted. You can stay with us for a week or two, but don't expect much sympathy from Jane and Jess.'

'Thanks, Ed. For standing by me, I mean.'

'You were always there for me during my marriage to Angie and I'll never forget that. But I love Sammy, too and I'll support her as much as she needs. Shall we stop for breakfast? Services are coming up.'

* * *

As they stood in the queue at Watford Gap, Roy took out his wallet to pay for the breakfasts. He pulled out a credit card to find it had been cut in half. Horrified, he pulled out the next one and the next. All of them cut neatly in two.

Eddie, spotting Roy's stricken expression, quickly took charge and handed the assistant his own card while Roy carried the tray over to a vacant table and sat down.

'She's certainly been busy,' Eddie said, taking a seat.

Roy checked his wallet again. He pulled out several folded bank notes. They too had been neatly cut in half, re-folded to look whole and then replaced back in the wallet. 'Can you believe it?'

'I can. Jane would no doubt do something similar. I think Sammy's trying to show you that she means business with the scissors. It's a symbolic gesture. I'd keep my wits about me if I were you. Make sure you lock the bathroom door when you're taking a shower.'

'She must have gone downstairs and wreaked havoc while I was sleeping. My wallet was in my jacket pocket. It's the only jacket she hasn't ruined, apart from the cream one at the dry cleaners.'

'You're very lucky to still have it then,' Eddie said, tucking hungrily into his eggs and bacon.

'It was my last birthday present from her. She designed it and had it specially made.' Roy looked sadly at the black, soft leather thigh-length jacket, with its equally soft, red leather lining. 'Oh, Ed, how on earth can I make amends? Livvy told me to go back to Sammy the other night. When I got home, I apologised. We talked; Sam was on the verge of forgiveness, until I made the big mistake of kissing her. She pushed me away, said she could smell Livvy on me and ran off before I could stop her. She threw up, and that was it. She's hardly spoken to me since. Now she's wrecked my clothes, my car and my cards. And *you* tell me she's already filed for divorce.' Roy's eyes were bright with unshed tears.

'Roy, come on, pull yourself together, man. Eat your breakfast. It's not very hot to start with.'

Eddie was conscious of the stares of a group of middle-aged women who were sitting at a nearby table. He heard one of them mutter, '*It is them! I'd know them anywhere.*' 'Maybe she'll change her mind,' he said. 'Who knows what the next few days will bring. At least you're away from both of them for a while. Here, have a fag and let's try and concentrate on the job in hand. We'll stop at Brent Cross and get you a change of clothes. I'll put them on the company credit card and you can pay the business back for your personal spending later.'

'Thanks, Ed, you're a real pal,' Roy said and tried to eat the congealing fried breakfast.

* * *

Jess was packing and addressing the winter mail-order catalogues on Friday afternoon when the office phone rang. 'It might be Nick for me,' she said as Sammy answered and passed the receiver over.

'It *is* Nick, for you. Let me speak to him before you hang up, love.'

Jess, 'yes-ed', 'no-ed' and then, 'Oh, that's a great idea, Nick, see you later. Love you, too.' She handed the phone back to Sammy.

Sammy spoke to Nick and replaced the receiver. 'Now that's a lovely thought.'

'What is?' Jane glanced up from her invoices.

'The party Jess and Nick were going to tonight's been cancelled so they're taking us out for a meal instead.'

'Oh, lovely,' Jane said. 'Who's paying?' She looked at Jess, one eyebrow raised.

'We are of course, Mother. What do you take us for?'

'Just going off your track record, darling,' Jane teased.

'I'll go home a bit earlier, get ready and drive over to your place,' Sammy said. 'We can relax over a couple of G&Ts and then Nick and Jess can pick us both up from there.'

'Stay over tonight then. You can have your old room. Ed and Roy are not coming back until tomorrow. Ed phoned last night and confirmed it. Did Roy call?'

'Roy who?' Sammy said dismissively.

Jane rolled her eyes. 'You have to talk to him next week. This situation is crazy. You still love him and *he* loves you. Ed said he's in bits, can't concentrate on anything. He sat in the hotel bar on his own last night and got legless. He wouldn't even go out for a meal with Ed and the lads from Perry's Dream. That's not like Roy. He loves to be involved as a rule.'

'He was probably sulking about his car, or hoping to pick up another blonde bimbo,' Sammy said. 'Talking of bimbos, I wonder if *she's* had her solicitor's letter yet. Roy's came this morning. It's waiting for him at home.'

'We can ask Jon later,' Jane said. 'She's bound to have confided in him now that it's out in the open. I'd better call him, make sure he's going to be home tonight and ask him to look after the kids.'

'Can't your mum and dad do it?' Sammy asked.

'They've gone to Gloucester for the weekend to see our Pete and his wife,' Jane said, dialling Flanagan and Grey's number. 'I dropped them off at Wilmslow Station this morning.' She pulled a face as the phone was answered. 'It's her,' she mouthed at Sammy. 'Can I speak to Jon, please? It's his mum.' Putting her hand over the mouthpiece she said, 'She sounds really miserable.'

'Good,' Sammy said. 'Serves her right.'

'Hi, Mum,' Jon said.

'Hi, Jon. Are you free to babysit tonight while Nick and Jess take me and Sam for a meal?'

'Yes, no problem. Can Helen stay over then? I'd arranged to take her out.'

'Of course she can, if you're sure her mother won't object. I'll treat you to a takeaway and you can help yourself to a bottle from your dad's wine cellar. Oh... have you?' Jane raised her eyebrows and looked across at Sammy. 'How did she know where you were working? I see. Oh well, we'll discuss it over the weekend when your dad gets home. See you later. Bye, love.'

'What's up?' Sammy asked.

'Jon's had a call from his Aunt Sally, Angie's sister. Angie's dad's died and the family wants Jon to go to the funeral next Monday. One of Sally's sons discovered that Jon works in Flanagan and Grey's and told his mother. Sally took a chance and called him. I don't expect she wanted to contact him through Ed.'

'Will it pose a problem?' Sammy frowned.

'God knows. Ed hates him having any contact with them for obvious reasons. But at the end of the day they *are* Jon's family and they always remember him on his birthday and at Christmas.'

'Bloody hell, there's always something to worry about.' Sammy sighed.

* * *

Jane drove home as quickly as she could in the Friday rush-hour traffic, stopping on the way to collect Katie and Dominic from Lucy's house. With her mum and dad away as well as Eddie, it meant she had to do all the organising *and* the morning school run. Thankfully, Lucy's mum had offered to care for the children after school today.

Back home, Jane fed the hungry pair and settled them in front of the television while she took a quick bath and washed her hair. Jon arrived with Helen and Jane met them on the landing as Jon was ushering Helen into his room.

'This is okay, isn't it, Mum? Helen sharing my room, I mean?'

'Yes, of course. I'm just finishing getting ready.' She grinned as her strapping stepson gave her a bear hug.

Helen smiled at the pair. 'Going somewhere nice, Jane?'

'Jess and Nick are taking me and Sam out for a meal. When your dad rings later, Jon, tell him to call me back about midnight, please.'

'Will do.'

Jane rushed back into her bedroom. She dried her hair, applied her make-up, fastened her gold chain and locket around her neck and slipped into her red silk Chinese dress. The Mandarin neckline hid the locket, but as long as she could feel it next to her skin she was comforted. Eddie had given it to her on their wedding day and she treasured it. She missed him, hated him being away. Still, the only alternative was to live closer to the recording studios in London and that was something she'd always refused to do.

When Sammy arrived, Jane poured their favourite tipple and they waited in the lounge for the arrival of their offspring. Jess had called earlier, confirming that she and Nick would be there for seven thirty. The table at Rozzillo's was booked for eight.

Jon and Helen sauntered into the lounge, holding hands. They smiled as they greeted Sammy. 'How are you, Sam?' Jon asked, bending to kiss her cheek.

'Fighting fit,' she replied with a wry grin.

'So I believe. Mum told me what you did to his car and clothes. That was brave. Bet he was livid.'

'If your dad hadn't taken him away on Thursday morning, we'd have ended up killing each other,' Sammy said. 'By the way, has Livvy said anything to you?'

Jon shook his head. 'Not really. She's been very withdrawn the last few days, even before all this blew up. She seems to be a bit off colour.'

'Not off colour enough to stop her sleeping with Roy,' Sammy said. 'Your mum tells me Aunt Sally's been in touch.'

Jon nodded. 'My grandfather passed away and the family

want me to go to the funeral. I'm not sure that I want to go really, but I suppose I should.'

Jane patted his arm. 'It's up to you, love. I don't think your dad will be too pleased, but at the end of the day it's your decision.'

'I've got the weekend to think it over. I'll go and collect our takeaway. I presume you'll be gone by the time I get back, so enjoy yourselves and I'll see you later. Say hi to Nick and Jess. Tell them if I don't see them tonight, I'll see them on Tuesday at the college gig.'

'You'll see them later, won't you? They'll come back here with us,' Jane said.

'Err, depends what time you get back. Helen and I were planning an early night,' Jon said as Helen blushed.

'Jon, you're embarrassing Helen. Go and get your meal,' Jane said.

'Would you read us a story, Helen?' Dominic held out a book, a hopeful expression on his young face.

'Of course I will, Dom.' She ruffled his hair affectionately.

Katie, looking puzzled, planted herself in front of her mother, hands resting on her hips. She'd been watching TV with one ear tuned to the earlier conversation. 'I thought Grandpa had gone to see Uncle Peter with Grandma,' she began.

'He has, Katie, they went this morning,' Jane replied.

'Well then, why did you say he was dead?'

Jane gasped. Katie had obviously taken in every word she'd overheard. Jane looked across at Sammy for inspiration, but Sammy shook her head and shrugged. Jane took a deep breath. 'Jon has another grandpa and grandma, Katie. Well, he *did* have, but the grandpa died this week.'

Katie looked even more puzzled. 'Are they my grandpa and grandma, too?'

'No, they're not,' Jane replied.

'I bet they're Jess's then.'

'No, they're only Jon's.'

'Why?'

Jane sighed. 'Because Jon had a different mummy to you.'

Katie's eyes opened wide and she grinned at the joke. 'Don't be silly, you're Jon's mummy.'

'No, darling, I'm not his real mummy,' Jane replied patiently, thinking that Ed was never around when things like this needed explaining properly.

'Well, is Daddy Jon's real daddy?'

Sammy gasped and looked away.

Jane hoped Helen hadn't heard the gasp. *Out of the mouths of babes*, she thought. She swallowed hard and lied. 'Yes, darling, Daddy is Jon's real daddy.'

'So, if *you're* not his mummy, who *is* his mummy?' Katie persisted.

'Her name was Angie. She died when Jon was a little boy.'

Katie raised her eyebrows and Jane could see the cogs whirring.

'So... does that mean Daddy had a different wife before you?'

'Yes, Katie, it does. Now stop asking questions, please. Go and watch out of the window for Nick and Jess, they'll be here soon. Actually, they're leaving it a bit late, aren't they?' Jane turned to Sammy, desperately trying to change the subject.

But Katie wasn't satisfied. 'So, who is Jess's mummy?'

'Me, darling,' Jane replied patiently.

Narrowing her eyes, Katie nodded knowingly. She folded her arms across her chest. 'So... that means Daddy twinkled his naughty bits at Angie to get Jon and then twinkled them at you to get Jess. That's really rude! Doesn't he know that you're only supposed to twinkle with one lady?'

Jane tried hard to hide her amusement. 'Katie, that's quite

enough. I promise that Daddy will explain properly about Jon's mummy to you another time.'

Sammy and Helen were struggling to keep their faces straight at this mother and daughter exchange. Car tyres crunching on the gravel created a diversion. Katie ran to the window and Jane breathed a sigh of relief.

'It's Jon,' Katie announced. 'He's got the takeaway, Helen.'

'I wonder where they are.' Jane looked at her watch: it was ten to eight and there was still no sign of Nick and Jess.

'Jon, you've got a different mummy, but she's dead!' Katie greeted him as he walked into the room.

Jon raised an enquiring eyebrow in Jane's direction.

'She heard us talking about your grandfather and thought we meant my dad. You can guess the rest. Be prepared for a barrage of questions,' Jane warned. 'Get her to bed as soon as you can or you'll find yourselves talking about twinkles and men's naughty bits all night.'

'Is she still on about that?' Jon laughed and swung Katie up into his arms. 'Bed for you, young lady. You too, Dom, come on.'

'I want to wait up for Nick and Jess,' Katie protested.

'Bed – now,' Jane said. 'As soon as Nick and Jess arrive, we'll be leaving. We're already very late for our reservation as it is.'

'I thought you'd be gone by now,' Jon agreed.

At eight, Jane called Nick and Jess's flat to make sure they hadn't been delayed, but there was no reply.

'If they knew they were running late, surely they would have called,' Sammy said, frowning.

'I wonder if the car's broken down somewhere,' Jane mused, replacing the receiver.

'Surely not, it's brand new. Anyway, they would have called from a phone box to let us know.'

Jon came back downstairs after settling Katie and Dominic. 'Do you mind if me and Helen go through to the kitchen to eat?' he asked.

'Go ahead, don't let us spoil your meal,' Jane replied. 'Would you like another G&T, Sam?'

'Please, just a small one.'

The phone rang just before nine and Jane sprang up to answer it. It was Eddie. She told him that she and Sammy were waiting for Nick and Jess to pick them up but that the pair were very late. She also told him about Jon's grandfather's death and the coming funeral. She held the phone away from her ear as Eddie exploded. 'What did I tell you?' she mouthed to Sammy. 'Have you quite finished, darling? He's not really that keen on going, but he feels he should because they expect it of him. Okay, well you can discuss it with him over the weekend. I think Nick and Jess are here, I can hear crunching gravel. I love you too, Ed. Call me about midnight. How's your other half, by the way? Oh dear, is he? Well, I'll talk to you later.' She hung up and looked at Sammy, who was staring out of the window, her face pale in spite of her carefully applied make-up.

'Sam, what is it?' She hurried across the room to stand beside her.

Sammy silently pointed to the car that had pulled up on the drive.

'Police!' Jane felt the hairs on her neck prickling. 'Oh my God! Something must have happened to Nick and Jess.' She flew to the front door before the two officers had a chance to ring the bell. 'What is it, what's happened?'

'Mrs Mellor? Can we come inside, please?' The taller of the two spoke.

'Yes. Yes, of course.' Jane's legs felt all wobbly as she led the officers into the lounge.

'Mrs Cantello?' The other officer spoke to Sammy, who nodded.

'Sit down, ladies, please.' He spoke kindly to them as they dropped side by side on the sofa.

Jon appeared in the doorway, followed by Helen. 'Mum,

what's happened?' He laid a hand on Jane's shoulder. 'What is it, Officer?'

'I'm afraid we've some bad news. Nicholas and Jessica have been involved in a road traffic accident. They've been taken to Stockport General. We'll take you both there right away.'

'Are they okay?' Jane asked, feeling her cheeks draining.

'It's hard to say at this stage, Mrs Mellor. Jessica was talking to us; she was able to give us your name and address and told us we'd find Nicholas's mum here as well. I'm afraid he was unconscious at the time.'

Sammy gasped in horror. 'No! Oh no, please tell me he's okay.'

'They're both alive, that's the important thing,' the officer replied kindly.

'Let me just ring the hotel before we leave. Both their fathers are in London,' Jane explained.

She ran to the phone, dialled the hotel number and was put through to Eddie's room. He answered immediately.

'Jane, calm down, love. What is it? Oh God, no! Right, we're on our way home. Be with you as soon as we can.'

'Please drive carefully, Ed. We'll meet you at the hospital.' Jane replaced the receiver as Sammy gripped her hand. 'They're on their way.'

* * *

Eddie rushed out into the corridor and banged on Roy's door. Roy opened it a crack and peered out, bleary-eyed and unshaven.

'I told you, Ed, I don't want to go out. I can't face it.'

'Get ready,' Eddie ordered. 'We're going home. Nick and Jess have been in a car crash. Move yourself, Roy.'

Roy held onto the doorframe, staring blankly at Eddie, who shook him gently by the arm.

'Roy, come on, the girls need us. Pack your stuff. I'll give you five minutes.'

He hurried back into his own room and threw everything haphazardly in his case. What next? One minute he was looking forward to a quiet meal and an early night. Now, he had this nightmare dash up the motorway and had to try and keep his wits about him. He knew Roy wouldn't be able to share the driving. He'd been drinking constantly since they arrived and today had been no exception – he'd drunk his mini-bar dry before seven tonight.

Leading Roy by the arm, Eddie steered him to the hotel reception area and checked out.

He threw their bags in the car boot, helped Roy into the passenger seat and fastened his seat belt. He clambered into the driving seat, lit two cigarettes, put one between Roy's lips, fired up the engine and began the longest car journey of their lives.

17

'Come with me, ladies, we've a room free. I'll organise some tea for you.'

Sammy and Jane followed the young nurse down a narrow corridor and into a small but pleasant room that was simply furnished with two comfortable chairs and a low coffee table piled high with magazines and newspapers. The nurse switched on a lamp, closed the sash window and drew the faded cotton curtains.

'Can we see Nick and Jess?' Jane asked tearfully, helping Sammy onto a chair.

'Not just yet. Jess is in theatre and the doctor is with Nick. Someone will be with you very shortly to explain what's happening. I'll go and get the tea.'

She came back with a tray, closely followed by a white-faced Jon and Jason.

'Helen's staying with the kids and I tracked down Jason at Jules's house,' Jon said as the nurse left the room.

'Any news, Mum?' Jason put his arms around Sammy's shoulders.

She shook her head and related what the young nurse had

told them. 'We're waiting for someone to come with an update. At least they're both alive, thank God. The policemen who brought us here said Nick had to be cut free from the car – it was wrapped around a tree.'

'Jesus Christ!' Jason exclaimed. 'Our Nick's a really careful driver. I know that car was fast, but he could handle it. Does Dad know about the accident?'

'Dad and Roy are on their way home,' Jon told him. 'When I spoke to the officers before they brought Mum and Sammy here, they told me that a car had overtaken Nick and Jess on a bend, then swerved back in front of them to avoid hitting a lorry coming the opposite way. Nick must have slammed on his brakes, lost control, hit the tree and the other car drove off.'

Another two hours passed slowly before a serious-looking, white-coated doctor entered the room.

'Mrs Mellor?' He addressed Jane. 'Jessica is stable and comfortable. She has a fracture to the right wrist, a broken right ankle, which we've pinned, and a few cuts and bruises, but she *will* be okay. You can see her now.'

Jane stood up, tears coursing down her cheeks.

'What about Nick, Doctor?' Sammy asked.

'I'm afraid it's too soon to say. He's still unconscious. He has several fractured ribs, a punctured lung and a broken ankle, but his other limbs are intact. It's his head injuries we're very concerned about. He's being transferred to ICU as we speak, Mrs Cantello. I'll arrange for you to be taken up there right away.'

Sammy looked up as the young nurse who'd brought the tea re-entered the room.

'Nurse Hammond will escort you and I'll speak with you both later,' the doctor said.

Nurse Hammond smiled sympathetically as Jason put his arm around his mother and helped her to her feet. 'I'll take Mrs

Mellor to Jessica and then we'll continue up to ICU to see how Nicholas is doing.'

* * *

Jess was sleeping peacefully, but her lovely face bore the brunt of being thrown against the windscreen. There was a deep cut above her right eye, her chin had been stitched in several places, her nose swollen, and the start of two black eyes was apparent.

Jane bent over the bed and gently stroked her daughter's face. She turned to Jon, who held her tightly while she sobbed against his chest.

'Mum, come on, she'll be alright, she has to be.' He swallowed hard, fighting back his own tears for the sister he adored, who was lying so pale and still. 'You need to be strong for Sammy.'

Jane touched his cheek. 'Jon, what would I do without you? I might not be your real mum, but I love you so much.'

'You *are* my mum.' He hugged her. 'In every sense of the word you are my mother. Shall I ask if I'm allowed to see Nick?'

'Yes, please, tell Sammy I'll be with her shortly. I just want to sit with Jess for a while.'

As Jon left the room, Jane looked at her watch. Where had the time gone? It was almost midnight; Eddie and Roy would be with them soon. She prayed that Ed was driving carefully. One road accident tonight was enough to cope with. What an awful week it had been, she thought: first, Roy and Sammy and now this.

As Jane sat holding Jess's hand, her eyelids flickered open.

'Mum,' she uttered weakly.

'I'm here, darling.'

'Mum, where's Nick?'

'He's okay, love. Sammy and Jason are with him at the moment.'

Jon re-appeared and sighed with relief on seeing Jess with her eyes open. 'Thank God! Hi, sis, how are you?' He kissed her forehead and gently stroked her cheek.

'I don't know,' she said tearfully. 'What happened, Mum?'

'You had a crash on your way to pick up Sammy and me. Don't you remember?'

Jess frowned. 'Will you go and see if Nick is alright, Mum, please? Then come back to me.'

'They wouldn't let me in,' Jon whispered to Jane.

'Okay.' She stood up. 'I'll see what I can do. You stay with Jess, please, Jon.'

* * *

Jon took Jess's hand and sat beside the bed. He felt sick inside at the thought that he'd almost lost her. She was the most precious thing in the world to him and at that moment, he longed to tell her that he loved her, that he'd always loved her and always would. Instead, he was forced to live a lie and pretend that he was happy with Helen and life was hunky-dory. He smiled as Jess looked at him, her lips trembling.

'Will Nick be alright? I couldn't bear it if anything happened to him.'

He nodded and swallowed hard. 'They're doing everything they can, Jess.' He hoped he sounded reassuring. 'You just concentrate on getting well.'

* * *

Jane hurried down the corridor to ICU and was shown to Nick's room, where a team of staff were attending to him.

Sammy told her there was little response from Nick. 'He's not even breathing on his own, he's all wired up to that machinery. They're waiting for brain scan results. I wish Roy was here,

I can't cope with this,' she said tearfully as Jason put his arms around her, his lips trembling.

'They won't be long, Sam,' Jane said. 'Just hang in there. I've left Jon looking after Jess. She's opened her eyes and she's asking for Nick. What shall I tell her?'

'Tell her he's alright. She doesn't need to know any more for now,' Sammy advised.

Jane squeezed Sammy's arm and left.

* * *

Tired and weary, Eddie asked at reception where their respective families were. He was taken to Jess's room and Roy to Intensive Care.

The tears that had threatened all night tumbled freely down his cheeks as he stood by his daughter's bed. Jane, who had been dozing in a chair, looked up as he sobbed.

'Ed, thank God you're here.' She stood up and he threw his arms around her, holding her tightly. 'I've been on my own since Jon took Jason back to our place for the night.'

'Is she going to be okay?'

'Yes, thank God,' she whispered. 'But I'm not so sure about Nick.' She explained the situation.

He nodded wearily. 'Roy won't be able to handle this. He's in a terrible state as it is. He sobered up a bit on the way home but he's still a mess.'

* * *

Sammy turned as Roy was shown into Nick's room. She gasped at his gaunt and unshaven appearance. His usually twinkling eyes held a haunted expression as he stared in disbelief at the still form of his son. He collapsed onto his knees, crying.

Sammy dropped down beside him and cradled him in her

arms. 'Roy, come on, you have to be strong for me. Don't you *dare* go to pieces, Cantello. I can't handle this on my own. I need you, Roy.' She shook him by the shoulders.

He looked up through his tears. Sammy took a tissue from her pocket and wiped his eyes and nose as though he were a small child. 'Roy, help me through this, please.'

He nodded and stood up, pulling her into his arms.

Strong until that point, Sammy broke down and let the tears flow. At that moment she felt she could forgive Roy anything, just as long as Nick survived.

'What have they said?' He spoke quietly, smoothing her hair from her face.

'Very little.' She related what the doctor had told her earlier. 'It's just time, I suppose. The scans will show if there's any brain damage and we'll have to cross that bridge when we come to it.'

'I want the best treatment money can buy.'

'Money's not the answer to this, Roy. They're doing everything they can.'

'Mr and Mrs Cantello, go and stretch your legs and get yourselves a coffee,' Nurse Hammond said. 'There's nothing you can do at the moment. I'll come and find you immediately if there's any change.'

'Come on, Roy.' Sammy took his arm. 'I bet you could use one after that long journey.'

They found a little café in reception, where Sammy ordered two coffees, a ham sandwich and a packet of chocolate biscuits. She carried them to a table tucked in a corner in the hope of avoiding the curious stares from several people who, she guessed, were trying to place Roy's familiar face.

'Here, get those down you. You look as though you haven't eaten for days.'

He nodded, absent-mindedly stirring his coffee. 'I haven't, not since Rozzillo's on Monday. I've no appetite. I've lived on booze and fags for the last couple of days. Do the police know what happened? Was the crash Nick's fault?'

Sammy told him what the police had told Jon.

He took a sip of coffee and grimaced. 'Ugh, cheap crap!' He looked at her. 'I wish I'd never bought him the bloody car. This is all my fault.'

'Roy, he would have used the BMW or my Porsche tonight anyway and they're both fast cars. The accident could still have happened. Don't blame yourself, please. It doesn't help anyone.'

He took her hand across the table. 'He has to survive, he just has to. I'm so sorry for what I've done, Sam. You and the boys are everything to me. I know you want a divorce, Ed told me. I don't blame you, but won't you reconsider?'

'Roy, at the moment all I can think about is Nick. What's happened between us doesn't even come into the equation. I feel numb right now. I'm not going to lie and promise you that it will be okay. Let's get through the next few days and then we'll see.'

'I love you, Sammy,' he said, adding, 'with all my heart.'

'And I love you too, Roy, but it's not that simple.'

They walked back down the corridor and popped their heads around Jess's door. Eddie was sitting on the one comfortable chair in the corner of the room, Jane sleeping on his lap, her head resting against his chest. He smiled at the pair as they walked in.

'How is she?' Roy whispered.

'Sleeping. Whatever they've given her for pain has zonked her out.'

'Poor Jess.' Sammy bit her lip. 'She'll go mad when she looks in the mirror. I hope that cut on her chin doesn't leave a bad scar.'

'That's the least of her worries,' Eddie said. 'How's Nick?'

'No change,' Roy replied. 'His face is a bit of a mess and there's no response. He's still not breathing unaided.'

Choking back tears, Eddie shook his head as Roy and Sammy said their goodbyes and returned to their bedside vigil.

* * *

After sitting in one position for hours, Eddie had developed pins and needles in his left leg and was desperate for a pee, but didn't want to disturb Jane. His mind wandered over the earlier news she'd imparted, about Angie's father's death and the family wanting Jon to attend the funeral. He really hoped that Jon wouldn't want to go.

What if Angie's sister showed him photographs of his late mother and Richard? There would be sure to be some lying around the family home. Would Jon spot the likeness between him and Richard Price and put two and two together? Or more likely, would Sally spot the likeness between the now-adult Jon and Richard? They were identical. Eddie sighed. He'd tried so hard to hide the truth, but at the back of his mind there had always lurked the dread that one day something would happen and consequences would need to be faced.

* * *

When Jess was discharged from hospital her parents drove her back daily to visit Nick. She sat by his bedside silently cursing her pearl engagement ring and the old wives' tale about pearls and tears. She was convinced it was contributory to the accident and wished desperately that she'd chosen something else. She brought books and read to him, played tapes of his favourite singers and groups, Sting, The Cure and Queen.

She sang along to a tape of some of their own songs, fully expecting him to open his eyes and join in. She brushed his hair, telling the nurses how fussy he was about the way he liked it styled. His facial injuries had healed and he looked as handsome as ever, but was still wired up to the equipment that was keeping him alive. She talked to him about their forthcoming wedding, the honeymoon in the Maldives and the possibility of having a family in the future. But Jess knew in her heart these things were unlikely to happen now.

Once hospital staff realised whose teenagers they were looking after, word quickly spread. The newspapers printed a front-page report of the accident and showed a photograph of Roy and Eddie receiving an award for their recent songwriting achievements. Flowers and gifts were delivered to the hospital from fans and there were always a couple of reporters on hand waiting for a news update, but Jess avoided them when she could. She was unable to share her grief with strangers.

Two more weeks ticked slowly by and as Nick showed no signs of recovery, Jess slipped further into the depths of despair. 'He's not going to make it,' she sobbed against Jon's chest.

'He will, you mustn't give up hope,' Jon said, wiping Jess's eyes.

Jon and Jess were taking their turn with the twenty-four-hour vigil Sammy had insisted upon. She wanted to be certain that if Nick showed the slightest response to anything, someone close should be there to witness it.

Jess shook her head. 'I've had a feeling for months that something was going to happen. Something bad, I mean. The recurring dream and the feelings I had in France and at his birthday party. They were premonitions, I suppose. Whenever I've tried to picture me and Nick married, I can't, no matter how much I try. It's been like looking at a blank photograph: it's not there in my head. I said on his birthday he would always be eighteen and I was right, he's going to die.'

Jon swallowed hard, took her in his arms and buried his face in her hair. 'I wish I could take the pain away.'

'You just being here with me helps,' she said. 'I need you. I couldn't do this without you, Jon.'

In the last week of August, Nick developed a chest infection, which quickly turned to pneumonia, and Jess realised her fears were to become reality.

A distraught Roy called them all to the hospital: Nick was not expected to last the night.

Numb with grief, Jess sat by Nick's bedside holding his hand. She couldn't cry tonight for some reason, but felt she'd shed more tears lately than she would ever have imagined it possible to shed in one lifetime. She gazed round at them all. Her dad, tears in his eyes, holding Mum, who was sobbing. Roy and Sammy, a truce declared, divorce proceedings on hold, devastated beyond belief, clinging to one another. Jon, his arm around Jason, who was crying heartbrokenly, was a rock.

Nick passed away just after 3 a.m. The consultant told them he would have remained in a permanent vegetative state even if he'd survived the pneumonia. At that point, Jess knew it wouldn't have been right for such a vibrant and lively young man and she laid her head on his chest and said her goodbyes. Jon led her out of the room, following their parents, leaving Sammy, Roy and Jason to say their goodbyes in private.

* * *

Nick's funeral was a family and friends affair and afterwards he was laid to rest in Ashlea Churchyard, alongside Roy's late Italian grandparents. A memorial service held the following week in Ashlea Church, where Nick and Jess had been planning to marry, was attended by family, friends, fans of The Zoo and staff from the hospital.

Following the service, the congregation was invited back to Roy and Sammy's home for a celebration of Nick's life. As Roy, Sammy, Jason and Jess left to walk the short distance to Jasmine House, Eddie spotted the lone figure of Livvy Grant, standing by the side of the church.

'Jane, go on ahead with the others. There's someone I just want to have a quick word with.'

'Okay,' Jane said, following Jon and Sammy's parents out of the churchyard.

Eddie waited until they were out of sight and strode over to Livvy. She looked up at him, blue eyes anxious in her pale face.

'What are you doing here, Livvy?' he asked her gently.

'I came to pay my last respects to Nick,' she replied, eyes brimming with tears. 'He used to be my friend.'

Eddie patted her shoulder. 'I know, love, and I understand. But don't you think it was a bit insensitive to turn up today? Sammy's had enough upset to last her a lifetime these last few weeks.'

Livvy nodded. 'Yes, I'm sure. Jon told me Sammy had done some awful things to Roy when she found out about us.'

'She did. But Nick's death made the problems they had pale into insignificance,' he replied.

Livvy's lips trembled and she dug her hands deep into her jacket pockets. She looked around at the congregation, who were slowly dispersing and leaving the churchyard.

'Is everyone going back to Roy's house?'

'Yes. How come you're not at work? Jon, Sean and John Grey are all here. Who's looking after the store?'

'Ian from Instruments is in the record department until I get back. It's my lunch hour. I just wanted to say goodbye to Nick, that's all.'

'Go back to work now you've done that,' Eddie advised. 'Whatever you do, don't contact Roy. Keep your distance. Let him and Sammy have a chance to get their heads around things.'

'I really need to speak to Roy,' Livvy said, looking directly at Eddie.

'No, you don't,' he said, a little more sharply than he intended. 'Just leave him alone.'

'Before Nick's accident, Roy was going to call me when he

got back from London. Obviously, he hasn't done because of what's happened,' she said.

'Your affair's over. It's time to put it behind you. Get on with your life, let Roy and Sammy get on with picking up the pieces of theirs.'

She folded her arms across her chest and looked away. 'I *do* need to speak to Roy,' she repeated. 'I've something to tell him. Will you ask him to call me, please?'

'No, I won't. Now stop this and go back to work.'

'Don't patronise me, Eddie. If you won't ask him to call me, perhaps you'll be good enough to pass on a message, or I'm going to have to phone him myself.'

Realising that he didn't have much choice, Eddie nodded. 'Listen, I have to go or I'll be missed. What's the message?'

'Just tell him I'm pregnant,' she replied quietly, then turned and walked away.

Eddie felt as though someone had snatched the ground from beneath his feet and hit him between the eyes with a cannon ball. Had he heard right? 'Livvy,' he called, running after her. 'Livvy, wait.'

She spun round, defiance etched on her pale face.

'What did you say?' He grabbed her by the shoulders and looked at her tear-stained face.

'I'm pregnant,' she sobbed, 'with Roy's baby.'

'Oh, Christ!' Eddie clapped his hand to his forehead. 'I don't believe it. That's all we fucking need! Are you sure?'

She nodded. 'It was confirmed the day Nick died. I'm three months gone.'

'I can't tell Roy this, I just can't. Not today anyway.' He racked his brains for a temporary solution, one that would prevent Livvy from contacting Roy. 'What day are you off next week?'

'Monday,' she replied. 'Why?'

'Right then, I'll call you on Monday morning. We need to talk about this. I presume you know what you want to do?'

She nodded and the tears started again. 'Yes.'

'Don't worry. I've been in this position myself. It's scary, I know, but these days you have choices, which is more than me and Jon's mum had.'

Livvy smiled weakly, looking a bit more cheerful for confiding in him.

'Listen, I tell you what; I won't phone you. I'll come and see you on Monday after I've dropped Katie and Dom at school. It'll probably be about nine thirty. For God's sake don't tell a soul, not even our Jon. Jane will kill me if she finds out I've even been talking to you. I must go, I'll see you Monday, okay?'

Livvy nodded, thanked him and walked towards her car.

As he left the churchyard, Eddie's mind worked overtime. He wouldn't say a word to Roy about Livvy's pregnancy until he'd spoken to her on Monday morning. For fuck's sake, Roy was forty-two, contraception was available everywhere you looked and he'd *still* managed to put her in the club. He sighed as he crunched up the long gravel driveway of Jasmine House.

Bloody hell! The press will have a field day if this ever gets out so soon after Nick's death.

* * *

Roy met Eddie in the hallway and handed him a whisky. 'Where've you been?'

'Talking to someone,' Eddie replied cagily.

'Was it Livvy by any chance?'

'What makes you think that?'

'Because Jason told me he'd spotted her near the church, but obviously he couldn't go and speak to her. Don't tell Sammy she was there.'

'What do you take me for, Roy?'

'Is she alright? I haven't been able to give her much thought these last few weeks. I've been so upset over Nick that nothing else mattered but as everyone keeps telling me, life must go on. I suppose I should call her, see if she's okay. After all, Nick was *her* friend too – they were fond of one another before I messed things up.'

'She's fine. She wanted to pay her last respects to Nick, that's all. Don't call her, concentrate on things here with Sammy. Livvy will get over you eventually if you don't get in touch.'

Roy nodded. 'Did she ask after me, give you any messages for me?'

'No,' Eddie fibbed. 'She realises it's over and you're back with Sammy.'

* * *

Eddie went to find Jane, who was sitting in the lounge with Sammy and Sean's wife, Tina, all three wearing expressions of grief. He couldn't begin to imagine the pain that Sammy and Roy must be experiencing.

Jason and Jules were sitting with Jess and Jon, telltale signs of tears on their faces. Jon caught his dad's eye across the room and walked over.

'Where've you been, Dad? I was beginning to get worried.'

'I just met someone I know at the church and got chatting,' Eddie replied.

'Livvy?' Jon whispered. 'Jason saw her too.'

'Yes, it was Livvy. Don't tell your mother or Sammy, for God's sake.'

Jon looked closely at his dad. 'You know, don't you? She's told you.'

'I presume we're talking about the same thing?' Eddie said, pulling Jon into the hall.

Jon nodded. 'I guessed last month and so did Sean. She was constantly checking the calendar and throwing up. We promised we'd support her while she decides what she wants to do.'

'She doesn't have a choice, not with circumstances like these,' Eddie replied.

Jon looked startled. 'Dad, of course she has a choice. I'm surprised at *you* for saying that. There's always a choice.'

'No, she doesn't. If Livvy goes ahead with the pregnancy, it wouldn't take long for Sammy to put two and two together and work out that she's carrying Roy's baby. Change the subject, here he comes.'

'You two alright for a drink?' Roy peered at their glasses. 'Top up, Jon?'

'No, thanks, Roy. I'll drive home, give Mum and Dad a chance to have a drink and unwind a bit.'

'What were you talking about just then?' Roy asked Eddie.

'Oh, nothing really, were we, son? Just about Jon getting in touch with Angie's family. He was supposed to go to his grandfather's funeral but with the accident it went out of our minds. I've suggested he ring Angie's sister and explain what happened.'

Jon nodded his agreement. 'She may have read about the accident in the paper. I'll call her. Not this week though, I can't get my head around anything at the moment.'

'Fair enough,' Eddie agreed. 'Do it when you're ready.'

'What's going to happen to Jess and Nick's flat? She's not been back since the accident,' Jon asked.

Eddie shrugged. 'I'll have to let the estate agent know she won't be back. We'll empty it soon and put her things in storage. She's told your mum she wants to stay at home. Anyway, she can't manage to do anything for herself until her arm and foot are out of plaster.'

'Poor kid.' Roy looked across at Jess. 'Her whole future

ruined just because some soddin' arsehole couldn't wait two bloody minutes. If I ever find out who they are, I'll kill them, I swear it.'

Roy was getting upset again. Eddie patted his shoulder in a comforting manner. The grief came in waves – one minute he was coping and the next, flying off the handle or crying.

'What really gets me,' Roy continued, 'and I know they mean well, of course, is when people say it was for the best. How can it be for the best? I've lost my eldest son. That can't be right, can it? I know he would have stayed in a coma, but where there's life there's hope. Now there's nothing, just this bloody big black hole with no bottom. It's the worst nightmare in the world. No parent expects to attend their child's funeral, do they?'

Eddie swallowed the lump in his throat. 'I realise how lucky Jane and I are to still have Jess, even though at this moment she wishes she was with Nick. She says she's nothing to live for and listening to her crying herself to sleep at night crucifies me. I'd like to get my hands round that bastard driver's neck and wring the fucking life out of him!'

The phone rang out at that moment and Molly hurried to answer it. She came back into the lounge and spoke quietly to Roy.

'That was your old friend, Stuart Green. He's on his way over. He's only just heard the news about Nick. He's been away and got back home yesterday. He called to see his mum this morning and she told him what had happened.'

'It'll be really nice to see him again,' Roy said. 'Sammy tried to contact him about the funeral and left a message with his mum.'

'Go and tell Sammy,' Eddie suggested. 'She always got on well with Stu, and if it hadn't been for him and John Grey, there might not be any of us.'

'That's true,' Roy said. 'Mind you, the way Sammy feels

about *me* at the moment, she probably wishes we'd never met at all.'

'Well, I can't say I blame her for *that*.' Molly looked pointedly at her son-in-law before sitting down again.

'I thought things were improving between you?' Eddie frowned.

Roy snorted. 'You must be joking! She won't let me near her. I'm allowed in the same room and bed on the condition I keep to my side and don't touch her. I've held her while she's cried and she's held me, but that's as far as she'll allow it to go. There's been no intimate contact between us for weeks, not even a kiss.'

'Give it time,' Eddie said.

'I killed everything we had that last time I was with Livvy. I can't ever see Sammy forgiving me for that. I'm walking on eggshells all the time at the moment. Nick's death hasn't made any difference to how she feels about *me*. The night the accident happened I blamed myself. I insisted on buying him the bloody car. Sammy said Nick could have been driving any of our cars and it might still have happened but last night she flipped and said the accident *was* my fault and that maybe Nick's mind hadn't been on his driving, that he was upset about us splitting up. I'm definitely not flavour of the month at the moment, not with Sammy, her mother, or *my* mother either, come to that.'

18

Sick at the thought of going behind Roy's back, Eddie pressed the intercom to Livvy's flat.

She let him in and invited him to sit on the sofa. As she curled up on the armchair opposite, with her baggy dungarees, hair scraped up into a ponytail and face devoid of make-up, she looked like a vulnerable child.

His heart went out to her.

'Would you like a coffee?' she asked.

'Please, Liv, no sugar, just a dash of milk. Do you mind if I have a fag?'

'The ashtray's on the windowsill.'

'Do you want one?' He held out the packet.

'No, thank you. I've given up – it's not good for the baby,' she said as she left the room.

He stared after her. What the fuck was she on about? He lit up and puffed smoke above his head. He picked up a pamphlet from the coffee table: *You and Your Baby*. He shook his head and put it down.

Livvy reappeared minutes later, carrying two mugs, and handed one to him. She sat down and took a sip.

'What do you mean?' he asked. 'Not good for the baby.'

'It can do all sorts of damage,' she said and pointed to the pamphlet. 'It tells you in there – I got it from the antenatal clinic when I went to get checked over.'

'But, Livvy, you can't have this baby,' Eddie began. 'You have to get rid of it. I'll pay for the abortion. You can have it done privately and no one need ever know. I thought that's what you'd want.'

Eyes wide with shock, she banged her mug down on the table and leapt to her feet.

'No way! It's our baby, mine and Roy's. You've no right to tell me to get rid of it.' Flopping down next to him, she burst into tears.

He took her in his arms. She was tiny and it was almost like holding Katie. She sobbed against his shoulder. He realised, apart from the problem in hand, the pent-up grief of the last few weeks was coming out: she'd lost a friend and needed to mourn, like everyone else.

'I'm sorry, Livvy. I came here to give you support, not to upset you.'

She looked up through her tears. 'I can't get rid of it, Ed. Please try and understand how I feel. I love Roy, this baby's all I've got now.'

He nodded. 'Let's start at the top. First, how will you cope on your own? Where's your family? Will they help? What will you live off when you give up work? How will you support a baby *and* yourself? I'm not being deliberately hard, I know what I'm talking about. I was eighteen when Jon was born. We really struggled, there were two of us to look after him, and our parents to help out. It wasn't easy. For the most part it was a bloody nightmare. I'd like you to think hard about your decision.'

She sniffed loudly and he handed her a tissue. 'I think about nothing else. I've no family. I've got some money in the bank. I'll be able to take paid maternity leave. When the baby arrives and I go back to work, I'll find a childminder. I could do some singing at night to earn a bit extra.'

'And who'll look after the baby then?'

She shrugged. 'I don't know. A babysitter – or maybe Roy would help out occasionally.'

Eddie took a long drag on his cigarette and mentally counted to ten.

'Livvy, you can't tell Roy about this baby. He's gone through enough. He's trying to work things out with Sam.'

'Well, he'll find out sooner or later. I can't hide it much longer and he has to take *some* responsibility. He was happy enough to jump into bed with me.'

'Do you have any idea what this will do to Sammy? She's just lost her precious son and here *you* are, pregnant by her husband. How the hell do you think she's going to cope with that? Then there's the press. This isn't a big town. Roy and Sam are very well known and respected here. You'll find yourself hounded by reporters and so will they. It's not a pleasant experience. Do you really want to be known as the woman who destroyed Roy Cantello's wife? No one will have sympathy for you. If you want the child, go back to Glasgow and keep your mouth shut about who the father is.'

Livvy sat silently, chewing her thumbnail. She appeared to digest all that he'd said to her, but made no comment.

He stood up. 'I'm off. All we're doing is going around in circles, with both of us getting upset and angry. I'll call you Wednesday morning before I take the kids to school. You can tell me then if you've changed your mind.'

* * *

Eddie made his way into Manchester. Jon and Sean knew Livvy better than anyone else and might be able to offer advice.

Sean greeted him enthusiastically. 'Hi, mate, how you doing? Take a pew.'

Eddie joined Sean behind the counter. Jon, coming out of the staffroom, arms loaded with LPs, smiled to see his father perched on the stool.

'What's up, Dad? You look a bit brassed off.'

'I've a confession to make,' Eddie began. 'Don't think too badly of me, I only did it because I thought it was the right thing: I've been to see Livvy.' He went through what had happened at Livvy's flat.

'I'm not surprised she wants the baby,' Sean said. 'What you have to understand, Ed, is that Olivia's had her own share of problems. She was adopted as a baby, ten when her parents split up, then she lived alone with her father. He physically and mentally abused her and she was taken into care.'

'Bloody hell, I didn't know that,' Eddie said.

'She was left to fend for herself at sixteen,' Sean carried on. 'She came to Manchester to start a new life. She began working for us, met your kids and the rest, as they say, is history.'

'I feel awful,' Eddie said. 'I'd no idea about the abuse.'

'Well, you wouldn't,' Sean said. 'She confided in me, Jon and Roy. When I sussed her affair with Roy, she told me he made her feel safe. Roy's her first and only lover and I reckon she also sees him as the father she never had. The reason she wants her baby, apart from the fact it's his, is because it's the start of a family she can call her own.'

'It's a messier situation than I first realised,' Eddie said. 'She must think I'm a right bully, telling her she has to get rid of it or else.'

Jon spoke up. 'Don't you think Roy has a right to know?'

'I don't know what to think, son. Give me a couple of days. I told her I'll call her Wednesday morning, see what she's decided. Don't expect she'll change her mind now, do you?'

Sean shook his head. 'If she decides to get rid then there's no need for Roy to know. If not, then he'll have to be told. She can't be expected to shoulder the responsibility on her own.'

'Okay,' Eddie agreed, glad he'd shared the problem.

'Dad, did you know "Let's Love a While Longer" is being released next Monday?' Jon changed the subject.

'I had a call from Spencer Philips last week,' Eddie replied. 'What with the memorial service and everything, it slipped my mind. Perry's Dream is supporting Spandau Ballet on tour next month and the song should get plenty of airplay. It'd be nice to have a number one again. It's been over a year since that happened, although we've had a few top-tenner's this last twelve months, so I'm not complaining.'

'When Tim and Pat come home, have you firm plans to reform The Raiders?' asked Sean.

'Yeah, definitely. Roy needs something to occupy him and *I'm* ready for performing live again.'

Sean grinned broadly. 'Well, that's some good news for a nice change. Do you fancy lunch, Ed?'

'Don't mind if I do, seeing as I'm in town anyway.'

'Right, I'll take an early lunch, Jon. We can go now. The pubs will be just about opening and I could murder a pint.'

'After this morning, so could I. See you later, Jon.'

'Bye, Dad. Remind Mum that I'm going for something to eat with Helen and I'll be home about nine thirty to sit with Jess. By the way, I'm calling Aunt Sally this afternoon.'

'Are you? Well... it's up to you.'

Sean glanced at Eddie as they left the shop. 'You okay, Ed? Don't you like the idea of him getting in touch?'

Eddie shook his head. 'No, I don't. They've hardly bothered with him, apart from sending cards and money for his birthdays and Christmas. They wanted him at Angie's dad's funeral, but with the accident, it slipped our minds.'

'Well, surely it won't do any harm. It's not as if they're

fighting for custody. They'd have done that when he was a nipper.'

Eddie smiled wryly. 'Over my dead body. But you're right, of course. What harm can it do?'

Eddie knew Sean would be shocked if he knew the real reason behind his concerns.

* * *

'Thanks, Molly.' Jane accepted the mug of coffee Sammy's mum handed her. 'I'm really in need of this.'

It was their first full day back at work since the accident and there was a backlog of paperwork to do. Supervisor Ruby had taken control during the last couple of weeks, with Jane and Molly popping in whenever they could.

Halfway through the morning, Jane called her mother. Eddie had announced at breakfast that he had some business to attend to after the school run. Her mum had volunteered to help Jess with showering and dressing. The plaster cast was due to come off Jess's wrist on Thursday, so at least she would have one injured limb free.

'Hello, Jane love,' her mother answered after a few rings. 'Yes, Jess is fine. She's gone out for a little walk with your dad and Lennon. No, she's not on her crutches. It's too much of a struggle. I don't know why on earth they gave her crutches in the first place. What on earth were they thinking of with a broken wrist? Your dad's put her in that wheelchair we borrowed. No, she didn't object – she wanted to go, she asked. Stop fussing, love; she'll get there. I'll see you later.'

Jane hung up. Mum was right, she was fussing too much. Jess was usually so independent, but with limbs in plaster she'd no choice but to be looked after.

Molly walked through with a pile of invoices. 'You okay, Jane?' she asked, dumping them in Jane's tray.

Jane smiled. 'Mum just told me to stop fussing over Jess. Dad's taken her out in a wheelchair. Can you believe it, Jess going out willingly in a wheelchair?'

Molly sighed. 'It must be very hard for her. She and Nick were devoted. It's going to take her a long time to get over this. When my Samuel was killed, I didn't want to go on living, I just wanted to die and be with him. But I had to think about my girls and carry on for their sakes. It was very hard, but they pulled me through and then I met Tom and fell in love again. Jess needs something to keep her going. I know they didn't have kids but The Zoo was Nick and Jess's baby – they lived for that band as well as each other.' Molly wiped a tear from her eye and continued. 'Jason popped in to see us the other night with Jules. He said the group will probably never play again. Tom and I think that's sad, because they're all so talented. Eddie and Roy shouldn't let it go to waste. It would give Jess a focus and while I'm still angry with Roy about the affair, managing the group again will give *him* an extra focus, too.'

Jane smiled. 'You could be right, Molly. It might help, but I don't know how Jess will cope without Nick beside her. They did all the vocals and harmonies and it would be like Eddie without Roy, they'd be lost. We'll have to see, but it's worth thinking about.'

'Hello, hello, hello... Shirking instead of working, Mrs Mellor?' Sammy popped her head around the door, closely followed by Roy.

'Hello, you two,' Jane said. 'What are you doing here? I thought you were taking this week off, Sam?'

Sammy gave a wan smile. 'I'm fed up at home. I can't settle to anything. Roy's going over to see Ed, so he brought me here. He's going to wait at your place for me and I'll go home with you, Jane, if that's alright.'

'That's fine, so long as you feel up to being here. You can eat with us tonight, we'll send out for something.'

'That would be lovely. Jason's going to Jules's for tea, so we don't need to worry about him.' Sammy turned to Roy, who was standing silently behind her, looking uncomfortable. 'You go now, Roy, I'll see you later.'

Roy made a move to kiss her on the lips, but she turned her head away and he brushed her cheek. Sammy's frown and Roy's injured expression didn't go unnoticed by Jane and Molly, but neither commented.

As Roy left, Molly slipped back into her own office, closing the door behind her.

'So, how are you?' Jane asked, taking in Sammy's pale face and the dark circles beneath her eyes.

'So, so. How's Jess?'

Jane shrugged. 'Up and down, you know how it is. How are things with you and Roy?'

Sammy blinked back tears. 'I hate him. I can't even stand to be in the same room. He's fussing round, trying to make amends, and all I can think about is him shagging the bimbo! It's eating away at me.'

'Oh, Sammy.' Jane stood up and put her arms around her. 'What the hell are you going to do?'

'I'm not sure yet. I've decided to go and see her, try and lay a ghost. I haven't a clue what I'll say or even when I'll go, but it'll be very soon. Keep it to yourself, Jane. I don't want Roy to find out. I can't move on or even *begin* to build bridges with him until I've confronted her.'

'I won't tell a soul, but are you sure you're doing the right thing? Wouldn't it be better to let sleeping dogs lie?'

'No,' Sammy said with feeling. 'It's something I have to do.'

* * *

Eddie and Sean walked companionably down the street towards Flanagan and Grey's, each with their own thoughts on the Livvy situation. They'd chatted comfortably over lunch and a couple of pints, and as they were parting company near the shop, Sean pointed at two young lads further down on the opposite side of the road.

'Isn't that young Jason and his mate, what's-his-name?'

'Jules?'

'Yeah, that's it, Jules. I'm sure it was those two.'

'Jason's supposed to be back at college today.' Eddie frowned. 'Maybe it wasn't them.'

'I hope it wasn't.' Sean raised an eyebrow. 'That pub they've disappeared into is a well-known haunt for gays.'

'Is it? Won't be Jason then, going into a gay pub. Lads all look the same these days with their poncey hairstyles. Jon takes longer than Jess does in the bathroom and *her* hair's almost down to her backside.'

Sean laughed. 'Anyway, Ed, you and Jane must come over and have a meal with me and Tina one night, if you can find the time.'

'Thanks, Sean, we'll make time. We'll do it before The Raiders re-form and while we can still call time our own. Get the girls to fix it up. See you soon, mate.'

* * *

Eddie carried on his way down the street, glancing into the pub doorway as he passed. The door was propped open and standing by the bar, sideways on, drink in hand, was the unmistakable figure of Jason. Standing by his side, his hand resting on Jason's shoulder was Jules. The pair were talking animatedly, completely oblivious to the fact that they were being observed.

Eddie hurried on his way before either boy spotted him. Sean was obviously wrong about the pub he thought; it wasn't just a hangout for gays. Oh well, whatever – Jason and Jules must have decided to skip college and have a pint instead. The only crime the lads were committing was underage drinking and they'd all been guilty of that in their time.

* * *

Jess and Roy were sitting at the table drinking coffee when Eddie arrived home.

'Where have you been, Dad?' Jess smiled. 'You look kind of mellow.'

'I had lunch with Sean. The mellowness is probably due to a couple of pints of lager.'

'Lucky you.' Roy sighed. 'You should have given me a call, I'd have come with you. I need to get out of the house. Being cooped up with Sammy all day's driving me crazy. She's blaming *me* for the accident now.'

Jess's eyes opened wide with shock. 'Roy, it wasn't your fault. Why on earth is she blaming *you*?'

'She says Nick wasn't concentrating. That his mind was probably on *our* problems.'

'That's just not true. Nick *was* concentrating. It was the stupid driver who swerved in front of us that caused the accident. Nick braked hard to avoid crashing into the back of him and for some reason, the car spun out of control. I remember everything quite clearly now. Nick cried out, "Hold on tight, Jess." Those were the last words he ever said to me, just like in the dreams I used to have.' She placed her hand over Roy's, blinking back tears. 'Roy, don't torture yourself. If anything, Nick's mind was on the gig we were due to play at the college. We were discussing the playlist before we crashed, honestly, and he was *definitely* concentrating. If we hadn't been on a blind bend, if that twat behind had waited a few seconds, if that lorry hadn't been coming towards us... See, Roy, it's all ifs; we were in the wrong place at the wrong time. No matter what went on between you, Livvy and Sammy, the accident would still have happened because of where we were.'

Jess took a deep breath and continued. 'If only the party we should have been going to hadn't been cancelled or we had arranged to pick up Mum and Sammy earlier or later. See what I mean, Roy?'

Roy nodded, his face crumpling. Tears coursed down his cheeks and he put his arms around Jess.

Eddie spooned coffee into three mugs and wiped his eyes with the back of his hand. He thought about Livvy, sitting on the chair this morning, looking so small and lost. He also thought about the baby she was carrying. Poor kid, she must be thinking he was heartless. He made up his mind that when he called her on Wednesday morning, if she really wanted to go ahead and have the baby, then he would tell Roy immediately. He handed Roy and Jess fresh mugs of coffee and joined them at the table.

'What do you want to do this afternoon?' he asked Roy.

'The body shop called this morning. My car's ready to collect. Would you run me over to pick it up and I'll take it home and garage it? Then we could come back here. Sammy's coming home with Jane.'

'No problem,' Eddie replied. 'By the way, "Let's Love a While Longer" goes on release next week.'

'Oh, that's good. Well, let's hope it takes off,' Roy said.

'James Perry from Perry's Dream is really good-looking. With him fronting the band, it should go straight to number one and, of course, they're singing a song written by two of this country's best songwriters, whose names slip my mind for the moment,' Jess teased.

'Cheeky madam.' Eddie was pleased to see her smiling again.

It would be short-lived. There would be tears again before the night was through.

***

Leaving the now-immaculate Lamborghini safely garaged at Jasmine House, Roy and Eddie set off for Hanover's Lodge. As Eddie pulled out onto the main road, Roy spotted Jason and Jules getting off a bus. He asked Eddie to pull over and opened the car window.

'Why aren't you at college, Jason?' Roy called as the boys walked across the road.

'Err, we've got a free afternoon, Dad,' Jason said, looking sheepish, as did Jules.

'You've only just returned. Surely you've a lot of catching up to do?'

'Well yeah, but that's in my own time.'

'Have you been drinking? Don't deny it, son, you're slurring your words.'

'I had half a pint at lunchtime, that's all,' Jason said, swaying slightly.

'And the rest,' Roy said. 'You'll be getting into bother for underage drinking if you're not careful.'

'Oh, and like *you* never drank underage?' Jason sneered.

'That's got nothing to do with anything. That was then, this is now. Your mother will go mad if she finds out. If you've deliberately skipped college, she won't be happy about that either. You'll fail your exams and you won't get into university.'

'I don't care about anything at the moment. Nothing's worth bothering about any more.' Jason was getting upset now. 'I really miss Nick, but no one's taken my feelings into account. It's all about how you and Mum feel. *She's* always blaming you and *you're* always shouting at her. I don't know why you don't just go away and leave us alone. She doesn't want you there, not after what you've done. Nothing's changed. Nick's death hasn't made your affair go away.'

Roy leapt out of the car. 'That's enough! You're upset, you

don't know what you're saying. I'm sorry if you think we've ignored your feelings. It wasn't intentional.'

'I don't want to talk to you, Dad. You make me sick and you make Mum sick too. I'm going home. Come on, Jules.' He turned his back on Roy and walked away.

Jules looked at Roy and shrugged. 'He's upset, Roy. He's finding it very difficult to cope.' He followed Jason around the corner.

Roy got back into the car and turned to Eddie: 'You heard all that?'

Eddie nodded as Roy continued: 'Sammy hates me. What Jason said confirms it. I can't go on like this, Ed. I'm going to check into a hotel for a while, give us both some space. I'll tell her tonight.'

'Good idea, mate,' Eddie agreed and kept it to himself that he'd seen Jason drinking in town earlier.

* * *

Lying in her bath, Livvy clasped her hands over her rounded stomach, trying to imagine what the baby would look like, blonde, like her, or dark like Roy. Was it a boy or a girl? She was still reeling from Eddie's earlier suggestion that she should have an abortion. This was *her* child and she wanted it. She clambered out of the bath and stood towelling herself dry in front of the mirror, checking herself from every angle. She was showing already and her breasts had filled out.

She quite liked her newfound curves. The only thing she didn't like were the more prominent veins on her breasts and the way her nipples, which Roy had likened to strawberries, had darkened. Still, it was a small price to pay. When Eddie got in touch, she would tell him she definitely wanted to go ahead and have the baby. What she didn't relish, apart from telling Roy that she was pregnant, was admitting to him that she'd forgotten her pills on a couple of occasions. He'd be thinking she'd done it on purpose. She took a deep breath; she needed to be strong to face Roy's wrath as this baby could not be hidden for much longer.

* * *

Jane opened a bottle of chilled white wine and poured two glasses, carrying them through to the lounge. The kids were in bed early and already asleep and Jess was having a lie-down in her room. 'Come on, Sam, relax while Ed and Roy are out getting the food.'

Sammy kicked off her shoes and sat on the sofa opposite Jane, tucking her feet up underneath her bottom.

'Now are you going to tell me what's on your mind?' Jane asked. Sammy had been quiet for most of the afternoon, brooding almost.

'Nothing gets past you, Jane Mellor,' Sammy said. 'I'm worried about Jason, if you must know. I heard him crying in the early hours, couldn't sleep myself and I went to sit with him.'

'Is he missing Nick?' Jane clapped her hand to her forehead. 'What a bloody insensitive thing to say, of *course* he's missing Nick.'

'He's missing him desperately. Lucky he's got Jules to support him. That lad's been good for Jason. Roy and I have been so wrapped up in our own grief that we've not really taken Jason's pain on board.' Sammy took a sip of wine and looked at Jane over her glass. 'There's a bit of an issue though. I'm not quite sure how to handle this one.'

'What's that?' Jane frowned.

'Jules is gay!'

Jane nodded. 'I *did* wonder.'

'Hmmm,' Sammy said. 'Nick was always hinting at it.'

'Does it matter?' Jane asked.

Sammy shrugged. 'Not at all, but Jason thinks that *he* might be gay, too.'

'Oh, right.' Jane put down her drink. 'So how do you feel about that?'

'I don't know.' Sammy shrugged. 'I feel a bit numb. Like you can throw *anything* at me now, anything at all, and nothing else can possibly hurt.'

Jane sighed. 'What did you say to Jason?'

'I held him and told him I love him; that he's my son, no matter what. I said I would support him. I also suggested that maybe he's wrong and perhaps it's all to do with the grieving process. He told me he felt more comfortable with Jules than he'd ever felt with girls. He said Jules understands him. He also said that he'd always felt different to Nick. Actually, looking back, a lot of things fall into place. Roy always said I babied and fussed Jason too much, but he needed it. He's so tidy and careful, nothing at all like Nick and Roy, just different.'

Jane smiled. 'I remember when they were all little, Jason was always the one who didn't like mud on his clothes or sticky hands. Sammy, how will you tell Roy this?'

Sammy stared at her. 'Jane, are you mad? I've told Jason not to say anything for now. They're not getting on at all, so their paths won't be crossing too often. Don't tell Ed, not yet anyway.' Sammy knocked back the rest of her wine.

'I won't. Like you say, it could be the grief. He might be enjoying the attention he gets from Jules. He seems a nice enough young lad and Jason needs a confidante.' Jane got up and reached for Sammy's empty glass. 'I'll get us another drink.'

* * *

Just before leaving work, Jon had called his Aunt Sally. The phone was answered by an elderly woman. Jon asked to speak to his aunt.

'She's not here at the moment. Can I take a message?'

'This is her nephew, Jonathon Mellor, Angie's son. Could you ask Sally to call me tomorrow at work, please?'

The woman drew in a sharp breath. 'Jonathon, this is your grandma, Angie's mother.'

'Oh... hello,' Jon stammered, his hand on the receiver going hot and sticky. 'I'm sorry I didn't make it to the funeral.'

'It doesn't matter, love. We read the report of the accident in the newspapers. Please don't worry. How's your sister, Jessica?'

'She's getting there, thanks. She's still in plaster, of course, and grieving for Nick,' Jon replied.

'I know how that feels, believe me. There's not a day goes by when I don't think of Angela. It never quite goes away, but it gets easier to live with as time goes by.'

'I'm sure it does,' Jon said.

'Well, Jonathon, are we going to meet up soon? I'd love to see you before I go back home. You were only a little boy the last time we met and we knew you as Jonny. I expect you've grown out of that.'

Jon chuckled. 'It's Jon now, and I'm over six foot tall, so be prepared for a shock. I'll come on Wednesday night if that's okay with you?'

'Come for dinner. Sally will be delighted. We'll see you about seven thirty then. Goodbye, Jonathon.'

'Goodbye, Grandma.' Jon hung up and let out a deep breath. Well, that hadn't been too bad. He was dying to know a bit about his late mother's family. He felt that something was missing from his life and it was probably all down to this link with Angie's past. He'd managed to piece together odd bits he'd gleaned from Sean and his godmother, Cathy. That Dad had dated Angie *and* Jane and when Angie discovered she was pregnant, she and Dad had been rushed into marriage.

Jon was aware that his father regretted the mistake and when the marriage had broken down, he'd gone back to Jane and his mother to Richard Price, who'd died alongside her. That was all he knew, but he had a feeling in his bones that there was a lot more. Hopefully, Sally would fill in some of the gaps on Wednesday.

* * *

'I'll see you tomorrow, Jane,' Sammy said as she and Roy left Hanover's Lodge. She ignored Roy as they drove down Ashlea Road and he glanced at her.

'I've been thinking,' he began nervously.

'Really? Well, let's hope you've used your brains this time!'

Roy chose to ignore her and continued: 'I'm moving out tomorrow for a few weeks. I'll book into a hotel and then look for a flat. We can't go on like this, it's destroying everything between us.'

Sammy nodded, it was exactly what *she* had in mind, but because of Roy's vulnerable state she hadn't suggested it. This way it was *his* decision and it also meant that Jason could relax a bit more at home while he tried to come to terms with Nick's death and his own sexuality.

'Are you sure it's what you want to do, Roy?' she asked, her tone gentler.

'Yes, I think it's for the best. We're going to end up splitting up for good if we don't put some space between us. Jason told me he wanted me out when I saw him earlier today.'

'When did *you* see Jason?'

'Eddie took me to pick up my car from the body shop. I drove it back to the house. Jason was on his way home with Jules. He'd skipped college and he'd been drinking.'

'He's very down,' Sammy said. 'He needs time and *you* need to be patient with him. He's lost without Nick. It's a good job he's got Jules to rely on. He's been a very good friend to Jason.'

Roy grunted and pulled a face. 'He's a bit effeminate if you ask me. All that bloody eyeliner and earrings and his hair resembles a badger.'

'It's the fashion these days,' Sammy said, sighing. There was no way on earth that Roy would begin to understand Jason's dilemma. He was too much a man's man, or a woman's man, as the case may be.

* * *

'You okay, Jess?' Jane popped her head around Jess's bedroom door.

'Have Sammy and Roy gone?' Jess struggled to sit up.

'Yes. Didn't you hear Sam calling bye to you?'

'No, I had the telly on. Will you help me shower and wash my hair before Jon gets back?'

'Course I will. You'll have to stand in the shower cubicle and I'll squeeze in with you. I'll go and put on some old clothes.'

Jane tied plastic bags around Jess's casts and getting wet through in the process, she did the best she could in the limited space. She wrapped Jess in her towelling robe and sat her in front of the dressing table mirror.

'I'll go and get into something dry.' Jane nipped across the landing to her own room. Eddie was lying on the bed reading *Rolling Stone* magazine and he looked up as she walked in.

'What happened to you? Been taking part in a wet T-shirt contest?'

'Watch it, you,' she threatened, peeling off her top.

'Or else?' He put down the magazine and stared at her half-naked body.

'Or else I'll chuck this at you,' she said and threw the wet T-shirt as he ducked out of the way.

'Right, lady, you're for it now.' He leapt off the bed and caught her arms, pinning them down by her sides. 'Kiss me, Jane,' he whispered, grinding against her.

'If I kiss you, you know what might happen.'

'No, I don't. Show me.'

'Yes, you do and Jess will *never* get her hair blow-dried tonight.'

'Well, kiss me anyway.' He put his arms around her and nuzzled her neck. She kissed him and slipped her hand down the front of his jeans, oblivious to footsteps on the stairs.

'Ooh-oh, sorry, you two,' a voice said, and they jumped guiltily apart.

'Oh, it's you, Jon.' Remembering she was in a state of undress, Jane folded her arms across her breasts while Eddie discreetly turned his back. 'It's not what you think, I was wet from showering Jess and err...' Jane gabbled.

Jon held up his hands. 'You don't have to explain your antics to me. Where's Jess now?'

'In her room, waiting for me to blow-dry her hair. I was getting changed when your father accosted me.'

'I'll dry her hair. I've come home early to be with her anyway. You and Dad relax and finish what you started.' He winked and discreetly closed the door on the pair.

Eddie turned the key and laughed. 'That boy of mine's one in a million, you know.'

'I *do* know,' Jane said. 'Anyway, he's as much my boy as he is yours. Come here, you.' She pulled him down onto the bed beside her and yanked off his jeans. Her wet hair flapped in his face and made him gasp.

'God, woman, you're wet through and your jeans are soaked. You'll have to take them off or you'll catch your death,' he said laughing and peeled off her clothes.

'Any excuse,' she said, rolling into his arms.

* * *

'Jess,' Jon called softly as he knocked on her bedroom door.

'Come in, Jon, *you're* early. Where's Mum got to?'

'She was getting changed out of her wet clothes when Dad pounced on her. That's the last you'll see of her tonight, I shouldn't wonder, so I offered to dry your hair instead.'

She laughed. 'They're worse than teenagers but at least they're happy. You'll have to brush the tangles out of my hair first. How's Helen?'

Jon picked up the hairbrush and sighed. 'We've had a falling out. She's annoyed with me for leaving her early again. I told her she's being selfish. I meet her every night just after six and don't usually leave till nine. So what's the difference between doing that or meeting her at eight and dropping her off at eleven?'

'Well, there isn't,' Jess said. 'It's the same length of time when all's said and done.'

'Exactly. Anyway, she didn't even say goodnight. Just got out of the car, slammed the door and flounced off, so I drove home. I'll call her later.'

'She's very silly. Supposing something had happened to you on the way home? She'd find it hard to forgive herself for not saying goodnight.'

He put his hands on her shoulders and smiled at her reflection, longing to hold her close. He couldn't care less if he never saw Helen again. Just to spend time with Jess, to have her needing his company, was enough. 'I know. I think she's a bit too young for me. She's lovely, but she can be very immature and it winds me up. She's as petulant as Katie sometimes.'

'Talking of immature, how's the marriage wrecker?'

'She's not that bad, Jess. I know you never really hit it off, but she's alright, is Livvy.'

'She's a little cow. How can you say she's alright? First, she makes a play for Nick and when she can't have him, she goes for his dad.'

'She *didn't* make a play for Nick. She was sitting close to him while they were listening to the tape playing back and it was Roy that made the pass at *her*.'

'But she knew he was married. She could have said no.'

'How easy is it to say no and mean it?' Jon raised an eyebrow. 'I reckon Roy's a very persuasive man when he gets a notion in his head. Anyway, what's done is done. Let's get this hair dried. Then I'll make us some hot chocolate and tell you about the conversation I had today with my grandma, Angie's mother.'

'You spoke to her? Oh wow, Jon. It's a deal.'

He switched on the hairdryer and smiled. At least tonight and in spite of the mention of Nick – so far – Jess wasn't in tears.

* * *

Lying in bed with Roy snoring softly beside her, Sammy thought back to the Monday night in August, before she discovered his affair. She'd traced her fingertips around his face after making love, wanting to treasure the moment for always. How could so much have happened in so short a space of time? Why had it all gone wrong? A break was the best thing. They could meet up, have meals out; date one another like they used to do. They'd both changed over the years; they needed to rediscover what they'd lost. She still loved and wanted him and she knew he still loved her. But the trust she'd had in him was buried beneath a mountain of pain and betrayal.

She sighed and turned her back on him. There was a time

when that never would have happened and they'd lain in one another's arms all night, spent from passionate lovemaking. She closed her eyes, but sleep wouldn't come. She turned on her back, stared up at the ceiling and made up her mind to go and see Livvy on Wednesday morning before work. She wasn't after a confrontation with the girl, more to let her know that although she and Roy would be living apart, it didn't mean he was available. Livvy mustn't get any ideas that Roy was free for her benefit. Decision made, Sammy drifted off to sleep.

19

Roy tossed clothes and toiletries into a small suitcase. He'd booked a week in The Grand Hotel in Wilmslow and once he found a place to rent, he'd collect the rest of his stuff.

Sammy had left for the factory just before eight. She'd told him she planned to leave work early to get the spare rooms ready for Pat, Tim and their daughters, who were due to arrive from Nashville on Saturday. The original plan that they stay with Eddie and Jane had changed now that Jess was back home. It wouldn't be much of a homecoming for his in-laws, Roy thought, not with his and Sammy's problems, but their presence would create a welcome diversion.

He dropped his suitcase by the front door, picked up the post and glanced through it. A Visa bill for Sammy, a guitar catalogue for him and a bank statement for their joint account. He put the mail on the kitchen table. Jason appeared behind him, immaculate as always.

'So, you're moving out?'

Roy nodded. 'Just for a while to give me and Mum some space. Would you like a lift into college?'

'No, thanks. I'll get the bus to Jules's place and we'll take the train into Manchester.'

'Okay, whatever.'

Jason hitched his college bag onto his shoulder. 'Bye then, Dad. No doubt I'll see you around.'

'No doubt you will, son,' Roy said, blinking back tears. The last thing he needed was to break down in front of Jason. The lad had little respect for him these days as it was.

* * *

'Katie, Dom, come on down for breakfast,' Jon called up the stairs.

'Where's Mummy and Daddy?' Katie demanded, plonking herself down at the table as Dominic slid onto the chair opposite.

'Having a lie-in,' Jon said and handed them each a glass of orange juice.

'Shall I go and wake them?' Katie said.

'No, leave them in peace. What do you want for breakfast, cereal, toast or both?'

'Coco Pops, please,' Dominic replied.

'Rice Krispies for me.' Katie nodded.

Jon served up their cereal and made Jess toast and coffee while they tucked in.

'I'll drive you into school today, let Mum and Dad have a rest,' he told them. 'Mum's not working until lunchtime. Finish your breakfast while I take Jess's up to her.'

'I'll need my bobbles putting in my hair,' Katie said. 'I can't do it by myself, Daddy usually does it for me.'

'I'll do your hair,' Jon called over his shoulder.

Katie finished her breakfast and went to clean her teeth. She came downstairs with the hairbrush and bobbles. Jon carefully brushed her long hair and divided it into two sections as he'd seen Dad do. 'I can't do plaits, Katie, you'll have to have pigs' tails or whatever they're called.' He wound the coloured elastic bands three times around the divided sections and stood back to admire his handiwork. Not bad for a first time, he thought. The two bright-pink plastic balls of each bobble were sat in the right place and there were no loose strands of hair hanging down. Ready to leave, the threesome knocked on their parents' bedroom door.

'Thanks, Jon. We haven't had a lie-in for ages,' Eddie said as he and Jane hugged Katie and Dom.'

'You're welcome, Dad. Will you be free tonight? I need to talk with you, it's important.'

'Yes, son, of course. What's wrong, have you got a problem?'

'Not really, but we *do* need to talk. Jess's got her breakfast by the way, so have fun.' He shepherded his siblings out of the room and closed the door.

* * *

Jane smiled. 'Jon's such a sweetheart.'

'Yeah, he is, and he certainly didn't inherit *that* from his mother,' Eddie replied.

'Maybe Richard was a nice guy, who knows?' Jane mused.

'Or maybe it's that a little of you has rubbed off on him,' he teased, tickling her ribs.

'Stop it, Ed.' She squirmed away. 'You know how much I hate being tickled.'

'I'll stop on one condition,' he bargained.

'What's that?' She leant up on one elbow and smiled.

'That you make mad, passionate love to me again,' he said.

'What about Jess?'

'She'll be fine, she's got her breakfast. She's hardly likely to walk in on us, is she?'

'Go and check she's okay first then I can relax.'

Eddie leapt out of bed and pulled on his towelling robe. He popped his head around Jess's bedroom door. 'Alright, love?'

'Fine thanks, Dad,' she said. 'How come you're not up yet?'

'Jon's taken the kids to school. Your mum's not in work until lunchtime. We thought we'd have a lie-in. Will you be okay for a while?'

'Yeah. Jon helped me to the loo and brought me breakfast, so I'm fine. Go on back to Mum and relax.'

He grinned and went back to Jane. 'She's alright; I told you she would be. She seems to be getting a bit, I don't know, I suppose the word's calmer.'

'Yeah, she does.' Jane nodded. 'Jon's been a tower of strength. I don't think she'd have got through the last few weeks without him.'

'He's always had time for her. He adored her from the moment he first set eyes on her and *she's* looked up to *him* all her life,' Eddie said.

'So do Katie and Dom, he's a smashing big brother. I know you had a miserable time when he was a baby, Ed, but he's been worth all of that.'

He nodded. 'I just wish to God he was my own flesh and blood. I don't mean that my feelings towards him would be any different, it's just to protect him.'

'I know you're worrying about him getting in touch with Angie's family,' Jane said. 'Maybe that's what he wants to talk about tonight. He's probably arranged a visit and he's bothered about telling you.'

Eddie nodded. 'We've gone all these years without the boat being rocked. I suppose we've been lucky. It's been a crap year so far, what with Pat's cancer, the accident, Nick's death and Roy's affair. I hope nothing else goes wrong, especially when you consider the implications of Jon meeting up with Angie's family.'

'Let's put everything out of our minds for at least an hour,' Jane said, snuggling up to him.

* * *

Sammy parked her Porsche around the corner from Livvy's apartment and put on her shades. She sank low into the driving seat so she could observe the car park entrance without being seen. Fifteen minutes later, her patience was rewarded when she saw Livvy pull out and turn in the opposite direction. Good, if she arrived around the same time tomorrow morning, she would be sure to catch the girl before she left for work. Satisfied, Sammy started up the engine and drove across town to the factory.

When Jane came in later that day, she planned to go home. She hoped Roy would be gone by then; she couldn't face seeing his hangdog expression. If she really looked into his eyes, she'd be lost. But that would mean giving in and he didn't deserve it. She'd continue to support him through his grief as much as she could, but his affair with Livvy was something else.

* * *

Jon arrived in the staff car park at the same time as Livvy. He clambered out of his car and greeted her with a hug. 'You okay, Liv? You look a bit pale.'

'I'm alright,' she said.

Sean smiled as they ran up the stairs. 'Get that kettle on, Liv, and *you*, Jon, phone Helen. She called a couple of minutes ago, sounding really miffed.'

'Oh fuck, I meant to call her last night. I was talking to Jess for ages and I forgot.' He picked up the phone and dialled Helen's number.

'Helen, it's me.'

'Oh, hi.' Her tone was clipped. 'Why didn't you call me?'

'I was going to, but Jess needed me.'

'You're always with Jess. I need you too, Jon. What are we doing tonight?'

'I can't see you tonight. I need to talk to my dad about something important.'

'That sounds like an excuse to me.'

'It's not an excuse at all,' Jon said. He raised an eyebrow at Sean and shook his head.

'Well, I'm fed up of hanging around waiting for you to spend time with me instead of Jess.'

'If that's the way you feel then we might as well call it a day. Jess needs me, I'll spend as much time with her as I can. Why can't you be a bit more thoughtful and think about what my sister has been through, instead of thinking about yourself all the time?'

'I've been very tolerant these last few weeks. You're my boyfriend, but you're not acting like one any more. You're so wrapped up in your sister, anyone would think you fancied her.'

Jon sucked in his breath. 'Right, that's enough. I've had a lot on my plate lately, I don't need this. I expected more support from you, not all this nagging. We should cool it until you grow up a bit.'

Obviously stung by this remark, Helen's reply was furious and Jon held the phone away from his ear as she shrieked, 'I'm grown up enough when you want to sleep with me! Well fine, if that's how you feel, then there's nothing more to say, goodbye.' She slammed down the phone, leaving Jon sighing.

'Bloody women!' He replaced the receiver and shrugged his shoulders.

'Trouble?' Sean asked.

'Why do women think they own you once you sleep with them? Helen was fun to be with at first, before she started getting clingy and serious. Now she's telling me I spend too much time with Jess. She's just accused me of *fancying* my own sister. Anyway, she can stew for a while. I'll be glad of the break. I haven't been home from work for dinner for ages.'

Livvy appeared behind them with a tray and handed them both a coffee.

'That's a bit of a sexist remark,' she said.

'What is?'

'About women thinking they own a man once they've slept with him. More often than not, it's the other way round.'

'Sorry, Livvy, I'm not pointing fingers.'

'I know, but the remark is out of character for you. Isn't it, Sean?'

Sean nodded and ruffled her hair. 'What about you, young Liv, have you decided what you're doing about this baby?'

'I'm having it,' she replied.

Jon saw the challenge in Livvy's eyes as Sean replied, 'Are you sure?'

'Dead sure!'

Sean tapped his fingers on the side of his mug and gave a low whistle. 'You do realise you'll be starting World War Three when Sammy finds out?'

'Yes, but it's my baby. It doesn't matter who fathered it, I'm the one carrying it. No one has a right to force me into any decision I don't want to take.'

Sean held up his hand. 'Okay, being a good Catholic, I agree with you and you'll have my support. But Sammy's been my friend for many years and she's gone through hell recently, so don't expect an easy ride. Being pregnant and single's one thing, but to be pregnant by Roy Cantello will attract all sorts of unwanted attention. I hope you'll be able to cope with it. When are you going to tell him?'

'I don't know; when I pluck up the courage, I suppose. It's my own fault I'm pregnant. I missed a couple of my pills.'

'Ye Gods, Livvy!' Sean shook his head. 'Rather you than me,

love. He'll be livid, but you'll have to tell him sooner rather than later, because you're looking rounder by the day, so you are. As soon as he claps eyes on you, he'll see you're in the club.'

Livvy patted her tummy proudly. 'I know. I had to move the button on my skirt this morning. Right, if you've finished...' She picked up the mugs. 'I'll go and wash these.'

Sean stared after her as she waltzed into the staffroom. 'Is *she* for real or what? I don't fancy being caught in the crossfire of this little lot, do you?'

Jon shrugged. 'I don't think we've much choice. We're bang in the middle of the bloody firing line.'

* * *

'Oh, those look nice.' Jane admired the mountain of brightly coloured corduroy and brushed-cotton fabric samples that Sammy was looking at. She picked up a pastel pink and grey check that was pinned to a piece of pink jumbo cord and ran her fingers over the soft, velvety pile.

'I thought they'd make up into toddler outfits,' Sammy said. 'They're hard-wearing and there's a selection of primary colours too. What do you think, Jane?'

'Brilliant.' Jane nodded. 'Where have the samples come from? It's not our usual supplier, is it?'

'No, it's someone Stuart Green knows. They're actually American fabrics, but they're reasonably priced. Stuart brought them over this morning. We had coffee and a chat and he left them with me to browse through. He's acting as a rep for a friend and he's hoping to set up in business by importing fabric from the States and Europe.'

'So, Stu's back in the rag trade after his foray into selling records?'

'He is, but he's not designing any more,' Sammy replied.

'He's got some really good contacts, so *we* might do well out of it.'

'We're too late for the winter catalogue and the fabrics are too warm for summer so when do you plan on using them?'

'What do you reckon to a Winter/Spring supplement? We could add a few more items to the range. Perhaps some smocked dresses in the checks and maybe jackets and long pants in the cord?'

'Yeah, great idea.' Jane was so pleased to see Sammy looking animated again that she would have agreed to anything.

'I'll do some sketches tomorrow and we'll take it from there,' Sammy said. 'How's Jess?'

'Okay, we're getting there very slowly. We didn't have tears last night, or this morning, but she won't have the radio on or listen to any records at the moment. Anything she and Nick used to sing triggers her off. She's spending a lot of time with my mum and dad, then she just goes to her room and waits for Jon to come home. He's brilliant with her, but it's causing him problems with Helen. Anyway, how are you and Roy? How did it go when you got home last night? Eddie told me Roy might be moving out for a while.'

'He is... today. He's booked into a hotel. Don't know which one, I didn't hang around to find out. He said he'd find a flat to rent until we're sorted,' Sammy replied, almost dismissively. She looked at her watch. 'I'll leave now. I want to pop into Kendals to buy new bedding to brighten up the guest rooms for Pat and Tim. I'm so excited, I can't wait to see them again.'

Jane looked at Sammy. 'Roy's going to be really lonely. He's lost Nick, now he's losing his home, you and Jason.'

'He should have thought about that before he jumped into bed with Livvy. I've no sympathy for him.'

Jane sighed. 'But he's never been unfaithful before. He wasn't seeing her for very long. He hasn't even been in touch with her since the night it finished. Can't you find it in your heart to forgive him?'

'Could *you*, if it were Ed?'

'Yeah, and I did. Ed hurt me more than I would ever have thought possible when he married Angie but I forgave him. *You're* still in love with Roy, you know you are. You're throwing away a lifetime over one mistake.'

'He might do it again, Jane. How can I ever trust him?'

'He won't. He's a broken man, you can see it in his face. He's desperate to make amends but you're not even willing to try.'

'We need this break. It's better this way. I can't stomach him near me. My mind conjures up the smell on him that night. It's awful, I know, but I can't help it, I really can't. It isn't doing *him* any good either, my constantly rejecting him.'

'Well, I still think you should try a bit harder. How's Jason?'

'I don't know. He wasn't home last night when we got in and he was still in bed this morning when I left the house. I want to try and preserve a bit of normality for *him* if possible. Ah, normality!' Sammy snorted. 'Who the hell am I kidding? One son dead, the other struggling with his sexuality, and a songwriting adulterer for a husband.' She shook her head and continued. 'The whole time Roy and Ed were in the spotlight we tried to live a fairly normal life and we managed it most of the time. None of the kids, apart from Jon, realised their dads were famous. The group was a job, like the songwriting is. It's a means of support at the end of the day. But since the accident and Nick's death, there's been bloody reporters prowling round the lane again. If they get wind of Roy's affair with airhead and they suss Jason out as gay, then God help us. They'll be raking up all sorts from the past and normality will fly out the window. Oh dear, Pat and Tim don't know what they're coming back to.'

'They do,' Jane said. 'Ed spoke to Tim and put him fully in the picture. No one knows about Jason, of course, just you and

I. But if he and Jules are always together, and unless they're very discreet, then like you say, God help us.'

Sammy stood up and stretched. 'Well, I'm off. I'll leave things in your very capable hands. Will you have a quick word with Ruby? See what she thinks about these fabrics and my ideas for them. I'll call you tonight. Bye, Jane.'

'Bye,' she called, staring after Sammy's departing back.

* * *

Eddie could hear sobbing and called up the stairs. 'Jess, are you okay?'

'Dad, can you come here, please?' Jess yelled a note of hysteria in her voice.

He raced upstairs two at a time. Jess was sitting on the landing, tears pouring down her cheeks. 'Darling, what's the matter? Why are you out here?' He cradled her in his arms.

'I fell over, I want Nick, Dad. I want Nick, I can't bear this.'

Eddie swallowed the lump in his throat. 'Jess, I wish I could give you what you want, I really do. I swore when you were born that you would have everything you ever needed, but the one thing I can't give you is Nick.' He held her tightly, kissing the top of her head. He really thought that she'd been making a bit of progress, but now they appeared to be back to square one.

'What triggered this?' he asked gently, wiping her eyes and nose with his hanky.

'I was looking at the photos of Nick's eighteenth and Brittany. I shouldn't have done it – it's too soon. I was lying on my bed thinking about the way we used to be and I suddenly couldn't picture his face. It was gone from my memory so I panicked and looked at the photographs. Then I thought back to that day in Brighton when you and I had a fight and I ran to the beach. Nick came and found me and we sat on the pebbles, holding each other. He told me he'd never leave me and that we had a whole lifetime of loving in front of us.

'We only had four more months, Dad, only four months and now he's left me and it's all gone. All I have is this awful emptiness and the photographs.' She took a deep shuddering breath and looked up, her blue eyes pleading. 'Help me, Daddy, please.'

Eddie covered his eyes with his hand. 'I don't know how to, Jess.' Only once before in his life had he felt this inadequate and that was when Mark Fisher, Jane's ex, kidnapped Jess.

Lennon ambled upstairs and placed his paw on her shoulder. Whimpering, he licked her salty tears away.

'Lennon, what do you want?' She stroked his silky ears. 'I can't even take you walkies at the moment. Do you need to go outside?'

'The front door's open. He'll find his own way out if he needs to go.'

'Eddie, Jess,' a voice called from the hall.

'We're up here, Gran,' Jess said.

Enid walked slowly up the stairs and looked at father and daughter, sitting on the landing with their arms around one another. 'Hello, you two, bad day, is it?'

Eddie sniffed. 'I'm afraid so, Enid.'

Jess sighed and looked at her grandmother through her tears.

'Come on, love. Do you want to come next door, or would you rather stay here with your dad? Let's go downstairs while you have a think about it.' Enid helped Eddie to lift Jess from the floor and they made their way downstairs and into the kitchen.

Roy was sitting at the table with his head in his hands. He raised his eyes wearily as the trio approached. 'I heard you upstairs with Jess, so I came in here. I didn't want to disturb you. Are you having a bad day, Jess love? Join the club, kid.'

'Oh dear, what will I do with you all?' Enid shook her head.

'It's not getting any easier to live with, like everyone keeps telling me it will,' Roy told Enid.

'I don't suppose it is, Roy,' Enid replied as she busied herself, making a pot of tea. 'And your problems at home aren't helping you very much either.'

'I don't have a home any more,' Roy said. 'I left this morning. I'm staying at The Grand in Wilmslow for now and I'm going flat hunting tomorrow. I've made a couple of appointments to view places.'

'I'll come with you, if you like,' Eddie offered.

'Thanks, mate. I was hoping you'd say that. It's a shame our original flat in Wilmslow isn't available. We could have had a real nostalgia trip down memory lane.' Roy had a faraway look in his eyes. 'Do you remember all those wonderful nights we spent there with the girls before we were married?'

Eddie signalled frantically with his eyes while Jess smiled through her tears.

'What? Oh shit! Sorry, Enid,' Roy apologised, clapping his hand over his mouth and blushing as she plonked a mug of tea in front of him.

'That's the first time I've ever seen you blush, Roy Cantello, in all the years I've known you. At least you've put a smile back on our Jess's face. Hey, and you needn't think I'm that daft either. I knew what went on in that flat and so did Molly. We used to call it "The Den of Iniquity" and we weren't far wrong, were we? Well, I'll leave you to your reminiscing. Get your dad to bring you over to ours, Jess, when you're ready.'

'Thanks, Gran, I will.'

As Enid left the house, Jess turned to Roy and smiled. 'Roy, only *you* could have got away with that in front of Gran. I bet you had some fun at that flat.'

Roy nodded. 'We certainly did, didn't we, mate?'

'Yeah, we did,' Eddie replied. 'Especially as I was seeing

your mum again. The time without her wasn't so nice, so I do know a *little* of what you're going through, Jess, believe me.'

Jess sighed. 'Dad, I know you don't like talking about Angie, and you obviously have your reasons, but what was Jon's mum *really* like? I mean, she can't have been that bad or you wouldn't have dated her. Don't you think it's time you told Jon a bit more? He's dying to know, but doesn't want to upset you by asking.'

Eddie looked at Roy for inspiration. 'Roy will tell you what Angie was like.'

Roy blew out his cheeks. 'Well, she was a fit bird. Everyone fancied her. We were all in the same year at school. She was the prettiest girl by far, but she only had eyes for your dad.'

Eddie nodded and took up the tale. 'Yeah, *she* fancied me and I suppose *I* fancied her. We started dating when we were fourteen.'

'Were you serious?' Jess asked.

'We were – well, sort of. She was always telling me she loved me. I couldn't say it back and mean it, because I didn't really love *her*.'

'Was she very popular?'

'She was. Like Roy said, everyone fancied her. She had long curly hair, like Jon's but not as dark, green eyes, a cute smile and a very sexy figure. She was a brilliant dancer and a bloody good kisser.' He grinned, remembering a few passionate clinches with Angie in Norman's Woods after school. 'But then I met your mum and that was it. I fell in love, although I didn't realise it right away.'

Jess looked puzzled. 'So, you dated them both at the same time?'

'Not really, I started dating your mum and I kind of finished with Angie.'

'Except he didn't tell her he'd finished with her,' Roy said, grinning. 'And then he wondered why she wouldn't leave him alone.'

'I *did* tell her,' Eddie protested, 'eventually.'

'Well, you must have got back with her because you married her and you had Jon. How did that happen and what went wrong with Mum?'

'She dumped me,' her dad admitted.

'Why? I thought she'd always loved you? This bit you've never told us is what puzzles Jon and me.'

'I'm embarrassed by what happened,' her dad replied.

Roy carried on for him. 'He was dating Jane for a few months, but he saw Angie one night with Richard and was jealous. The following week, he walked Angie home and afterwards, Angie threatened to tell your mum he'd slept with her.'

'*I* told her instead,' her dad continued. 'She was upset and walked out on me, but we got talking a couple of months later and she agreed to see me again.'

'I can't imagine you two-timing Mum. You and Roy are tarred with the same brush,' Jess teased.

Her dad grimaced and continued. 'We had a couple of dates the same week and then she came to our gig that weekend. Afterwards we went back to my mum's. We made love for the first time and I told her I loved her and asked her to marry me. She was only sixteen, but she said she would marry me when she was eighteen.' Eddie sighed, remembering the night as though it were yesterday.

'So what happened, Dad, how come you ended up married to Angie?' Jess frowned.

Eddie wondered if he should go on. He'd opened the can of worms now, but Jess wasn't out to judge him. She just wanted to know the truth, well... as much of the truth as he was prepared to impart.

'We were lying around talking and Angie walked in on us.'

'You're joking!' Jess's hand flew to her mouth.

'There's worse to come,' he said, cringing inwardly. 'She went mad, told us she was pregnant and I was the father.'

'Shit! Poor Mum, she must have been devastated.'

'She was. I don't know how she managed to forgive me but she never stopped loving me, or I her. I married Angie in July, as you know. Jon was born in December. The marriage lasted less than three years. I got back with your mum in February 1964, Angie started seeing Richard Price again and soon after that, they were killed in a car crash. I took custody of Jon and your mum moved into the flat with us. We married in November that same year and you were born the following June. You don't need to work it out, Jess; you were already on the way. You've always known that anyway, the strange thing is, *we* hadn't a clue! What I'm trying to tell you is that we didn't rush into the marriage because of you, it was because we loved one another. You were the icing on the cake.'

Jess looked at her dad and took his hand. 'Thanks, Dad. It took some guts to tell me that. I know you don't like to talk about your time with Angie, but Jon's very curious. He thinks that because you won't discuss his mum with him, something must have been really awful about her. Now is that it? You've told me the whole story?'

'That's it, Jess.'

'Well, can we tell Jon? It'll put his mind at rest. He's got it into his head that his mum was a real ogre but she was just a teenager who made a mistake like thousands of others. Poor Angie, and poor Mum.'

'*You* can tell Jon if you like,' her dad said. 'He can come and ask me questions if he wants to. But one thing I have to add, Jess, is that from the minute Jon was born, I never regretted having him. I love him and I'm very proud of him. I always have been. Make sure you tell him that. I'd hate for him to think otherwise.'

'I will. Take me over to Gran's now, please.'

'Don't mention this to your gran, Jess. She's been told an edited version and that's enough.'

'Your secret's safe with me,' Jess said, giving him a kiss. She hugged Roy, said goodbye and Eddie gave her a piggyback over to Enid's house.

* * *

Jon went straight up to Jess's bedroom when he arrived home from work. She looked up and smiled as he walked in.

'You're home early again. Not seeing Helen tonight?'

He shook his head. 'Nope, it's over.'

'Why? I thought you really liked her?'

'She was getting too demanding of my time,' he replied with a dismissive shrug.

'You mean she was fed up of you being with me and not her, I suppose?'

He flopped down on the bed beside her. 'Something like that. Don't worry about it, we weren't really right for one another anyway. So, what sort of a day have you had then?'

'Very interesting, actually.' Jess told him how she'd been upset over Nick and about her conversation with their dad and Roy.

When she'd finished, Jon lay back with his hands behind his head and sighed.

'So, she didn't have two heads then, this mother of mine?'

'Don't be silly.' Jess smiled. 'I don't understand why he hasn't told us before really, why it's all had to be kept so secret.'

'Maybe to protect Mum's feelings,' Jon said. 'He'd already hurt her enough without him keep dragging it up.'

Jess nodded. 'You're right, of course. I never thought of that.'

'Shall we go downstairs and get something to eat? The kids are in the kitchen talking Dad's socks off – well, Katie is – and Dom's hard pushed to get a word in. Mum's just home from work. Come on, you, up you get.' Jon lifted her easily and Jess slung her un-plastered arm around his neck and held on tightly. He smiled; Jess felt good in his arms, so right in fact and better than Helen had ever done.

'Don't drop me!'

'As if,' he said, carrying her downstairs and sitting her at the kitchen table.

'I'll take these two up for a bath,' Jane said, looking at Jon and Jess's faces.

'I'll read you a story later,' Jon called out to the kids as Jane hurried them upstairs. 'Dad,' he turned to Eddie, 'thanks for telling Jess about Angie.'

'I should have told you ages ago, Jon. Truth is I was a bit embarrassed. What must you both think of me?'

'Dad, you were a kid,' Jess reassured him.

'Yeah, a *stupid* kid who thought he was God's gift.'

'Well, it's in the past now and at least I know a bit more about my real mum,' Jon said. 'I called Aunt Sally yesterday. She wasn't in but I spoke to Angie's mum, my grandma. I'm invited for dinner tomorrow. I hope you don't mind.'

'You've a right to know your mum's family, Jon. How was the old— erm, your grandma?'

Jon grinned. 'I presume you and she didn't get on?'

'That's the understatement of the century. Lydia Turner and I hated one another. She called me a tearaway and threatened to have me castrated on many an occasion.'

'Oh dear, I'll try and keep your name out of the conversation then.'

'You'd be very wise to.'

20

Sammy couldn't believe she had slept soundly for at least eight hours. Jason had stayed over at Jules's and she'd had a quiet night on her own. Roy, sounding doleful and drunk, rang to let her know where he was in case she needed him, and she'd called Jane for a chat. A long soak in the Jacuzzi bath, a bottle of chilled white wine and she'd retired to bed, refreshed and relaxed. She shed a few tears on Roy's pillow, breathing in the lingering scent of his aftershave. She thought about Nick and the vibrant young man he'd been, and she'd recalled Jason's earnest face the night he confided he might be gay. What on earth had she done to deserve all this in one fell swoop? Surely nothing else could go wrong now?

As she drove to Livvy's, Sammy rehearsed what she would say. She swung into the car park, wondering if Livvy was looking out of the window. The girl certainly wouldn't let her in if she rang the intercom. She'd hang around and wait for someone to go in or come out of the building. As she pondered, she spotted a postman making his way across the car park. She leapt from her car and followed him. As both she and the postman arrived at the door, a young woman, pulling a toddler by the hand, held the door for the postman and Sammy nipped in behind. A brass plaque on the wall by the stairs proclaimed that flats five to eight were on the next floor. She ran up the stairs and across the landing to the red door. She knocked and waited. The door opened a few inches and Livvy, wrapped in a pink bath towel, peeped out. Her jaw dropped when she saw Sammy.

'Roy isn't here,' she began as Sammy pushed past her and walked into the flat without waiting to be asked.

'I know he isn't. But you and I have a few things to discuss.' She marched into the lounge as Livvy followed.

'Sit down.' Livvy gestured to the sofa. 'I'll put some clothes on.'

* * *

Livvy rushed into the bedroom and sank down on the bed. Her legs were shaking. Why was Sammy here? Had she found out about the baby? She took a calming breath and pulled on underwear and a big loose T-shirt, hoping it would hide her baby bump. She skirted past the lounge and into the kitchen.

'I'm making tea, would you like one?' she called, popping her head around the lounge door. Sammy didn't look angry, just pale and sad-eyed.

'Please, no sugar,' Sammy replied.

* * *

Sammy looked around the small, but neat lounge. She pictured Roy seducing Livvy on the sofa. Her stomach rolled and she swallowed hard. She closed her eyes to blank out the scene as Livvy carried two mugs through and placed one on the table in front of her. She sat on the opposite chair, pulling her T-shirt down.

Sammy took a sip of tea. 'It's not easy for me, coming here,' she began, wishing she hadn't. All she wanted to do was run out of the place. 'But I need to talk to you. Roy and I have separated. It's a temporary measure. We need some time apart.'

'I see.' Livvy looked at the floor.

'What I'm trying to say,' Sammy continued, 'is that it doesn't mean he's available for *you*. If he comes to see you, I want you to send him away. We're going through an awful time, as I'm sure even you can imagine. I want to try and bury the past and start again. Roy and I can only do that if he has no further distractions.'

'I haven't seen him for ages now,' Livvy said. 'I won't let him in if he comes round. I'm seeing someone new.'

'Let's hope he's not married this time. That's all I've come to say. I'll go now.'

* * *

As Sammy moved towards the door, the phone rang and Livvy remembered that Eddie was supposed to be calling her that morning. She couldn't take the call in front of Sammy, just in case it *was* him.

'Would you excuse me? I'm expecting a call from my boyfriend. I'll take it in my bedroom.' She ran to her room and snatched up the receiver, hoping that Sammy would see herself out.

'It's Eddie,' the caller said.

'Hi.'

'I can't talk long. Have you decided?'

'Yes, I'm keeping it.'

'And you're sure it's what you want?'

'I'm positive.'

'Okay then. It's your decision and I'll stand by you. We'll get together this week and I'll decide how I can best help you.'

'What about your suggestion that I go back to Glasgow and not tell anyone who the father is?'

'Forget I said that. I'll call you when I can. Bye.'

'Bye, Ed, and thanks for offering to pay for the termination. But more than that, thank you for standing by me.'

'Think nothing of it.'

Livvy hung up. At least she had someone on her side, other than Jon and Sean. How she wished she could confide in her best friend Sheena in Glasgow. Maybe later in the year she'd do that. She took several deep breaths as her stomach lurched. The last thing she needed was to give the game away by puking while Sammy was around.

* * *

Sammy glanced at a pamphlet on the coffee table. She frowned as the heading *You and Your Baby* leapt out at her. She could hear Livvy talking to her boyfriend and crept down the hall. She heard Livvy say 'I'm positive.' There was silence as Livvy obviously listened to what the caller was saying. Then Sammy heard her say, 'What about your suggestion that I go back to Glasgow and not tell anyone who the father is?' There was silence again as her stomach tied itself in knots. Livvy must be pregnant, she thought. But why would her boyfriend want her to go back to Glasgow? What Sammy heard next sent a chill down her spine. 'Bye, Ed, and thanks for offering to pay for the termination. But more than that, thank you for standing by me.'

As Sammy heard Livvy replace the receiver, she hurried back to the lounge. Livvy was pregnant and Eddie was the father. Oh my God! She must have started seeing him after Roy finished the affair.

'Sammy, are you okay?' Livvy asked, walking back into the room. 'Would you like another cup of tea?'

Sammy nodded. Her hands were shaking and she knew she

was incapable of driving at the moment and facing Jane after what she'd just learnt. Maybe the new boyfriend was called Ed too? That would surely be the answer. But then why would he ask Livvy to keep his identity secret and why would she have to go back to Glasgow when she had a nice little flat and job here? Something didn't add up.

Livvy brought more tea through and stood in front of Sammy. 'I'm going to get ready for work; I won't be a minute. I need to go soon or I'll be late and I'll have Sean to answer to.'

'Okay.' Sammy sipped her drink, her mind working overtime.

Livvy reappeared five minutes later, wearing a suit. The jacket strained at the buttons across her swollen belly. Sammy's eagle eyes raked over her and narrowed.

'Who's the father?'

'I'm sorry?' Livvy looked at her, wide-eyed.

'You're pregnant. Who's the father? I saw the pamphlet on the coffee table and overheard your conversation with your so-called new boyfriend. How far gone are you?'

'About seven weeks.'

'Is that all?' Sammy did a quick calculation. Roy hadn't seen Livvy since early August, or so he'd told her and it was now mid-October. So that just about let him off the hook. She breathed a half-sigh of relief then remembered what she'd overheard.

'So, who's the father? You still haven't told me.'

'My new boyfriend,' Livvy replied, blushing furiously.

'And the new boyfriend's called Ed, is he? Coincidence, wouldn't you say? Seeing as Roy's best mate is called Ed, too. Why were you thanking him for offering to pay for a termination? Didn't he want you to have the baby?'

'Not at first,' Livvy faltered. 'But he does now.'

'Well, *you* didn't waste much time, considering Roy told me you don't sleep around.'

The phone rang again.

Sammy looked at her. 'Aren't you going to answer it?'

Livvy remained where she was, frozen to the spot.

Sammy marched over and snatched up the receiver. Before she had a chance to speak, a softly spoken male voice informed her he could see her at lunchtime today. They'd have a bite to eat and talk properly then. He told her not to worry and said goodbye.

'Bye,' Sammy replied quietly and hung up. She turned to Livvy, who was staring at her with a terrified expression in her eyes.

From Sammy's horrified facial changes as she'd listened to the unknown caller, Livvy had convinced herself it was Roy. She waited for the onslaught.

'Eddie will see you later,' Sammy announced. 'He'll take you for lunch and then you can talk properly. Oh, and he also said not to worry!'

Livvy stared into space.

'So, is Eddie the father?' Sammy asked her.

'Of course not, my boyfriend is,' Livvy stammered.

'And your boyfriend just happens to sound exactly like Jane's husband on the phone. What sort of a girl are you? You obviously get a kick out of sleeping with your friends' fathers. Are you trying to destroy our families for some reason?'

Sammy was furious, she just wanted to batter the hell out of the girl, but knew she ought to leave the flat before she did something she might regret. She picked up her bag and walked to the door.

'I don't fancy your chances when Jane finds out about this, she'll make mincemeat of you,' was her parting shot, before slamming the door.

She stormed downstairs and out to her car. She headed towards the factory, rubbing her forehead with the heel of her left hand. Something was nagging at the back of her mind.

Something that didn't quite add up, but she couldn't for the life of her think what it was. She went over the phone call word for word. It had definitely been Eddie Mellor; there was no mistaking that softly spoken voice.

She turned on the radio and pulled up at the traffic lights on the road just around the corner from the factory. She tapped her fingers on the steering wheel and stared out of the window. As she waited for the lights to change, it came to her in a blinding flash: Eddie had had a vasectomy shortly after Dom's birth. The baby couldn't possibly be his. Relief washed over her, but was quickly replaced by another rush of consternation. Why then, was *he* involved? Shit! The baby must be Roy's and he'd roped Eddie in to help him sort things out.

Sammy thought back to Livvy's swollen belly. That was bigger than a seven-week pregnancy – more like four months. 'Oh, Roy,' she muttered, 'you stupid idiot.' He'd assured her Livvy was on the pill. The girl must have either forgotten to take it, or she'd deceived him all along. Bloody hell, if it wasn't one thing it was another.

An impatient tooting from behind made her realise the lights had changed. She set off, head whirling. She'd have to phone Roy, get him to come to the house later. They would need to talk seriously now. As far as she was concerned, this well and truly put the tin hat on their ailing marriage.

* * *

Eddie had been packing Katie and Dominic into the Jeep for the school run when a thought had occurred to him. He'd some running around to do this morning, but he could meet Livvy for lunch, before picking Roy up later for the viewings. He told the kids to fasten their seat belts and dashed back into the house. Jane was drying her hair and Jess was still in bed. He quickly dialled Livvy's number and, giving her no time to speak, told her of his intentions then hung up, frowning. Had he dialled the right number in his haste? It didn't sound like Livvy saying bye. Ah well, never mind, he'd call in the shop anyway and see if she was free. He rushed back to the Jeep and set off on the school run, oblivious to the fact that he'd just spoken to Sammy.

* * *

Following Sammy's departure, Livvy tried to calm down. All this upset wouldn't be good for the baby. She dreaded the day ahead. Sammy would be sure to tell Jane of her suspicions and then what? All hell would break loose. She'd have to warn Eddie at lunchtime and give him the opportunity to get his story straight before Jane confronted him. Poor Eddie, all he'd tried to do was help her and he'd got unwittingly caught up in the middle of the mess. If only she knew where Roy was staying, she would pluck up the courage to call him and tell him about the baby; after all, it was *his* mess too. She looked at her watch: it was after nine and she would be late into work now. Sean wouldn't be too pleased about that.

* * *

Roy lay on his bed in his luxury hotel suite, staring at the ornate ceiling. He was depressed and felt he had nothing to live for. He'd been awake ages and had showered and dressed. He'd drunk himself into a stupor last night, smoked the last of his dope and been violently sick in the bathroom. Earlier in the evening he'd toyed with the idea of calling Livvy then decided against it and phoned Sammy instead. She'd been polite, but cool, answering with a yes and a no as necessary.

He swung his legs off the bed and decided to pay his parents a quick visit. No doubt his mother would give him earache when he told her he'd left Sammy, but he could probably weather that. He just needed to see a familiar face and who better than his own mum? She'd been devastated by Nick's death and he knew that it was only right that he should explain to her what was going on before someone else told her.

The phone rang as he was about to leave the room. It was Sammy, asking him to meet her later at Jasmine House. She needed to talk urgently, she said. He told her he had a couple of flats to view this afternoon and could they meet tonight instead. She agreed and said to come after six. He wondered what she wanted to talk about that was so urgent. Maybe she wanted him back? But pigs might fly, he thought as he left his suite. 'I'm just popping out. If anyone wants me, I'll be back around lunchtime,' he informed reception.

'Okay, Mr Cantello, we'll see you later.' The red-haired girl smiled at him. As he left the desk, he heard her say to her blonde colleague, 'Bloody hell, he's still a dish. I wouldn't mind jumping *his* bones tonight!'

'Sharon, he'll hear you and then what will he think?' the blonde said with a nervous giggle.

Roy smiled to himself. Girls were so forward today, not like when he was younger and you really had to be an expert in the art of chat up and persuasion. Not that he'd had much luck until Sammy and it had taken a few cracks of the whip before she'd finally succumbed to his charms. 'Oh, Sammy, what have I done to us?' he murmured. He climbed into the car and put his head on the steering wheel.

* * *

Livvy found herself making one mistake after another that morning. When a second customer complained about being short-changed, Sean put his hands on her shoulders and ordered her to take a break. She went willingly as he shook his head after her. She'd told him she'd overslept, which was why she'd been late in. Every time the phone rang, she expected it to be Jane and had managed to avoid answering it so far. She sat in the staffroom sipping a glass of water, wishing she'd never set eyes on Roy Cantello.

Jon popped his head around the door moments later. 'Want to talk, or would you rather be on your own? I'm due a break for ten minutes if you need an ear to bend.'

She nodded, glad of his support.

He sat down opposite her. 'Fire away; you've been a nervous wreck all morning. Are you having second thoughts about the baby? Only you haven't got very much time to change your mind. You're almost too far gone now to terminate it.'

'I still want it,' she said. 'Sammy came to see me this morning. She guessed I'm pregnant. Your dad called me while she was at the flat and she overheard half the conversation, put two and two together and came up with five. Then he called back and she actually picked up the phone. He thought it was me and told her he'll take me out for lunch so we can talk. She hung up without saying a word to him other than bye, so he won't have realised it was her. But she went crazy with me. Now she thinks your dad's the baby's father.'

'For fuck's sake!' Jon's mouth fell open. 'Why didn't you tell her it was Roy's? It can't be Dad's anyway. He's had a vasectomy, Sammy must have forgotten. But if she says anything to Mum, *she'll* realise he's been in touch with you and all hell will break loose.'

'I know and I feel awful. Eddie's only trying to be supportive. I made up a tale that I've got a new boyfriend and that it's his baby, but Sammy didn't believe me. I couldn't tell her it was Roy's. She came round to warn me off, told me he'd moved out so that they could have some space. How could I drop a bombshell like that on her? I promised her if Roy gets in touch, I'd send him away.'

'I'll call Sammy and tell her not to say a word to Mum, if she hasn't already.' Jon rushed back into the shop, pushed past Sean, grabbed the phone and dialled the factory, muttering that it was an emergency. He got straight through to Sammy.

'It's Jon, is Mum there?'

'No, she's on the factory floor talking to Ruby. What's wrong, Jon, you sound agitated?'

'Livvy just told me you called round this morning and you think the baby is Dad's,' he gabbled. 'Dad had a vasectomy ages ago. Don't tell Mum he's helping Livvy, please. She'll go apeshit with him for keeping secrets.'

'Calm down, love. On the drive back to work I remembered about your dad's vasectomy. I've already worked out why he's helping Livvy: it's because the baby's Roy's.'

'Yes,' Jon admitted. 'It is.'

'I presume Roy knows she's pregnant and wants nothing to do with it?'

'No, he doesn't have a clue.'

'Really? So, Eddie's offer of help is to protect Roy?'

'Yes, he thought it best not to tell him if she wasn't going ahead with the pregnancy, but she is. She's too scared to tell Roy though.'

'Right. I'll tell him tonight. He's a big boy, Jon, and an idiot, but he's got to face up to his responsibilities. I'm not happy about all this, I can tell you, but to be honest I'm past caring and Livvy won't be able to cope on her own without financial help. I take it there's no one close, no family she can turn to?'

'She has no one.'

'Okay. Well, tell your dad when he collects her at lunchtime that I know about the baby and that Roy and I will take over the responsibility, and you'd better tell Livvy as well. I think I scared the life out of the poor kid this morning and she doesn't need that in her condition. How far gone is she? I need to know for when I present his lordship with the facts.'

'Nearly four months. Sammy, you're being unbelievably calm about this.'

'It's the calm before the storm. I'm in shock, but I'm trying to think practically. Your mum's on her way back into the office; I can hear her talking to my mother. Don't worry, I won't say a word. Bye, Jon.'

Jon put the receiver down and looked at Sean, who was shaking his head in disbelief.

'Bejesus! Is that right? Sammy thought it was Eddie's kid? Talk about tangled webs!'

Jon nodded. 'I'd better tell Livvy that Sammy now realises the baby is Roy's.'

'Better than any bloody soap opera this.' Sean grinned. 'I tell you, Jon, since I started working with your mother back in the sixties, I've never been short of entertainment where your family and their friends are concerned! But this little drama takes the biscuit.'

Jon smiled wearily. 'You've heard nothing yet. Dad told Jess the saga of himself, Mum and Angie yesterday.'

'Oh, I know most of that one, I told you some of the tale myself. It caused quite a stir back then. But at the end of the day, your dad's one of the best, so he is. Never forget that, Jon.'

'Thanks, Sean; he's the best alright. That's why I feel guilty about going to see Angie's family tonight. It hurts him. He thinks they abandoned me because of him, but maybe it was because they felt it best to let sleeping dogs lie. I doubt Dad was very approachable at that time and it was Jane who brought me up. He was always on tour or doing something with The Raiders. Maybe Angie's family felt they would be interfering or something. Anyway, I'll go and tell Livvy that Roy is to be told about the baby.'

Livvy took Jon's news with a certain amount of relief. 'Thank God for that, although I know he'll go crazy with me for getting into this mess in the first place.'

'It takes two, Liv; you didn't do it on your own.'

'But he specifically said that he didn't need this sort of complication in his life.'

Jon put his arm around her shoulders and pulled her close. 'Well, it's too late for recriminations. You'll both have to face up to it.'

* * *

Over lunch, Livvy told Eddie the events of the morning.

'Trust Sammy to get hold of the wrong end of the stick! Ah well, we'll let *her* tell Roy. She knows him better than anyone, so she'll approach it the way she thinks best.' He looked at Livvy, who was pushing her pasta around her plate. 'Come on, Liv, eat up. You're feeding two now.'

She smiled. 'Thank you for everything; you're a wonderful man. Jon and Jess are so lucky to have a father like you.'

'And thank *you*.' Eddie swallowed the lump in his throat. 'Have you ever thought of tracing your natural parents?'

'Occasionally, but I wouldn't know where to start. All I know about them and my past is that I was born in Glasgow, my parents were called Gina and Peter and they were both sixteen. My adoptive grandmother knew Gina's family. She told me that after the adoption, they moved to Canada and Gina went with them. I presume she's still there. I know nothing of Peter's whereabouts. I just wish they'd kept me. What I went through was far worse than being brought up by penniless teenagers.'

Eddie sighed, twiddling the stem of his wineglass. 'There were so few options in those days. You either married the girl, as I did Angie, or the baby went up for adoption. I'm sure they wouldn't have parted with you willingly.'

Livvy nodded. 'Maybe you're right. I might think about trying to find them after I've had my baby. I just feel I've enough on my plate to cope with at the moment.'

Eddie signalled to the waiter for the bill and escorted Livvy back to work. 'I'll call you tomorrow, see how things are,' he said.

'Thank you so much for your support, and thanks for lunch.' She stood on tiptoes, kissed him lightly on the cheek and walked into the shop.

Eddie smiled as he made his way back to the car. She was a lovely girl and he could fully understand why Roy had been smitten.

21

Roy told the receptionist he was expecting a visitor who could be sent straight up to his room. He flirted briefly with her and her colleague and then went on his way, mulling over the berating he'd received from his mother over lunch. His father had shown a bit more sympathy, but only after his mother left the room. Roy hadn't dared argue back – if it made her feel better then so be it. She ranted and raved about what a good wife and mother Sammy was and what a lot she'd had to put up with during the early years of their marriage, when Roy was never around. How she didn't deserve any of this, especially after losing Nick. She also said that if he didn't go back to Sammy, and he took up with that young woman again, she would wash her hands of him once and for all!

He'd tried to explain that Sammy didn't want to live with him at the moment and that it was over between him and Livvy, but found it hard to get a word in edgeways and had wisely chosen to stay quiet. He was glad to escape back to the sanctuary of the hotel. The chambermaid had just finished cleaning his suite as he approached and he winked as she pushed her trolley up the corridor. Pity she wasn't wearing a

French maid's outfit like they wore in the *Carry On* films, Roy thought wistfully, checking out the drab grey uniform *his* particular chambermaid was wearing. Definitely a turn-off in anybody's books.

* * *

'Can I help you, sir?'

'Roy Cantello's room, please.' Eddie smiled at the girl on reception, whose eyes opened wide when she recognised him.

'Err yes, room 125, up the stairs and to the left.'

'Avril, Avril, come here quick,' she whispered. She pointed after Eddie's departing back. 'It's another one of the group that our mums like. He's going up to Mr Cantello's room.'

'Was *he* good-looking as well?'

'I'll say he was. You should have seen his big blue eyes. Bloody hell, they've aged much better than The Rolling Stones!'

'I'll stay out on the desk for a while, see if they come down,' Avril decided, shuffling bits of paper around in an effort to look busy.

They didn't have long to wait; within five minutes Roy and Eddie strolled through the reception area and smiled at the girls as they left the building. Avril and Sharon gazed after them with longing. Sharon grinned knowingly. 'Perhaps Roy Cantello is on the lookout for a new wife, we'll have to wait and see. Play your cards right, girl, and you never know.' She patted her hair into place as the phone rang, and switched on her receptionist's voice: 'The Grand Hotel Wilmslow! You're speaking to Sharon. How may I help you?'

* * *

'Where's the first flat?' Eddie asked as they pulled away from the hotel.

'Just a couple of roads down from here, we could have walked.'

'Oh, I can't be bothered walking, I've just had lunch with L — err, Jon and I'm full.' Eddie stopped himself just in time. Shit, he knew he shouldn't have had the wine; it had addled his brains. Still, pasta without a couple of glasses of red was unthinkable.

'Why didn't you tell me you were going out for lunch? That's twice this week you've been into town and not told me,' Roy grumbled.

'Sorry, mate. Jon wanted to discuss his mum and things. We can't really talk at home because of Jane. I don't like to bring the Angie subject up too often in front of her,' Eddie lied.

'Oh, right, fair enough. I had lunch with my folks,' Roy said.

'That was nice for you.'

'Was it? I got a right earbashing from my ma. She talks to me like I'm sixteen and still a kid.'

'Well, you *are* a kid, in her eyes anyway. My mother was always like that, bless her. She never thought I was capable of doing anything for myself, even though I was married and supporting a family at eighteen.'

'Whoa, slow down,' Roy said. 'The first apartment block is to your left. Oh, I don't like the look of these,' he added, staring up at the soulless, three-storey brick and pebbledash building. 'Looks like a prison without the bars.'

'Might be alright inside.' Eddie got out of the car and looked around the car park. 'There are a couple of decent cars. The people who live here are probably okay. Anyway, you never bother with neighbours, so it wouldn't matter if the Addams Family lived next door. Let's go take a look.'

Roy nodded reluctantly. 'The agent's meeting us inside.' He pressed the intercom for flat number ten. 'Mr Cantello to view,' he informed the answering female voice.

'Ah yes, please come up, Mr Cantello.'

An open lift beckoned in the corner of the reception hall, but Eddie pushed Roy towards the staircase. 'The exercise will do you good.'

'This isn't the sort of exercise I like,' Roy protested. 'The flat's on the top floor.'

'Well, you're not getting any other exercise at the moment, so move it.'

A grey-haired woman answered the door. Her severe navy suit gaped wide across an ample bosom. 'Mr Cantello, do come in.' She smiled, displaying a row of teeth that Roy thought wouldn't look amiss in Red Rum's mouth. She shook him firmly by the hand.

'This is my friend, Mr Mellor.' Roy flinched and flexed his precious guitar playing fingers. The woman had a grip like a vice.

'I'm Miss Osborne.' She stood back in the narrow hallway as they struggled past her bulk. Once in the lounge, she picked up a folder from the coffee table and handed it to Roy. 'Here you go, Mr Cantello. You'll find all details regarding room dimensions, utilities, rental and maintenance charges and so on in there.'

Roy took a quick look at the details. He'd already decided the flat wasn't for him. 'It's too small,' he muttered to Eddie. However, out of courtesy, he followed the woman as she waxed lyrical about the wall-mounted electric fire with its glowing log effect and the neat, but boring, fitted kitchen with the built-in appliances. The tiny white bathroom was cold and clinical. Not a patch on his luxury bathroom back home, where he and Sammy used to lie each end of the Jacuzzi, legs entwined, glasses of chilled wine to hand.

The woman gave an apologetic cough. 'And this is the bedroom. I'm afraid it's quite small, not really enough room for two.' She looked pointedly at Eddie, who was slower on the uptake than Roy. He'd realised, from her tone of voice, that she assumed they were partners.

Sitting on the bed and bouncing up and down, Roy caught Eddie's eye and grinned. 'I'm sure we'll manage,' he said. He grabbed Eddie by the hand and pulled him down. 'What do you think, sweetie?' he simpered, draping one arm loosely around his shoulders.

Keeping a straight face, Eddie looked into Roy's eyes. 'It's divine, darling, but I think the two of us may have a bit of a squeeze in the bathtub, you've such long legs. We'd be better off with a corner bath.'

'You're probably right, honey bun.' Roy looked at the woman and fluttered his long dark lashes. 'I want him to be really happy with where we choose to live,' he said with mock sincerity. 'On reflection, I don't really think this is the place for us. Isn't that right, sugar plum?'

Eddie smiled and ran his hand suggestively up and down Roy's thigh.

'Well, thank you for taking the time to view anyway, Mr Cantello.' The woman appeared anxious to be rid of them. She moved out of the bedroom as quickly as she could and stood by the open front door as they squeezed past, holding hands. She shut the door behind them with a horrified gasp as they collapsed with laughter on the landing outside.

'That was wonderful,' Roy chuckled. 'What a performance. Any more of that thigh stroking and you'd have had me as horny as hell!'

'Did you see her face as we passed her in the hall and you squeezed my arse?' Eddie wiped the tears of laughter from his eyes with the back of his hand. 'Oh dear, we needed a laugh. That was brilliant. Where to next, sweetie-pie?'

Roy looked at his list, still grinning from ear to ear. 'It's only ten minutes from here, the first floor of an old house. I quite like the sound of this one.'

'Is someone meeting us there?'

'Yeah. Not the same woman, thank God. It's a different agency. Take the first road on your right here and the house is called The Cedars.'

Eddie pulled onto the semicircular gravel driveway of a large detached house and Roy nodded with approval. 'This looks more like it.' He clambered out of the car and looked around at the mature gardens. The large, double-fronted house sported elegant bay windows both upstairs and down and was fronted by a huge lawn with neat flowerbeds. The driveway had a separate entrance and exit gates. Roy ran up the front steps to the burgundy-red front door and rang the bell for Flat Two.

Footsteps echoed in the hallway and the door was thrown open by an attractive, smartly dressed woman, who Roy took to be in her mid-thirties.

'Hello, I'm Sarah Caldwell, from Jones and Jones.'

'Roy Cantello.' Roy shook Sarah's outstretched hand and introduced Eddie. *This was more like it*, he thought, catching Eddie's look of approval.

'Follow me, the flat's upstairs,' Sarah announced, leading the way and giving Roy the opportunity to admire her slender legs.

The house was Edwardian with many original features. 'Nice floor,' Roy said, admiring the cream, blue and terracotta tiles in the hall. 'And a perfect banister for sliding down.' He ran his hand over the gleaming mahogany wood. Sarah opened a door to the left of the landing and led them into a spacious room that looked down onto the front garden.

'Hey, nice big lounge,' Roy said. 'What do you think, Ed?'

'It's great. Love the fireplace. The furniture looks good quality.'

'The fireplace is original,' Sarah said. 'Have a look at the kitchen.'

Roy smiled, not that he would be using the kitchen very

often. He would dine out, live off takeaways or eat at Ed's place before he would cook and wash-up. They followed Sarah back through the lounge, where another door led across a partitioned corridor to a large well-fitted bedroom, containing an antique brass bed. Roy looked at Eddie and grinned, remembering the poor woman they'd just left at the other flat.

'Very nice,' Eddie said.

Sarah opened a door in the bedroom to reveal a spacious en suite bathroom, complete with period-style fittings and a large bath on clawed feet. She stepped back to let Roy take a look.

'Oh, this is great, plenty of room for two in that bath.' He winked as she blushed.

'There's a fully tiled shower cubicle, too,' she said, composing herself. 'And as you can see, the flat's been newly carpeted throughout in the oatmeal Berber.'

'Yeah, it's nice. I'll take it on a six months lease,' Roy said. 'When can I move in?'

'Early next week,' she said. 'We'll have the lease drawn up and we'll need references from your bank and employer.'

'Bank should be no problem, but I'm self-employed. Would a reference from my accountant do you?'

'Of course. What line of business are you in, Mr Cantello?'

'We're songwriters,' Roy said.

'Oh, right.' She looked closely at them. 'I thought I recognised you when you came in and your name's so familiar. Were you in a group?'

'The Raiders ring any bells? Ed here was our drummer.'

Sarah smiled. 'Yes. I bought your records when I was at school. "My Special Girl" always made me cry. I was sorry to read about your recent bereavement, it must have been a very difficult time for you and your family.'

Roy sighed. 'It was, Sarah; and it still is, believe me.'

Eddie pointed to a further door, running off the corridor. 'Is that another room?'

'Oh, I'm sorry, I almost forgot. You can actually access it from the bedroom too. Let me show you.' Sarah led them back into the bedroom and opened one of the fitted wardrobe doors. At the back of the cupboard was another door. She opened it and they stepped through into a pleasant little room, simply furnished with a single bed, small chest of drawers and a nursing chair.

'There you are: a spare bedroom. It's actually a nursery, but I don't expect you'll need it for that purpose, will you?'

'I doubt it.' Roy grinned. 'I can keep my guitars and amps in here. *They're* my babies these days.'

Eddie stared silently out of the window as Roy arranged an appointment with Sarah to sign the lease.

'You're miles away, mate. You okay?' Roy asked.

'Yeah,' Eddie replied. 'Just a bit tired.'

They said goodbye to Sarah and drove back to the hotel in companionable silence.

'Come on in, Ed. I'll have them send up coffee and cakes,' Roy suggested.

'That'll be nice, but I can't stay too long, I've got to get Katie and Dom. Lucy's mum's collecting them from school and taking them home with her for an hour. I don't like to take too much advantage.' He followed Roy into the hotel reception area.

'Okay, well half an hour then.' Roy approached Sharon with a smile.

'Yes, Mr Cantello?'

'May I have a tray of coffee and Danish pastries sent up to my room, please?'

'Of course, right away, sir.'

'Sharon?'

'Yes, Mr Cantello?'

'For God's sake, call me Roy, please!'

'Oh, okay, err, Roy. I'll see to that straight away... err, the coffee, I mean.'

'C'mon, Ed, let's go up.' Roy led the way, leaving Sharon staring open-mouthed after them.

'Did you hear that, Avril? He called me Sharon and asked me to call him Roy!'

Avril tutted behind her back and ordered the coffee and cakes from the kitchen.

'Come down off your cloud, he was just being friendly. Maybe he prefers to be called Roy. I mean, he's hardly your suited and booted businessman type and he's not at all stuffy and boring.'

* * *

Eddie stretched out his denim-clad legs on Roy's bed and looked around the elegant suite.

'It's not too bad. You've loads of space and it's nicely decorated and furnished.'

'Yeah, it's okay, I suppose. A bit girly though, don't you think?' Roy said, looking at the mainly pink décor and carpet. 'It'll do until I can move into the flat. I should have asked Sarah if she knew anything about my neighbour. I hope it's not some old battleaxe who doesn't like loud music or I'm in big trouble.'

'I doubt it will be. The rent's quite steep at four hundred a month. It'll probably be a yuppie couple, someone with a decent income.'

'Hopefully, or it might be a nice woman on her own. Who knows?' Roy had a gleam in his eye. 'That Sarah was fit, wasn't she?'

'Don't you think you've enough problems with the two women you've got?' Eddie spoke without thinking.

Roy stared at him thoughtfully. 'Which two? It's over with Livvy and I don't think Sammy wants me any more.'

'Didn't you say you were going to see Sammy later?'

'Yes, she wants to talk to me about something. She's given me no clues as to what. Do you think she wants me back?'

'Who knows? Ah, the door... coffee and cakes no doubt.' Eddie welcomed the diversion of room service. Sammy had plenty she wanted to talk to Roy about, but he was quite sure she hadn't any immediate plans to ask him to go back home.

Roy opened the door and let in a young girl bearing a tray. He tipped her a fiver as she left the room, shooting them both a shy smile.

They tucked into the Danish pastries and the pot of fresh coffee.

'I really must join a gym.' Roy licked his sticky fingers. 'Otherwise I'll start putting on weight with the lack of physical exercise I'm temporarily experiencing.'

'We should *both* join,' Eddie said. 'If we're planning to do live shows again, we need to be fit, otherwise we won't be able to cope. I tell you what, let's go swimming tomorrow.'

'Great idea. I'll go back home when you leave, sort out my swimming gear and the rest of my clothes before Sammy gets in. Not that I've many clothes since the massacre. She used to buy me something new most weeks at one time, you know,' Roy said wistfully. 'Ah well, those days are gone, for now anyway.'

'Right, I'm off.' Eddie stood up. 'See you tomorrow then.'

'Yeah, I'll come over after lunch.'

22

Jane looked up as Sammy replaced the receiver.

'Who was that and why are you smiling so mysteriously?'

'Wouldn't you like to know?' Sammy teased.

'Yes, I would, especially as you've arranged to go out to Rozzillo's tomorrow night. It's obviously not Roy, because *he* certainly hasn't put a smile on your face for the last few weeks. Come on, Sam, tell, we don't have secrets.'

'It was Stuart Green, actually,' Sammy replied, her cheeks flushing.

'Was it now? Well, well, well!'

'Don't you go reading anything into it; it's just a business meeting, that's all.'

'You could have had that here.'

Sammy shrugged. 'We could, but it'll be nicer over a candlelit dinner and a bottle of red.'

'Benito will get a shock when he sees you with another man.'

'Won't he just?'

'I wonder why Stu never married,' Jane mused. 'He's had a lot of women. There never seemed to be anyone serious.'

'I think he enjoys being single, to be honest,' Sammy said. 'He's lived all over the place, Germany, the States, a long spell in Oz. When he brought those samples in the other day, he told me he's fed up of travelling and has decided to settle in England. He's bought a small cottage just outside Wilmslow.'

'Really? That's great. So we'll be seeing a lot more of him then? By the way, when are you next seeing Roy?'

'Tonight actually.' Sammy sighed. 'There's something we need to discuss, something serious.'

'You mean about Jason and Jules?'

'No, not yet. Listen, I'll tell you, but be prepared for a shock. Close those doors so Mum doesn't hear us talking and whatever you do, don't yell out with surprise.'

Jane leapt up and pushed the adjoining doors to. 'What is it, Sam?'

'Sit down again, otherwise you'll fall down. You know when I said the other night that you could throw anything at me and it wouldn't hurt, because I've been hurt so much already?'

She nodded, wondering what was coming next.

'Well, today I got the absolute, ultimate smack between the eyes.'

'What, for God's sake?'

'I went to see Livvy before I came to work.'

'Oh God, Roy was with her!' Jane gasped.

'No. If it was just that, I don't think I would feel so bad.'

'Well, what then? What could possibly be worse?'

'Are you ready for this? Livvy's pregnant.'

Jane's jaw dropped and she was glad she was seated. 'No! Are you sure?'

'Oh, dead sure. She's got a nice little belly full of arms and legs courtesy of my adulterous husband.'

'I don't believe it. Is it definitely Roy's?'

'Yes, absolutely definitely.'

'But, Sammy, remember how Angie duped Ed?'

'I know, but this baby is Roy's.'

'How can you be so sure?'

'Your Jon confirmed it and the timing is bang on.'

'Jon told you? How come he hasn't mentioned it to us then?'

'Because he was sworn to secrecy.'

'Oh my God! So, you're going to tell Roy tonight?'

'That's the plan. For one thing he's got a right to know and for another, Livvy can't be expected to cope on her own. He's going to have to offer her some support. It's his responsibility, although to give Roy his due, he thought she was on the pill.'

'The stupid girl must have forgotten to take it, or maybe she lied in the first place and was never taking it at all,' Jane said.

'That's probably more like it.'

'I bet she planned it to get money out of Roy,' Jane continued. 'She'll have seen him as a lifelong meal ticket. Oh hell, what if she contacts the papers? They pay a fortune for kiss and tell stories, especially if there's a baby involved. You can just see the headlines: *Randy Raider Roy fathers secret love child with girl young enough to be his daughter!*'

Sammy smiled wearily. 'That's why I want Roy to sort it out now before she *does* do something like that. Otherwise, we can kiss goodbye to any privacy for months to come.'

* * *

Roy let himself into Jasmine House. Sammy wouldn't be home until at least five thirty, which gave him half an hour to sort out a few things. He busied himself packing the remainder of his clothes. In the music room he picked up several boxes of tapes and guitar leads and packed them all into the boot of the family BMW. He loaded in his favourite Fender Strat, an amp and finally squeezed in his keyboard. If he was going to be stuck in the hotel room for a few days, he might as well be productive and write some lyrics.

His stomach began doing cartwheels at the thought of seeing Sammy again. It was only a short time, but he was missing her so much he felt like his right arm was gone. He passed Jason's room, heard a slight sound and stopped to listen. It hadn't dawned on him that Jason might be home. There was usually evidence of his presence by the sound of loud music blasting from the hi-fi. The sound came again, a muffled sigh and whispering. Roy smiled. It sounded like Jason had a girl in his room. He tapped the door gently, not wishing to disturb them, but to warn Jason that they weren't alone. He opened the door a crack and peeped inside.

What he saw shocked him to the core and the room swam before his eyes. He clutched the doorframe for support. His son and Jules were lying on the bed, locked in one another's arms. Jason was crying, Jules stroking his hair and caressing his back.

Roy sprang forward. He grabbed Jules by the hair and yanked him off the bed. 'You little pervert, get your hands off my son!' Jules screamed as Roy punched him hard in the face, knocking him out onto the landing. He fell to the floor, howling.

Jason leapt off the bed, a look of horror on his face. 'Dad, what the fuck are you doing? You bastard, you've broken his nose!' He ran out of the room, knelt by Jules and helped him to a sitting position. Blood spurted from Jules's nose, over the landing carpet and down the front of his white shirt. Jason ran into the bathroom, grabbed a towel, dunked it in cold water and held it against Jules's face. Roy sat down heavily on Jason's bed, staring at the pair through the open door.

His son was in tears, cradling Jules in his arms. The lad moaned with pain as Roy heard the front door open and close.

* * *

'Roy, are you upstairs?'

'Mum, we're here,' Jason said. 'Dad's flipped!'

Sammy ran upstairs and gasped. Guessing immediately what had happened, she looked at the distraught young men and Roy, his face a mask of horror, and shook her head.

'Roy, come here.' He came forward silently. 'Go and sit in our room, go on.' Sammy gave him a push. 'Jason, get Jules a clean shirt and I'll run the pair of you to Casualty. I can't leave your dad alone for too long, he's in shock.'

'Okay, Mum.' Jason helped Jules into his bedroom.

Sammy ran downstairs, tipped a liberal measure of brandy into a glass and took it up to Roy, who was now sitting on their bed, still wearing the same horrified expression.

'Stay there, I won't be long.'

He looked at her with haunted eyes. 'You knew, didn't you? You knew what was going on and you never thought to tell me.'

'Not now, Roy. I need to get Jules to Casualty. Be back as soon as I can.' She patted his shoulder and left the room.

* * *

Sammy was back within half an hour. She'd given Jason money for a taxi home rather than have to venture out again. A few brandies wouldn't go amiss for her, she thought, never mind Roy, while she geared up to telling him about Livvy.

She collected the brandy bottle and a glass and went upstairs. He was still sitting where she left him, still looking numb, and clutching the now-empty glass. She poured him another drink and took his cold hand. 'Roy, I couldn't tell you, not so soon after Nick's death,' she began. 'It would have been too much for you to cope with.'

He turned to her. 'Why has this happened? I mean, he's *my* son; he shouldn't be gay. We Cantello men have *never* been gay. Nick wasn't. What's gone wrong with Jason?'

'There's *nothing* wrong with Jason, Roy. He's a lovely boy.

He's got all your nice qualities about him, he can't help the way he is.'

'But people will point him out in the street and laugh at him. His life will be hell. God, even Eddie and me were pratting about this afternoon, pretending to be a gay couple to wind up the estate agent. He'll be a figure of ridicule.'

'He won't. People these days are more understanding about homosexuality. But the understanding has to start at home – with his parents. He's very discreet and so is Jules.'

'Sammy, if the papers get to hear of it, they'll make Jason's life impossible. You can just imagine the bloody gutter press, can't you? So soon after Nick's death it will have more of an impact. Then they'll find out *we've* split and they'll be digging deep for more muck, making mountains out of molehills as usual. For fuck's sake, Sammy, there'll be no bloody peace!'

Sammy took a deep breath. 'Well, before you get on *too* high a horse about Jason, there's something else you ought to know. Something *you're* responsible for, Mr Squeaky Clean!'

'What?'

'Livvy's pregnant!'

'Say that again.'

'Livvy is pregnant, with *your* child.'

* * *

Roy stared at Sammy as her face spun out of focus. The blood rushed through his ears, the room swam before his eyes and Sammy's voice, echoing, asking him if he was okay, was the next thing he was conscious of. He was on his back on the bed and she was bending over him, a look of concern on her face as she pushed his hair out of his eyes.

'Roy, Roy, are you okay? You fainted.' He stared blankly up at her. 'I think it was the shock of everything. God, you fool, you scared the life out of me! I thought you'd died. Can you sit up now? Come on, try.'

He sat up slowly. His eyes wandered briefly to his flies. Still zipped up and no pain. She was sitting calmly by the side of him, having just informed him that he'd put Livvy in the club, and he was still alive and in one piece. Why? It didn't seem to make any sense to his befuddled brain.

'She *can't* be,' he uttered weakly.

'She is, believe me.'

'Well, it's not mine then.'

'Of course it's yours.'

'But she was taking the pill. I haven't slept with her since August, so it *can't* be mine,' he finished confidently. 'She must have been with someone else since then.'

'Roy, whether she was taking the pill or not, she's pregnant. She's almost four months. It's now October, so some time between late June and early July, *you* got her pregnant. You can't wriggle out of it, I'm afraid – it's *your* baby.'

'Have you been to see her then?' he asked, still reeling.

'Yes, this morning, and I'm afraid I got hold of the wrong end of the stick. I thought it was Ed's baby and I accused her of all sorts, she was very upset.'

'Hey, hang on, why on earth would you think it was Ed's? What's *he* got to do with it?'

Sammy explained what had happened and how Eddie came to be involved. 'He was trying to protect you and got caught up in the mess. Now that's a really loyal friend for you and don't you ever forget it. Eddie, bless him, was trying to save our marriage.'

Roy shook his head. 'He had all that on his mind today and he never let on. Does he know about Jason?'

'Not yet, but Jane does and she'll probably tell him tonight. I had to confide in someone. She also knows about Livvy.'

Roy let his head fall back against the pillows and stared up at the ceiling for a long moment.

'So, what do I do now, Sam?'

'Well, for starters, you have to go and see Livvy. I suggest you go tonight when you leave here. What you decide to do after that is up to you. Come on downstairs, I'll make us something to eat. Will a stir fry do you?'

He nodded. 'Thanks. My stomach's churning. I'll just go to the loo and join you in a minute.'

* * *

Roy splashed cold water on his face and looked at his pale complexion in the mirror. He just couldn't understand why Sammy wasn't going absolutely crazy. Maybe she'd done all her crying in private. She was certainly being strong for both of them. After all, he thought, as he trudged wearily downstairs, somebody needed to be.

He sat opposite Sammy at the kitchen table, silently eating his meal. 'I'll go when I've finished this,' he said as she toyed with her food.

'Okay. Go before Jason and Jules get back. You have to make some time to talk to Jason, perhaps over the weekend. He'll need to be told.'

'I will. I've found a flat by the way, Sam.'

'Oh, and is it nice?'

'Very.' He told her where the flat was located and described it in detail.

'I know the old house, it's beautiful. That'll be really nice for you. I'll sort you out some crockery and linen. Come over Sunday and collect them. In fact, come for lunch. Pat and Tim will be here, of course, and I plan on inviting Ed, Jane and the tribe. You should be here for the reunion.'

He was conscious of her searching his face. She still loved

him, it was there in her eyes, and some inner sense told him she was dreading the outcome of his pending visit to Livvy's.

He reached across the table, took her hand and gently kissed each finger. Spurred on by the fact that she didn't jerk her hand away, he pulled her to her feet and took her in his arms, his body aching with longing.

He tilted her chin with his forefinger, kissed her, gently at first and then with passion. He pulled her nearer, pressing his body against her. This was the closest they'd been for weeks and he was scared to even breathe in case it stopped. He desperately wanted more. 'Sammy, I *do* love you. I need you so badly,' he said softly.

He looked into her eyes again, she wanted him to. He led her through into the lounge and they sank onto the sofa. He unbuttoned her linen shirt. She tugged off his T-shirt and ran her hands down his back. His hungry mouth sought her breasts and his eager hand wandered up her skirt to the tantalisingly warm area of bare flesh between her stocking tops and her French knickers. If there was one thing guaranteed to blow his mind, it was Sammy's long legs clad in silky stockings.

She groaned as he caressed her. 'Roy, I love you, I need you. I shouldn't, but I do.'

'I love you too, Sam.'

He unzipped and released himself, feeling ready to explode; it had been so long. They made quick, passionate love on the sofa and she dug her fingernails into his buttocks as she moved beneath him. Her orgasm was quick and explosive and Roy followed suit. He gasped with pleasure at the welcome release of weeks of pent-up frustration.

'Jesus Christ, we've never come so quickly in our lives!' he exclaimed.

'We have,' Sammy reminded him, sitting up as he rolled off her.

'When?'

'Our first time,' she said. 'That Sunday afternoon, back at your mum's place.'

He grinned, remembering. 'Oh yeah, but if you think back, half an hour later we lasted ages and you told me I was the best lover in the world.'

'Roy, you're the *only* lover I've ever had. I've nothing to compare you with.'

'Well, I hope it stays that way.' He looked at her, his head on one side. 'Thank you for that, Sam, I *do* love you.'

'I love you too. I can't quite believe we did that. It's the most ridiculous and bizarre situation. We're separated; you've just punched the lights out of our son's gay friend. I tell you your bit on the side's having your kid and then we screw one another like there's nothing wrong. What's happening here, Roy?'

He smiled and shook his head. 'I'd say we still have a lot of feelings and love for one another, wouldn't you?'

'We have. But what about all the mess in-between, what do we do about *that*?'

As Roy opened his mouth to reply, he heard the front door opening. 'Shit, Jason's back!'

Sammy straightened her clothes. Roy zipped up his jeans and looked around for his T-shirt, but along with Sammy's French knickers, it had been tossed over the back of the sofa.

Jason wandered into the lounge, announcing, 'The taxi driver dropped Jules at home.' He stopped and stared at his dad's bare chest and his mum, buttoning up her blouse and trying to smooth her crumpled skirt down, guilt written all over their faces.

Roy felt like a teenager whose parents had caught him in the act.

Jason shook his head in disbelief. 'Mum, you fool! How *could* you?'

'Don't you dare speak to your mother like that, have some respect,' Roy began.

Sammy laid a hand on his shoulder. 'Leave it, I'll sort it out.'

But Jason hadn't finished and spat out, 'Respect? You don't know the meaning of the word. Do you know Livvy's pregnant, Mum? Shall I give you three guesses who the father is?'

Sammy sighed wearily. 'Yes, I know she's pregnant, so does your dad.'

'Well then, for God's sake why have you just done that with him? You make me sick, both of you.' He burst into angry tears and fled from the room.

Sammy made to go after him but Roy pulled her back. 'Leave him alone for now, Sam. Talk to him later when I'm not here. I'd better go and see Livvy, get it over with. Is it too late for an abortion?'

'She won't have one. Ed tried to talk her into it and even offered to pay. She wants the baby, she's adamant about that. You're going to have to offer her some financial help. By the way, Jane knows nothing about Ed's involvement in this, so remember that and keep quiet about it in her company.'

'I will.' Roy pulled on his T-shirt and picked up his jacket. 'Thanks, Sam, for everything.'

She smiled. 'I should hate you for all you've put me through and everything you've done, but I can't. Phone me tomorrow and let me know how things go with Livvy tonight.'

He nodded. 'Come and have lunch with me at the hotel. We could have room service and then one another for dessert – again.'

'You never give up, Cantello. I *might* join you. I need to regain my trust in you, but I wasn't banking on the extra complication we now find ourselves with.'

'I'm sorry, Sam, I really am. It was the last thing I wanted to happen. I'd have done something about it myself if I'd known she wasn't protected.'

'It would have been far simpler not to have had the affair in the first place. But you did and we have to deal with the fallout.'

Roy shrugged. 'I'll talk to you tomorrow. I'm taking the BMW, by the way. I've loaded the boot with guitars and stuff. I'll bring it back when I collect my car. Hope Jason will be okay. I can't get my head around that one just yet, I'm afraid.'

'You will. It'll take us both time to get used to it, but we will.'

'Do you think Jules will report me to the police for assaulting him?'

'Would you blame him if he did? We'll have to wait and see. Good luck, Roy, might see you tomorrow lunchtime.' Sammy kissed him lightly on the lips as he left.

* * *

Jon drove out of town in the heavy traffic. Once he hit the Mancunian Way, he could put his foot down. Aunt Sally lived in Styal Village out near the airport and he wanted to be on time for this important first meeting. Feeling slightly apprehensive, he supposed it was understandable, given the circumstances.

He switched on the radio, singing along to Nik Kershaw's 'Wouldn't It Be Good', thinking that it wouldn't be so good to be in Livvy's shoes at the moment.

His thoughts turned to Helen and how he wasn't even missing her. Then he thought about Jess and grinned. His preoccupation with Jess made him feel permanently hot under the collar and he wondered if she felt the same. They'd become even closer since Nick's death and helping Jess get her life back on track was his main priority these days.

Several times recently he'd walked into her bedroom while she'd been in varying stages of undress. He always knocked first, but Jess called him in regardless. She'd asked him to button up her top the other day and it was all he could do to stop his hands from straying underneath.

He knew he had to sort himself out, but he didn't know how – he just wanted to spend every waking minute with her. He glanced at the scrap of paper on the passenger seat and checked the address: he was nearly there. Five more minutes and his life could possibly be about to change.

* * *

Driving home, Jane's mind was in a whirl over Sammy's latest revelations. She spotted Lennon waiting patiently for her on the lane, opened the passenger door and he leapt up beside her, licking her face in greeting. 'Hello, precious boy. Oh, you've got muddy paws. Ed will go mad.'

She leapt out of the car and ran inside to find a cloth before Eddie saw the mess and told her off. He was standing in the kitchen by the Aga and judging from the delicious aroma, cooking up something good. Her mouth watered as she dashed past him and into the utility room.

'What's the matter with you?' He frowned, as she rushed back out again.

'Nothing,' she called over her shoulder. She wiped the mud and left the cloth in the car rather than carry the evidence inside. Ed had told her time and again that Lennon wasn't to get into the Porsche or his Ferrari with muddy paws.

Back in the kitchen, a glass of chilled Chardonnay was standing on the table.

'Oh, Ed, what would I do without you?' She wound her arms around his neck. 'I love you.'

'Love you too, babe.' He kissed the top of her head. 'Give your mum a call and ask if Jess's coming home, then I know how much rice to cook.'

'Okay, it smells good.'

'Chicken curry,' he announced. 'All my own work. No tins or packets *and* I ground my own spices.'

'You sound like Fanny Cradock,' she teased as she dialled her mother's number.

'Surely you mean Johnnie?'

'Do I?' She giggled at his raised eyebrows. 'I could never really be sure which one was which.' She spoke quickly to her mother and hung up. 'Jess's staying over until Jon comes home. I'll get out of this suit and into my jeans, then I'll come and talk to you and have *I* got some news for you.'

* * *

Livvy was working until eight. She was tired and had been hoping to finish at six, but Jon had asked if she would mind covering for him while he visited his late mother's family. She felt she could hardly refuse such a request and had reluctantly agreed.

Sean had given her a couple of hours off in lieu that afternoon and she'd fallen asleep in the old armchair in the staffroom. She'd woken with a stiff neck, which had now developed into a headache. She put her hands on her aching back and took a deep breath.

'Liv, go on home, you looked whacked.' Sean patted her shoulder.

'Would you mind?'

'Not at all. Go on, I can manage. There's only another hour to go and it's not that busy. See you in the morning. Come in a bit later seeing as you've done extra tonight.'

'Thanks, Sean.'

* * *

Yawning, Livvy ran herself a bath. She sank gratefully into the bubbles, fighting back the tears that insisted on flowing freely down her cheeks. Roy must surely know about the baby by now.

Dear God, what would he say? He'd be assuming she'd done it deliberately. But a baby had not been in her future plans, nor had an affair with a married man. All she'd wanted was a foot on the bottom rung of a singing career.

She'd hoped her job at Flanagan and Grey's would help her meet musicians and like-minded people. Never in her wildest dreams had she expected to meet Roy Cantello, let alone become involved with him.

* * *

Sammy knocked on Jason's bedroom door.

'Go away,' came the muffled response.

'Jason, it's me. Let me in, darling, please.'

There was a shuffling noise and the door opened a fraction. Sammy took one look at his tear-stained face and burst into tears. 'I'm so sorry, Jason.' She put her arms around him and held him while he sobbed against her shoulder. 'Come downstairs, we'll have a brandy and a chat.' She gently stroked his cheek.

He nodded and followed her. 'The carpet's all messy where Jules bled on it,' he said.

'Don't worry, love, I'll clean it off later, I can't be bothered right now.' She handed him a small brandy, helped herself to a larger one and sat down on the sofa next to him.

'Dad will never understand, will he?'

'He will. It was such a shock to him, that's all. You have to give him time.'

'What's happening with you two then? Are you going to let him come back home already?'

'No. He's found a flat and he's moving in next week.'

'Oh!' He looked up with surprise. 'So what was all that about earlier? You're supposed to be separated.'

'He's my husband, I still love him. I needed him and he needed me. You'll understand one day.'

'What about Livvy and the baby, what's he gonna do about that?'

'I don't know. I haven't an answer to that one. I don't want to lose your dad to Livvy, but at the end of the day there's now a child to consider. What about Jules? Is his nose broken?'

'No, fortunately not. They X-rayed him, cleaned him up and said he could go home. He'll have two lovely black eyes tomorrow.'

'What on earth are his parents going to think when they see the state of him?'

'He's only got a mum. She wasn't home when the taxi dropped him off. He said he'd tell her he got into a fight. Jules's mum knows he's gay and that sometimes lads who can't handle it pick on him – she won't think a bloody nose is anything too out of the ordinary.'

'Will he be pressing charges against your father?'

Jason shook his head. 'Course not. I asked him if he wanted to and he gave me his word that he wouldn't. Jules and I don't want our friendship to be common knowledge, Mum. We haven't done anything wrong. It's against the law till we're twenty-one and we want to wait. We just like being together, it's comfortable.'

Sammy ruffled his hair and smiled. 'Thanks for telling me that, it makes me feel a bit better. Maybe you'll change as you get older.'

'It's not something I'm going to grow out of.' Jason rolled his eyes. 'You might as well get used to it.'

'Oh, Jason, it doesn't matter. You're my son and I love you so very much. So does your dad. It might not be apparent by his recent actions, but he does, believe me.'

Jason finished his brandy and stood up. 'I'm going to have a bath and an early night. See you in the morning, Mum.'

'Goodnight, love.' She kissed him and watched as he left the room, his head held high.

* * *

Livvy was settled on the sofa with a cup of tea when the intercom buzzed impatiently. She froze, cup halfway to her lips. 'Oh no,' she moaned softly. She knew it would be Roy. Most people pressed it once. It buzzed again and again. Sitting glued to the sofa, she hardly dared breathe in case he heard her. He would know she was home; her car was in the car park. She sat for what seemed like ages and then jumped out of her skin as something hit the lounge window with a resounding thud.

'I know you're up there, let me in!' Another clod of earth hit the window and he shouted again. He sounded really angry, she thought, sick to her stomach. She jumped up and peered through the window. Roy was standing on the path below, looking up with a furious expression on his face.

'What are you playing at? Let me in, for God's sake! The woman in the flat opposite has just threatened to call the police if I don't stop shouting. Oh, fuck off, Mrs!' Roy turned his attention to the downstairs window and gestured rudely.

'Go to the door,' she mouthed and released the catch.

He was upstairs in seconds, burst into the flat, marched past her and sat down on the sofa. With an angry gesture, he flung his jacket on the floor and lit a cigarette. She followed him into the room.

'Sit down!' he ordered, pointing at the chair to his right.

Livvy meekly obeyed, not daring to look at him. She felt him staring at her with his dark broody eyes while she nervously pleated the hem of her oversize T-shirt. She wished she'd put on more clothes now, she felt vulnerable and half naked as Roy's eyes bore into her.

'Well?' he demanded. 'What have you got to say for yourself?'

She bit her trembling lip and tried not to cry, but the tears ran unbidden down her cheeks.

'I really trusted you, and you've let me down big time.'

'Sorry, Roy,' she mumbled, still avoiding his gaze.

'So, what the fuck are we going to do about this mess? Are you too far gone to have an abortion?'

Livvy felt very sick and took a deep breath to calm her churning stomach. This wasn't what she wanted to hear from him at all, but it was no more than she'd expected.

'I'm not sure, probably,' she faltered.

'Right, well first thing tomorrow you'd better find out and if it's not too late, we'll make the arrangements,' he said, puffing frantically on his cigarette.

'I don't want to get rid of it.'

'What? You can't possibly want it. Think of all the problems you'll have bringing it up alone. You needn't think I'll be around to help you because I won't be. You said you were on the pill. I can't believe you deceived me over something so important. I told you I didn't want complications like this the last time I was here, didn't I?'

'I was already pregnant then, but I didn't really know, Roy, honestly.' She planted herself firmly in front of him, arms folded across her swollen belly, courage coming from somewhere deep inside. 'I'm not asking you for anything. I didn't even really want you to know. I only told Eddie 'cos I was scared. If Sammy hadn't paid me a visit, I was going to pretend it was someone else's baby. You have absolutely no right to come into my home and tell me what to do with my body. You once told me that no baby is ever unwanted. Well, I'm having this baby, whether you like it or not. I can't believe I ever thought I loved you. You're as selfish as the next man. You only wanted sex. Just get out of my sight, I hate you!'

She turned and ran into her bedroom, slammed the door behind her, flung herself down on the bed and sobbed into her pillow.

* * *

Roy lit another cigarette and remained seated. Seeing Livvy standing there in front of him, with her arms folded protectively over her bump, telling him what she thought of him, had taken him by surprise. He'd never had her down for a feisty little piece before, but she was certainly one tonight. He supposed it was the mother hen protecting her chick thing. Hell fire, and now she thought he'd only wanted her for sex. That wasn't true, he loved her, but he also loved and wanted Sammy.

What the hell was he supposed to do? He'd come here with the intention of keeping a stiff upper lip, persuading Livvy it was in everyone's best interests to abort the baby, handing over a cheque for the cost and then he could wash his hands of the whole bloody mess. But who was he kidding, exactly whose interests was it in the best of? Certainly not Livvy's, probably not his own either, and Sammy had already accepted the fact that Livvy wanted to keep the child. He finished his cigarette and tapped on Livvy's bedroom door: 'Liv, can I come in, please?'

There was no reply so he pushed the door open. She was lying face down on the bed, sobbing. He sat by her side and gently touched her shoulder. She looked at him, nose running, eyes swollen and her face blotchy. Tendrils of hair, sticking to her wet cheeks, made her look like a child who was crying because she'd broken her favourite dolly.

'I told you to go-o a-way,' she sobbed.

'Do I *ever* do anything anyone tells me?' He pulled her into an upright position.

'No, I don't suppose you ever do.'

'Well then, that's why I'm still here.' He took her in his arms and cradled her.

'I'm sorry, Roy, really I am. I *did* take the pill, I can show you the packets. But I missed a couple and that's how this happened. I know I should have told you, I'm so sorry.'

'I'm sorry too. I shouldn't have had a go at you like that. You getting so upset can't be good for the baby.' He pulled up her T-shirt and ran his hand gently over her swollen belly.

'It's quite big already,' he said. 'I didn't realise. How long have you known for sure?'

'Ironically, the results came back the day Nick died,' Livvy sniffed.

Roy swallowed hard. 'When did you tell Ed?'

'The day of Nick's memorial service.'

'He told me he'd spoken to you. Did you ask him not to tell me?'

'No, I wanted you to know at that point. I asked him to give you the message that I was pregnant, but he said he couldn't because you and Sammy were in a bad way.'

Roy sighed. 'I realise he thought that was for the best, but I wish he'd told me. You shouldn't have had to cope on your own.'

'It wouldn't have made any difference, I would still have decided to keep it.' A note of defiance had crept into her voice.

'Okay, okay.' He held up his hands. 'So, when is this baby of ours due?'

'March the tenth,' she replied.

'When are you planning on giving up work?'

'Probably after Christmas, I should think.'

'Right, well, let me get my head around things for a day or two. I'll need to talk it over with Sammy, but I'm sure we can come up with a plan to help you financially. We'll pay the rent on your flat for starters, buy all the baby stuff you'll need and make sure you have enough to live off once it's born. You won't have to struggle. How does that sound?'

'Thank you, it's very generous of you.'

'I can't offer to marry you or anything. Sammy and me... well, we're trying to patch things up. I'm staying in a hotel for now and I move into a flat on Monday. We've got family problems with Jason as well as coping with Nick's death. Sammy and Jason need me right now and I really need them.'

Livvy nodded. 'I understand. Will Sammy object to you doing all those things for me?'

'I doubt it, she's not an ogre. She's a wonderful woman and it took guts for her to come here and face you like she did.'

'You're right, it did. I couldn't have done it. Would you like a cup of tea? I'd made one before you arrived, but it'll be cold by now.'

'I'd love one.' He lifted her off the bed. 'You'll look like a little barrel in a few weeks if this baby keeps on growing at the same rate.' He kissed her gently and in spite of just having had sex with Sammy less than an hour ago, there was a familiar twitching. 'I *do* love you, Livvy. I've told you that often enough, but I'm torn between the devil and the deep blue sea. I'll be around and I'll do everything financially to help that I can, but I can't marry you. You *do* understand that, don't you?'

As she nodded, he continued. 'There's one thing that you must promise me and it's more to protect Sammy and Jason than me. You have to keep it to yourself that I'm the baby's father, certainly for the time being anyway. It'll come out soon enough, but we'll be stronger to cope with the backlash by then.'

'I will, but you told me earlier that you wouldn't be around for me.'

'I was angry. I'll be there for you, I promise, and we will look after you both.'

* * *

As Jon left Aunt Sally's, a huge weight lifted from his shoulders and a bit more of his life jigsaw had fallen into place. The family had made him more than welcome and he'd felt instantly comfortable with them. His cousins, Sally's offspring – Brian, Kevin and Grace – all older than him and married with families of their own, had extended invitations to visit their homes at any time. Furnishing Jon with addresses and phone numbers, they were all pleased to formally meet at last the mysterious cousin they'd heard so much about, whose father was the famous rock drummer and songwriter, Eddie Mellor.

His grandma, a tiny lady with a blue-rinsed Margaret Thatcher hairdo, was nothing like the formidable ogre his dad had painted her, and indeed, she'd even asked after Eddie and Jane's health. She'd invited Jon to visit her at her East Sussex home and told him to bring Jess with him if she would like. Jon thanked her and said that if Jess felt up to it, he was sure she'd be pleased to accept the invitation and they'd visit in the not too distant future.

Sitting on a chair next to a teak wall unit, Jon spotted a framed photograph of a familiar face. 'May I?' he asked as Sally nodded. He picked up the frame and stared at the photo.

'That was taken in Angie's last term at school, the year before she married your dad,' Sally told him.

In her school uniform, Angie looked young, pretty and full of fun. Her light-brown hair fell in soft curls on her shoulders, her green eyes sparkled with happiness and a dimple in each cheek highlighted her mischievous grin. Jon studied his mum closely, biting his lip to stop the tears.

'She doesn't look old enough to be almost married and a parent,' he said.

'She wasn't and neither was your father,' his grandma said. 'They were foolish kids who should have known better. Still, they weren't the first to make that mistake and they certainly won't be the last. But Eddie and Jane have done a wonderful job of bringing you up, Jonathon. Angie would have been very proud of you. I want you to pass that on to Eddie and to let him know that I'd like bygones to be bygones. We never saw eye to eye. He always had a bee in his bonnet that I blamed him solely for Angie's pregnancy. But my daughter was a wild one and it took the pair of them to tango. I couldn't get close to Eddie, he was always on the defensive. Their marriage was doomed from the start, they were better apart. Eddie was happier with Jane, and Angie with Richard. It's a pity Angie and Richard didn't have more time together. Will you pass my condolences on to Roy and Sammy over the loss of their son? Rebel that he was, I always liked Roy Cantello. He had a caring heart and he looked after Eddie like a brother.'

Jon nodded. 'I'll do that.' He got to his feet. 'I'm sorry to leave so early, but I like to spend time with Jess before she goes to sleep. She's very depressed at the moment – she and Nick had planned to marry in December.'

Sally nodded sympathetically. 'Well, Jonathon, don't be a stranger. Come and visit us again and bring your sister. Have you any more sisters and brothers by the way, or is it just you and Jess?'

Jon grinned. 'No. After Dad finished touring with The Raiders, he decided he wanted to add to the family. He and Jane got busy and we have Katie who's eight and Dominic aged seven. They're a handful, especially Katie. Dad's a house husband, he looks after them and Mum runs a clothing business with Roy's wife, Sammy.'

'I can't picture Eddie in a flowery pinny.' Sally laughed. 'Leather jackets and drainpipe jeans used to be more his style.'

'He's not *quite* at that stage,' Jon said. 'He and Roy still write songs and they're re-forming The Raiders when Tim and Pat come home from the States.'

'Oh, so young Tim's in America, is he?' his grandma said.

'I forget that you obviously knew them all,' Jon said. 'He's back home on Saturday after years of living in Nashville. He and Pat have two young daughters now. Pat's had breast cancer recently, so they've decided to return to England.'

'I hope she makes a full recovery,' his grandma said. 'Our Angie used to follow that group all over the show when they first started out. It was your father she was after, of course, and she was determined to win him. She achieved her goal, even if it did all backfire in the end. Ah well, youth never learns, does it? Go on, Jonathon, off you go. Get back to that sister of yours. We'll look forward to seeing you again soon.'

23

'How did it go?' Eddie searched Jon's face for clues that he might have discovered the truth.

'Fine, Dad. They're a really nice bunch. Grandma talked a lot about Angie and you as well. She said she'd like to make her peace with you.'

'There's a turn up for the books. She used to be a right old witch.'

'She's a little old lady with a blue rinse now. She's invited me to her home and the offer extends to Jess, too.'

'That's nice of her,' Jane said, walking into the room.

'Hmm. *I* thought so. Is Jess upstairs?'

'She is, she's waiting for you. Her plaster comes off her wrist tomorrow, so your dad's taking her to the hospital and then he's going swimming with Roy.'

'Bloody hell, how come?' Jon grinned. 'I thought you'd given up on the keep fit after the jogging nearly killed you.'

'We need to build up our stamina before we start performing live again,' his dad said. 'Anyway, Roy has a distinct lack of physical activity in his life at the moment.'

Jane raised an eyebrow. 'Not any more. I've just been speaking to Sammy.'

'They're back together?' Jon asked.

'Not that you'd notice. Roy's sleeping at the hotel later. He ate with Sammy this evening and shall we say they reached a mutual understanding. He's gone to see Livvy now, supposedly to sort out a plan of action to help her.'

'More exercise then?' Jon quipped.

'Oh, Jon, trust you. Even Roy wouldn't stoop *that* low. Would he?' Jane turned to Eddie.

'I don't know, love. I'm not his keeper. But let's hope not, eh?'

* * *

Jon tapped on Jess's door and walked in. She was reclining against the pillows, reading a magazine.

'Hi, Jess.' He bent to kiss her cheek and felt the heat rush to his face.

'Hi, you. Sit me up.' She held out her arms.

He lifted her into a sitting position. His hands brushed against her breasts through the thin cotton of her nightdress and he jerked away.

'What's wrong? Do I make you nervous?'

'Of course not.' He took a deep breath. Maybe it was time to tell her how he felt. Keeping it to himself was killing him inside. She might understand, or more likely tell him to get lost. She was looking at him, head on one side. What if he spoilt the closeness they shared? She might never speak to him again. 'It's me,' he began, feeling his eyes fill. 'For a while now, I've been having these weird feelings when I'm close to you. It's freaking me out.'

'What kind of weird feelings? You're all flushed. Come on, tell me.'

He looked up at the ceiling for a long moment and sniffed. 'Well – they're very un-brotherly feelings. I shouldn't be getting them and I'm embarrassed that I am.'

Jess looked away and sucked in her cheeks.

'Say something, Jess, for God's sake. Tell me to stop being stupid.' She remained silent. Jon wished he'd kept his mouth shut. Then she spoke quietly, not looking him in the eye.

'I have very un-sisterly feelings towards you, too,' she mumbled.

'What do you mean?'

She blushed. 'After that time in France when you said you wished you were Nick, I've often wondered what you're like naked and how it would feel to kiss you properly on the lips.'

Jon blew out his cheeks. 'Maybe we're attracted to one another because we're half-siblings and not fully blood-related.'

'I don't know.' Jess shrugged. 'It's very wrong to feel like this. Maybe it's because I'm missing Nick or something. But even when I was *with* Nick, it never stopped me feeling jealous when you were with one or other of your girlfriends, especially Helen. I used to think hey, that's my big brother you're snogging. I always wondered what she was feeling while you were kissing her.'

'I was irrationally jealous of Nick,' Jon confessed. 'When he told me you'd first slept together I wanted to thump him and wipe the smile from his face, even though he was my best mate. I couldn't bear the thought of him touching you like that. I had a job keeping my feelings under control that day.'

'I saw it in your face,' she said. 'He was always jealous of our closeness. Poor Nick, I think maybe he was a little insecure with me, which is probably the reason he wanted us to marry quickly.' She reached out and stroked his cheek with her plastered hand.

He took hold of it. 'This is coming off tomorrow.'

'It is, thank God.'

He uncurled her fingers. 'It will feel really strange for a while.'

She nodded.

He wrapped a tendril of her hair around his finger. 'I want to kiss you,' he said softly.

Jess closed her eyes and sighed. 'Jon, we can't, can we?'

'We shouldn't, but we can.'

'And if we do, then what?'

'We might not like it,' he teased.

'That's true.'

'Well, then?'

'Well... then.' She looked at him.

He took her in his arms and kissed her gently on the lips. She responded, kissing him back.

'Well?' He smiled, pulling away.

'*Well!*' she replied, nodding.

He kissed her again and held her close, feeling the warmth of her body through her nightdress.

'Oh, Jess,' he whispered into her hair.

She ran her good hand through his curls and smiled. 'That was wonderful. I had good reason to be jealous of Helen.'

'Did you?' He lowered her back against the pillows and lay beside her, kissing her again. He undid the buttons down the front of her nightdress and slid his hand inside, touching her breasts. She gasped and kissed him harder, moving her body closer as his tongue probed hers.

'We'd better stop, before we go too far,' she said as his hand brushed down across her stomach towards her thighs.

'I know. I don't want to though, it feels so right.'

'It does, but it scares me. We shouldn't feel this way. It's incestuous and against the law.'

He sighed. 'Not only that, Dad would kill me. I'd better sit away from you, you're making me horny.'

'Tell me about Angie's family, that will take your mind off things.'

'You reckon?' He lifted her into a sitting position and re-buttoned her nightdress.

'I bet you've never done that before, buttoned anyone up.'

'Just the opposite,' he said, grinning. He told her about his visit to Aunt Sally's. 'So, do you fancy coming to Hastings with me for a few days?' he finished.

'I'd love to. My ankle plaster comes off next week and I start physiotherapy. So what about going at the end of November? My ankle should be strong enough to hobble around on properly by then.'

'That sounds fine. I can let Sean know a week or two before we go. I need to take the time off before Livvy finishes for her leave.'

'Is she going on holiday?'

'Oh shit! I forgot, you don't know.'

'Don't know what?' Jess frowned.

'She's pregnant. She's on maternity leave soon.'

'No. Bloody hell! *She* hasn't wasted much time finding someone else, has she?'

'Jess, the baby's Roy's.'

Jess's jaw dropped. 'Fuck! Sammy will kill him when she finds out.'

'She knows. Roy's visiting Livvy tonight to discuss what she wants to do.'

'I can't believe it. How does Roy feel? He's forty-two, he's far too old to be bringing kids into the world.'

'Well, obviously he's not. It would appear that he's still in good working order.'

'Nick would have had something to say about this. Does Jason know?'

'I don't know. I haven't seen much of Jason recently, he's always with that Jules guy.'

'I just can't believe it.' Jess shook her head.

'I'm going to bed now, Jess. I'll see you in the morning before I go to work.' Jon leant over and kissed her gently on the lips again, but she pulled him close and kissed him back, running her fingers through his curls.

'I wish you could stay with me and hold me all night. I haven't been held all night since the accident,' she said, a catch in her voice.

'I wouldn't be able to trust myself,' he responded truthfully. 'We'd end up *really* breaking the law.'

'But we're not doing any real harm just kissing and cuddling, are we? As long as we don't get *too* carried away.'

Jon grinned. 'It's a deal. See you in the morning. Goodnight, Jess.'

'Night, Jon.'

* * *

Jane ran upstairs and found Jon leaning with his back against Jess's bedroom door, his eyes closed, breathing deeply.

'Jon, are you okay?' she asked, taking in his flushed cheeks and haywire curls.

'Fine, Mum. Just a bit tired. It was quite an emotional time at Aunt Sally's.'

'I'm sure. You off to bed now?'

'Yes, I've said goodnight to Jess. I'll nip down and say goodnight to Dad.'

'Okay, love.' Jane stared after him as he ran lightly down the stairs. She shook her head and knocked on Jess's door.

'What have you forgotten now?' Jess called out in a teasing voice.

Jane opened the door and peeped in. 'It's me, Jess, not Jon.'

'Oh hi, Mum. Come in.'

'Is the radiator too hot in this room?' Jane said. 'You look flushed and so did Jon.' Jess's cheeks had a bloom to them and her eyes sparkled for the first time in weeks.

'I'm alright,' Jess replied. 'Jon was telling me about his mum's family and how his grandma's invited us both for a visit.'

'When you consider the bad feeling between her and your dad, I think it's a very nice gesture,' Jane said. 'It shows she's willing to put the past behind her. Do you fancy going with Jon?'

'Yeah, definitely. It will give me something to look forward to. Hey, Mum, what about Roy, then? If it weren't such a serious matter I'd laugh. Fancy slipping up at his age! What will Pat and Tim make of it all?'

'Heaven knows.' Jane rolled her eyes 'Right, I'll check on the kids and then your dad and I are going to bed. See you in the morning, love.' She bent to kiss Jess goodnight. 'God, you reek of Jon's cologne.'

Jess smiled. 'Well, he kissed me goodnight before he left the room. Probably went over the top, splashing it on before he went on his visit.'

Jane nodded and left the room. She frowned as she went into Katie's room and pulled the curtains across. Jon's musky cologne had smelt strongly on Jess, more so than a fleeting kiss would have left behind. There was his flushed face, too and his usually neat curls standing on end. Maybe Jess had had a weepy session and he'd cuddled her for a while, although she certainly didn't have swollen eyes or a blotchy face. In fact, she looked chirpy tonight, more animated than she'd looked since the accident. Had she and Jon been kissing properly?

Jane pushed the unbidden thought to the back of her mind. Things like that didn't happen in families like theirs. Jess and Jon were close, like brother and sister should be. *Ah, but*, the thought mocked, *they're not brother and sister*, and Jane was aware that there had always been an attraction between them. From the moment he'd clapped eyes on her, Jon had been devoted to Jess and she in turn had always been a flirty little madam around her brother. She shook her head and closed Katie's door. Dom was flat out and she swept his fringe from his eyes and smiled. She mustn't think along those lines. It was a ridiculous notion anyway and one she certainly wasn't going to share with Ed – he'd think she was cracking up.

* * *

Sally was pleased with the way her nephew's visit had gone. It was strange, but wonderful, seeing Angie's child again after all the years apart. He was tall and handsome and had lovely manners. At long last Eddie Mellor had redeemed himself in her mother's eyes. He'd brought Jonathon up to be a decent young man.

Sally had fully expected Jon to resemble Angie in looks, but he hadn't and he certainly didn't look like her distant memories of Eddie. He hadn't the vivid blue eyes or Eddie's straight, glossy brown hair. Jon's curls, similar to Angie's, were dark and abundant and his eyes, fringed with thick sooty lashes, were a deep penetrating green.

With her mother settled in bed, Sally took out a photograph album from the cupboard. It was her 'Angie album' filled with snapshots of her sister. There were photos of Angie and Eddie before and after their marriage and then with Jon. She'd planned to show Jon the album during his visit, but had decided against it and was keeping it for a time when maybe she could see him on his own. He must have been dying to ask questions about his mother, but there had been too much going on with her own brood here too and he'd been quite shy at first. Still, that was only to be expected – he hadn't known any of them from Adam.

Martin brought her a cup of tea and sat down opposite.

'I'm just looking at my "Angie album",' she told him. 'It's

tragic really, looking at all these photographs and thinking back to how vibrant and lively she used to be. There's a photograph here of her taken at an early Raiders' gig with the group and her friend Cathy. Angie's draped all over Eddie, she really loved him at that time.' Sally shook her head sadly and turned the page. There were more photographs of Jon and his mother alongside Sally's own children. Another photograph, taken at Jon's second birthday party, showed the ever-widening gulf between his young parents. They looked like distant strangers, posing with their son as he blew out the candles on his cake.

She turned to the last page, which contained photographs from the spring following the couple's separation. One, taken at her son Kevin's birthday party, showed a beaming Angie sitting on a garden bench with Jon on her knee. Next to her, his arm protectively around her shoulders, was Richard Price. Sally smiled, remembering how very happy Angie had been at that time, with plans to marry Richard as soon as their respective divorces were granted. As Sally looked closely at the photo, trying to recapture some of her sister's lively presence, she was conscious of a prickling sensation on the back of her neck and gave an involuntary shiver.

'What's wrong, Sal?' Martin looked closely at her face.

'Nothing,' she replied, closing the book quickly. 'Just a little ghost running over my grave.'

'Okay, well I'm off to bed now. I'll leave you alone with your memories for a while. Don't stay up too late.' He bent to kiss her and left the room.

Sally opened the album again. She took the photo of Angie, Richard and Jon from beneath the protective plastic cover and carried it over to the standard lamp. She studied it intently and gasped: Jonathon was Richard's double. She sat back down on her chair. Why hadn't she noticed it before? The dark curls were an instant giveaway and she remembered now that Richard's eyes had been a very definite shade of green.

There could be no other explanation, it was staring her right in the face. Richard was surely Jon's father and not Eddie Mellor, as Angie had led them all to believe. Sally rummaged in her cupboard and took out a packet of photographs. Sifting through them, she selected three of her sister and Richard. She held them under the lamp and scrutinised them. One was very clear, a close-up of Richard with three-year-old Jon on his shoulders, and even at that tender age the likeness was apparent. But the now-adult Jon was so much the image of Richard back then that Sally was convinced she couldn't possibly be mistaken – the pair could easily pass as twins.

Her heart thudded so loudly she was sure her mother and Martin could hear it upstairs. Had Angie herself known? If so, she certainly hadn't confided in Sally. There was probably only one other person in the world who would know for sure and that was Cathy, Angie's best friend, and Sally didn't have an address or phone number for her. Maybe Jonathon would know, after all, Cathy was his godmother and Sally also remembered from past newspaper reports that she had married one of The Raiders: Carl Harrison, the keyboard player. Eddie and Jane would be sure to keep in touch with them.

Sally decided that she would call Jonathon in the morning and ask for Cathy's phone number on the pretext that her mother wished to see her again for old time's sake. She put away the photographs, not relishing the thought of her mother looking through them tomorrow and coming up with the same conclusion. Thank goodness she hadn't brought out the album while Jon was here. Her daughter Grace never missed a trick and would be certain to have spotted the likeness immediately.

* * *

'Thank God for that,' Jess said as she and Eddie strolled out of Outpatients.

'You okay, sweetheart?' He slung his arm around her shoulders.

'Yes, Dad. Just glad to get out of there. This place doesn't hold very happy memories for me.'

'Not for any of us, Jess. It's where Angie died, too.'

'Dad, I'm so sorry, I had no idea.' She squeezed his arm. 'I'll have to grin and bear it again next week when I have my ankle plaster removed, but then that's it. I hope I never have to set foot in there again.'

'Did the clinic confirm the physiotherapy appointment?'

'Yes, I start next Tuesday for my wrist and the following week for my ankle. I'm looking forward to going back to work once I've built up some strength – I'm getting bored at home all day.'

'I tell you what, let's pop home first while I call Roy and then we'll go into town, surprise Jon and take him out for lunch,' Eddie suggested.

'Err, oh okay,' Jess said.

'What's the matter? Don't you want to go? I thought it would make a change for you.'

'It's fine, honestly.' Jess felt her cheeks warm. There had been a slight awkwardness when Jon had popped his head round her door to say goodbye this morning, neither of them meeting the other's eyes. He'd not even pecked her on the cheek as he normally did and now she was wondering if he was already regretting last night's kisses and cuddles.

Back home, Eddie rang The Grand to speak to Roy.

'I'm sorry, sir, Mr Cantello has given instructions that he doesn't wish to be disturbed until after eleven. I can pass on a message if you like?' the receptionist offered.

'Thanks. Tell him Ed called and I'll meet him at The Lodge about two thirty.' He hung up and turned to Jess. 'Roy's not available. Shall we set off for town and have a wander round the shops before lunch?'

'Yeah, I might buy myself something new to wear and I'm almost out of perfume. Can we go to Kendals first?'

'That's more like it, girl. C'mon, I'll lift you into the Jeep. Do you need your crutches?'

'No, I'll lean on you, if you don't mind. I can put a bit more weight on my ankle now they've fitted this boot thing over my cast. I feel a right prat on the crutches!'

* * *

Jess and Eddie wandered around her favourite clothes shops, emerging with several bags containing sweaters, tops, underwear and perfume. Eddie purchased a large flask of Jane's favourite Chanel No5, and then they made their way to Flanagan and Grey's.

Leaning heavily on her dad's arm, Jess laboured up the stairs and emerged at the top, puffing and panting. A delighted Sean took her in his arms and hugged her.

'Jess, it's good to see you out and about, so it is,' he said, kissing her on both cheeks.

She waved her un-plastered arm triumphantly in the air and looked across to the counter where Jon was standing. He stared at her for a long moment then walked over and hugged her.

'So, sis, how does it feel to be plaster-free?'

'Really good. Dad wants to take us out,' she said.

'Oh, nice one. Can I go for an early lunch, Sean?'

'No problem. Livvy's just arrived, so I can manage. Not that she'll be much help, she looks half asleep this morning.'

'Maybe she didn't sleep much because of the outcome of seeing Roy last night,' Jon said.

* * *

Livvy strolled out of the staffroom and caught them all standing in a huddle. Guessing correctly that she was the topic of their conversation, she felt her cheeks warming when she saw that Jess was with them. Jon came to the rescue by telling her that Jess had just had the plaster cast removed from her wrist.

'How are you, Jess?' she asked, looking directly at the girl.

'I'm getting there, slowly but surely,' Jess replied.

'I'm so sorry about Nick, really I am.'

Jess nodded. 'Congratulations.' She looked pointedly at Livvy's baby bump.

Livvy felt her cheeks heat further. 'Thank you, although I wouldn't have said that congratulations were really in order, would you?'

'Well, you want it, don't you? Otherwise, you would have got rid of it, or made sure it didn't happen in the first place.'

'Of course I want it. I'm just not sure that everyone else thinks I *should* have it.'

'You have to admit it's an awkward situation for everyone,' Jess said. 'Your timing could have been a little better.'

'I didn't plan to get pregnant, it was an accident. Anyway, Roy wants me to have the baby. He's standing by me and he's offered all kinds of support.'

'Bet he hasn't offered to marry you though, has he?' Jess's reply was laden with sarcasm.

Livvy's eyes filled and Eddie stepped in to diffuse the situation.

'Jess, that's enough,' he ordered gently.

But Jess hadn't quite finished. 'He hasn't, has he? And he never will. He'll never, ever divorce Sammy for *you*, no matter how often you open your legs for him!' She turned away as angry tears sprang to her eyes and ran down her cheeks.

* * *

Jon led Jess into the staffroom. He shut the door behind them, sat her down and handed her a glass of water. 'Calm down, you.' He knelt in front of her and took her hand. It was cold and lifeless after weeks in plaster and he rubbed it gently.

'What does Roy see in her?' Jess sobbed. 'She's a calculating little bitch who got pregnant to trap him. She likes what she's seen on her visits to our homes and she wants to be part of it. Roy's such a fool for falling for that one.'

'It goes a bit deeper than that, Jess. Roy *loves* Livvy, but he also loves Sammy and he's a very mixed-up man at the moment. Whether we like it or not, Livvy's carrying his kid and he's taking responsibility for it.'

Jess sniffed. 'Well, at the end of the day, it's no one's business but Roy, Livvy and Sammy's. God though, I'd want to scratch her eyes out if I was Sam.'

'Well you're not, so stop fretting about it. You and I have a far more pressing problem of our own.'

'Do we?' Her lips trembled, her smile wary.

Jon nodded. 'You know we do. I couldn't face you this morning, I was embarrassed. Then when I got here, I was annoyed with myself because I probably upset you by not saying goodbye properly.'

'Well, I did wonder,' she replied.

'The truth is, I *wanted* to kiss you again this morning, but I didn't dare. Everyone was up and about and it would have only taken Katie to come barging in and we'd have been in deep shit.'

'So now what?'

'Maybe we should avoid being alone together.'

'Is that what you want?' Jess looked at him with tear-filled eyes.

'Of course not. I'm terrified of voicing what I *really* want because we can't do that and I'm damn sure if we're alone, it'll happen.'

She was silent for a moment. 'Yes, it would. I can't believe this is happening to us, Jon. We're brother and sister; we're from a normal family. Things like this don't happen to people like us.'

'Hardly a normal family, with everything that's happened in the past and having a famous dad. Circumstances have brought us closer as well with Nick's death.'

'I've come to rely on you so much. I don't want us to be frightened of our being close, but we need to keep our feelings under control.'

'That's easier said than done. Are you ready to face them all again? Dad will be wondering what's going on. Let's go and have lunch.' He kissed her on the lips and hauled her to her feet. 'Lean on me.' He took her arm and together, they went back into the shop.

* * *

'Alright, you two?' Eddie said as Jon and Jess emerged from the staffroom. With them out of the way, he'd managed to speak to Livvy about Roy's reaction and the promises he'd made her.

Jess nodded. She turned to Livvy and smiled. 'I'm sorry, I had no right to be rude to you. It's a difficult time for everyone. I'm sure you'll do what's best for you and the baby and I hope things work out for you.'

Livvy smiled wearily.

Between them, Jon and Eddie lifted Jess under the arms and whisked her down the stairs, closely followed by an obliging Sean, carrying the packages.

'I'd join you, but I can't leave Livvy alone,' he said. 'I'll see you again.' With a wave of his hand, he strolled back inside the store.

'Pub lunch or Italian?' Eddie asked.

'Pub lunch, please,' they chorused.

'Right you are. Let's go to the Rose and Crown, they do decent food.' Eddie led the way, carrying the shopping, while

Jess held on tightly to Jon as they followed their dad down the road. As he disappeared through the pub doorway, several yards ahead of them, Jon turned and kissed Jess on the lips.

'I'm sorry, I couldn't resist that one,' he said and led her into the pub.

They made their way to the bar, where their dad was chatting to the barmaid, a pint of lager already in his hand. 'Come on, you two. What do you want to drink?'

'Same as you please, Dad,' Jon replied, winking at the barmaid. 'Alright, Carol?'

'Not so bad, Jon. And yourself?'

'Overworked and underpaid,' he said, smiling.

'Aren't we all?' Carol pulled a neat pint and handed it to him.

'Have you decided, Jess?' her dad asked.

'Pint of cider, please.'

'Ah, our favourite tipple from schooldays.'

Jess tutted with mock disapproval. 'And *you* used to go on at us about underage drinking.'

'I was trying to be a protective father.'

Jon found an alcove and Jess slid onto a seat. Jon squeezed in next to her.

'They've done this place up a bit,' Eddie said, putting the shopping bags down and looking round at the fresh cream décor, mahogany floor and red velvet upholstery. 'Bit fancier than it was in the sixties – your shoes used to stick to the old carpet.'

'What have you been buying?' Jon peered into one of the shopping bags. 'Oh, that looks nice.' He half pulled out a black lacy item.

'Jon, put it back,' Jess hissed, taking the bag from him and blushing furiously. 'I don't want everyone to see it.'

'Sorry.' He grinned. 'I thought it was a dress or something.'

'No, it's not. Now can we please stop discussing my underwear in public?'

'Here, choose something to eat.' Eddie handed them the menu, grinning at Jess's comments. 'I'll just have a sandwich. I'm supposed to be swimming later. If I eat too much now I'll sink, never mind swim.'

'Steak for me,' Jon said and Jess chose the same.

With his father out of earshot at the bar, Jon whispered in Jess's ear, 'I wouldn't mind seeing you in that black lacy thing sometime.'

'Pack it in, Jon, Dad will hear you. This is going to have to stop.'

'But you don't really want it to, do you?'

'You know I don't.'

'What are you two whispering about?' Eddie made them jump as he appeared beside them. 'Would you prefer chips or a baked potato with your steak?'

'Chips please, Dad,' they chorused.

As Eddie walked away, Jon squeezed Jess's hand.

'You're treading dangerous ground.' She pulled her hand away.

'I know.' He took a sip of his drink. 'But it doesn't feel wrong.'

'It *is* wrong though,' she said.

'What is?' Eddie sat down and picked up his drink.

'Oh, Roy and Livvy,' Jess replied quickly.

'Well, it's certainly a mess but it's happened and he needs to do the best he can for all concerned. Now I wanted you both together to tell you something. It mustn't go any further because of the delicate nature, but I'm telling you two as I know you'll offer support.'

Eddie lowered his voice and told them about Jason and Jules. He sat back and looked at their faces. 'It's a bit of a shock, I know. I found it hard to take when your mum told me last night. The whole family have a lot on their plates at the moment and they need us, and that includes Roy, Jess, so don't give him a hard time when he comes over later.'

'I did wonder – you know, about Jason, I mean,' Jon said. 'He has that sort of look.'

'What look?' Jess frowned. 'Well whatever, he's our mate and always will be. I like Jules a lot, too. He's really good to Jason.'

'Roy thumped Jules last night and nearly broke the lad's nose. He's lucky he isn't facing an assault charge today. Poor Roy, it wasn't his night. Sammy told him about Livvy and the baby and he fainted clean away.' Eddie shook his head.

'Bloody hell! So he didn't know about the baby until last night?' Jess said.

'No, only me, Sean and Jon knew, but Roy didn't and neither did Mum or Sammy until yesterday, so don't you dare let on to Mum that I knew before her.'

'I won't, but how come *you* knew?'

'I saw Livvy in the churchyard after Nick's service. She told me then.'

'Oh!' Jess was shocked. 'So, in all fairness to Livvy, the baby *was* genuinely an accident and she's kept it to herself all this time?'

Eddie nodded. 'She asked me to tell Roy. She was frightened and unsure what to do. Anyway, to cut a long story short, Sammy went to see her and that was that.'

'Why did Sammy go and see her?' Jess asked.

'To tell her to send Roy packing if he turned up. She spotted Livvy was pregnant, hit the roof and you know the rest. Come on, sup up, here's the food. Same drinks again?'

'Please, Dad.' They spoke in unison as Eddie strolled to the bar, leaving them staring at one another.

* * *

'Ignorant cow!' Sammy slammed the phone down and turned to Jane.

'Who is?'

'That bloody receptionist at The Grand. She said Roy doesn't want to be disturbed until after eleven. I told her I'm his wife and it would be quite in order for me to speak with him, but she was adamant, said she'd pass on a message.'

'Oh well, let's have a coffee and then you can be on your way. Give her a piece of your mind.'

* * *

Sharon called Roy's room just after eleven and conveyed both Sammy and Eddie's messages to him. He jumped out of bed, stretched and lit a fag. Feeling much better for the extra sleep, he ran a bath, shaved and splashed himself liberally with Sammy's favourite aftershave. He pulled on his usual Levi's and T-shirt, then deciding he should look a bit smarter, chose a cream cotton shirt instead to show her he'd made an effort. He lay back on the hastily made bed, flicked idly through the TV channels and waited.

* * *

Sharon's jaw dropped at the sight of the coolly elegant woman standing at the desk. With her pale-green linen suit, white silk top, shiny brown hair falling neatly to her shoulders, her make-up immaculate, she looked the epitome of a successful businesswoman. Her cool blue eyes raked over Sharon, who smiled in a friendly manner.

'Yes, can I help you?'

'Mr Cantello's room, please.'

'I'll just check that he's receiving visitors.' She dialled Roy's room number. 'Whom shall I say?'

'Mrs Cantello – his wife,' the woman replied pointedly.

'Mr Cantello,' Sharon said as the call was answered, 'I have your wife in reception. Thank you, goodbye. Room 125, through the double doors, up the stairs to the first floor and turn left,' Sharon instructed. She stared enviously as Mrs Cantello walked away. She noted her long slender legs elegantly clad in shiny stockings and looked down at her own short ones. Her mother had always told her that she must have been at the back of the queue when God handed out legs. Roy Cantello's wife had obviously been right at the front. She was certainly an attractive woman; she looked cool and frosty though. Maybe that was why he'd left her. Perhaps she was cool and frosty in bed and he needed someone warmer and more spontaneous.

* * *

Sammy grinned as she walked away from reception, knowing she was being scrutinised. The receptionist seemed to be taking her duties a bit too seriously where Roy was concerned. Still, it didn't worry her; the girl was no competition. Short, dumpy redheads had never been his type. She knocked on the door of room 125.

* * *

'You look gorgeous, as always.' Roy pulled Sammy close and kissed her.

'And *you* smell gorgeous,' she said with a smile. 'You know what that aftershave does to me.'

'Why do you think I'm wearing it? I need all the help I can get,' he quipped. He took her hand and led her into the middle of the room. 'Chair or bed?'

'Chair.'

'Oh!' He looked crestfallen.

'Idiot, as if,' she teased. She removed her jacket, hung it over the back of the chair and sat down on the bed.

'Do you want to eat first or afterw...?' he trailed off as Sammy smiled at him.

'Jumping the gun as usual, Cantello!' She patted his hand. 'I'm starving, let's eat first.'

He nodded and called reception for room service. He ordered a tray of assorted sandwiches, a fresh fruit platter and a bottle of chilled white Chardonnay.

'Right, before the food arrives, tell me quickly how you got on with Livvy last night. I was going to call you around midnight but I fell asleep. I rang this morning but the snotty cow on reception wouldn't put me through, because you'd asked not to be disturbed.'

'I was just tired, you know, with everything that happened yesterday,' he told her, thanking God he'd come home and not stayed at Livvy's last night. He outlined his plans to help Livvy and Sammy nodded her approval.

'And when the child arrives, are you going to want access?'

'I hadn't thought that far, to be perfectly honest. We'll cross that bridge when we come to it.'

She smiled. 'Now let's concentrate on Jason and us. Our son needs us more than Livvy does at the moment.'

'Well, Jason isn't here right now, but we are, so let's concentrate on us today.' Roy stroked her thigh through her skirt, kneading the little bumps of her suspenders. 'Stockings and suspenders again. You certainly know the way to a man's heart, girl.'

'I know the way to yours,' she said, pulling him down beside her. She undid the buttons on his shirt and buried her face in the dark, curly hairs on his chest. A knock on the door made them both jump.

'Room service,' a voice Sammy recognised as the redhead's called out. She straightened her clothes and sat on the edge of the bed while Roy opened the door. The girl waltzed in and blushed furiously at the sight of Roy's open shirt and hairy chest beneath. 'I'm sorry to disturb you, Mr Cantello,' she stuttered.

'It's okay, you didn't,' Roy said, smiling at her. 'We ordered the food, so we were aware it would be arriving soon.'

'We're short of chambermaids today. This isn't my usual job,' she informed Sammy, her words tripping over one another as she placed the tray down on the dressing table.

'Really?' Sammy arched an eyebrow.

As the girl left the room, Roy hung a 'Do Not Disturb' sign on the door. He grinned, picked up a corkscrew and the bottle of Chardonnay. 'I think we embarrassed her. Drink?'

'Please,' Sammy said, helping herself to a sandwich. 'Serves her right for being nosy. What are you doing later?' she asked.

'Swimming with Eddie.' He wolfed down a dainty sandwich. 'I've no plans for tonight. What about you? Fancy eating here and spending the night with me?'

'I can't, I'm going out for a meal.'

'Who with?'

'Stuart Green, actually.'

Roy frowned, another sandwich halfway to his mouth. 'Stuart?'

'Yes, Stuart.'

He looked deflated. 'Oh, I didn't think you would, well... you know...?' he tailed off.

'You didn't think I'd what, go out with someone else?' Sammy challenged.

'Well, yes.'

'It's a business meeting.'

'Well in that case, couldn't you have had it at work during the day?'

'God, you're as bad as Jane. Stuart asked me if I'd like to go for a meal and I accepted. We've things to discuss.'

'You and Stu used to be very friendly,' he said jealously and took a long slug of wine.

'I like Stuart. I've known him all my life.'

'You'd have gone out with him if I hadn't come on the scene, wouldn't you?'

She shrugged and bit into a strawberry. 'It was probably on the cards. But you *did* come on the scene and we fell in love.'

He gazed down into his glass, blinking furiously.

'Roy, what's wrong?' She saw the tears in his eyes. 'Oh, for heaven's sake, it's not a date! Come here.' She took his glass, put it down on the bedside table and pulled him into her arms. 'You're upset, why?'

'I just can't bear the thought of you going out with anyone else, for whatever reason.'

'Well, I can't just cancel without a good excuse. Stuart thought it would do me good with everything that's been going on lately.'

'Does he know about Livvy and me?'

'Not about the baby, but he's aware you had an affair that's over. He knows you've moved out while we sort ourselves out.'

'Does he also know that I want to move back home and that I still love you?'

'Of course he does. He's not going to make any moves on me and he also knows that *I* love *you*. Give me some credit where it's due. I think I've handled things quite well so far, Nick's death, Livvy, the baby, Jason, and us, but just because I appear cool and calm on the outside doesn't mean that I'm not churning up and in bits here.' She banged her chest. 'When you left me to go to Livvy's last night I felt so sick, especially after what had happened between us. I know you had to try and sort out what to do for the best, but I was terrified of letting you go in case she managed to wrap you around her little finger again. The pain I feel knowing Livvy's carrying *your* baby when I've just lost one of mine is indescribable, Roy. I worry that when it's born she's going to have such a hold over you that you'll leave Jason and me properly and go off with her. After all, *I* can't give you another child.'

Roy looked at her face and could see the grief and pain bottled up. If he could take it from her and bear it himself he would. No matter what promises he'd made to Livvy last night, never again would he go alone to see her. Any further contact could be made by telephone or at Flanagan and Grey's. Sammy and Jason must be his priority now or he'd lose them for good. His earlier promise, to look after Livvy and the child financially, still stood, but Sammy needed him and he needed her. He kissed her and pulled her down on top of him.

'I won't ever leave you or cheat on you again. *You* wanted the break from *me*, remember? You made me feel like I couldn't do anything right around you, even though I tried so hard to make amends. I don't want to be in this hotel room, Sam; I hate it. I don't want to live in that lonely flat, nice though it is. I want to be in *our* home with you. I want to be in our room and our bed. But until you feel ready to have me back, I haven't got a choice, have I?'

She looked down at him and he almost expected her to say, 'Come home' but she kissed him instead. 'Win back my trust, Roy. You can do it if you really try.'

He rolled her onto her back, touching and kissing with such frenzy that she cried out for him.

They lay in one another's arms for what seemed like hours afterwards. He leant up on one elbow and looked at her. 'I love you so much. I don't deserve you, I know that, but believe me, Sam, no one could ever love you more than I do. I'll never hurt you again, I promise.'

Her eyes filled with tears. 'Roy, there's never been anyone else for me, you're all I've ever wanted.'

'I know.' He wiped her eyes with a napkin from the sandwich tray.

She struggled into a sitting position. 'I'd better go back to work, Jane will wonder where I've got to. Look at the state of my skirt, it's all creased. I should have taken it off.'

'Well, I was going to do that, but you didn't give me the chance. You kept saying, "I want you now, Roy!" And who am I to argue?'

She sat on the edge of the bed, her hands over her eyes, shoulders shaking.

'Sammy, love, why are you crying again? What have I done now?'

'I'm not crying,' she said, shaking with laughter. 'You'd try the patience of a saint, Roy Cantello! How anybody else would want to put up with you, I just don't know. What on earth will the girls on reception think when I walk through there, looking like this?'

'Oh, sod them! Come and have a shower with me. If you hang your skirt up in the bathroom, the creases should fall out with the steam.'

'How do *you* know that?' she asked. Roy had never been in the least bit domesticated all his life.

'It was a lazy trick we learnt on the road. If we hung our stage suits up in the bathroom while we had baths or showers, we hardly ever needed to press them.' He picked up the phone and dialled for an outside line.

'Who are you calling?' Sammy asked, putting her skirt on a hanger. She retrieved her silk top and underwear from the floor.

'Jane,' he replied. 'Hi, it's Roy. Sam's gonna be a bit late getting back to work.'

'Okay,' she replied. 'Is everything alright?'

'Fine, thanks. She just needs a bit more time, I expect she'll explain later. Bye.'

Next, he called Eddie: 'Ed, can we cancel the swimming?'

'Yes, sure. Are you okay?'

'Couldn't be better. I'm just spending a bit more time with

Sammy. I'll see you later after you collect the kids from school.'

'Roy, you didn't need to cancel your swimming,' Sammy protested as he hung up.

'I wanted to. Truth is, Sammy, I don't want this lunchtime to end. I hate the thought of you going home later and out with Stuart.'

She sighed. 'Would it make you feel better if I cancelled? I can call Stuart from here.'

'No, that would make me feel worse.'

'Well, what's it to be then?' She looked at his doleful face.

'Oh hell! What right do I have to tell you what to do any more after my performance? Of course you must go out for dinner with him, he's *my* friend too. He's hardly going to make off with my wife, is he?'

'No. Now are we having that shower or what? I *do* have a business to run.'

* * *

By the time Roy walked Sammy through reception and out to her car, her clothes were fairly wrinkle-free, but her immaculate hairstyle and carefully applied make-up were no more. He slung his arm affectionately across her shoulders and winked at Sharon and Avril on the desk as Sammy nodded and said goodbye.

Roy watched Sammy drive away, his heart pounding. He trusted her implicitly, but was still concerned about her going out with Stuart Green. He remembered the way Stu used to look at her when they were younger, always with a hunger in his eyes.

He glanced at his watch as he went back to his suite: there was half an hour to kill before Ed would be home from collecting the kids. He picked up his Fender and began to strum softly, humming the chorus of 'My Special Girl'.

24

'Do you feel better now that Roy knows about the baby?' Jon asked Livvy, who was filing records on the shelves, wearing a dreamy expression.

'Much better. At least I know now where I stand. He told me he won't divorce Sammy, but once the wee one's here I'm sure he'll change his mind. He'll want to be with us, be a proper family.' She walked over to a customer and asked if she could help.

Jon glanced at Sean, who shrugged. 'That's all she's gone on about while you've been out. How much Roy loves her and what he's gonna do.'

'Shit!' Jon said. 'He's trying hard to put things right with Sam. Should I call Dad, tell him what she's been saying, then he can warn Roy?'

'Wait until she's finished serving and I'll send her out for lunch. By the way, your Aunt Sally rang. She'd like Cathy's phone number, if you have it.'

'Not on me. I'll get it off Dad.'

* * *

'Hi, you.' Jess grinned into the receiver. Her dad was upstairs, looking for Jon's godmother's phone number.

'Hi, yourself,' Jon replied. 'Will you be okay on your own while Dad goes swimming?'

'He's not going. Roy cancelled. Right, Dad's here now. Any chance we can see Jason tonight?'

'Yeah, that would be nice. We'll have a drink with him. I'll call him when he gets in from college. Bye, Jess.'

'Why does Sally want Cathy's number, Jon?' Eddie asked curiously after he'd given it to Jon.

'Grandma wants to see her before she goes home.'

'Oh, I see.'

'I believe the swimming's off?'

'Yeah, Roy's spending time with Sam.'

'Listen, Dad, Livvy's got hold of the wrong end of the stick where Roy's concerned. She says he'll want to marry her when the baby arrives. Warn him that his problems are far from over.'

'Bloody hell,' Eddie said wearily. 'Leave it with me.'

'Problems, Dad?' Jess handed him a coffee. He sat down at the kitchen table and lit a cigarette.

'It's this bloody Livvy affair.' He told her what Jon had said. 'It's never-ending.'

* * *

Sally stared at the telephone for ages after Jon returned her call. Dare she contact Cathy, or would she be opening up a can of worms? She looked at the photograph in her hand. She'd been carrying it around all day in her pocket, checking it in different lights and from all sorts of angles. No matter how hard she tried, she couldn't change the image of Richard's face: Jon was his double. There was no doubt in her mind that Richard was Jon's father. Sally wondered if Angie had realised whose baby she was carrying, plumping for Eddie as a safer bet because Richard had been engaged to someone else.

Angie would have been terrified of their parents finding out. Her sister, younger by ten years, had rebelled against the strict upbringing they'd had. Once Angie set her sights on Eddie Mellor, she'd thrown caution to the wind.

Sally had warned her she was playing with fire and would end up in trouble one day. The problem now was *who* exactly had got her into trouble? Judging from the photo evidence, it was Richard. Sally had to find out the truth. She'd keep it to herself, but she needed to know for her own peace of mind or it would eat away at her. She dialled Cathy's number before she changed her mind.

* * *

Jane was finishing her lunchtime sandwich as Sammy crept into their shared office. 'Bloody hell, you look like you've been dragged through a hedge backwards! So how did it go?'

She smiled. 'Do I really look that bad? He told me his plans for Livvy and the baby. He's promised financial support and that's it, for now anyway. Hopefully he won't need to see her again. He doesn't really have any reason to, he can do everything through our solicitor. I must remind him of that.'

'What about when the baby's born, will he want to see it?'

'I asked him and he said he'll cross that bridge when he comes to it.'

Jane nodded. 'Are you bothered by that? That he may want to be a father to it, I mean?'

'Of course I am. She'll always have a hold over him and it freaks me out.'

'You'll have to see what happens over the next few weeks.'

'That's all I can do. How did Jon get on with Angie's family last night?'

'Very well, apparently. Mrs Turner invited him to visit her in Hastings and she's extended the invite to Jess as well.'

'Very thoughtful of her,' Sammy said. 'Is the plaster off Jess's wrist now?'

'Yep, Ed took her to the hospital this morning. He called me a few minutes ago after he took Jess and Jon out to lunch. I spoke to Jess too and she told me they're planning to see Jason tonight.'

'That'll do Jason the world of good,' Sammy said.

'It'll do those two good to get out of the house, too. They're spending far too much time cooped up in Jess's room.'

'Is that a problem?' Sammy said as a look of concern crossed Jane's face.

'Not really, but there was something about them last night that I just can't put my finger on. I could have sworn they'd been kissing. Properly, I mean, not their usual pecks on the cheek. And another thing, Jess smelt very strongly of Jon's cologne.'

Sammy's eyes widened. 'Surely you're not suggesting something's going on between them? They're brother and sister, for God's sake.'

'Oh, but they're not,' Jane said.

'Shit! Of course they're not.' Sammy clapped her hand to her mouth. 'I forget sometimes. Well, they've been brought up as brother and sister anyway. They wouldn't do anything, would they?'

'They've become very close since Nick's death. Too close for comfort *I* think. Jon will do anything for her. He dries her hair, helps her to dress and carries her up and down the stairs. There's always been an attraction between them. But I sense an intimacy that wasn't there before. *I've* noticed it, but I don't think Ed has. I'm not sure how to handle it, Sam. I can't say anything to them, because what if I'm wrong and it's my overactive imagination?'

'You're usually very astute, Jane, not much passes *you* by. I'd keep on observing for now and if you feel there's cause for concern, say something to Eddie. Don't leave it until it's too late.'

She nodded. 'Don't we have some bloody awkward problems? We should have married someone spotty and dull from school, like Doug Murray or Georgie Green. Then we'd have had dull and spotty kids too.'

Sammy chuckled. 'Yeah, but just think how boring life would have been. At least we've seen the world and had fun with Roy and Ed. It's been a good life, most of the time anyway.'

* * *

Sally pulled up outside the large detached house on an exclusive, tree-lined road in Wilmslow. She got out of her car, admired the attractive Tudor-style frontage, strolled up a drive flanked by well-stocked gardens and rang the doorbell. A loud barking erupted from within, making her jump. A female voice called out for quiet. There was scuffling and whimpering and then the door opened.

'Hello, Cathy,' Sally began nervously.

'Sally.' Cathy held out her arms. 'How lovely to see you again. Please come in. I'll let Ben out. I've put him in the kitchen, but he'll scratch the door to bits if he's shut in for much longer.' She opened the door and the owner of the bark, a red brindle Boxer, shot into the hall, clattering on the parquet flooring. He leapt up and down like a mad thing as Cathy tried to grab his collar.

'He's a complete loony, I'm afraid,' Cathy said. 'Behave yourself, Ben, for God's sake!' The over-excited dog ignored her commands. 'He'll settle down in a minute or two. We always have this performance when we have visitors. Carl got him to keep me company when he's away.'

Sally laughed as she tried to pat Ben's head. He squirmed and wriggled with delight, his stumpy tail wagging frantically.

'I'll put him in the garden for a while. Go on, Ben, find the squirrel.' Cathy pushed him out and closed the back door. 'Carl's in London and his mum, who lives with us, is asleep upstairs, so we've got some peace.'

'I'm surprised anyone can sleep through that dog barking.' Sally laughed, following Cathy into the stylish kitchen.

'She takes her hearing aids out,' Cathy said.

'So, what's Carl been up to since The Raiders disbanded?'

'He's a session pianist. Works with everyone you can think of, Rod Stewart, Eric Clapton, you name them and he's probably played on their albums at some time or other. He misses the lads though and he's looking forward to the band re-forming.' Cathy picked up a tray. 'I'm all organised, see. Come on through to the lounge and get comfortable. You said you had something to ask me and I'm intrigued.'

The lounge overlooked the large rear garden and Cathy invited Sally to sit on one of the two cream sofas, placed either side of a marble fireplace.

Sally gazed in awe around the tastefully furnished room, taking in the deep pile beige carpet and blue washed Chinese rug. She thought about the damp and squalid flat, with its threadbare carpets and hand-me-down furniture, that Eddie, Angie and their baby had been forced to live in. This house was a million miles away from those days and made Sally realise just what a lot her sister had missed out on. 'You have a beautiful home, Cathy.'

'Thank you,' Cathy said, pouring coffee into china mugs. She handed one to Sally. 'It's all down to Carl's hard work.'

'And your good taste in furnishings.' Sally smiled at the poised and elegant woman, fashionably clad in black linen trousers and a cream silk shirt. Her well-cut, light-brown hair fell neatly to her shoulders. There was a time when Cathy had been the plain girl, always in Angie's shadow. *How things change*, Sally thought.

She delved into her pocket and took out the photograph. She held it out to Cathy, who smiled as she took it and looked at her late friend Angie, Richard Price and the young Jonathon. She looked enquiringly at Sally.

'I had a visitor last night,' Sally said.

'Who?'

'My nephew, Jonathon.'

'Oh, I see. I saw him recently at Nick's memorial service.'

Sally nodded. 'I hadn't seen him for years. My dad died recently and Mum thought Jon should know.'

'I'm sorry to hear that,' Cathy said.

'Kevin, my eldest, found out where Jon works and we got in touch. He didn't make the funeral because of Nick and Jess's accident. But he called me and came to visit last night.'

'He's made a smashing young man,' Cathy said. 'Angie would have been very proud of him.'

'She would. He's lovely. Tall and dark, not a bit like Eddie.'

'He takes after Angie with his curls and everything,' Cathy said. She took a sip of coffee.

'That's funny, Cathy, because *I* don't think he looks anything like Angie.'

Cathy frowned and chewed her thumbnail. She looked at the photograph again.

'He does, a little bit.'

'Take a really close look at Richard, then look at Jon again.'

Studying the photograph, Cathy wriggled uncomfortably.

'Jon was three years old when that photo was taken,' Sally said. 'But there's a definite resemblance even then, wouldn't you agree? Now *you* saw him recently at Nick's service, so you're well aware of how he looks today. He's the double of Richard Price.'

Cathy's eyes filled with tears and she walked across the room to stare out of the window.

'Tell me, Cathy, please, is Jon Richard's son?'

Cathy nodded. 'Yes, he's Richard's.'

Sally's hand flew to her mouth. 'I knew it.'

'I'm sorry, Sally. It must be an awful shock to you.'

'Why didn't Angie tell me? How long have you known?'

'Since he was born I suppose, even before. When Angie found out she was pregnant, she didn't know who the father was, but of course she blamed Eddie. He married her and Richard's name was kept out of it.'

Sally leant back on the sofa, speechless. She couldn't believe her sister would be so deceptive. 'So, when did she realise the baby wasn't Eddie's?'

'As soon as he was born,' Cathy said, sitting back down.

'And she still led Eddie to believe it was his child?'

'Yes, Ed doted on Jon. She couldn't bring herself to say anything to him.'

'So all this time, Eddie's brought Jon up as his own, never realising he was someone else's?' Sally shook her head in disbelief.

'Well, actually, no. There's more, and it might be a bigger shock than what I've already told you,' Cathy said.

'I don't think I can be any more shocked than I am now, but go on.'

'The police gave me back a camera Angie borrowed. It was in the car following the crash and was undamaged, so I used up the film at Jess's christening. I had it developed and Carl looked through the photographs. He spotted the likeness between Jon and Richard immediately. He assumed Richard was your brother, Jon's uncle. I couldn't handle it any longer. I broke down and told Carl the truth. I was certain he may mention the likeness to Ed one day in passing and Ed of course knows you don't have a brother. Carl was horrified and insisted I told Ed and Jane right away.'

Sally nodded as Cathy continued.

'We went to see them that night and I told them everything. They were devastated, but couldn't bear the thought of losing Jon. He was happy, settled in a lovely home and calling Jane, Mummy. We made a pact never to tell a soul and we never have done, until now.' Cathy broke down sobbing, while Sally sat silently, tears pouring down her cheeks.

'Sally, I beg of you, don't tell Jon. Can you imagine what the shock would do to him? I'll have to let Eddie know that I've told you. The only other people who know are the Cantellos and the Davises. The eight of us were at Hanover's Lodge the night the pact was made. It's been the most closely guarded secret and not even Phil Jackson, the other Raider, knows.'

Sally sat silently for a while, gathering her scattered thoughts. 'Thank you for being honest with me, Cathy. There's no need to upset Eddie and Jane, I promise I'll take the secret to the grave. Eddie's been a wonderful father to a boy who's not his own. I reckon he had enough to put up with when he married Angie in the first place. What with *her* moods and the stick my mother gave him, the man deserves a bloody medal! I just needed to know the truth for my own sake, otherwise it would have eaten away at me forever.'

Cathy nodded tearfully. 'I understand. Would you like more coffee?'

'Please,' Sally said, thinking that Cathy might appreciate a moment or two on her own. Left alone, Sally gazed around the room, her eyes alighting on a framed colour photo in pride of place on the wall: The Raiders accepting an award. Sally leant forward to look at their smiling faces. Eddie looked so happy, his blue eyes shining brightly, standing next to a jubilant Roy, who held the award above his head. A world of difference from the teenage tearaway who'd married her sister. There was no doubt in Sally's mind that Angie would have denied him all the fame he'd achieved if they'd stayed together. As much as she'd loved Angie, Sally would be the first to admit that she'd been selfish and thoughtless to take away Eddie's freedom. No matter how frightened she had been of telling their parents, what she'd done was inexcusable and to carry on the charade after Jon's birth was unforgivable.

Cathy arrived back with a fresh tray of coffee and sat down. 'I knew one day it would all surface again,' she began. 'You can't keep something like that a secret forever. But you have to understand how much Eddie loved Jon. To lose him to yourselves, or maybe even Richard's family, who were total strangers to Jon, was more than he could bear.'

Sally nodded. 'I understand. I just wish Angie had confided in me – I thought we were close in spite of our age difference.'

'She was embarrassed and said you'd be really angry with her for getting into such a mess. The guilt made her withdraw from Eddie and also *he* was still in love with Jane, so the marriage didn't stand a chance.'

'Poor kids, all of them,' Sally said softly.

'There's one more thing. The day Angie and Richard died, they were going to tell Eddie that same night that Jon wasn't his.'

'I never thought I'd ever hear myself say this, Cathy, but sometimes things happen for all the right reasons, if you know what I mean.'

'I've thought that myself over the years. God moves in mysterious ways, as Carl's mum's always telling us.'

'I suppose I'd better go home,' Sally said. 'I don't want Mum or Martin to get wind of this. They'll wonder where I am if I'm away any longer.' She stood up, put her arms around Cathy and hugged her.

'Are you sure you wouldn't like me to tell Ed and Jane that you know?' Cathy said.

'There's no point in causing them any upset,' Sally said. 'They've had enough to contend with recently with the accident. Thanks again for being honest with me. I'll see you sometime soon, I hope. Goodbye.'

* * *

Roy leant back on his chair and frowned. He'd arrived at The Lodge earlier than planned. Eddie was still out on the school run and Jess had just asked him how he felt about the prospect of being a father again at his time of life.

'Am I really that old in your eyes, Jess?'

She shrugged. 'Not old exactly, it's just a bit of a shock, that's all.'

'Well, it was to *me* as well. I still can't quite get my head around it, I fainted when Sammy told me.'

'Yeah, Dad said. Livvy thinks that you love her. Do you?'

Roy lit a cigarette and took a long drag. 'In a way. I feel responsible for what happens to the baby.'

'But you won't ever divorce Sammy?' Jess asked anxiously.

'Never. I love her more than anything. She's my life, my whole world,' he replied.

'Your special girl,' Jess sang out.

'Absolutely.' Roy smiled, glad the mood was lightening. Jess's questioning was making him feel decidedly uncomfortable.

The back door flew open and Katie bounced into the kitchen. 'Uncle Roy,' she squealed and jumped onto his knee.

He grimaced. 'Careful, Katie, watch where you're putting your knees!' He tickled her and she squirmed and giggled.

Eddie strolled in, carrying the bags, Dominic on his heels.

'Katie, go and take off your uniform and hang it in the wardrobe. Don't dump it on the floor like you did yesterday. I had to press her skirt this morning, all those bloody pleats,'

Eddie complained as Roy looked at him with an amused expression.

'Don't you laugh at me, it's hard work looking after kids and the home, and then there's Jane demanding dinner on the table at six thirty every night and woe betide me if it's not ready.' Eddie rolled his eyes in a mock gesture of a put-upon housewife and folded his arms below an imaginary bosom.

Roy roared with laughter. 'Ed, shut up! You look and sound just like your old mum.'

Eddie grinned broadly. 'Heaven forbid! Jess, keep an eye on the kids for a while, give them juice and biscuits when they come downstairs. We need to talk,' he told Roy.

'Why, what's happened?'

'Livvy,' Eddie replied. 'I'll tell you in a minute. Come on, let's go up.'

Roy frowned and followed him up to the music room. He flopped down on a chair by the mixing desk. Eddie handed him a cigarette and lit one himself.

'So, go on, what about Livvy?'

'Well, for starters, she told Jon and Sean that you went to see her and promised her the earth for her and the baby.'

'Yeah, I did. I went to try and sort things out. Listen, Ed, before I go any further, I know that you tried to help and I appreciate what lay behind it. Thanks, mate, I owe you one.'

'It's okay. I never intended to interfere. At the end of the day I'm only interested in what happens to you and Sammy. I had a quick word with Livvy earlier and she said you were going to support her financially after the baby's born.'

'I haven't a choice. If I help her voluntarily, then she's less likely to sell her story for money.'

'Good point. I know you've other problems as well. Jane told me about Jason and what's going on there. But you need to be aware that Livvy's convinced once she's given birth, you'll want to be with her and live as a proper family. She told

Sean and Jon all this and Jon was concerned enough to call me.'

'Bloody hell! I never made her any promises to be with her permanently and I told her I couldn't marry her. I thought I'd made it quite clear that all she will get is financial help. She's obviously taken things the wrong way.' Roy took a lengthy drag and coughed. 'I won't let Sammy down again. Ed. Things are going well now, just as long as I don't blow it again. She's going out with Stuart Green tonight for a meal and it really bothers me.'

'Why? Jane told me their meeting was purely business.'

'Yeah, so she says. I was hoping she'd spend the night with *me*. It's the last night she'll have free before Pat and Tim arrive. Tomorrow she'll be busy getting sorted and grocery shopping. Oh well, maybe she'll find time for me next week.'

'You can live in hope, mate.' Eddie patted his shoulder. 'Eat with us tonight, if you like.'

'Thanks, I will,' Roy said. 'It'll help keep my mind off things.'

* * *

Jon grinned when he saw Roy's car on the drive and he wondered what he'd been up to that afternoon. He called out a greeting as he walked into the warm kitchen where his dad was slaving away over the AGA, making what smelt suspiciously like his special bolognese sauce. Roy, Jane and Jess were seated around the table, knocking back red wine. Jon took a seat next to Jess and let his knee touch her leg. She responded with gentle pressure and smiled at him.

'Hi, love,' Jane said. 'Would you like a glass of wine?'

'Please, Mum.'

Jane pushed a glass and the bottle across the table. 'Help yourself. Had a good day?'

'Fine, thanks. Did Dad tell you Sally rang for Cathy's number?'

'He did.' Jane caught Roy's raised eyebrow. 'Did Sally say *why* she wanted to speak to Cathy?'

'Yeah. Grandma wants to see her before she goes home.'

'I see. I believe you and Jess are going out with Jason later.'

Jon nodded. 'We haven't seen him socially for weeks now and it'll be good to get out.'

'Hmm. You've been cooped up in Jess's bedroom for so long you'll take root,' Jane said.

'I'll go and get changed before we eat, save me doing it later.' Jess struggled off the chair.

Jon sprang immediately to her aid. 'I'll carry you.' He scooped her up in his arms and walked out of the kitchen.

* * *

Jane stared after them, biting her lower lip.

'Something wrong, Jane?' Roy asked.

She shook her head. 'I hope he doesn't give himself a hernia, carrying Jess upstairs like that.'

Eddie turned from the AGA. 'She's light as a feather and a big lad like Jon won't strain himself.'

'You're right, of course.' Jane swallowed the last of her wine and opened another bottle, pushing unbidden thoughts away.

* * *

Puffing slightly, Jon made his way into Jess's room, kicked the door shut with his foot and sat her on the bed. 'Good job that door was open,' he said and knelt in front of her. Taking her face in his hands, he kissed her. She put her arms around his neck, returning his kisses with fervour. He looked at her, eyes burning into hers. 'You tell me that didn't feel right and I'll never do it again.'

Jess smiled and stroked his cheek. 'It was perfect, so *very* right in fact. Oh God, but it's not, is it?'

'I'm falling in love with you, Jess.' Before Jon could say any more, a knock at the door made them jump apart.

Jane popped her head in and frowned at their flushed faces. 'Are you two okay?'

'Fine, Mum, thanks. I banged my wrist on the headboard when Jon put me down and he was rubbing it better for me. It's made me feel sick and it's upset him 'cos he thinks it was his fault.'

Jess plucked the lie from somewhere and Jon hoped she sounded convincing.

'Oh dear, let me have a look. Do you want a couple of your painkillers?'

'No, I'm okay, really,' Jess insisted. 'You can help me get changed if you will, save me struggling alone.' She smiled at Jon. 'Thanks for carrying me upstairs.'

He took the hint. 'I'll take a shower.'

* * *

'What do you fancy wearing?' Jane opened the wardrobe and looked at the vast array of clothes.

'I've got new sweaters in that bag over there,' Jess said.

Jane rummaged in the bag and pulled out a short, blue and grey striped cotton sweater with long sleeves. 'This one's nice? What else did you buy?'

'A couple of tops, underwear and perfume,' Jess replied. 'Dad bought you some Chanel No5. It's a surprise, so don't let on I told you.'

Jane smiled. 'He must have noticed I'm almost out, bless him. What are you going to wear with this sweater?'

Jess frowned. 'Well, normally blue jeans, but I can't get them over my plaster. It'll have to be a skirt. The denim one maybe, or what about that pale-grey leather one Nick bought me earlier this year? I've hardly worn it.'

Jane removed the skirt from the wardrobe, taking into account that Jess had mentioned Nick without even flinching. She helped her into the skirt and pulled the sweater on. The blue set off her eyes perfectly and the pale-grey stripes were an exact match for the leather skirt. Jane brushed her long hair until it shone and Jess applied a sweep of blusher and kohl-rimmed her eyes.

'What about your legs?' Jane said. 'You'll be cold after living in jogging bottoms for weeks.'

'Well, I can't put tights on and I'm not wearing socks, for goodness' sake. I'll be okay. We'll be in the car and the pub most of the time and my legs are still quite brown from the summer.'

'Okay, well I'll go down and see if your dad needs a hand with dinner. I'll ask Jon to carry you back downstairs.'

Jane knocked on Jon's bedroom door. 'Come in,' he called and she found him lying on the bed, an unfathomable expression on his face. 'You alright, Jon?'

'I'm fine.'

'Will you carry Jess downstairs, please?'

'Of course.'

* * *

Jon breathed a sigh of relief as his mother left the room. He was so sure she'd been suspicious of him and Jess. He told himself it must be guilt – she'd no reason to be suspicious at all. He jumped up and went back to Jess.

'That was a close shave,' she said as he shut the door.

'I know. I meant what I said before she interrupted. I'm falling in love with you.'

Jess swallowed hard. 'What the hell do we do now?'

He shook his head. 'I don't know. How do *you* feel?'

'I'm falling for you too, Jon. Do you think it's too soon after Nick to feel like this?'

He kissed her and swung her up into his arms. 'I don't think time has anything to do with it. We'll talk later when we're out, either before or after we've spent time with Jason. I like the sweater, by the way. Is it one of the new ones?'

'It is.'

'Don't suppose you've got that black lacy thing on underneath?'

'No, I'm saving it for a special occasion.'

'What special occasion?'

'The one where you take me out for a meal after I've had my ankle plaster off and I can dress up properly.'

His eyes lit up. 'I'll look forward to that.'

* * *

Sammy lay on her bed. She was supposed to be getting ready to go out with Stuart, but the last thing she felt like doing was dressing up and putting on fresh make-up. Her hair needed a wash after the ravages of being with Roy. She smiled as she thought back to lunchtime. He never changed, still thought he was twenty-one. Mind you, he had the body and stamina of a much younger man.

Jason knocked on the door and strolled in, carrying a china cup and saucer. 'Thought you might fancy a cup of Earl Grey, Mum. You still going out with Stuart tonight? You look fit for nothing!'

She sat up and took the cup. 'Thank you, love; I *am* going out with Stuart, but I feel really tired. It's been a funny week all round. Everything that's happened has left me drained.'

'I'm not surprised. Did you see Dad today?'

'I had lunch with him at The Grand.'

'Was he okay?'

'He's fine. He'll want to talk to you over the weekend. Make some time for him, he's sorry for what happened with Jules. How is he, by the way?'

'A bit of a mess. His eyes are going black, but he'll be okay. Mum, what happened with Dad and Livvy last night? Did he sort things out?'

'Yes, he's offered her financial help.'

'Will he want to see the baby? I mean, it'll be my half-brother or sister.'

Sammy sighed and sipped her tea. 'I don't know if he'll want contact. I hope he doesn't, but that will be up to him.'

'I suppose we'll have to wait and see then.'

Sammy drained her cup and handed it back. 'What time are Jess and Jon coming over?'

'About eight. I'm looking forward to seeing them. It's been weird, them not being around. I've felt very lonely.'

'Do you think that's maybe why you've turned to Jules?' she asked gently.

Jason shrugged. 'No, Mum, and don't get the wrong idea. Jules isn't around because I'm lonely, Jules is around because I want him to be.'

'Of course he is.' She patted his arm affectionately. 'I'd better get in the shower and wake myself up a bit. If Stuart arrives early, show him into the lounge and offer him a drink. There's a bottle of your dad's single malt in the drinks cupboard, I remember him being rather partial to a drop of that.'

* * *

Stuart's eyes lit up as Sammy walked into the room and he gave a low whistle. He placed his empty tumbler on the table next to the sofa and stood up to greet her. 'Wow! You look absolutely stunning, Sam.' He admired her cream silk shift and navy jacket with the padded shoulders. 'Very Alexis Colby! One of your own designs?'

'Jacques Vert, actually,' she said, blushing slightly, a fact that didn't go unobserved by Jason, Jon and Jess, who exchanged knowing looks. 'Thank you, Stuart. I'll see you kids later.'

'Have a nice meal, Mum.' Jason kissed her cheek as she and Stuart left the room.

'Enjoy yourself, Sammy,' Jess called after her.

* * *

'New car, Stu?' Sammy asked as he helped her into his silver Honda Accord and shut the door.

'Yes.' He slid in beside her. 'Not as upmarket as yours, but it's new all the same. Are you alright, Sammy? You seem a bit preoccupied.'

She smiled as he swung off the drive onto Jasmine Lane. 'I'm a little tired. It's been a busy day and I spent a hectic couple of hours with Roy this afternoon...' she trailed off, feeling her cheeks warming.

Stuart chuckled. 'Say no more. I know Roy of old. I warned you about him years ago and what did you say at the time?'

'I want some fun!' they chorused, laughing together.

'Well, you've had plenty of that.'

'I have. It's just lately everything's fallen apart – Nick's death, Roy's affair and now this baby.' She remembered too late that Stuart didn't know about the baby.

'Baby?' He frowned. 'Has he put Livvy in the club?'

'Unfortunately.'

'Shit! How do you feel about that?'

'Not very happy.'

'Christ, I bet you're not! Is that why he's moved out?'

'He moved out before we knew about the baby. We needed

a break while we sort our heads out. He's hoping I'll allow him home eventually, and I will, because I love him very much. I don't want to lose him to her.'

'I understand. You've been together since you were kids. It's a lifetime. But you're a very forgiving woman. Most would have killed for a lesser crime.'

'Don't think I haven't been tempted!' Sammy related what she'd done to Roy's clothes and car earlier in the year.

Stuart grinned and pulled into the restaurant car park. He helped Sammy out and took her arm as they walked inside. She glanced at his profile as they waited to be seated. He was still good-looking. Tall and slim with light-brown hair, he'd always had nice twinkly green eyes and an attractive dimple in his chin.

Benito recognised Sammy at once and came over, looking behind her for Roy.

'He's not with me tonight,' she told the puzzled head waiter.

'Okay. Follow me.' He seated them in a private alcove, where the table was set for two, and lit the candle decoration.

'I take it this is your usual restaurant?' Stuart said.

'It is, but we haven't eaten here since I found out about Roy's affair. Then Nick and Jess had their accident at the end of that week. So all in all, we haven't been out anywhere for ages, other than to Ed and Jane's place.'

'It must have been a very difficult time.'

Benito brought over a carafe of wine and the menus. 'Is red okay, Miss Sammy?'

'Perfect, thank you, Benito.' She smiled at the little man.

'Mr Roy, he is not ill, I hope?'

'No, no, he's fine, really,' she assured him. 'This is my friend and business colleague, Stuart Green.'

Benito nodded, seemingly happy with her explanation, and left them alone to study the menus.

'What you were saying just then, Stu, about it being a difficult time... it was, it still is. Our family life, as we knew it, is over forever. I can't quite believe it sometimes. I wake up in the middle of the night and Roy isn't next to me. Then I worry about Nick and Jess and hope that they're okay in their little flat, and then it hits me: Nick's dead. Then there's Jason's little problem.' She lowered her eyes as her voice trailed off.

Stuart frowned and looked at her. 'What about Jason? He seemed fine when he let me in earlier.'

Sammy looked around to make sure no one could overhear her. 'He thinks he's gay,' she whispered.

'Really?'

'He's got this friend, Jules, he met at college. Yesterday, Roy found them together in a bit of a compromising situation and thumped Jules.'

'Jesus Christ, Sam! How have you kept your sanity with all this going on? You look so cool and collected.' Stuart shook his head and took a swig of wine.

'I'm not cool inside,' Sammy admitted. 'I only found out about Livvy's pregnancy yesterday. I told Roy last night. He was so shocked, he fainted clean away. I tell you, Stuart, it was like a scene from a Brian Rix farce! And to top it all, Pat and Tim will arrive home on Saturday right in the middle of this mess.'

Stuart smiled at Sammy's description of her problems.

'And how are Jane and Ed these days? Any more shocks in store for me?'

'Oh, everything's rosy in their court,' she said, smiling. 'Still as love-struck as they've always been.'

After Benito refilled their glasses and took their order, Stuart told her he'd spent yesterday evening in the company of John and Margaret Grey, who'd suggested having a welcome home party for Pat and Tim sometime in the next week or two.

'That would be wonderful. I haven't seen anyone socially for months now, not since Nick's eighteenth birthday party.

They were all at his memorial service, of course, but I wasn't really in a fit state to talk to anyone.'

'Well, John said he would call you over the weekend and arrange a time,' Stuart said.

The food arrived and in-between courses, Stuart asked Sammy if she would like to accompany him to a textile exhibition at Earl's Court in November.

'The companies I represent from the States and Italy will be having stands to launch their new designs and I'm sure you'll enjoy mixing with like-minded people.'

She nodded. 'I'd love to, I haven't been to a textile show this year.'

'I'll book the accommodation then. The exhibition starts mid-week until the weekend. If I book for Thursday and Friday nights, will you be able to organise the time off?'

'Yeah, no problem. Jane will look after the place. I'm afraid I've let things slide a bit since the accident. Fortunately, I've good, loyal staff in both the shops and the factory. The business runs quite smoothly. All I really need to do is the designing and choosing the right fabrics. Mum does the accounts and Jane and Jess run the mail order side of things.'

'I didn't realise Jess worked for you, too. It's a real family affair then.'

'Jess works part-time, although she hasn't been in for weeks. I suppose you noticed the plaster cast on her ankle and she's only just had the one on her wrist removed.'

'Jess reminds me of Jane. It's the long dark hair, but those blue eyes and dimples are pure Ed.'

'You should see Katie, their youngest – she's the spit of Jane and so is Dom.'

'How old are their younger two? I've lost count.'

'Katie's eight, going on eighteen. Dom's seven. They keep Ed busy. He and Jane swapped roles. Ed's a house husband and Jane works.'

'He and Roy are still writing songs though, aren't they?'

'Yes, of course. There's a new single out on Monday by a band called Perry's Dream. Jason tells me it's tipped for the top. There's a plan afoot to re-form The Raiders as soon as Tim arrives.' Sammy took a sip of wine and Stuart topped up their glasses. 'We've hardly discussed business, Stu. I've waffled on all night about my problems, you should have stopped me.'

'I think you needed a fresh shoulder to cry on. And it's been nice to catch up on what everyone is up to. We can discuss business anytime.'

'How come you never married, Stu? Didn't you meet the right girl?'

He smiled and took her hand. 'I met her alright, but by the time I realised it, she'd fallen in love with my friend, Roy.'

'Stuart,' Sammy faltered, 'you never said a word.'

'Well, before I had a chance to say anything, Roy already had the hots for you. The day I told Ed that Jane fancied him, Roy asked me about you. I told him you liked him and I promised to introduce you at the coffee bar that Saturday night. He went on and on about your legs all the time, drooling like a lovesick puppy. I hadn't the heart to tell him that *I* fancied you as well. Anyway, once you set eyes on Roy that was it: you were glued to one another's lips for most of that night and no one else stood a chance. What Roy wanted, he got, end of story!' he finished with a grin.

Sammy smiled, remembering back to the night he was referring to. 'That was January 1959, so long ago, yet I can remember it as though it were yesterday.'

'So can I. You had long hair almost down to your bottom, legs to die for and you could jive superbly.'

Sammy grinned. 'I bet I couldn't do that today if I tried. You *also* used to jive well, if I remember rightly.'

'When we go to London, I'll take you to a club. We'll have a few dances for old time's sake, pretend we're kids again.'

'Yeah, why not?' she yawned and put her hand over her mouth. 'Oh, I'm sorry, Stuart, I feel so drained.'

'You're whacked. I'll get the bill, it's been quite a week for you.'

'It's certainly not one I'd like to repeat in a hurry,' she admitted.

Stuart settled the bill and they left the restaurant. 'Thank you for a lovely evening and your delightful company,' he said as he pulled up outside Jasmine House.

'Would you like a nightcap?' Sammy asked, her stomach fluttering slightly as he gazed into her eyes.

He touched her cheek gently. 'No, thank you, you're shattered. Another time, maybe? I'll call you over the weekend, make sure Tim and Pat are back safe and sound. Maybe we could go out for a meal with them one night next week?'

'That would be lovely and thank you for listening to my problems.'

He leant over and kissed her lightly on the lips. 'My pleasure. Goodnight, Sammy.'

As she stood on the steps watching Stuart drive away, the door opened behind her and Jason popped his head out.

'I heard the car. Had a nice time, Mum?'

'Very nice, thank you. Very nice indeed. Have Jon and Jess gone home?' She followed him indoors.

'Yeah, they dropped me off a while ago. We went for a drink and had a good talk. When Jess gets some strength back in her wrist and can play her bass again, we're gonna do a bit of jamming. Jules sings quite well, not so good as Nick did, but there's always room for improvement and Jon and Jess are okay about him joining us. If it works out, we might have ourselves a new band.'

'Oh, Jason, that would do you all the world of good, give you a new lease of life.'

'Mum, you're all flushed. Is that the wine or is it down to Stuart's company?' he teased.

'The wine, cheeky! Stuart's just a friend. Anyway, I'm going up to bed. I promised your dad I'd call him as soon as I got home.'

'Why? Doesn't he trust you?'

'He's terrified of losing me, Jason, that's why,' she replied, willing him to understand how insecure Roy was feeling.

'He should have thought about that before he jumped into bed with Livvy.'

'He knows that and he regrets it.' Sammy stuck up for Roy, knowing she probably shouldn't.

'He's an idiot,' Jason declared. 'Anyway, I'm off to bed. See you tomorrow, Mum.'

'Goodnight, love.' Sammy kissed his cheek and he sauntered off up the stairs.

* * *

Sammy was put through to Roy's room. He answered immediately, as though he had been sitting on top of the phone.

'Sammy?'

'Well, who else are you expecting at this time of night?' she teased.

She heard a sigh of relief. 'Oh good, you're home then?'

'I am.'

'Did you have a nice time?'

'Lovely, thank you; Stuart's very good company.'

'Oh, I see.'

'Roy?'

'Yes?'

'I love you, you idiot!'

'Oh, Sam, I love you too. Do you fancy having lunch with me again tomorrow?'

'Yes, I do. Then I'd like us to take flowers to Nick's grave. I think I can handle a visit now.'

'Okay, love. We'll do that. I feel ready too.'

'Goodnight, Roy.'

'Goodnight, darling.'

She replaced the receiver and lay back against the pillows. At least she knew for certain where he was tonight and could go to sleep with peace of mind.

25

'Where are we going?' Jess asked as Jon turned the Jeep in the opposite direction to home.

'Somewhere we can have a bit peace,' he replied.

They travelled in silence down a few miles of country lanes before Jon turned into the gateway of a rundown farm. He killed the engine, dimmed the lights and drummed his fingers on the steering wheel.

Her stomach looping, Jess reached over and touched his cheek. 'What is it, Jon?'

He turned, his eyes burning into hers. 'I've been longing to touch you all night, but there were too many people around who knew us.'

'Well, we're alone now,' she whispered.

He released her seat belt, pulled her into his arms and kissed her. She responded, running her fingers through his hair. Tugging his denim shirt from the waistband of his jeans, she undid the buttons and nuzzled her face into his dark, curly chest hairs. That musky cologne – how she loved the smell of him.

'Shall we get in the back of the car?' she suggested. 'I can't get close enough to you here.'

'We'd be better with somewhere we can lie down,' he said. 'With your ankle and lack of space, it might be a struggle. There's a barn in that field,' he said. 'Come on, I'll carry you.'

He leapt from the car and ran round to her side. She flung her arms around his neck as he lifted her out. The gate was ajar and he squeezed them through. The old barn was over to the left and the narrow path, leading to it, was lit by silvery moonlight.

'What if there are cows in the barn?' she said. Cows weren't her favourite farm animal since a herd had chased her and Dad when she was small.

'It's usually empty.'

'Ah – so you've been here before?' She raised an eyebrow. 'And who was the lucky lady?'

'No one *you* know. And it was years ago.'

'You can put me down now.' She struggled out of his arms as they drew level with the ancient stone building. 'I can walk here, the ground's quite flat.'

Jon swung open the barn door and they peered inside. It was empty except for a few bales of hay and some rusting farm machinery.

'This'll do fine.' Jon led her in and pushed the door closed with his foot. 'It's dry and quite warm and there's no one to disturb us.'

Jess sniffed the air. 'Doesn't smell of cows,' she said, feeling relief. 'In fact, it smells quite nice.'

Jon spread a bale of the sweet-smelling hay on the floor at the back of the barn. He wiped his hands on his jeans and turned to her. 'Your bed awaits,' he said, looking anxious.

Jess smiled and reached up to pluck pieces of straw from his hair. 'The Worzel Gummidge look is not for you,' she said, looking into his eyes.

He grabbed her and crushed her to him, then dropped to his knees, took off his shirt, spread it on the hay and lowered her onto it. She pulled him down and he lay beside her, kissing and caressing her.

'I love the scent of you, Jon,' she said as his hands slid under her sweater. 'Front fastening,' she whispered as he unhooked her bra and pulled her sweater over her head.

'*Your* scent drives *me* wild,' he said, tracing her nipples. 'You're so beautiful.'

He rolled on top and she loved the feel of his naked chest against hers. When his hand wandered up her skirt, she pushed it away. No matter how tempting, they couldn't – it wasn't right, they'd be breaking the law. 'No, Jon, this is as far as we go. We can kiss and touch as much as we want, but nothing below waists.'

He sighed and kissed her again, tongue searching her mouth, pushing against hers. She responded, frantically kissing him back. Then he was squeezing and kissing her breasts and her nipples stiffened against his tongue. She moaned, feeling a familiar tugging in her tummy. She wanted him so badly and it was all she could do to keep her hands from straying to his crotch, where his erection twitched impatiently against her.

Jess felt like she was floating. Her senses were heightened. The sweet scent of the hay, Jon's musky cologne, the taste of his kisses, the scrabbling that she was certain must be field mice, the moon shining through the grimy, cracked windows, throwing mysterious light on their semi-nakedness.

'I've dreamt about this so often,' he whispered as she ran her hands over his slim, muscular body, stopping at the waistband of his jeans. 'I need you, Jess.'

Then his hand, soft and warm, was up her skirt again, stroking her thighs and his fingers caressing insistently through the soft lace of her knickers. She groaned as he pushed her legs apart, *she* needed *him*, too, but...

He knelt up as she moaned with pleasure. Her skirt and knickers were off and tossed to one side. His lips moved down her body, raining kisses, teasing as she writhed in ecstasy. She was powerless to stop him and reached out to unzip and push his jeans off.

'Jess,' he groaned as she held and caressed him and arched her back to draw him in. 'Jess, I love you.'

'I love you, too,' she said as he slid into her.

His long, slow strokes were confident, loving and sensual and she moved with him, enjoying sensations she'd never felt before. As their breathing deepened, he slipped his hands beneath her, pulling her ever closer; his thrusting urgent. She saw his face, his gentle green eyes full of love, looking deep into hers. Her shuddering orgasm sent Jon to an explosive climax. He collapsed on top and buried his face in her neck, whispering her name again and again. She ran her fingers through his curls and burst into tears.

'That was amazing,' she said. 'It was so... so loving.'

'I know.' He stroked her hair from her face. 'But why are you crying?'

'Because it was so wonderful,' she sniffed. 'How can it be wrong?'

'Oh, Jess,' he said, wiping her tears with the back of his hand. 'I love you so much.' He kissed her again and held her close until her tears subsided.

* * *

As he held Jess, Jon reflected on the last hour. How could a love like theirs possibly be wrong? *Nothing* had ever felt more right to him in his life. He'd always loved her and she was *his* now. He wanted to love her and protect her for eternity. There had to be a way to be together. It saddened him to think they could never have a normal relationship, hold hands in public, get engaged, married, have kids. But for him, to be with Jess and experience love like they'd just shared would be enough.

He felt tears welling and they tumbled down his cheeks. He wiped them away with his hand. No matter what the future, holding her tonight, kissing her, touching her, the scent and taste of her would remain with him forever. She stirred in his arms and looked up at him.

'You okay?' he asked, caressing her cheek.

She nodded, smiling.

'Me too.' He bent to kiss her again.

* * *

'How was your night out with Stu?' Jane asked as she handed Sammy a mug of coffee at their morning break.

'Very nice,' Sammy replied.

Jane grinned knowingly. 'Stu always had a soft spot for you, but *you* only had eyes for Roy.'

'I did and I'm having lunch with him again today. I might be a bit late back.'

'Is that right?' Jane raised an amused eyebrow.

'Jason told me he, Jon and Jess enjoyed themselves last night,' Sammy changed the subject. 'They're planning to do some jamming when Jess can play her bass again.'

'That sounds positive. I haven't seen Jon and Jess today. They were late home last night. When I got up, Jess was still in bed and Jon was leaving for work.'

'They must have gone on somewhere,' Sammy said. 'Jason was home when I got back and it was only around eleven, if that.'

Jane frowned. 'Where would they have gone? The pubs would be closed and if they'd gone to a club, surely they would have taken Jason? Jess can't dance at the moment anyway, so clubbing seems unlikely.'

Sammy shrugged. 'Maybe they met up with friends on the way home.'

'Maybe.' Jane nodded thoughtfully.

'What is it?' Sammy saw a look of concern cross her friend's face.

'Nothing, I'm being stupid again. My imagination's working overtime.'

'Do you still feel there's something going on?'

'It horrifies me that I think that way, but yes, I do. I popped into Jess's room last night, before they went out. Jon was kneeling in front of her and they were both flushed. She said she'd banged her arm on the headboard and he was rubbing it better, but I'd swear they'd been kissing.'

'You should tell Ed your suspicions before it gets out of hand.'

'I can't, Sam, he'd go absolutely mental.'

'Well, *I* bloody would, before something happens.'

'What if it already has?' Jane chewed her lip. 'Last night I was awake when they came home. It was after twelve thirty and you said they left yours before eleven so they'd been on their own for well over an hour. They might have parked up somewhere.'

'Talk to Ed, Jane, you have to. They've been brought up as brother and sister. It's incestuous.'

'It's not though, is it?' Jane said. 'They're not related. What if they're in love? I've seen the way he looks at her. Even when she was with Nick, he looked at her in a certain way and she's *always* been very close to him. I knew something like this would happen one day. We should have been honest with Jon when he was old enough to understand. If I say something and I'm wrong, it will spoil that closeness they share and then they'll be afraid to show their feelings.'

'Well, you know *my* opinion on the matter, but if you're not ready to discuss it with Ed until you've made further observations, just make sure they're not alone together.'

Jane nodded. 'I'll make sure Katie gets in their way as much as I can.'

'That shouldn't be too difficult. Do you want to go home when I get back from seeing Roy? Spend a bit of time with Jess?'

'Yeah, okay. Maybe I'll take her shopping.'

'You do that.' Sammy put on her jacket and picked up her handbag. 'I'm off. See you later.'

* * *

Roy made a mental note of things he needed to do as he drove into Manchester. He'd taken the references and deposit to the estate agents earlier and Sarah told him he could collect the keys to the flat on Monday morning. Guitar strings from Flanagan and Grey's and a quiet word with Livvy were next.

Sean greeted him with a broad grin. 'Hi there, Super-Stud, long time no see.'

'Leave it out, Sean,' Roy said good-naturedly. 'Is Livvy in today?'

'She's in the staffroom, making a brew for us overworked and underpaid slaves. Isn't that right, Jon?'

Jon nodded, but had a look on his face that told Roy he hadn't heard a word Sean had said.

'Wake up, lad.' Sean winked at Roy. 'I think he's in love.'

'Is he now?' Roy joined in the banter. 'Who's the lucky lady, then? Thought you'd dumped Helen?'

'I have,' Jon grunted. 'There's no lucky lady. Sean's got the wrong end of the stick – as usual.'

'Well, something's bothering you,' Sean said. 'You're not normally so head in the clouds – that's Livvy's domain.'

'I'm tired, that's all. Jess and I were out with Jason last night. We were late home and then I couldn't sleep.'

'Oh well, that explains it,' Roy said, grinning. 'Okay if I pop through and have a private word with Livvy?'

'Feel free.' Sean nodded.

* * *

Livvy was pouring milk into a mug as Roy popped his head around the door. She jumped and slopped the milk onto the tray.

'Jon, now look what you've made me do!' She turned, an annoyed expression on her face. 'Oh, it's you. I thought it was Jon. He's always sneaking up on me, making me jump.'

'*You're* a grumpy cow this morning,' Roy said. 'I need a word and Sean said it was alright for me to come through.'

'Sit down while I take them their coffees.' She picked up two of the mugs. 'You can have mine if you like.'

Roy parked himself on the old armchair as she left the room and he sipped her coffee. She came back in and made herself another.

'Why don't you come to the flat after I finish work?' she said, sitting on a small chair opposite.

'I can't come to the flat again,' he said. 'I promised Sammy I wouldn't and I've no intentions of breaking the promise. She's in full agreement with me about the money side of things, that we should support you, but she doesn't want me to have contact with you. Get your bank details for me and I'll transfer some money and set up a standing order. I'll keep in touch, make sure you're okay, but I can't see you alone again, Livvy.' Roy held up his hands as she began to protest. 'I don't want to hurt Sammy further. *You* chose to stay pregnant. I own up to fathering the kid. I'll help financially, like I said, but that's it. I'm sorry, I have too much to lose if I see you again.' He stood up and patted her shoulder. 'Get me those bank details.'

She looked at him. He wasn't meeting her eyes. This wasn't

what he wanted, she was certain. She'd bet her life that this was what Sammy was telling him to do. 'Stay in town, Roy. Have lunch with me, we could talk a bit more.'

'Sorry, no can do. I'm having lunch with Sammy,' he replied. 'Besides, there's nothing else to say. I know you told Jon and Sean that I'll feel differently when the baby arrives, but believe me, I won't. I want to stay with my wife, Livvy. I've never stopped loving her; I made sure you knew that right from the word go. If *you'd* been honest with me, we wouldn't be in this mess. I never wanted to bring another kid into the world. But like you told me the other night, I've no rights over your body and what you choose to do with it.'

She blinked back tears. 'You're right. I've no reason to expect anything of you. It's my fault I'm pregnant and I'm grateful for the offer of support.' She rummaged in her handbag for her chequebook, wrote the numbers down and handed over the piece of paper. 'I'll see you around, I expect.'

'If you need me, contact Ed or Jon. Don't call the house. I don't want Sammy upset at any cost.'

'Are you moving back home then?'

'Not yet, Sammy needs more time. I'm moving into a flat on Monday.'

'Can I have the phone number for there? In case I have any problems.'

'It's best if you don't. Call Ed if it's urgent. He'll let me know right away and I'll get straight back to you. I'm going now or I'll be late for Sammy.'

Livvy nodded as he stood up. 'Bye then,' she said quietly.

'Bye, Livvy.'

* * *

'I'm sorry to take up her working time, Sean,' Roy apologised as he went back into the shop. He felt awful, hurting her like that,, but there was no other option if he wanted to save his marriage.

'That's okay. Is she alright?'

'She's a bit upset. She had to face a few home truths and I know I've really hurt her, but at the end of the day, it's her decision not to have a termination. I hope I've got through to her and this time it sinks in.'

Sean shook his head. 'It's a mess, Roy. I don't envy you one little bit. I sometimes wonder if Livvy's not quite all there, you know. Two sandwiches short of a picnic, as Tina said.'

'Why do you say that?' Roy asked, frowning.

'Sean's right, Roy,' Jon chipped in. 'She doesn't always listen to what you're telling her. Like Granddad Ben says, she's two sheep short of a flock, half the time. She hears what she wants to hear and it's not always what you've told her.'

'For God's sake, are you two trying to tell me she's fucking loopy?'

'Not loopy exactly,' Sean reassured. 'A bit strange now and again, but not really loopy.'

'You don't think she'll do anything stupid, do you?' Roy asked, concerned. 'I mean anything to harm herself or the baby?'

Jon shook his head. 'No, well, I hope not anyway.' He broke off as the staffroom door opened and Livvy walked out, eyes red-rimmed.

'I thought you'd gone!' She glared at Roy. 'You said you had to get back for Sammy.' She almost spat the name out.

'I'm going now.' He headed towards the stairs. 'I need some guitar strings.'

Sean followed him downstairs and led the way to the display of strings and accessories. 'I need a quick word,' he said to Roy.

'What's up?'

'Find out if Jon's got a problem at home. What with him and Livvy, between them they're doing my bloody head in.'

'What sort of problem?' Roy frowned and handed Sean two packets of strings. 'I ate with them last night and they were all fine then.'

'I don't know.' Sean shrugged, giving the strings to the girl at the till. 'I wondered if the meeting he had with Angie's family might have upset him.'

'From what I understand, that went off alright. Leave it with me. I'll ask Sam, see if Jane's said anything. I'll call you later.' Roy paid for the strings and slipped the packages into his pocket.

'I'd appreciate that, thanks,' Sean said.

* * *

Sammy's Porsche was already in the hotel car park and Roy swung alongside it. As he hurried through reception, Sharon told him his wife was in the bar. He thanked her and joined Sammy. He bent to kiss her lightly on the lips and attempted to push Livvy's hurt expression to the back of his mind.

'Do you want another drink down here, or shall we head upstairs?' he said, gazing into Sammy's eyes. He'd been so looking forward to this and the look she was giving him told him she was feeling the same.

'Guess?' she teased as Roy caught her hand. She looked good enough to eat. Her neat shiny hair was just begging to be messed up and that glossy pink lipstick could be kissed off in seconds.

'Upstairs, woman!' he ordered, laughing. 'I'm not guessing, I'm telling!' He picked up her drink and pulled her to her feet.

'Roy, I love it when you take charge,' she giggled. 'The food can definitely wait till later.'

***

Jess stared at the page in disbelief, burst into tears and chucked her diary across the bedroom. It hit the wall and landed by the dressing table. She fastened a plastic bag around her ankle cast and hobbled into the shower. The hot water splashed over her shoulders and mingled with her tears. If last night had been wonderful, then why, this morning, did she feel so consumed with guilt? Jon had popped his head briefly around her door before going off to work. She could tell by the way he avoided her eyes that he was feeling guilty, too. But there was no going back.

She wrapped a towel around herself and removed the plastic bag. Her pale-faced reflection in the dressing table mirror stared back at her: *Oh, Jess,* what *have you done?* She bent to pick up the diary and stared at the page. It hadn't changed, it was still the same date. Her period was due in exactly two weeks. Last night, in the throes of passion, she and Jon hadn't taken precautions. She needed to speak to him, tell him her fears.

Grabbing her bathrobe, she limped across the landing to her parents' bedroom. Mum was at work and Dad had told her he was going grocery shopping after the school run. She picked up the phone and dialled Flanagan and Grey's number, hoping Jon would answer, but it was Livvy. Jess asked to speak to him.

'Hi, Jess! Everything alright?'

Her stomach fluttered at the sound of his voice. 'Hi, Jon. Err, not really. I need to tell you something,' she began, feeling more tears welling. 'It's important.'

'What's wrong?'

'Last night,' she said. 'We didn't use anything.'

'Well, there was no need.' He lowered his voice. 'You're on the pill.'

'Not any more. I stopped taking it when Nick died.'

'Fucking hell, I had no idea!'

'I didn't think to say. I'm sorry. It's bad timing, too. I'm right in the middle of my cycle.'

'Shit! We'll just have to keep our fingers crossed.'

'But what if the worst has happened? What will we do?' she wailed, wanting reassurance.

'Don't get upset. Listen, I can't talk right now, but try not to worry. We'll talk tonight when I get home, I promise.'

'Jon, do you love me?'

'You know I do.' His voice was barely a whisper.

'You didn't say it this morning.'

'I couldn't. Mum and Katie were on the landing.'

'Oh, okay. I'll see you later then. I love you, too.'

* * *

Jon sighed and put his head in his hands. He knew he'd upset Jess that morning by not speaking properly. Driving to work, he'd felt bad about that. He'd hardly slept a wink. He felt guilty, but not sorry that it had happened. Shit though, what if he'd knocked her up? He turned to find Sean standing behind him, eyebrows raised.

Jon looked away and muttered, 'Where's Livvy?'

'I sent her for early lunch. What's going on?'

'Nothing.'

'I've known you since you were three years old, I can guess when something's bothering you. I also know that was Jess on the phone. Livvy told me before she went out.'

Jon nodded.

'Is she in some kind of trouble?'

'Of course not. What makes you say that?'

'I overheard you telling her not to worry, you'd keep your fingers crossed. In my day it usually meant one thing. Is Jess in the club?'

Jon gasped at Sean's directness. 'No, she hasn't even got a boyfriend.'

'Is something going on between you and Jess?' he persisted.

Jon looked down at his shoes. How on earth could he admit the truth to Sean?

'Jon,' Sean said gently, 'what's the matter?'

Jon closed his eyes. The guilt was eating away and he needed to unload. He glanced around: the shop was empty. He took a deep breath. 'I slept with Jess last night.'

Sean's jaw dropped. 'For fuck's sake, she's your sister!'

'Half-sister,' he said. 'She's my half-sister.'

'Well, that doesn't make it right. You're still blood-related.'

'I'm in love with her.'

'Oh fuck, have *you* got problems!'

'I've an even bigger one. I didn't use anything, thought she was on the pill.'

'Sounds like shades of Livvy.' Sean rolled his eyes. 'You dozy sod!'

'I know.' he shrugged. 'All we can do is hope for the best.'

* * *

Jess flung down the phone. She sobbed into her dad's pillow and that's how he found her, ten minutes later.

As he struggled into the kitchen with loaded bags, Eddie heard cries of anguish and followed the sounds into the bedroom.

'Jess, darling, whatever's wrong?' He knelt beside the bed and stroked her hair. She looked at his kind, gentle eyes and concerned expression and wanted to confess everything.

'Hey, hey, love, come on. Nothing can possibly be this bad, surely?'

She sat up, tears streaming down her cheeks.

'What is it, Jess? Tell me, please.'

'It's nothing.'

'Of course it's something, you don't cry like this for nothing. Are you missing Nick?'

At the mention of Nick, she went completely to pieces. She sobbed, screamed and tore at her hair. Eddie picked up the phone and called Jane at the factory. He asked her to come home right away. He'd no idea what to do with Jess. Even directly following Nick's death her emotions had never been so out of control. He sat and held her until Jane arrived.

Taking one look at her hysterical daughter, Jane took her in her arms and hugged her. Jess was incoherent and neither Jane nor Eddie could understand a word she was saying, except what sounded like, 'Nick, Jon and I'm really sorry!'

'What do you think's wrong?' Eddie asked worriedly.

'Not a clue,' Jane said. 'But it's something to do with Nick. She's obviously missing him a lot more than we realise.'

As Jess's sobs subsided, Jane lay her back on the pillows and covered her with the duvet. Jess closed her eyes and fell into an uneasy sleep.

* * *

'Let's go downstairs and have a cup of tea while she has a little sleep,' Jane suggested. 'I think she's just overtired. God knows where she and Jon got to last night after they left Jason, but they weren't home until half twelve.'

'Must have met up with some mates,' Eddie said as they left the room. 'I think they could do with a holiday, Jess especially. A week in the sun, Spain maybe, would do them both good.'

'Well, *we* can't go away at the moment,' Jane said, following him into the kitchen. 'Not with Tim and Pat back on Saturday, and I don't want to take the kids out of school mid-term.'

'I didn't mean us,' Eddie said. 'They can go on their own.

Jess will be fine with Jon, he'll look after her. We'll discuss it with them tonight.'

Jane turned away as she brewed a pot of tea. She'd obviously been mistaken about Jess and Jon. Jess being so inconsolable about Nick just proved there was nothing going on other than sibling support.

* * *

Jess searched her dad's face for evidence that he might have guessed her guilty secret. Maybe she'd yelled it out during her attack of hysteria but there was nothing other than a concerned smile as he handed her a cup of tea and sat down on the bed next to her.

'Thanks, Dad,' she said. 'Gran's cure-all!'

'Feeling better for that little nap?' He smoothed her hair from her face and gently stroked her cheek.

'Yes, thank you,' she said, his gesture bringing a lump to her throat.

'Your mum and I think you need a holiday. When Jon gets home from work, we'll have a chat about sending you off to Spain for a week. How do you feel about that?'

Jess stared at him, wide-eyed. They couldn't possibly go away together, but she nodded her agreement as her mother walked into the room, looking anxiously at her.

'Are you feeling better, love?'

'Yes, thank you, Mum, much better.'

'Well, I *was* going to finish work early anyway. Would you like to go shopping, maybe into Stockport? We could have afternoon tea at Tiffin Time.'

Jess smiled and licked her lips. 'Their cakes are wonderful. Could we buy a plant or something and take it to Nick's grave? I'm ready to go and visit him now.'

'Of course. Sammy and Roy are going today, too. *They* say

they feel ready now. You all need to take things one step at a time.'

'Maybe we could pick up some travel brochures while we're in Stockport. Jon and I can browse through them later, see if there's anything we fancy,' Jess said, thinking it was best to play along with her dad's suggestion for now, until she had a chance to speak to Jon.

'It's a deal,' said Jane. 'There's a nice new travel agent just opened on the corner of Mersey Square. We'll try there. Finish your tea and I'll help you get dressed.'

* * *

Jon parked himself on a bench in St Peter's Square, chain-smoking and wondering what the hell he would do if Jess was pregnant. He should call her from a phone box before he went back to the shop. She'd sounded really upset earlier and with hindsight, he realised he hadn't been very reassuring. He checked his watch and realised he would be late back to work if he stopped to call her now. There was a phone in the staffroom out of Sean and Livvy's earshot. He'd use that to tell Jess he really did love her and they'd talk tonight.

He ground out the butt end of his cigarette and stood up. So absorbed in his thoughts, he'd been oblivious to the fine drizzle which had soaked his hair and was trickling down the neck of his leather jacket. He flicked up his collar, thrust his hands deep into his pockets and headed back to work.

* * *

Sean looked up from serving a customer and smiled at Jon. He followed him into the staffroom, telling Livvy to hold the fort for a minute. He closed the door and told Jon to sit down.

'While you were out, Roy called. I asked him to find out if

you had a problem at home. This was before your earlier confession.'

'And?' Jon frowned.

'Roy's spoken to Sammy and she told him your mum half suspects something's going on between you and Jess.'

'Fucking hell! You didn't tell Roy what we've done?'

'Don't be daft! I wouldn't betray your confidence, you should know that. But you and Jess are going to have to be very careful from now on, because Jane may be watching your every move.'

Jon shook his head. 'I can't believe this. I've really fucked up! It's my fault entirely, not Jess's. I should have listened to her when she said no. I'm gonna call her, I need to know she's okay. She was upset earlier and I wasn't very reassuring.'

'You do that and I'll keep Livvy out of the way for a few minutes.'

'Thanks, Sean, and thanks for not blowing us out to Roy.'

'Well, that's what mates are for. I don't for one minute condone what you've done but I understand how feelings get in the way of common sense. I've been there myself, although I might add, *not* with my sister!'

* * *

Jess wasn't home. Dad told Jon that Mum had taken her shopping. Jon listened, feeling even guiltier as Dad explained how Jess had been hysterical. He also told him that he thought a week in Spain might do the pair of them the world of good. Jon, his mind in a whirl, agreed, said goodbye and hung up. Reeling, he strolled into the shop and looked at Sean.

'We need to talk,' he mouthed over Livvy's head.

'Leave us alone for a few minutes, Liv,' Sean said. 'Go and help Ian in Instruments. What's wrong?' he asked as she left.

'You're not going to believe this. Mum and Dad want to

send me and Jess to Spain for a week. They think it will do us both good. Jess had a hysteria attack. Mum's taken her shopping and to pick up travel brochures. It doesn't make sense after what Roy told you.'

Sean stared open-mouthed. 'Jon, you can't possibly go away together. You'll have to think of a good excuse not to.'

'Yeah, but what?'

'Tell them you can't take time off. You've had two full weeks off for France and that week in Brighton.'

He nodded. 'I'll need a few days off in November too when I go and visit Grandma. I'll tell them I've used most of my annual leave; that should do it.'

'Well, you have, more or less. You wouldn't get paid if you took any extra time off this year. Mind you, that wouldn't matter to your dad, would it? He'd make sure you weren't out of pocket.'

'True, but he also knows I like to be independent. I'll try and explain tonight, see how it goes.'

'Tell him I can't spare you because Livvy needs time off for her antenatal clinics and stuff. You'll think of something convincing, I'm sure.'

* * *

Sammy knelt beside Nick's grave and removed the wilting flowers from the marble urn. Roy's parents were regular attendees and they'd brought fresh flowers each week until she and Roy were able to do it themselves. The marble headstone had been removed so that Nick's name could be added alongside Roy's Italian grandparents. At least Nick wasn't totally alone, she thought, as she arranged the fresh flowers in the urn and topped it up with water. She glanced at Roy, who was kneeling beside her and saw his face crumple. She put her arms around him as he sobbed heartbrokenly on her shoulder.

'It's not getting any easier,' he sniffed, wiping his eyes with the back of his hand.

'Not really,' she said. 'I can go for a few minutes without him on my mind and then wham, it hits me that I'll never see him again.'

They walked slowly back to the car park, their arms around one another.

'Are you going back to the factory, or are you going home?' he asked.

'Back to the factory. I told Jane to take time off to spend with Jess. Drive me back to the hotel to get my car, then take yourself off to see Ed.'

As they approached Roy's car, Jane's black Porsche swung into view. They watched as she leapt out and helped Jess up from the passenger seat. Jess carried a potted plant and smiled as she limped towards them.

Jane took Sammy to one side as Roy greeted Jess with a hug. Sammy listened as Jane told her about the hysteria attack and how Eddie had decided that Jess and Jon should take a short holiday. Sammy nodded, looking at Roy and Jess, who were talking.

'Poor kid, it takes time. Roy's just broken down, too. So, do you reckon now that you were definitely mistaken about her and Jon?'

Jane nodded. 'I honestly think I was. Jon's being supportive and concerned, like a loving brother should be. I told you I've got an overactive imagination. Fancy me thinking something like that about my own kids. She was in such a state. Ed was worried to death.'

Sammy gave her a hug. 'Give her time and lots of support. I'll get back to work and I'll see you at the airport tomorrow. You and Ed take the Jeep, I'll take the BMW and Mum and Tom will take their car, too. Pat and Tim will have loads of luggage, so we'll need as much boot space as possible.'

Jane nodded excitedly. 'I really can't wait. It's so nice to have something good to look forward to after the last few weeks.'

Sammy linked her arm through Jane's as they walked across to Roy and Jess.

'Ready, Sam?' Roy smiled.

'I am.' She took his hand and squeezed it. 'See you two tomorrow.' She waved as arm in arm, Jane and Jess made their way towards Nick's grave.

* * *

Jess was dozing, the holiday brochures on the floor beside her bed, when Jon knocked on the door.

'Come in.' She struggled to sit up and he was immediately by her side, lifting her easily and plumping up her pillows. He sat beside her, taking her hand.

'Hi.' He smiled.

'Hi, yourself,' she said with a wistful grin as he leant in to kiss her.

'I love you, Jess,' he said, stroking a straying lock of hair from her face.

Jess felt her stomach flip as she gazed into his eyes. 'I love you, too.'

'So what happened today?'

'I lost the plot. Everything crowded in on me – Nick's death and what's happening between us. It was all too much.' She stroked his cheek. 'And also I just needed to know that you really love me.'

'Oh, Jess, you silly girl! Of course I do, that's the whole point. Last night wouldn't have happened at all if I *didn't* love you. I've thought about nothing else all day. I want us to be a couple. Driving home tonight, I've been racking my brains, trying to work out how the hell we can do it. I think I've come up with a solution. I don't know what you'll think of my idea, and we don't have to do it yet, but it's there for the future.'

'What?' she asked, intrigued. Jess hadn't considered that she and Jon could *ever* have a future.

'Well,' he began, 'the way I see it, the only way we can do it is to move away. We could flat share. It's not uncommon for brothers and sisters to move away from home together. If we got a two-bedroomed flat, it would look like we're innocently sharing the rent and bills, etcetera. What do you think? We'll have to get new jobs, of course, but I've got the bulk of my inheritance from Celia to tide us over and you've still got a fair bit of yours.'

Jess stared at him. What he said made perfect sense; they could be together. 'Let's do it, but we'll wait until after Christmas and plan it properly. It's best if we're around this year, for Sammy, Roy and Jason and it's Pat and Tim's first Christmas home, too.'

Jon hugged her. 'Okay. There's something I have to tell you though. Sean overheard my conversation with you this morning. I told him what had happened. He more or less guessed anyway and I had to tell someone, the guilt was killing me. He won't say anything, but Roy told him that Mum spoke to Sammy about us and she suspects there's something going on.'

'No!' Jess was shocked. 'She can't possibly. Why would they suggest we go away to Spain on our own if Mum thought that? Roy and Sammy were at the graveyard earlier when Mum and I took a plant for Nick. Then Roy was here with Dad when we arrived home with the brochures. No one said a word to me that would suggest they'd any suspicions along those lines. Whatever Roy told Sean, it can't have been that.'

Jon shrugged. 'Well, whatever, we have to be very careful from now on.'

She smiled. 'I know.'

'We can't go on this holiday. It's not that I don't want to, because believe me, there's nothing I'd like better than to spend a whole week just loving you. But it wouldn't be right, Dad paying for it and everything.'

She nodded. 'Now all we have to do is convince the parents,' she said as Jane called upstairs to tell them dinner was ready.

* * *

Over dinner, Eddie had his own suggestion to help relieve Sean's staffing problems when Jon told him he couldn't be spared at work.

'I could do your job for a week. I've done it before and it would be a nice change,' he enthused.

'Ed, you can't,' Jane protested. 'Who'd collect the kids from school? No, if Jon can't take time off, then they can't go and that's that.'

'I need a few days off in November to visit Grandma,' Jon reminded them. 'Jess will be coming with me so it will be a nice little break for us.'

Jess nodded. 'I wouldn't be able to swim or anything if we were abroad and my wrist and ankle would miss out on physiotherapy for a week. Better if we leave it until next year.'

Her dad smiled and patted her hand. 'It's okay, I don't mind. I just thought it would do you both good. Actually, you could do me a favour while you're down in Hastings.'

'What's that?' Jon asked, tucking into his lasagne.

'Drive over to Brighton and check on Celia's place. Make sure the agent's doing his job properly. I'll treat you to a night or two in a hotel. The Ship Inn's nice, it's right on the front opposite the pier. The band always stayed there when we played The Pavilion.'

'Brilliant, Dad,' Jon said. 'We'll spend a couple of days with

Grandma and then a day or two in Brighton. Is that okay with you, Jess?'

'Perfect,' she replied.

'When are you going to take the house off the market, Dad?' Jon asked. 'All you've had are silly offers.'

'I don't know. I signed a contract on a no sale, no fee basis, but the property had to be on for a full six months. I'll get the paperwork out later and have a look at what date I signed it. You can go and see the agent, ask how the property market's doing. If it doesn't sell soon I'll keep it, have some work done and let it for the holiday season.'

Katie and Dominic, who had been having tea with their grandparents, arrived back at that moment, with Lennon on their heels, creating a noisy diversion.

'Right, you kids, bath and bed,' Jane ordered, getting up from the table. 'Will you clear up, Ed, and load the dishwasher, please?'

'Yeah, sure. Do you two fancy a bit of a jam session?' he asked Jon and Jess. 'Give your wrist a bit of exercise, Jess.'

They nodded enthusiastically.

'Right then, give me a hand with the dishes and we'll go and rock!'

26

Lying in the bubbles, Livvy reflected on Roy's visit to the shop. Initially upset, as the day wore on, her feelings had been replaced by anger and his refusal to allow her a contact number really hurt.

What the heck did he think she'd do? If she wanted to make a nuisance of herself, she could call his home. Anyway, until he moved into his flat he'd be easy enough to track down if the hotel he was staying in was local. The more she tossed the idea around, the more she liked it. Now she'd had all afternoon to mull things over there were things she wished she'd said to him. Clambering out of the bath, she wrapped a towel around her middle and made for the lounge.

She grabbed the *Yellow Pages* from under the coffee table and turned to hotels. Ruling out the larger establishments near the airport, she concentrated on smaller but exclusive hotels where Roy might seek more privacy. She tried two without success, but when the receptionist at The Grand in Wilmslow offered to put her through to Mr Cantello's room, she hung up, smiling.

She hurried to her bedroom, carefully applied her make-up

and pinned her hair up on top, leaving a few curly tendrils round her face. She pulled on black lacy knickers and a matching bra, then, having second thoughts, took the bra off. She slipped into a black, below-the-knee dress with a seductive side slit. Silky hold-up stockings and black high-heels finished the look.

She checked her appearance in the full-length mirror. Another week or two and she'd be unable to wear this dress. It clung to every curve, accentuating her baby bump, and the low-cut neckline showed off her new cleavage to perfection. Picturing Roy's face when he set eyes on her, she grabbed her car keys and handbag and before her nerve deserted her, dashed out to the car and drove the few miles to Wilmslow.

She could see Roy's car halfway down the car park. A quick glance around told her Sammy's Porsche wasn't here. She parked her Mini at the bottom behind a van. If by any chance Sammy arrived later, the car would be out of sight. Sammy would have no forewarning of her presence and may even find her and Roy together at the bar. On the other hand, what if she was already here? Roy might have picked her up. She may even have arrived by taxi. They could be having dinner together right now in the hotel restaurant. 'Stop being a wimp, Liv,' she muttered as she climbed out of the car. She smoothed her dress over her bump and went inside. A round-faced redhead on reception eyed her up and down.

'Good evening. Can I help you?'

'I'm looking for Roy Cantello.'

'Mr Cantello's in the bar.' The girl pointed to double glass doors opposite the desk.

'Thank you.' Livvy turned and walked towards the doors, feeling the girl's eyes burning into her. Dare she go in? She hesitated momentarily. Sod it! Why shouldn't she? As far as *she* was concerned, there was unfinished business between her and Roy. She pushed open the doors and strolled boldly through.

***

She spotted Roy immediately. He was sitting alone on a small sofa, reading a newspaper. He had his back to her, giving her an advantage. She saw him reach out to the table in front and pick up a glass. She waited until he'd taken a sip and returned the glass before she approached him.

She tapped him lightly on the shoulder and he spun round, frowning.

His eyes widened with shock. 'How the hell did you find me?'

'I let my fingers do the walking!'

'Huh?'

'*Yellow Pages.*'

'Oh. Right. But why? I thought I covered everything this morning.'

'You might have had *your* say, but *I* didn't. Do you mind if I sit down?'

'Feel free.' He moved over and made room.

Heart pounding, she sat beside him, crossing her legs. Her slit skirt revealed a lacy stocking top, which, she observed, didn't go unnoticed.

'Would you like a drink?' He knocked back the remainder of his brandy. 'I could do with another.'

'Orange juice, please.'

He frowned. 'Oh, of course, no alcohol.'

Her eyes followed him as he walked to the bar. He looked good in smart black trousers and a cream shirt. Her palms were sweating and she wiped them on the sofa's plush velvet pile. She smiled as he came back, placed the drinks on the table and sat down beside her, draping his arm across the back of the sofa.

He touched the loose tendrils of hair on the nape of her neck.

'It's a bloody good job Sammy's not here tonight!'

'If her car had been outside, I wouldn't have come in.'

He stared at her cleavage. 'You look nice, all round and womanly. So... have your drink, tell me what you want to say and then you'd better go, just in case Sam *does* decide to turn up.'

She leant forward to pick up her drink. Her breasts jiggled with the movement and she could feel her nipples stiffening as they rubbed against the fabric of her dress. 'Is that likely?'

He shrugged. 'Probably not, but you never know.'

'I'll take my chance.'

'Suit yourself.' He peeled his eyes away from her, picked up his drink and knocked it back. 'Should have got a double. I'll get another.'

As he went back to the bar, she took a sip of her drink. He was nervous, she could tell, but *she* was feeling braver by the minute.

'Come on then,' he said as he sat back down. 'What is it you want to say?'

'You upset me today,' she began, forcing a tear. 'I can't believe you don't want to see me again after everything we've been to one another.' She took a tissue from her bag and dabbed her eyes. 'I'm carrying your child. Doesn't that count for anything?' She watched as he gulped down a mouthful of brandy and twiddled the stem of his glass.

'Of course it does. But I'm terrified of losing Sam and Jason, and everything I've worked for. It's over between us, Livvy. It has to be.'

'I don't want it to be over.' She took another sip of orange juice, she could see beads of sweat on his top lip.

He was silent for a few seconds before replying. 'Well, it is. I've nothing more to say.' He finished his drink and stood up. 'Come on, I'll walk you to your car, then I'm having dinner and an early night.'

'*I* haven't eaten yet,' she said, fanning herself with her hand.

'I feel quite faint actually. It must be the stress of coming here.' She forced more tears as he helped her to her feet.

'You need some fresh air,' he said, leading her towards the door, but she pulled back.

'It's food I need, not fresh air.' She shrugged his hands away and watched his face as his jaw tightened.

'Go home then and get something to eat. You shouldn't have come here. Like I told you, it's over, there's nothing more to say.'

She glanced around. The bar was fairly crowded and people were watching them. Perfect, he wouldn't want a scene in public.

'How can you treat me this way?' she wailed. 'The least you can do is buy me dinner.'

Roy's eyes darkened and he pushed his hands in his pockets. 'No... I can't. Please go home.'

'I'm hungry,' she said, raising her voice. 'One meal, I'm not asking for much.' She lowered her voice slightly. 'After all, thanks to *you*, I'm feeding two!' She patted her bump.

Roy steered her out to reception. 'What the hell are you playing at?' he said, shaking her arm. 'Everybody's looking at us.'

'I'm not playing at anything,' she cried. 'Nobody heard me. Anyway, they'll probably all think you're my dad!'

'Hardly. People know who I am and that I don't have a daughter. It'll be all round bloody Wilmslow tomorrow. That's not going to do much for Sammy and Jason, is it?'

'Sorry, but I'm hungry.' She could see the redheaded receptionist staring at them as Roy ran his hands through his hair. 'Would it kill you to eat with me? If anyone asks, you can say I'm the daughter of a friend.'

'Okay,' he said. 'Just calm down. We'll eat and *then* you go. Right?'

She smiled through her tears. 'I'll pop to the ladies' and tidy my face. Will you wait here for me?'

'No, I'll be in the restaurant. Join me when you're ready.'

She nodded as he went through the swing doors. She turned to the redhead: 'Ladies' room?'

The girl pointed towards a corridor. 'Two doors down on the right.'

'Thank you,' Livvy said and hurried away.

* * *

Livvy looked around and smiled. The ladies' room was plush with marble sinks, soft pink towels and fresh flowers. She could get used this. She dabbed her cheeks to remove the mascara smudges and touched up her lipstick, pulled down a few more curly tendrils and adjusted her cleavage, pleased that she'd chosen to wear her best dress. A quick spray of perfume, a deep breath and she was ready to join him.

* * *

Roy ordered their food while Livvy gazed at her surroundings, taking in the elegantly dressed windows and richly patterned red carpet. The restaurant was fairly quiet and they were seated in a private alcove. She turned to Roy, who was staring at her. There was something in his eyes. She wasn't sure what, but he seemed more relaxed now than he'd been in the bar.

'You okay?'

She smiled. 'I've never been anywhere this posh before. Have you?'

'Frequently. When the band was at the height of its fame we stayed in some of the best hotels in the world. It's boring after the first half dozen or so. Hotel living can be very lonely.'

'Poor Roy.' She reached for his hand. 'It's my fault you're here.'

He jerked his hand away as the waiter brought over a bottle of wine.

'Madam?'

'Just a drop, please.' The waiter half-filled her glass and turned to Roy.

'Fill it up. Don't worry about me,' he said to her as the waiter walked away. 'I'm a big boy now, I can look after myself. How's work been today? Are Sean and Jon still being supportive?'

She nodded as another waiter placed a prawn and melon starter in front of her.

'Jon's been a bit on edge today about something. Sean kept sending me out of the way, so I couldn't find out what was going on. Jess called Jon this morning and after that, he seemed worse.'

'Really?' Roy raised an eyebrow. 'Perhaps he and Jess had a falling-out. You know what siblings are like.'

'Actually, I don't. I'm an only child.'

'Of course. Sorry, I forgot. Is there no one at all you can turn to besides me?'

'You know there isn't. You're so bothered about losing everything. But me, well – I've *nothing* to lose.' She toyed with her starter, poking it around the plate.

'Thought you were hungry,' he said. 'Better get stuck in.' He knocked back his wine and picked up the bottle. 'Want another?'

She shook her head.

'All the more for me then.'

After the main course, Roy finished the last of the wine and ordered coffees and a double brandy.

Livvy glanced at her watch: it was after ten. He'd hardly said a word during the meal, but was mellow and smiling now. He lit a cigarette and looked at her through a cloud of smoke. His eyes spoke volumes.

'I suppose I'd better go.' She pushed back her chair.

Roy stood up. 'I'll walk you to your car.'

She sighed as he took her arm and led her outside. He seemed distant again as he strolled beside her. Tonight wasn't going to end the way she was hoping it would. She unlocked the car door and stood on tiptoes to kiss his cheek.

'Is that all I get?' he teased as she moved away.

'It's all you deserve.'

He sighed and pulled her into his arms; he held her close and spoke into her hair.

'I'm sorry. I know I've hurt you but I don't know what else to do.' He tilted her chin and planted a gentle kiss on her lips.

She seized her moment and kissed him hard. She clung to him as his hands ran down her back and he grabbed her buttocks, pulling her close.

'Christ!' He stepped back. 'That wasn't supposed to happen.'

She moved in for another kiss. She could feel him twitching against her and ran her hand over his crotch. He lifted her off her feet, kissing her again.

'Now look what you've done,' he said. 'You'd better go.'

She smiled into his shoulder. 'Are you sure?' She looked into his eyes, searching his face.

'No!' He stared at a place above her head. She held her breath.

'Stay with me,' he whispered.

'Will it be okay?'

'Yeah. Sam's collecting me in the morning around eleven, but you'll be gone before then.'

'I'll leave early to go home and get ready for work,' she said. 'I've nothing with me. No clothes or shampoo, not even a toothbrush.'

'There's shampoo in the room and you can use my toothbrush,' he said.

'It's a deal.'

'Let's go. I'll ask for an alarm call.' He took her hand and led her back inside.

'An alarm call and two room service breakfasts for seven thirty, please, Sharon,' he said to the redheaded receptionist. 'And no calls to my room tonight.'

'Certainly, Roy,' she replied.

* * *

'Oh, it's gorgeous,' Livvy gasped as she stepped into his suite. 'Pink's my favourite colour, it's so... so me!'

'Yeah, it's not bad. Bit fussy for my taste, but it serves its purpose. There's a Jacuzzi in the bathroom. Go fill it and we'll jump in together.'

'Okay.' She hurried into the bathroom and turned on the taps. She smiled at her refection in the mirror. Just this one night with him and she'd be able to persuade him there should be more. She didn't object to being his mistress. What she *did* object to was no contact at all and she was sure now that that wasn't *his* choice. It was no doubt Sammy laying down the rules. She strolled back into the room. He was rummaging in the mini bar and produced a small bottle of brandy. After unscrewing the top, slugged it from the bottle.

'I need to call Sammy in a minute,' he said.

'Unzip me.' She stood with her back to him and he kissed the nape of her neck as he pulled down the zip of her dress. She stepped out of it, slipped it on a hanger and hung it in the wardrobe. She could feel his eyes burning into her, taking in her stockings and skimpy lace knickers. She turned and smiled as he knelt in front of her.

'Livvy, for God's sake, woman, you drive me crazy!' He caressed her breasts and kissed her rounded belly. He tugged at her knickers, pulling them down slowly, teasingly, with his teeth.

'Roy, make your phone call first,' she said, pushing him gently backwards.

'Okay.' He sighed, tearing himself away. 'Go and wait in the bath for me, I won't be a minute.'

* * *

As she lay in the bath, Livvy could hear Roy speaking to Sammy, who, from what he was saying, appeared to be already in bed. He talked for a few minutes about the arrangements for tomorrow and finished with, 'I'm just about to jump in the bath and have an early night myself. See you in the morning. Yeah, I love you, too.'

She heard him hang up and he was quiet for a moment. She guessed he was feeling guilty. Sammy trusted him and here he was, about to betray that trust again. Well, she thought, there was sod all they could do about it. She was here, in the bath, waiting. There was no way he would tell her to go home now. She smiled as he hurried into the bathroom, throwing off his clothes.

* * *

Sammy woke early and leapt out of bed. She stretched in front of the full-length mirror and smiled at her reflection. At last she could see light at the end of the tunnel. Pat was on her way home and Roy – well, he would be with her later and she was so looking forward to seeing him again. She took a quick shower, dried her hair and was about to go downstairs when the bedside phone rang. She glanced at her watch: 7:00 a.m. Who could be calling so early? Roy? A shiver ran down her spine as she snatched up the phone.

'Hello.'

'It's Jane,' an excited voice told her.

'You're up early.' Sammy smiled into the receiver.

'Couldn't sleep, I'm on such a high! I've checked on TV and listened to the news on the radio and there's been no plane crashes, so that's promising, isn't it?'

'Jane! For crying out loud, what are you like?' Jane hated flying and was like a cat on hot bricks while anyone she knew was in the air.

'I can't help the way I am. Did you see Roy last night?'

'No, I stayed home and relaxed. I went shopping straight from work. I've filled the fridge and freezer and topped up the drinks cupboard and wine racks so we won't go short over the weekend. You and Ed must come for dinner tonight. I'm toying with the idea of asking Roy to stay over this weekend and then he can move straight into his flat from here on Monday. You're all coming for Sunday lunch, too, aren't you?'

'Yes, we'll be there. I'll get Jon and Jess to babysit tonight. Roy will be so happy if you ask him to stay. I'd better finish getting ready. See you later, bye.'

Jane rang off and Sammy decided to call Roy before making breakfast.

* * *

Roy sat up, signalling frantically to Livvy, who was wrapping herself around him, to be quiet. They were in the middle of making love and Livvy groaned at being disturbed. She lay quietly on top of him, eyes opening wide as he mouthed it was Sammy and not the alarm call coming early.

'I'm sorry, did I wake you?' Sammy asked.

'No, I was already half awake,' he replied. 'What's up, why have you called so early?'

'Would you like to check out of the hotel this morning and

spend the weekend at home with us? I'd really like you here. That's if you want to, of course.'

He gasped as Livvy disappeared under the bedcovers. He took a deep breath and tried to concentrate on what Sammy was saying. His voice came out an octave higher as Livvy's mouth worked its magic.

'Yes, Sam, that would be great,' he panted, trying to fight the wonderful sensations Livvy was giving him.

'You okay, Roy, you sound a bit odd?'

'I'm fine, really. Got cramp in my left foot. I'll go now, try and get rid of it. See you later.' He hung up and dived under the covers to drag Livvy out. 'You little minx!' He rolled her onto her back. 'You get me into some bloody trouble, you do. Let's finish what we started before breakfast arrives.'

She grinned and wrapped her legs around his back, sighing blissfully as he slid into her again.

'What would be lovely?' she asked when Roy eventually cried out and rolled off her.

'What?' He lay back against the pillows, panting.

'What you said to Sammy while I was under the covers.'

'Oh, so you could still hear what I was saying, could you?' He pulled her into his arms. 'You'll get me hung, drawn and quartered one of these days.'

'Well, *what* would be lovely?' she repeated, snuggling closer.

He sighed. 'You won't like it. Sam wants me to stay at Jasmine House this weekend.'

'Will you be sleeping with her?'

'We'll probably be in the same bed.'

'That's not what I meant, Roy. Will you be making love to her?'

He shrugged. 'I don't presume anything any more.'

'But if Sammy wants to, will you?'

'Stop it, Livvy! I don't want this conversation. Let's not spoil what we've just enjoyed by arguing.'

'Okay, I'm sorry. Can we do it one more time before I have to go?'

'I can't, Livvy, not so soon. I'm forty-two, remember, not twenty-two like you. I need a rest in-between these days and we haven't the time. You've got to get out of here before Sammy arrives. Come on, get up.'

'Please, Roy, just try.' She reached down but he grabbed her hands.

'No, I'm knackered. You wore me out last night and finished me off just now. I thought you'd have had enough yourself. You're more randy than ever now you're pregnant!'

'But I don't know when I'll see you again, do I?' she said wistfully.

He shrugged. 'Let's play it by ear. I don't want to cause problems at home with Pat and Tim staying there. I'll try and call you over the weekend or early next week and I'll transfer that money into your account on Monday, so you can go shopping for some clothes. That dress just about fitted where it touched last night. God knows what people must have thought.'

'Will the receptionist tell Sammy I stayed with you?'

'It's more than her job's worth. Anyway, Sammy won't need to come inside. I'll meet her in the car park.' He climbed out of bed, dragging Livvy with him. 'Shower, go on, get in and I'll join you. Breakfast won't be long.'

* * *

Sammy frowned as she replaced the receiver. Roy had sounded really odd and he'd rung off abruptly. The hairs on the back of her neck prickled. Something was wrong: he wasn't alone, she just knew it. But who could he be with? Surely not Livvy? He wouldn't dare, would he?

She rummaged in her handbag and found the piece of paper with Livvy's phone number. She dialled and it rang and rang. The girl might be in the shower and couldn't hear the phone ringing, or maybe she'd already left for work.

She waited five minutes and dialled again; still no reply. She pulled on a pair of jeans and a sweater, grabbed her handbag and keys and ran out of the house. Jumping into her car, she shot off towards Wilmslow. In the hotel car park, her headlights picked out Roy's car in the morning gloom. Down near the bottom, her sharp eyes spotted a red Mini. She pulled up alongside it and clambered out.

Sammy could see nothing through the windows that would identify the vehicle as belonging to Livvy. Anyway, it probably wasn't her car and she was overreacting. Not answering the phone didn't necessarily mean the girl was here with Roy.

'Get a bloody grip,' she muttered. 'You may as well join him for breakfast now. Tell him you wanted to surprise him.' She walked into reception, where the redhead was filing her nails, dashed past her, ran up the stairs and knocked on the door of Roy's suite. 'Room service!' she called. He threw open the door, a towel around his waist. His jaw dropped as she marched in and pushed him out of the way. Her eyes took in the rumpled bed and clothes strewn on the floor. Roy stood holding his head in his hands as Livvy strolled out of the bathroom, naked.

'Is that breakfast? I'm starving.' She stopped, eyes widening in horror.

'You little bitch!' Sammy lunged as Roy sprang between them.

'No, Sammy, no! She's pregnant, leave her alone. It's not her fault. I invited her over for dinner because I was lonely and I asked her to stay.'

Sammy rounded on him.

'Lonely! How the fuck are you lonely? After everything we've done together this week and everything you've promised me.' She turned to Livvy. 'Has he told you I've been coming here at lunchtime and we've been making love? No, judging by the look you're giving me, he hasn't.'

'She knows I've seen you at lunchtimes,' Roy faltered as Livvy's face crumpled.

'He's using us both, Livvy,' Sammy ranted. 'Two stupid women who can't resist him! What an ego booster, you bastard! Well, that's it as far as I'm concerned. You're welcome to him. You'll both be hearing from my solicitor next week. I never want to set eyes on you again, Cantello, as long as I live. Don't you dare come near me, Jason, or the house again!'

Giving him one last burning look, Sammy turned and marched out of the room.

With shaking hands, Roy closed the door, walked across the room and collapsed onto the bed. That final look had contained such anger, hurt and betrayal it would remain etched in his memory for ever.

* * *

The rush of adrenaline carried Sammy down the stairs, past the receptionist and out to her car. She started up the engine and drove to Hanover's Lodge on automatic pilot. Climbing out of the car, she spotted Lennon cocking his leg against Jane's Porsche. He ran back indoors. She followed him into the warm kitchen and surprised Eddie by collapsing into his arms.

He called for Jane to come quickly and she raced downstairs in her towelling robe, freshly washed hair flapping around her face. She looked in dismay at her friend's pale and stricken face and led her to a chair. 'Tea!' she ordered Eddie. 'Put plenty of sugar in it.'

'She doesn't take sugar,' he began.

'Just do it, Ed. What is it, Sam? Has there been a plane crash?'

Sammy shook her head.

'What then? For God's sake, what's wrong?'

'Roy,' Sammy uttered in a strangled voice.

'What about him?' Jane shook her gently. 'What about Roy? Has something happened to him?'

Sammy opened her mouth but nothing came out. She closed it and burst into tears.

* * *

Eddie grabbed the phone and dialled The Grand. 'Room 125, please.' His eyes opened wide as the phone was answered. 'Livvy? It's Eddie, is Roy there?'

'He can't talk right now,' Livvy sobbed down the line. 'Sammy just came to the hotel and found us together.'

'It's okay, you don't need to say any more. Tell him I'll call back later and he'd better have a bloody good explanation.' Eddie hung up, looking at Jane's shocked face over the top of Sammy's head.

'No!' Jane shook her head in disbelief.

'Yes!'

She blinked back tears and sat down in front of Sammy, taking her friend's cold hands into her own. 'Why?'

Sammy shrugged. 'I don't know,' she whispered. 'We were so happy yesterday. I don't understand it. I called him after I spoke to you earlier and asked if he'd like to stay over the weekend. He sounded odd, sort of breathless; his voice was different. He told me he'd got cramp in his foot and hung up quickly. Oh God,' Sammy looked at Eddie and Jane in despair, 'it's just dawned on me – he was screwing her. I wouldn't have been any the wiser if I hadn't called him. She'd have been long gone before I picked him up and he would have been sharing *my* bed tonight. I bet he's never stopped seeing her and after all the promises he made me this week. I can't believe I've been so bloody stupid to fall for all those lies about loving me and not letting me down. I wouldn't have slept with him again if I'd known he was still seeing her.

'Christ, I feel dirty, used. He told me yesterday no one could love me like he does and then... this.' Her hands shook as she took the mug of sweet tea Eddie handed her. 'The marriage is over now, believe me.'

* * *

Livvy put down the phone and looked at Roy, who was lying on the bed, staring silently up at the ceiling. She felt helpless and didn't know what to do or say so busied herself making coffee from the hospitality tray. She placed them on the bedside table, lay down next to Roy and put her arms round him.

'I'm so sorry. Why did you take all the blame? It was my fault, not yours.'

He looked at her and shook his head. 'No, Liv, I asked you to stay when I should have told you to go home.'

'But Sammy said she doesn't want to see you again and she sounded as though she really meant it.'

'She *did* mean it, believe me.' He sat up. 'Shit, what a fucking mess I've made of things!'

'I shouldn't have come here,' Livvy said tearfully. 'I only wanted one more night with you. Now I've ruined everything for your family.'

'Stop it! Think of the baby. It won't do any good to get upset. I should have sent you packing, but I didn't. What about you? Now you know I've been sleeping with Sammy again.'

'She's your wife. You were trying to patch things up.'

He rubbed his eyes. 'Well, that's it, my marriage is over. She's made the decision for me. I'll have to speak to Ed next time he calls. Sam's obviously gone to his place. He and Jane will look after her.'

Livvy sighed. 'I'd better go home, I need to go to work soon.'

'Don't leave me,' he begged. 'I don't want to be on my own today. Jon will know what's happened and he'll tell Sean you're with me.'

'Well, I'll have to get clothes from my flat,' she said. 'I can't wear that black dress all day. I need clean underwear and my make-up and stuff.'

'We'll go shopping later and I'll buy you some new clothes. Your things are too small for you now anyway. Just give me a bit of time to compose myself. Breakfast will be here soon. You need to eat and look after that baby.'

As he spoke, there was a knock on the door. Roy let in the receptionist, carrying a tray.

'Breakfast, Mr Cantello,' she said as Livvy turned away from her curious gaze.

'Thanks, Sharon.' Roy handed her a five-pound tip and closed the door.

'Maybe Sammy will change her mind when she's had time to calm down,' Livvy said, parking herself on the bed and buttering a slice of toast. 'I could try talking to her, tell her it was my fault.'

'It won't do any good. She gave me one last chance and I blew it. I knew I was skating on very thin ice when I asked you to stay.'

'But, Roy, you *should* talk to her. Don't you even want to try?'

'I couldn't face it. But I guess the least I can do is call Ed, make sure she's alright.'

* * *

Jane answered Roy's call. '*You've* got a bloody nerve,' she said and handed the phone to Eddie.

'Roy, I'll go upstairs and talk to you privately. Hang on a

minute, mate. Jane, put that phone down when I pick up in our room,' Eddie ordered.

She nodded and slammed down the receiver as soon as she heard Eddie's voice.

Sammy drained her cup and sighed. 'I suppose I'd better go back home and finish getting ready.'

'Don't you want to wait and hear what Roy has to say?'

'No! I want nothing more to do with him. I don't think I can ever forgive him for this. I'm totally devastated, more so than I felt the other day when I found out she was pregnant. I honestly thought we'd turned a corner. I mean, yesterday at Nick's grave Roy cried and we held each other. We had a lovely lunchtime and yet he *still* had to spend the night with her. I just don't understand it. She obviously means more to him than he realises.'

Sammy stood up to go and Jane put her arms around her and hugged her.

'I'm so sorry, Sam, I really am. This is the last thing we need, today of all days.'

Jon strolled into the kitchen, making them jump. 'Hi, Sammy, you're up early. What's up?' He frowned at their tear-stained faces.

'You tell him, Jane. I'll go home. Jason will be up soon and he'll wonder where I am. I'll see you at the airport in a couple of hours. Meet me in the arrivals hall.'

Sammy left as Jon poured coffee and popped a slice of bread into the toaster.

'So?' He raised an eyebrow at Jane.

'Can't you guess?'

'I've a pretty good idea. Roy and Livvy?'

'She spent the night at the hotel with him. Sammy had her suspicions, went to the hotel and caught them together first thing.'

'You're joking? Fucking hell! Oh, sorry, Mum.'

'It's alright, Jon. I feel like swearing myself.'

'What the hell is he playing at? He came into work yesterday and told Livvy he couldn't see her on her own again. Now you tell me they spent the night together. He's crazy.'

Eddie walked into the kitchen, shaking his head.

'Well?' Jane asked.

'I wash my hands of him for now, I can't be doing with it.'

'What did he say?'

'Just what Sammy told us. He asked Livvy to spend the night with him. Sam called him this morning and then she turned up at the hotel shortly afterwards. I told him she doesn't want him back. He said he realises he's well and truly blown it this time. Livvy's staying with him today and he'll catch up with us later. Obviously, he wants to see Pat and Tim, if they want to see him, of course.'

'Pat won't.' Jane folded her arms. 'I can tell you that now. You and Tim can meet up with him later but don't bring him here 'cos I'll bloody kill him!'

Jon finished his breakfast and stood up. 'Right, I'm off.'

'Bye, Jon. Oh, will you and Jess look after the kids tonight while we spend some time with Tim and Pat?' Jane called as he opened the back door.

'Yeah, no problem. See you later.'

* * *

Jon unlocked his car and could feel the grin splitting his face. Fantastic, a night alone with Jess. Get Katie and Dom to bed as early as possible, crack open a bottle of Dad's wine, relax together and see what happens.

27

Sammy, Tom and Molly were standing in arrivals as Jane and Eddie arrived.

Sammy waved them over and pointed to the flight arrivals board. 'There, it's landed, just.'

'Thank God for that.' Jane let out a huge sigh and flung her arms around Sammy. 'I can relax a bit now.'

'They'll be ages in baggage reclaim and customs. Shall we get a coffee while we wait?' Eddie suggested.

'Good idea, black for me,' Sammy said. 'I'm off to the ladies'. Coming with me, Jane?'

Molly stared after Sammy and Jane, then turned to Eddie, who'd found them a table. 'So, where is he?' she demanded as Tom went off to order drinks.

'What's Sammy told you?' Eddie replied cagily.

Molly frowned. 'Nothing, other than that he can't make it. What's going on? I've bitten my tongue for long enough over the mess those two are in. Something's very wrong. Roy's been looking forward to this day for ages. Sammy told me last night that she was collecting him from the hotel, now suddenly he can't make it? He's seeing that bloody girl again, isn't he? Don't bother to deny it, Ed. Just wait till I get my hands on him, he'll wish he'd never been born!' Her voice shook and Tom, who had returned with a tray of mugs, patted her shoulder.

'Molly, love, don't jump to conclusions. He might have been genuinely delayed.'

'How could he be? Sammy was picking him up. What could possibly delay him? Roy wouldn't miss this for the world unless there was a damn good reason.' She narrowed her eyes and turned to Eddie: 'Did Sammy go to the hotel for him?'

'Yes.'

'Well, where is he then?'

Eddie sucked in his breath. 'He wasn't alone.'

'What? You mean he had *another* woman with him? How many bloody affairs has he had?'

'It wasn't another woman, it was Livvy.'

Her jaw dropped. 'So he *is* seeing her again? No wonder Sammy's upset. Well, she needs to divorce him good and proper now.'

Eddie spotted Jane and Sammy and waved them over. 'The girls are back, change the subject.'

* * *

Sammy smiled warily as she sat down and reached for a mug of coffee. No doubt her mum had pounced on Ed and given him the third degree as soon as her back was turned. She was gratified to see him wink reassuringly at her. She glanced across to the doors, where several passengers, laden with luggage, were filtering through. 'Do you think this lot is from Pat and Tim's flight?'

'I wouldn't have thought so,' Tom said. 'Drink your coffee and relax for a few minutes. They'll be here soon enough.'

Sammy sighed as she put down her mug. Feeling calmer, she tried to blank out the caring look on Roy's face earlier when he'd protected Livvy from her wrath. Sammy had almost felt like the other woman for a few minutes. It should have been *her* he was protecting, not that little bitch. 'Let's stand by the barrier,' she said after another fifteen minutes had ticked slowly by and her thoughts were turning positively murderous.

Standing beside the barrier, scanning every face for a familiar one, she and Jane spotted Pat simultaneously. 'There she is!' they shrieked, leaping up and down.

'Bloody hell, look at the length of Tim's hair!' Eddie exclaimed as Tim, long blond hair swept back in a ponytail, appeared.

'Oh, look at the girls!' Molly, who hadn't seen her blonde-haired, blue-eyed granddaughters in over two years, swept Kim and Abby into her arms. 'How grown-up you are.'

After much hugging, kissing and backslapping, Tim looked around. 'Well, where is he?'

Sammy bit her lip. 'I'll explain when we get home.'

Pat looked at her stepsister with concern. 'Oh, Sam,' she said, her blue eyes brimming.

Sammy put on a brave smile and took Pat's arm. 'No tears. He's not worth it. Come on, let's go home and start our new lives.'

* * *

Roy and Livvy left the hotel together. She insisted on driving back to her flat for a change of clothes before he took her shopping.

'I'm taking my car home first,' she said as they strolled through the car park. 'Do you want to follow me?'

Roy nodded. 'You go home and wait for me. There's something I need to do first.'

She looked at him, eyes wide. 'Are you going to go and see Sammy, after all?'

'I wouldn't dare. After last time she'd probably finish the job off good and proper with the scissors! I'm going to visit my folks. I need to tell them what's happened, before Sammy does. I'll also tell them about you and the baby. I owe them that much.' He sighed and continued. 'I don't suppose they'll be too pleased with me but at least it will give them time to get used to the idea of becoming grandparents again.'

Livvy rested her hand on his arm. 'Roy, I *do* love you, I *really* do. I feel bad for taking so much away from you.'

He pulled her close. 'Livvy, I love you too, never doubt that. It's my own fault that I've lost everything. Are you quite sure you want to be stuck with an old geezer like me for the rest of your life? You're so beautiful, you could have anyone you want, baby or no baby.'

'Roy, it's *you* that I want and only you. I always have done. Age doesn't come into it. I don't regret our affair, and I certainly don't regret carrying your child. I just want to make you happy, that's all.'

He stroked her cheek. 'I'm not an easy man to live with. I can be real hard work at times. I'm untidy and noisy, I get totally paranoid and chain-smoke if things aren't going right when I'm working on new songs.'

'I think I can learn to live with that. You're also very loving and kind and I like those qualities in a man.'

'Well, at least we've got a basis to work with. I'm willing to give us a go if you are. Sammy will throw the book at us and we'll probably end up all over the papers. Can you cope with it?'

'Why would that happen? No one knows about us other than your close friends and people at work.'

'And the people at the hotel who saw us together last night and today when we go out shopping. I'm a face that people recognise, Livvy. I try to ignore it, but it doesn't go away. There are often reports in magazines and papers about what Ed and I are up to. When Nick died, there were reporters all over the place – they don't miss a bloody trick. I'm trying to protect you here,' he said, seeing the panic in her eyes. 'Just keep your head down and don't speak to anyone you don't know, no matter how persuasive they are.'

'I'll be fine,' she said. 'Go and see your parents now, get that out of the way first.' She kissed him and they went their separate ways.

* * *

Roy spotted his mother on the opposite side of Chatsworth Road. He pulled onto the drive of the bungalow he'd bought for his parents. Monty the Third, an overweight Springer Spaniel, who'd replaced Roy's boyhood pet *and* his predecessor, was dragging her along the road.

'Hello, Mum,' he called, getting out of his car. He kissed her as she reached him.

'Hello, son,' she said as Monty wriggled on his back with delight by Roy's feet. He bent to tickle the dog's tummy as his mother continued, 'I thought you'd be at the airport.'

'Err, no, change of plan,' he stammered. His mother always had the knack of making him feel like a naughty schoolboy and the frown crossing her chubby face now meant business.

'What do you mean, change of plan? What have you been up to? You've guilt oozing from every pore, I can smell it!'

'There's something I need to talk to you about,' he said, stomach looping as they walked towards the front door.

She pursed her lips in time-honoured fashion. 'Well, you'd better come in then. Your dad's out, he's taken some rubbish to the tip. Come through to the kitchen and I'll put the kettle on.'

Roy sat on a stool at the breakfast bar, Monty by his feet. His mother switched on the kettle and reached into the cupboard for mugs and a jar of Nescafé.

'Well, come on, out with it.'

'I've got a surprise for you, Mum.' He stared at her back, cringing as she paused, a spoonful of coffee granules poised above a mug. 'You're going to be a grandma again.'

She turned, mouth agape. 'What?' She dropped the spoon into the mug and smiled. 'It's a miracle. You never let on that Sammy had had her sterilisation reversed. Were you keeping it a secret in case it didn't work? Oh, love, you must be over the moon.' She went on and on in the same vein as Roy rolled his eyes heavenward.

It had never crossed his mind that his mother would think it was Sammy who was pregnant. God Almighty, was the woman an idiot, or was she in denial? She knew about his affair with Livvy and his estrangement from Sammy, so why wasn't she putting two and two together like she usually did? Roy took the mug of coffee she handed him and sighed.

'What is it, Roy? Aren't you happy about the baby? It's what you both need, it will bring you closer.'

He braced himself. 'Mum, you've got the wrong end of the stick. Sammy isn't pregnant. It's Livvy, my girlfriend. Me and Sam, well, it's over.'

She sat down heavily on a stool, the colour draining from her cheeks.

'Roy... no! How could you? Sammy must be devastated.'

'She doesn't want me, Mum.'

'Well, can't you talk her round? Surely you can't be serious about Livvy? She's only a bit of a kid. Are you quite sure it's your baby?'

'Yes, of course it's mine. I *am* serious about her. She's *not* a bit of a kid and Sammy won't be talked round under any circumstances.' He wasn't prepared to tell her of the morning's happenings. She looked shocked enough without him making things worse.

'So, where is this girl, then?'

'At her flat; I'm joining her later. I love her, Mum. I also love Sammy and would prefer to stay married to her, but she doesn't want to see me again. I'm going to try and make a go of it with Livvy. She needs looking after, she has no one except me.'

His mum sucked in her breath. 'You're a bloody fool, Roy, but you're my lad at the end of the day and blood's thicker than water. God help you when this gets out! You need to keep a low profile for a while to let the dust settle.'

'That's impossible. We're re-forming the band and hoping to put out a new single as soon as we can, and go on tour. I don't know how Eddie and Tim will feel about working with me at the moment though.'

'You lads always stick together, have done since you were kids. They'll stand by you. Here's your father, you can tell him your news while I visit the bathroom.'

Roy smiled as his dad strolled into the kitchen.

'Our Roy's got something to tell you, Bob,' his mother called over her shoulder.

'Oh, and what's that?' Roberto Cantello, dark eyes twinkling, grinned at his only son and offered him a cigarette.

'You'd better sit down, Dad.' Roy held out his lighter and lit up himself.

'Oh, oh, sounds serious. What have you been up to now?'

He told his tale and Dad took the news better than Roy thought he would.

'I suppose we'd better meet this young lady. Where's she from and how did you get involved with her?'

'She's from Glasgow, she was a friend of Nick and Jason's.' Roy took a lengthy drag on his cigarette as his father's eyebrows shot up his forehead.

'So she's younger than you?'

'She's twenty-two, Dad,' Roy said, feeling the heat rush to his cheeks.

'You lucky bugger,' Dad said, lowering his voice. 'The times

I've tried to trade your mother in for a newer model, but never one as young as that.'

'I'm not lucky. Like Mum says, I'm a fool. I've lost the best wife in the world, my eldest boy's dead and Jason doesn't want to know me. I'll also lose a fortune, because Sammy will demand half of everything.'

'Well, face it, Roy, you're not short of money and Sammy's worked hard, keeping you on the straight and narrow. You'd have lost every penny to drink and drugs in the past if she hadn't been behind you.'

'I know that, but if Ed says he doesn't want to work with me, God knows what I'll do for the future. I might end up having to write songs on my own.'

'Ed will stand by you, like you've always done for him.'

'Let's hope you're right. Livvy has a brilliant voice and I've plans to manage *her* career. She can support me and the kid if needs must,' Roy quipped as his mother reappeared.

'So, when's this baby due?' she asked.

'Beginning of March.'

'She's four months gone already and you've only just decided to tell us?'

'I only found out myself on Wednesday night. She was keeping it from me – she knew me and Sam were having problems and didn't want to add to them.'

'What made her decide to tell you then?' his mother persisted.

'Livvy didn't tell me, Sammy did.'

'You mean she told Sammy first. Well, the devious little madam!'

'Mum, the details don't matter. I don't want to keep going over it again and again – it's been a painful week all round.'

'It will be even more painful if Sammy uses her dressmaking shears on you,' his dad said.

Roy smiled weakly and stood up to leave.

His mother put her arms around him. 'You'll never learn, will you, Roy?' She shook her head wearily. 'We'd better meet this Livvy, then. Bring her for lunch tomorrow, about two.'

'Okay, Mum. Thanks for not being too angry with me.'

'What's the point? You've made your bed.' She patted his shoulder. 'There's been enough heartache this year without us turning our backs on you. Both you and Sammy need our support and you'll get it. We won't take sides. But try and grow up a bit now, son, for this new baby's sake if no one else's.'

* * *

'So, what now, Sam?' Pat asked as she, Jane and Sammy were comfortably ensconced in the lounge at Jasmine House. Pat had learnt the full extent of the week's happenings as well as that morning's and was horrified by Roy's betrayal and the news of Livvy's pregnancy. Tim had disappeared with Eddie to Hanover's Lodge, Abigail and Kim had been taken by their grandparents to visit relatives, leaving the threesome to catch up.

Sammy shook her head. 'I've no choice now other than to divorce him.'

'You do,' Jane said. 'Earlier this week, you said you'd fight to keep him.'

'That was before today, Jane. I mean, finding out about the affair was one thing and the baby was a horrendous shock. But to see them together this morning in that room, the rumpled bed, their clothes on the floor and the pair of them fresh out of the shower... That's when it hit me for real. They looked a couple. Right and comfortable with each other and suddenly *I* was the outsider. I've never seen them together before, apart from onstage at Nick's party. It was an awful shock, even though I suspected she was with him.' Sammy took a deep breath and continued.

'*She* looked as horrified as *I* felt. When Roy defended her, well, that was the worst thing. I made a lunge at her. I was going to slap her across the face and he stepped in between us. He told me to stop because she's pregnant. He was protecting her like she's his property, which I suppose she is. She was really shocked when I told her Roy and I had been sleeping together. It's pathetic, but I had to have a dig at her and that was all I could come up with.'

Pat sighed. 'Maybe it will put her off him. Make her realise what a bastard he is.'

'I doubt it. They don't seem able to stay away from one another. Can you just imagine how it will be when that baby arrives? There's no way Roy will be able to resist seeing it. He loves kids, he's a big softie at heart. He's lost Nick, Jason doesn't want to know him. The baby will be all he's got. I might as well let him go now rather than face all the inevitable pain and heartache next year.'

'Put like that, I suppose you've got a point,' Jane reluctantly agreed.

'I have to face it, it really *is* over.' Sammy's eyes filled with tears that tumbled down her cheeks.

Pat and Jane stared helplessly at one another. Neither knew quite how to console Sammy.

'I'll make a fresh pot of coffee,' Jane announced and escaped to the kitchen as Jason strolled into the house, followed closely by Jules.

'Hi, Jane. Are they here?' Jason grinned good-naturedly.

'Tim's out with Ed. Pat's in the lounge with your mum. Tread carefully, please, Jason. There's been an incident with your dad this morning. I expect your mum will explain later.'

Jason's good looks darkened. 'What's the bastard done this time?'

'Wait until later, Jason, please,' Jane pleaded.

'Okay. C'mon, Jules, we'll go through.'

Sammy looked up through her tears as the boys walked in.

Pat leapt up and threw her arms around her nephew. 'You look well, Jason, and who's this young man?'

'This is my friend Jules,' he replied. 'Jules, meet my Auntie Pat. She's married to Tim, The Raiders' bass player. And where's Dad?' Jason raised his eyebrows enquiringly.

'Not here,' his mum replied.

'So *where* is he?'

She shrugged. 'At the hotel with Livvy, I presume.'

'Mum, you've got to call it a day.'

She nodded. 'First thing on Monday, I'll see my solicitor. I promise you. I'm divorcing him.'

'You should go out with Stuart again, Mum, he really likes you. I could tell by the way he looked at you on Thursday night.'

Sammy blushed while Pat looked at her, eyebrows raised.

'You went out with Stuart Green? You never said.'

'I haven't had a chance yet,' she replied.

'Jules and I will go up to my room while you three have a good gossip. I bet if you talked for a whole year, you still wouldn't catch up,' Jason teased.

'Cheeky monkey!' Sammy smiled, tears forgotten for the moment. 'By the way, Jules, the black and purple eye colouring is very fetching. It matches your shirt.'

'I don't bear him any grudges, Mrs Cantello,' Jules said. 'It must have been quite a shock for him. But Jason tells me you gave him an even bigger shock later.'

'You can say that again. It wasn't Roy's night. Anyway, we'll see you boys in a while.'

'So, come on, you.' Pat turned to Sammy as the boys left the room. 'What happened with Stuart, then?'

Jane waltzed in with the coffee pot and grinned. 'Tell her what he said about you being the right girl for him, before you started dating Roy.'

Pat smiled knowingly as Sammy related her night out with Stuart 'I knew he always had a soft spot for you, but *you* could never see it.'

'That's what I said.' Jane grabbed the phone from the side table. 'Call him, ask him over tonight.'

'I can't do that, Jane. Can I?'

'Course you can. Tim would love to see him again and so would Pat, wouldn't you?'

Pat nodded enthusiastically.

'He might think I'm chasing him.'

'So what if he does? Start as you mean to go on. Call him, or I will.' Jane thrust the phone at Sammy.

Rolling her eyes, Sammy dialled Stuart's number. 'Hi, Stu, it's Sammy. Yes, they're back safe and sound.' She smiled at Pat. 'Would you like to come round tonight for dinner? Brilliant. See you about eight then. Bye.' She replaced the receiver, smiling broadly.

Jane grinned at her. 'See, that was dead easy, wasn't it?'

'Don't you go reading anything into it,' Sammy said. 'We're just good friends, that's all.'

'He's asked you to go to London with him,' Jane said slyly.

'Well, that's business, not pleasure.'

'You'll be staying in a nice hotel. The trip could turn to pleasure if you wanted it to.'

'Oh God, I couldn't! It's too soon. I've only ever been with Roy, I wouldn't know what to do!' Sammy exclaimed.

'Well, they're all built to the same design. There's no mystery. Anyway, with what you've learnt with Roy over the years you could give Stuart a brilliant time in bed. He'd think it was Christmas and his birthday rolled into one!'

'Jane!' Sammy blushed furiously as Jane grinned and continued.

'I bet Stuart would give his right arm to spend a night with you.'

'Pack it in. I won't be able to look him in the eye tonight. You can be so brazen at times, Jane Mellor. Where *do* you get it from?'

'Years of being with Ed, I suppose,' she said, winking at Pat, who was grinning broadly.

'So, you and Ed are still getting on well?' Pat asked.

'They're always at it,' Sammy chipped in, making Jane blush this time. 'They're worse than rabbits! If there's no peace at home, they drive to Norman's Woods, don't you?'

'Sometimes,' Jane admitted. 'If the house is full and needs must.'

Pat laughed. 'Some things never change. Good old Norman's Woods. Tim and I had a bit of a strange time while I was ill. I hated him seeing me without my breast – I felt ugly and I wouldn't go naked in front of him. But now I've got my new boob, we're back on track.'

'I can't get over the length of Tim's hair and it's so blond. I expect that's the sun,' Sammy said. 'Makes his eyes look bluer than ever. Your hair looks lovely, short like that,' she added, admiring Pat's new hairstyle. 'Very chic.'

'It's growing back quite well,' Pat said, running her hand over her head. 'I like *your* hair in that bob-style, Sam, and even *you've* gone a bit shorter, Jane.'

'Yeah,' Jane said. 'I'm not as brave as Sam. Ed likes my hair long and I think he'd be really upset if I got it cut any shorter, so I struggle with it for his sake.'

'How's Jess doing? Is she coming to terms with losing Nick?' Pat asked.

'She's getting there slowly.' Jane sighed. 'It was a bad day yesterday, she was hysterical.'

Sammy's eyes filled with tears again at the mention of Nick.

'Oh, Sam, I'm sorry,' Pat apologised.

'I'm okay; it comes and goes. I was just remembering Roy at

the grave yesterday afternoon. Not twenty-four hours ago and look what's happened.'

'Sammy, please talk to him before you see the solicitor,' Jane pleaded. 'I've been thinking, have you considered that Livvy might have taken it upon herself to go to the hotel last night? Roy probably didn't invite her at all.'

'Well, why did he tell me he had?'

'Probably to stop you belting her one,' Pat said. 'He knows what you're capable of.'

'He'll never bloody give her up, no matter what.' Sammy sighed wearily. 'I can't stand sharing him. Anyway, he must have invited her to stay the night and you're not telling me they just lay side by side, holding hands. I know my husband better than anyone in the world and he can't keep his hands to himself.'

'See,' Jane said, 'you just called him your husband. You still love him and I know damn well he still loves you. Talk to him, just one more time before you throw it all away.'

'I'll see. But don't expect a miracle, because I *really* don't think I can ever forgive him for last night.'

28

'So, what's the latest on the Roy situation?' Tim asked as he and Eddie travelled to Hanover's Lodge. 'I didn't like to ask too many questions. Molly was bristly when I asked where he was and Sammy looked as though she'd just had the stuffing well and truly knocked out of her.'

'Well, obviously you know about the affair,' Eddie began. 'After the accident, Roy stopped seeing Livvy. Anyway, she turned up at Nick's memorial service, told me she was pregnant and asked me to tell Roy.'

Tim's eyes widened. 'She's pregnant? No way!'

Eddie filled Tim in on the events of the last few weeks, finishing with that morning's escapade. 'And that, my friend, is as far as we've got. Sam came straight to us, totally devastated. Roy phoned later, told me what had happened, but by then Sam had made up her mind: she's had enough and wants a divorce.'

Tim whistled through his teeth. 'And who could blame her?'

'The stupid thing is though, he really loves Sam. Doesn't want a divorce. If he'd stayed at home, none of this later stuff would have happened. But she made it impossible, pecking his head all the time. He needed space and so did she, and while I don't for one minute condone what he's done, I understand it.'

Tim nodded. 'So, tell me, Ed, what's she like, this Livvy? She must be something special to win Roy from Sammy.'

'She's pretty fit. Petite, blonde curls, big baby-blue eyes, very sexy body and twenty-two to boot.'

'Ah well, nice little package then, eh?'

'Very nice little package, but don't you dare repeat that to Jane. She doesn't know of my involvement with Livvy over the baby either, so don't drop me in it, for God's sake.'

'My lips are sealed,' Tim said as Eddie pulled up outside Hanover's Lodge.

Lennon ran over to greet them, bounding round like a mad thing.

'Who's this fine fellow, then?' Tim bent to stroke the dog, who wagged his tail with delight.

'Goes by the name of Lennon,' Eddie said. 'Jane's baby substitute. Oh, oh, here comes trouble!'

The back door flew open and Katie hurtled outside, followed by Jess.

'Daddy!' Katie leapt up and down. 'Hello, Uncle Tim, where's Uncle Roy?'

'In the doghouse,' Eddie replied, without thinking.

'What doghouse? Where is it? Can we go see it? Are there lots of doggies there?'

'Only Uncle Roy at the moment. Stand still a minute, Katie.'

Tim looked at the little girl hopping from foot to foot.

'Hi there, Katie. Miniature Jane,' he said to Eddie.

'And twice as bossy!' Jess said.

'Hi, Jess. How are you?' Tim took his goddaughter in his arms and hugged her. 'Boy, you've sure grown up in the last couple of years. You look just like your dad but with your mom's long hair.'

Jess smiled. 'Where's Roy, Dad? Thought the three of you would be stuck together like glue.'

'I'm not quite sure where he is, but I'm going to call the hotel in a minute to see if he's there. Your mum's staying at Sammy's for a few hours. They've got mountains of gossip to catch up on. Is Dom at your gran's?'

'Yeah, she gave him and Katie lunch and said they can stay there this afternoon. Molly rang Gran and she's bringing Kim and Abby over later so I'll go and see them when they arrive and take Katie with me. Jon called me earlier, he said Livvy hasn't turned up for work, so Roy might be at her flat if he's not at the hotel.'

'Thanks, love. We'll clear off to the music room and try and locate him. See you later.'

'She sure is pretty,' Tim said as he followed Eddie upstairs.

'Yes, she is,' Eddie said proudly. 'Nick worshipped her. They were such a lovely couple and you should have heard them sing. Their harmonies were superb. I've got some tapes of songs that Roy and I wrote with Nick earlier this year. I'll play them for you later.'

Tim shook his head sadly. 'You'd think losing their boy would have brought Sammy and Roy closer, wouldn't you?'

'Well, it did and it didn't. Sammy blamed Roy, not for buying the fast car, but for Nick's mind being on their problems rather than his driving. It wasn't, of course, but you say things you can't take back sometimes, don't you?'

'Very true. You got an English ciggie, Ed?'

Eddie winked. 'I can go one better, I got fresh supplies from Mac.' He reached into his desk drawer, took out a small package, the tobacco tin and papers and rolled a joint. He lit up and passed it to Tim, who drew deeply and smiled.

'Ah, home sweet home. Call Roy, get him over here.'

Roy wasn't at the hotel, nor was he at Livvy's flat. Livvy told

Eddie he had gone to visit his parents and she'd ask him to get in touch as soon as she could.

Eddie called Roy's parents at Tim's insistence and his mother told him that Roy had just left. 'He's got himself into a right mess, Eddie,' she said.

'He certainly has,' Eddie agreed, grinning at Tim.

'We've told him we won't take sides but he needs to sort himself out for everyone's sake. He acts like a teenager instead of a responsible, middle-aged man. He's forty-two, for heaven's sake, it's time he grew up!'

Eddie agreed again and said goodbye. He related to Tim what Roy's mum had said.

'She's always treated him like a big kid,' Tim said.

Eddie laughed and put on a demo tape of the Perry's Dream song.

Tim listened as the strains of 'Let's Love a While Longer' filled the room. 'Excellent,' he said as the powerful rock ballad came to an end. 'Hey, you've still got it.'

'Well, it's tipped for number one, so fingers crossed.'

'What's the plan regarding The Raiders?' Tim handed the remains of the joint to Eddie.

'I'll call a band meeting for next Wednesday, so we can air some ideas.'

'You're still in contact with Carl and Phil?'

'We see Carl regularly, when he's not working in London, but Phil hardly ever. We hear from him at Christmas and we've got an address, so I can easily get in touch.'

'I wonder what *he's* been up to since we disbanded. Is he still with Laura?'

'I don't think so. He bought that place just outside Ashlea in the sixties, Apple Tree House. It was a bit of a commune for a while. He lived there with Laura and his kids, but I guess they've split up as he's back with his mum. Laura might still be living in the house. We don't hear from *her* at all.'

'Ah well, no doubt we'll find out when we have our meeting. I need to work to get out from under Pat's feet. As soon as we've found a house we like, I'm all yours. Pat wants to start looking right away. On the way over here, I saw The Old Vicarage in Ashlea has a For Sale board outside. I wouldn't mind looking at that for starters. It would be good for Pat to have Sammy close to hand when we go out on tour and it'd be less of a worry for me. It's a massive place; the board also said paddocks and the kids love riding. Pat promised them new ponies – we had to sell theirs when we sold the ranch.'

'How *is* Pat?' Eddie asked. 'I mean, her state of mind and everything.'

Tim sighed. 'She's getting there. We went through a rough patch after the op. She was convinced I wouldn't fancy her any more but I was just so grateful to still have her, boob or no boob. Now she's been rebuilt, she's getting her confidence back. The biggest shock for me was her hair.' He snapped his fingers. 'All that lovely, long blonde hair, gone, just like that. But it's growing again and I quite like it short.' He blinked rapidly and stared up at the ceiling for a long moment. 'Ed, thanks for listening to me. It's been hard with no one close by to offload on – the guys in the band weren't really into that sort of talking.'

Eddie patted his shoulder. 'Any time, Tim. I can't imagine what you must have gone through.'

He nodded. 'Are you going to play me something by Jess's group now?'

'Yeah.' As Eddie reached for the tape, the phone rang out. 'Grab that while I put it on.'

'The Mellor residence, Tim Davis speaking. Well, hello there, Mr Cantello. Congratulations, you randy old stud! You coming over? No, the girls are at your place. There's just Ed, me and Jess around. Come and share a joint. We've had one, but we'll wait for you before we skin up again. See you in ten.'

Eddie switched on the tape and as they listened to the

lovely harmonies, Tim's eye caught a movement by the door: Jess was standing perfectly still, blinking hard.

Tim smiled at her as the song came to an end. 'Beautiful.'

'Thank you,' she said. 'It's the first time I've heard the songs since the accident.'

'So, Jon plays drums, like his dad?' Tim turned to Eddie.

'He does. And Jess plays bass, like Uncle Tim.'

'Are you up there?' a voice yelled from the bottom of the stairs.

'Come on up,' Eddie called back.

'Hi, Jess.' Roy winked as he strolled past her.

'Hi, Daddy Roy.' She winked back.

'Stop it, you,' he warned playfully. 'You'll never let me live it down, will you?'

She grinned as Roy flung his arms around Tim and hugged him.

'Fucking hell, Tim! Look at the length of your bloody hair, man. Don't they have barbers in Nashville?'

'Not that you'd notice,' he quipped. 'Oh, Roy, it's so good to see you again. What have you been up to? Apart from the obvious, of course.'

Roy smiled wryly. 'I expect Ed's told you I've found a flat and I move in Monday. I've just been to see my folks and told them about the baby.'

'We know,' Eddie smirked. 'I called your mum. She's not taking sides, she said.'

'She's bloody barking.' Roy sighed. 'She thought Sam was in the club. I wish she was, life would be a lot easier.' His face clouded. 'Is she okay, Ed? I feel awful, I can't believe she turned up like that. Why *did* she, do you know? I'd just spoken to her and agreed to stay for the weekend. I got a bit distracted, I suppose, and I guess Sammy must have sensed something from my voice. Next thing, she's knocking at the door, shouting "room service". I tell you that was the worst moment of my life, opening the door and her walking in just as Livvy walked out of the bathroom – starkers. The looks on their faces, they were both gobsmacked. Sammy went for Livvy and I stopped her, which obviously made matters worse. God, it was awful, talk about piggy in the middle!' He shuddered at the memory. 'Roll that joint, Ed. Boy, do I need it! You're sure the girls won't show up like a lynch mob?'

'Relax, they're at your place. Jess, don't tell your mum Roy was here, please.' Eddie looked at his daughter, who was shaking her head at Roy's story.

'I won't, on one condition,' she bargained.

'What?'

'Share your joint with me.' She limped over and sat down beside Roy.

'I can't do that. You're only a kid!'

'I'm nineteen,' she retorted. 'Don't be such a meanie, Dad!'

'One toke, but don't tell your mother.'

'Well, *she* smokes weed.'

'Only occasionally, and she doesn't like you kids to know she does.'

'Two tokes for my silence, or it's no deal,' she bargained and took the new joint from Roy.

She took a long drag and inhaled deeply, a blissful expression on her face as Eddie rolled his eyes.

Tim laughed. 'Ed, she smokes a joint the same way you do. What a chip off the old Mellor block!'

'She is,' Eddie said as Jess grinned.

* * *

Livvy lay on her bed and stretched her arms above her head. She felt smug, like the cat that drank all the cream. It had been painful, but worth it, and now she'd got him and they could adjust to being a couple before the baby arrived. He'd left the flat like a gleeful schoolboy for his reunion with Eddie and Tim. She felt a bit disappointed they weren't going shopping after all, but he said he'd take her next week instead and she didn't want to start off by being too clingy. He loved her; that was the main thing. He'd be back later to collect her to spend the night at the hotel.

She was looking forward to being officially seen in public on his arm. No more sneaking around. He'd told his mum and dad about the baby and they wanted to meet her tomorrow. She wasn't looking forward to it, but it would be interesting, to say the least, she thought as she turned on her side, closed her eyes and drifted off to sleep.

* * *

Stuart drove into Manchester, a broad smile splitting his face. He was looking forward to being in Sammy's company later. He'd worshipped her from afar since his teens and although he'd had many partners over the years, no one had ever quite measured up to her so he'd made a choice to stay single.

He parked his car on Chorlton Street car park and strode the few blocks to Flanagan and Grey's. He ran lightly up the stairs and was greeted by Jon and Sean.

'Give us a hand, Stu,' Jon called. 'We've been rushed off our feet and we haven't had a brew for hours. I'll make the coffees if you'll help Sean.'

'Sounds like a good deal to me,' Stuart replied, taking his place behind the counter.

Five minutes later, they took a breather and drank the welcome mugs of coffee.

'I don't know why they all come in at once,' Jon grumbled.

'There's nowt so funny as customers, as John Grey is fond of saying.' Stuart grinned. 'Where's your young girl today?'

Sean raised an eyebrow. 'You might well ask but we know

where she was last night *and* this morning. She called earlier, told me she couldn't leave Roy on his own. He was in too much of a state.'

'What's she doing with Roy?' Stuart's eyes widened. 'I know she's expecting his baby, but I thought the relationship was over. Sammy said she and Roy were getting back together. So, what's happened since Thursday night when I last saw Sammy?'

Jon told him what had gone on that morning.

'Wow! It's a wonder he's still around to tell the tale. Sammy called me a short time ago and invited me over tonight. She was with Pat and Jane at Jasmine House. So... I guess Roy won't be there?'

'Not unless Sammy's serving him up balls first on a skewer.' Jon laughed. 'I'll call home, see what the latest news is.'

'Go ahead,' Sean said. 'I love every minute of this ongoing saga.'

Jess answered Jon's call. 'Hi, Jess. What's happening? Give us an update. You sound a bit giggly. What's all that noise?'

'It's Dad, Tim and Roy having fun. They're jamming old rock 'n' roll stuff and sharing a spliff. Roy's singing "Summertime Blues" at the moment.'

'Sounds good, wish I was there,' Jon said enviously. 'So, Roy's still in one piece? How's Tim?'

'Roy's still intact and Tim's just great. Hair down to his shoulders, really cool and laid-back. They're having a rare old time. God knows how Dad's going to drive Tim back to Sammy's place later to pick up Mum. I think I'll insist Tim takes a taxi – I don't want Dad to drive until his head clears. He might have an accident and that thought scares the life out of me.'

'Good idea. You haven't by any chance been smoking, have you?'

'Just a couple of small tokes. I haven't to tell Mum that

Roy's here, so Dad and I did a deal: my silence for a share of their joint.'

'Well, you sound a lot more cheerful anyway,' Jon said. 'I'll see you later. I presume you know we're babysitting tonight.'

'Yeah, Mum mentioned it. I'm looking forward to that,' she whispered. 'See you later. Love you.'

'Yeah, me too,' he whispered back and hung up. He turned to Sean and Stuart, who'd just finished serving customers: 'They're having a wild old time back there. Jamming all their old stuff and smoking spliffs!'

'Good for them.' Sean laughed. 'They must be over the moon to be together again.'

'A lot of water's gone under the bridge since they last played,' Stuart said. 'So, what's on the cards then? For The Raiders, I mean.'

'A reunion, definitely,' Jon said. 'They're re-forming and going out on tour.'

'And Roy and Sammy, what do you think will happen there?'

'She's divorcing him. That's what she said earlier. I honestly can't see her changing her mind again. So if *you* fancy Sammy, the coast is clear,' he added with a knowing grin.

Stuart smiled. 'How do you know I fancy Sammy?'

'The way you looked at her on Thursday night was a good giveaway,' Jon said.

'He's always had a soft spot for Sam, haven't you, mate?' Sean said.

'Yeah, but I never stood a chance with Roy hanging around. Sammy was besotted with him from the word go.'

'Well, she's no longer besotted, Stu, so you're in with a chance,' Jon said.

Stuart nodded. 'I'm off now. Thought I might see if my old mate Mac still hangs around Tommy Ducks. I want to get Tim a little welcome home gift for tonight.'

'Mac's always in Tommy Ducks,' Jon said. 'Dad and Roy still see him.'

'Great, see you both soon then,' Stuart called as he left the shop.

* * *

Stuart stopped to buy three bouquets of pink roses from a street flower vendor, then made his way to Tommy Duck's public house and spotted Mac immediately.

'Bloody hell, Mac, you don't change one bit,' he said to his old college chum, who thumped him on the back and bought him a pint.

'Neither do you.' Mac's dark gypsy eyes twinkled below his thatch of black curls. 'You still single?'

'For now,' Stuart said, leading the way to a small table. 'And you're still with the lovely Jackie?'

'Yep, we've got four kids now. Don't know how Jackie puts up with me, but she does.'

'You've been together a long time – like Roy and Sammy,' Stuart said.

'Built to last, you see.'

'Not Roy and Sammy. They've split up. I'm surprised you don't know.'

'I thought something was going on,' Mac said. 'I've seen Roy in here with a little blonde piece. Brings her in for lunch occasionally. She's very young, half his age.'

'She's also very pregnant,' Stuart said, offering Mac a cigarette.

'Get away! Bloody hell, Sammy won't stand for that. Christ, *I've* had flings but if I brought that kind of trouble to the door, Jackie would sling me out, no messing.'

'Sammy has done – slung Roy out, I mean.'

Mac looked closely at Stuart. 'So, now it's time for you to make your move.'

'And how do you know I want to make a move?' Stuart took a long drag on his cigarette and blew a smoke ring above his head.

'Because you've always wanted Sammy. You missed your chance in the sixties. Don't miss out again, mate. Those roses are a good start.'

Stuart smiled. 'They're for Pat and Jane, too, and I need a little gift for Tim. He and Pat arrived home from Nashville today. Got any?'

'Do bears shit in the woods?' Mac grinned and slid a small package across the table. 'On the house, to welcome Tim home. Tell them to re-form The Raiders. They've no excuse now he's back.'

'They're doing just that. Thanks, mate.' Stuart smiled and dropped the package in his jacket pocket. He finished his pint, shook Mac by the hand and left the pub, his thoughts tumbling over one another.

Sammy was free; an opportunity like this came once in a lifetime. He made up his mind that he'd take a chance on getting hurt if she decided to take Roy back. He'd already booked the hotel for the trip to London and planned to tell her later, if the opportunity arose. He made his way to his car, a happy man, mind firmly made up.

* * *

Roy let himself in with the key Livvy had given him. He called her name, but there was no reply. He checked the lounge and then pushed open the bedroom door.

She was on the bed, her cheeks flushed from sleep and her blonde curls haloed across the pillow. Roy felt his heart contract with love for her. She looked like a vulnerable Goldilocks and must have been so tired to sleep all afternoon. He lay beside her and placed his hand protectively over her stomach, gently caressing.

He felt tired too; it had been a draining day. The good and noisy time he'd just had with Tim and Ed added to his tiredness. He closed his eyes and snuggled closer. She wriggled and put her arms around him.

'Hello, handsome,' she muttered.

'Hello, beautiful lady,' he said, kissing the tip of her nose.

She leant up on one elbow. 'Have you been drinking? Your eyes look strange. You shouldn't have driven if you've been drinking, it's dangerous.'

'I haven't touched a drop,' he said truthfully. 'I shared a couple of joints with Ed and Tim, that's all.'

'I see.' She pursed her lips.

'Do you have a problem with it?' He was surprised by the look on her face.

'Well, I don't know. I've never considered drugs, to be honest.'

'I've smoked dope almost all my life. It relaxes me. It's the only stuff I do these days. Don't worry about it.'

'Okay.' She frowned as he kissed her again.

'I'm sorry I wasn't around to take you shopping, but we've got all the time in the world. I'll take you Wednesday. You can help me move into my flat Tuesday. I need to buy bedding and towels and stuff like that. Tell you what, why don't I fly us to Paris? We can buy my stuff, get you some decent clothes and stay over a couple of nights while the dust settles here. The shops out there will knock your socks off.'

'I'll be working next week.'

'Bollocks! Call Sean on Monday and tell him you're not coming in again.'

'Roy, I can't do that. I need my job, I can't afford not to work.'

He sat up and stared at her. 'Livvy, are you for real? I'm a fucking millionaire! You don't need the job, I'll be looking after you from now on. You call Sean on Monday and tell him you're leaving. I want no arguments, you need to get some rest before the baby arrives.'

She lay back on the pillows, staring up at the ceiling, a mutinous expression on her face.

'What is it, what's wrong with you?'

'What if you go back to Sammy and I've burnt all my boats?'

'She wouldn't have me back, there's no question of it.'

'And that's the only reason you want me? Because Sammy won't have you back?'

'No, I want you because I love you. I want to look after you properly, and you're expecting my kid.'

'I was expecting your kid before all this happened today and *you* wanted to stay married to Sammy. I've always been independent, running my own life since I was sixteen. I've got my flat, my car and my job and I hadn't planned on giving any of it up.'

'So what exactly are you saying, Olivia? That you don't want me and I've fucked up my marriage for nothing?' Roy looked at her, a stricken expression on his face.

'No, Roy, I *do* want you. But we should take it one day at a time. I'm not quite as impulsive as you are, except maybe last night when I needed to see you. I'm not giving up my flat or my job just yet. I'll stay with you at night, that way I know where you are. If it works out between us then we can move in together after the baby arrives. Once you start to play and tour with the lads again, I'll need to get used to being alone and I'd rather be under my own roof.'

He shook his head. She was a stubborn little madam, but she obviously knew her own mind. 'Okay, if it's what you want, then that's fine. But it seems a bit daft, keeping two flats going. When you decide you're ready to move in with me, I'll buy us a new house. You can choose where you want to live, somewhere spacious for our little family.' He patted her bump.

'There's only one in there, we won't need anywhere *too* big.'

'There can be another one on the way as soon as that one arrives. One a year if you like.' He grinned and pulled her close. 'Smoking dope makes me randy.'

'You don't need dope to make *you* randy, mister,' she giggled, rolling into his arms.

29

Stuart clutched the bunches of pink roses and rang the doorbell, stomach looping, hands sweating. Sammy threw open the door with a welcoming smile and invited him inside. Nerves settling, he smiled back. 'There's a bunch for each of you,' he said as she led him into the lounge. She kissed him lightly on the cheek and he saw Jane and Pat exchange knowing glances.

'Thanks, Stu, they're lovely. I'll pop them in a bucket for now. Take a seat, won't be a mo.'

He sat on the sofa opposite Pat and Jane. Eddie and Tim were sprawled on the rug in front of the fire and they called out a greeting.

'Now, what would everyone like to drink?' Sammy said, hurrying back into the lounge.

'G&T for me, please,' Jane said.

'And me,' said Pat.

'Any single malt, Sam?' Eddie asked hopefully.

'I certainly have.' She walked over to the drinks cabinet. 'There's a couple of bottles, and seeing as his lordship won't be drinking it, you can come and help yourself. No doubt Tim will join you.'

'Same for me, Ed,' Stuart said as Eddie jumped to his feet and proceeded to slosh generous measures into cut-glass tumblers. 'So,' he asked casually, 'where's Roy tonight?'

'Who knows?' Sammy shrugged. 'More to the point, who bloody well cares? But I would hazard a guess he's entertaining his bimbo.' She handed Jane and Pat their drinks and raised her glass. 'Cheers, everyone. Welcome home to Tim and Pat and here's to our brand-new futures.' She clinked glasses with Stuart and flopped down on the sofa beside him.

Stuart turned to Eddie. 'I've heard a rumour you're re-forming The Raiders.'

'Yeah, we're having a band meeting next week. By the way, you okay for Wednesday, Tim? I spoke to Phil and Carl earlier and they can do that night. I'll check with Roy, but I'm sure it won't be a problem.'

'Wednesday's good for me. Can't wait to see the others and get cracking.'

'Will you still be writing your own stuff?' Stuart placed his glass on the coffee table.

'Yeah, we've loads of half-finished songs to work on. Enough to put out an album at least and Tim's written a few country ditties.'

'Country rock, that is,' Tim said. 'Eagles style.'

'Brilliant!' Stuart said. 'I'll look forward to the first single. Good luck, lads, although I'm sure you won't need it with the reputation The Raiders already have.'

Sammy leapt to her feet. 'I'll check on the pasta.'

'I'll give you a hand.' Stuart stood up and followed her.

'What's going on there?' Tim's eyes narrowed as the door closed.

'Nothing, yet!' Jane said.

* * *

Sammy was standing in front of the sink, her shoulders shaking. Stuart hesitated momentarily and then put his hand on her arm.

'Sammy?'

She turned to face him, eyes glistening with tears.

'Oh, Sam, come here.' He took her in his arms and held her close as she sobbed against his shoulder.

'I'm sorry, Stu. Band talk brings back so many memories.'

'That's okay, I understand.' He took a handkerchief from his pocket and wiped her eyes. How could Roy do this to her? If she was *his*, he'd never hurt her or make her cry.

She lifted her face and smiled through her tears. 'Thanks.'

He pulled her closer, folding his arms protectively around her. Her arms crept around his waist and she leant into him. He lifted her chin with a finger and kissed her lightly on the tip of her nose, waiting for a response.

When it came, the response was warm and encouraging as she kissed him on the lips.

'Wow! Now that was worth waiting all my life for,' Stuart whispered.

'Was it?'

'Most definitely.' Bending to kiss her again, he crushed her to him.

'Oh, oh, I'm sorry.' Jane's voice broke them apart.

'It's alright, Jane,' Sammy said.

'Ed's spilt his drink on the coffee table. I need a cloth, I didn't mean to disturb you.'

Sammy threw her a J Cloth and Jane left the room.

Stuart pulled her back into his arms. 'Now, where were we?'

'Like this, I think.' Sammy smiled and lifted her lips to his.

* * *

'Catch.' Jane chucked the cloth at her clumsy husband.

'What's up with you?' Eddie frowned, wiping up the spillage. 'You look smug.'

'Do I?' She winked at Pat.

'Where are Sam and Stuart?' Tim said. 'I'm really starving, I thought they'd gone to sort out the pasta.'

'They're doing just that – and one or two other things besides,' Jane said gleefully.

'Bloody hell!' Eddie said. 'Roy won't like that.'

'It's got nothing to do with Roy,' Pat bristled.

'It's got everything to do with Roy,' Tim replied. 'She's his wife.'

'Really?' Pat raised an eyebrow. 'It's a pity Roy didn't think about his wife when he was screwing Livvy this morning. Anyway, Tim, I refuse to fall out with you over him. As Sammy said earlier, he's not worth it.'

'Roy's burnt his bridge at both ends,' Jane said, folding her arms. 'Sammy's free to do as she wants, when she wants and with whom she wants.'

'Okay, Jane, enough,' Eddie said. 'Let's not spoil the night by arguing.'

'Well, you two stop sticking up for Roy then,' she said.

'Truce!' Tim held up his hands. 'But I'm still starving. Another drink, Ed?'

Sammy popped her head around the door, looking flushed and cheerful. 'Foods ready. Do you want to sit at the table or eat buffet style?'

'Buffet style,' they chorused, following her into the dining room, where they helped themselves to seafood pasta and green salad.

'Stu, would you open the wine, please?' Sammy handed him a bottle and a corkscrew.

'Certainly, madam,' he said, holding her gaze.

Jane looked on with a smile, guessing correctly that Stuart

would have been quite happy to stand in the kitchen kissing Sammy all night if it hadn't been for his hungry mates.

* * *

Roy sat in his flat, glass of whisky in hand, looking round with a certain amount of pride. It would do for the next few months until he found a place to call home with Livvy. They'd shopped for linen and towels yesterday and she'd been so excited, choosing bargains carefully, until he'd told her to forget the price – if she liked it, he'd buy it. But the trip to Paris was off. The stubborn little madam wouldn't take time off work.

On reflection, it was perhaps as well because Ed had organised a band meeting for tonight in the Royal Oak. Roy finished his drink and smiled. With a bit of luck, they'd be out on the road in a couple of months. Adrenaline surged through his veins at the thought. Not much else in his life felt right at the moment. He loved Livvy dearly, but he wasn't *in* love with her, not like he was with Sam.

He thought about Sam all the time. He wanted to call her desperately, needed to hear her voice, make sure she was okay, but he didn't dare. Ed had told him she was fine and had been happy enough over the weekend. He'd also mentioned in passing that Stuart had been at Jasmine House on Saturday night. Roy felt angry and jealous. Sammy had enjoyed last week's night out with him and he was sure that if Stu thought there was a chance with her, he'd grab it.

He reflected on his own weekend; Sunday lunch at his parents' place had been a big mistake. His mother had dropped Sammy's name into every conversation. Framed photographs of him, Sammy and the boys had been purposely placed on every available surface, his mother tactlessly pointing out to Livvy when they'd been taken.

Their wedding portrait was in pride of place, with Sammy

looking stunning in her cream silk wedding dress. Pictures of them both as proud new parents, holding their tiny babies.

Roy's eyes filled with sudden tears as he thought of his wife and his precious boys. What a fool he was to lose everything. He shook his head and muttered, 'Snap out of it, Cantello. The Raiders might make it big again.' He stood up and stretched. Might as well have a kip in readiness for the drinking session tonight's meeting would probably turn into.

* * *

'Penny for them!' Sammy sat herself on the desk in front of Jane, who was staring into space.

'What? Oh sorry, Sam, they're not worth a penny.'

'You've been miles away all day. What's bothering you?'

Jane shook her head. 'Nothing – well, not really. It's that overactive imagination at work again.'

Sammy frowned. 'Jon and Jess?'

'Yeah, but I'm probably worrying over nothing as usual.'

'What's happened to add fuel to the fires of your imagination *this* time?'

Jane took a deep breath. 'I always empty the wastepaper bins in the bedrooms before the cleaner comes in.'

'And?' Sammy prompted.

'Jess's bin had two empty condom wrappers in it. They weren't even hidden, just sitting on top for me to see.'

'Did you say anything to her?'

'No. It would have looked as though I was prying.'

'Are you absolutely sure she isn't seeing someone?'

'Who and when? She never goes out anywhere without Jon. As far as I know, she doesn't have anyone round during the day and anyway, Ed's at home with her most of the time. She was alone with Jon for hours on Saturday night while we were at yours. There was an empty wine bottle in the kitchen. Ed had left a joint rolled for when we got home, but it had gone. Ed laughed it off. Called them a pair of rum buggers, but I was thinking they'd be all chilled and relaxed and well, you know.'

'I do. It was one thing when you thought they'd been kissing, but now you've reason to think they're sleeping together. You need to discuss this with Ed, and pronto.'

'How can I tell him? He'll go crazy.'

'Well then, *you'll* have to say something to them. You can't let it go on, Jane.'

Jane put her head in her hands and muttered, 'What if I'm wrong?'

'Well, someone's using condoms and unless they've been blown up to amuse Katie and Dom, I can think of only one other use.'

'You're right, of course. Any idea how I can broach the subject?'

'God, I don't know, Jane. I really don't.'

'Oh well.' She shrugged. 'I guess I'll just play it by ear for now. Oh, by the way, have Pat and Tim been to view The Old Vicarage yet?'

'They were going this afternoon. I'll call and see if they're back. Do you fancy coming over tonight to have a drink with us? Tim and Ed will be at the band meeting.'

'Yeah, that will be nice. It means leaving Jess and Jon alone though.'

'Well, it's up to you,' Sammy said. 'I'll give Jason and Jules the money for a taxi, they can go and join them. That'll keep them *all* out of mischief.'

'Good idea.' Jane laughed. 'Ed said Roy's going to the meeting tonight. Have you spoken with him yet?'

'No,' Sammy replied. 'I've nothing to say. The solicitor can do all my talking for me. That's what I'm paying him for. Roy's mum called last night. Told me they met Livvy on Sunday and weren't that impressed. Irene thinks she's tarty and out to trap

Roy for his money. She told me I should fight for my rights and get him back. I told her I didn't want him. She made him out to be a right little angel and Livvy the seducer. Can you believe it? She's never really known her son, has she?'

Jane smiled. 'Not really. But then, do I know *my* kids?'

Sammy picked up the phone. 'Let's have a change of subject. Take that design I've just finished through to the pattern cutters and I'll call Pat.'

* * *

Pat ran across the kitchen and grabbed the phone. 'Hello. Hi, Sam, I was about to call you. We've just walked in from the viewing. We loved it. It's brilliant, needs a bit of an overhaul, but otherwise it's fantastic. Yeah, six bedrooms, so Tim can have his all-important music room. Similar layout to yours downstairs and the gardens are fabulous, absolutely huge, in fact, and there's the paddock so the kids can have ponies. Tim's really keen to put a cash offer in today. With the money we made on the ranch, we could buy the place twice over, but of course we need new cars and furniture, too.'

'Well, make them a much lower offer than they're asking and then you can go up a bit if they refuse. The market's slow at the moment and a cash offer on a house that price is unusual. They should bite your hand off!'

'We will,' Pat said. 'I feel happy and positive about the future now. The house feels so right, I can picture us living there already.'

'Go for it then. Call the agent now, put in the offer and good luck.'

'Will do. See you later.'

* * *

Sammy smiled as she hung up. Pat's excitement had rubbed off on her. Having her stepsister around had definitely taken the edge off Roy's departure and Sammy was also enjoying the attention she was receiving from Stuart. The two of them had been out for a meal on Monday night and on the way back, Stuart had parked the car on a quiet country lane and taken her into his arms.

'We never got the chance to do this as teenagers,' he'd told her. She'd responded to his kisses and caresses with more enthusiasm than she ever imagined she could do. They'd talked about the planned exhibition trip to London and although Sammy was slightly apprehensive, deep down she was also a teeny bit excited. She knew that if Stuart got his way, they'd end up spending the night together, even though he'd told her he'd booked two rooms. It wasn't that she didn't want to spend the night with him, she was worried about disappointing him. Roy going off with Livvy had dented her confidence. She was convinced her performance in bed was to blame. Why else would he have had an affair? Every other aspect of their married life had been good and she had always assumed she was everything Roy wanted in a woman. But she'd obviously been mistaken.

'Did Pat like the house?' Jane's voice broke through Sammy's thoughts as she strolled back into the office.

'Yes, they both loved it. Tim wants to put an offer in today. It'll be handy to have her close by, especially when Tim's away with the lads.'

'When are you seeing Stuart again?'

'Friday, I think. He suggested we all go out for dinner. Is that okay with you, Jane?'

'Yeah, great. Roy's going to feel so left out of everything, isn't he?'

'Well, it's tough. He's made his bed. I wonder how he went on moving into his flat yesterday. I promised to sort him out some linen and towels. I forgot all about it after the performance on Saturday morning. He won't have a clue what to buy, he thinks you just open a cupboard and everything's magically there.'

'See, you're still worrying about him. You still care.'

Sammy rolled her eyes. 'Of course I care. I told you, I love the stupid fool to bits, but I *can't* forgive him. Last Saturday morning just finished it for me. You can't blame me, Jane, I was willing to give him that one last chance and I was so sure it was what *he* wanted, too. But no, Roy had to have his bloody cake. Like I said, once that baby arrives, he'll be besotted whether he wanted it or not and *I* won't stand a chance.' She took a sip of coffee and grimaced. 'Ugh, it's gone cold! I'll make us a fresh one. Anyway, I have to admit that I'm rather enjoying Stuart's attentions.'

'Are you now?' Jane raised an amused eyebrow.

'We were like teenagers on heat the other night.' Sammy grinned. 'Stuart parked up. I haven't snogged like that for years. He's got wandering hands like Roy, too.'

Jane laughed. 'You sound like the girls from the factory floor. Next thing you'll be coming in with Hide 'n' Heal on your love bites.'

'I'm not looking for anything serious, it's too soon, but I reckon I'm due some fun after the last couple of crappy months, don't you?'

'You are, Sam,' Jane agreed. 'If anyone deserves it, you do. Stuart's lovely and he's good company.'

* * *

Eddie and Tim were first in the Royal Oak. They were shortly after joined by Phil and Carl and there was much hand shaking and backslapping.

'I think Phil shares your aversion to barbers, Tim.' Eddie

laughed as he admired Phil's lengthy blond locks. 'Mind you, he always had the longest hair of us all in the sixties.'

'He did,' Carl said, laughing. 'I hated him for it. My awful ginger thatch was an embarrassment compared to his flowing mane.'

Tim went to the bar and they'd downed their first pints when Roy strolled in.

'Same again, lads?' he called.

'Please, Roy. Lager all round,' Eddie replied.

Roy strode across to the alcove and placed a laden tray on the table. He shook hands with Phil and Carl and sat down, beaming from ear to ear.

'What's up with you?' Eddie asked.

'I just feel happy, that's all.' Roy took a drink of his lager and offered his cigarettes round.

'Have you just come from Livvy's place?' Tim narrowed his eyes.

Roy shrugged and held out his lighter. 'Might have.'

'The poor kid's been at work all day and you go jumping her bones as soon as she gets home.' Eddie shook his head.

Phil looked from one to the other, puzzled. 'Would somebody mind telling me what's going on? Who the hell's Livvy?'

'Yeah,' Carl said. 'Who's Livvy?'

'Roy's new bird,' Tim informed them. 'You'd better tell them what's happened in the last few weeks, Roy.'

'I will. But first of all, a toast.' He lifted his glass. 'Here's to the return of The Raiders.'

'Here, here,' said Tim.

'And all who sail in her!' Eddie grinned.

'Right, come on, Roy, tell us what you've been up to before we get down to any serious band talk,' Phil insisted.

'Well, briefly, I had an affair and me and Sam have split up,' he began. 'We're getting divorced. I've moved into a flat for now until I buy a house for Livvy, me and the sprog.'

Phil spluttered into his lager and Carl almost dropped his pint. They stared at Roy.

'Fucking hell!' Phil exclaimed. 'I thought you and Sam were for life? You *never* played away from home. What went wrong?'

'I don't really know,' Roy replied lamely. 'I met Livvy, got her pregnant and Sam doesn't wanna know me.'

'Well... congratulations, I suppose, on the sprog, anyway,' Phil said. 'But I'm sorry to hear about you and Sammy, I really am. I thought you'd have had enough traumas this year with losing your lad.'

Roy sighed. 'These things happen, Phil. What about you and Laura?'

'Divorced,' Phil replied. 'I got married again but that didn't work out either. We split up three months ago. That's why I need to work again, and as soon as possible. I've got mega commitments. Two exes and six kids!'

'Fucking hell!' It was Eddie's turn to splutter into his lager. 'How did *that* happen?'

'You mean no one's ever explained the facts of life to you, Ed?' Phil said, grinning. He took a sip of lager. 'Laura and I had two girls after the twins and then like Roy, I had an affair. I was half living with Jo and half with Laura till Laura slung me out. I've got two girls with Jo. So there you go, that's six last time I did a head count. Big commitment, believe you me.'

'To some bloody tune,' Eddie agreed. 'So, you're a single man again?'

'And newly vasectomised,' Phil said. 'So I'm raring to go.'

Roy grimaced. 'Sounds painful. What about you and Cathy, Carl? Do you plan on having kids?'

Carl smiled shyly. 'We'd like them, but it just hasn't happened.'

'Oh well, plenty of time.'

'Not really,' Carl said, blushing as red as his carroty hair.

'Cathy has problems. Time's running out, so I got her a dog instead.'

'Very wise,' Tim said kindly. 'Less trouble all round, if you ask me.'

'It would have been nice to find that out for ourselves, but Jon comes to see Cathy occasionally and that keeps her happy.'

'She's always had a soft spot for Angie's lad,' Tim said.

'Hey, doesn't Ed get a mention here?' Phil said, 'Jon's *his* boy, too.'

'Well, of course,' Carl stuttered and picked up his pint.

Eddie, sensing Carl's discomfort over the touchy secret subject, quickly changed tack. 'How old are your kids with your second wife, Phil?'

'Three and two,' he replied.

'So, Jo's a few years younger than you?'

'No, Ed, same age. Forty-one now, like me.'

'Why did you split up?' Eddie asked curiously.

'She accused me of being a womaniser,' Phil said. 'Can you believe that?'

The others laughed bawdily. Phil had been the biggest womaniser on the planet when The Raiders were in their heyday.

'How old's *your* new bird, Roy?' Phil asked.

'Twenty-two,' he replied sheepishly.

'Bloody hell!' Phil's glass hit the table with a thud.

'I know, I know. I'm old enough to be her father.'

'No, mate, it's not that. I envy you. Has she got a friend?' Phil grinned wickedly.

'Right, enough about our problems, let's get down to some serious business.' Eddie tried to bring order to the meeting as the others nodded. 'We're in agreement that re-launching the band is what we all want so we need a plan of action. I suggest we get together on Friday at my place and have a session, see how we sound these days. Me and Roy have written some new stuff we can try and we'll jam some of the oldies. I'll give Frank James a call tomorrow and let him know our plans.'

'Is Frank still in the business?' Phil asked of their old agent and manager.

'He is,' Roy said. 'Are you under any contracts you can't get out of, Carl?'

'No, free as a bird at the moment,' he replied.

'And you are, Phil, obviously.'

'I'm all yours.'

'I'll have to get a new bass and amp to be going on with,' Tim said. 'All my stuff's on its way with the shipping company, but it'll be another week or two. I've got a brilliant fretless bass, the sound's rich and deep.'

'Fantastic,' Roy said. 'I love a fretless bass. We'll nip to Flanagan and Grey's tomorrow then and pick up some gear.'

'Actually, Sean would probably loan you the stuff,' Eddie said. 'It seems daft buying new gear when you've got umpteen guitars on the way. I'll call him in the morning.'

They continued drinking and making plans for the next few hours until the landlord threw them out just after midnight.

30

'Who were you saying that to?' Eddie spoke quietly as he watched Jess replace the receiver, a smile playing on her face.

'Oh, Dad, you made me jump,' she said, colour rushing to her cheeks. 'In answer to your nosy question, that was my big brother. We always say "I love you", it's what brothers and sisters do.'

'Is it? I wouldn't know, I never had any,' he said yawning. He sat down at the kitchen table. 'Make me a black coffee, Jess – I feel knackered.'

'Hungover, more like,' she said. 'You've got bloodshot eyes. Good night, was it? Get everything sorted with the lads?'

'We did,' he said, lighting his first cigarette of the day. 'But I feel terrible. Never again. Lager gives me horrendous hangovers.'

'You shouldn't have drunk so much then, should you?' Jess showed no sympathy for her dad's self-inflicted ills as she spooned coffee granules into two mugs.

'To be honest, I didn't realise *how* much we'd drunk until Phil offered to get in his second round, which would have made it ten pints each. So we stuck at nine and I struggled with that.'

'How *is* Phil? I haven't seen him for years. What's he been doing since you disbanded?'

'Getting married, twice, *and* he's fathered six kids to boot,' he replied as Jess pushed a mug of strong black coffee across the kitchen table.

'Six! Wow, that's some responsibility.'

'He's desperate to work. Needs money badly. He's just split from his second wife, so he's got massive financial commitments. He's had to move back home with his old mum, can't even afford to rent a flat.'

'What's he done with all the money he made with The Raiders?'

'All gone! Phil was a big spender, generous to a T where women were concerned. Roy and I got the lion's share, because we're the songwriters. Tim wrote a few and he's had a fair bit of success in the States, so he's pretty comfortable. Carl works constantly, of course, so he's also financially stable. But, Phil... well, he hasn't done anything except spend and breed, it would appear. He still owns a couple of nice houses in the area,' he continued. 'Laura, you remember her, redhead, had twins. Well, she lives in Apple Tree House with four kids and his other ex, Jo, is in the second house with two more. Phil's only other possessions are his guitars and a fairly clapped-out Mercedes.'

'Poor Phil! So he's starting again from scratch?'

'He is. We're meeting here tomorrow, so you can pass on your sympathy then, seeing as you're not giving me any for my bad head.'

She laughed. 'What are your plans for today, Dad?'

'I'm gonna give Sean a call in a minute, see if he'll loan Tim a bass and amp from the store. Then we'll collect them. Do you want to come with us?'

'Yeah, I'll take a quick shower while you ring him.'

'Okay,' he said, and took a long swig of coffee.

'By the way, Dad, that call from Jon was to say Perry's

Dream is on *Top of the Pops* tonight and also that F&Gs have sold out of the single.'

'Excellent! It'll be number one next week with a bit of luck. We'll watch TV tonight then. Don't let me forget.'

'I won't. I want an eyeful of James Perry for myself!' she replied over her shoulder.

Eddie smiled. Jess was showing definite signs of improvement. After last Friday's hysteria attack, she seemed so much calmer and relaxed. On Sunday at Sammy's, she'd appeared on top of the world. She and Jon had laughed and joked with Jason and Jules. It had been good to see them all smiling again, but he hoped Jess wasn't blocking her pain and grief by denying herself a reasonable mourning period. He stood up and stretched as Lennon whimpered and butted his leg: 'Want your breakfast? Come on then, old son.'

* * *

Roy hadn't told Livvy he was going into town today and he was lounging against the wall in the Instruments department when she arrived back from lunch.

'Hi, Liv,' he greeted her.

'What are *you* doing here?' She walked towards him, clutching a Kendals' carrier bag.

'Thought I'd surprise you. Come and say hello to Tim.' He placed his arm around her shoulders and led her to a tall man with long blond hair: 'Tim, meet Livvy.'

Tim spun round, eyes widening as he took in Livvy's beauty, her tumbling blonde curls and big blue eyes. 'Well hello, Livvy, nice to meet you at last. Congratulations, by the way.'

'Thank you, Tim.' She shook his outstretched hand. 'Nice to meet you, too. I've heard such a lot about you from Roy.'

'All good, I hope?'

'Oh, absolutely. I'd better go upstairs and do some work.'

She held up the carrier bag. 'I got us some lovely china mugs for the flat, Roy.'

'Tell me how much I owe you later.' Roy bent to kiss her. 'See you soon.' He stared after her, smiling.

Tim, Sean and Eddie looked at one another, eyebrows raised.

'Very nice, Roy.' Tim voiced his approval.

'She is,' Roy said proudly. 'She does wonders for my battered ego.'

'Right, Tim, which one do you fancy?' Eddie turned his mind back to the more pressing subject of choosing a bass.

'Hmmm.' Tim frowned and scratched his chin. 'The Fender Precision, I think. It sounds fine. I'll take that Marshall amp as well, Sean.'

Sean nodded. 'I'll throw in a couple of extra leads and some strings. Just make sure me and Tina get front row seats for the first gig.'

'It goes without saying,' Tim said. 'I really appreciate this.'

'Think nothing of it. Right, let's go upstairs, have a coffee, and then I'll help you load up. I presume you're in the Jeep, Ed?'

'Yeah, I'll bring it round to the loading bay when we're ready to go.'

* * *

Livvy was alone behind the counter.

'Where's Jon and Jess?' Sean asked her.

She nodded towards the staffroom door. 'They're making coffee for everyone.'

'I'll go and hurry them along,' Sean said. He tapped on the door. Jon and Jess sprang apart guiltily as he slipped into the room, closing the door behind him. 'It's a bloody good job it's me and not your dad.'

'Sorry, Sean,' Jon apologised, hanging his head as Jess blushed furiously.

'Be careful, you two. You're playing a very dangerous game. Have you finished brewing?'

'We'll be out in a minute,' Jess said.

'Well, hurry up then.' Sean nodded and left them to it.

* * *

'Sean wasn't very pleased then.' Jess stared at the door. 'You don't suppose he'll say anything to Dad?'

'No, he won't,' Jon reassured her. 'When are Mum and Dad going out again, have they said?'

'Tomorrow night, I think. I'll ask Dad in a minute. We can always go back to the barn.'

His face lit up. 'Okay. If they don't go out tomorrow, we will. Right, let's take the tray through. Get the door for me.'

* * *

'Coffee on the house, this brings back memories,' Tim said, a faraway look in his eyes. 'But not in this shop, of course. I mean the old Stockport branch. Oh, happy days, when our cares were few and our needs were simple.'

Roy sighed. 'Weren't they just! I often think about those times. Ten Woodies, the latest records and meeting Sammy, Pat and Jane in the shop after school and then walking them to Mersey Square to catch the bus home.'

'And you, lusting after Sammy, hoping to drag her off to Norman's Woods,' Tim said. He suddenly remembered Livvy standing behind the counter. 'Sorry, Livvy,' he apologised. 'I didn't think.'

'It's alright, Tim, everyone has history,' she said coolly. '*Some* more than others!'

'That's because some of us are older,' Tim quipped in an effort to lighten the mood.

'Dad, are you and Mum off out tomorrow night?' Jon tactfully changed the subject.

'Yeah, why, is there a problem with you babysitting, or something?'

'No. Jess and I said we'd go out with Jason if you were staying home, that's all.'

'Well, if you don't mind, we're off out for a meal. Is that right, Tim?'

'Yep, Jason and Jules are actually babysitting for us tomorrow. Stu's booked a table for eight thirty. I'm not sure where, you'll have to check with Sammy.' Out of the corner of his eye, Tim saw Roy's jaw tighten.

'So, who else is going?' Roy asked.

'Just the six of us, I believe,' Tim replied.

Roy's eyes grew dark and he gripped the edge of the counter until his knuckles were white. 'Six of you?' He looked at Eddie. 'Is Sammy seeing Stuart?'

Eddie shook his head. 'Not in the way *you* mean. They're just good friends.'

'Don't give me that just good friends load of bollocks! He's always fancied Sam, *you* know that. Has she been out with him, apart from that so-called business meeting last week?'

Eddie sighed and looked at Tim for support.

'Well... has she?' Roy demanded.

'He took her out for a meal on Monday night, Roy, that's all. Just a meal, don't get upset about it.'

'And it never entered your head to tell me? My wife goes out with another man and my best mate says nothing!'

'Roy, stop it, you're upsetting Livvy.' As Eddie looked at Livvy's stricken face, she fled into the staffroom, slamming the door behind her.

'Now look what you've done,' Sean raised his voice. 'If you

can't handle Sammy seeing Stuart, you should have thought twice before you screwed Livvy again.' He followed her into the staffroom.

Roy shook his head. 'Shit! I'm sorry, I can't deal with this at the moment. I'm going back to my flat. I'll jump in a cab and I'll talk to you and Tim later, Ed.'

He shot off down the stairs, leaving the others staring after him.

'He still loves Sammy,' Jess stated. 'He looked really hurt and upset just then.'

'Of course he still loves Sammy and she still loves him. But there's Livvy and the baby to consider, too. Think how she must be feeling right now,' Eddie said.

'And now Roy knows a little of how Sammy must also feel,' Tim said.

Sean strolled out of the staffroom, shaking his head. 'Bloody hell, I feel like I'm walking on eggshells! She heard what I said to Roy about him screwing her. I've just been told in no uncertain terms that Roy made love to her, he didn't screw her!'

Tim rolled his eyes heavenward. 'Well, whatever she wants to call it, the end result was the same. Bingo! For Christ's sake, this is a good start to our Raiders' reunion.'

'Come on, Tim, I'll drop Jess and the gear back at The Lodge and you at Sammy's,' Eddie said. 'Then I'll go and see Roy. He's still very cut up over losing Nick and the least little thing upsets him.'

'Will Livvy be okay, Sean?' Jess asked. 'Would you like me to talk to her?'

'Don't worry, Jess. Jon can take a break and go and sit with her for ten minutes after I've helped your dad load the car.'

'Can you manage the stairs, Jess?'

'Yes, Dad, but you lot go down first and I'll meet you at the front door in a couple of minutes.'

***

Jess held Jon's gaze as their dad led the way downstairs. The record department was customer-free as Jon took her in his arms and kissed her tenderly.

'I love you, Jess, but everything's a bloody mess. All these dilemmas.'

'Well, *we'll* be okay,' she said, smiling reassuringly.

'But *we're* having an incestuous relationship. We've got to get away after Christmas.'

She nodded. 'I'd better go, Dad will be waiting. See you later, Jon.' She touched his cheek gently and went downstairs.

***

Jon knocked on the staffroom door. Livvy opened it a crack.

'Come on out,' he said.

'Have they gone?' Her lips wobbled slightly as she looked at him. 'He still loves her, doesn't he? It's not going to go away, baby or no baby. He'd go back to her tomorrow if she'd have him.'

'Well, you've known that all along. He never told you anything different. He's loved Sam from the day they met and they were inseparable, until you.'

'So, what do I do now?'

'I don't know. Wait for him to calm down, I suppose. Sammy won't have him back, she's made that perfectly clear. All you can do is hang in and see what happens. Were you supposed to be staying with him tonight?'

'I was, but I'm gonna go straight home. He can call me if he wants me.'

'Very wise,' Jon agreed. 'Give him a chance to get his head around the Stuart thing.'

'I guess I need the patience of a saint where Roy's concerned.'

'I guess you do,' he said.

* * *

'Come in, Ed. Do you want a drink?'

'Please.' Eddie followed Roy into the lounge. 'A small one.' He sat down on an armchair. 'What was all that about earlier?'

Roy poured a glass of single malt and passed it over. 'I can't stand the thought of Sammy with Stuart. She's mine, she's always been mine.'

'You gave up that right last weekend.'

Roy let his head fall back against the sofa. He stared at the ceiling, his eyes burning with unshed tears. 'I know, and it hurts like hell.'

'I see Livvy's been busy,' Eddie said, looking at the pink and cream cushions, which matched the pink and cream Chinese rug in front of the fire.

Roy nodded. 'She has. Pink's her favourite colour, although *I* could live with a bit less of it. The red roses on the table are my touch, in case you're wondering. Romantic bastard that I am!'

'She's doing her best, Roy. You have to give her a chance. You can't keep lifting her up, then letting her down.'

'Do you think if I went down on bended knee, Sammy would forgive me?'

'Not this time, mate. I wish I could say differently. Anyway, Livvy and the baby aren't going to go away.'

'I've made a right fucking pig's ear of everything. I'd better give her a call before I lose her, too. I *do* love her, but not in the same way as I love Sammy.' He refilled his glass and topped up Eddie's. 'If I ask you a question, Ed, will you be absolutely honest with me?'

'Ask away,' he said, slugging back his whisky.

'Is Sammy sleeping with Stuart?'

'Not that I know of. She would have told Jane, and as a rule, Jane tells me everything. Sammy's only been out with him the once when all's said and done. Anyway, she wouldn't rush headlong into a relationship without first weighing up the pros and cons. You should know that.'

Roy nodded. 'This has been the worst three months of my life. It's an effort to get up each morning and I feel so depressed.'

'You seem happy enough when you're with Livvy.'

'Well, yeah, most of the time I am. I just have to get on with it and make the best of a bad job.'

Eddie drained his glass and stood up. 'The sooner we get the band organised, the better. Get you out in front of a screaming audience again. That'll take your mind off your problems.'

'I can't bloody wait.'

* * *

Jane drove home from work, her mind going over the previous night's conversation with Pat and Sammy. They'd both urged her to speak to Ed about her worries over Jon and Jess. She felt sick at the thought. If she was mistaken and Ed tackled the pair, it could destroy the family closeness. But on the other hand, if she chose to stay quiet and they *were* in a relationship, then what? The family closeness would still be destroyed. Ed would have to come clean about Jon's parentage and then Jon might lose all the trust he had in the family. Whichever path she chose would be a nightmare. And then there was tomorrow night when she and Ed would be out again and Jon and Jess would be alone once more.

Maybe she could feign illness halfway through the meal and have Ed drive her home. She shook her head and mumbled, 'Not a good idea, Jane.' What if they caught them at it? All hell would break loose and she couldn't handle that. She glanced across to the stationary driver beside her at the lights. The woman turned her head and smiled as she caught Jane's eye. Jane smiled back. 'Bet *she's* going home to a perfectly normal family,' she muttered, envious of the unflustered-looking woman with the friendly smile. The lights changed and Jane roared away, leaving the little car and the woman with the normal life behind.

As she turned into the private lane, Jane pushed these thoughts to the back of her mind and switched on her glad-to-be-home smile. She walked indoors, where Eddie and Jess were seated at the kitchen table, passing a cigarette to and fro. Jane frowned at Jess's welcoming smile: 'Jess, you know I don't like you smoking. I thought you'd given up? Ed, you shouldn't encourage her.'

Jess rolled her eyes. 'Mum, I'm stressed. I just fancied a quick drag.'

'Well, you were okay over the weekend. You didn't appear to be stressed then,' Jane said, aware that she was being unreasonable, but unable to stop.

'Jane, that's not a very nice thing to say after everything she's been through. What's the matter with you?' Eddie frowned as Jess's face crumpled and she fought to blink back tears.

Jane sighed and shook her head. 'Sorry, Jess, just ignore me. It's been a funny day all round.'

'We know all about funny days, don't we, Jess? We've had one ourselves,' Eddie said.

'Oh, why's that?' Jane helped herself to a glass of red wine and sat down beside him, kicking off her shoes.

'Roy threw a wobbler about Sammy seeing Stuart,' Jess said.

Jane listened as Eddie told her the events of the afternoon.

'I could bang Roy and Sammy's bloody heads together,' she

snapped. 'Today, Sammy was concerned that he wouldn't have a clue what type of linen to buy, etcetera, and she's worrying how he'll manage on his own.'

'Livvy's been shopping with him and sorted him out on that score,' Eddie said.

'It's not taken *her* long to get her feet under his table. So, *is* he alright, Ed?'

'No, he's not. He's depressed and hitting the bottle again. I just don't see what more I can do to help, other than get him concentrating on The Raiders.'

Jane nodded and sniffed the air appreciatively. 'Lasagne?'

'And garlic bread,' Jess said.

'Oh, wonderful! I'm starving.'

Eddie went to the oven and checked his lasagne. 'Done to perfection. Jon shouldn't be long now and then we can eat.'

Jess wobbled to her feet. 'I'm going to the loo.'

'Sammy's going to London with Stu next month,' Jane said as Jess left the kitchen. 'He's arranged to take her to a textile exhibition at Earl's Court.'

'Oh shit! Is she? That'll upset Roy. When you say going with him, you mean staying together in a hotel?' He ran his hands agitatedly through his hair, leaving it standing on end.

Jane reached up and smoothed his locks down with her fingers. 'Well, he's booked separate rooms, but you only have to observe the way he looks at Sammy to know that he wants to take things further.'

'I obviously don't notice these things, being a mere male. Pour me a glass of wine, Jane, will you, while I set the table.'

The phone rang out as Jane picked up the bottle and she grabbed the receiver.

'Oh, hello, Mrs Turner.' She raised her eyebrows at Eddie, who turned and frowned. 'Jon isn't home from work yet, he shouldn't be too long. Okay, well I'll get him to call you. Goodbye.' Eddie stared at her as she hung up. 'She wants to speak to Jonathon.'

'I wonder what the old battleaxe wants. Call your mum and ask her to send the kids home. Jon's here now, I can hear his car on the drive.'

It was a noisy family dinner, during which Jane tried to observe Jon and Jess's reactions to one another. But she couldn't pinpoint anything untoward.

'So, did Grandma Turner say anything other than that she wanted to speak to me?' Jon asked, helping himself to a chunk of garlic bread.

'No, just that,' Jane replied.

'I'll call her later then, when the kitchen's quiet.'

'If you want some peace, use the phone in our room,' Eddie suggested.

'Okay, thanks. But make sure you save me some seconds, don't let greedy Katie finish all the garlic bread.' Jon stood up and teasingly pulled on Katie's pigtails.

'I'm not as greedy as you and Dad,' she said, glaring at Jon.

'Yes, you are.' He laughed, ducking out of the way as she hurled her Barbie doll at him. It hit the dresser with a thud, knocking one of Jane's antique plates on the floor, where it shattered into small pieces.

'Katie, Jon, behave yourselves,' Jane yelled. 'Now look what you've done – that was one of my favourite plates.' She knelt to retrieve the pieces and Jon knelt beside her to help.

'Sorry, Mum,' he apologised. 'I'll buy you another, I promise.'

She smiled at his worried expression. 'You'll have a job. That was a one-off, hand-painted, that I found in a French flea market years ago. It doesn't matter, go and call your grandma before I box your ears.'

His eyes sparkled. 'You haven't done that for years.'

'Only because I can't reach! But you're the right height

while you're down on your knees, so you watch your step, my lad!'

He leapt up, grinning. 'Back in a minute.'

Jane placed the broken pieces of china in the kitchen bin and yawned loudly.

'One more glass of wine and then I'll bath these two and take a shower. I need an early night. We'll be out late tomorrow and you woke me up last night when you came in drunk, stumbling all over the place.' She glared accusingly at Eddie.

'I couldn't get my jeans off,' he said. 'They were stuck on my feet.'

'That's because you didn't take your boots off first, you idiot!'

'I realised that this morning when I fell flat on my face as I tried to stand up. How come *you* didn't help me take them off?'

'You fell asleep as soon as you landed backwards on the bed. I just threw the duvet over you, I was too tired to help you.'

'See how she neglects me sometimes,' Eddie said to Jess as Jon strolled back into the kitchen, frowning. 'What's up, son, problems?'

'Not really. Grandma has to go into hospital for a hip replacement at the end of November. She'd like Jess and me to visit next week, a bit earlier than planned. I'll ask Sean for time off. Will you be okay, Jess? I mean, you only get your ankle plaster off tomorrow and you'll miss your physiotherapy.'

'What time are you planning on going? My physio's at ten on Tuesday. We could go straight after, spend some time with your gran and then go to Brighton for a couple of days like Dad suggested.'

'Okay, that sounds fine.' Jon nodded. 'Sort out the papers and keys for Celia's house, Dad, and we'll attend to that while we're down there.'

'I've decided to take it off the market for the time being,'

Eddie said. 'I'll give you a letter of authority to hand to the agent so that you can sign any paperwork.'

'Okay.' Jon nodded. '*Top of the Pops* is due to start. Shall we go through to the lounge?' He swept Jess up in his arms as she shrieked with laughter. 'She wants to ogle James Perry, don't you?'

'Leave bathing the kids for now, Jane. Come and see this new band. Tell me what you think of them,' Eddie said.

'Can we have some more ice cream then?' Dominic asked hopefully.

Jane smiled. 'Don't you two want to watch the band sing Daddy and Roy's new song?'

Katie shook her head, wrinkling her pert little nose. 'They're always singing Daddy's songs on the TV. I'd rather have more ice cream, please.'

* * *

Eddie strolled into the lounge and joined Jon and Jess on one of the sofas. 'Katie's not the least bit impressed by my fame, she prefers ice cream.'

'Does Roy know they're on tonight?' Jon asked.

'I forgot to mention it. I'll ring him now. Shout me if they come on.' He dashed back to the kitchen.

Livvy answered his call. 'He's in the shower, Ed. Would you like him to call you back later?'

'No, it's okay. Just tell him Perry's Dream's on *Top of the Pops* tonight.'

'He knows. I told him earlier. I'm just cooking him something special for supper to cheer him up a bit.'

'Have you made up then?'

He heard her suppress a giggle. 'We have. Well, you know Roy – there's only one way he knows to make up after a disagreement!'

'Yes, I *do* know Roy, only too well.' Eddie said goodbye and hung up as Jane raised an enquiring eyebrow. 'Don't ask. Come on, let's watch *Top of the Pops* before we miss it.'

Back in the lounge, Simon Bates was introducing Perry's Dream. Jess gazed lustfully at the tall, blond, good-looking James Perry: 'God, he looks so sexy in that cream suit.'

Jon dug her playfully in the ribs. 'He's alright, I suppose. Bit of a smoothie if you ask me.'

As the song came to an end, Eddie turned to his family: 'Well?'

'Brilliant, Ed, as always.' Jane hugged him tightly. 'You're so clever.'

'And Roy,' he reminded her.

'Yeah, and Roy. What was all that about on the phone earlier? You looked a bit angry.'

'I'm not angry, what's the point? Livvy answered the phone. Said they'd made up and she was cooking him supper. He was in the shower.'

'It didn't take *him* long to get over his upset about Sammy. Mind you, if Livvy went round offering it on a plate, he's not going to refuse.' Jane stood up and stretched her arms above her head. 'Come and help me bath the kids, Ed. I'm really tired tonight.'

He stood up and put his arms around her. 'Come on then, *I'll* load the dishwasher while you run the bath and then I'll join you.'

* * *

Alone at last, Jon turned to Jess, eyes shining: 'Two whole nights together in a hotel, I can't wait.'

'Shhh, they'll hear you! It'll be wonderful. The only problem is I'm due my period on Monday, but it's sometimes a day or two late. Why don't we go to Brighton first, spend

Tuesday and Wednesday night there? Go and see your grandma Thursday and Friday, then come home on Saturday?'

'I was hoping we could spend some of the weekend in Brighton, too,' Jon said. 'Anyway, it doesn't matter just this once and let's face it, we should be welcoming it with open arms, rather than complaining about the inconvenience.'

Jess nodded. 'Once we know for sure I'll start taking the pill again, no more worrying.'

* * *

'What's on your mind, sweetheart?' Eddie asked as Jane lay stiffly beside him. 'You've been prickly on and off all night.'

'Oh, it's nothing.' She turned to face him. 'I suppose I'm worrying about Sammy and what's going to happen there. She and Roy shouldn't be apart, it's ridiculous.'

'I know it is, but what can we do? Sam's adamant she doesn't want him back and you told me she quite likes Stuart. By the way, and don't bite my head off for asking this, has she slept with him?'

'That's Roy wanting to know, not you, isn't it?'

'Of course it is.'

'No, she hasn't. But I think she may do soon. They had a steamy-windows session in the car on Monday night.'

'Did they now?'

'Well, you can't blame her, can you?'

'Not at all. But I know how Roy feels – I used to feel sick at the thought of you with Mark Fisher.'

She smiled at him. 'And *I* felt exactly the same when you were with Angie and Sammy feels like that about Livvy. It's a horrible feeling.'

'It is, but apart from worrying about Roy and Sammy, is everything else okay? Are you concerned about me being away when we go on tour next year?'

'I haven't even given it a thought, to be honest,' she replied. 'I won't be able to tour with you like I've done before.'

'You will, occasionally. You can join me for the odd night, surely?'

Jane sighed. 'We'll see; it's not as easy as it used to be, when we packed Jon off with your parents and took baby Jess with us. Katie and Dom are too much for Mum and Dad for any length of time and Jon and Jess will be working. Well, I hope she'll be back at work by then.'

'She will be, she seems fine most of the time and going away next week with Jon will do them both good.'

'Hmm, maybe,' Jane said quietly.

He frowned and tilted her chin. 'What?'

'Nothing,' she said, looking away.

He sat up and pulled her with him. 'Out with it, come on! Something's been bothering you all night.'

'I don't know how to tell you,' she said, lips trembling.

'Try from the beginning.'

'I'm probably making a mountain out of a molehill and you'll be really annoyed with me...'

'Jane, for heaven's sake, what is it?'

'It's Jon and Jess.'

'What about them?'

'Well, don't you think they're a bit too close for brother and sister?'

'What do you mean?'

'Well, they're together all the time, like they're very close, if you know what I mean?'

He shook his head. '*You* think Jon fancies Jess? Jane, what bloody planet are you on? She's his sister.'

Her eyes filled with tears. 'It's not a joke, Ed. And Jess is *not* Jon's sister, in case you've forgotten. Haven't you noticed how lovey-dovey they are with each other?'

He could see she was serious by the set of her mouth. 'I'm

sorry, Jane, I'm not joking, and no, I haven't noticed anything untoward between them. But then again, I haven't been looking either. It's perfectly natural for brothers and sisters to be close, isn't it? *You* should know about closeness between siblings – you've got Peter, I'm an only child. Jess was telling Jon that she loved him only the other day. She told me it's what brothers and sisters say. Am I being naïve here, Jane, believing that to be true?'

She shook her head. 'No, you're not. *I* love our Peter, of course I do.'

'Then don't you think you might be overreacting where Jon and Jess are concerned? He's given her the strength to carry on after Nick's death. You saw the state she was in last Friday. She still loves Nick. Jon's a big support, she needs him. It would set her back weeks if she thought for one minute that you were having doubts about her relationship with him.'

Jane nodded. 'There's something else – I found condom wrappers in Jess's bin the other day.'

'She's probably been clearing out her handbag. They'll be from when she was with Nick, before she went on the pill. Stop worrying about everyone else and worry about me instead. I feel neglected!'

She smiled. 'You want to make love?'

'Don't you?' He pulled her down beside him and caressed her through the silk of her nightdress.

'Oh, Ed,' she sighed, 'I missed your cuddles last night, you drunken lump!'

'Sorry. It was a good lads' night out, but I can't drink like that any more. I'm getting too bloody old.' He rolled on top and kissed her. 'I just hope I never get too old for this.'

31

Eddie lit a cigarette and called Lennon to heel.

'Walkies, fella,' he said as they entered the lane. He'd just waved Jess and Jon off on their trip to Brighton. Since last week's conversation with Jane, he'd secretly observed the pair, but had seen nothing untoward. They were comfortable together, but then they'd always been that way. He shook his head and smiled – Jane's imagination was more than fertile at times.

Back indoors, he checked his watch, slapped ham and tomato between two slices of bread and made a pot of coffee. Roy would be arriving soon to work on songs for the proposed stage set. If all went according to plan, the first gig of the tour would be scheduled for next March.

The meeting with Frank James yesterday had gone well. The Raiders had been the most successful band on Frank's books and he'd told them he was looking forward to working with the group again. He'd suggested they play the main theatres and auditoriums in the UK followed by a European tour.

Roy said he was keen to tour the States, Tim and Phil

fancied Oz. Frank had sprung into action immediately and booked a new studio in an old converted Stockport factory. Tomorrow afternoon, they were having their first full-blown rehearsal since the mid-seventies.

Roy arrived, finished Eddie's sandwich and helped himself to a mug of coffee.

'Would you like me to make you a sandwich of your own?' Eddie asked.

'No, thanks, yours was very nice,' Roy quipped.

'You're a bit more cheerful today.' Eddie offered him a cigarette.

Roy lit up and blew a wobbly circle of smoke above his head. 'Hey look, a crooked halo!'

'I wonder why that would be.'

'Who knows? Anyway, yeah, I *am* feeling happier. I made a big effort with Livvy at the weekend. She stayed over, did all the cleaning and my laundry.'

'Sounds like *she's* the one making the effort.'

Roy ignored the jibe and continued. 'We've chosen names for the sprog. She bought one of those books but we couldn't agree. Anyway, we narrowed it down to two of each and she picked Joshua for a boy and I picked Harley for a girl.'

'Nice.' Eddie nodded. 'Our favourite bike.'

'That's why I chose it. She's certain it's a girl, but who knows?'

'Jane was the same when she was carrying Jess, *and* she was right.'

'Oh well, maybe Livvy's right, too. Women have a sixth sense about these things,' Roy said and swigged the last of his coffee.

'Talking of sixth sense, Jane's got a bee in her bonnet that Jess and Jon are getting a bit too close for comfort.'

Roy sighed. 'Actually, mate, Jane mentioned to Sammy a while ago that she thinks Jon's got the hots for Jess.'

'You're joking? Fuck! I've just waved them off on a trip to Brighton. I've booked them into The Ship for a couple of nights before they visit Angie's mum.'

'Don't worry, Ed. Like you say, Jane's probably got it all wrong. It hasn't been an easy ride for Jess recently. Jon's just being supportive from what I can see.'

'That's what *I* said.' Eddie pushed his concern to the back of his mind. 'Right, let's get to work. We've a busy few months in front of us.'

* * *

In spite of heavy traffic, Jon and Jess arrived in Brighton just before six and checked into the hotel. Jess held onto Jon's arm as they followed the porter with the cases down a plush carpeted hallway to their adjacent rooms.

'Dad could have saved some money if he'd known we'll be sharing the same bed,' she said quietly as they went into her room.

'What he doesn't know won't hurt,' Jon said and slipped the porter a couple of pounds. 'We'll unpack first then call home. Come to my room when you're ready.'

As Jon left, Jess gazed out of the window. It was dusk and the fairground lights from the Palace Pier were reflected on the sea. Directly opposite lay the stretch of beach she'd walked on in April, following the argument with her dad. She swallowed the lump in her throat as she remembered sitting with Nick on the pebbles. She drew the curtains and sighed. Then she thought of Jon, waiting next door, and smiled.

She unpacked a short black dress, hung it in the wardrobe and put the rest of her clothes in the drawers. Jon had promised to take her for a special meal in The Lanes tomorrow night and she planned to wear the dress over her new lacy underwear.

Her case empty, she pushed it under the bed and went to his room.

'You okay?'

She nodded. 'I felt a bit sad when I looked out the window, I remembered sitting with Nick on the beach.'

'Come here.' He took her in his arms, kissed her gently and held her close. 'Feel better now?' he whispered into her hair.

'Much.'

'I'll call home, let them know we've arrived.'

Jess checked her watch: 'Mum should be home from work now.'

'Have a bounce on the bed, it's very comfy,' he said, grinning. 'The bathroom's really nice, too. Have you got a bath or a shower cubicle?'

'A shower cubicle. Why, what have you got?'

'Both. We could take a bath together later, if you like.'

Jess smiled. 'I *would*. Ring home then it's done and we can relax properly.'

* * *

Eddie popped his head around the lounge door and smiled at Jane, who was lying on the sofa. 'They've arrived. The rooms are nice and they've got sea views.'

'Good. But I still feel anxious about them,' she said as he strolled into the room.

'Well, there's absolutely no need. Stop worrying. Here, have another drink.' He topped up her glass with Chardonnay and sat down, lifting her legs across his knee. 'It's nice to have the lounge to ourselves.' Katie and Dominic were in bed and Lennon was snoring softly on the rug in front of the fire.

'Oh, that's lovely,' Jane said as he massaged her feet. 'How was your afternoon with Roy?'

'Great, we got loads done. Three new songs are ready for Friday's rehearsal. I'll play them for you later.'

'That'll be nice. Are they ballads?'

'Two are rockers, right up Roy's street. He absolutely belted them out, and the other has a waltz rhythm. How was Sam today?'

'Fine, she was out with Stuart again last night.'

'Getting to be a regular thing, dates with Stuart.'

'She's seen him every night since we went out on Saturday. He seems really smitten. She's going to his place for a meal tonight and he's promised to cook for her.'

'Bit cosy, isn't it?' Eddie frowned.

'What do you mean cosy? Why shouldn't he cook her a meal?'

'Not so much the meal, but her going to his place. Things might move forward.'

'I hope they do. Sammy needs to feel loved again.'

'Hmm.' He wasn't convinced and switched on the TV. 'We'll watch this film, then listen to the songs.'

'Sounds good to me,' she said, snuggling up to him.

* * *

Sammy stirred in her sleep and turned over. There was an arm lying around her waist and for a moment she wasn't sure where she was. She opened her eyes and looked around. It definitely wasn't her bedroom and the arm wasn't Roy's. She inclined her head to see Stuart's gentle green eyes looking into hers.

'Hello.'

'Hi!' he said. 'You look kind of puzzled.'

She smiled and reached to stroke his cheek. 'I thought I was dreaming for a moment.'

'I'm sure *I* am. I'll wake up soon and find out that this is all just a dream.'

'You won't, because *I'm* right here and it wasn't,' Sammy said, her thoughts returning to the previous night. They'd eaten the chilli Stuart had made and shared a bottle of wine, sitting side by side on the rug in front of the fire. They'd held hands, reminisced about the sixties, and listened to music.

Stuart made coffee accompanied by brandy and by the time Sammy stood up to drive home, although not feeling drunk, she realised she'd had more than she should.

Stuart had drunk as much, if not more, than she, so *he* wasn't capable of driving either. He suggested calling her a taxi and picked up the phone while Sammy flopped back down beside him. They were locked in one another's arms in seconds, kissing passionately, the phone back on its cradle.

Sammy looked into his eyes, willing him to ask her to stay. When he did, he offered her his bed, telling her he'd sleep on the sofa. She kissed him and unbuttoned his shirt, saying she was happy to share with him. Stuart hauled her to her feet, asked if she was sure and when she nodded, he led her upstairs.

They tumbled onto the bed and he slowly undressed her and she him. She felt no shyness as he looked at her and told her how beautiful she was. She admired his physique and his body felt good under her hands.

He was a skilful and passionate lover and she was amazed how easily and often he brought her to orgasm. Being used to Roy and his ways she never expected another man's touch to have quite that effect. They made love most of the night and eventually lay spent in each other's arms.

She sat up and yawned. 'What time is it, Stu?'

'About six. Surely you don't want to get up yet? You've only had an hour's sleep.'

'Of course not, but I'll need to leave about seven thirty. I have to go home and get ready for work. I haven't even got a toothbrush or clean knickers with me. I bet Pat will be wondering where I am – I should have called her last night.'

'She'll have guessed you stayed over. I've a spare toothbrush, but I can't help you in the knickers department. Anyway,' he said, pulling her back into his arms, 'I'd rather have you without.'

'Men,' she said, kissing him on the nose, 'you're all the same!'

'Well, can you blame me when you are so deliciously irresistible? Can I make love to you again?' He circled her nipples lightly with his fingertips, his mouth seeking hers.

She sighed as he nibbled her ears and ran his hand over her stomach. 'You don't have to ask,' she said. His politeness was so refreshing after Roy expecting sex as his right. Sammy pushed the sudden image of Roy's face away as Stuart's hand slipped between her thighs. Why on earth had she thought about him? She closed her mind and concentrated instead on the wonderful feelings she was experiencing as Stuart's fingers explored.

* * *

Pat was at the kitchen table reading a newspaper as Sammy sloped in and sat down opposite.

'No need to ask what you've been up to!' Pat raised a neatly plucked eyebrow. 'So?'

'So!' Sammy flicked her hair back and pouted. 'Did you know I'm deliciously irresistible?'

'Are you now? I didn't realise you were going to spend the night with him.'

'Neither did I. It kind of took us by surprise. But I'm glad I did. He was wonderful and I'm feeling on top of the world.'

Tim sauntered barefoot into the kitchen, put his hands on Sammy's shoulders and kissed the top of her head. 'The wanderer returns.'

'She spent the night at Stuart's,' Pat told him.

'As in "spent the night"?'

Sammy nodded. 'Same as.'

'And?' Tim said, taking a seat.

'It was a wonderful night, of course.'

'Good for you, girl. Play Roy at his own game, eh?'

'Oh, Tim, trust you.' Pat glared at her tactless husband. 'She didn't do it to get back at Roy, she did it because she wanted to. Didn't you, Sam?'

'That's right. No strings, no hang-ups and no false promises. You can stick love as far as I'm concerned. If last night was pure lustful sex, then I want more. It causes no pain, no hurt, just pleasure.' She stood up and stretched. 'Right, I'm off to have a soak before I get ready for work. I'll call Jane first and let her know I'm going to be a bit late in.'

* * *

'Sorry, love, didn't mean to put my foot in it,' Tim said. 'I'm glad she enjoyed herself. It kinda worries me though, this no love thing. I suspect Stuart's more than a little in love with our Sam, and at the end of the day, *she's* still very much in love with Roy.'

Pat sighed. 'Maybe, but we'll have to wait and see. No doubt someone will get hurt along the way, but I have a feeling that it won't be Sammy this time.'

He nodded in agreement. 'I'll call the estate agents later, see if the vendor's accepted our offer. If they haven't, I'll go up a couple of grand, no more for now.'

'Well, I'm off for a shower so I'll leave you to it,' Pat said.

* * *

'Morning, Jane.' Sammy smiled wanly as Jane placed a mug of strong coffee and a chocolate donut in front of her.

'So, come on, don't keep me in suspense. Why are you late? Why so tired and what did Stuart cook for you?'

'You're a nosy cow, Jane Mellor,' Sammy said as her mum's head popped around the door.

'Morning, girls, everything okay? You look tired, Sam, didn't you sleep well?'

'Like a log,' she replied. 'But I was late going to sleep and early waking up.'

'I see... Well, I'm going to get stuck into that pile of invoices on my desk. See you later.'

'You stayed over at Stuart's, didn't you?' Jane whispered as Molly closed the door.

Sammy nodded. 'I did, and to answer your question, he made a fabulous chilli.'

'Well, you obviously had a good time. How was he... you know?'

Sammy smiled. 'Great, *bloody* great in fact!'

'Really? So... you weren't disappointed, I mean, after Roy?'

'Not at all. I thought Roy knew every trick in the book, but Stuart had a few surprises up his sleeve. He was so polite, too. Actually asked if he could make love to me again this morning, didn't just assume it was his right because I was in his bed.'

'He's such a nice guy. How do you feel about him?'

'I really like him, obviously. I wouldn't have slept with him otherwise. But I don't feel love for him.' Sammy bit into her donut as Jane frowned.

'Well, I think he loves *you*, the way he looks at you and everything.'

'Jane, I love Roy, and in spite of the fact that he's hurt me, I'd take him back today if Livvy could be guaranteed to be out of his life forever. When I was driving home from Stuart's this morning, I felt more on an even footing with Roy. I hope that doesn't sound like I'm using Stuart for sex. I wanted to sleep with him because it felt right and I needed to know that it wasn't me being crap in bed that pushed Roy into Livvy's arms. After last night, I know it wasn't.'

'You shouldn't have felt like that anyway. Roy still wanted you. He asked Ed if you'd slept with Stuart and Ed asked me. You hadn't then, so I said no. He told Ed he couldn't bear the thought of you sleeping with Stuart or anyone else.'

Sammy took a sip of coffee. 'Really?'

'Really. Sam, don't divorce him. It's such a waste. Live apart like you're doing, but don't divorce him.'

She shrugged. 'We have to be legally separated for two years before we can get divorced anyway.'

'I'd think twice about the whole thing. If you still love him and he still loves you, it doesn't make sense to me. He'll be away with the group for weeks on end next year and she's not going to like it one bit. She won't be able to go with him in her condition and then with a new baby to look after. He's going to spend a lot of nights on his own.'

Sammy nodded, feeling a rush of guilt. If she hadn't forced Roy to move out, Livvy wouldn't have been able to spend any more nights with him and the relationship might have fizzled out. But then, she thought, why should she feel guilty? She'd only done what Roy had done. Maybe if she hadn't drunk so much wine, or accepted that final brandy, common sense would have told her to go home. But she'd really wanted to stay with Stuart. So why were doubts crowding her head?

Taking a deep breath, she reached for the phone. She dialled a number that she'd never dialled before, but one that was firmly etched in her mind.

'Hi, it's me. Did I wake you? Sorry, I shouldn't have called. No, no, I'd better go, I'm sorry.' She hung up quickly.

Jane stared at her. 'Did you just call Stuart?'

Before Sammy could reply, the phone shrilled out. She stared at it as though it would bite her.

'Answer it,' Jane ordered, but Sammy shook her head. Jane sprang across the office and snatched up the receiver. 'Hello,

Cantello Designs! Oh hi, Roy. No, she's here, just a minute.' Jane held out the phone but Sammy shook her head.

'I can't,' she mouthed. 'I think she's with him.'

Jane spoke into the receiver again. 'Are you alone? Okay, hang on. He's on his own. You woke him up.'

Sammy chewed her lip and took the phone while Jane tactfully left the office.

'Hi, Roy. Just wondered how you were doing.'

'I'm fine, Sam, but I'm missing you so very much. How's Jason and how are things with you and Stuart?'

'Jason's okay and me and Stuart are just good friends,' she replied, swallowing hard. 'Well, um, it was nice to talk to you. I just wanted to say good luck with the rehearsal this afternoon. I know getting the band back together means so much to you all.'

'Thanks. Sammy?'

'Yeah.'

'I'm so sorry for everything. I still love you, darling.'

'Oh, Roy, don't, please.' She wished she hadn't called him now. Hearing him say that was so painful.

'But I do love you, you know I do.'

'It's too late for all that.'

'It's not too late. I've never stopped loving you. And why would you bother calling me if you didn't care? Come over and see me, Sam, please.'

She hesitated. Roy must have sensed her hesitation and tried again: 'Come to the flat for lunch. You haven't seen it yet, I'd really value your opinion.'

'I'm not sure. I don't know that I want to be alone with you.'

'For God's sake, Sam, it's me, your husband. Speaking to you has made me realise just how much I'm missing you. Sammy, I beg you, please come.'

'What time do you have to leave for your rehearsal?'

'I have to be at the studio for two. If I leave here around one thirty, it should give me plenty of time.'

'I'll see you about twelve then. Bye.' She hung up and leant back in her chair. What the hell was she doing and why? She could hear Jane out in the corridor, talking to Ruby. 'Jane,' she called. 'Come in here, quick.'

Jane popped her head around the door. 'What's up?'

'Close the door,' Sammy mouthed. 'I'm going to see Roy's new flat at lunchtime. For God's sake, *don't* tell my mother. She'll be really angry with me. If Stuart calls, tell him I've gone to the bank. I'll ring him back later.'

Jane nodded. 'I'm sure you and Roy can work things out if you really want to. I know he's been a stupid fool but you can find it in your heart to forgive him. As far as *I'm* concerned, Livvy, the baby and even Stuart don't come into the equation.'

* * *

Sammy's finger hovered over the bell as the door flew open, startling her. She felt her stomach looping as Roy stood there smiling.

'Hi,' she said, smiling back.

'I spotted your car from the window. Come on in, you look very nice,' he said, admiring her black suit and cream sweater. 'But then, you always do.' He bent to kiss her cheek.

'Thanks.' She followed him up the stairs and into the flat. 'I could say the same of you. That shirt's lovely, is it new?'

Roy glanced down at his brown, needlecord shirt. 'I bought it this week.'

'It suits you, matches your eyes. Did Livvy choose it?'

'No, I did. Take a seat.' He gestured towards the sofa.

'I will, in a minute.' She slipped off her jacket and threw it over a chair. 'Show me round the flat first. This lounge is beautiful, and the fireplace is stunning, although I'm not too sure about the cushions and that rug – plain cream or gold would have been classier.'

'Ah, well, *those* are Livvy's choices, I'm afraid.'

'Why am I not surprised?' she said, following him into the kitchen. 'Very well equipped.'

He led her down the corridor to the bathroom. She smiled at the towels on the floor. He picked them up and threw them over the towel rail. 'Sorry, I forgot about those.'

She picked up a bottle of aftershave, minus its top. The evocative aroma made her smile. 'That scent brings back a million memories,' she said as she screwed the top back on.

'Good memories or bad?' He stared into her eyes.

She shivered. 'Mainly good.'

'Would you like to see the bedroom?' He raised a teasing eyebrow and smiled.

She shrugged. 'Might as well.'

The brass bed had been hastily re-made, the duvet lying not quite straight, and Roy's cast-off clothes were in an untidy heap in one corner of the room. She was heartened to see nothing of Livvy's in evidence.

'It's a lovely room. Don't you have a laundry basket?'

'No point. I never used ours at home, did I?'

'True. But you actually have to lift up the lid, the clothes don't jump in by themselves.'

'I know.' He laughed. 'But that's work for women!'

Sammy tutted. 'Your mother has a lot to answer for, she never house-trained you.'

He smiled lazily, his dark eyes holding hers. 'Fancy some lunch?'

'I'd love a sandwich. Have you any juice?'

'I'll see what I can find. Take a seat. Will cheese and ham be okay?'

'Lovely.' She sat down on the sofa and glanced around.

Livvy's touches were everywhere. Sammy shook her head and smiled. The girl was obviously enjoying playing house, but funnily enough, it didn't hurt like she'd expected it to. It was almost as though making love with Stuart had had a cathartic effect.

Roy reappeared, carrying a tray laden with sandwiches and two glasses of orange juice.

'Very domesticated,' she said as he placed it on the coffee table. 'Have you been taking lessons from Ed?'

'Don't be sarky.' He flopped down beside her. 'I can do things when I have to.'

'The flat's lovely, I can see you're quite comfortable. Err, Livvy not moved in with you?'

He shook his head. 'No. She stays over, but says there's no point in us getting used to living together just yet, when I'm gonna be away with the band.'

'Hmm.' Sammy nodded, glad to hear that. 'Are you looking forward to being on the road again?'

'I am actually,' he said and bit into a sandwich. 'In bed the other night, I was thinking back to our first tour. When we were bottom of the bill and me and Ed wrote "My Special Girl".'

'Then soon you were top of the bill and the song went into the charts,' Sammy said with a catch in her voice as the memories of that exciting time came flooding back.

'I wish we could go back to those early days,' Roy said wistfully.

'Do you?' She looked at him.

He nodded. 'They were wonderful times, full of discovery and simple pleasures.'

'Jane and I often say that we wish we could go back, too, but knowing what we know now.'

'Would you change anything?'

'Nothing – except for the last few months.'

'Same here,' he said quietly.

Sammy sighed. 'Oh, Roy, what went wrong? We were so happy together.'

He put down his sandwich and took her hands. 'Me, that's

what went wrong. It was never you, Sam. You put up with a lot from me over the years; drugs, boozing, my being away all the time. Bringing up the boys on your own, working hard at your business and me expecting you to drop everything and give me your full attention the minute I walked through the door, as though no one else mattered. I'm sorry for everything I've put you through. This bloody mess I've got into now is just about the most disastrous thing I could have done to us and at the worst possible time.'

She looked at their hands entwined on her lap and at Roy's contrite expression. His eyes held hers for a few seconds before his arms crept around her and his lips sought hers. She clung to him, returning his insistent kisses. His hands slid under her sweater. The phone rang out, making them jump apart.

'Ignore it,' he whispered, moving back towards her.

'What if it's important? Maybe it's Ed changing the time of your rehearsal, or something.'

'Nothing is more important to me at this moment than kissing you, not The Raiders, not anything.' The phone stopped ringing as Roy pulled her onto his knee. She unbuttoned his shirt, snuggling into him.

'Love the scent of your body.'

'And I love the scent of yours,' he said, yanking off her sweater. As they slid down onto the rug, he said, 'Better take off your skirt. This rug sheds like crazy and you'll be covered in pink fluff.'

She slipped out of the skirt and threw it onto the chair with her jacket, pushing the thought that she was mad to be doing this with him from her mind. The look in his eyes as he gazed longingly at her was enough.

'Sam, you know nothing gets me more excited than the sight of you in black stockings and French knickers. Did you put them on specially?'

'No. How on earth could I have done that, when I didn't

know I was going to be seeing you? And I certainly didn't have *this* in mind when I called you earlier.'

'But you want to?' His eyes held such a pleading expression that she knew she was powerless to refuse.

'Yes.' She reached up and kissed him. Nothing else mattered to her at this moment other than pleasing him. The phone rang again as he slid into her. They let it ring and rolled together on the rug, frantically swapping positions, lost in their urgent lovemaking.

'Sam, we've still got it, girl,' he whispered, stroking her hair.

She lay quietly, waiting for her breath to return, hardly able to believe what she'd done. *How* had she made love like that after spending the night in Stuart's bed? She could feel her cheeks warming and hoped Roy would think it was the result of their passion.

He cradled her to him, dropping kisses all over her. 'I love you, Sammy; I love you so much it hurts. I can't believe that just happened. I thought I'd never get to make love to you again. I really thought you didn't want me any more.'

She swallowed hard. 'I love you too, Roy, more than you know. So, what now?'

'God only knows. What do *you* want?'

'Everything to be as it was before you met Livvy, but that's impossible.'

The phone rang a third time and Roy reached over to answer.

'Hello. Oh, hi, Ed. No, I've been here all morning. I heard the phone ring, yeah, but Sammy's here so I ignored it.' He was quiet for a moment and then, 'Okay, thanks for that. See you soon, bye.'

Sammy smiled as he hung up. 'What did he want?'

'Livvy called him. She wondered where I was when I didn't pick up – it was her ringing the first couple of times.'

'Thank God you didn't. That would have really put me off.'

'I suppose I'd better give her a call, see what she wants. Do you fancy a shower? I'm sweaty and we're covered in pink fluff.'

'Yeah, in a minute. I'll brew up while you make your call. Can I borrow a T-shirt?'

'I'll get you one from the bedroom. Any particular colour?'

'You choose, so long as it covers my bottom.'

He handed her a white T-shirt and she pulled it over her head while he watched her, head on one side.

'What?'

'Nothing, just checking it covers your arse!'

'And does it?' She twirled in front of him.

'Just about. Anyway, no one can see us up here. We're well set back from the road.'

'I'd rather not take any chances. Make your call and I'll put the kettle on.'

* * *

Sammy smiled as she spooned coffee granules into two china mugs decorated with pink and blue butterflies. 'She's no bloody taste,' she muttered. The kettle boiled and she popped her head around the door to see if Roy had finished his call.

He was seated on the floor, leaning against the sofa and she could see the scratches on his back from her fingernails. He was still talking and her heart leapt as she gazed at his body, long legs stretched out on the rug.

He hung up and turned his head. 'She's out to lunch. That was Sean wishing the band good luck for the rehearsal. How about that shower? We can have our coffees later.' He stood up, held out his arms and she moved into them.

* * *

Livvy parked her Mini in the staff car park. She turned off the engine and rested her head on the steering wheel. She was late back from lunch and Sean would be mad. They were short-staffed as it was with Jon away. She'd called Roy twice this lunchtime and when he didn't answer, she called Ed, who didn't know where he was either. She'd driven to the flat to see if he was okay, convinced he'd fallen in the shower and knocked himself out.

As she swung onto the semicircular drive of the big old house she saw Sammy's Porsche parked next to his car and her stomach heaved. She sped off the drive, pulled up around the corner, leapt from the car and was sick in the gutter. What was going on now? She had a key but couldn't face walking in on them, even if they were only talking, which she very much doubted, otherwise he would have answered the phone. Heart pounding, she drove back to work.

As she stomped up the stairs, Sean looked at her and frowned. 'Now what's up and why are you late back? Roy called you a few minutes ago. He's probably left the flat by now, but he said he'll see you tonight.'

'Oh, did he?' Livvy stormed into the staffroom, took off her jacket and washed her face. She flounced back behind the counter and sat down on the stool. 'He'll be lucky.'

'Why?'

She told him what had happened.

He patted her shoulder sympathetically. 'I'm sorry, Liv. There's only going to be one winner in this mess. If it had been anyone other than him, I would have said there may be good reason why he wasn't answering his phone.'

'But because it's *him* you can only think of the obvious.'

'Yeah.'

'Maybe she went to see him over something to do with the house, or Jason, or the business?' She knew she was grasping at straws.

'Well, there's always that, but it doesn't explain why he didn't answer. I'm not trying to hurt you, I'm trying to help you face facts.'

She nodded and grabbed the phone.

'He'll have left the flat by now,' Sean said, looking at his watch.

'I'm trying to catch Ed before *he* leaves,' she said. 'He can pass on a message for me. Hi, Ed, it's Livvy again. Yes, I know he was at the flat, thanks. I don't want to speak to him now, but would you tell him I won't be round tonight, or any other night for that matter, and I hope he enjoyed his lunchtime with Sammy. If he denies she was with him, you can tell him I saw her car on the drive. Thanks.'

She slammed the receiver down and sat back with her arms folded. 'That's the last time the Cantellos make a fool of me.'

32

'I'm back,' Sammy announced as she dodged past her mother's office and into hers and Jane's.

Jane looked up as Sammy closed the door. 'Why are you wearing shades in November and what's happened to your hair?'

Sammy removed the glasses and took a mirror and small vanity case from the filing cabinet.

Jane tapped her chin with a pen and watched as Sammy applied make-up and fastened her hair back with a large slide.

'That's better. I took a quick shower with Roy, my make-up washed away and my hair got wet. He doesn't have a nozzle on his dryer, so I couldn't blow the ends under properly.' She realised she was babbling and fell silent as Jane stared at her, eyebrows raised in amusement.

'A shower with Roy, eh? So, what's going on now?'

'Oh God, I don't know. I really don't know.'

'Well, I hope this is the start of you two getting your acts together. What will you say to Stuart? You can't mess around with his feelings.'

'I don't intend to. Stuart knows how I feel about Roy and I hope he'll see last night as nothing more than a drunken mistake. I love Roy, *he* loves me. We've just had the most amazing time. Took us both by surprise; I honestly had no intentions of that happening. It just did and it was incredible.'

'Did you tell Roy you slept with Stuart?'

'God no! He'll go crazy when he finds out.'

'He's bound to find out sooner or later.'

'Not unless someone tells him and there's only you, Pat and Tim know.'

'And Ed.'

'How did Ed find out?'

'Tim told him, and Ed rang to ask if it was true.'

'They're as bad as a bunch of old women for gossiping.' Sammy tutted. 'Well, I hope they don't say anything to Roy.'

'They wouldn't do that.'

'I feel fit for nothing now and I've got loads to do this afternoon. Has Ruby been in with the children's samples in the cord and check?'

'No, but I'll go and chase her up while you catch your breath.'

'Thanks, Jane. I need to get them into the shops next week, see how they go before I order more fabric.' Sammy slumped in her chair and yawned loudly. 'Oh, sorry, I just want to sit here for a while and calm down, my heart's racing. Dear God, I can't believe what I've done. It's almost like sleeping with Stuart made me feel guilty and I had to make things right with Roy, without him knowing why. Isn't that mad when you consider what he's done to me? I can't make any sense of it at all.'

Jane smiled. 'Well, at least it's made you realise you can't let him go that easily.'

Sammy nodded. 'But it doesn't make Livvy and the baby disappear. The flat's full of blonde bimbo stuff. Naff cushions, a pink rug that sheds fluff everywhere. What was Roy thinking, letting her choose things like that?'

'Well, like you said yourself, he wouldn't have a clue.'

'Did Pat call while I was out?'

'Yes, she's dropped Tim at our place and then she's taking the girls for their school uniforms. They start next Monday. God help Manor Banks with two more Raiders' kids to educate. By the way, Phil Jackson's got two exes and six kids!'

'I'm not in the least bit surprised.'

'He's free again now and he's had a vasectomy,' Jane said. 'So he's raring to go.'

Sammy laughed. 'Well, *he'll* certainly enjoy himself on the road!'

* * *

Eddie was standing by his Jeep, finishing a cigarette as Roy pulled into the car park of the factory conversion where the rehearsal studio was situated. He leapt out, grinning like the proverbial Cheshire cat, and slid down the wing of his BMW.

'Hi, Roy,' Eddie greeted him. 'Do you recognise this place?'

'Should I?' Roy frowned, looking up at the three-storey building that also housed craft studios and artists' workshops. 'Oh yeah, I do! It's the old paint factory where you used to work when you were married to Angie.'

'It certainly is. I've come a long way since *those* days.'

'Bloody hell, mate, you're not wrong there!'

'My gear's inside. Give us a guitar to carry.'

'Thanks, Ed. I've brought three, you take the Strat.'

'There's an old lift up to the third floor, where we're rehearsing,' Eddie told him, leading the way. 'Everyone's here. I warned them you might be a bit late. So, have you been discussing stuff with Sam?'

'Amongst other things,' Roy replied airily as the lift door opened.

In the lift, Eddie glanced sideways at Roy's beaming face. 'What other things?' he asked, pressing for the third floor. 'You mean...?'

Roy nodded. 'The most mind-blowing lunchtime ever.'

'But I thought...' Eddie trailed off.

'Thought what?'

'Nothing, I presumed you were just talking, that's all.'

'So did we. She called me, I invited her over, made us lunch, we got talking about old times and that was it, we couldn't help ourselves.'

'What about Livvy?'

'Oh, *she* wasn't there,' Roy quipped. 'It was just the two of us.'

'Stop pissing about!'

'Sorry, Ed, couldn't resist. I don't honestly know. All I *do* know is that I love Sam, *she* loves me and I think I've got a final chance with her. There has to be a way of resolving this mess, because I want Sammy back more than I've ever wanted anything in my life right now.'

'Sounds fair enough to me, but we'll talk some more later,' Eddie said as the lift creaked to a standstill. They alighted and made their way down a long, carpeted corridor to the rehearsal studio, where the rest of the band was tuning up.

'This is a brilliant place, Ed!' Roy exclaimed, looking round. The studio, run by two ex-professional musicians, was well equipped. In the corner, Carl was entertaining them all, doing Jerry Lee Lewis impersonations on a brand-new piano. 'Plenty of space to move around and the ceiling height's just right. We should get a great sound. We could have used their PA system, too, save lugging ours with us.'

'Frank's booked it for three afternoons a week until Christmas,' Eddie said. 'We can re-book in January if we feel the need. And we can always run through stuff at my place. Right, let's get cracking.' He picked up his drumsticks and looked at Roy, who was removing his Fender from its case and chatting animatedly to Phil. It was obvious that Sammy had not mentioned her night of lust with Stuart. Roy was too happy for one thing. *Ah well, she must know what she's about*, he thought.

'Ready, lads?' Roy called. 'Let's warm up with "Summertime Blues". Two, three, four!'

They launched into the old Eddie Cochran favourite, closely followed by Chuck Berry's 'Sweet Little Sixteen', with Roy in his element, duck-walking up and down the room.

Dave and Geoff, the studio proprietors, were laughing at his antics and cheered loudly as the song finished.

By the end of the first set, sweat dripped from them all. Eddie stripped off his top and rubbed himself down with a towel. He delved into his bag for a clean T-shirt and a bottle of Lucozade. 'Shit! That was brilliant,' he said and slugged back his drink. 'But I'm really out of condition. My back and shoulders are killing me.'

'We're all out of condition,' Roy said. 'We need to join a gym or we'll never cope with the pace of playing night after night for weeks on end. But I really enjoyed that. We'll slow the pace a bit and do a few ballads when we catch our breath. Have you got a spare drink, Ed? I completely forgot to bring anything with me, I was in such a rush to get here.'

'In the bag. Help yourself.'

They started the second set with 'My Special Girl', Roy and Eddie's voices filling the room with their harmonies.

'Sounds as good as it ever did,' Phil said. 'That'll get 'em all weeping and chucking their knickers on stage!'

'Well, it never fails to move Jane, Sammy and Pat,' Eddie said.

'Not Sammy any more, surely?' Phil looked at Roy.

'I think I can safely say it will still have an effect on Sammy,' Roy said, smiling.

Tim caught his brother-in-law's eye: 'Have you and our Sammy been up to something?'

Roy shrugged. 'What do you mean?'

'You know full well what I mean. You and Sam, what's going on?'

'We love one another.'

'Well, in that case sort yourselves out and get back together. Loads of guys have affairs, they even father kids, but they don't break up their marriages.'

'It was Sammy's choice, not mine. I never wanted us to split up in the first place.'

'Well, you've obviously made a move to patch things up today,' Phil chipped in. 'Don't let her slip through your fingers again. You're making the same mistake I made – I let Laura go instead of fighting for her. My second marriage failed because I'm still in love with Laura.'

'Really, are you?' Eddie looked at Phil, who was usually so flippant in his comments about marriage and women.

Phil nodded sadly. 'It kills me when I go and visit the kids and she's there with her new bloke. I could throttle the bloody life out of him. The grass might appear greener, but believe me, Roy, it's not.'

'I'll second that,' Eddie said. 'Right, before we continue, are we all agreed that Roy should be back with Sammy, where he belongs?'

'Yes!' The group was one voice.

'Okay, okay, if she'll have me,' Roy said.

At the end of the rehearsal and as they loaded their cars, Eddie took Roy to one side. 'Come back and eat with us tonight.'

'What about Livvy? She's coming over later. I need to talk

with her. Though Christ knows what I should say. I promised her the earth the other day, a new home, more kids.'

'She's not coming to the flat. When she couldn't get an answer to her calls, she was worried. She drove to your place and saw Sammy's car on the drive.'

'Shit! So she called *you* again and told you that, did she?'

Eddie nodded. 'She put two and two together, said to tell you she won't be round tonight, or any other night for that matter!'

Roy sighed heavily. 'Right, well I suppose I might as well follow you home then. Do you think I should call her or leave it for now?'

'Leave it; you've screwed her up enough. I don't know how much more she can take.'

'Maybe you're right.'

* * *

Livvy dug out her address book. She looked up a number and dialled it before she had a change of heart. The call was answered by a woman whose voice she didn't recognise, but guessed it was Tim Davis's wife, by the slight American accent. The woman told her Sammy was working late. Livvy scribbled down the number she was given. This time Jane answered the call. Spurred on by the friendly tone in Jane's voice, she asked to speak to Sammy.

'Hold on, I'll pass you over.'

'Olivia.' Sammy's tone sounded shocked but cool.

'I'd like you to pass on a message to Roy.'

'Why can't you speak to him yourself?'

'Because no doubt you will see him before I do.'

'Oh... will I?'

'Well, you saw him at lunchtime. Your car was on the drive. You just won't let him go, will you? You say you don't want him, yet you're determined to keep him from *me*. We love one another; *I'm* having his baby. He wants it no matter what he tells you. We've even chosen names. I can't cope with being messed around any more. Tell Roy I'm going back to Glasgow, I might let him know when the baby arrives. You can have him back, Sammy. *You're* the one wanting your cake and eating it, not Roy. I know you've also got Stuart in tow. He called in the shop this evening. I overheard him telling Sean that everything's great with the two of you and that you spent last night together. You and Roy are tarred with the same brush, messing about with people's feelings.'

Livvy felt close to hysteria then Jane's voice came soothingly down the line: 'Calm down, Livvy, I can hear you over the other side of the office. Now listen to me: all this shouting is not good for your baby. Are you at home? Okay, me and Sammy will be with you shortly. Sit on the sofa, relax, and take some deep breaths.'

* * *

'Come on, we've got to go to Livvy's place before she miscarries that child,' Jane ordered. 'She was in a right state just then. You can tell me what she said on the way over. Grab your bag and get in my car. Go on, Sam, move yourself.' She handed Sammy the car keys, switched off the lights and pushed her out of the door.

'So, come on, what did she say?' Jane said as they headed for Jackson's Heath. 'You're white as a sheet.'

'She knows I spent the night with Stuart. She'll tell Roy, he'll hit the roof.'

'Hey, hang on! Get it into perspective, you're not the one at fault here.'

'It doesn't matter, he'll never forgive me. I'll lose him to her again.'

'Not if he's got any sense,' Jane muttered grimly. 'Where is he tonight?'

'At the flat, I presume. We didn't actually make arrangements to meet up, I suppose we thought it wasn't necessary. I was going to call him later.'

'I'll stop at that phone box down the road and call Ed. He should be home from the studio by now, he'll know where Roy is.'

'Don't tell him we're going to Livvy's. I don't want Roy turning up until I've persuaded her to keep her mouth shut. Though God knows how I'm going to do it.'

Jane stopped at the phone box and jumped out of the car. She was back in minutes and restarted the engine. 'Roy's at our place with Phil. Ed wondered where I was. Forgot to tell him I was working late. I told him we're taking some stock to the Wilmslow shop and he suggested we go back for something to eat after we've finished.'

'Oh, that's good. Right, let's get to Livvy's and sort this mess out.'

* * *

Sammy pressed the intercom and the catch was released. The door to flat seven stood ajar but Sammy knocked before they entered. Livvy was in the bedroom, throwing things into a suitcase. Sammy noted her pale, tear-streaked face and shaking hands.

'What are you doing?' she asked as Jane went into the room and put her arms around Livvy's shoulders.

'I told you, I'm going back to Glasgow.' Livvy sobbed. 'I can't stay here with all this mess going on around me.'

'Well, whose fault is it? This mess, I mean?' Sammy said from the doorway. She couldn't bring herself to step into the room where Roy had spent time with the girl.

'Sammy!' Jane warned as Livvy's shoulders shook even more. 'Livvy, come and sit down and I'll make us a nice cup of tea.'

Sammy walked ahead into the lounge, her stomach churning. Seeing Livvy again with Roy's child growing inside her tore her heart to pieces and she wished with all her being that she could have another baby with him. She sank down onto the sofa before her legs gave way. Livvy flopped onto a chair opposite her and folded her arms protectively over her bump as Sammy's eyes bore into it.

Jane came in with three mugs and sat down beside Sammy.

'I haven't sugared them,' she announced, handing them round.

'I don't take sugar,' Livvy muttered.

'Neither do we,' Jane said. 'We're sweet enough!'

'That's what Roy said, first time I made him a coffee.'

'Did he?' Sammy felt sick as she pictured her man, sitting on the sofa drinking coffee, long legs stretched out in front of him. She shook her head to clear the vision. 'Right, Livvy, we need to get a few things straight. I'm going to ask some questions. Do me the courtesy of being absolutely truthful.'

She nodded. 'I'm sick and tired of lies.'

'Well, that's something we agree on. On the Saturday morning when I walked in on you and Roy at The Grand, had he invited you over or did you go to find him of your own accord?'

Livvy looked her in the eye. 'I phoned a few hotels; he was easy enough to track down. He wasn't expecting me. As far as I was concerned, we had unfinished business.'

'I see, and then what happened?'

'He bought me a drink, asked me to join him for a meal.'

'And afterwards?' Sammy swallowed hard.

'He asked me to stay the night.'

'Didn't it occur to you to say no?' Jane asked.

'Why should it? I knew he would ask me. He can't resist me, you see.' She stared defiantly at Sammy.

Although she felt like shaking Livvy's head off her shoulders, Sammy kept her cool and continued: 'I suppose he told you I was collecting him to go to the airport the following morning?'

'Of course he did. He asked me to run a bath while he called you to make the final arrangements, before he joined me in it.'

Livvy seemed to be enjoying rubbing salt in her wounds and Sammy saw red. She stood up and paced the room. 'Right, lady, that's enough. Thanks for being honest with me. Now I'll be honest with you. If I can forgive Roy for everything he's done with you, don't you think that me spending one night with Stuart is small potatoes by comparison? I told Roy earlier that I'd slept with Stu,' she fibbed. 'It doesn't make a blind bit of difference to how he feels about me. You can't have him, Livvy. I'm not divorcing him and he's so thrilled to have another chance that he can forgive me anything.

'He's moving back home so you can't hold my night with Stuart over my head, because it simply won't wash. Stu knows I love Roy. Deep down, he also knows that he and I are just good friends.' Sammy took a deep breath and sat down again, looking at Jane for further inspiration.

'I think you should speak to Roy before you go rushing off to Scotland, Livvy,' Jane advised. 'You can't just up sticks and go like that. Roy has rights to his child.'

Livvy jumped up and stared white-faced at them. 'Roy Cantello's ruined my life. He has no rights, no rights at all. I didn't plan to fall in love with him, or have this baby, it just happened. If you two are back together then what happens to *me* now?' she directed at Sammy.

'What do you mean, what happens to *you*?'

'Sit down, Livvy,' Jane said gently, giving Sammy a warning look. 'What plans did you have before you got pregnant?'

Livvy dropped back onto her chair and sighed. 'To sing professionally. Roy promised to help me.'

'And you still could. Why not have the baby adopted and carry on with your life?' Sammy suggested.

'Roy would never allow that.'

'Have you discussed adoption with him?' Jane asked.

'No, he wants this baby. The other night he lay with his head on my tummy, singing to it. He told it little stories and the names we've chosen.'

Sammy smiled faintly. She could picture him doing just that – he'd done exactly the same thing during both of *her* pregnancies.

'What names have you chosen?' Jane asked.

'Harley and Joshua,' Livvy said proudly.

'Roy's favourite bike,' Sammy said.

'And Ed's.' Jane smiled.

'What bike?' Livvy frowned.

'Harley-Davidson. The lads loved them when they were teenagers,' Jane replied.

Livvy tutted softly. 'Trust Roy! Fancy wanting to name your daughter after a bike. So, what now?'

'I don't know what to suggest,' Sammy said. 'But I think you should stay around until the baby arrives and then make a decision about your future. Did Roy transfer money into your account?'

'Yes, thank you. More money than I ever expected.'

'We promised we'd look after you and the child. But I want my man back and this time I'm keeping him. Do you understand what I'm saying?'

'Yes.' Livvy nodded, wringing her hands.

'Roy and I will come here together and talk to you next

week. We'll discuss things further then.' Sammy stood up and Jane took her cue.

'Goodbye, Livvy.' Jane patted her arm gently.

'Bye, Jane, and thank you.'

'You're welcome,' Jane said as she and Sammy left.

'Thank God that's over,' Sammy muttered, closing her eyes as she sank into the passenger seat.

'You do realise what you said to her, don't you?' Jane said as she switched on the engine.

'Yes.' Sammy sighed loudly. 'I've now got to face Roy and tell him I slept with Stuart and ask him to move back in with me. Not such a tall order, is it, Jane?'

'I'm sure he will be fine,' she said reassuringly.

* * *

After Sammy and Jane left, Livvy lay on her bed, her mind going over their suggestion of adoption. If she was honest with herself, it made a lot of sense. How the hell was she supposed to cope on her own? Mind you, even if they were together, Roy would be away a lot of the time anyway. She felt strangely calm about the whole thing. It was never going to work with him. There would always be the worry that he'd go back to Sammy. Her child needed two parents, but what if the adoptive parents were as bad as the ones *she'd* ended up with? The whole thing needed a lot of thinking about. Tomorrow she was having dinner with Sean and Tina. She'd share her problems with them, see what they thought about the adoption idea.

* * *

A very noisy party was in progress at Hanover's Lodge with Katie, sitting on Uncle Roy's knee, and singing along with him. Dominic was hammering a saucepan with two of his dad's old drumsticks and Phil was banging on the kitchen table with spoons. Eddie was leaning against the dresser, smiling indulgently.

Sammy stuck her fingers in her ears as she and Jane walked in.

'Hi, Phil,' they shouted above the racket. 'Good to see you again,' Sammy added.

'Auntie Sammy, Uncle Roy told me you're his special girl,' Katie called out.

'Did he now?' Sammy smiled at Katie and Roy.

Roy winked at Sammy and put Katie down. He walked across the kitchen, slung his arm around her shoulders and whispered, 'I love you.'

He'd been drinking or smoking pot, Sammy couldn't decide which, but he was definitely mellow. *Strike while the iron's hot*, she thought. 'Love you too, Roy.' She took his hand. 'Can we go back to your flat? We need to talk.'

'Only if you promise to stay the night.'

'I will,' she said, feeling in his jacket pocket for his keys. 'My car's at the factory, we'll use yours. But I'll drive, you don't look very capable.'

'Whatever you say. You're all witnesses to that.' Roy smiled gleefully at the others. 'She's promised to stay the night. Lead the way, Sam.'

'Bye, you two,' Jane called after them and closed the door.

* * *

'You're a flighty little piece, Katie Mellor,' Jane said as her daughter clambered onto Phil's knee. 'Flirting with Uncle Roy, and now Uncle Phil.'

'Uncle Phil's got four little girls,' Katie announced, '*and* he's got twin boys,' she directed meaningfully at her dad.

'Don't start that again about not being born a twin with Jess,' he warned.

'Well, Phil did it properly!' She ducked out of the way and shot across the kitchen as Eddie playfully tried to grab her arm.

'That little monkey's getting to be more than a handful,' he said.

Jane laughed. 'God help us! Go and get ready for your bath, Katie. You too, Dom. Pour me a G&T, Ed, while I sort them out. Did you think to save me any supper?'

'It's in the oven. There was enough for Sam, too.'

'I'll have Sam's,' Phil said. 'You make a mean chicken curry, Ed. I could manage another plateful.'

'So, how's Phil doing?' Jane asked, bending to kiss his cheek.

'Phil's just fine,' he said, giving her a hug. 'In fact, he's raring to go.'

'So I heard. Have vasectomy, will travel, eh?' She laughed.

'Something like that, Jane. I need to find me a new woman and soon, before I go crazy.'

'Roy's got one going spare,' she quipped. 'Oops, sorry, I didn't mean to be so flippant about Livvy. Poor kid, she was in a bad way tonight when we called at her flat.'

'What?' Eddie said, handing her a drink. 'You've been to see Livvy? I thought you were going to the shop? You'd better explain what's going on, Jane.'

Eddie and Phil sat back on their chairs as Jane told her tale.

'So Sammy's actually prepared to tell Roy she slept with Stuart?' Phil exclaimed. 'He won't like that.'

'He'll be gutted,' Eddie said. 'But at least it will put it all behind them. He wants Sammy back more than he's ever wanted anything in his life. He admitted that this afternoon.'

'If that's the case, he'll find it easy enough to forgive her. After everything *he's* put *her* through, it's not really a big deal,' Jane said.

'So what's Livvy going to do?' Phil asked curiously.

'Don't know. Sammy suggested they get together to talk next week. We'll have to await the outcome of tonight first and see what happens.'

* * *

'I'll need to leave early in the morning to get ready for work,' Sammy announced as she swung onto Roy's drive. She felt a rush of heat to her cheeks. This was two nights running that she'd spent away from her own bed without so much as a toothbrush.

Roy took her hand as they ran up the staircase to his flat. He swung her up into his arms and carried her over the threshold.

She giggled as he put her down, huffing and puffing. 'I'm not as fit as I used to be,' he panted.

'And I'm probably a bit heavier than I was the last time you carried me over a threshold.'

'Never, you're as slim as you ever were.'

'Probably the stress of the last few months.'

'Come here.' He took her in his arms and kissed her. 'I'm going to spend the rest of my life making that up to you.'

She kicked off her shoes and he pushed her jacket off her shoulders and threw it over a chair. He pulled her down onto the sofa. 'I've been floating on clouds all afternoon.'

'Have you?' She stroked his cheek. 'How was the rehearsal by the way?'

'Brilliant! Fucking brilliant! Even after all this time we were still shit hot.'

'Stop blowing your own trumpet, Cantello,' she teased.

'I'm not. We were, honestly. Anyway, what do you want to talk about? Or was that just an excuse to get me alone so that you could have your wicked way with me, again. I hope it's *us* you want to talk about?'

'Yes, us, Livvy and Stuart.'

She saw his jaw tighten and he raised a wary eyebrow. 'Where does Stuart fit into this?'

She took a deep breath, get the worst bit out of the way first. 'You know that I've been seeing him, don't you?'

'Yeah. Well, I know you've been out with him a couple of times for meals – Ed and Tim told me.'

Sammy looked at him and took another deep breath. She felt sick. 'There's no easy way to tell you this: I slept with Stuart last night.'

She watched his colour drain and his eyes widen in horror. He pushed her away and stood up, fists clenched. She shrank back against the cushions waiting for the onslaught. Instead, he turned and hurried out of the room, slamming the door behind him. She heard the bang of his bedroom door and then silence. Her heart thudded in her ears and she sat for what seemed like ages but in reality was a minute.

Should she go to him, or stay put until he came back to her? She stood up and walked to his bedroom door. She needed to be with him and she sensed he needed her, too. He was face down on the bed, sobbing broken-heartedly into his pillow.

'Roy.' She touched his shoulder gently. 'Roy, please don't cry. I'm so sorry.'

He leant up on one elbow, his stricken eyes gazing into hers. 'No, Sam, *I'm* the one who's sorry. *I* drove you into Stuart's arms.'

'Oh, Roy,' she said, 'I love you, I really do.' She lay down beside him and he clung to her, fresh sobs racking his body.

'You're *my* girl, Sam. You've always been mine. Don't ever leave me again.'

'You still want me, even after what I've just told you?'

'Want you? I'll show you how much I want you.' He tore off her clothes and made love to her with a wild urgency that surpassed their lunchtime session. Afterwards he held her and kissed her like he'd never let her go. 'You're *my* woman, mine, not Stuart's,' he said.

'And you're my man, not Livvy's. I want you to move back home immediately.'

'Really?' He stared at her. 'Are you sure? What about Jason?'

'Jason could move in here for the rest of your lease while things settle down. It will give him some space and maybe Jules could share with him.'

'That's a good idea. There's only one proper bedroom though. Jules would have to sleep in the little nursery.'

'That will be up to Jason and Jules to decide, not us,' Sammy said pointedly. 'Roy, Jane and I went to see Livvy tonight. She called the factory and was hysterical because she saw my car here at lunchtime. She's threatening to go back to Glasgow, but she's agreed to wait until she's spoken to you. I told her we'd go together and see her next week. She said you really want the baby and that you've chosen names.'

He sighed. 'We have. I certainly want to be a father to it anyway. But Livvy and I would never have worked out in the long run because I want to be with you.'

Sammy nodded. 'We need a fresh start. How would you feel about retaking our marriage vows?'

He smiled. 'I'd love to, very much in fact. Let's do it soon, start as we mean to go on. Put the last few months behind us.' The bedside phone rang out, making them jump.

'What if it's her?'

'Well, what if it is?' Roy grabbed the receiver said, 'Hello' and smiled. 'Hi, Pat. Yes, she's right here beside me, hang on.'

'Hi, Pat,' Sammy said. 'Were you worrying about my whereabouts? What? Mum's with you? Oh shit! Well yes, you can tell her I'm with Roy. Don't tell her I'm in bed with him, she'll go barmy! Yes, I know I'm nearly forty and I'm married to him, but even so, she won't approve. Tell her we're talking – anything that sounds innocent will do.' She smiled at Roy, who was nibbling her ears and stroking her thighs. 'No, I'm staying here with him tonight. Yes, he knows about Stu. There are no secrets between us now. We're going to retake our marriage vows and he's coming home with me tomorrow for good.'

Roy took the receiver from her. 'Bye, Pat, me and Sam have some catching up to do. See you tomorrow.' He hung up smiling.

33

'The A529 takes us straight into Hastings,' Jess said, running her finger across the map.

'Okay.' Jon turned to smile at her. 'Have you enjoyed yourself?'

'Very much. Have you?'

'Best time of my life. I'd like to spend every night with you from now on.'

'Me too, I'll miss you tonight.'

'There may be a chance. Grandma might go to bed early.'

Jess nodded, her mind going over the last forty-eight hours. Both nights they'd dined in The Lanes followed by drinks in the hotel bar. The first day had been mainly taken up with visits to the estate agent and checking over Aunt Celia's place. The house had smelt musty from being closed up. As Jess wandered from room to room, opening windows, she had an idea. She called to Jon, who was in the attic checking for roof leaks and burst pipes.

'Everything seems okay,' he said, joining her in the lounge, where she was sitting on the window seat. 'What is it?'

'We could live here. Why didn't we think of it before?'

'Here?'

'Why not? It's ideal. We can redecorate, fit new carpets and replace the kitchen. I'll bring the furniture from my flat down. Jason and Jules could join us for college holidays, maybe even live with us when they finish their art courses. They could go to university down here. There's a big gay community that I bet they'd love to be part of.'

'Hmm.' Jon nodded. 'What would we do for work though? Have you thought about that?'

'Yeah, pub and college gigs. I could get a daytime typing job. Maybe there's a music store looking for staff. We'd have no rent to pay. We can caretake the place and just pay the bills. Maybe take in B&B guests if we did up a couple of rooms nicely. I'll even learn to cook properly! We could make it work if we really tried.'

Jon grinned at her eager expression. 'You're serious about this, aren't you?'

'Yes. It's a way we can be together. We'll tell Dad and Mum we want a fresh start and we need to get away from Cheshire.'

'Okay. We'll talk it over with them when we get home.'

Jon's voice brought Jess back to the present. 'I wonder how The Raiders' rehearsals are going. We must remember to ask next time we call home.'

She pointed to her right. 'Your gran's place is on the next block. There it is, number seventy.'

Jon pulled onto the narrow drive of a white bungalow with tubs of colourful autumn pansies by the door. The spotless net curtains twitched then the glossy red front door flew open. Jess stared curiously at the elderly lady, with the blue-rinse perm, who had put the fear of God into her dad. She looked harmless enough now, she thought, as she waited for Jon to help her out. He was hugging his grandma and planted a kiss on her cheek. He ran round to the passenger door and helped Jess to her feet.

She shook his grandma's outstretched hand as Jon introduced them.

'Come inside out of the cold, Jessica. Can you manage, or do you need Jonathon's arm to lean on?'

'She needs my arm, Grandma,' Jon said.

'Well, come into the lounge then.' They followed her down the long hall and into a large, pleasant room, where French doors overlooked the neat back garden. 'Sit yourselves down. Would you like something to rest your foot on, Jessica?'

'No, thanks,' Jess said. 'And you can call me Jess.'

Jon's grandma smiled. 'What about a nice cup of tea?'

'That would be lovely.'

'Need any help?' Jon said as his grandma left the room, leaning heavily on her walking stick.

'I'll call when it's ready and you can carry the tray through.'

Jon joined Jess on the sofa. She gazed round the airy lounge and her eyes alighted on a black and white framed photograph on the sideboard: a girl in school uniform.

'Is that Angie?' she whispered.

'Yes.' He picked up the frame and passed it to her. 'It's same as the one Aunt Sally has – it was taken the year before I was born.'

Jess took in the pretty face, mischievous smile and curly hair of Jon's mum. 'She's so young, only a kid.'

'I know. She was lovely, wasn't she?'

'Very pretty,' Jess said. 'Nothing like I expected. That christening photo you have does her no justice. Roy told me she was the prettiest girl in class. She looks like she might have been fun, full of mischief.'

'She was that alright.' Jon's grandma limped back into the room. 'The tray's on the worktop, Jonathon, if you wouldn't mind.'

'Yes,' she continued as he left the room, 'one thing you can safely say about Angela is that she was mischievous. But then, she had a good teacher, didn't she?'

'You mean Dad?' Jess grinned.

'I do, and may I say you look just like him. I'd know those big blue eyes anywhere.'

'Everybody says that,' Jess said proudly.

'Regular little tearaways, him and that Roy Cantello. Still, they've done very well for themselves. As I said to Jonathon the last time we met, Eddie and Jane have done a wonderful job of raising him. Angie would have been very proud of her boy.'

Jon strode in with the tray and placed it on the coffee table. 'Shall I be mother?'

'Please, dear. No sugar for me. Cut that cake into slices and give Jess a piece. I tell you what I've got that you might find interesting. In the sideboard cupboard is an old chocolate box. Pass it over please, Jonathon.'

Jon obliged and handed her the box. She lifted the lid, sifted through a mound of photos and handed one to Jess.

'Can you spot Angela and your father?'

Jess studied each fresh young face on the black and white class photo. 'Yes, and I can see Roy and Tim, too. Look, Jon. How old were they when this was taken?'

'Fourteen. This was a year later.' She handed another class photo to Jess. 'The final-year photo is the individual one in the frame – Angela was sixteen then.' She handed the box to Jon.

Jess looked into the box and picked out another photo. She swallowed the lump in her throat as she gazed at the very youthful faces of her dad and Angie on their wedding day. Her dad looked as though he carried the woes of the world on his shoulders and Angie's smile seemed forced. Silently, she handed the photo to Jon.

'That's one wedding that should never have taken place,' Jon's grandma said. 'It was a disaster from start to finish. They were a silly pair to get into such a mess. Still, they weren't the first and they certainly won't be the last. I'll get off my soapbox now, because without *their* mistake, Jonathon wouldn't be here.'

Jess grimaced as she wondered what on earth Jon's grandma would make of *their* secret relationship. 'Dad's a wonderful man, Mrs Turner. He may have been a bit of a rebel, but he's the best dad in the world. I'm very proud to be his daughter.'

'I'm sure you are, Jess. You're a lot like him in many ways, sticking up for what you believe is right. That's a good quality in a person. If you've finished your tea, I'll show you to your rooms and you can unpack while I prepare lunch. I made chicken soup last night, it just needs reheating.'

Jon and Jess followed her to their adjacent bedrooms.

'I'm just across from you, Jess. The bathroom's next to me, opposite Jonathon's door.'

'Thank you,' Jess said as Jon nipped out to the car for their cases.

He dropped his outside his door and laid hers on her bed, pushing the door closed with his foot.

'I think we can say goodbye to any nooky under *this* roof,' Jess said. 'She'd have you strung up by the balls and me stoned to death if she had any idea we're lovers.'

Jon grinned. 'Let's see how it goes. Maybe we could leave tomorrow morning and stay in a hotel tomorrow night. I'll tell her we have to go early because there's a problem at work and I need to be back for Saturday, or something.'

'Brilliant idea. I think we'll have had enough by then.'

'Any sign yet?' he asked, raising an eyebrow.

'Nope.'

'Do you feel pregnant?'

'Jon, how the hell would I know? I've never *been* pregnant.'

'No, of course. It was a stupid thing to say. But you're four days late.'

'Well, I don't feel sick or anything, just a bit bloated.'

'Lunch is ready,' Jon's grandma called.

They took their places at the dining table. Jon's grandma ladled soup into bowls from a large tureen.

'What did my grandfather look like?' Jon asked, taking a bowl from her.

'He was a handsome man in his youth and very dashing in his naval uniform. I've a lovely photo of him, if you'd like it.'

'Thank you, I *would* like,' he replied, tucking hungrily into his soup.

'This is lovely,' Jess said, smacking her lips.

'Thank you, Jess. I love home-made soups, they're so filling.'

'So do we. Dad makes a fabulous leek and potato and a cracking French onion. Doesn't he, Jon?'

'He certainly does.'

'Yes,' Jess continued, 'he does most of the cooking and shopping and looks after our little brother and sister *and* he still finds time to write hit songs with Roy.'

Jon's grandma smiled. 'I know he does, my dear – Jonathon told me. Don't feel you have to convince me of Eddie's worthiness. I knew him better than he thought I did. I've something else for you to take home. It's in the loft so you'll have to get the ladder out after lunch.'

'What is it?' Jon asked curiously.

'A box of Angie's bits and pieces. School reports, pop records, that sort of stuff. They'll only get chucked out when I die. I'd like you to have them because apart from you, they're all that's left of your mum's past.'

'Thanks, that's brilliant.'

'Now, who'd like sherry trifle?'

'Oh, please,' they chorused.

Jon smiled at Jess as his grandmother left the room. 'See, she's not so bad really.'

'She's okay, but I don't like it when she has a pop at Dad. She's calling you, Jon.'

He jumped up, returning seconds later carrying a large cut-glass dish.

'Help yourselves,' his grandma said, placing a jug of cream on the table.

Jess dug in, filled a bowl to the brim and smothered the trifle with cream. 'Mm.' She rolled her eyes in ecstasy.

'It's good to see a young girl tucking into her food and not worrying about her figure,' Jon's grandma said. 'Do you see much of Cathy, Jon?'

'I haven't seen her since Nick's memorial service,' he replied. 'I should visit more often, but I never seem to have time. *You* saw her though, Gran, when you were at Sally's.'

His grandma looked puzzled. 'No, dear, I didn't.'

'That's odd. Sally asked me for her number. Said you wanted to see Cathy before you went home.'

'Did she? Well, she never mentioned it. I'll ask her about that next time we speak. Anyway, let's clear the table and then we'll have a little stroll on the promenade.'

Jon stood up and collected the dishes. 'Oh, by the way, Gran: we'll have to leave tomorrow, I'm sorry. It's earlier than we planned, but I've been called back to work to help with the stock take.'

'Oh well, never mind. You can always come again.' She shuffled out of the room as Jon squeezed Jess's hand.

* * *

By lunchtime the following day, Jon and Jess had checked into a hotel in Northamptonshire as Mr and Mrs Mellor and were lying in each other's arms.

'This is bliss.' He kissed her. 'We'd better make the most of the next few hours, they have to last for ages. Well, until Mum and Dad go out at the weekend.'

Jess smiled. 'Let's order room service tonight and picnic in bed.'

'Sounds good to me. We can look through Angie's box, too.' Jon glanced across the room to where the box, covered in pink and blue floral wallpaper and bearing a white label – *This Box Belongs to Angie Turner. PRIVATE, KEEP OUT* – stood. 'Right, Jess Mellor, I'm gonna make love to you like you've never had it before,' he said, crushing her to him.

* * *

'Poor old Ted, all battered and worn.' Jon held a balding, one-eyed teddy bear in his hands. He and Jess were sitting in bed surrounded by half the contents of Angie's box. He reached in, pulled out a scrapbook and opened it. Pasted inside were newspaper cuttings of Buddy Holly's plane crash and on the next page a report of Eddie Cochran's death. There was also a poster advertising a local gig at a Stockport club with The Raiders top of the bill.

Several records were neatly stacked to one side, still in their original sleeves. 'Wow, look at these! Buddy Holly, Elvis, The Everly Brothers, all in mint condition. These are worth a few bob now,' Jon enthused.

A large brown envelope held swimming certificates and school reports, each declaring that Angie had been a bright pupil. A lock of brown hair, fastened up with a blue ribbon and stored in a yellowing envelope, bore the message *Eddie's hair, November 1959*.

Jess smiled as she lifted out several exercise books, each bearing the legend – *Angie Turner loves Eddie Mellor*. 'She was really into Dad to some tune, wasn't she?'

Jon nodded and picked out a handful of black and white snapshots. 'Here she is with Cathy and some other girls. It's written on the back where it was taken. *"Mario's Club, Xmas*

1959." Here's another one dated the same time with Dad, Roy and Tim. Angie's sitting on Dad's knee. Well, they certainly looked happy enough then.'

Jess lifted out an oblong tin box, fastened at the front with a small padlock. The box was labelled, *Keep Out, Very Private*.

'Is there a key?' Jon frowned, peering in the box.

'Not unless it's fallen to the bottom. Probably her crown jewels.'

'No, this is her jewellery box.' Jon held up a small, wooden treasure chest and opened it. Inside was a collection of trinkets – a silver charm bracelet, clip-on gold earrings and a silver locket and chain.

Jess prised open the oval locket and smiled. Inside were tiny photos of her dad and Angie. 'I wonder if Dad gave her the locket, like the gold one he gave Mum on their wedding day.'

'Who knows? But I don't fancy asking him,' Jon said. 'In fact, I'm going to keep this box in the staffroom at work. It might upset Mum and Dad if they see it. I'll leave it in the car boot for the time being.'

'Good idea. How can we get into this box?' Jess turned it over and over.

'I could unscrew the hinges or try and prise the padlock open – there's a set of screwdrivers in the car.'

'Go and get them then.' Jess smiled as he leapt up, pulled on some clothes and dashed from the room, returning minutes later with a small toolbox.

He tried one of the screwdrivers. 'Damn! It's rivets, not screws. I'll have to force the padlock.' He pushed and poked and eventually managed to break it. He looked inside: 'Notebooks. But why lock them away?'

Jess lifted out the top book and caught her breath. Printed inside the cover in a neat hand were the words, *Diary 1959*. 'They're her diaries, Jon. These will give you an insight into her thoughts and the kind of girl she was.'

Jon nodded silently. He shivered.

Jess ran her hand down his arm. 'What's wrong?'

'I don't know. Maybe we're prying into something very private.'

'Would you rather we didn't read them?'

He shook his head. 'We've come this far. I want to know everything there is to know about Angie, *all* about her.'

Jess turned over the first page and began to read out loud.

'January 7th 1959: *Back to boring school today. I'll get to see Ed again. Haven't seen him since Boxing Day. He's always too busy playing and rehearsing new songs with the group.*'

Jess turned a few pages. 'She hasn't written an entry for every day. You can read them properly yourself when you get some time. Here's a bit where she's actually dating Dad properly. August 10th 1959: *School hols. Met Ed, Roy, Tim and Sue on the rec. Went back to Roy's and drank his mum's sherry. Necked with Ed all afternoon. Sue and Roy went upstairs.*'

'Ah, bless! All very innocent.' Jon laughed. 'Sue must have been Roy's girl before he met Sam.'

'Hmm, innocent, you reckon? Listen to this. November 20th 1959: *Babysat for Sally with Ed. We got a bit drunk and he asked me to go all the way but I said no.*'

'Randy little git!' Jess grinned.

Jon picked up the next book and opened it. 'This is 1960, the year Dad met Jane. January 3rd 1960: *Babysat for Sally with Ed. Roy and Sue came round and brought a bottle of horrible red wine. Me and Ed went upstairs and we had a big row. He said I tease him and don't love him, but I do. He said prove it and go all the way. I said I would next time.*'

Jon looked at Jess and shook his head.

'Look, here's an entry about Mum,' Jess said. 'April 12th 1960: *Ed's seeing someone else. He hasn't said anything, but he's been very off with me for the last few weeks. I think it's one of those snooty Mersey Square girls. Cathy said she'd find out who it is.*

August 20th 1960: *The Raiders played at Mario's tonight. Eddie's girlfriend came back from her holidays today and he kissed her right in front of me. He did it on purpose. Richard Price gave me a lift home and Eddie saw me getting into his car.*

August 21st 1960: *Cathy told me that Eddie asked her if I was seeing Richard and she told him to mind his own business.'*

As Jess leafed through the rest of the diary entries for that year, they confirmed what her father had told her. How Jane had discovered that he was seeing Angie behind her back and finished with him. After that, and according to Angie, she and Eddie seemed to be inseparable for a while then he went back to Jane. Jess picked up the diary for the following year and leafed through it.

> May 1st 1961: *I'm almost six weeks late. I'm sure I'm pregnant and I don't know what to do. Cathy said I have to tell Eddie, but I'm scared he'll go crazy and say it's not his baby.*

Jon looked up as she finished reading aloud. 'They must have got back together. But why would Dad say I wasn't his?'

Jess frowned and shook her head. 'Don't know. Have we missed something?' She flicked back a few pages and studied each entry, her eyes opening wide.

'What is it?' Jon took the book from her.

> March 15th 1961: *Ed was on his own tonight and he walked me home from Mario's. He came in and we did it on the rug. When I told him that I love him, he was really odd with me and rushed off home. He's probably worried that I'll tell Jane what we did.*
>
> March 22nd 1961: *Ed's been ignoring me so I went out*

with Richard to dinner in a posh restaurant. I really fancy him. We went for a drive and then we made love in his car.

'Do you think Dad knew that she slept with Richard?' Jess frowned, taking the book from him.

'Well, she doesn't actually say she went all the way, just that they made love. In those days it might not have meant full sex.'

'Oh, come on, Jon! She was no angel, she fancied Richard; she said so. Dad must have known what she was like, or else why would she be so worried that he'd say the baby wasn't his?'

Jon shrugged and lay down with his hands behind his head. 'Read me some more.'

'April 7th 1961: *Jane's dumped Ed. He told her he'd slept with me behind her back because I said I was going to tell her. I thought he'd come back to me but he won't even speak to me now.*

July 10th 1961: *Still haven't told Ed I'm pregnant. Cathy said I have to do it tonight after the gig, but I don't know who the father is.*

Back from the gig and I still haven't told Eddie. Jane was there tonight looking very sexy and he couldn't keep his eyes off her. Cathy said Mac's girlfriend told her they're back together. That's all I need, him back with Jane. I'm going to go round to his parents' place now and get it over with. I'll tell him I'll go away until the baby's born and then get it adopted. Mum will go mad. She wouldn't let me keep it anyway. Ed can stay with Jane and we can all get on with our lives.'

Jess bit her lip and looked at Jon, whose face had drained of colour.

'July 11th 1961: *What have I done? I went to see Ed and he was in bed with Jane. He told me they were back together for good and she'd agreed to marry him. I told them I'm pregnant and he's the father. I don't know why I said it. Jane was hysterical and Ed said it couldn't be his. I can't tell him about Richard now, I just can't. I'll have to go along with it and hope that it is Ed's.'*

Jess put down the book. 'Do you want me to carry on?'

He looked at her, pale-faced, and nodded. 'Please. Now we've started, I need to know everything.'

The diaries were dated up to 1964, the year Angie died. Jess leafed through a few more pages. 'Well, the outcome is as Dad told me. Their parents rushed them into marriage and you were born in December. They lived in an awful little flat in Stockport, had no spare money and argued all the time. God, Jon, it sounds horrendous. Poor kids, because that's all they were.

'January 10th 1962: *I'm convinced Jonny is Richard's. He looks exactly like him. His eyes are deep green and his hair is dark and curly, he's nothing like Eddie. What can I do? I feel trapped and so does Ed. He hates being married to me, but he loves Jonny.*

February 12th 1962: *Cathy also thinks Jonny looks like Richard. She says I should be honest with Eddie and tell him the truth, but I can't.*

July 8th 1962: *Richard has married Louise and gone to live in Wales. Jonny even smiles like him now. I can't tell Ed the truth. He already hates me for trapping him, he'd kill me if he knew. He misses Jane and the group and all his friends. I miss my job and I feel like doing myself in some days.*

December 10th 1962: *I overheard Roy telling Ed that Jane is going steady with Mark Fisher now and he's been horrible ever since. He's always threatening to leave me but I tell him I won't let him see the baby if he does that. I know he'll never desert Jonny.'*

'Jon, this is a mess.' Jess looked at his stricken face. 'Are you sure you want me to carry on?' She put her arms around him and hugged him. His safe, secure world was crumbling around him, but he was compelled to know the truth and nodded bravely.

'Skip up to the time Dad actually leaves her, see why he goes.'

'Okay.' She leafed through the diary for 1964.

'February 28th 1964: *Eddie got the sack from his job last week and he's joined The Raiders again. I'm sure he's seeing Jane. He goes missing for hours on his motorbike and he smells of perfume when he comes home. Richard's marriage hasn't worked out and he's back at the salon. We went for a drink after work. I want to tell him about Jonny. He'll only have to look at my little boy to know he's his father. I don't know why Eddie can't see it. Maybe it's because my mother is always saying Jonny looks like my dad as a child.*

March 10th 1964: *Eddie has started working at Flanagan and Grey's record store with Jane. He's admitted they're having an affair and he's guessed about Richard and me seeing each other again. He told me he wants a divorce as soon as possible.*

March 15th 1964: *Eddie's left me. He wants custody of Jonny. Richard's told me he loves me. I think he may have guessed that Jonny is his. He hasn't said anything, but I saw him looking at Jonny the other night as though he'd guessed. I don't think he'll be too disappointed.*

April 12th 1964: *Cathy told me Ed and Jane are engaged. They'll have a long wait to get married. Our divorce will take forever. Ed's complaining about his access to Jonny. He says he wants him all weekend. He's never satisfied, always causing trouble. Richard said it's gone on long enough, he has to be told the truth sooner rather than later. I'm pregnant again. Richard is really excited.*

May 1st 1964: *I've moved in with Richard and we're so happy. I still have a problem with telling Ed about Jonny. He dotes on him and I think he will want to kill me.'*

Jess looked at Jon, who was on his back, staring at the ceiling.

'June 7th 1964: *We're going to Wales for the weekend. We got engaged and Richard is taking me away to celebrate. Jonny is staying with Cathy. When we come home, we'll go together to Eddie's and tell him the truth. I can't face him on my own.'*

That was the final entry. Angie and Richard had never returned home from Wales.

* * *

'I can't believe it, Jess. I feel numb.'

'It might not be true,' she said hesitantly.

'But why would she lie? It all ties in with what Dad told you. Well, the only way to find out for sure is to ask Cathy. She was the only other person to know the truth.'

Jess nodded. 'And then what? How on earth do we tell Mum and Dad? They'll be devastated.'

'I know,' Jon said, taking her hand. 'Everything I've ever had from my dad – home life, car, Aunt Celia's money – has never been mine by rights. What about Grandma Turner and Aunt Sally? They don't know either and poor Dad, taking all the blame for something he didn't do.'

'By pure fluke!' Jess smiled wryly.

'This guy, Richard, my biological father, we don't know anything about him. I've probably got relatives in Stockport. Maybe he had kids from his first marriage. I might have more brothers and sisters. If Angie had lived, I would have had at least one.'

'Angie doesn't really say that much about his background. There's no mention of his family or that they were aware of your existence. You'll have to go and see Cathy as soon as possible, see if she can throw any light on things.' Jess placed the diaries back in the tin box. 'If it *is* all true, you and Dad could have blood tests to make absolutely sure.'

Jon nodded. 'We'll go and see Cathy on the way home tomorrow.'

'It's been an awful shock for you, Jon. Shall I go down to the bar and get some brandy?'

He sat up and pulled her close. 'In a minute. There's something we need to talk about first, something that we haven't even considered. If Richard really *is* my father, we're not in an incestuous relationship.'

She stared at him, eyes wide.

'We could even get married,' he continued.

Jess nodded slowly. 'We could. And if I'm pregnant?'

'Then we keep it. I wouldn't allow you to abort our baby when it isn't necessary.'

Jess slid her arms around his neck and kissed him. 'I love you so much, Jon.'

'I love you too, Jess. What will I do if Dad disowns me when we tell him I'm not his son?'

'Dad would never do that. He thinks the world of you. You *know* that.'

'That's because he thinks I'm his flesh and blood. It might be a different story when he knows the truth.' A frown crossed his face. 'A horrible thought just occurred to me.'

'What?'

'If Angie hadn't lied, you and I may never have met, especially when you consider she wanted to have me adopted in the first place.'

'There's always a reason for everything, Jon.'

'So it would seem,' he said, and kissed her.

* * *

'Carl, will you take your mum and Ben out for a couple of hours?' Cathy asked, as Carl strolled into the kitchen, a pile of sheet music in his hands.

'Do I have to? I've got all these arrangements to work on for the tour. Why can't *you* take them out?'

'Jon just called. He's been to see Angie's mum and needs to discuss something. He wouldn't say what, but I have a horrible feeling that it's about Richard and Angie. I don't want your mum here if the shit hits the fan. He's on his way with Jess and sounded very upset, so something isn't right.'

'You're probably barking up the wrong tree. How the hell can he possibly have found out? Angie and Richard took the secret to the grave. Sally swore she'd do the same and Ed and Jane have stayed mum all this time.'

'I don't know how, but *something* tells me he knows. I need to get my wits about me before he arrives.'

'Right, I'll take Mum for afternoon tea in Kettleshulme. Ben will have to stay in the car, but he'll go to sleep.'

'Thanks, Carl.'

* * *

Cathy rushed around tidying up, plumping cushions and straightening the rug. She combed her hair and slicked on lipstick. She was dreading Jon's visit. Almost all her life she'd worried about him finding out the truth from someone other than Ed and Jane. It was her opinion that they should have told him years ago, no matter how difficult. Coming from them at an earlier age, he would have long ago accepted things and put it behind him. By the time she let in Jon and Jess, her nerves were at breaking point and she almost wished she'd called Ed and warned him.

She sent them into the lounge and brought a tray of coffee and biscuits through. She looked at her godson with pride. Such a handsome boy, Angie's child had always held a special place in her heart.

'Well, sunshine, I haven't seen *you* for ages. What's bothering you? You both look worried.'

'Will you please tell me who my father is?' Jon came straight to the point.

Cathy swallowed hard. 'Eddie, of course. What a strange question to ask.'

Jon looked at Jess, who held the tin box on her knee. She pulled out the diaries. They had folded down the pages with the entries where Angie had written about her and Richard planning to tell Ed of Jon's true parentage and the entry where she had first realised she was pregnant.

Silently, Jess handed the diaries to Cathy, who balked at the sight of her late friend's handwriting.

'Where did you get these?'

'From Grandma Turner. They were locked away in that tin box,' Jon replied.

Cathy read through some of the entries, her eyes filling with tears.

'So, Cathy, who is my father?' Jon asked again. 'Please tell me the truth.'

'Richard Price,' she whispered, not meeting his eye.

Jon nodded, took Jess's hand and kissed it, placing his other arm around her shoulders. Cathy stared at the pair.

'What's going on?'

'Would you help us please, Cathy?' he asked. 'There's no one else we can turn to.'

'Of course, if I can. What is it?'

'Jess and I are lovers,' he began. 'We thought we were in an incestuous relationship, which of course we knew was wrong. But if Eddie is definitely not my dad then we're not breaking the law.'

'Richard was your father, Jon, that's the truth. You and Jess are not blood related in any way. I presume Eddie and Jane are unaware of what's going on between you?'

He nodded. 'I haven't a clue how to tell Dad about what's in the diaries. What do you know about Richard Price? Do you have any photographs of him?'

Cathy went to a desk near the bay window. She opened a drawer, took out a box and handed Jon a photograph of Richard, Angie and himself as a small boy.

Jess's eyes opened wide. 'Jon, you look exactly like him. Oh my God, it's spooky! You and Dad won't need blood tests!'

'You're the image of him, Jon,' Cathy said. 'Richard wasn't much older then you are now when he died. You're so alike, you could be twins. I think we should call your mum and dad and ask them to come over. There's a lot more you need to be told and I don't think that's up to me.'

Cathy called Eddie and Jane, and without saying why, asked them to come over to the house as soon as they could.

She sat down in front of Jon and Jess and smiled. 'I suppose I've been dreading this for years, but I wasn't expecting the added complication of the pair of you being lovers.'

'How can we tell them about us, Cathy?' Jon asked worriedly. 'Dad will kill me for this, I just know he will.'

'Well, here they are, so we'll soon find out and if the worst comes to the worst, you'll have to come and stay here with me and Carl for a while. Now don't worry, let's play it by ear. Listen first to what they've got to tell you, okay?'

Cathy let in a puzzled Jane and Eddie.

'Hi, Cathy,' Jane said. 'Is that Jon's car on your drive? Are they here – Jon and Jess, I mean?'

She nodded. 'In the lounge. They know about Richard and Angie and want some answers,' she whispered.

'Oh shit!' Eddie exclaimed. 'How the fuck did they find out?'

'*They'll* explain, go on in. I'll make a fresh pot of coffee.'

* * *

'Hi, kids,' Eddie greeted them. Jane followed him and sat down on the sofa opposite. 'So, what's up? Come on, out with it.'

'We've got Angie's diaries, Dad. We've read most of them. Everything you told Jess is logged in them, exactly as you said it happened.'

Eddie nodded and sat down next to Jane. 'But there's something else?'

'She says Richard Price is my father, not you.'

Eddie swallowed the lump that had risen in his throat. 'Does she, son?'

'You don't seem surprised, Dad.'

'I know that Richard was your *biological* father, Jon. I've known for a very long time, since you were four years old, in fact. But it's never made any difference to me. As far as *I'm* concerned, you are and always will be, my boy.'

Jon stared, mouth open. 'You've brought me up all these years knowing Angie conned you into believing you were my dad and you just accepted it?'

'What *else* could I do? I thought you were mine. Had every reason to *believe* you were mine. Why should I have treated you any differently when I found out the truth? It certainly didn't alter my feelings for you.'

Jess looked at her mum. Jane's eyes were tear-filled as she took Eddie's hand.

'Jon, we both love you very much. When we discovered that Richard was your father, we were devastated, but there was no way we could have let you go, even though we had no legal rights to you. Ed's name's on your birth certificate. No one was going to contest that and take you away from us. You were our little boy and we wanted to keep you. Maybe what we did was wrong. We denied you your real family, Richard's family. But I don't think that they even knew you existed. They still don't, of course. It will be up to you if you want to try and trace them. Please don't think too badly of Eddie and me for what we did.'

Jon, tears streaming down his face, knelt in front of Jane and took her hand. 'Mum, you and Dad have been the best parents any kid could have. I love you very much. I don't have any wish to get in touch with Richard's family at all. Does anyone else know about this besides you two and Cathy?'

'Roy, Sammy, Pat, Tim and Carl,' Eddie replied. 'We made a pact not to tell a soul. It's been the most closely guarded Raiders' secret in the world. Not even your grandparents know.'

Jon nodded and went back to sit beside Jess. He took her hand without thinking and Jane caught her breath. She smiled at the bewildered pair. 'Now *our* secret's out in the open, what about you two? Have you got something you'd like to share with *us*?'

Jon nodded. 'Yes. Me and Jess, well, we're in love.'

Eddie looked at Jane, eyebrows raised in amazement. 'You were right, as usual.'

'Mum, you knew?' Jess's tone was incredulous.

'I had my suspicions. I saw the way you looked at one another, the way you're so comfortable together. More like lovers than brother and sister, which of course you now know you're not.'

Eddie smiled as Jon and Jess exchanged looks of relief. Poor kids, they must have gone through hell, trying to hide their feelings. 'You'll need to be discreet in front of the little ones for now until we find a way to explain things to them. Dom will have a holy fit if he thinks you end up with your sister forever.'

'Thanks for everything, Dad, Mum and you too, Cathy,' Jon said as Cathy popped her head around the door.

'Yes, thanks, Cathy,' Eddie added. 'I've always lived in dread of this day, as I know you have, but it's not been half as bad as I was expecting it to be. Not even with the extra complication.'

'You're all very welcome,' Cathy said. 'To be honest, I think the extra complication makes it easier for Jon to cope with.'

He nodded. 'I don't care about Richard Price and his family, that's all in the past now. My main concern has been for Jess. Now I know for sure that I'm not her half-brother, we can go home and start planning a future.'

'Well, good luck to you all,' Cathy said. 'Life's never dull at your place. How are things with Roy and Sammy, by the way?'

'Oh, wonderful,' Jane replied. 'They're together again. Roy's moved back to Jasmine House. They're planning to retake their marriage vows before Christmas.'

Jess and Jon stared at Jane. 'We've only been away since Tuesday and all this has happened, honestly?' Jess asked.

'Honestly, they're really back together, thank goodness. Anyway, come on, let's go home and we can talk some more.'

34

DECEMBER 1984

Blinking back tears, Jane held Eddie's hand as they sat side by side in the front pew of flower-bedecked Ashlea Church.

Roy, wearing a cream linen suit and brown silk shirt, looked into Sammy's eyes as he pledged his love. Sammy, blue eyes shining, looked every bit the blushing bride in her long, cream silk dress. A simple circle of cream rosebuds topped her shoulder-length hair and she held a small bouquet of matching roses.

Jane glanced along the pew at Dominic, quietly studying his hymn book, with Katie next to him, fidgeting as usual. Jess and Jon were seated either side of their siblings. Jane caught Jon's eye and he winked. She winked back, noting how happy and relaxed he looked. Jess, smiling wistfully, seemed serene enough, but Jane knew that in her daughter's mind was the knowledge that next weekend, she would have been marrying Nick in this very church.

Three weeks after the discovery of Angie's diaries, Jon had revealed that Jess was pregnant. At almost ten weeks she was blooming and had developed a very rounded bump. Looking at her daughter's profile now, Jane knew they had to tell people the truth sooner rather than later.

Jane nodded at Bob and Irene Cantello across the church. Irene dabbed her eyes and gazed proudly at the happy couple. Tom and Molly Mason were seated behind them, alongside Jason and Jules. Pat, Tim and their daughters, Cathy, Carl and Phil were silently listening to the vicar blessing Roy and Sammy's new rings.

* * *

As the guests filed outside, cameras flashed and congratulations filled the air. Roy took Sammy's hand and they went to Nick's grave. She laid her bouquet by the newly engraved headstone and they stood quietly for a moment with their arms around each other.

Roy brushed a hand across his eyes and whispered, 'You okay?'

She smiled through her tears.

'Come on then. Keep smiling and make a beeline for the car.'

A crowd of press photographers was waiting by the church gates as they ran to the vintage Rolls.

'Can you tell us why you decided to retake your marriage vows, Roy,' one called out, snapping away.

'To show the world that I love my wife,' he said as they climbed into the car.

'Is it true you had an affair with a girl half your age?' another shouted.

'No comment,' Roy said as the Rolls pulled away.

'Cheeky sod!' Sammy muttered as she sank back into cream leather luxury. 'How the hell did he find *that* out?'

'God knows. But don't let it spoil our day.'

'What if they know about the baby?'

'How can they? Livvy's been sworn to secrecy and only close friends and family knows it's mine.'

'Ours!'

'Ours,' he echoed and took her hand. 'You're still sure about it?'

'I can't wait.'

Roy squeezed Sammy tightly. His thoughts returned to the week he'd moved back in with her. They'd paid a visit to Livvy. She made them coffee and outlined her plans. Afterwards, Sammy sat back on the sofa, mug halfway to her mouth while he dropped his on the floor.

Livvy calmly mopped the carpet then sat opposite, fingertips steepled together and smiled. 'Well, what do you think?'

Roy gathered his wits first. 'Olivia, do you realise what you're saying?'

'Yes, and I've thought long and hard. It makes perfect sense. Sammy and Jane suggested adoption. Who better than you two? You told me Sammy regrets not having more children. It might be a girl – Roy said you always wanted a daughter.' She looked at Sammy.

White-faced, Sammy nodded.

'Well, there you are then, and before you say anything, this isn't a whim. *I* can't give it the upbringing you two can. I'm going back to Glasgow after the birth. I don't want to take it with me, I'd rather it go to you two than strangers.'

Roy frowned. 'For fuck's sake, Livvy, this is our kid we're discussing, not a bloody puppy!'

'Exactly, *ours*, yours and mine! No matter how hard it will be to give it away, it will be harder still for me to raise it as a single parent. Please, Roy, can't you see? It's for the best all round.'

Sammy chewed her lip and looked at Roy. 'We need to think about it. It's not a decision we can make on the spot. I wasn't expecting this at all. All *we* wanted to do was make sure you're okay for money and support.'

'I'm fine for both, thanks,' Livvy said. 'I'm leaving this flat and moving into Sean and Tina's spare bedroom next week. Tina said she'll take care of me.'

'You've got it all planned.'

'I haven't had much choice, Sammy. You made that quite clear the other night. I accept that you and Roy want another go at making your marriage work. *I* need the chance of a fresh start, too.'

Roy took a deep breath and stood up. 'We'll go now – Ed and Jane are expecting us for dinner. I'll call you over the weekend when we've had a chance to discuss things.'

Livvy nodded. 'Okay. I'll be here for a few more days and then you can contact me at Sean's or work. I'll see you out.'

'Well,' Sammy muttered as they made their way to the car, 'that's a turn up for the books!'

'You can say that again. But it's out of the question: *we* can't bring the kid up.'

'Why not?'

'Because it wouldn't be fair on you. I've put you through enough, I couldn't expect you to raise the child as well.'

'I'd love to help you bring up your baby, Roy.'

'What?'

'You heard! If *she* clears off back to Glasgow, you'll have sole custody and we can bring it up together. If she stays around and expects you to be a part of its life, then I'll never have peace of mind.'

'You're really willing to do that for me?' He pulled her close and kissed her. 'You're one hell of a woman, Sammy Cantello! If you're sure, we'll do it. But I want it all legal. I'll see our solicitor and get him to draw up some sort of document, one where she gives up all rights. We'll make her a one-off payment to help her get her life back on track. How does that sound?'

Sammy smiled, eyes bright with tears. 'Let's go and tell Jane and Ed the news.'

'What about your business and how will you cope when I'm on tour?'

'We'll cross all those bridges as and when we come to them.'

* * *

Sammy turned to Roy as the Rolls purred to a halt outside The Grand.

'You were miles away. Not having second thoughts already, are you?' she teased.

'Not at all. I was thinking about the honeymoon and stuff.'

'I can't wait. Paris, here we come!' Sammy grinned, as Roy helped her out of the car.

'It would have been nice to go further afield,' he said. 'But with the tour coming up and recording the new album, it will have to wait for another time.'

'I don't care. It will be so good to be away, just the two of us.'

'I wonder if Sharon will be on reception,' Roy said as they ran up the steps to the entrance doors.

'What on earth will she make of all this!' Sammy exclaimed as he swung her up into his arms and pushed open the door with his backside.

'We'll soon find out. Here she comes.'

Sharon was awaiting the wedding party in the reception hall and her eyes widened.

'Sharon, how nice to see you again,' Roy greeted the bewildered girl. He put Sammy down. 'Meet the wife.'

'Don't be confused.' Sammy laughed. 'We've retaken our wedding vows. The reception is booked under my maiden name of Hardy.'

Sharon's right hand flew to her breast. 'Oh, Mr Cantello, err, Roy, that's so romantic. I'll show you to your function room. If you'd like to follow me.'

They followed her down a corridor and into a large room

and Sammy's eyes lit up as she took in the elegant candle and floral displays that decorated the centre of each table. Pine garlands, strung with twinkling fairy lights and red and gold bows festooned the top table. A large decorated tree took pride of place in the corner of the room, beside a grand piano.

'It looks very beautiful,' Sammy said. 'We're really lucky it's almost Christmas, we've got all the extra trimmings.'

Sharon smiled. 'It looks stunning, doesn't it? I'll leave you now and get back to reception to direct your guests as they arrive.'

'Thank you,' Roy said. He turned to Sammy as Sharon departed and took her in his arms. 'You happy, Mrs C?'

'Very. But we mustn't forget that next week would have been Nick and Jess's wedding day.'

'I know. I said a silent prayer for him and one for Jess, too. I wonder what was going through her mind as she was watching us.'

Sammy shook her head. 'I honestly don't know. She's been through the mill lately, but she's got a good future with Jon. He adores her and they've got the baby to look forward to. They'll be just fine.'

* * *

'Congratulations, you two,' Jane greeted the pair as she and Eddie strolled in with their family.

'Thanks! Grab a drink,' Sammy said, grinning with delight.

Roy signalled to a waiter, who walked over with a laden tray and handed round glasses of mulled wine.

'That was a lovely ceremony and *you* look gorgeous, Sam, just like a real bride,' Jane said, clinking glasses with her.

'It *was* nice, short but sweet. You two should do it sometime.'

'We might, one day. We have to sort out Jon and Jess first. They want to marry at some point, don't you, my love?'

Jess nodded. 'Eventually, after I've given birth.' She looked down at her swollen belly.

Sammy smiled. 'You're enormous for your dates. Have you told your mum and dad yet, Jane?'

'No. I'm dreading it, to be honest. Ed and I are a right pair of wusses!'

'Well, what's done is done. Once you explain the facts to them they'll accept it, you know they will,' Sammy said. 'Think how hard it was for Jon and Jess to tell you and Ed. Get it in proportion.'

'Are *you* looking forward to *your* baby, Sammy?' Jess asked.

'I am, very much. The time will fly, what with Christmas and the group away recording and getting ready for the tour. Delivery day's only ten weeks off.'

'Well, it doesn't show,' Eddie teased, playfully patting Sammy's flat stomach.

'What a bloody bizarre situation we're all in,' Sammy said. 'How did life ever get this complicated, Jane?'

'We've Ed and Roy to thank for that. None of it's our doing,' Jane said dryly.

'Here come the mums,' Roy muttered. 'Talk about something normal, like the weather or the price of eggs.' He greeted his mother, mother-in-law and Enid and handed them each a glass of mulled wine.

Enid, clutching her handbag in one hand and her glass in the other, looked at her daughter and smiled. 'That was a lovely little ceremony, wasn't it, Jane?'

'Yes, Mum, lovely,' Jane agreed.

'I hope they'll both be very happy this time.'

'Mum, they always *were* happy. It's just this last year that's been difficult for them. What with the accident and...' Jane trailed off as her mum pursed her lips in time-honoured fashion.

'They'll be well rid of *that* little madam! It's very good of Sammy to offer to bring the baby up for Roy. Not many wives would do that.'

Jane stared at her mother for a long moment. 'I brought Jon up for Ed.'

'Yes, dear, of course you did. I haven't forgotten.' Her mum glanced around as though to make sure no one was eavesdropping and lowered her voice. 'I've been meaning to have a word with you about our Jess.'

Jane stiffened slightly. 'What about her?'

Again, her mum's eyes darted from side to side and she whispered, 'She's putting on a fair bit of weight!'

'So, she's eating better.'

'No, I don't mean that sort of weight. I mean... she's putting weight on. You know!'

Jane suppressed a giggle. 'What *do* you mean, Mum?'

'Do I have to spell it out? I thought you of all people would have spotted it.' Her mother was getting agitated now and her straw hat wobbled indignantly.

'Spotted what?' Jane teased.

'I think our Jess is, well...' Her eyes went down to her stomach and up again. 'You know, in a bit of trouble!'

'Ah... I see. You think Jess is pregnant?'

'Shhhh! Don't let Ed hear you. It'll give him the shock of his life.'

'Mum, Jess *is* pregnant, and Ed already knows. We've both known for a while.'

'Well, why hasn't anyone had the decency to tell me and your father?'

'Because it's complicated, that's why.'

'Is something wrong with the baby? Was it damaged during the accident?'

'What? Oh, Mum, you think it's Nick's baby?'

'Well, of course I do.'

Jane shook her head. 'There's nothing wrong with the baby, or Jess, but it's not Nick's. That's where the complication comes in. I don't think now is the time and place to be discussing this.'

'Okay, Jane. But I have a very strange feeling that I know what you're going to tell me.'

'You do?'

'I'm not daft. I've seen the way he looks at her. He worships her, always has done.' She inclined her head towards Jon and Jess, who were talking animatedly, his hand on the small of her back. 'So, how will you cope with this little lot?'

'Same way I always cope. With Ed's help,' Jane replied. 'It's not as bad as you think. I'll tell you everything tomorrow, I promise.'

'Okay, love.' Mum smiled, patted her on the shoulder and signalled to Molly, who came to stand beside her.

'Problems?' Molly whispered.

Jane stifled another giggle as she overheard her mother mutter, 'Isn't there always with this lot?'

* * *

The wedding planner made his presence known and invited the guests to take their places at the tables.

Roy waited until everyone was seated and then clapped his hands to gain their attention. 'Welcome. This little speech is out of the normal order of things, but before we begin our meal, I want to thank everyone for their love and support over the trying times of the last few months. If you've all got a glass of champagne, I'm going to ask you to raise a toast to my darling wife for standing by me. To Sammy, the most understanding woman in the world.'

'To Sammy!' Everyone in the room took up the toast as Sammy smiled at Roy with adoring eyes.

***

Leaving their guests still celebrating, Sammy and Roy left the hotel in a taxi and headed home.

'Are you sure you're okay to drive to the airport, Roy?' Sammy asked anxiously as he dragged the suitcases onto the landing.

'Yep. I only had a couple of glasses of champagne and the mulled wine.'

'Well, you can relax on the flight to Paris and have as much to drink as you like,' she said.

He pulled her back into the bedroom and took her hand. 'Actually, Sam, I don't quite know how to tell you this, but there's been a slight change of plan. I forgot to pay the balance of the flights and the travel agent cancelled the booking.'

She stared at him. 'Oh, Roy, how could you forget? Why didn't you just pay for the flights in full when you booked?'

'I booked on impulse and didn't have my cards or chequebook with me. I only had enough cash for the deposit and I completely forgot about the balance. I'm sorry, sweetheart, really I am. But they offered us an alternative to make up for the disappointment.' He threw a packet down on the bed.

She tutted and picked it up. 'So where are we off to then, Blackpool?' She opened the envelope, pulled out the contents and squealed. 'Oh my God! Two weeks in Mauritius. Roy Cantello, you sneaky, lying bastard!'

'That's no way to speak to your husband when he's just given you the trip of your dreams.'

She flung her arms around him. 'I love you, Roy.'

'I know you do,' he grinned, 'and I can't say I blame you!'

She giggled and punched him playfully on the chest. 'What about clothes? I've only packed warm things for Paris.'

'All sorted. Your case is in the car boot, courtesy of Jane and Pat. They've packed bikinis, sarongs and shorts. What you haven't got, you can buy when you get there. Mauritius, here we come!'

* * *

'Didn't I always say Jon could be the milkman's?' Enid said as Eddie and Jane finished telling her and Ben their tale.

'You did.' Eddie smiled and helped himself to a bacon roll. 'Well, he was the head stylist's actually!'

'You poor lad, and what a way for our Jon to find out. Bless him. The shock must have been awful, and for Jess, too.'

Eddie nodded. 'He's taken it far better than I ever thought he would do and I wish now we'd told him years ago.'

'Well, with what's going on between him and Jess, it's a bloody good job he *isn't* your natural son!' Enid said.

'Isn't it just!' Ben offered Eddie a cigarette. 'So, what do they want to do?'

'Ed's having the barn at the back of our place converted to a bungalow like yours,' Jane said. 'The plans are drawn up and we're waiting to hear if they've been accepted. Then we'll get the builders in and Jess and Jon will make it their home. They want to get married, but we're not sure how that can be arranged. Both birth certificates state that Ed's their father. That in itself will cause complications, I'm not even sure where to start making enquiries.'

'The Registrar of Births, Marriages and Deaths, I suppose,' Enid suggested.

'Probably,' Jane agreed. 'Anyway, we'll see. They've all the time in the world. Jess needs to relax and rest properly. Her nerves are shot to pieces and her dodgy ankle keeps giving way with the extra weight she's carrying.'

'How are you going to explain things to Katie and Dom?' Enid asked.

'As truthfully and simply as we can,' Eddie replied.

'There'll never be secrets again in our household. If we'd been completely honest with Jon, he and Jess wouldn't have had all that worry.'

'True, but you might have lost him ages ago,' Enid said. 'He may have wanted to trace his natural father's family. You did the right thing, don't have doubts about that. He's a smashing lad and a credit to you both.'

'Thanks, Enid, and you too, Ben – for being so understanding, I mean,' Eddie said.

'Very little shocks us these days.' Enid smiled. 'That's what comes of being surrounded by you young rock 'n' rollers!'

Jane grinned and stood up. 'Thanks for breakfast, Mum. We'll go and tell Jon and Jess they can relax now. No doubt they'll come and see you later.'

Strolling back up the garden, Jane grabbed Eddie by the hand.

'Come here, you young rock 'n' roller!' She kissed him.

'You looking forward to being a grandma?' he asked.

'Yeah. What about you, Grandpa?'

He laughed. 'It's bloody ironic though. The Italian Stallion's about to become a father again. I'm going to be a grandpa and *he's* older than me.'

'Ah, but *he'll* have the sleepless nights and bags under his eyes, we won't,' Jane said. 'Mind you, two weeks in Mauritius should set him up nicely for all of that.'

* * *

'You enjoyed yourselves, then?' Jane asked as she and Sammy sat in the office with the first mug of coffee of the New Year.

'It was the most wonderful, blissful time I've ever had.' Sammy sighed dreamily. 'You've got to get Ed to take you there, it's beautiful.'

'When the tour finishes and I can be sure that Jess and the

baby are okay, I think Ed and I will be ready for a holiday ourselves.'

Sammy stretched out her slender tanned legs and grinned. 'I feel really happy.'

'After everything that's happened, it's good to hear you say that.'

'I'm so excited about the baby, too,' Sammy said. 'I just can't stop talking and thinking about it. I'm really hoping it's a girl. I'm praying that Livvy won't change her mind.'

'Have you spoken to her since you came home?'

'Roy has. He called her yesterday and she's fine. She can't wait to get it over with. She asked him to be at the birth.'

'You're joking! How do *you* feel about that?' Jane frowned and took a sip of coffee.

'I'm not too keen, if I'm honest. But since he was at the conception, he might as well be at the finishing post.'

'How does Roy feel, though? He missed Nick's birth by minutes and passed out at Jason's,' Jane said. 'He's never actually seen a delivery.'

'He's not too keen, either. He's very squeamish at the best of times and he'll be more of a hindrance than a help. He's actually suggested we both be there. Chances are he'll be touring when she goes into labour. Unless the group is somewhere reasonably close it'll be impossible for him to get home in time. Anyway, we said we'd play it by ear. Livvy told Roy that Sean and Tina have been marvellous with her, really looking after her, which we're very grateful for.'

Jane smiled. 'They're a smashing couple. I hope Livvy will be okay. I mean, giving your baby away is a very brave thing to do. I just hope it doesn't send her over the edge.'

'I'm sure she's thought it through. We've decided to stick with the names they've already chosen, but I'm going to add Nicholas or Nicola as a second name, in memory of our Nick.'

Jane blinked away sudden tears and put down her mug. 'Sammy, that's lovely. Oh, I've gone all goosy.'

'Don't start, Jane, please. I had Roy in tears when I suggested it and then *I* started bawling too. We were lying on a beautiful beach, sobbing our hearts out. People must have wondered what on earth was going on. Can you imagine having to explain all that to a stranger?'

'Bit complicated,' Jane agreed. 'Was Roy recognised while you were away?'

'Funnily enough he was. By people our own age, who must have been fans in the sixties. We had a meal one night with a lovely couple who live just outside London. Roy told them the band had re-formed and were set to tour this year. They said they'd catch the show when it's in their area. Roy took their phone number and he's promised to call them and send them a backstage pass.'

'Well, they're off to London next Wednesday to record the new album. Eddie said they'd be releasing a single from it to coincide with the start of the tour. He's earmarked "I'm Gonna Change the World" as his favourite.'

'Roy loves that one. He was singing it all the time we were away.'

'Right, do you want to go through the diary now, see what we've got on this week?' Jane said. 'There's not many appointments with it being early in the New Year, but I *have* got a confession to make.'

'What have you done now?' Sammy drained her coffee mug.

'Stuart phoned while you were away. He's got new samples for you. How do you feel about seeing him again?'

'Oh God!' Sammy blushed. 'I don't know. I haven't seen him since the night I slept with him. I've only spoken to him the once to tell him Roy and I were back together. But I know I can't avoid him forever.'

'I'm sure he's got over it. He's no doubt put it down to too much wine and the heat of the moment. It happens. Anyway, Ed saw him in the pub just before Christmas with a young blonde hanging off his arm so I wouldn't worry about him if I were you.'

'Young blonde, eh? Another Livvy, maybe?'

'Probably.' Jane laughed.

'Okay then,' Sammy said. 'Arrange an appointment, but promise me you'll stay with me. Dare I tell Roy?'

'We'll arrange it for when the group's in London and Roy will be none the wiser.'

'Good idea. Roy doesn't hold Stuart a grudge or anything, but he would feel a bit insecure if he thought I was meeting him alone for whatever reason.'

'That's fair enough,' Jane agreed. 'You're still building bridges. Right, I'll call Jess, make sure she's okay, then I'll get on with some work. Don't forget I'm taking this afternoon off to go with her to antenatal.'

* * *

Jess yawned and stretched her arms and legs. 'Come in,' she called as someone knocked lightly on her bedroom door.

Gran's smiling face appeared. 'Cup of tea and some toast, Jess?'

'Oh, thanks, Gran. You shouldn't be waiting on me hand and foot like this.'

'Well, somebody has to and with your dad out and your mum and Jon working, who else is there? Your mum just called to ask if you're okay.' She sat down on the edge of Jess's new double bed. 'How are you feeling today?'

'Fat!' Jess groaned. 'Look at the size of me and I'm not even four months yet. Jon's already complaining I take up most of the bed.'

'It'll no doubt be a big baby, love. Jon's a strapping lad; he weighed over nine pounds at birth.'

'Thanks, Gran! Cheer me up, why don't you? The very thought makes me cringe. I'm never having any more.'

'We all say that. I reckon we women are gluttons for punishment. Sammy's doing it the right way this time, letting someone else have the baby for her.'

'Grandma! What a thing to say. I bet Sammy wishes *she* was carrying it. Much as I hate being pregnant, I couldn't bear the thought of Jon going with anyone else.'

'No, I'm sure. I'm only joking, love,' Gran said, patting Jess's arm. 'Eat your breakfast now and then I'll help you with your shower, unless you prefer to do it by yourself.'

'I can manage on my own now, thanks all the same. But you could help me dry my hair if you will then I'll be ready for Mum.'

'Give me a shout when you're ready.'

* * *

As Enid hurried away, Jess sat back against the pillows and sipped her tea, reflecting over the last few weeks. After the revelations at Cathy's house, she and Jon had mulled over how to tell his grandma and Aunt Sally. Then Cathy had called and told them that Sally already knew, but had promised to keep it to herself.

'We'll have to go and visit Sally,' Jon had suggested. 'Tell her about the baby.'

Their dad agreed. 'She's already in the picture about Richard. It shouldn't be too difficult. Invite her to the wedding and christening. Perhaps she can think of an easy way to explain it to her mother.'

Sally had welcomed them with open arms, telling Jess how much she looked like her dad with her big blue eyes. Jess warmed to Sally immediately and wondered if she in any way resembled how Angie might look now if she'd lived. But she couldn't equate the picture of the youthful schoolgirl with the plump and motherly Sally.

'Now then, Jon, how did the visit to my mother go?' Sally asked. 'I know you only stayed one night and guessed you'd had enough after that.'

He blushed slightly and glanced sideways at Jess.

'Sally, Jess and I know that Ed's not my real dad,' he said.

Sally gasped, hand flying to her mouth. 'Oh my goodness, who told you?'

'No one. Grandma gave me Angie's diaries. Except of course she has no idea that she gave them to me. They were locked away in a tin box that was stored in another box of Angie's belongings. With hindsight, it's probably as well, considering the information they contained. Dad, Mum and Cathy confirmed everything she'd written.'

'I had no idea she kept diaries,' Sally replied, her face pale. 'It must have been a terrible shock for you, Jon. I know that it was for me. But you are *so* like Richard that I knew I couldn't be mistaken.'

'It knocked me for six,' he admitted. 'But, to be honest, it's the best thing that could have happened for Jess and me.'

Sally looked puzzled as Jon took Jess's hand and laced his fingers through hers.

'This will come as another shock: Jess is expecting my baby.'

Sally sat back on her chair, mouth agape. She quickly composed herself and shook her head. 'Well, I can see she's expecting, but I didn't think... Oh, Jon, how have your parents taken it?'

'They're fine. Mum suspected something was going on between us and they already knew that Richard was my father. It's just a pity they didn't tell *us*, it would have saved us a lot of worry.'

Sally nodded. 'I expect they did what they thought was best at the time. What about you two, were you already involved before you found out you weren't related?'

Jon smiled sheepishly. 'Yes. We planned on leaving the area so that we could live together.'

Sally sighed and shook her head. 'If our Angie weren't already dead, I swear I'd throttle her for her lies and deceit! It's had such far-reaching consequences for years.'

'To be honest, Sally, she was terrified of telling anyone,' Jess said. 'Her diaries tell the tale of a very mixed-up teenager who got involved with Richard and ended up pregnant after a one-night stand.'

'She should never have deceived Eddie. That was very wrong of her and to keep it up when she realised Jon was Richard's was unforgivable,' Sally said.

'We know.' Jon smiled. 'But she *was* my mum and at the end of the day she was so young. Look what I've done. I'm my mother's son alright! But I can put all those wrong things to bed and forgive Angie for everything now. Because of what she did, I can now rightfully marry my "sister"! There's just one more thing, Sally.' He grinned as she looked enquiringly at him.

'What's that?'

'Who's going to tell Grandma?'

'Oh my Lord!' Sally exclaimed. 'Do we have to?'

'Well, she wants us to visit her again and we'd love to, but Jess can't hide her bump. Not only that, we plan to marry next year. She'll have to be told sometime.'

Sally puffed out her cheeks and shook her head. 'I'll do it. You two youngsters have quite enough on your plates. Leave it with me, I'll let you know how I get on.'

'Will you come to our wedding and the christening?' Jess asked.

'I'd love to. It's a chance to buy a new hat.'

Two weeks after the visit, they received a letter from Jon's grandmother. Enclosed was a cheque for five hundred pounds to put towards a pram, cot and whatever else they needed. She congratulated them, said she wasn't surprised as she'd guessed they had feelings for each other and wasn't it as well that Richard was Jon's father and not Eddie. She admitted to being shocked at first, but was now looking forward to her first great-grandchild and the wedding.

Jess waved the cheque in front of her father.

'*She's* obviously mellowed in her old age,' he said, reading the letter Jon handed to him. 'There are no recriminations, or "how could you's?" Jon, you are obviously her blue-eyed boy.'

'Don't you mean green?' he quipped as Jess laughed at them.

'At least you don't have to sell your drum kit like poor Dad did to buy you a cot and pram,' she said.

A scratching at the bedroom door broke Jess's daydreams. Lennon pushed his way in, jumped up on the bed and held out his paw.

'Hello, old fella. Want some toast?' She broke off a corner and scratched his silky ears. 'There won't be much room in the bed for *you* to snuggle up to me soon if the baby keeps on growing at this rate.'

35

FEBRUARY 1985

The Raiders' UK tour began with a gig at The Apollo Theatre in their home city of Manchester. The venue was sold out over two nights. Their family members, who occupied most of the circle's front row, attended the first night's show. Sean, Tina, and a heavily pregnant Livvy were seated close by.

Support act Perry's Dream opened the show. When the handsome James Perry stepped into the spotlight, Jon nudged Jess.

'If you hadn't got involved with me, Dad could have introduced you to him later.'

'He's so handsome, but I think he'd be more interested in Jason and Jules than me,' she whispered.

'You're probably right there.' Jon squeezed her hand.

Perry's Dream finished their spot with the number-one hit 'Let's Love a While Longer', written by Roy and Eddie, and took a bow. As they left the stage, the theatre lights came up and Katie tapped her feet impatiently.

'When's Dad coming on?'

'Soon,' Jon said. 'Just be patient and don't speak with your mouth full. You're spitting popcorn everywhere.'

'I'm tired,' Dominic complained. 'Can we go home?'

Jon rolled his eyes. Their dad's fame washed completely over Katie and Dominic's heads. But then again, they'd only ever known him as Daddy who was home all day and looked after them. 'We can't go home yet, Dom. Dad would be really disappointed if we missed the show. Have a jelly baby and pass one to Katie and Abby. When the lights go down again, the group will come on stage.'

Dominic sighed and sat back on his seat. He pulled a cellophane bag from his jacket pocket and begrudgingly held it out to his sister and Abby. 'Only take one each,' he said to Katie, who grabbed a handful.

'You're such a meanie with your sweeties,' she said. 'You've eaten nearly all Abby's popcorn and *she* didn't complain.'

'Don't you two start,' Jane said as the lights dimmed and a hush fell over the audience.

Katie leapt to her feet, sweeties forgotten for the moment. 'Is it now? Is Daddy on now?'

A ripple of amusement sounded as people turned to look at the excited little girl.

'Yes, Katie, any minute,' Jane said.

In the dark, silent theatre the audience held its breath. A small circle of light fell on the stage and picked out a hand, poised to strike a chord on a white Fender Stratocaster.

Sammy's breath caught in her throat as Roy's hand crashed down on the strings and coloured spotlights picked out the members of The Raiders as they launched into their raunchy rocker, 'You Give Me That Feeling'.

The theatre erupted as for the first time in over twenty years the band belted out their old number-one hit in time-honoured fashion. Katie, Kim and Abby were up on their feet, clapping and dancing. Jane, Sammy, Pat and Cathy breathed a collective sigh of relief and smiled at one another as the song ended to tumultuous applause.

'They're back!' Sammy grinned.

'They look wonderful in those cream suits,' Cathy said. 'Thank God they decided on the brown shirts and not the pink. Carl looks hideous in pink with his red hair.'

'They look almost fanciable from up here!' Jane laughed.

Roy stepped forward, a big smile splitting his face. 'The next song is our new single and will be on sale from next week.'

'I'm Gonna Change the World' was a slightly slower tempo and it was the first time the girls had heard the group perform it.

'Number one that! I bet you anything,' Sammy whispered to Jane. 'It's fabulous when you hear it properly.'

'I reckon you might be right about number one,' Jane said, clapping along to the song. Eddie was drumming and shaking his head from side to side with the rhythm. He looked exactly the same as he'd always done, except he no longer had a floppy fringe to flick from his eyes. Roy was on top form, dancing around, and cracking jokes with the audience when the number ended. He handed his guitar to the roadie for a string replacement as requests for favourite Raiders' songs flew thick and fast. The band ran through their repertoire, playing their own songs and a selection of rock 'n' roll favourites.

'Will they sing "My Special Girl"?' Katie asked.

'Of course they will,' Jess replied, smiling at her little sister.

'Because I'm Daddy's special girl now that you've got Jon,' Katie said smugly, folding her arms.

'We're *all* special to Dad,' Jess replied, grinning.

As the show drew to a close and the audience members, who had left their seats to dance in the aisles, went to sit down, Roy squinted up at the circle and waved at Sammy.

'Our final song tonight is the very first hit we ever had, way back in 1965. Eddie and I wrote it for three very special ladies. Tonight, we sing it not just for *our* three special girls, but also for our daughters, and special girls everywhere.'

Sammy felt the familiar tears start. She glanced at Jane and

Pat, who were wiping away their own tears. She looked at Jess and Jon, who were holding hands, and smiled at Abby, Katie and Kim, who were sitting on the edge of their seats as though knowing that the song was being sung just for them.

Livvy, sitting next to Sean, put her hand protectively over the wriggling bump that she was so sure was a girl and whispered, 'This is for you too, Harley. That's your daddy out there singing for you.'

Sean smiled. 'This was always mine and Tina's favourite.'

The audience erupted again as the beautiful ballad came to an end. The whole theatre was on its feet, clapping, whistling, stamping and cheering as The Raiders assembled at the front of the stage and took a bow.

* * *

Roy turned to Eddie and flung his arm across his shoulders. 'That was brilliant, but I'm absolutely knackered!'

'Me too,' Eddie nodded, 'and we've got the encore to do yet.'

'I need a pee first,' Roy whispered as they filed off stage while the audience yelled 'MORE!'

'Phew!' Carl grinned delightedly. 'That went down great. God, I feel fantastic.'

'So do I,' Phil said as Roy disappeared into the bathroom. 'You almost had me in tears out there, Roy.'

'Why?' Roy called from behind the closed door.

'All that sob stuff about special girls. Laura and our daughters are here tonight. I gave her a pass for later, so I hope they'll come and meet the rest of you.'

Roy reappeared, zipping up his flies. 'That's great, Phil. Come on, let's rock some more and then we can grab something to eat and drink backstage. "Summertime Blues", here we come!'

They ran back on stage and took their places, launching into the old rock 'n' roll classic with renewed vigour. Ending on a triumphant note, they bowed and waved their way off stage.

As they peeled off their damp clothes and changed into jeans and T-shirts, their agent and manager Frank James strolled into the dressing room, carrying a crate of champagne.

'Come on, lads, there's a crowd of women out there, claiming they're all someone's special girl. Come and sort out whose is whose.'

Roy grinned and led the way to the hospitality area, where a cold buffet awaited, along with a crowd of pressmen and photographers. After giving a brief interview and posing for photographs, the group greeted their families and tucked hungrily into the food.

Sammy flung her arms around Roy and kissed him. 'You were brilliant! I'm so proud of you, darling.'

'I'm knackered, Sam,' he said wearily. 'God knows how I'll cope with the whole tour. Believe it or not, all I want to do right now is go home and go to be – to sleep, I might add.'

'That's not like you, Roy.' She handed him a glass of champagne. 'You were always at your most randy after a gig!'

'I know, love. It worries me. I'm getting old, Sam.'

'Don't be silly, you're in your prime. Livvy's over there with Sean and Tina. We should go and say hello, ask how she's feeling. She looks really pale tonight, she's only got a week to go now.'

Frowning, Roy turned to look across to where Livvy was standing. He caught her eye and she raised her hand. 'She *does* look pale,' he said and crossed the room to Livvy's side, Sammy following.

'Hi, Liv.' He smiled at her. 'How are you?'

'Fine, thanks,' Livvy grimaced. 'Well, I think I am. I feel very uncomfortable, like it's going to drop out any minute.'

'Is that normal?' Roy turned to Sammy.

'Perfectly normal. You men don't know you're born! Why

don't you sit down, Livvy? You look really tired. There are some chairs over there. Come on, I'll sit with you and Roy can wait on us hand and foot.'

As Sammy led the way, a gush of water shot down Livvy's legs and splashed onto the floor. She pulled on Sammy's sleeve and whispered, 'My waters have broken.'

Sammy quickly took charge. 'Oh no! Right, keep calm, I'll go and find Jane. We came in the Jeep, we can use it to get you to hospital.' She turned to a worried-looking Roy. 'Stay with her. I'll explain what's happening to those who need to know.'

Sammy dashed across to Jane. 'Livvy's waters have broken. We need to get her out of here. Can you take us to the hospital right now?'

'Of course. Just let me tell Ed where I'm going and then he can see to the kids. Grab a handful of clean towels from the lads' dressing room and meet me by the stage doors.'

Sammy got the towels and went back to Roy and Livvy, who were both looking terrified. Between them, they helped Livvy out of the crowded room and down a corridor followed by Sean and Tina.

'What if there are fans waiting at the stage door?' Roy said.

'Oh God, I never thought of that,' Sammy replied. 'Well, they'll be looking for autographs, won't they? You'll just have to sign a few programmes while Jane and I settle Livvy in the Jeep and then you can make a run for it. Just divert their attentions away from what we're doing.'

'Okay,' Roy muttered as Livvy let out a howl of pain.

Tina frowned and took her hand. 'You've been having pains all night, haven't you?'

Livvy nodded. 'All day really, but I didn't want to miss the show. I need to go to Sean's house for my case,' she told Sammy.

'It's okay, we can do that,' Roy said as a screech of brakes sounded outside the doors. 'Sounds like Jane's here.'

Sean opened the doors a crack and peered out. 'It *is* Jane

and there aren't that many people outside. It's chucking it down, so that will have seen a lot of them off. Drape a towel over your head, Roy, and make a run for it. Jane's got the car doors open. Go on quick, we'll see to Livvy.'

Roy did as he was told and threw himself into the back of the Jeep. Sammy handed him the towels and told him to spread them across the seat. Then she and Sean helped Livvy to clamber up next to Roy.

'Me and Tina will go home now,' Sean said. 'The doors have shut behind us anyway, so we can't go back to the party. Call as soon as there's any news.'

'We will, thanks for your help,' Jane said as she and Sammy climbed into the front of the Jeep.

'Get your foot down, Jane,' Roy said as Livvy yelled again.

'Ow-ow-ow-ow-SHIT!' she screamed, clutching Roy's hand.

'It's okay, Liv, it's okay, I'm here,' Roy said soothingly as Jane sped off down the road.

'For fuck's sake, Roy, it's not okay! It hurts like hell and the water's still running out all over Jane's car!'

'Don't worry about that, it'll clean up,' Jane said. 'I wish I had a blue flashing light so we could skip through the traffic lights.' She headed towards Sean and Tina's place to collect the case. Roy chatted to Livvy to try and keep her mind off her pains, which suddenly seemed to be coming very quickly.

'I don't think we've time to get to the hospital,' Jane whispered to Sammy.

'We have to, she's booked in there,' Sammy said, with a look of panic.

'That baby's going to be here any minute. I'm telling you, Roy will be delivering it himself.' Jane stopped the Jeep next to a phone box and turned to look at Livvy's screwed-up face. 'Call an ambulance and the hospital, Sam. Let them know she's on the way.'

'I need to push!' Livvy shrieked as Sammy leapt out of the car and ran to the phone box.

Jane climbed over the seats into the back. 'Get behind her shoulders, Roy, and support her properly while I have a look at what's happening.'

Looking worried to death, Roy moved quickly, pulling Livvy round so that she was lying against him. She was crying and sobbing, saying she wanted to push. Jane peeled off her wet trousers and underwear and gasped with shock.

'She *does* want to push. Roy, the head's crowning.'

'Is it? Oh, Jesus Christ!' Roy said. 'What the fuck does that mean? You've had three, Jane, you must know what to do!'

Jane looked at his stricken face. 'Yeah, Roy, but I was at the other end!'

Sammy ran back, opened the passenger door and climbed aboard, taking in the scene. 'The ambulance is on its way.'

'So's the baby, the heads nearly out,' Jane said. 'We'll have to cope the best we can. Roy, I'll need your T-shirt to wrap it in. Pull it over his head, Sam, if you can reach him.'

Sammy knelt up on her seat and leant over. She yanked Roy's T-shirt off as Livvy screamed again and pushed hard at Jane's instructions.

Roy held Sammy's gaze, his eyes echoing the fear in hers. He whispered silently, 'Please, God, don't let me lose another child.'

At fifteen minutes past midnight, Harley Nicola Cantello slithered into the world, seconds before the ambulance arrived. Jane breathed a sigh of relief as the tiny bundle opened her rosebud mouth and wailed in protest. For her father it was all too much and he fainted clean away.

Jane wrapped the baby in Roy's T-shirt and laid her on Livvy's stomach. Sammy, tears pouring down her cheeks, was frozen into a kneeling position on the front passenger seat.

The two ambulance attendants, who looked in on the scene,

smiled as they congratulated a tearful Jane on the safe delivery. They cut the cord, checked the baby's airways and delivered the placenta before Roy came round.

Sammy smiled at her pale-faced husband as he struggled to sit up. Livvy was still lying against him and she tilted her head backwards.

'Hello, Daddy,' she said wearily. 'It's another special girl for your harem!'

Jane lifted his daughter, who was now wrapped in a clean white sheet, and held her up for Roy's inspection. He smiled as the crumpled little face, with a mop of jet-black hair and dark button-eyes, studied him unblinkingly.

'She looks a bit annoyed,' he said.

'Are you surprised?' Jane said. 'It's not a very dignified start for her.'

'She looks exactly like Nick and Jason did,' he said softly, looking at Sammy.

'Doesn't she just?' Sammy agreed, tearfully.

'Hold her, Sammy,' Livvy urged. 'She's *your* daughter too.'

Sammy took the baby from Jane and gazed in awe. 'She's beautiful. Thank you, Livvy. Thank you *so* much.'

'You're very welcome. I just hope she helps you put the past to bed.'

Sammy smiled tearfully and nodded, too choked for words.

'Right then, let's get this little lady and Mummy to the hospital,' the elder of the two attendants spoke up.

'She's booked into The Melville Private Maternity Home and they're expecting her,' Sammy told him.

'What about you, Dad? Aren't you getting in with them?' asked the younger attendant as Livvy and Harley were settled comfortably in the ambulance.

'Err,' Roy hesitated and looked at Sammy.

'Go on, Roy. We'll follow in the Jeep,' she said.

'You sure?' he whispered.

'Positive. They can't go alone. What would it look like? Go on!' Sammy pushed him towards the ambulance doors. 'See you soon.'

He climbed in and sat down besides Livvy, taking Harley in his arms as the doors closed and the ambulance sped off into the night.

* * *

Livvy looked up at Roy and smiled. 'What do you think of your daughter, Mr Cantello?'

'She's gorgeous, absolutely gorgeous,' he said, tears running down his cheeks. 'I'm so proud of you, Livvy. I can't believe how quickly she came.'

'I was actually in labour all day,' she confessed. 'But like I told the others, I wasn't going to miss your show for anything. I sat through it, counting contractions and deep breathing.'

'You crazy girl! Did you enjoy the show, in spite of the pains?'

'Very much. It was brilliant! It's been quite a night all round, hasn't it?'

He kissed the baby's head. 'You can say that again!'

* * *

'How do you feel?' Jane asked as she and Sammy followed the ambulance.

'Stunned! I'll feel better when I'm with Roy again. I had to let him go with her, didn't I? I feel sick at the thought of it. Supposing he decides he wants to be with them now. I mean, going through all that together may bring them close again.'

'He won't want that, believe me. He did very well, considering he'd only just finished the show. He's probably worn out now and desperate to get home.'

'What about you, Jane? You were wonderful back there, I can't thank you enough.'

'Oh, it was nothing,' she said modestly. 'Livvy did most of the work. I still can't believe how quickly she gave birth.'

* * *

Livvy and Roy were taken to a private suite, where Livvy was made comfortable while Harley was examined by a paediatrician who declared her a fit and healthy six pounds four ounces. The hospital staff had been made aware of the situation regarding the baby's parentage and when Jane and Sammy arrived, they were taken immediately to Livvy's suite. After a last cuddle all round for Harley, they said goodnight to Livvy and promised to visit the next day.

On the way back to the theatre, Jane reflected that the whole trip had taken less than ninety minutes, but had felt like a lifetime. Meantime, Eddie had sent Katie and Dominic home in a taxi with Jon and Jess. Tim, Pat and their sleepy daughters had also left for home. Only Eddie, Phil, Carl and Cathy, along with Frank James, remained.

The theatre management was waiting to lock up and go, but let in Jane, Sammy and Roy, who were greeted with enthusiasm.

'We've decided to go to our place for a nightcap,' Eddie told them. 'You can tell us what happened when we get there. Just tell us one thing to tide us over. Boy or girl?'

'Girl!' Roy announced, a big grin from ear to ear.

* * *

Livvy traced her finger around her daughter's face and smiled. She was waiting for Roy and Sammy to collect one-week-old Harley and take her home. After today there would be no further contact with her baby. She'd signed a document, drawn up by Roy's solicitor, and a cheque for fifty thousand pounds was sitting in her handbag. Roy said it would help her get on her feet in Glasgow. Well, that much was true, but it still felt like blood money. She was planning on calling her friend Sheena once she was back at Sean and Tina's place – Sheena would put her up for a few weeks while she decided what she wanted to do.

Maybe Sheena would like to re-form their duo and sing in pubs and clubs. Roy had also given her a few contact numbers and the tapes he'd recorded with her singing solo. It would be up to her, he'd said, whether she tried to get an agent interested. He could help her no further.

Harley stirred in her arms and opened her eyes. 'Hello, baby girl. You're going home soon with your new mummy and your daddy. They'll take great care of you. Your big brother Jason will spoil you rotten. You're a lucky little lady because you'll never want for anything.'

Tears dripped onto the baby's face and she blinked. Livvy gently wiped them away with her fingertips. 'Your daddy will tell you all about me one day. Why I left you behind with him. But trust me, this is for the best.'

There was a gentle tap at the door and Roy popped his head around, followed by Sammy 'You okay, Liv?' he asked.

'I guess so,' she replied. 'She's all ready for you. She's wearing Tina's new outfit and I've packed all the other gifts in that bag over there.'

Sammy picked up the small holdall. 'You are sure about this?'

Livvy nodded. 'Sean and Tina will be here in ten minutes to take me home. Best if you go before they arrive. Tina said if you change your mind, *she'll* have her!' She smiled through her tears.

'I'm sure she would,' Sammy said. 'She'll be able to come

and visit whenever she wants to and we're going to ask her and Sean to be godparents, along with Ed and Jane.'

'Well, that's lovely. They'll be thrilled to bits. Right then, here you are, Roy.' Livvy handed him the shawl-wrapped bundle. 'Tell her that I did this for *her*.' She turned away as he looked into her eyes. She thought she could see something there and she didn't want to acknowledge it. 'Just go now, please.'

'Livvy!' Roy put his hand on her shoulder. 'Thank you. I'll tell her all about you as soon as she's old enough.'

'Leave it until she's ten.'

'If that's what you want,' Sammy said.

Livvy nodded. 'I do. I'll leave my friend's address with Sean. Will you send me a photograph occasionally?'

'Of course we will. Goodbye, Livvy. Thank you so much. We'll love her to bits and I'll send you progress reports. Come on, Roy. Let Livvy get ready for Sean and Tina.'

As Roy and Sammy closed the door behind them, Livvy threw herself onto the bed and sobbed into the pillow.

* * *

Jess lay on the couch at her antenatal appointment as the doctor frowned. 'Is something wrong?' she asked anxiously as he gently palpated her tummy. Her blood pressure was normal and her urine sample and weight okay, the nurse had said so. Why then was he looking concerned?

'I'd like you to have an ultrasound scan,' he said, scratching his chin. 'You're rather big for your dates. If you just wait there for one moment, I'll see if we can fit you in now.'

'Okay,' she said and stroked her lump as he left the room. 'Trust you to be a big one,' she said. 'Just my luck!'

He was soon back. 'They can fit you in right away,' he announced.

In the scan room, Jess climbed onto yet another couch. She

lay back and hoisted up her baggy top. The doctor spread gel onto her bump. It felt cold and she shivered.

'I'm just going to roll this transducer across your tummy,' he said. 'If you look at the screen beside you, you'll be able to see your baby.'

Jess turned her head and stared at the image of a little alien doing gymnastics. She frowned. 'What's that thing behind it?'

The doctor's face broke into a big smile. 'That's its brother or sister. You're expecting twins, Jessica.'

'What?!'

'It's twins,' he repeated. 'Look, two sets of arms and legs, two heads and those two black pulsating dots are their beating hearts.'

'Oh my God!' Jess stared at the aliens as they waved at her. She started to laugh. 'No wonder I'm so huge. Are they okay?'

'They look fine to me. We'll book you in for another scan at your next appointment. Bring your partner with you.'

Jess left the clinic in a daze. Her mum was the undisputed heroine of the hour for her midwifery skills and she and Jon had jokingly suggested they book her to deliver their baby. What on earth would she say when she learnt there were two?

She made her way back to Hanover's Lodge and called Jon at work.

'You'd better sit down,' she told him.

'Why, is something wrong with the baby?'

'Err, babies,' she corrected him, 'and no, there's nothing wrong with them, they're doing just fine.' There was silence. Jess heard a clatter and then Sean's voice came breezily down the line.

'Jess, is that you, love? Is everything okay? Jon's white as a sheet and he dropped the phone.'

'Ah well, that would be because I just told him we're expecting twins.'

'Bejesus, you're not?'

'We are.' She giggled.

'Hang on a minute, Jess. Jon's come back to the living.'

'Jess.' He sounded shocked.

'Yes, Jon?'

'Did you say babies?'

'I did.'

'How many?'

'Just the two!'

'Two! How on earth will we cope?' His voice held a note of panic.

'We'll be fine, don't you worry,' she reassured him.

'How can you be so calm?'

'I don't know, I just am.' She grinned, picturing his face, which she was sure must be ashen. 'I'm gonna call Dad now, see if I can catch him at the hotel in London to tell him and I'll call Mum at work. I'll see you later. Get Sean to make you a nice cup of tea and put plenty of sugar in it! Jon?'

'Yes?'

'You don't mind, do you? It'll save us having another later. We can get it all out of the way in one go.'

'I don't mind at all. It's you I'm worried about. You've had so much to cope with the last few months and now this.'

'I'm fine, Jon. I've got everything to look forward to, haven't I? And I love you so much.'

'I love you too. I'll see you later. Bye.'

Jess called both parents with her wonderful news. They were thrilled and when Eddie called Jane later, they laughed together over how Katie would take it. Her brother would be a hero in her eyes for doing twinkles right!

* * *

Jane called Sammy, who was at home looking after Harley. Roy's mother had stepped in to help them while Sammy was working and Roy was away touring, but today Sammy was taking time off.

'How are you coping?' Jane asked.

'Great. She's so placid, considering all the rows and upheaval the poor little mite went through before she was born. Jason and Jules are besotted, they won't put her down. She's the spit of Roy. I'm so glad she's not blonde like Livvy – I don't know if I could have handled that, to be honest. But she looks just like my own babies did and it's been so easy to take to her. How are you today?'

'Fine, thanks. I've got some news for you: Jess is expecting twins.'

'No! Whatever next? How does she feel about that?'

'Okay, I think. She said Jon sounded shell-shocked. Ed's over the moon. It just goes to show you what a one-night stand can amount to.'

'What one-night stand?'

'Well, if you think about it, all this stems from Angie and Richard Price's one-night stand and we're still counting the cost, not to mention the babies!'

36

JULY 1985

'Down by the orchard, please.' Jane directed the suppliers to the exact spot where she wanted the marquee erecting. As she went back indoors, the phone rang out.

'I'll get it!' Katie shot across the kitchen and snatched up the receiver. She chatted for a few minutes, then, 'Mum, can I go to Lucy's house and watch *Live Aid*? Her mum said she'd come for me because she knows you're dead busy today.'

'Yes, that would be great. Get you out from under my feet,' Jane replied and Katie excitedly told Lucy she could come and dashed off upstairs to get ready.

Jane smiled after her. Her youngest daughter was becoming as music mad as the older kids. After seeing The Raiders' concert earlier in the year, it had suddenly dawned on Katie that having a famous dad could be quite useful. She'd recently acquired a coveted Wedding Day Barbie from a classmate in exchange for James Perry's autograph. She'd also sold several copies of the same for a pound a time.

Katie reappeared in the kitchen in an outfit from Sammy's summer collection. The short skirt of the pink and white, candy-striped rah-rah dress flipped out as she did a twirl.

Jane peered closely at her and frowned. 'Are you wearing lipstick and perfume, madam?'

'Only a bit of lipstick, Mum. It's from my Girls World, it's not the real stuff like you and Jess wear.'

'No, but that smells like my real Chanel No5!'

Katie went all coy. 'I didn't think you'd mind.'

'So... who's this little effort for then?' Jane raised an amused eyebrow. 'Not Lucy, *I'll* bet.'

Before Katie could reply, Jon strolled into the kitchen and whistled in her direction. 'Morning, Mum, Katie. Wow, don't you look nice, Katie?'

'She's off to Lucy's to watch *Live Aid*,' Jane told him.

'I see, and is young Toby Johnson going as well?' he teased as Katie glared at him.

'Who's Toby Johnson?' Jane asked as she poured two mugs of coffee and handed one to Jon.

'He's a new boy at school,' Katie replied sheepishly. 'I'm going over to see Jess and the twins.' She dashed out of the kitchen before Jane could question her further.

'She can't possibly be interested in boys yet. She's only nine, for goodness' sake!'

'Nine and a half,' Jon said, sitting at the table. 'Don't forget the all-important half. What time are you expecting Dad home?'

'Anytime soon. They were leaving Nottingham first thing. How's Jess this morning?'

'Fine, thanks. The boys slept for five hours in a row last night, so we feel like we've actually had some proper rest.'

Jon and Jess's four-week-old boys were always hungry, it seemed. The new parents had spent the last month in a whirl of feeding and nappy changing. Help was always available, but there never seemed to be enough pairs of hands.

'It'll get easier, Jon,' Jane said. 'Me and Sammy have decided to sell the business and take a very early retirement.

She's got her hands full now and wants to spend time with Harley and Roy, when he's home. I want to spend more time with your dad and give some help to you and Jess.'

'That will be brilliant, Mum. We feel like zombies at the moment, we've hardly had a minute to ourselves since the babies arrived.'

'Next week should be easier. Your dad will be home until Thursday and he'll help. Why don't you book a table for Tuesday night? Take Jess out and spoil her. We'll look after Jack and Nathan and keep them overnight.'

Jon's face lit up. 'Mum, you're an angel. Thank you.' He stood up and planted a kiss on her cheek. 'I'd better go back and see if Jess needs any help. She was feeding one or the other as I came out. I'm still struggling to recognise which is which.'

'Oh, that's easy.'

'How?' He looked puzzled. 'They're identical.'

'Well, Nathan looks you directly in the eye and Jack's a bit coy,' Jane said, smiling as she thought of her grandsons' little ways.

'They both look at me almost accusingly, as if to say, we weren't ready for all this! But they're here now and I wouldn't swap them for the world.' He drained his mug. 'Right, I'll see you later.'

Jane waved goodbye as he strolled across the garden towards his new home.

* * *

Jon stopped briefly to speak to the men who were erecting the marquee for tomorrow's joint christenings of the twins and Harley.

Jess was seated beneath a tree feeding Nathan – or Jack. Jon stood for a few seconds, observing her. Katie sat on the grass beside her, cuddling Jack – or Nathan. His sisters and his sons, for he still thought of Jess as his sister, as well as his future wife. It was a strange set up in anyone's eyes, but he was sure that there was no happier man in the world than him at that moment.

As he approached, Jess looked up, blue eyes shining. He bent to drop a kiss on her lips before flopping down next to Katie.

'Do you want me to take him?' he asked, looking at the sleeping baby on Katie's knee.

She nodded. 'I'd better go home and wait for Lucy.'

'Thanks for nursing him to sleep, Katie,' Jess said. 'Enjoy *Live Aid*.'

'I will. See you later.' Jon took the baby and she jumped up, brushing bits of dried grass from her skirt.

'Have fun with Toby,' he teased.

'Who's Toby?' Jess asked.

'Someone Katie fancies at school,' Jon replied as Katie stood in front of him, hands on hips.

'No, I don't! Anyway, Lucy tried to snog him last week and he couldn't do it. That's no good to a girl, is it?' She turned and ran across the garden, leaving Jon and Jess laughing.

'Oh, dear!' Jess wiped the tears from her eyes. 'Toby had better buck his ideas up if he knows what's good for him.'

'Mum's offered to babysit next Tuesday night,' John said. 'The boys can stay over. Do you fancy going out for a meal?'

Jess beamed. 'Brilliant! I'm desperate for some time together, no babies or visitors. We could park up and go to that barn on the way back,' she suggested, a glint in her eyes.

'Hey, remember what happened last time we did that?' He gestured to the twins. 'We got a bit more than we bargained for!'

Jess laughed. 'It's funny though, when you think of it, these two conceived in a barn and Harley born in the Jeep.'

'Oh, hilarious!' Jon raised an ironical eyebrow. 'I can't quite believe the last twelve months. When you think back to this time last year, we'd just come back from France. I was with Helen, you were engaged to Nick. Do you regret any of it? I mean, apart from Nick's death, of course.'

'I don't regret a thing, well, apart from Nick's death, as you say. That was tragic, but I have a funny feeling deep down that he and I would never have married.'

'Really? Why?'

'Don't know why.' Jess shrugged. 'Just this funny feeling.'

'Well, everything that's happened seems to be for a reason,' Jon mused. 'Harley was surely meant to be, maybe to help soften the blow of losing Nick for Roy and Sammy. And then the two of us and these boys of ours, how weird is that? Angie's son and Eddie's daughter, it must have been meant to be.'

'The Lord moves in mysterious ways, as Gran's so fond of saying,' Jess said. 'Maybe he made Nick our guardian angel and *he* decided to give us a double dose for our sins, hence the twins!'

'Nick always did have a warped sense of humour.' Jon laughed. 'I'm glad we gave Jack his name. Jack Nicholas, do you think he might take up golf one day?' he quipped.

Jess rolled her eyes. 'Very funny.' She looked at her sleeping baby and stroked his soft cheek. 'We really have to do something about reviving our band again now the babies are here. I can't keep putting it off. First, my wrist and ankle, and then my huge bump getting in the way of my bass.'

'We'll sort it. Get Jules and Jason over and launch Zoo Two. The Raiders' renewed success has fired my enthusiasm and I'm dying to get cracking again,' he said.

* * *

Relaxing in the kitchen with a sandwich and a pot of coffee, Eddie smiled as Sammy and Pat strolled through the open back door, arms laden with silk flowers and bags of ribbons. 'Come to decorate the marquee, girls?'

'Yep,' Sammy replied. 'How are you, Ed? You look a bit tired.'

'Absolutely knackered! Touring's hard work these days. That's the problem when you're older and been away from it for as long as *we* have.'

'Roy said the same. He went straight to bed to recharge his batteries. Tim's looking after the baby and Kim and Abby.'

'I bet Tim's as tired as Roy is.'

'He is, but he's watching *Live Aid* with the girls and Jules and Jason. If he nods off, they're on hand to take over.'

'I'll leave you to get on with your decorating and I'll go and watch *Live Aid* with Jon and Jess,' Eddie said. 'Do the doting grandpa bit at the same time.'

* * *

'Only me,' Eddie called out as he strolled into the kitchen.

A harassed-looking Jon poked his head around the lounge door. 'Dad, you're just in time to help with feeding. Jess's in the bath and they've both fired up together. Grab a twin and a bottle.'

Eddie picked up a screaming baby and sat down on the sofa opposite the TV. He popped a teat into the demanding mouth as Nik Kershaw walked on stage. 'Rather him than me,' he said. 'Geldof called Frank, but we've been so busy, with the tour and promoting the album. Which baby is this?' He looked down into vivid blue eyes that mirrored his own, little mouth sucking in a contented fashion.

'Err, not sure.' Jon frowned. 'Is he looking you directly in the eye, or acting coy?'

'What on earth are you on about? Coy, I suppose, but how would I know?'

'Well, if he's coy, then it's probably Jack.'

'How do you work that one out?'

'It's what Mum said this morning.' Jon sat the baby he was feeding forward. The child belched loudly and opened his eyes wide with surprise. 'This is definitely Nathan Edward. Sounds just like his namesake!'

Eddie laughed, looking at Jon's proud face. 'You've taken to this father lark much better than I first did.' *Mind you*, he thought, *having your family with the woman you love has a lot to do with that*, as he'd found out when he and Jane had Jess. As if his thoughts had conjured her up, Jess appeared in the doorway, dressed casually in T-shirt and shorts.

'Ah, now there's a lovely sight, all my favourite males in one room,' she said.

'Hi, sweetheart, how are you?' Eddie greeted her.

'Fine, Dad. How's the tour going?'

'Fantastic, Jess. Every theatre's sold out. Can you believe that women are still screaming for your old dad? I'm so tired, I'm glad to be home for a few days.'

'How are the others coping?' Jon asked.

'Same as me, knackered! Sammy told me Roy's gone to bed and that's not like him.'

'Not on his own anyway,' Jon said.

'Quite!' Eddie laughed. 'Phil's back with Laura. It's early days, but he's spending the next few nights at Apple Tree House with her and the kids. Fingers crossed for them. They're coming tomorrow afternoon, so we can see for ourselves how they're doing.'

'Laura's a nice lady,' Jon said. 'You got on well with her when you met her backstage after the first show, didn't you, Jess?'

Jess smiled. 'Yes, she was lovely, really friendly and she's so pretty. Phil's lucky to be given another chance with her. Hope it works out for them. I'm going over to help Mum,

Sammy and Pat decorate the marquee. Can you two cope alone?'

'Of course we can,' Jon replied. 'Dad's a dab hand. They're asleep now anyway, so they can go down in their baskets for a while and we'll grab a couple of beers and watch *Live Aid* in peace.'

* * *

Jess found her mum, Sammy and Pat sitting on the lawn by the side of the marquee, sipping glasses of white wine.

'Alright for some,' she said, grinning.

'Help yourself,' Sammy said. 'Grab a glass and join us.'

'Thanks, I will.'

'She looks well,' Pat said as Jess strolled towards the house.

'She's so slim already,' Sammy said. 'I couldn't have got into shorts that skimpy so soon after having Nick. My extra weight hardly shifted at all.'

'That's because you were pregnant again.' Jane laughed.

Sammy rolled her eyes. 'Don't remind me. But then again, thank God I was because I wouldn't have had Jason.'

'How are he and Roy getting along these days?' Jane asked, pushing her sunglasses up her nose as Jess came back and flopped down beside her.

'Really well; better than I dared hope. That's definitely down to Harley, bless her. She's brought them so close.'

'Have you heard from Livvy?' Jess asked.

'Yes, we had a letter from her last week. I've written back and sent her a couple of photographs of Harley. I know we said at first we wouldn't have any contact, but she looked so sad when we were taking Harley that I couldn't do it to her. The odd letter won't hurt. I mean, she's given me her child. You can't get more generous than that.'

'Do you think she'll ever come back for her?' Jess, who had

every admiration for Livvy these days, asked. The girl had been so brave in giving up her daughter that Jess couldn't imagine how empty she must be feeling right now.

'I don't think she would somehow, Jess,' Sammy replied. 'She wrote that she's met up with her old boyfriend, Danny McVey.'

Jess nodded and twiddled the stem of her glass. 'Good luck to her.'

'Shall we make a start on getting this marquee decked out?' Jane jumped to her feet.

Sammy yawned loudly. 'Oh God, *I'm* so tired, never mind Roy, Harley was awake at six this morning. Can you see the bags under my eyes?' She ran her fingers over her wrinkle-free face.

'Oh yeah.' Jane laughed. 'Bloody big holdalls they are, too!'

37

Eddie lay in the half-light with Jane dozing in his arms. He kissed her forehead, rolled her onto her side and extracted his arm.

She opened her eyes and smiled sleepily. 'Oh, you *are* here? Last night wasn't a dream then?'

He arched an amused eyebrow. 'Hey, lady, I hope you're not in the habit of having dreams like that or you won't want the real thing when I come home.'

'I'll *never* stop wanting the real thing.'

'It *was* pretty wonderful,' he said. 'Makes such a difference when the kids stay at your mother's.'

'The whole night was wonderful. The meal out was good, and then all of us back here.' She leant up on one elbow. 'What time is it, Ed?'

'Almost eight,' he replied, leaping up. 'Would you like breakfast in bed? Then we'll share a bath.'

'Mmm, sounds good. Toast and coffee for me, please.'

'What time are the caterers due?' he asked, pulling on boxer shorts and a T-shirt.

'About one.'

'Roy and I are really looking forward to today. It's kept us going all week. It's one thing being admired by fans night after night, but we like nothing better than being home with our families.'

'Talking of families, have you remembered that Angie's mother accepted her invitation to the christening?'

'Yes,' he said. 'But I don't care. What can she possibly say now after everything that's come out? She owes me a bloody big apology really.'

'I doubt you'll get one. You still slept with her daughter. Jon could have been yours. You were just bloody lucky!'

'How do you work that one out? *I* took the blame, married the girl *and* brought up the kid.'

'You wouldn't be without Jon for anything.'

'I'm joking, Jane. *I'm* the lucky one. It was worth it in the end. We've got the start of a new band with Jack and Nathan.'

'Yep, and they're so beautiful, just like you and Jess with their big blue eyes. Poor old Jon never got a sniff where looks were concerned, except for those wispy curls.'

'Maybe their next one will look like him.'

'There won't be a next. Jon's promised he'll have the snip as soon as he can. Jess says she doesn't want any more.'

'They're a bit young to be making drastic decisions like that.'

'It's their lives, we can't interfere. They've got their hands full with the twins. Jess wants to enjoy herself, not get bogged down with more babies. No, a vasectomy is definitely the answer.'

'You wouldn't say that if you were a man!' He grimaced. 'It's agony, *I* should know.'

'No more than childbirth. When I delivered Harley, I saw all that pain and fear in Livvy's eyes. I couldn't go through that again. No wonder Roy passed out, but at least he actually saw a child of his coming into the world.'

'He's so in awe of you. He says he'll never forget it as long as he lives.'

'Nor will I,' Jane said. 'Right, are you going to make that toast for me while I call Sam? I know it's early, but she'll be up.'

Sammy sounded bright and breezy when she answered.

'Hi, Jane. You're awake early, considering you're in a kid-free zone.'

'I'm still in bed,' Jane replied. 'Ed's making breakfast. Wasn't it nice to have them home last night?'

'Wonderful. Roy's taken Harley out for a stroll in her buggy. They've got flowers to put on Nick's grave. He wanted to go on his own with her.'

Jane detected a slight catch in Sammy's voice. 'Oh, Sam, that's lovely. Jon and Jess went last week. They told Nick about the twins. Jess said she would hate him to feel left out.'

'I thought they had,' Sammy said softly. 'I saw the flowers when I went on Thursday. At least he has plenty of visitors. Jason and Jules go every weekend, so do Roy's mum and dad.'

'Are we meeting at your place before church?' Jane asked.

'Yeah, about two. We can have a drink before we set off. I hope the press doesn't show up, I hate our private lives being invaded.'

'We've kept things low-key by doing it ourselves,' Jane said. 'The only outsiders are the caterers and marquee people. It should go smoothly. Jon and Jess are nervous as well, so you're not on your own.'

'Ah well, fingers crossed. Well, we'll see you later. Bye, Jane.'

'Bye, Sam.' Jane replaced the receiver as Eddie carried a tray into the bedroom.

'You okay, love? Why the serious face?'

'Sammy hopes the press won't show up at the church.'

'Well, unless the vicar's sold his story to *The Sun* for the church roof fund, there's no reason for them to be there.'

'Yeah, but look what it was like at the hospital after Nick and Jess's accident and the church after Roy and Sammy's ceremony. If it gets out about Jon and Jess, the papers will make it sound so sordid.'

'If that's the case, I'll tell everyone the truth. We've nothing to be ashamed of. Roy's got more to hide than me, passing Harley off as his and Sammy's kid.'

Jane took a sip of coffee and sighed. 'I know, I can't help worrying though, it's in my nature.'

He ruffled her hair affectionately. 'Enjoy your breakfast while I run a bath.'

* * *

'Which way does this hat go?' Jon was dressing Nathan ready for the christening. He'd managed the white romper suit, with a blue N embroidered on the front, but the little white hat defeated him. It looked exactly the same, whichever way he turned it.

'Either way, Jon. It sits on top of his head. Pull the brim down and slip the elastic under his chin,' Jess replied from across the room, where she was feeding Jack.

'Like this?' Jon held out his son, complete with hat.

'That's it. He looks so cute. Ah, bless him. You go and get changed now while I get Jack ready. I won't put my new dress on until the last minute in case one of them pukes on it.'

Jon placed Nathan in his Moses basket and left the room. Jess popped Jack on the changing mat and picked up his romper suit. He looked at her, blue eyes wide, and gave her a lopsided smile. She gasped and smiled back. 'Jon, quick, Jack just smiled.'

Jon shot back into the room and stared at his tiny son, who stared back unblinkingly, without the least trace of a smile. 'Probably wind.'

'It looked real enough to me,' Jess said.

Jon put his arms around her and pulled her close, kissing her slowly. 'I feel like carrying you off to the bedroom.'

'We haven't got time,' she said. 'Later, maybe, if these two go to sleep for a few hours.'

'I can live in hope,' he called as he dashed away.

Jess finished dressing Jack and laid him in his basket. She looked up as Jon came back into the room.

'You look nice in that shirt. The pale green suits you, it echoes the colour of your eyes.'

'Thanks. Now *you* go and get ready and I'll keep an eye on these two,' he said, rushing to answer a knock at the door.

Enid, wearing a peach two-piece and matching hat, asked if they needed any help.

'You look lovely, Gran.' Jon held the door open for her. 'Come on in, Jess is getting changed.'

'We've an hour before we need to be at Sammy's, so why don't we take the babies to ours? You and Jess can have a bit of time to yourselves,' Enid suggested.

'Brilliant!' Jon's face lit up. He lifted a Moses basket in each hand and followed her across the garden.

Jess was sitting in front of the dressing table putting on her make-up when Jon returned and pulled her onto the bed.

'The boys are with Gran and Grandpa. We've just under an hour together. What would you like to do?'

'Hmm, now let me think...' She laughed as his face lit up.

* * *

'Where are they?' Jane looked at her watch. 'You said they were getting ready.' She looked accusingly at her mother and father, who had carried the twins across in their baskets. 'Honestly, you give them an inch.'

'Jane, get off their case and don't have a go at them,' Eddie said. 'They haven't had a minute to themselves lately. Here they are now, see.' Jon and Jess, flushed and smiling, walked into the kitchen, holding hands. 'Everything alright, kids?'

'Wonderful, thanks, Dad,' Jon said, winking at Jess.

'Good. Shall we get on our way then?'

* * *

The convoy left Hanover's Lodge, with Jon, Jess and the twins in Jon's car. Eddie, Ben, Enid and Dominic were in the Jeep. Jane and Katie brought up the rear in Jane's Porsche.

Katie chatted excitedly on the way to Sammy's house. She was still trying to work out how Aunt Sammy had managed to have a baby without getting fat. She'd asked several times lately why Livvy didn't babysit any more.

She'd spotted Livvy at The Raiders' concert and between her, Kim and Abby had decided that she was pregnant. Then Livvy had suddenly disappeared with Uncle Roy, Aunt Sammy and Mum, never to be seen again.

Nothing had been said in front of Katie and Dominic about Harley's arrival. But Kim and Abby had overheard snatches of conversation between their mum and Sammy and the young detectives had decided that Uncle Roy and Aunt Sammy were looking after Livvy's baby because Livvy must be ill.

What they couldn't quite fathom, but didn't dare ask, was why Harley looked so much like Uncle Roy. Abby suggested that maybe Uncle Roy was Harley's dad, but Katie said that Uncle Roy had told her Sammy was *His Special Girl* and she was quite sure he wouldn't have done any of that twinkling stuff with Livvy. So where Harley had actually come from, remained, for the time being at least, a mystery.

'Who's gonna be Harley's godparents, Mum?' Katie asked for the umpteenth time, hoping to extract another clue.

'Me, Tina, Sean and your dad,' Mum answered, stopping at

the traffic lights. 'And before you ask, Tim, Phil and Pat are Jack's, and Sean, Carl and Cathy are Nathan's.'

'Yeah, I know all that,' Katie said, twisting a strand of hair around her fingers. Mum was giving nothing away, as usual.

'What time are Lucy and Toby coming over?'

'Five o'clock, I think,' Katie replied, feeling her cheeks warming at the mention of Toby.

'I see you're wearing lipstick and my perfume again,' Mum teased. 'Is that for Toby's benefit?'

Katie rolled her eyes and stared out of the window while Mum sniggered at her own silly comment.

* * *

Ben and Eddie accepted generous measures of whisky from Roy. Sammy handed Jane a glass of chilled Chardonnay and smiled broadly.

'Everything alright, Jane? You look a bit frazzled.'

'I'm fine, just had the third degree from madam.' She nodded her head towards Katie, who was running towards Abby and Kim.

'About Harley? When they're a bit older, we'll explain.'

'If they don't suss it out for themselves,' Jane said. 'The caterers arrived to set up just before we left so it should be easy going when we get back. Where *is* Harley, by the way?'

'Upstairs with Jason and Jules, listening to music,' Sammy replied. 'Honestly, they talk to her as though she understands every single word. But then, she probably does. She's four months going on fourteen years! She looks at us as though she's been here before. I wonder sometimes if she's not a reincarnation of Nick.'

'Right, are we ready?' Eddie called from the front door. 'Grab the babies and let's go.'

***

The guests were waiting in the churchyard and Jon spotted Aunt Sally, Martin and Grandma Turner talking to Cathy and Carl. He waved and walked over, carrying Nathan. He kissed his aunt, Grandma and Cathy and shook Martin and Carl by the hand.

'Well, who have we here?' Lydia Turner smiled at the tiny boy in her grandson's arms.

'This is Nathan, and,' he turned as Jess appeared by his side, 'this is Jack,' he finished proudly.

'Jess, my dear. Congratulations! You look so well, considering.'

'Considering what?' Jess frowned.

'Well, considering the position you're in. Two babies and no ring on your finger!'

Jess gasped at her directness. 'It doesn't matter in the least. Jon and I love one another.'

Jon nodded. 'What's a ring and a bit of paper got to do with anything?' he said. 'Jess and the babies are my world. We'll marry when we're ready.'

Eddie caught the tail end of the conversation between his children and Angie's mother. He placed himself between them and slung protective arms around their shoulders. 'Problems?' he asked.

'No, Dad,' Jon replied. 'It's okay. Err, you remember my grandmother, don't you?'

'How could I ever forget?' Eddie smiled politely at the woman who used to scare him witless and held out his hand.

She shook it firmly. 'It's good to see you again, Eddie. You're looking very well. Congratulations on becoming a grandfather. Now isn't it ironic that Angie's child and your child should produce these two beautiful boys?'

'Oh, very ironic!' he agreed with a hint of sarcasm. 'But

you're forgetting that Angie's child is very much my child, too. I brought him up.'

'And a wonderful job you did, Eddie. I'm Sally, remember me? This is Martin.'

Eddie turned as Sally stepped in to diffuse the situation. 'Hi, Sally, Martin.' He shook their hands warmly. 'Good to see you both again, and under much pleasanter circumstances this time.' Eddie hadn't been in the company of Sally, Martin or Lydia Turner since the week following Angie's funeral. But now that Jon wished to keep in touch with them, he had to put his anger and bitterness to one side and try and get along. 'So, what do you think of our beautiful boys?' he said proudly.

'They're gorgeous! You're a very lucky man,' Sally replied, '*and* you deserve it. In fact,' she whispered, glancing at her mother, who was fussing over her great-grandsons, 'you deserve a bloody medal!'

Eddie grinned and called out to Jane. 'You've met my wife, haven't you?' He put an arm around her shoulders. 'Jane, you remember Mrs Turner, Angie's mother – and Sally and Martin.'

'Of course.' Jane shook hands with them all.

* * *

Roy called out to Eddie and Jane from the porch, where he'd been in conversation with the vicar. 'Come on, we're going in now. Ah, Mrs Turner, Sally and Martin, how are you all?'

'Roy Cantello, well, well, well! What a smart man you've turned out to be. A nice change from the leather-jacketed tearaway who used to come to my house,' Lydia greeted the handsome man standing in front of her.

'Congratulations on your new daughter, Roy,' Sally said, shaking him by the hand.

'Thanks, wait until you see her, she's a real beauty,' he said proudly.

'If she's anything like her mother, she'll be lovely.' Lydia nodded in the direction of Sammy, who was taking Harley from Jason.

'Err, actually, she's nothing like her mother,' Roy said. 'Sam, bring Harley over here, love. You remember Angie's mother, don't you? She wonders if Harley resembles her mum!' He prodded Sammy meaningfully in the back as she turned the baby to face Lydia.

'Oh, my goodness! She's the image of you, Roy. Oh, look, Sally, isn't she?'

Sally nodded and smiled at the lovely dark-eyed baby, who beamed back.

'Yes,' Sammy said. 'All our kids have been the image of Roy. You would think I'd had nothing to do with them!'

'Right, come on before the vicar has kittens,' Roy said. 'He came out looking for us ages ago. Everyone else has gone into church except us and the babies and without them, there's no christening.'

* * *

Nathan and Jack behaved impeccably at the font. Harley didn't like the water on her head and wailed miserably throughout the short service.

'I think she may be teething,' Sammy whispered to Roy. 'She's been a bit grumpy for the last couple of days.'

'Typical female,' Roy whispered back as his daughter grizzled against Tina's shoulder. 'Probably getting in some early PMT practice.'

'Roy, stop it, you fool, be serious!' Sammy suppressed a giggle. 'Baby girls are not as laid-back as boys, you ask Jane.'

'I don't need to. I've already sussed that for myself. She only has to look at me and I'm putty in her hands. But woe betide when she's not in the mood, she certainly lets me know.'

Sammy smiled. Roy was enjoying every minute with his daughter. Thank God for Livvy's selfless decision. She offered a silent prayer for the young woman, who must surely wonder, every minute of every day, what her baby was doing.

As the service ended, the christening party filed outside for a photo session.

Roy's mother stood beside him and Sammy, head on one side. 'That old woman over there, who is she?' Her large blue hat jerked in Lydia Turner's direction.

'It's Mrs Turner, Ed's ex ma-in-law, and she's no older than you!' Roy replied.

She ignored his barbed comment and pursed her lips. 'So... she's Angie's mother, Jon's grandma?'

'That's right,' Sammy said.

'Hmm, well I wonder what *she* makes of this Jon and Jess affair.'

'Mum, stop gossiping.' Roy tutted. 'She knows Ed's not Jon's father. Jess and Jon have every right to be together. I explained it all to you ages ago.'

'There's no need to talk to me as though I'm senile. All I'm saying is that it's as well they're not related, considering what's happened. And don't *you* go getting on your high horse with me, Roy Cantello, not after what *you've* been up to!'

'I'm not, Mum, and hey, listen, don't you dare say a thing about Livvy to anyone. Those who need to know already know and those that don't, don't matter. As far as Mrs Turner's concerned, Sammy is Harley's mother. You know how your tongue loosens after a couple of drinks.'

'Credit me with some sense, Roy. Talk about tangled webs. It gets worse with you lot as you get older.'

* * *

'Katie, Dom, I'd like you to meet Jon's grandma,' Eddie introduced his children to Lydia Turner. 'These are my youngest,' he told her.

Katie studied the old lady for a moment or two before saying bluntly, 'Are you Angie's mum, then?'

Lydia gasped and smiled. 'Yes, my dear, I am.' She looked at Eddie. 'So, you've told them about Angela?'

He nodded. 'Of course! They know Jon had a different mum to them.' He arched an ironical eyebrow and continued. 'They also know he had a different dad, too, and that is the *only* reason it's okay for him to live with Jess and have babies with her.'

Lydia nodded slowly. 'That must have taken some explaining.'

'You can say that again!'

'I owe you a big apology.' Her eyes filled with tears as she looked at him.

'You two go and find Mum and I'll be with you in a minute,' he urged Katie and Dominic. Katie didn't need to hear what he suspected Lydia was about to say. 'No, you don't. What's done is done, we can't turn the clock back. Jon could have been mine. As it happened, he wasn't, but I couldn't love him more. I did wrong by keeping the truth to myself when I found out about Richard, but I didn't want to lose Jon, not to anyone. It was my one big dread that you'd take him away from me. When Jane and I married, as well as being very much in love, it was to give him a stable home, never guessing that Jess was already on the way. But look at the pair of them now. Have you ever seen a happier-looking couple? Whatever lies Angie told me have long been cancelled out by the wonderful family I have today. You're very welcome to be part of it.'

He handed Lydia a handkerchief and she wiped her eyes and smiled at him. 'When Jess came to visit me, she told me she was very proud to be your daughter. I can see why she said that. You're a remarkable young man, Eddie Mellor.'

'Not so young these days,' he said.

'Oh, I don't know. When you were on *Top of the Pops* the other week I had my friends over and we watched you. I told them you used to be my son-in-law and you're Jon's father and I was very proud of that fact. They were green with envy. They've got strait-laced families with son-in-laws in boring jobs,' she finished, grinning impishly.

'How've you explained the situation between Jon and Jess to them?' he asked.

'I haven't, not yet. They can work it out for themselves. It'll get the grey matter working overtime when I go home armed with the christening photos and they see them together with the babies, won't it?'

Eddie threw back his head and laughed. 'You're not so bad, Mrs T!' He bent and kissed her lined cheek.

'That's the first time you've ever kissed me. I hope it won't be the last.' She smiled and touched his hand.

'I'm sure it won't. Take my arm. I'll escort you to Sally and Martin and they'll bring you to our house for the party.'

Jane, who was chatting to Sally, stared in astonishment when Eddie appeared by her side, with Lydia on his arm.

'Alright, love?' she asked, looking at his smiling face.

'I'm fine, darling. I've just been laying a ghost or two with Angie's mum.'

'And do you feel better for it?'

'I do,' he said and bent to kiss Jane lightly on the lips.

* * *

Phil laughed as he overheard Abby and Katie, who were standing by the entrance to the marquee, discussing who was the better-looking of his twin sons. His twelve-year-olds were similar, one being slightly taller. Both blond and blue-eyed with dimples and a lopsided grin.

'I think Matt's nicer,' Abby said, head on one side.

Katie screwed up her face. 'No, definitely Zak!'

'Let's see if they'd like a glass of Coke,' Abby suggested.

'Hello, Abby, Katie,' Phil greeted the pair.

'Hello, Uncle Phil.' Katie smiled sweetly. 'Would your boys like a glass of Coke?'

Phil turned to his sons. 'Do you wanna go with the girls, get yourselves a drink?'

They nodded shyly. 'Well, go on then.' He gave them a gentle push and turned to smile at Laura, who was looking amused.

'They start young these days,' Phil said. 'Our girls are a different kettle of fish.' He looked at his daughters, the image of Laura, with auburn hair and green eyes.

'That's because they came along after your initial bout of fame,' Laura said. 'They haven't been exposed to it like Ed and Tim's children. It goes over the tops of their heads. When they saw you at The Apollo, they couldn't believe it was Daddy on stage and seeing you on *Top of the Pops* finished them off. They need time to get used to it, like *we* both do.'

'I know, but time is something we have plenty of now,' he said, taking her hand. Having Laura back by his side was Phil's dream come true.

'We've all the time in the world, Phil. I want us to get it right this time. Here comes Jess with one of the twins.' Laura greeted the young mum with a sympathetic grin. 'You okay, Jess? You look a bit tired.'

Jess suppressed a yawn. 'I'm fine thanks, Laura. They're getting a bit more settled as the days go by.'

'It's a long haul, but you get there. If you need any help during the day, call me. Believe me, *I* know all there is to know about raising unexpected twins. Don't I, Phil?'

'She certainly does,' he said proudly.

'I just might take you up on the offer,' Jess said. 'With Dad away, Mum working and Jon back to work next week, I don't know how I'm going to cope.'

'Well, now you do, and I really mean it, Jess. I'd love to help.'

'Thanks. I'm just off to feed Jack and settle him down in Mum and Dad's bedroom and then I'll come back for Nathan. Jon's grandma has taken charge of him for now.'

'How did your dad get on with her earlier?' Phil asked curiously. 'I saw him chatting to her, I remember there was no love lost between them.'

'Actually, they've made peace. I'm glad, because it puts an end to all that bitterness. All we need now is to sort out a way for me and Jon to get married. Mum's made enquiries and been told Jon's birth certificate can have an amendment inserted to state that he was a child of the marriage, rather than that he's Dad's son. As soon as it's all sorted, we'll plan our wedding.' Jess excused herself and took Jack indoors.

Laura smiled at Phil. 'When's your divorce through?'

'Soon, I hope, why?'

She shrugged. 'Oh nothing, I was just wondering.'

'Would you consider re-marrying me?' He looked into her eyes.

'I might. If we get along okay for the next few months, I just might. You'd better behave yourself though. Cheat on me just once and it's all off, I mean that.'

'I wouldn't dare,' he said. 'Anyway, who wants five old geezers like us when the likes of Paul Young and Simon Le Bon are available?'

'*Who's* an old geezer? Speak for yourself, Jackson!' Roy walked up behind him, carrying Harley. 'Here's living proof that *I'm* not past it.'

'Didn't Charlie Chaplin father a child in his seventies?' Laura teased.

'Probably,' Roy agreed wryly. 'Are you enjoying yourselves?'

'Very much,' Phil replied. 'Katie and Abby have made off with our sons. Do you think they'll be okay?'

Roy laughed. 'Ask me that in a couple of years and the answer will be a definite no, but for now, I don't think you need have any worries. Although I must say Katie's quite a forward little hussy, much like her mother here.' He nodded at Jane, who had appeared by his side.

'Hey you!' Jane took Harley from him. 'Watch your step, I was never a hussy.'

'Not at first, Jane,' he teased, 'but you soon caught up.'

'Sammy wants to give Harley her tea and your mother's looking for you, Roy.'

'Oh God! What have I done now?' He smiled and waved at the blue-hatted figure striding purposefully across the lawn.

'Roy, isn't anyone going to make a speech?' she greeted him, bumping into Phil with her hat brim and knocking his drink flying from his hand.

'No, why? It's not a wedding. You don't make speeches at christenings, do you?' He turned to Phil, who was picking up his empty glass.

'Search me. I didn't when ours were christened.'

'See, Mum, it's not really necessary,' Roy said. 'I never made a speech at Nick and Jason's christenings.'

'Yes, you did.' The hat bobbed indignantly.

'Well, *I* don't remember.' He looked blankly at her.

'Oh, you're getting old, Roy! Your memory isn't what it used to be.' She turned and walked away, hat brim quivering

'For God's sake, what's this obsession with my age? I'm forty-three, Ma, not eighty-three,' he yelled after her. 'She's doolally half the time and that bloody hat looks like a flying saucer's landed on her head.'

'Uncle Roy, Jess wants you,' Katie called out to him.

He excused himself and joined Katie by the marquee entrance. 'Where is she?'

'In the kitchen.' She pointed to the house and ran back to Abby, Zak and Matt.

* * *

Roy frowned as he walked into the house, wondering why Jess was indoors. She was standing by the kitchen dresser, holding the phone.

'You okay, Jess?'

She nodded. 'Close the door, quickly.'

'What is it? You look worried to death,' he asked as she covered the mouthpiece with her hands.

'It's Livvy, she wants to talk to you.'

'Shit! What does she want?'

Jess shook her head, close to tears. 'She wants to know how the baby is, of course. What else can you expect, Roy?'

He puffed out his cheeks and took the phone. He sat down on a nearby chair, his stomach lurching and hands shaking. He took a deep breath. 'Hello, Livvy, what can I do for you?'

'Roy, hi. I'm sorry to call, but I really couldn't help myself. I got Sammy's letter with the photos this week. She mentioned the joint christening was today, so I guessed you'd all be at Eddie's place. How's our daughter?'

Roy swallowed the lump in his throat and passed his hand over his eyes. 'She's fine, Livvy,' he replied. 'She's beautiful. Well, you can see that from the photos, can't you? How about you? Are you alright?' There was a silence and Roy could hear her sniffing as he blinked tears away.

'I'm okay, Roy. I've met up with Danny again, I told you in my letter. He's asked me to marry him and wants us to move to the States.'

Roy took another deep breath as she continued.

'I told Danny about Harley and that's she's been adopted by a wealthy couple. I didn't tell him who, of course. I never will.'

'Have you told Danny that you'll marry him?'

'I said I'll think about it. Before I give him my answer, I need to ask you a question.'

'Ask away.'

'Are you still happy with Sammy? I mean, really happy, Roy?'

He smiled into the receiver, swallowed hard and let go of the past. 'Yes,' he said truthfully. 'I'm very happy, very happy indeed.'

There was silence for a moment. 'That's all I needed to hear. It sets me free to move on.'

'I wish you all the luck in the world, Livvy. Be happy yourself, won't you? I'm sorry for the pain I caused you and I can't thank you enough for Harley.'

'Look after her, Roy,' she said, her voice breaking before saying goodbye.

Roy sighed heavily as Jess replaced the phone on its cradle.

'You okay?' She touched a hand to his shoulder.

'Yes, thanks, Jess,' he replied. 'That was quite emotional. But can we keep this to ourselves? For obvious reasons I won't tell Sammy she called – I don't want to spoil her day.'

'Of course we can. Was she alright?'

'I guess so.' He told her what Livvy had said.

'Well, I hope she'll be very happy but somehow I think it will take her a lifetime to get over you.'

He nodded. 'I did care for her, you know. It wasn't just a casual fling. If she'd chosen to stay around and keep Harley, I think Sammy and I would have struggled to cope. I'd be torn in two. But Sammy must never know that, it would break her heart. My love for her is on a different level to what I felt for Livvy.'

'I understand what you're saying because of my relationships with Jon and Nick. It's funny how things turn out. I always thought you and Sammy would be my parents-in-law one day. Instead, my own parents will now be my in-laws and I don't even have to change my name. How weird is that?'

Roy smiled and took Jess's arm as they made their way back to the party. 'We've always been a bunch of weirdos, you ask my ma! Why change the habits of a lifetime? You've quite taken to this motherhood lark, haven't you, Jess? From wild rock chick to almost tame mother in less than a year. Who'd have thought it?'

'Hey, the almost tame mother bit is just temporary. You wait until we start our new band and I'm back in my leather jeans again. I'll show you, I'm no stay-at-home mum. And another thing, you'll *never* catch me wearing a daft hat like the one your mother's trying to decapitate Carl with!'

Roy chuckled. 'She's a bloody liability with that hat. There'll be no Raiders left at this rate, she's already attacked Phil with it.'

Sammy walked up the garden with Jon to greet Roy and Jess as they strolled arm in arm, laughing. 'Hello, you two, you look very chummy. Everything alright?'

Roy took her hand. 'Everything's just fine, Sam. Better than it's been for a long, long time,' he replied as Jess moved into Jon's outstretched arms.

'Good,' Sammy said, smiling at him. 'That's just what I needed to hear.'

A LETTER FROM PAM

Dear reader,

I want to say a huge thank you for choosing to read *The Daughters of Mersey Square*. If you did enjoy it, and want to keep up to date with all my latest releases, just sign up at the following link. Your email address will never be shared and you can unsubscribe at any time.

www.bookouture.com/pam-howes

To my loyal band of regular readers who bought and reviewed all my previous stories, thank you for waiting patiently for another book. Your support is most welcome and very much appreciated.

As always, a big thank you to Beverley Ann Hopper and Sandra Blower and the members of their Facebook group, Book Lovers. Thanks for all the support you show me. Also, thank you to Deryl Easton and the supportive members of her Facebook group, Gangland Governors/NotRights.

A huge thank you to team Bookouture, especially my lovely editor Maisie Lawrence – as always, it's been such a pleasure to work with you again – and thanks also to copyeditor/line editor Jane Eastgate and proofreader Jane Donovan for the copy edits and proofreading side of life.

And last, but definitely not least, thank you to our amazing media team, Kim Nash, Sarah Hardy, Jess Readett and Noelle

Holton, for everything you do for us. You're 'Simply the Best' as Tina would say! And thanks also to the gang in the Bookouture Authors' Lounge for always being there. As always, I'm so proud to be one of you.

I hope you loved *The Daughters of Mersey Square* and if you did, I would be very grateful if you could write a review. I'd love to hear what you think and it makes such a difference helping new readers to discover one of my books for the first time.

I love hearing from my readers – you can get in touch on my Facebook page or through Twitter.

Thanks,

Pam Howes

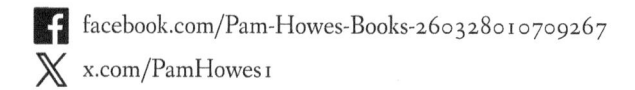

facebook.com/Pam-Howes-Books-260328010709267
x.com/PamHowes1

ACKNOWLEDGEMENTS

As always, for my partner, my daughters, grandchildren, great granddaughters and all their partners/spouses. Thanks for being a supportive and lovely family.